NICOLA THORNE

Yesterday's Promises

This edition published 1995 for
Parrallel Books
Units 13–17 Avonbridge Industrial Estate
Atlantic Road
Avonmouth, Bristol BS11 9QD
by Diamond Books
77–85 Fulham Palace Road
Hammersmith, London W6 8JB

First published in Great Britain by
Grafton Books 1986

ISBN 0 261 66707 6

Set in Times

Printed in Great Britain

Nicola Thorne is the author of a number of well-known novels which include *Pride of Place*, *Where the Rivers Meet*, *Bird of Passage* and The Askham Chronicles (*Never Such Innocence*, *Yesterday's Promises*, *Bright Morning* and *A Place in the Sun*). Her most recent novel is *Champagne Gold*. Born in South Africa, she was educated at the LSE. She lived for many years in London, but has now made her home in Dorset.

By the same author

The Girls
In Love
Bridie Climbing
A Woman Like Us
The Perfect Wife and Mother
The Daughters of the House
Where the Rivers Meet
Affairs of Love
The Enchantress Saga
Champagne
Pride of Place
Bird of Passage
Champagne Gold

The Askham Chronicles:
Never Such Innocence
Yesterday's Promises
Bright Morning
A Place in the Sun

CONTENTS

PART 1

Echoes of the Past
1920–1921

CHAPTER 1

When Bobby Lighterman was twenty-one he became one of the richest young men in England. Through his paternal grandfather he inherited the vast fortune that Sir Robert had accumulated from humble beginnings.

On the night of his birthday ball in March 1920 Bobby stood with his family at the top of the grand staircase of Lighterman House in Manchester Square, greeting his guests. Everyone who was anyone in London was there, the hospitable doors of his grandmother's home flung open to receive the rich and titled, celebrities from all walks of life.

'So glad you could come.'

'Glad you could come.'

'How are you, dearest Melanie, you look so *well*.'

'I remember Bobby when ...'

'Adam, you'll soon be a judge. Your speech at the House ...'

'Thank you, thank you ...'

'Dearest Susan, sure to be a beauty.'

And so the patter kept up, hands pumping up and down, soft cheeks inclined to be kissed.

'How do you do, Sir Dermot? Yes, isn't the news about Martha marvellous, though I don't know how she'll handle twins ...'

'And *dearest* Betty. Of course you haven't seen Bobby since he was a *baby*. How clever of you and George to miss the War in South Africa.'

If there was a little irony in Bobby's mother's voice as her eyes followed George and Betty Bulstrode down the line it was not surprising. By birth Lady Melanie was an Askham and, among their other considerable achievements, her family and their kin had not been backward in offering their sons over the years to die for England. Lady Melanie's first husband, Bobby's father, had been killed at Omdurman in the year before Bobby was born.

No Askham, or anyone related to an Askham, would be proud of people who had put saving their skins before service to their country. It was simply that the Bulstrode family were too interwoven with the Askham family to be left off the list.

Finally, when the last guest had come up the stairs and Bobby looked over the balustrade to see if any more loitered in the hall, a man came through the front door with whom he was unfamiliar. The stranger was a tall, slightly rakish-looking man, a little on the heavy side, with sleek black hair neatly parted in the middle and a fine moustache. He looked Edwardian, a relic from the past. Bobby watched him give his coat to the butler and run his hand over his head as he peered at the mirror in the hall and, as he squared his shoulders preparing to make his way upstairs, he glanced upwards and saw Bobby.

'Someone I don't know,' Bobby murmured to his mother, who looked up. As she did, something happened which Bobby rarely saw on that perfectly groomed countenance. Lady Melanie blushed.

'Lord Denton Rigby,' the *major domo* announced in a sonorous voice as the stranger whispered in his ear.

Bobby was aware of a stir in the family ranks at the mention of the name. There was an imperceptible rustle along the line as if memories were awakened by something that had happened long ago. Bobby thought that maybe it was fanciful, or maybe it wasn't. Lord Denton bowed low over Melanie's hand, pausing for a second to say something to her, looking into her eyes and, as he did, she turned to Bobby.

'You won't remember Lord Denton Rigby, Bobby. He is a very old family friend.'

'I remember you, young man,' Lord Denton said heartily. 'You'd have been about seven or eight.'

10

'I think I do remember you, sir,' Bobby politely shook hands. 'I'm sure I recall you coming to this very house.'

'Indeed I did.' Lord Denton glanced again at Melanie before passing on to her husband who shook his hand perfunctorily without saying a word. Adam Bolingbroke was a distinguished lawyer and politician who, although for many years estranged from his wife, still shared a home with her for the sake of appearances, of what people would think. From his impassive countenance it was hard to believe he had ever seen, or heard of, Lord Denton before.

This was not the case with Lady Askham, Melanie's mother, who was an old familiar of Denton's father and wanted to know where he was and how he did. She kept her hand tucked in Denton's before passing him to Bobby's grandmother, Lady Lighterman, who seemed inclined to ignore him too, as did Bobby's two aunts, Flora and Rachel. Both gave him distant, almost disapproving looks.

It was odd, Bobby thought, as he took his mother's arm and, with her, led the family parade into the drawing-room where those assembled were being offered champagne in tall, fluted glasses by a small army of servants resplendent in the yellow Lighterman livery.

'Who is Lord Denton?' he whispered as they walked at a measured pace through the beautiful salon dominated by a portrait by Sargent of the late Sir Robert Lighterman in Alderman's robes.

'An old flame,' Melanie whispered back. 'More a family friend.'

'His name wasn't on the list.'

'He only just came back to London from abroad.' Melanie waved to an acquaintance. 'I knew you wouldn't mind.'

'It occurred to me that no one seemed to like him. Did something happen?'

'Oh darling, what could *happen*?' Melanie's fabled blue-green eyes opened innocently and Bobby knew that, for the time being, he would learn no more.

11

It was a splendid party. No expense had been spared by Mabel Lighterman, who had shared humble origins with her husband, but knew quite well by now how to entertain and flatter the rich. Indeed she was richer than most people in the room, despite the fact that her father had been a carter in Brixton. Her one son, Harry, had astonished but gratified his family by his marriage to an earl's daughter; but, alas, it only lasted a few weeks before his death in battle. It said quite a lot for Lady Melanie, who was an arch snob, that she was as fond of her mother-in-law as she was. The fact that she preferred her to her own mother was quite well known and, in the early years of her widowhood, she had seen more of Mabel than Lady Askham. Bobby knew Lighterman House as home more than any other place.

Melanie and Dulcie Askham had always been rivals for the attention of others, especially of men. But since the war Dulcie had withdrawn from the absurd social combat leaving the field clear for Melanie. Grief and age had taken their toll of a woman whose looks and vivacity had dominated London in the eighties and nineties, a mantle that her daughter had inherited during the brief but splendid reign of Edward VII.

But the War had changed everything. Now there were no pre-eminent hostesses or society beauties, as Melanie and Dulcie had been, just a crowd of frenetic people, young and not so young, survivors from the War, desperate to have a good time.

There were plenty of young people at the party, Bobby's friends, Susan's friends. After Bobby had opened the dancing with his mother, the staid old-fashioned waltzes were abandoned for the more lively tunes that had come out of America since the War.

Dulcie took her seat near the dancing with a group of her older friends who usually sat with her on occasions such as this to chat and gossip, to reminisce about the past. Dulcie was corseted and upholstered in a blue gown bedecked with bows, plumes and feathers, the fashion of the 1880s when she had been a London belle. Now in her sixty-eighth year she was a handsome, formidable woman; controlled, disciplined, her hair – elaborately arranged under her diamond tiara – still auburn, her clear eyes that brilliant blue-green she had handed down to her children. She sat ramrod straight with a pronounced bosom like her friend Queen Mary who, however, was her junior by a number of years. Dulcie had always enjoyed the favour of the Royal Family, was an intimate of Queen Alexandra, and it showed in her detached, regal manner, her graciousness to underlings, her often chilling remoteness towards familiars.

Dulcie Askham was much loved, but also feared. She was typical of an age that was past, a style that had gone out with the War. There were very few left like her. One of them was the dear old Duchess of Quex, whose lorgnette was seldom far from her eyes, raking the room to provide her with fresh items for gossip.

'Everyone's here,' she said approvingly. 'I haven't seen the Plomley-Pembertons for years.'

'Oh, is that gal here?' Dulcie's eyes were bright with interest. 'Grace. She wanted to marry Bosco and even came to Egypt to try and hook him.'

'So *many* people wanted to marry Bosco,' the Duchess sighed, allowing her lorgnette to drop on to her capacious bosom. 'Alas. But Rachel *is* a dear,' she added as an afterthought.

'Rachel *is* a dear,' Dulcie affirmed. 'A very good daughter-in-law she's been to me.'

'Pity she has such funny ideas,' the Duchess sniffed. 'Left-wing. I hear they call her the "Red Countess".'

'That's exaggerated,' Dulcie said in the firm voice of one intent on quashing rumours. 'She does have one or two funny notions but, at heart, she's a good person. Susan loves her better than her own mother, which is hardly surprising.' Dulcie frowned as she looked about for her younger daughter.

13

'Maternal feelings never being strong among Melanie's virtues.'

No, Melanie had few real virtues, the Duchess thought, singling her out in the crowd dancing with a subaltern in the Guards young enough to be her son, though she was still a beauty at forty-two; tall for a woman, auburn-haired, a complexion whose quality had inspired poets. The men seemed to flock towards Melanie as they had to Dulcie when she was part of the Prince of Wales's set that danced and played cards at Clarence House and many secret rendezvous in London, unknown to the Princess of Wales.

Susan, on the other hand, took after her Aunt Flora, her mother's sister. She was not exactly plain but, like Flora, she did not make the best of herself. She was gauche and rather awkward, aware that her hair was too thin and the wrong colour and that she was a Bolingbroke rather than an Askham. She would grow up, of course, because she was not yet seventeen. But a beauty? The Duchess slowly shook her head, passing from Susan, dancing with her father, to her brother.

'Do you think Bobby is interested in the Lawler girl? He's danced with her twice.'

Dulcie emphatically shook her head.

'Certainly not. Bobby is going to be like Bosco and surprise us all. You can be sure that anyone his mother or grandmother invites for him to meet he's never interested in. Bobby is a law unto himself.'

Meanwhile, on the floor, the subject of all their speculation, Bobby, thought Emily Lawler pretty but dull. He was not, actually, particularly interested in women. He didn't run after them as some of his friends did, and accordingly they ran after him. Bobby was considered a great catch by many of the mothers of eligible daughters and a lot of thought had been given to ensembles for this party, dresses and hairdos and make-up, though it was still not considered the thing for well-bred girls to wear it.

14

But others thought that attractive, rich young men like him were dangerous because they were in love with themselves. Filling his card between dances Bobby flitted from girl to girl like a bee from flower to flower. His eyes were vaguely on his mother, his mind preoccupied with Lord Denton Rigby and something that had happened years ago which he could dimly recall, but not bring clearly enough to mind. It was like grasping at something apprehended but unseen, that mysterious happening in the past that had brought blushes to his mother's face.

Eventually he made his way towards a group of younger women in a far corner of the room who included his aunts Flora, and Rachel, the widow of his Uncle Bosco. Unlike her mother-in-law, Dulcie Askham, Rachel did not have a special coterie because most of her contemporaries regarded her as odd. She was uninterested in Society, having strong left-wing views; she was a newspaper owner and – that horror of horrors among women – an intellectual! Most young society matrons carefully skirted round her as though she had some form of virulent disease. As her sister-in-law, Flora, shared the same affliction, being a distinguished scholar and Egyptologist, they were firm friends and invariably sat out at parties, chatting.

'Heads together,' Bobby taunted, standing in front of them wagging a finger. 'Chat, chat. Can I get you anything, Aunts? If I didn't know you I'd think you were pulling Davina Wellbeloved to pieces. Too well beloved if you ask me.'

Rachel, who loved him, pulled him down beside her. She thought Bobby was talented, fun and charming. Also sad. Bobby shared with Susan a streak of melancholy that doubtless had its roots in their unsettled family life. It had not been hard to mother him and Susan, taking Melanie's place. Melanie was invariably absent from home – out every day; at a ball, party or dinner every night, and a vigorous attender at country house weekends. Her beautiful home lacked a mother's interest and her children were, in a way, as deprived as any offspring of the poor. Rachel had visited them at school,

15

had them for holidays, taken them abroad with her own children, the eldest of whom was fourteen.

'Bobby, don't be a gossip,' she said.

'I *did* want to gossip, Aunt Rachel, as a matter of fact.' Bobby carefully displaced his coat tails as he sat down. 'I wanted to ask you about Lord Denton. It seemed to me no one liked him, and yet he made Mother blush.'

Rachel looked lost for words momentarily, but Flora grimaced.

'No one does like him much.'

'Why? I've *never* seen Mother blush. Was it something that happened long ago?'

Flora and Rachel looked at each other and then Rachel carefully studied her fingernails.

'You should ask your mother these things, Bobby. Not us. It's not fair.'

'Then there was something? Would she tell me if I asked her?'

'She might.' Flora looked doubtful.

'There was something between them?'

'Bobby, we can't gossip about your *mother*,' Rachel protested. 'Be reasonable.'

At that moment Melanie glided past them in the arms of Lord Denton who had been hovering all evening on the fringes of the great crowd waiting for just such an opportunity.

'Do be careful, Denton,' Melanie said, smiling graciously at Bobby as they passed him. 'Bobby's suspicious about you, I can tell. Don't hold me too close.' Immediately she drew away from him.

'I'm sorry.' Denton contrived to look crestfallen, an expression that was difficult for so vain and self-confident a man to muster. 'Anyway, I can't bear the dancing. Everyone *is* staring,' he said, looking over his shoulder. 'It's as though they all *know*.'

'Well, they don't. Only my family. Let's go and get a glass of champagne, anyway. I'm frightfully thirsty.'

Susan didn't like Lord Denton. She could tell he was a cad. He had bedroom eyes and made her uneasy, not that she and her brothers hadn't lived lives of unease and suspicion for years in the company of their incompatible parents, their knowledge of their mother's special 'friends'.

Yet, as children do with parents who don't get on, Susan loved them both passionately, wanted both to adore her, beloved father and exciting, indifferent mother, whom Susan would so like to have resembled but did not. How she would like to have been an Askham and not a Bolingbroke with her thin, mouse-coloured hair and pasty, unhealthy complexion blemished, now, with adolescent spots. Everyone said it would pass, this awkward period, but when? She hated dancing; she was alarmingly tall and kept on tripping over her partners' feet, squads of correct well-connected young men whom the family had ensured filled up her card even before the dancing began. It would never do for Bobby's sister to be a wallflower.

But when it was Bobby's turn he led her on to the floor just before supper.

'It's a super party,' Susan said lamely.

'I can tell you're not enjoying it.'

'I didn't think you were, much, either.'

Bobby smiled and pressed her briefly to him. Half-brother and sister, more of age than the younger brothers, they had always been close, or as close as Bobby allowed himself to get to anyone.

'One has to go through these things. It's a sort of initiation. You will, too. It's just so that the family can be seen to spend a lot of money in the company of all the right people.'

'You're frightfully cynical, Bobby,' Susan pretended to chide him. Then, suddenly: 'Do you like Lord Denton?'

'Why do you ask?'

'I saw you looking at him in a funny way.'

'He's an old flame of Mother's.'

'I know.'

'Oh? How?' Bobby looked at her with interest.

17

'Your grandmother told me he used to take her out.' 'Your grandmother' meant Lady Lighterman, who was sitting with her own particular set, rather lower down in the social scale: wives of minor politicians, or the *nouveaux riches* of whom there were a good many since the War. Many had even made fortunes out of death – Sir Robert Lighterman among them. He had become an armament king, rivalling Krupp in Germany.

'Then she must have been married to your father at the time.'

'Mummy has always been married. Hasn't she?'

'Mother has always been a flirt,' Bobby observed, not without bitterness. 'I shouldn't worry about Lord Denton.'

When the music stopped the company in the ballroom streamed towards a buffet which was of such lavishness that it could quite easily have fed a couple of thousand hungry people. Most of it, however, would be collected the following morning by the rubbish cart which collected refuse in Manchester Square. The buffet was set in yet another drawing-room (there were four) in the huge eighteenth-century house which had been reconstructed by Colin Campbell, who had remodelled Lord Burlington's house in Piccadilly.

The house had been furnished with no regard for expense by Sir Robert who, like many men born poor, had developed a connoisseur's eye and judgement as soon as circumstances allowed him to gratify them. It was full of treasures, most of them locked away tonight – not because of fear of theft, but fear of breakage by the firm which had been brought in as caterers. The buffet table ran from one end of the room to the other and, as some took seats at the many small tables arranged round the room, others went to the groaning buffet to select morsels to tempt the palates of their partners. Footmen in the Lighterman livery circulated with glasses of champagne, or cordial for the few who preferred it.

Bobby led Susan to a larger table where his two grandmothers were seated next to Adam and Flora. All already had

18

food. Dulcie was looking distractedly about her as Bobby and Susan appeared, saying:

'There you are! Now where's your mother? She really should be here when Bobby cuts the cake.' Dulcie saw Rachel chatting to a Member of Parliament and signalled her over.

'Have you seen Melanie, Rachel?'

'Do you want me to go and look for her, Mother?'

'I'll go.' Susan, who had just sat down, jumped up again, but Bobby expostulated.

'Don't be silly! Mother will make her own way here in her own good time.'

Adam looked at him with approval and raising his glass said: 'Happy birthday, Bobby.'

'Dearest boy. Happy birthday.'

As the family raised their glasses everyone seemed to think that this was the signal for the cutting of the cake and before Melanie was found, or the order given, the Master of Ceremonies gave the command, and it was wheeled in, its twenty-one candles aflame, by the chef from Searceys who had made it. The five piece string orchestra, which had played diligently and without rest all evening, struck up the chords of 'Happy Birthday' and everyone rose to their feet. The hatted chef presented Bobby with the knife with which, taken unawares, but accepting the *fait accompli*, he promptly cut into the cake, at the same time extinguishing all the candles in one blow.

Everyone sang 'Happy Birthday' again and cheered, before rounding off the ceremony with the refrain of 'He's A Jolly Good Fellow' which, Dulcie remarked to her close friend the Duchess, she thought rather common: a sign of the times.

Bobby gracefully acknowledged the applause of the crowd as his stepfather rose and put out his hand for silence. He then made a very short speech, laudatory yet to the point, extolling Bobby's virtues and concluding: 'I have had the privilege of standing in for many years for Bobby's father, Harry, whom we also honour tonight. Harry Lighterman, ladies and gentlemen, and, for you younger people who do not know, was a hero who died at Omdurman, giving his life for a friend. That friend Bosco, Lord Askham, my brother-in-law, later gave his life for me. Without him I wouldn't be here.' Adam paused for a moment, the muscles of his face hard at work to suppress his emotion, and then he continued, 'The Askham family has always honoured its heroes of whom it is very proud. The Askhams, yes, and the Lightermans and Bolingbrokes as well have honoured them. But tonight, especially, I want to honour Bobby's father, Mabel's son, and say how much I wish he could have been here on this day.'

Mabel's ready handkerchief was pressed to her eyes as Adam sat down, the joyfulness of the occasion suddenly dampened. Mabel clasped Adam's hand and even Dulcie dabbed at a tear as Bobby rose to thank his stepfather for his gracious speech and, particularly, the tributes to his father and uncle, concluding: 'I can only say, dear Adam, that you have always been a real father to me, taking the place of the one I never knew, and I thank you and my mother for seeing me to my majority.'

As Bobby sat down the crowd resumed its ebullient spirits, few seeming to notice the absence of Melanie, and cheered him again while champagne corks popped and the orchestra burst into the merry rumpus of 'Ain't We Got Fun?'

But the family were annoyed about Melanie and, as the party got going again, started speculating among themselves as to her whereabouts.

'I'm *sure* I can hear the "Happy Birthday", Denty darling,' Melanie said anxiously, breaking away from his embrace to cock an ear towards the door.

'Never mind.' Denton clasped her passionately to him again.

'But, dear, I *do* mind. It's Bobby's birthday. He must be blowing out the candles. People will wonder where I am.'

'Let him do it again.'

20

'You're very *naughty*, Denton, irresponsible.' Melanie tapped his nose flirtatiously. 'People will talk.'

'Let them. They did before. Remember those dinners at Ciro's?'

'And Quags? Do I not,' Melanie sighed loudly, breaking away once more and lifting her glass which, the champagne inside it by now a little flat, stood on the table in the soundproofed library.

'But there'll be no talk when we're married,' Denton said with all the assurance and pride of a man who had just proposed as the strains of 'Happy Birthday' reached them.

'Providing Adam agrees to a divorce.' Melanie's colour was high and the sparkle in her eyes had not been seen by anyone for years.

'Why shouldn't he agree?' Denton wondered if he was about to be misled all over again, prompted to rash action by a misinterpretation of the signs. Melanie was such a tease.

She shrugged. 'You know, appearances, the children, that kind of thing.' Impishly she smiled at him. 'On the other hand I think he just *might* be glad to get rid of me.'

'Rid of you? Preposterous!' Denton was shocked. 'The most angelic woman in the whole world? Darling, if you knew how I longed for you...'

Denton drew her pert mouth up to his and, as they kissed, neither of them was aware of the door opening and a very astonished, even frightened young woman gazing at them from the doorway. She was about to withdraw when Melanie, sensing movement, broke away from Denton and turned, her hand flying to her mouth.

'Susan!'

'Mother!'

'Susan, you're snooping.'

'I'm not.' Susan covered both her hot cheeks with her hands. 'You're standing there, looking. It's *hateful*.'

'What you're doing is hateful, too. Oh Mummy, how *can* you, on this day of *all* days? *Everyone* wonders where you are.'

21

The shock and tension were too much for Susan who, collapsing into a leather armchair a few feet away from her mother and Lord Denton, burst into tears.

Instead of caressing her and comforting her, as perhaps a thoughtful mother might have, Melanie seized her daughter by the shoulders and shook her until her teeth chattered.

'Little snoop! Prying, are you?'

'*Please*, Melanie.' Denton, rather appalled at the behaviour of his beloved, attempted to take her by the shoulder too; but she shook herself free, her face contorted with anger.

'If there's anything I hate it's a snoop. Couldn't you have knocked?'

'I didn't know anyone was here,' Susan blubbered. 'We were looking for you, Aunt Rachel and I. Bobby has blown out the candles and cut the cake. You've spoiled *his* evening and now ... this.' Susan's tragic face stared balefully at her mother as Rachel, coming swiftly into the room and appraising the situation, closed the door behind her, carefully locking it.

'All you needed to do was turn the key,' she remonstrated. 'It could have been anyone.'

'We never thought people would come snooping in here.'

'It's not snooping! Bobby has cut the cake. Everyone missed you.'

'We didn't hear a thing.' Melanie's voice began to betray her guilt. 'It's not my fault.'

'Whose is it, then?' Rachel put an arm tenderly round Susan's shoulders as she stared angrily, accusingly, at Melanie and Denton.

'It's no one's fault,' Melanie said. 'It's one of those things.'

'Nonsense! But it's typical of you, Melanie, if I may say so.' Rachel clasped Susan more firmly. 'Always thinking of yourself, never of anyone else. Like that day ...' She stopped, looking first at Melanie then at Susan, about to betray what happened in the past. Then she said: 'Oh, never mind. You ought to come back into the party and make some sort of

22

apology to Bobby. As it is you've ruined the evening, everyone is anxious.'

'Don't you dare make that insinuation.' Melanie had recovered her aplomb. 'I have not ruined anyone's evening. I shall do as I please. I'm old enough.'

'But not responsible enough,' Rachel began but, before she had time to proceed, Melanie's hand shot out and hit her across the cheek.

'Oh, I say!' Denton, his puffy face puce with fresh embarrassment, produced a handkerchief. Susan began to bawl again and someone started banging on the door, asking if everything was all right.

Rachel clasped her hand to her cheek, her eyes smarting with tears of anger as she tottered rather unsteadily towards the door.

'What an evening to remember,' she said, shakily turning the key and opening the door, as the mob surged in, like greyhounds on the scent.

CHAPTER 2

All London society was agog at the thought of a divorce in the eminent Askham family. Of course like all large, old families it had had its black sheep, its skeletons firmly locked in ancestral cupboards. As recently as the year 1913 the splendid Bosco, eleventh Earl of Askham, in a libel suit brought by him, had been revealed in the High Court as an adulterer, possibly a coward. For a while after that the Askhams had temporarily gone to ground; Dulcie retired to the country and even Melanie's name was erased from the lists of fashionable hostesses when the 1913 season began. However, a year later the War intervened to make such matters appear trivial and unimportant and Bosco very quickly redeemed himself in battle, where he won the Victoria Cross.

The subject of Bosco's act of heroism during which he died was his brother-in-law, Adam Bolingbroke, who now found himself in the ignominious position of being sued for divorce by a faithless wife despite the fact that, unlike her, he had never once deviated from the matrimonial path. But Adam was a gentleman, middle-class maybe in the eyes of his mother-in-law, but a gentleman nevertheless. In 1920 one of the only ways to freedom through divorce was by means of adultery and, naturally, Lady Melanie did not expect to find herself in such a compromising situation. Whatever blame might attach to her in private, it would never do for a lady of such distinguished ancestry to be cited for divorce. In the eyes of society, Bolingbrokes were nothing. An Askham had accompanied Henry II to France in his war against Louis IX. Yet the idea of Melanie being innocent was laughable, and her peers enjoyed the joke.

24

As it was, the divorce would do Melanie, blameless or not, enough harm already. She would be barred from court, from Royal Ascot and, for a family who had always been close to the monarch and Royal Family, this was not a privilege that a lady, fêted and admired, lightly surrendered.

Why then did Melanie so wish to be free of her loyal, faithful husband; to change him for a man who was rather feckless, not in the least wealthy and had once raped her? Many years ago, misinterpreting the signs he thought she gave him, he had taken her by force and the result had been a child, Jordan, and his self-imposed exile in the West Indies.

Lord Denton didn't know about Jordan until he returned to England in 1919. He felt an immediate thrill, not only at being a father, but at having sired a son by Melanie. It revived all his old ardour for her and she, always a flirt and attracted by dangerous men, found the idea of one who had once violated her unexpectedly appealing. They realized how alike they were and began again; resuming a relationship that, he persuaded her, only a simple misunderstanding had interrupted twelve years before.

Lord Denton Rigby was a weak man. He had the attraction that weak, handsome men have for some women. They are preferred, God knows why, to hard-working, sober, earnest, devoted men like Adam who somehow lack sparkle. He, who did nothing for a living, was weak enough to let Adam jeopardize his own considerable career for Melanie, by pretending to commit adultery with a woman he had never met until they were closeted alone together in a Bloomsbury hotel some time in the summer of 1920, six months after Bobby's birthday party.

By that time a lot of other things had happened. Adam had left home to live in a bachelor apartment in Gray's Inn. Bobby, more detached than the others, had gone to America to try and lure American engineers to his works in Wiltshire where the Askham motor car, started by Bosco and advanced by Sir

Robert, was being manufactured, incorporating a lot of new ideas.

Bobby was a keen businessman with the makings of a very good one. He was one of those people who, though rich, wanted to be richer; who regarded wealth as a means to power. Knowing that he had everything, Bobby did not intend to waste it. He wanted one day to be a very powerful man indeed; the sort of man to whom people deferred, whose opinions they sought, whose advice they took. He did not intend to throw away what his grandfather had gathered and nurtured with such care.

But Mabel Lighterman lived, as she was entitled to for life, in the magnificent house in Manchester Square, going at weekends to Robertswood on the banks of the Thames near Reading where her daughters and her grandchildren were invariably to be found in her company. It did not suit Bobby to share his grandmother's house, once he came of age. It did not match the picture he had of himself, and he bought a town house in Hill Street, Mayfair which he regarded as more suitable for a man of his independence and wealth. While he was away it was done up to the most exacting specifications, with a basement swimming-pool and a garden on the roof.

To all appearances, at the age of twenty-one, Bobby was a handsome, even striking young man; black-haired, blue-eyed, sturdy of build, not particularly tall. Ostensibly, too, he was a dutiful son, who loved his mother, was polite to his stepfather and venerated the memory of his grandfather.

Yet of Melanie's four children Bobby was least affected by the divorce. Despite the affection of his family and, particularly, the devotion lavished upon him by his paternal grandparents, he had grown into a self-possessed, self-contained man who seemed somehow untouched by love. Maybe it was this that made Bobby draw apart. Although Adam was a father figure he was a remote man, not very close even to his own children – a man rejected also by his wife – and the blame for Bobby's emotional coldness may perhaps be laid mainly at the door of that other iceberg in the Askham family, that spoilt, capricious creature: Lady Melanie.

For though throughout her life she attracted men who swarmed slavishly about her, she gave very little in return – content to be admired, worshipped as a goddess on a pedestal.

Bobby was devoted to his half-sister, Susan, as far as he was able, yet he patronized her. It was as though he was aware that he was good-looking and she was not; that it mattered; and that he was extremely wealthy, whereas she was merely comfortably off, although she had inherited from her grandfather, the tenth Lord Askham, a considerable sum that he'd left to all his grandchildren. With Bobby it only made him richer; with Susan it would make her independent as soon as she came of age, but not rich.

The Bolingbrokes had no money. Rachel and Adam's father had been a country solicitor who left an estate of a thousand pounds on his death in 1916. Rachel, of course, was now a very wealthy woman, having been left Bosco's entire estate; but Adam could almost be described as poor. He had never made money from the Bar, and the stipend of a Member of Parliament was now four hundred pounds a year. But he would never let Melanie keep him although, inevitably, as she became more wealthy with the deaths of her father and brother, she was not content to live on her husband's income. She bought herself a beautiful house in St John's Wood and Adam, who had always felt that he lived there on sufferance, was glad to move out.

Now as he stood at the window of his small flat overlooking the gardens of Gray's Inn he felt reflective, even sad. The divorce would be a cut and dried affair. He had provided the evidence required, even though he and the co-respondent provided by his lawyer had played cards in the hotel bedroom until the detective sent by the opposite party had found them. It had all been worked out beforehand, sordid and rather nasty. Now he would be branded an adulterer. He didn't care, or rather he cared but not in the way Melanie cared. He cared because there was one woman he would like to marry when he was free and she would not have him on the grounds of consanguinity; they were too close. Flora was his sister-in-law and, although for many years they had shared a love, they had never shared a bed. He was waiting for her now.

Flora was always prompt and as a clock in Holborn struck three there was a ring on his doorbell and a few seconds later his daily woman admitted her to his pleasant, book-lined study, with a large desk in the middle that he had removed from the house in St John's Wood.

Flora was a tall, angular woman who increasingly, in recent years, had made up in elegance what she lacked in beauty. She'd begun to care about what she wore, unlike the woman of pre-war years who had little regard for clothes; content, even proud, to be as nature made her without much embellishment. Flora had the rich auburn hair that she and her sister shared with their mother, and Susan so conspicuously lacked; but, otherwise, she had not the harmonious disposition of features that made her sister and mother such beauties – her nose was broad, her mouth wide, the blue-green Askham eyes direct and over-intelligent for most men, only slightly feline. Today she wore a belted coat and skirt which almost reached her ankles and a velour hat with a blue band and a broad brim, like a man's. She stood looking at Adam, swinging her handbag and then, as he held out his arms, she came into them and laid her head on his shoulder.

'Dearest,' she whispered, 'it has all been such a frightful ordeal. One wonders if it was really worth it.'

She raised her head and looked into his eyes, and he wondered how long he would have to endure the agony of wanting Flora without possessing her. They had loved each other now for so long; but Flora, out of principle, always resisted. To her it was physically impossible to sleep with her sister's husband. Would it change, now that bond was to be broken?

'One didn't have the choice,' Adam murmured, breaking away to take a cigarette from the box on his desk, tapping it on his thumb before lighting it.

'You had the choice of *not* allowing Melanie a divorce.'

'I didn't really.' Adam, who was a compulsive smoker, lit the cigarette, hungrily swallowing the smoke. 'You know Mel. What she wants she gets. People forget, Flora. They will soon forget that I was involved in a divorce case ...'

'I don't think your constituents will forget,' Flora said prosaically. 'Working people in the north can be very strait-laced, almost narrow-minded. But, dearest, what I have come to talk to you about today is not the past but the future.'

'About us?' Adam looked at her hopefully. 'Then it will all have been worthwhile.'

'About us, yes.' Flora's tone was guarded. 'But not *quite* in the way you think. Even with you and Melanie divorced, my dearest, I can never change the way I feel about you, in the sense you're thinking of – the physical sense.' She went up to him and linked her arms round his waist in a way he found tantalizingly provocative though, completely inexperienced as she was in sexual matters, she would never realize it. 'But you know, Adam, that I love you in a far, far higher, more important way. The longer I live, dear, the more convinced I am that the senses deceive people about the true meaning of their relationships. My sister is an example, my mother before her. You and I are united by a firmer, stronger bond than that. No, my dearest, what you have suggested, want, I know, in a carnal way, can never be. What I am proposing today is that I should buy a house in which you and I can live and which will provide a home for your family. After all, I am their aunt and no one would think it amiss.'

As Flora released him, Adam sat down abruptly and she followed him, perching lightly on the arm of his chair and curling her hand round his neck. These familiarities were permitted, but no other. It was as though she were quite unconscious of the effect of her physical presence, as though she gave no thought to it.

'I have just come from inspecting a delightful house in Bedford Row, a short distance from here, admirably placed for the Law Courts and Parliament. It is in excellent condition, needing very little doing to it, a lick of paint, some modernization of the downstairs and the kitchen. It could all be completed well before Susan leaves school, because it is Susan I am primarily concerned about and her unhappiness at the collapse of her parents' marriage.' She looked around his bachelor flat. 'This is no place for a girl on the brink of womanhood, and two younger boys. Indeed it is not. Melanie already has plans to move abroad when she and Denton are married. It may ease the situation between Melanie and Susan if she does, but what will become of Susan? What will she do?'

'Rachel ...' Adam began.

'She can't make a home for your children! She has got five of her own. It is too much. No, I will willingly purchase the house and make it a home for you and your children.' Flora held up a hand. 'And don't ask me what people will say. I don't care what they say. All I ask is that they leave us in peace. There now, Adam, my mind is made up. It all depends now on whether you like the house.'

She smiled tenderly at him but he didn't return her smile, remaining in his seat, his head sunk on his chest. He thought that it made no difference whether he liked it or not – like Melanie, strong-minded Flora too was adept at getting her own way. Sometimes, he thought, he hovered between the frying pan and the fire. Mentally he reprimanded himself for disloyalty.

Flora leaned over, staring gravely into his face. 'Doesn't it please you, Adam? A respectable spinster, the aunt of the children concerned, cannot possibly be a subject of scandal!'

'It's not the scandal I'm thinking about,' Adam sighed. But he knew she wouldn't understand.

* * *

Nevertheless, what Flora wanted came to pass as Adam suspected it would. And it was a nice house, even a lovely house, large and pleasant with a frontage on to the street and a small garden at the back. By Christmas the divorce was made absolute and in February of the following year Melanie was quietly married to Denton Rigby in Nice, with only her mother and Bobby of all her family present. For once there were none of the large flock of family relations that always came to Askham occasions, which had graced her second marriage in 1901. Melanie didn't mind. She felt now that she'd cut herself off from much of her past, that a new life was beginning.

Rachel read the announcement of the wedding in *The Times*. '*Between Lord Denton Rigby and Lady Melanie Bolingbroke, younger daughter of the Tenth Earl of Askham, in Nice ...*'

She put down the paper and, removing her spectacles, placed them on top. Now the gossips would start. The telephone would ring. There would be the usual excuses, evasions, half-truths. It's a wonder, she thought, that people tolerated a law that was so unfair, that so obviously and blatantly permitted people to be falsely accused of something they didn't do. Undoubtedly it would damage Adam's career although he pretended not to mind. Maybe one day, after a suitable interval had elapsed, she would write a leader on the subject of divorce reform in her paper. After all, why should people who didn't want to live together have to stay married? But adultery as the only means of divorce was clearly ridiculous; one must move with the times and, unfortunately, people were marrying more partners than they used to.

And there was the question of Flora ...

'Come in,' she called, aroused from her reverie by a tap on the door.

As Susan peeped into the room Rachel glanced guiltily at the paper as though seeing the announcement of her mother's remarriage would reinforce Susan's private agony. She had been staying with Rachel for half-term as her father's new

31

house was not yet ready. No one knew that Flora was paying for it, and only yesterday that she was moving into it.

Rachel composed her features into an expression of the sort of reassurance she felt Susan needed and put out a hand.

'Hello, dear. Did you sleep well?'

'Not at all.' Susan, still in her dressing gown, slumped on to the chair opposite her aunt, rubbing her eyes. 'I was thinking of poor Daddy ... I know he'll be upset about Mummy.'

'I doubt that he'll be too upset after all these years. It's no secret to you children that your parents didn't always see eye to eye.'

'And there was Aunt Flora, which I didn't know about.' Susan's tone was accusatory, the dark rings round her eyes bearing witness to not one but many sleepless nights.

'What about Aunt Flora?' Rachel's voice was purposely gentle.

'That she and Daddy have been in love for years.' Susan's lower lip wobbled. She'd been in an emotional state ever since the divorce, refusing to be reconciled to it.

'Who told you that?'

'Bobby. He found out from Mummy just before she left for France. It wasn't only Lord Denton, you see. Mummy had to tolerate that kind of thing too. Oh, I do think people are ... awful.'

Susan now burst into tears, bending her head and kneading her fists into her eyes. Rachel thought then how very young and vulnerable she was, immature for her years.

'Darling,' she got up and crouched by Susan's chair. 'That is not quite true. Not at all. Your father and Aunt Flora have been attached, it is true, but in a very correct and platonic way. They have never been lovers, I know that, because it is something neither of them wished. Your aunt was, and is, deeply attached to your father, but it is not a carnal sort of understanding at all. Not at all.' Rachel shook her head emphatically. 'It is really a true friendship and Flora has been of great help to Adam in his campaigns for women's suffrage, his help for needy people and so on. Matters that did not interest your mother at all.'

'Then why didn't he marry Aunt Flora?' Susan's stormy face was still stained with tears. Rachel nodded understandingly.

'Indeed, maybe he should have married Aunt Flora in the first place; but he didn't. It is true they had much in common and your Uncle Bosco, before he married me, certainly suggested it because he loved both Flora and your father and he saw how very well suited they were.' Rachel sighed. 'But, alas, you can't force people to do things they can't see for themselves and your mother was a very beautiful woman, as she is now. Adam was hopelessly in love with her, and she encouraged him. She felt vulnerable, a young widow with a small child. Adam was so caring and sweet. But it was not a good marriage, not a happy one.'

'Never?' Susan sounded agonized. 'Never, ever? Even when I was born, and Christopher?'

'Oh, my dear, don't misunderstand me.' Rachel impulsively clasped at her arm. 'Of course they were happy, and for many years. But their disparate interests drew them apart, and their unsuitability became more apparent.' Rachel didn't add that Melanie's flirtatious ways also helped to sunder the marital bond. It was only much later that Adam and Flora became interested in each other – a love never to be consummated, by Flora's express wishes.

'I feel so unwanted, Aunt, so unloved.' Susan's hand crept up to her eyes again and a single tear stole down her cheek. 'I know I'm a baby, but it is awful when the home breaks up, the only home I've ever known. The boys don't feel it so much as I do. They think it's fun to be spending holidays with Mummy in the South of France. I ... I hate it.'

'But, precious, you've got us.' Rachel's motherly arm stole round her niece's shoulder. 'You've got Daddy and Aunt Flora. The house will soon be ready. If you pass your exams at school you could think about going to university perhaps.'

'But that's just it. I don't *want* to go back to school! I hate it, especially when the girls see *that* ...' Susan flicked a hand at the carefully folded *Times* newspaper lying beneath Rachel's spectacles. 'They will laugh at me. They will know that Mummy and Daddy faked the divorce so that Mummy could marry again. You don't know how horrible it's been for me all term, the girls laughing and sniggering about Daddy being accused of adultery, sleeping with another woman.'

It was true the newspapers had made the best of the uncontested divorce – banner headlines in one of the evening papers: LEADING KING'S COUNSEL ADMITS ADULTERY. The fact that the Askham family were involved made sure of that. It reminded them all of the libel trial in 1913 when the papers went to town. The Askhams, or anyone connected with them, always made news.

Yet Rachel was rather surprised that, in the expensive school where Susan was a boarder, with all the young sophisticates it contained with similarly unsettled unfortunate parents, the girls had the nerve to be horrible to Susan, whose situation was not unique. Perhaps they were not so much horrible as derisory: sniggering, yes, at the suggestion of smut and sexual innuendo, cruel as only young people can be.

'Darling, I do think it important that you pass your sixth form exams, very important. It is quite fashionable now for girls to go to university, and a good thing too ...'

'Mummy didn't go! You didn't.'

'No, but it wasn't so easy or so popular in those days. Your Aunt Flora did and did very well indeed. I would like you to emulate her ...'

But Susan's work had fallen off. The situation at home had made it hard for her to concentrate.

'I don't want to go back to school, not after that! Please, please, Aunt Rachel, speak to Daddy for me. Let me stay here with you.'

Rachel took Susan's hand and held it. Then she spoke very gently, but firmly.

'Susan, darling, you know I love you as much as my own children. But you're also very much loved by your mother and father, by the rest of the family, too. You are a young woman, eighteen in July. Yet you seem so troubled by insecurity and doubt. Why do you doubt yourself so much, Susan? Why do you have to be constantly comforted and reassured? Believe me, I do sympathize with you. I lost my mother when I was about your age and the loss of parents in death, or the break-up of a marriage, is very hard to bear however old one is. I feel strongly that you should go back to school, at least for the rest of the term, and then we'll think again during the summer. Face the music. I am on your side and I love you, but I do think this is the best thing for you to do. Now go and get dressed because Charlotte and Em want you to take them out this afternoon. You know, as far as they're concerned, you're very grown-up. Just show them, now, how adult you really are.'

That afternoon Rachel had a visitor, Mrs Snowden, wife of a prominent Labour politician, who had served with Rachel on a number of committees, yet was giving her for the first time an account of her visit to Russia the previous year.

'If you think the Revolution is successful,' Mrs Snowden said, accepting another cake from Rachel, 'I can say that it is, but only up to a point. There are the most frightful things going on.'

'What kind of things?' Rachel crossed and uncrossed her legs.

'Dreadful atrocities, shootings, murders ...'

'But that is the aftermath of all wars ...'

'I assure you it's not a mere aftermath. It is deliberate policy. The Extraordinary Commission, known as the Cheka, is as ruthless as the secret police once operated by the Czar.'

'I find that very difficult to believe.'

'Nevertheless, believe it you must, Lady Askham. I saw many things to admire in Russia but many, many other things to criticize, some of them quite shocking – the poverty of the people, famine, the unfair distribution of food. Members of the Party live like the old nobility in special accommodation with special rations while the proletariat, the working class whom the Revolution was supposed to put in power, are worse off than before. There is starvation everywhere. Housing and clothing are inadequate. Much, of course, is due to the Allied blockade which has prevented much-needed goods and supplies entering Russia and I do blame the Allied Armies, including the British, for this. We had no business there.'

'There I certainly agree with you.' Rachel replaced her cup in its saucer and got up to stretch her legs, going to the long windows of her sitting-room overlooking St James's Square. Since the death of her husband she had closed most of the house because it was far too big for her needs. Except for young Hugo, whom she kept with her, the children were at school and her mother-in-law scarcely ever left Askham Hall now, the family seat in Wiltshire. She had a small sitting-room and dining-room on the first floor. The sitting-room had formerly been Bosco's study, and there were still mementoes reminding her of him: his pictures on the wall, trophies, relics of his Lancer days and Egypt – crucial for all the families involved, the place where he and she had first met.

There was a picture of Bosco with his brother Arthur at Eton, several other school photos and memorabilia and a very formal, untypical wedding-day photo which was one of the few they had of them together, except for a Holy Family style triptych when Ralph was christened.

The desk she used was Bosco's and the chairs they sat in had been used by him. Here more than anywhere else she was able to recapture the spirit, the feeling of one who had been dead for over five years.

Much of what Mrs Snowden told her was not new to Rachel who, fervent supporter of the Revolution as she was, found it very hard to believe that so much of the criticism she heard was true. Yet Mrs Snowden was a supporter, a fellow believer; so many critics were not. Her evidence, therefore, was all the more crucial, more damning. She had known many of the Bolsheviks who had lived in exile abroad before 1917, and numbered among her many correspondents the noted feminist Alexandra Kollontai, and Inessa Armand who had been the lover of Lenin in exile. Although Rachel was a Socialist and not a Communist she had come, like Alexandra Kollontai before her, to realize that Bolshevism, with its dedicated, almost fanatical adherents, was more likely to obtain results than the many factions of the Socialist Revolutionary parties, including the Mensheviks.

'I must go to Russia for myself,' she said. 'Lenin himself sent me an invitation when I wrote to congratulate him about the success of the Revolution. I think I will go in the summer and take my niece Susan, who would like the change. Maybe my nephew Bobby would come too and see whether he can sell his motor car in Russia.' The decision made, she beamed at Mrs Snowden, noticing her look of surprise. 'Have you not heard about The Askham? The Askham Society and The Askham Super are cars that my nephew is developing in the plant started by my husband, and supported and expanded by Sir Robert Lighterman. He is introducing some entirely new principle of suspension which I confess I don't understand. The Russians were very interested in motor cars before the war.'

'Alas,' Mrs Snowden sighed as she rose to go. 'Our party travelled in a motor belonging to the late Czar. It was a most uncanny experience to think that he, that poor murdered man, had once sat inside with his family.'

'I regret the murder of the Czar and his family, who would not?' Rachel agreed. 'But he was responsible for too many evils and his wife, the Empress Alexandra, actually had an *anti*-feminist movement to encourage women to stay at home and enhance the so-called virtues of being wives and mothers. I feel they should have been given sanctuary abroad but, alas, they were not. It is even hinted that King George did not wish to give them refuge in case their very presence should cause similar unrest in England. I don't know quite what the truth is, but my mother-in-law, who is close to the Royal Family, says...'

Rachel turned as the door suddenly burst open and an urchin of some eight years ran across the room towards her, his arms outstretched, a nurse in hot pursuit.

'Mamma, Mamma,' he cried, as she caught him in her arms and held on to him. 'I found a kitten but Nanny says I must not keep it. I have hidden it in my room.'

'It is full of fleas, Lady Askham,' Nanny said with disapproval. 'Master Hugo found it in the yard outside the kitchen door, where he is overfond of playing.'

'Mamma, it is a *tiny* little scrap of a thing,' Hugo said, his hands contracting to a tiny, imaginary ball, as he gazed at her with the sorrowful wide eyes Rachel remembered when she had first found him, like an abandoned kitten himself, a scrap of a thing playing in the overgrown garden of a run-down house in Brixton. He cupped his hands into a shape that would not be big enough to contain a tennis ball.

Rachel laughed and hugged him, then turned to her guest. 'Forgive this little domestic interlude, Mrs Snowden. I don't think you have met my son Hugo?'

'I don't think I have,' Mrs Snowden said with aplomb, skilfully and diplomatically disguising the fact that all London still speculated about the origin of this last member of the Askham household who joined it somewhat mysteriously after the death of Lord Askham. Needless to say, no one dared ask because had they done so they would probably have been told it was none of their business.

Unkind rumour had once said that he was the child of Lady Askham by an unknown man and her reputation suffered accordingly. Not that it worried Rachel, well known for her unconventional views, her dislike of being addressed as 'Lady Askham' so great that she asked acquaintances in the Labour Party and the feminist movement to call her Mrs Askham. Her radical views made her disdain even being a countess and her dress, deportment and plain speaking were not those associated with a member of the aristocracy, the wife of an earl and now the mother of one.

Mrs Snowden gingerly shook the grubby mitt extended to her by Hugo, who reminded her of some of the poor she met during her good deed forays to the East End of London. He had black curly hair which fell over his impish, rather dirty face, and blackened knees, that had seen a good many falls, above torn socks and scuffed shoes. His jumper, though not threadbare, looked as though it had been handed down from older siblings.

'How do you do, dear?' Mrs Snowden said in the kind of tone she reserved for the destitute. 'I think Nanny should have that kitty back, don't you?'

'Nah.' Hugo's accent was sometimes cultivated from the lesser fry he associated with in the kitchen, and the intriguing men who came to empty the dustbins in the back yard. 'She's not going to find it, either.'

'Come now, Hugo,' Rachel laughed with pleasure, as if completely and blissfully unaware of the unfavourable impression young Hugo, her darling, was making. Indeed, he could scarcely be parted from her and she found it hard to be long away from him. She ruffled his hair. 'Come and let's see Mrs Snowden out and then we'll go and see the pussy.'

'I *know* you'll let me keep it, Mummy,' Hugo said, his face at its most appealing, his tone of voice at its most trustful. 'I *know* you'll love it like I do.'

Rachel smiled and, from the light in her eyes and the way she looked at the child, Mrs Snowden was of the opinion the little boy would have his way. Clearly there was more than a smidgen of truth to the rumours about the Countess of Askham.

As Rachel accompanied the wife of the Labour leader to the door a few minutes later the Askham car drove up and out of it alighted Susan with her charges. As opposed to the tear-filled eyes and mournful countenance of this morning, Susan radiated cheerfulness, and Charlotte and Em tumbled out of the car behind her as if they were still romping in the nursery.

'Mummy, Mummy,' screamed Em, 'did you know that Nancy Lederha . . .' She stopped as she saw the matronly figure of Mrs Snowden on the steps behind her mother. 'Oh.'

'Mrs Snowden, I don't think you've met my daughters Charlotte and Emmeline.' Rachel brought them sharply to a standstill, her expression indulgent as the Labour Party dignitary, graciously thanking the butler who held the door open, followed her hostess down the steps. 'This is Charlotte, my eldest, and this is Emmeline, Freddie's twin. We call her Em. Susan I think you once met at Adam's house?'

'How do you do?' Mrs Snowden smiled and shook hands. 'I can see Charlotte takes after her daddy.'

Inwardly Rachel sighed. Whenever her daughters met someone for the first time Charlotte was always mentioned first. It was true that Charlotte was the eldest, but she was also a beauty, with Bosco's glossy dark chestnut hair, pale face and the blue-green Askham eyes. For a thirteen-year-old she was tall and seemed as mature as a girl of sixteen, and she had the relaxed, graceful manner of a young woman about to be launched on to the world. Em on the other hand looked not a day over twelve – a tall but rather awkward girl carrying too much weight, puppy fat. Like her mother and brother she was fair, her hair thick and wavy, a better texture than Susan's but not as blond as Rachel's. Like Rachel she too had blue eyes, a tilted chin and a snub nose. She looked jolly and was, a mischievous schoolgirl, whereas Charlotte was something quite different, special. Charlotte stood out. The girls exchanged pleasantries with Mrs Snowden, politely saw her to her car, then Em and Charlotte scampered up the stairs in front of their mother while Susan gravely followed behind.

'Enjoy yourselves?'

'Very much. Cold in the park,' Susan said, taking off her gloves and unfastening her muff. 'Lady Lederham's brother

40

was there. He went to the Antarctic with Captain Scott and had a very interesting tale to tell.'

'Well, how would you like to go somewhere cold – to Russia?' Rachel put her arm round Susan's waist, drawing her into the house.

'Russia?' Susan stopped and looked at her aunt. 'How? When?'

'I've been wanting to go ever since the Revolution. I've met many of the leaders, you know, who are now at the top, and Lenin himself has invited me but, of course, the last two years have been very busy for them as well as for me. Now things are settling down and I would like to see for myself. I hear such differing reports. I would also like a companion and as I know how restless you feel you could accompany me, if your mother and father agree. I'm sure they will. But there is a condition.' She looked merrily at Susan who was still staring at her. 'You must take your final exams. You will feel you've achieved something. I know that you will never be poor, but even if you are very rich you will always be glad of the company of the intellect which is without price.'

Susan was about to reply when Rachel heard a chorus from the two girls, who had preceded them, of 'ohs' and 'ahs' and knew what had happened.

'Isn't he *adorable* ...' Charlotte, always tender and loving with animals or humans, who found her naturally sympathetic, reached out for the tiny tabby kitten but Hugo, solemn and wistful, almost like the kitten himself, hugged him even closer.

'Where did you get him?' Em asked, also reaching out, but Hugo refused to yield him, his blackened hands almost completely enclosing his minute charge, and stared at Rachel.

'The dustmen found it in a bin,' Hugo said in a choked voice. 'One of them took pity on it and left it in the yard. If I hadn't found it ...' two large tears made grimy furrows down his face at the very thought. 'Mummy says I must give it up.'

'I never did,' Rachel said indignantly. 'I just wondered ...'

'Oh, Mummy, we *must* keep it,' Charlotte begged, stretching out a tentative hand to stroke it, almost as nervous of possessive Hugo as the kitten. Hugo, close, very close, to Rachel, had his own important niche in the household. Sometimes it made the others jealous. The kitten turned its little head to its saviour, eyes adoring, and emitted a faint but distinctly throaty purr.

'It's called Smokey,' Hugo said, timidly glancing again at Rachel.

'I think "Lucky" would be better.' Charlotte withdrew her hand from the kitten's chin and stroked the thin fur on its back. 'Lucky you found it, or rather the dustmen did. Fancy putting a *kitten* in a bin. Aren't people horrid?'

'But, darling, we don't know where it came from.' Rachel, too, tenderly stroked the tiny head with her index finger. The whole situation, finding the abandoned stray, did remind her of that autumnal day in 1915 when she'd found Hugo at the home of Bosco's former mistress, Nimet, playing alone in the yard in the care of a brothel keeper, his mother having gone home to Cairo and forgotten about him. Yes, she knew they would keep it as she had kept Hugo, though all the family thought her foolish. Maybe Smokey or Lucky, or whatever his name was, would be special to Hugo as Hugo was to her – the best beloved, maybe because he too was unwanted by his mother; not unnaturally subject to the jealousy of her own family, flesh of her flesh. Or maybe the mother had died and somehow given the little kitten life. No one would ever know, as few people knew the truth about Hugo.

As if divining her thoughts Smokey looked up at her with eyes so full of trust, of hope, that she wondered at the power humans had to give affection or withhold it; the power they had at their command.

She realized that the two most concerned about the fate of the kitten, Charlotte and Hugo, were looking expectantly at her, as though by the mere touch of her finger she could cause it to live or die. Her finger moved back and forward over the tiny furry body – even its coat was thin and unkempt beneath the light touch.

'Well, it must be defleaed,' she said at last, 'and Hugo must look after it entirely and be responsible for it, not tire of it and leave it to one of the servants.'

'Oh, Mummy, I won't.' Hugo catapulted himself into her arms, almost dropping his precious charge.

'And then I think you should give it a really important name.' She laughed with pleasure – maybe conscious of her own power to give or withhold love – as Hugo covered her face with wet kisses, almost drowning the sound of her voice.

'Like what, Mummy?'

'Like Lenin, say to give it a start in life.'

'Who's Lenin?'

'He's one of the most important men in the world in many ways,' Rachel said mysteriously, continuing to stroke the tiny scrap. 'And in the summer Susan and I are going to see him.'

CHAPTER 3

Petrograd had been built on marshland at the mouth of a river by Peter the Great as his new capital and, during the eighteenth and nineteenth centuries, as St Petersburg, it was a city of glitter and splendour. Yet it must always have had lowering skies and plenty of rain; and the breeze from the Neva made Rachel draw her cardigan closer round her shoulders. Opposite them the grim fortress of the Petropavlovsk stood like a great stone monolith to cruelty and tyranny. It was here that, within sight of the Winter Palace on the opposite bank, so many of the enemies of successive Czars had been imprisoned, tortured and sometimes murdered. The aristocratic Decembrists, whose ill-fated uprising in St Petersburg's Senate Square in December 1825 has sometimes been called the first Russian Revolution, had been imprisoned there before exile to Siberia. The novelist Dostoievsky had seen the inside of those grim walls and so had the anarchist Prince Kropotkin, as well as Bakunin and Breshskovskaya, the grandmother of the Revolution.

Before going to bed Rachel and Susan were standing on the balcony of the Narishkan Palace, built for the mistress of one of the Czars, and now used by the government to entertain its guests. Rachel and Susan shared a room which was only divided by a thin curtain from a corridor through which people seemed to tramp day and night. Hardly anyone appeared to sleep in Russia. Perhaps it was because there was no nightfall, but whatever the cause there seemed to be endless, perpetual activity unbroken by slumber.

Already they were tired after the rigours of the journey and the frantic pace of the sightseeing since their arrival four days before. It was the Petrograd Soviet which had really started the

Revolution in 1917. For two years Lenin had run it from the Smolny Institute, formerly, incongruously, a school for the daughters of the nobility, before transferring the headquarters of power to Moscow. But there was still plenty to be seen: the Tauride Palace, the home of the Duma, an assembly which attempted, without avail, to temper the power of the Czar before the Revolution; the beautiful Winter Palace and, next door, the huge Admiralty building with a frontage on the Neva for nearly half a mile. An hour's train ride over flat, grey country with sand dunes and a sprinkling of silver birches took the visitor to Tsarkoe Selo, literally Czar's village, where the Autocrat of all the Russias had lived in privileged seclusion with his family and entourage. The small Alexander Palace was kept in the same state as it had been before the Czar and his family left it for the last time in 1918 for Ekaterinberg.

In the Smolny Institute, and little bigger than a monk's cell, was the room where Lenin had lived and worked. It was preserved as he'd left it in 1919 with its white-grey walls, a deal wardrobe and two iron bedsteads for Lenin and his wife, Krupskaya.

But, despite shades of its former magnificence, the overall impression of Petrograd was of decay and desolation. It was not only that the War had several times threatened to overwhelm it by the sheer physical presence of the enemy on its outskirts – the forces of Yudenich were repulsed by the heroic effort of the Petrograd Soviet – but it appeared as a city without life; its streets dirty and deserted except for the shiftless masses of the inhabitants, reduced from two million before the war to a mere five hundred thousand. The bright shops that altered the face of devastated post-war Europe were missing in Petrograd, where everything was under the control of the government; and the few street traders who hastily tried to dispose of or barter goods were under constant threat by the authorities.

'There is so much contradiction here ...' Rachel voiced her

thoughts aloud, tucking her hand through Susan's arm. 'I hardly know where to begin my despatches.'

But Susan was enthusiastic. Everything she'd seen she'd approved of, except the people shuffling through the street with felt tied round their feet instead of shoes. In fact the Russians seemed obsessed by shoes and gazed at the extremities of visitors as if envying their well-shod feet. Once they'd passed a woman wearing a sable coat with her feet bound with felt. Everywhere in Russia there was a shortage not only of shoes but of consumer goods of all kinds and, of course, there was the terrible shortage of food that in parts of the country had reached famine-like proportions with thousands, some said millions, dying of starvation.

If there were certain things Susan didn't like – and no one liked poverty or hunger – she put it down to the blockade of Russia by Britain and its allies, the costly war against the Poles. She found little to blame in the Russian people or their rulers; but laid everything at the door of hostile outside forces. In her enthusiasm she was becoming more left-wing than her aunt who, as Mrs Snowden before her, had reservations.

'I believe you're becoming a true Bolshevik, Susan!' Rachel said, when Susan had finished telling her aunt where exactly to begin her despatches: the contrast between the old regime and the new, the freedom of the working class, previously oppressed by the Czar, the universality of education, the opportunities for people of all kinds, not just a privileged few.

'I want to agree with you,' Rachel said, squeezing her hand, laughing at her happy, transformed face. 'But it's hard. The people don't *look* happy; there is such gloom, such an atmosphere of deprivation ...'

'But, Aunt, the Russians have been fighting a war for seven years, not only against external forces, first the Germans, now us and the Poles, but a civil war too. The country has undergone a revolution of one hundred degrees. It has been turned right on its axis. It will take years and years to sort it all out.'

46

Rachel looked at her quizzically, noting how the experience of travel and seeing new sights, perhaps being far enough away from the family disharmony at home, had changed Susan from a discontented frump to an outwardly happy, vivacious girl in such a short time.

In fact, if anything, the transformation in Susan was the more remarkable because it had affected her looks. She glowed with vitality, her blue, intelligent eyes mirroring a new-found contentment with herself and all she saw around her. She was no longer gauche and pasty-faced, awkward with men and given to blushing easily; no longer spotty and self-conscious, wanting to hide behind people all the time. Susan seemed to have cut herself off, in a very short time, from all that had been holding her back, inhibiting her: in a few brief weeks she had become a woman.

'And do you really think it was worth it, all this upheaval?' Rachel made an expansive gesture towards the river which took in the entire city, maybe the whole country.

'Yes, I do, and so should you. I think you do in your heart, Aunt,' Susan said almost sternly. 'It's the Askham in you that makes you doubtful.'

'I haven't any Askham in me at all!' Rachel protested. 'I was born a Bolingbroke, like you. *You* are more Askham than I am.'

'I have rejected everything that Askham stands for, you know that. I don't mean I reject Mummy or Gran, or Uncle Bosco or my cousins, not as *people*. But I reject the theory of a landowning, inherited, privileged aristocracy and here in Russia they've done away with all that, and I don't think it will ever come back.'

'But they have done away with it very cruelly, Susan,' Rachel said quietly, as a man came up to them and stood to one side apparently listening. She thought how very radical, and positive, Susan had become in such a short time. In rejecting the family was she embracing a new faith? 'Former aristocrats are not only classed as "deprived persons" and given the most meagre rations. Their children, who are entirely blameless, are treated in the same way, deprived of a proper education, ejected from their houses ...'

'That's not entirely true, Mrs Askham.' The man emerged from the shadows and smiled. 'I hope you don't mind me eavesdropping but, like you, I am interested to know the truth.'

'And you don't think that's true, Mr Foster?'

'No, it isn't. I hear that Princess Narishkan, to whom this house belongs, still lives here and is doing good work for the Soviets.'

'*Only* if they throw in their lot with the government.' Rachel was glad that this member of their party, a quiet self-effacing man from Preston in Lancashire, had not heard their conversation about the Askhams. At least she hoped he hadn't, because she preferred to travel as 'Mrs Askham' and would have hated the truth to be known by their party of tourists. 'I assure you I am against cruelty of any kind, Mr Foster, whether to the poor or the formerly rich, especially to their children.'

'Did you talk to Kyril?' Mr Foster leaned against the balcony, his eyes on the grim Peter and Paul Fortress. 'I believe his family was a noble one.'

'Kyril Ferov?' Susan's voice was interested.

'Yes, our guide, and a dedicated Communist. I've heard his father was a prince. Do you know, Mrs Askham?'

Rachel shook her head. 'He seems a very nice, knowledge-able young man. I must ask him.'

'Oh, be very careful. He doesn't talk about it. Someone else told me. But I understand that he still uses the family house in Moscow. It may be interesting to quiz him if the subject comes up.'

'It's very late,' Rachel looked at her watch, 'and tomorrow we are to visit the Putilov Works, and some of the educational experiments on the outskirts of Petrograd.'

'When will you start writing your articles, Mrs Askham?'

48

'I think on the train to Moscow,' Rachel replied, wondering why he was so interested, 'or maybe before, if we get a moment. Good night, Mr Foster. Coming, Susan?'

'Yes, Aunt.' Susan smiled at Mr Foster, excusing themselves, and they both bade him good night and went inside.

'I think he likes *you*,' Susan whispered later as they lay in their beds pulled close together in a corner of what had once been a gracious salon. There were no curtains at the windows and the daylight of this curious Russian night made it hard to sleep. Yet the beds were comfortable, the sheets clean and the furniture, or what was left of it, good enough to have graced an Askham drawing-room. Rachel had been lying thinking about the contrasts between Russia and England, and what it all meant, when Susan spoke.

'Who?'

'Mr Foster.'

Rachel glanced across at her niece. 'What do you mean, *likes* me?'

'Well, likes you. He follows you around. Do you imagine he might be a spy?'

'Don't be absurd! What is there to spy on?'

'The members of our party might not know you're a countess, but the Russian authorities do. They must be very anxious to know whether you're going to try and smuggle former aristocrats out of the country.'

'I don't know any. I thought, anyway, that all those who could go had gone, and the rest stayed either because they wanted to or had to.'

'Would you help anyone leave the country if they asked you?'

'How could I? I might try, if I thought their case was bad enough, but I have no influence at all.'

'You do think, though, that the Party has treated them badly, don't you?'

'I don't like the category "deprived person" for anyone,' Rachel replied. 'They used to use such terms to discriminate

49

against the Jews. Now it is used for former aristocrats and others who have offended the Party. I'm reminded terribly of the French Revolution.'

'You're much more critical than I thought you would be, Aunt,' Susan murmured. 'You surprise me.' Her voice was already sleepy and Rachel, knowing her niece was on the verge of sleep, was silent. Susan had thrown herself so vigorously into everything that she would soon burn up all her nervous energy and then Melanie, who had been reluctant to let her go, would be annoyed with her if a pale, nervous, over-excited girl – to say nothing of one with Bolshevist sympathies – returned home. Would this transformation last?

But Rachel couldn't sleep. The light from the window, the noise of people continually passing on the other side of the flimsy curtain (where to? what for?) disturbed her. Besides, she was restless; the contradictions of Russia almost a torment to her neat, analytical mind anxious for facts. She, too, was also conscious of the presence of Mr Foster, always hovering, never far from her; but the thought that he might be a spy had never occurred to her.

At breakfast the following morning Mr Foster slid into the seat beside Rachel as she came down well before the others, having left Susan to sleep. If the Russians went to bed late they seemed to rise late too, and breakfast was from 9.30 onwards.

'Did you sleep well, Mrs Askham?' Mr Foster drew towards him a basket of black bread and offered it to her.

'No, I didn't. I can't get used to the light at night, and the people coming and going. Have you a room to yourself?'

'No, I share it with Kyril and two other members of the delegation, Mr Mars and Mr Barton. Very few people in Russia, apart from high Party members, have a room to themselves.'

'The Party members have become the new aristocracy.' Rachel began to spread on her bread some of the precious butter which few of the 150 million Soviet people could obtain.

A dignified servant hovered behind them who looked as though he might have been butler to the Prince Narishkan, and now served them with tea drawn from a large samovar into glasses.

'Not all of them, some of them only. You will always have some people who abuse the system, but you can be sure that in this equitable society they will be caught and dealt with.'

'And you approve of that too, I suppose?' Rachel placed a piece of smoked herring on her bread and butter and brought it to her lips. 'And the Extraordinary Commission which has taken the place of the Okhrana?'

'Oh the Cheka is nothing like that. Its purpose is not terror, but to stop the spread of counter-revolutionary ideas and practices. Whenever you have a revolution you have people who try and overthrow it. The Bolsheviks are determined not to let that happen. Lenin has said that they must rob the robbers, and they do and will!'

Mr Foster spoke with a fervour which disturbed Rachel, who listened to him raptly, her breakfast still in her hand. He was a tall, not unpresentable man of, she thought, about thirty-five, with a head of very thick, untidy brown hair which lacked the ministrations of a good barber, and a large untrimmed moustache. He looked slightly Slav himself, had piercing black eyes, and spoke with a northern accent. Usually he stood at the back of a group listening carefully to what was being said, asking few questions and saying little. He had more to say this breakfast time than at any time during the days she had known him; on the boat during the journey out to Reval, and on the train to Petrograd. She didn't know what he did except that most of the members of the party were either newsmen or women, or supporters of the British Labour Movement.

'Are you a Communist, Mr Foster?' Rachel carefully took a bite of her bread spread with herring and looked at him while she chewed it.

'I am not a Communist, Mrs Askham, but I am *very* sympathetic to the Russian Revolution. I was thrilled when it happened and I have remained impressed by the rise of the Bolsheviks and their achievements.'

'Including the way they seized power?'

'How do you mean, Mrs Askham?'

'By eliminating all their rivals? Ruthless suppression of all other revolutionary parties including the Anarchists and the Mensheviks. It was scarcely democratic. The more I learn the less, I confess, I like it.'

'But there were too many of these factions. They were all quarrelling helplessly with one another. If Lenin and Trotsky had not been firm the Whites would soon have been back in power.'

Mr Foster put a large piece of cheese on his bread and crammed both into his mouth. Then he took a gulp of tea as if to wash it down, an act which Rachel, despite her egalitarian instincts, could not help associating with the working classes. Maybe her unwitting disapproval registered on her face because Mr Foster gazed stonily at her, smiled and wiped his mouth on the back of his hand.

Rachel looked away, feeling ashamed of herself. She considered herself a Socialist; if not of the working class then in sympathy with them, the industrious poor. Yet her instincts were like those of her mother-in-law who had in her mind a series of little mental images of niches into which people fitted: working class, lower middle class (a terrible category this, the most despised of all), middle class, gentry or upper middle class, professional people, the untitled wealthy and, finally and most importantly, the aristocracy. She considered too that Mr Foster, for some reason or the other, liked provoking her and was doing so deliberately.

The dining-room was now full of other people also enjoying, regardless of cost, the hospitality of the State while the rest of Russia went without or starved; with inadequate accommodation, poor food or none at all and without the means to buy more. They were whisked around in cars while the ordinary Russian walked in his threadbare footwear, or travelled in the overcrowded trams or trains, always provided he or she could get a *propusk* – a permit. From the moment she had set foot in Russia, carried there in the special carriage for the delegates on a train bursting to the seams, she had been aware of this privilege. It was said that people stayed for days on railway stations hoping to board trains which ran infrequently and seldom on time. Many of those who succeeded in getting aboard, and then managed to find room on the roof of the train, were subsequently killed when the train rushed under a bridge which knocked them off. No one missed them except, maybe, a few relations who would never know what happened. People disappeared all the time. The overall impression of Russia was of a society which completely lacked compassion.

Like Mrs Snowden, however, Rachel too had travelled in one of the cars that had once belonged to the Czar, and she slept in beds the luxury of which few ordinary Russians knew.

Mr Foster was munching his breakfast happily while Rachel conducted this internal dialogue with herself when Susan came in with Kyril, the young Communist they had mentioned the night before.

He was a man of about twenty-five with an open, good-natured face, sunburnt from time spent in Odessa and places on the Black Sea with another delegation. He had sandy-coloured hair, blue eyes and he spoke very good English, a sign that he had been well educated and, thus, that he probably came from a wealthy or a noble household, because before the Revolution few of the working class or peasants went to school. He was of medium height and rather thick-set, of athletic build; his face was marked by a childhood scar, but still he was an attractive man. As they came in he and Susan joined together in laughter at some shared joke or comment they had found amusing.

'I think our young Communist friend likes your niece very much, Mrs Askham.'

'Maybe that's because there are so few young people in our

party,' Rachel commented, sipping her hot sweet tea served without milk, an almost priceless commodity in the city.

'Still, there is an attraction. Haven't you noticed it?'

'My niece is only eighteen,' Rachel said indignantly, conscious of sounding like her mother-in-law again; how strange it was to emulate so easily qualities one despised. So many things were changing on this visit – opinions and attitudes, previously cherished, were being turned on their heads.

'Still, she can like men, and they can like her.'

Mr Foster looked at her quizzically. He was interrupted by an excited Susan: 'Kyril says that when we come back from the tour today we are going to a reception at the Winter Palace given by the Petrograd Soviet.' Susan took the seat next to Rachel, which happened to be vacant, and seized her aunt's hand. Kyril sat opposite them, his face beaming with good-natured pleasure.

'I tell you we eat very well at these dinners. They are worth a year's rations to some people.'

Rachel was aware of Spencer Foster looking at her, but she made no comment except to the effect that it would all be very enjoyable. Then she excused herself to go upstairs to get ready for the rigours of the day.

That day and the days that followed were very rigorous indeed, and there seemed no end to them. An energetic tour of a factory, a nursery school, a home for crippled children and one for old people, would be followed by a banquet in the Winter Palace, a reception at the newly converted Assembly Rooms, or a concert at the Opera House where the British visitors were carefully displayed to the audience who rose to clap and greet them as they took their places in the boxes. Rachel was very conscious of the propaganda use to the Russians of the English delegation; and sometimes she was at pains to try and correct the false impression that they all approved everything done by the regime. But it was of little avail. Too many of the visitors were anxious to please their generous hosts by effusive words of praise, and little that she said or even wanted to say could counteract it.

During the days that followed Mr Foster's observation about the attraction between Susan and Kyril, Rachel came to realize that there was something in what he said. They seemed now to have split into two couples: Susan who was always with Kyril, and Rachel trailed by Spencer Foster. His presence was not unwelcome. He was unobtrusive and, on occasions, very knowledgeable. It transpired he was a trades union official from Manchester, a well-read, cultured man who was able to discourse about a performance of Gluck's *Orpheus* they saw at the Petrograd Opera. He was a lover of Arnold Bennett, an admirer of H. G. Wells, an activist who had thought hard about his commitment to socialism. He was altogether a charming and vigorous man, one not completely uncritical about what he saw in Russia. However, for all its faults, he was inclined to think that the Revolution was a good thing and, up to a point, Rachel agreed with him.

After ten days in Petrograd and trips to places around it they took a train for Moscow where they arrived after thirteen hours to find there was a problem of accommodation. Their visit coincided with the two congresses: The Third Congress of the Third International, to which some of their party were delegates; and the First Congress of the Red Trades Union International to which Spencer Foster was going as an observer. All the official delegates and observers had been quartered in the Hotel de Luxe which had been renovated as a foreign guest house, or the Hotel Delavoy Dvor in which Mrs Snowden had stayed the previous year and complained about bed bugs. The Hotel National, known as the First House of the Moscow Soviet, was also bulging at the seams, and Kyril spent the morning after their arrival bustling about to try and find accommodation for Rachel and Susan, a Mrs Gibson, who was a member of the Society of Friends trying to discover how much aid the Russians needed, and a Miss Rostron, a Baptist bent on discovering the official position of God in that atheistic regime. In addition there were a Mr and Mrs Tuke who were lifelong Socialists and supporters of the suffrage, and were the only people on the trip Rachel had known previously. She'd asked them to refer to her as Mrs Askham, a measure they approved of and with which they heartily concurred.

They all spent the morning waiting patiently by their bags at the station which resembled a football ground milling with people who were coming or going, or hanging about. Rachel noticed a lot of military in evidence, or men dressed in leather suits with guns in their belts who she was told were members of the Cheka. They wove in and out among the crowds, the would-be travellers patiently waiting for trains, checking permits, and twice they approached the English party, none of whom could speak a word of Russian. Spencer Foster had reluctantly been swept off to his hotel, promising to get in touch with Rachel as soon as he knew where she was. But Rachel felt no fear or alarm at their wait as she chatted to Mr and Mrs Tuke or tried to cheer up poor Miss Rostron who had seemed to benefit little so far from their tour, and kept on talking about her wish to return home. She was a slight woman of about forty-five, her fair hair always covered by a hat, even on the most informal of occasions. She did not accompany the party on all the excursions they made, and was said to spend a lot of time in what space she could find to be alone writing home to her parents and reading the Bible. Mrs Gibson, on the other hand, was a large robust lady who seemed to be undergoing a slow, albeit reluctant, conversion to the principles governing the Communist society, so impressed had she been by all that was seen – the schools, the nurseries, the crèches, homes for the elderly and so on. Rachel had warned her not to take everything she saw as typical of the true state of things in Russia, reminding her of the model villages which Potemkin had built solely in order to impress his empress, Catherine the Great, that all was well in her empire.

At just after noon Kyril returned waving a piece of paper. 'I have found accommodation for Mr and Mrs Tuke at the National, there is an unexpected vacancy as someone is ill. For you, Mrs Askham, Miss Bolingbroke and the two ladies I can only offer you a very inadequate room, though it is a roof over your head, where I live. There is a very large bedroom which, if you don't mind, you could all share.'

'I, for one, am relieved to be with Mrs Askham.' Miss Rostron, who had seemed at times close to tears, clutched Rachel's arm.

'I don't care where I am as long as I don't spend the next week on a railway station.' Mrs Gibson thankfully mopped her brow and looked expectantly at Kyril who summoned a porter, then helped him carry the heavier bags to a droshky waiting outside.

'I thought you'd like to see Moscow from a cab,' Kyril said, giving the driver instructions. 'Anyway, all the motor cars seem to have been commandeered by the official delegates.'

'This is lovely.' Rachel got into the horse-drawn carriage with Mr and Mrs Tuke while Kyril summoned a second which he got into with Susan and the other two ladies. Then he pointed to the driver who, flicking his whip, turned his horse to lead the way.

The first thing that Rachel noticed was that the people in Moscow seemed more cheerful, better fed than those in Petrograd. The streets were full and everyone seemed to have a purpose as they busily made their way along. There were the usual felt-covered feet and drab clothes; but there was a vitality to Moscow lacking in the former capital city of the Czars. And whereas Petrograd looked like a city which had barely survived a hurricane, the low buildings which lined the streets of Moscow were painted in soft colours while everywhere, above the roofs, rose the blue and gold domes of the hundreds of churches for which the city was famous.

One very strange phenomenon, with which they were familiar after Petrograd, was the absence of shops, all of which were boarded up, except for a few co-operative stores managed by the government, outside which stretched seemingly endless queues. Over the disused shopfronts were the signs of what they had formerly stocked in the days of free enterprise: a string of sausages on one, on another cakes and biscuits, a third, fourth and fifth had hand-painted signs depicting a gun, a bullock or a tall black hat, most of these lines only dimly visible now since the shops had been closed by the Revolution years before. What would happen to all these empty shops now, Rachel wondered? Would they be razed to the ground to provide much-needed homes for the dispossessed peasants who had flocked to the city to join the urban proletariat?

Droshkies passed them and, here and there, large limousines containing important officials of the Party or the visiting delegations swept past, sending up clouds of dust. They turned into a thoroughfare even more crowded than the narrow streets they had left, also flanked with boarded-up shops, many of which seemed to be undergoing the demolition Rachel had wondered about.

'This is Tverskaya Street!' Kyril called cheerily from the droshky in front. 'It is one of the main thoroughfares of Moscow. It is like your Regent or Oxford Street.'

'I didn't know he'd been to England.' Rachel looked at the Tukes with interest.

'He said he was there as a boy with his father.' Mr Tuke was attempting to light a cigarette as the carriage bowled along. 'I pressed him but he wouldn't elaborate. I don't think he cared to.'

'There's something funny about that young man,' Mrs Tuke said guardedly. In Russia one learned to watch one's words, even in the open. 'He's not like a worker, if you ask me.'

'I heard he was a prince,' Rachel smiled. 'Could it be true?'

'If he was a prince he wouldn't be here.' Mr Tuke made a grim gesture with his finger across his throat.

'I thought they shot them,' Rachel also looked grim. 'Or "deprived" them.'

58

'Oh, they don't shoot them.' The Socialist Mr Tuke, a convinced fellow traveller, was appalled at the very idea. 'I have heard there is no capital punishment in Soviet Russia.'

'But still, I've heard there is a lot of killing ...' Rachel began as Mr Tuke frowned; but what she was going to say was drowned by the cries of Kyril who was excitedly gesticulating ahead. As Rachel looked up she saw a two-way arch and over each passage was a pointed tower. Between them stood a church and, as they approached the passage and the view widened, a sight at once recognizable and yet unexpectedly spectacular confronted the eyes of the droshky's passengers. The bulbs, domes, pinnacles and turrets of the Kremlin with its high battlements – notched in the shape of swallows' tails – rose around them like some graphic realization of pictures from story books. Red Square lay before them and they crossed it slowly, gazing wonderingly at the sight of that colossal fortress, nearly eight hundred years old. Beyond it rose a number of great asymmetrical domes clearly identifiable as the Cathedral of St Basil, built by Ivan the Terrible to commemorate the conquest of Kazan. He is said to have gouged out the eyes of the principal architect so that he should not build another like it.

The Russian for Red Square, *Krasnaya ploshchad*, can also be translated as 'the beautiful square' and, indeed, the view was so awe-inspiring that they were still gazing behind them when the droshkies passed the Arsenal, then went through the Nikolski Gate and turned into Nikolskaya Street, which was one of the three main streets of the Kitai Gorod (literally Chinese City), the oldest part of Moscow. Abruptly they turned off into a quiet square where eighteenth-century buildings flanked a magnificent house set in its own garden which occupied an entire side of the square.

The iron gates to the house stood wide open; there was an air of bustle in the courtyard while from many of the open windows hung bedclothes or items of washing. It was a strangely incongruous sight, this palatial house which had yet

59

managed to lose its obvious exclusivity while retaining its grandeur, and even stranger to be taken through the gates by the droshky and deposited at the grand door which was open.

'We call this the ninth house of the Moscow Soviet,' Kyril explained. 'It was formerly the Ferov Palace and is where I live. It belonged to my family, and now my Aunt Varvara and I share it with many other people, as you can see.'

Smilingly, without apparent rancour, he gesticulated towards the many windows, from some of which appeared curious faces. When one of them looked to see what was going on he raised a hand and waved, calling back in Russian.

'Is that a relation too?' Rachel enquired as he helped her down from the carriage.

'No, he is a student at the university. We have many students here because the university is not far away. We have students and workers, people of all kinds. That is what Communism is about.' Kyril looked at her gravely as though he was aware of her doubts. Indeed publicly she often voiced them, to a critical reception from the converted who formed the majority of her group. 'We have no barriers at all now and we gladly welcome the members of the proletariat to share our house with us. Anyway, it no longer belongs to us, but to the State and I had to have permission to bring you here. Come and meet my Aunt Varvara. She will be delighted to see you, and the others too.'

His expression as he looked at them was kind, welcoming, and as he stood back, gesturing for them to precede him into the house, one could sense that, still, he felt himself the host.

In the years since she had married the heir to the Earldom of Askham, Rachel had seen the interior of many fine houses, not only in England but in France, Italy and, before the War, in Germany and Austria too. The English aristocracy tended to extend its branches as the Askhams had over the centuries; and there were cousins, aunts and uncles in most European countries. But, although the links between England and Russia were close before the War because the English and Russian

Royal Families were related, and many English made their homes in Moscow and St Petersburg, while many well-bred young women had come as nannies and governesses to the Russian nobility, Rachel had never been there before. She had missed the pre-war delights of Moscow and St Petersburg and now would never know them although, not long before she left England, Asquith had called Bolshevism 'a passing phase'. From what she had seen so far in Russia his pious hope was unjustified.

Thus, although Rachel had visited many of the grand homes in England and on the Continent she was hard put to name a building finer than the old Ferov Palace as she entered the massive entrance hall which, by some clever architectural feat, towered to the roof of the four-storeyed house, each floor arranged around the central staircase. Each storey had a rectangular balcony which overlooked the hall, and over which several pairs of heads were peering curiously down on them.

Once again Kyril looked up and waved in friendly fashion, just like the master of the house, before opening a door that led off the hall and conducting them along a corridor towards what once must have been the dining-room, or perhaps a drawing-room, overlooking the gardens.

'This room was occupied by a family who went to Odessa as one of the children was consumptive. You can see how compassionately the Soviet State looks after those in need. Previously the child would have died in some Moscow slum; now she is sent to a sanatorium on the Black Sea and her family with her.' Proudly he flung open the door and the four women saw a large, pleasant room that obviously once had been a study or lounge, but now contained six neatly made-up beds, a scrap of rug on the floor and a solitary, naked electric light bulb. There were two chests of drawers and one or two chairs which looked none too solid. It was the kind of accommodation they had come to expect in what they had seen so far of Soviet Russia, yet it was slightly more private than the Narishkan Palace in Petrograd.

'This *is* lovely.' Susan, reverting to schoolgirl behaviour, jumped up and down on one of the beds. 'Oops,' she cried as the bed creaked and sagged dangerously at one corner.

'You just be careful,' Kyril laughed, catching her hand, and holding on to it. 'These beds come from one of the barracks and have had much wear and tear from the heavy bodies of soldiers sleeping on them. We are lucky to have them at all.'

'How many people are there here?' Rachel enquired.

'In this house? About one hundred people. Don't forget when my family lived here they had up to fifty or so servants, and managed themselves to live in considerable comfort.'

'Don't you miss it?' Miss Rostron asked suddenly, looking at him with her pink-tinged, short-sighted eyes. Slowly, wearily, she sank on to one of the chairs. Despite the comfort of their apartment in the train she had not slept and felt tired.

'Miss what?' Kyril was about to light a cigarette, then looked round and changed his mind. His impeccable manners, his thoughtfulness for others, had been something that Rachel noted from the first day he became their guide.

'Living here with your family in the style you were accustomed to.'

'I miss my family, but the life they lived was doomed. As a boy I knew it was wrong and ... but I must not linger. I have to take Mr and Mrs Tuke to the National. I'll introduce you to my aunt and she will show you around. In the basement where the old kitchens were we have cooking facilities so that all those who live here can look after themselves. You will find it a struggle, as everyone wants to get first to the stove, but I am sure on many evenings you will be officially entertained. I already bring apologies from one of our senior comrades, Zinoviev, for putting you here instead of at the National or the Luxe.'

'I like it better here,' Mrs Gibson said firmly, sitting on a bed and easing off a shoe. 'Oh, my poor feet. I'm going to have a sleep, if no one minds. I didn't sleep a wink in the train, and it is all so different and exciting.'

'I'm going to sleep too.' Miss Rostron looked carefully around her, as though judging which bed was the most comfortable.

'*I'm* not going to sleep!' Susan protested. 'May I not come with you, Kyril?'

Kyril glanced at Rachel, who said: 'I think you had better let Kyril get on with his work, Susan, or he'll be expelled from the Party.'

'I'll see you here tonight, anyway,' Kyril answered. 'I'll bring you your rations. You're entitled to them as a guest of the Moscow Soviet. I'll see if I can get some white bread and a little meat and we'll have a feast. Come and meet Aunt Varvara.'

Leaving the other ladies in the room Rachel and Susan followed Kyril along the corridor back into the huge hall where they bade farewell to the Tukes. Then they mounted the vast marble staircase. It was embellished with beautifully carved motifs, and on the wall were the clear outlines of where large paintings had formerly hung. The top of the roof was made of frosted glass, and so the whole aspect of the house was one of light.

'Some of the pictures were by great artists and have been taken to safe-keeping. The mob stormed this house in the Revolution because the quarters where the Czar's servants lived, the Khamovniki district, is not far away.'

'Where were you when this happened?'

'I'll tell you later over dinner,' Kyril replied as they reached the broad landing, pausing to greet a young couple on the way who had come out of a room, leaving the door partly ajar. Rachel looked in and saw a scene very similar to the one downstairs, a number of functional bunk beds with the bedclothes rather disordered. She realized that the very young man and woman had come out of the same room.

'Do men and women share the same bedroom?' she asked, as they followed Kyril along another labyrinthine corridor.

'Only if they're in the same family.' Kyril looked over his shoulder and smiled. 'Or, rather, officially that's the case. Truthfully, no one checks. Here's my aunt.'

Reaching the end of the passage he knocked softly on a door and led them into a room that retained some of the elements of its former graciousness. It was a sitting-room with comfortable, well-upholstered chairs, polished tables, a heavily draped mantel with pictures and candlesticks over an empty grate. A stately-looking woman sat at an *escritoire* in the corner and, removing a pince-nez, came over to greet them, her hand extended. Aged about sixty, she was beautifully dressed in a silken afternoon frock that would not have currently disgraced a London drawing-room in the height of the season. On her feet were high-heeled shoes with a strap fastened by a small gold buckle, and her greying black hair was softly and fashionably waved.

'This is my Aunt Varvara Valkova, formerly Countess Valkova. She is my father's sister and we have shared this apartment since the Revolution. Aunt, Mrs Askham and her niece Susan …'

'Of whom Kyril has talked so much.' The Countess Valkova gazed at Susan with a knowing smile and then shook Rachel's hand. 'I believe you are an activist who runs a newspaper, Mrs Askham? That is excellent, a sympathizer with our cause, no doubt?'

Rachel was so dumbfounded by the whole scene, which seemed to contradict so much of what she knew and expected, that a few seconds passed before she could reply. Like Kyril the Countess spoke perfect, hardly accented English, and indeed she looked like an Englishwoman with her open, friendly, slightly horsey face, her beautifully coiffured hair.

'I am certainly very *interested* in what I have seen in Russia,' Rachel began cautiously. 'And, yes, I do own and run a newspaper, *The Sentinel*, which is sympathetic to socialism and feminism … but Communism is only a very tiny element in the politics of our country. I would not call myself a Communist.'

'We must change that!' Varvara Valkova looked as though she was about to hug her, and then changed her mind as she saw her nephew's expression. 'Kyril, must you not be off? Try not to be late for dinner. And don't worry about extra rations. I have plenty, except a little real coffee. If you could get some, that would be very nice. Now, why not take Miss Bolingbroke with you? I'm sure she would like to see inside the Kremlin where the Third International is being held.'

'Oh, I'd love that.' Susan's face went pink with pleasure. 'Is it all right, Kyril? May I, Aunt?'

'I suppose so, if you're not in the way.' Rachel was doubtful.

'I'll be very good. Maybe I'll see Lenin!'

'Maybe you will,' Varvara Valkova laughed. 'And maybe you won't. He is a very, very busy man and even we, who are his friends, scarcely ever get near him.'

'*You're* a *friend* of Lenin?' Susan looked impressed.

'And Trotsky, Zinoviev, Bukharin, Stalin ... well, not so much of Stalin perhaps.' Varvara's face clouded for a moment. 'But we did help to bring Lenin from Germany! Yes, it was my brother Vladimir, not Kyril's father, who went to Germany for secret negotiations and travelled with him in the sealed train. Off you go now, young people, enjoy yourselves!'

As Rachel doubtfully watched them leave the room Varvara pointed to a chair.

'Do sit down, Mrs Askham. Do you smoke?' She held out a silver cigarette case but Rachel shook her head. 'You don't mind if I do?' The Countess selected a cigarette and raised it to her lips with beautifully manicured fingers, lighting it with a silver lighter. Then she sat opposite Rachel and smiled. 'I can see you're very surprised. Shocked, maybe?'

'I thought all former aristocrats were either in exile, in prison or living in poverty, forced to beg on the streets ...'

Varvara gave a silvery laugh, blowing smoke into the air. She may have had Bolshevik views, but her features were decidedly aristocratic, with hooded eyes of a brilliant blue, a thin, haughty nose and a rather long upper lip. She had

65

probably never been beautiful or even very good-looking, but was now a handsome, imposing woman.

'Only those who deserve to be! Oh yes, Mrs Askham, the Revolution was their fault, make no mistake. Or rather, it was not the fault of *all* the aristocrats. My brother Vladimir and I, and several members of our family, have been anti-Czarist for years. One of our ancestors was a Decembrist, so revolutionary ideas are in the family. They are mostly on the Ferov side. Alas, my husband and his family were incurable monarchists.'

'And where is your husband now, may I ask?'

'Certainly you may. The answer is I have no idea. We are divorced and my only son died in infancy. My husband, I know, fought with Yudenich and then Wrangel and I think left with one of the last Allied boats to leave Odessa. Either that or he may be dead. But the Ferovs were very active against the Czar and a cousin of ours, Prince Boris Ferov, was shot by the Czar's secret police.' She made the announcement as one who was retailing something of which she was particularly proud. 'But Prince Alexei Ferov, Kyril's father ...' she raised a hand in a gesture of contempt and let it flop against her bosom. '*He* was an arch-Czarist. He was aide-de-camp to the Czar Nicholas, and our father was chamberlain to Nicholas's father Alexander! It gave me particular pleasure to move into the Ferov Palace after Alexei and his family left and turn it into a Soviet home for the workers. We have made a nice job of it, don't you think?'

'Excellent.' Rachel nodded. 'But I haven't seen it all.'

'We must remedy that!' Varvara Valkova stubbed her cigarette out vigorously and rose, taking hold of Rachel's arm as she too got up, and steering her to the door. 'We were given the contents of an army barracks when their old beds were replaced by new ones and we can sleep here about 100 to 150 people, more if it is winter and very cold. They have beds, clean linen, a room where they can gather for meetings, a social room where they can dance, and a court in the garden where they can play tennis. This is all paid for by the State, which owns the house. I offered my services to the government, but my dear friend and comrade, Lenin, asked me to stay here and also help to turn other houses belonging to the former nobility into homes for the workers. He said it was the best way I could help the State; the way I could best repay it for the sins of my family. He knew I was entirely blameless, but my husband was shamelessly a White Russian and I had to redeem myself, don't you see?' She opened a door that led into a long corridor. 'Naturally, I would have preferred a more important post like some of our women have been given. Alexandra Kollontai is so active on the women's commission but, of course, I never had her gifts.' Rachel thought the countess looked a little bitter. 'However, she has fallen foul of our beloved leader, Vladimir Ilich, by speaking out against his New Economic Policy at the Second International Conference of Communist Women in June. All our leaders were on the platform and I am glad to say that she got not one whisper of applause at the end. But then it is hard to take very seriously a woman who marries a much younger man, is it not?' Her tone was waspish, even malevolent.

'Who did she marry?' Rachel asked curiously. 'I once had the pleasure of meeting Madame Kollontai in London, but know nothing of her private life.'

'She married a sailor, Dybenko, *seventeen* years her junior. Imagine that! He has now been sent to the Crimea as Commander-in-Chief of the Western Black Sea Coast. Many say he is flagrantly unfaithful to her.' Countess Valkova beamed with satisfaction.

'She's someone I would much like to meet again.' Rachel ignored the hint of spite and gazed with approval at the long room into which Varvara led her, overlooking the palace gardens. It was comfortably furnished with deep chairs, polished tables piled with newspapers, and family portraits still hung on the walls. In one or two of them Rachel fancied she could see a likeness to Kyril.

'I will try and arrange it for you. I have access to all the high Party members. Why don't you stay a few months with us, Mrs Askham, and learn about Soviet Russia? The American Louise Bryant has been among us for some time and Emma Goldman, the American Anarchist, has served on an important commission. We have many foreign sympathizers with our cause. You'd be surprised.'

'I have a family *and* my newspaper,' Rachel perched on the arm of a chair and smiled at this odd woman who, somehow, did not convince her as the dedicated Party member she seemed to want to be. 'I can't leave either for long. But I assure you I'll return as often as I can.'

'Come, I'll show you the rest of the house.' The Countess beckoned, jumped up and led the way from the room.

After a while one room in the Ferov Palace was pretty much like another: functional, fairly clean, furnished with beds and chests of drawers. There was no evidence of any servants, though Rachel knew that the higher Party officials still had menials working for them, although it was supposed to be forbidden. The former Countess explained that everyone, including herself, was expected to do their own cleaning and demonstrated, as evidence of this, the huge kitchens in the basement which, although fairly untidy and chaotic, did not look unhygienic. Next to them was a dining-room with low trestle tables and benches running the length of the room.

The Countess occasionally said to whom this room or that had once belonged, and Rachel gathered that Kyril was one of several brothers and sisters, all of whom had gone into exile with his parents. When the Countess at last returned to her sitting-room and began to make tea from a samovar boiling in the corner, she asked: 'Doesn't Kyril miss his family? He's so young!'

'He is a man of twenty-five.' The Countess turned round and smiled. 'He was already a revolutionary at the age of sixteen and the secret police were looking for him. He was always a rebel. Luckily my brother Vladimir, the one who went to fetch Lenin, looked after him and hid him until the Revolution. No, Kyril was always a serious boy and a dedicated young man. He fell out with all his family on the question of the responsibility of the Czar for what was happening in Russia. His father never forgave him but his mother, of whom he was particularly fond, nearly died of a broken heart when the family packed up and decided to leave after the deposition of the Czar. Everyone knew what would happen. But I wanted to stay behind because of the close friendship I had with Sergei Petrovsky, who is now high in the Party, and because of my support for the Revolution. Kyril, who was twenty-one at the time and a student at the university, took part in most of the fighting in Moscow and was a Commander in the Red Guards. He helped to capture the Kremlin, fighting hand to hand with Yunkers who were defending the corrupt Provisional Government. Oh, those were heady, exciting days! I was alone in this place, listening to the sound of the guns, not knowing when I would see Vladimir or Kyril again, or any of the volunteers who had come here to take shelter.'

'What happened to your brother Vladimir?' Rachel sipped the hot, sweet milkless tea she was becoming so accustomed to.

'Alas, my Vladimir died of the influenza which swept over us after the war, as it did the rest of Europe. As if we had not all had enough! He would have been a very senior official in the Party now, had he survived. He was one of the earliest Bolsheviks when they were only a tiny minority and he would never permit anyone to call him "Prince". Now it is just Kyril and myself ...' The Countess looked sad, as though the achievement of one's aims didn't always bring happiness. Then, brightening, she smiled at Rachel: 'Tell me something about your niece Susan. What a dear girl she is.'

'She is a dear girl indeed, but so *very* young,' Rachel said firmly. 'And we are going home soon.'

She hoped that would be the end of the matter.

CHAPTER 4

Despite the chaos caused by the Revolution, the disruption to city life, the closing down of all private shops and buildings devoted to commerce, Moscow had made great strides in the last four years to pull itself together under the new order. Museums of art flourished, and collections devoted to the Revolution sprung up all over the place, impressively mounted and documented. As for the theatre, it was as if the Revolution had never happened, and nightly the theatres and operas were packed, though with a somewhat different audience to the one they'd had before 1917. Such entertainments as the Grand Opera, the Marinski Opera, the Little Theatre, the Hermitage Theatre and the Moscow Art Theatre nightly offered a wealth of spectacle and choice, with few writers as yet debarred from having their works put on; and the plays of Chekhov and Shakespeare still enjoyed a great vogue.

But it was to Stanislavsky's Moscow Art Theatre that Kyril and his aunt took Rachel and Susan to see a performance of *Night's Lodging* by the most approved literary hero of the Soviets: Maxim Gorky. This powerful drama, kept strictly within the bounds of socialist realism, was also perfectly acceptable to one educated in the traditions of the West. Spencer Foster had managed to escape from his official entertainment to join them, and outside the theatre they were met by a large, official-looking limousine which bore them swiftly to the formerly fashionable Arbat district of Moscow, close by the Novinski Boulevard, where it stopped before a large house almost as large as the Ferov Palace but discreetly tucked back from the road and surrounded by iron railings rather than a garden. To Rachel's surprise a leather-clad member of the Cheka, with a pistol in his belt, stepped out of the shadows to open the car door.

'Where are we going?' Susan looked at Kyril who smiled at her mysteriously, jumping out of the car to open the door for his aunt and Rachel.

'We are invited to dinner. Unfortunately our host couldn't be at the theatre with us, but he asked us to join him here.'

Unlike the Ferov Palace the interior of the house bore little trace of revolutionary fervour. The inlaid marble was polished and the wooden panelling shone with beeswax. However, instead of family portraits, the imposing figures of Marx and Lenin faced each other across sheaves of wheat surmounted by the hammer and sickle. There was a very low light in the wide hall, through which the Cheka member led them towards an ornate lift that resembled a large gilded birdcage. Half fearfully, Rachel stepped inside, reassured by the expressions of pleasant anticipation on the faces of the Countess and her nephew, the comforting bulk of Spencer Foster beside her.

As the lift stopped on the third floor the door was opened by a tall, distinguished-looking man whose arms were extended in greeting.

'Varvara!' The Countess flew into his arms to be enclosed in an embrace and then, being introduced to Susan and Rachel, he kissed their hands and shook those of Spencer Foster and Kyril, drawing them all into the hall of his apartment, where a uniformed maid stood waiting to take their coats. She gave a very western-style bob and disappeared with them into a side room while their host led them into an imposing drawing-room. This was lit by low lights, glowing against green velour curtains pulled tightly across the windows although, as in Petrograd, it was still light outside. Their host had kept a proprietorial arm round the Countess's waist and, as they all gathered in the large room, she put her own arm round him and said:

'This is my good friend, Sergei Petrovsky. He has been very anxious to meet you but, with all that is going on, he has had very little time. It is very good of you, Sergei, to invite us tonight.' She smiled up at Petrovsky, who beamed down at her, suggesting a meaning to their relationship that wasn't lost on the visitors. He was a large man with cropped hair and high Slav cheekbones, a rather short, bullish neck and a thick body. Although not conventionally handsome there was a definite attraction about him, a combination of strength and a certain magnetism.

'Comrade Petrovsky spent many years in exile,' Kyril said, going to a table which was full of bottles of alcohol, the first that Rachel had seen all the time she had been in Russia, as alcohol was banned by the Soviets. Beside her were plates of *zakuski* – Russian delicacies made from caviare, salmon and other products thought to be almost unobtainable in this famine-stricken land of 1921. She looked up at Spencer, who winked.

'In honour of our guests,' Petrovsky said, as if interpreting their signal and pointing to the table, 'we have vodka and wine tonight. The Moscow Soviet is very generous to those friends of Russia who come from abroad. Vodka for our guests, Kyril.'

Just then a wide door opened and a woman of about twenty, who bore an unmistakable resemblance to him, stepped into the room. Not fashionably dressed by western standards she was, nevertheless, much better dressed than the average Russian woman they had met, with the exception of the Countess. She wore a light summer dress with a low V neckline and a bow at the waist, her hair waved in the Amami style. Petrovsky drew her forward: 'This is my daughter, Anna. She has been interpreting all day for our guests on the Trades Union Congress.'

'I think I saw your daughter on the platform today.' Spencer Foster smiled and took her hand. 'How do you do?'

Anna Petrovsky shook his hand and was, in turn, introduced to Rachel and Susan. She paused for a moment to look carefully at the latter, then at Kyril who was unconcernedly pouring vodka into small, thick glasses. Carrying two carefully he gave one to the Countess and another to Rachel saying: 'Comrade Petrovsky was a great friend of my Uncle Vladimir. Together they planned to bring Comrade Lenin to Russia.'

'I spent many years in exile, happily with my wife and family, so I was not alone,' Petrovsky explained.

'That's how you speak such good English,' Rachel said.

'Yes, I was in England in 1912. My daughter Anna went to school in London. We lived near her school in Camden Town.'

'That must have been the North London Collegiate School for Girls,' Rachel said enthusiastically. 'It is a very well-known school.'

'We were there not only to be near her but because we were so poor. It was a district venerated by us because of its association with the great Karl Marx and his friend Engels who lived in Regent's Park Road. We came to know the area well – Hampstead Heath, where he took his family. In Paris I knew Karl Marx's daughter Laura and her husband Paul Lafargue. Unfortunately they killed themselves before they could see the joy of the Revolution, generated by Laura's father, realized throughout the world,'

'Not throughout the world surely?' Susan accepted her drink from Kyril and fingered the glass.

'Germany, France … America …' Petrovsky appeared to count the countries on his fingers. 'In ten years the whole world, or the greater part of it, will be governed by the proletariat. It is only a matter of time. Come, let us eat.'

As the maid opened the door through which Anna had appeared and bobbed again he put his arms jovially round the shoulders of his daughter and the Countess and led them into the dining-room. This was almost as large in scale as the drawing-room, furnished with a long mahogany table beautifully lit with candles, gleaming with heavy, old-fashioned silver. On the matching sideboard was a steaming tureen from which the maid was spooning soup into large bowls.

73

Petrovsky, seeing that his guests were seated and they all had a bowl in front of them, begged them to start, pointing to the cut slices of white bread in silver entrée dishes on the table, besides others containing cleverly formed whorls and curlicues of golden butter.

'Please eat. Masha will serve the wine.' He spoke to the maid rapidly in Russian, and she drew out from a large cooler on the sideboard a bottle of white wine which she carefully poured into the tall crystal glasses by the side of each place.

'From the Caucasus,' Petrovsky said, raising his glass to toast Varvara Valkova. 'It is thanks to our friend, the Countess, that we have this good wine. The Ferov estate in the Caucasus still produces this fine beverage, though it is, alas, not available to our people.'

'Is alcohol banned because it cannot be obtained or because it is thought bad for one?' Rachel crumbled her white bread, remembering the hungry people she saw drifting about the streets trying to dispose of some pathetic family heirloom for a morsel of hard black bread or a little salt.

'Both!' Petrovsky smiled showing, between his rather fleshy lips, several gold teeth. 'The success of the Red Army is thought to be due to the fact that alcohol was completely banned. It is certainly not good for people to drink too much and, alas, in times as hard as these that is all the Russian people would do if they had the chance. But for our guests ...' he made a bland gesture over the table, 'everything is possible. You know we normally do not live like this, even the highest Party officials have their rations. It is a treat for us too. So I raise my glass and say "To the Revolution in England!"'

'To the Revolution in England!' Susan echoed him, an enthusiastic smile on her face. Turning, she first raised her glass towards Kyril. Rachel sat with her eyes on her glass, while Spencer Foster made a half-hearted gesture, fiddling with the stem between his fingers.

Petrovsky drained his glass and then looked smilingly at Rachel.

'You do not drink, Mrs Askham, to the Revolution?'

'Not in England.' Rachel shook her head, raising her eyes to meet his. 'I'm afraid I can't. While I do think there is much to admire here – and in Moscow I have seen many fine schools, institutions devoted to the sick and elderly, and well-run factories – I do not think I would like to see the same thing happening in England. You see, we don't need it. We have had democracy since the eighteenth century. Our political system has evolved. It suits us better that way.'

'But your workers live in terrible conditions, Mrs Askham.' Anna Petrovsky spoke quite sharply. 'Have you not read Engels?'

'Indeed I have,' Rachel flushed. 'But Engels wrote about conditions sixty years ago! I don't say things are perfect in our country, but I don't think violent revolution is the means to change them.'

'But we don't have violence here.' Kyril spoke quite hotly. 'The Revolution, for such an upheaval, took place with remarkably little bloodshed.'

'We don't want *any* bloodshed at all,' Rachel said firmly. 'It is not necessary. I understand that only recently a number of sailors from Kronstadt which, after all, was where the Revolution began, were shot down when they tried to make a protest.'

Rachel was conscious of the silence which suddenly fell as those round the table eyed one another uneasily. She was aware, too, of the admiring eyes of Spencer Foster upon her.

'The sailors were misguided,' Petrovsky said stiffly. 'It is not an incident we would have wished, but they were led by counter-revolutionary agents. It had to be suppressed for the sake of the country as a whole.'

Rachel was determined to pursue her point despite the obvious disapproval of her hosts, all of whom were frowning as though she'd spoilt the evening. 'You will never restore democracy by ruthlessly cutting out all dissent. That's what we in England believe, anyway.'

'I assure you we have our dialogue too,' Kyril said earnestly. 'There is much discussion and criticism within the Party. But in a country of this size with so many disparate elements we have to have a united front, otherwise we are finished. There will be more disorder and chaos, absolute collapse. The country must be saved by the Party, by *force* if necessary. Russia is not England, Mrs Askham. It is 150 million people of very different attitudes, ideas, and even nationalities and languages. There are things about the Revolution we certainly regret. But things that have had to happen may not necessarily happen again. There will be an end to suppression, I assure you, and every soul in Russia will be free! That is our object, after all.'

'Amen to that!' Spencer Foster said, looking with pleasure at the large pieces of meat on the plate set in front of him, the white potatoes and green vegetables in silver dishes. Red wine, this time, was poured into fresh glasses and Spencer took advantage of the pause to toast his host.

'We of the English working-class movement send fraternal greetings to our Soviet comrades. Power to the Soviets!' he said and, the ice broken and good humour once more restored, Sergei Petrovsky seized the opportunity to make a lengthy reply, assuring the guests of reciprocal fraternal feelings from the great Russian people.

After dinner, coffee was taken in the drawing-room where sweetmeats and a fine French cognac were also served. It could well have been an occasion in a London house, and Rachel wanted to say so much more, but now she didn't dare. For one thing every time she opened her mouth, the neophyte, Susan, glared forbiddingly at her and she was already troubled enough by her niece's behaviour after the past few weeks not to aggravate the situation more.

She knew that Susan was captivated by their young Communist guide, never missing an opportunity to be with him. And opportunities there were in plenty. Rachel had her despatches to send – carefully calculated not to offend at this

76

stage; she might be more honest when she got back to England. The pace of everything also made her feel very tired, so that many of the excursions – to the Tolstoy Museum, the Historical Museum in Niglinnaya, the Horitonevsky Garden, the exhibition of peasant art in the Leontevsky Pereulok – she avoided and spent the time in her room instead. Not that she was ever alone for long. She had attended sessions of the Third International Congress held in the great rooms of the Kremlin and the Red Trades Union Congress in the House of Trade Unions. She had heard Lenin speak, and was suitably impressed, as was everyone who heard him. She had shaken hands with Bukharin, Sverdlov, Kamenev, Rykov and Stalin – all leaders of the party. She had been to so many functions where speeches were made and toasts drunk that it seemed to her she hardly knew anything about what she had come to discover: what Bolshevik Russia was really like.

That night after all the toasts, farewells and promises were made as the guests left, she said to Susan as they lay in bed: 'I would like to come back and take a long tour to the south; the Caucasus and the Crimea, Kharkov, Kiev, the Ukraine.'

'Kyril says we could go to Odessa next week. He is taking a party there.'

'But next week we are going home.'

There was silence. They spoke quietly because they were not sure whether their companions, who had been in bed when they arrived home very late, were really asleep or merely pretending. Inevitably the two ladies were a little jealous of the attention Mrs Askham and her niece received, the obvious preference they were given. Relations between them had cooled considerably since they had arrived in Moscow. Some days it was confined to 'Good morning' and 'Good night'. This evening it had not even been the latter.

'Aunt?' Susan's whisper made her hard to hear and Rachel moved closer to the edge of the bed.

'Yes?'

'Do we have to go back?'

'Of course we have to!'

'But do I?'

'Of course you have to, darling.' Rachel felt a sudden chill, as though her blood had inexplicably run cold.

'I'd love to stay on here, Aunt. I'm really happy ... for the first time in my life.'

'I know you would! I know you are.' Rachel paused, then added, even more quietly, 'Your real wish is to be with Kyril.'

'It isn't only that!'

'I think it's mostly that. I must tell you, I'm very worried about it, Susan.'

More silence, then: 'Well, you mustn't be.'

'He is a very attractive young man. He is also a revolution-ary Communist...'

'Well, so am I.'

'You most certainly are not! You haven't had a chance to think about the matter. You are bowled over by what you see here but mostly, I think, by Kyril.'

'He is also a prince, if you're thinking about what Mummy will say...'

'Susan!' Rachel sat up and leaned over to Susan's bed. 'You aren't serious, are you?'

'We do like each other a lot.'

'Has he spoken?'

Susan giggled in the half light. 'Oh, Aunt Rachel, don't be so old-fashioned! People just aren't like that these days! No one "speaks" formally, or anything, any more. I know he likes me. He wants me to stay on. I mean he would like you to stay on too, that's why he mentioned Odessa. He's sure he could get us on the trip.'

'I'm sure he could, with his connections. Don't you think it rather disgraceful, the conditions in which people like Petrovsky live compared to most of the ordinary people?'

'He is a very high Party official. I think he is a member of the Central Committee of the Party.'

78

'But what? What does he do?'

'I'll ask Kyril.'

'Susan, we have to leave on Sunday. Please tell him that. You can write. We can come back, but your mother and father are expecting you back in London next week.'

'Oh, are they? Do you think they care?'

'Susan, of course they care!'

'I thought they were too busy with their own lives. They always have been, why should it change now? I'm no longer at school, Aunt. Have you thought about what I'm going to do? I took your advice and sat my exams. What now?'

'I thought you might go to university.'

'I'm not sure I want to …' there was another pause, 'after being here.' She propped herself up on her elbow and in the strangely crepuscular light her face seemed to glow. No longer plain now; not exactly a beauty, but a girl under the spell of something – a girl quite clearly in love. 'It's not just Kyril … and liking him. It's the whole of Russia. I feel I am in a new and vital country. This is a land, a time of so much promise, Aunt. Compared to Russia England seems dormant, dead …'

'It is anything but dead or dormant,' Rachel said angrily. 'We are building too, after the War. Do you think I like half a million people unemployed, many of them ex-servicemen? Do you think I like the strikes, the industrial unrest, the poverty we have in our own country? We have a lot to work for in England too. But I don't want to go about it the way they have in Russia. I've spoken to many people who say that the Lubianka prison in Moscow and the Peter and Paul Fortress in Petrograd, the prison of Schlüsselburg on the Neva, are full of political prisoners, many of whom are never seen again. They are either shot or sent to Siberia. There is widespread corruption among Party officials who have the best accommodation, the best rations, as we saw tonight. If you think this is a perfect society, it isn't.'

'But neither is ours. I think the ordinary people here have more of a chance. After all, we have people living in terrible accommodation in *London*. Have you ever thought of throwing Askham House open to them, as the Countess has with the palace?'

'She had no choice.'

'Well, I don't think you should have either. It's quite ridiculous that you can live in that huge house by yourself, or that Gran lives at the Hall with about fifty servants to wait on her. It's unseemly. Now it seems to me immoral.'

'Yes, it is unfair,' Rachel said quietly. 'But don't you see, it gives a lot of people employment too. Better that than on the streets. Many of the peasants came from great estates in the country to Moscow and have no work. But that doesn't excuse what happens in England. We must try and do something about it.'

'But *will* you, Aunt Rachel? You'll talk, but *will* you?'

Would she, indeed? Rachel wondered but said nothing. There seemed, at that moment – a moment, in retrospect, fraught with all sorts of signals she should have interpreted and heeded – nothing more she could say.

Sunday was three days away and there was so much Rachel wanted to do, wanted to see. Kyril, ever attentive, planned everything for her and she thought, or imagined, that he seemed to pay less attention to Susan. But he had brought up Odessa, mentioning it to her, rather timidly, as they made a complete tour of Moscow in a droshky on their last day but one.

'It's very nice of you, Kyril, but I can't possibly. I have children, you know. They expect me back.'

'But Miss Bolingbroke ...' Kyril had glanced awkwardly at Susan, who deliberately avoided her aunt's gaze.

'Miss Bolingbroke is a young woman, under age, and in my care,' Rachel said, rather pompously. 'If I returned without her, her parents would be furious. She may come back, *I* may come back ... but I'm afraid, now, it is quite out of the question to stay.'

'I see, Mrs Askham,' and Kyril seemed to accept it.

It seemed everyone was leaving Moscow at the same time. The Congresses were over and the enthusiastic delegates were streaming home to spread the new gospel throughout Europe and the United States. Nothing had been left undone to impress them. They had seen all the sights, heard all the speeches, been flattered, feasted and fêted, given the best accommodation and food that they apparently thought everyone else was getting. How could they? Rachel had wondered as she moved among them exchanging fraternal greetings with this delegate and that, keeping her silence on controversial topics.

On the last night there was a huge banquet in the Kremlin and she hardly seemed to fall asleep before it was time to wake up again. Miss Rostron and Mrs Gibson were bustling about packing, and Susan ... She looked at Susan's bed but it was neatly made, almost as though it had not been slept in.

But she *had* slept in it, they had ... No, they had not! Rachel shot out of bed and sat on the side, rubbing her eyes and blinking, looking at her watch. They had not come in together because they had been separated by the great throng that streamed out of the Kremlin hall. She had come home with the Countess after dropping off Spencer and the Tukes, while Kyril had promised to see Susan home and Miss Rostron and Mrs Gibson as well.

'Have you seen Susan?' Rachel said in a voice resonant, she felt, with fear.

'Susan?' they both looked around as if Susan's whereabouts were a sudden mystery.

'Did she not come home with you?'

'No.'

'But I thought ...'

'She's in love with that young man, you know,' Mrs Gibson said a little tremulously. 'I expect they wanted a few moments together.' A romantic at heart, obviously, she gave a deep sigh.

'But she hasn't slept in her bed ...'

'Oh, surely ...' they both looked at the bed, then at each other, then at Rachel. What they were all thinking was impossible.

'Her case isn't here, either,' Miss Rostron said, a note, it must be confessed, of almost pleasurable anticipation in her voice. 'I'm *sure* it was at the end of the bed.'

'Yes, it was.'

Rachel tried externally to maintain her calm, but the fear now seemed to have reached her heart, her brain. She couldn't think. 'I don't know how you could have left her,' she said, 'I thought she was with you.'

'Mrs Askham, your niece isn't in *our* charge,' Mrs Gibson said loftily, accusingly, 'and if *you* haven't seen what's been going on under your nose, *we* have.'

'But she would never ...'

'Oh, wouldn't she, though?' Miss Rostron made a sound that was a cross between a cry of derision and a snigger. 'She's a very strong-minded young woman, if you ask me, and she is wholly in love with Communism, as well as with one of its representatives. I think you've been too busy with your own preoccupations, my dear, to see what's been going on.'

The implication, not lost on Rachel, who was rapidly dressing as the women spoke, was that she'd been preoccupied with Spencer Foster. And, although this was emphatically not the case, she could see how it might be misinterpreted. Having donned her underclothes and the two-piece linen suit she was travelling in, she ran a comb through her hair and hurriedly caught it up in the soft bun she wore at the nape of her neck, a rather old-fashioned pre-Raphaelite style that she favoured and which suited her. Then, without another word to her fascinated audience, she took up her handbag and ran from the room.

The Countess Valkova was breakfasting by the window as Rachel burst into her room, pausing only briefly to knock. Through the open window came the sound of birdsong and the Countess was eagerly perusing the pages of *Isvestia* with her pince-nez on the end of her nose, a cup of steaming coffee in her hand. It was a scene reminiscent of upper-class life in England, very far from the ideals of the Revolution. There were bone china and silver on the table, which was covered by a starched white linen tablecloth, edged with broderie anglaise. As Rachel came hurrying in, the Countess's welcoming smile turned to a look of consternation.

'Why, Mrs Askham ...'

'I'm sorry to burst in ...' Rachel stopped abruptly, aware of how idiotic her behaviour might seem if Susan's disappearance had a logical explanation, and drew a deep breath. 'Do you know where Kyril is?'

'Why, certainly. Kyril has already left with his party for Odessa. He went straight to the station from last night's dinner, I believe. Did he not say goodbye to you?'

'No, he didn't, and I think I know why.' The clamour of her heart made Rachel breathless and, perching on the arm of a chair, she tried to draw great gulps of air into her lungs. 'I think my niece has gone with him.'

'Miss Bolingbroke! But, surely not?'

The Countess too began to look concerned and, removing her spectacles, she neatly folded the paper and placed it on the table before getting up and coming over to Rachel. Clearly she was a woman who seldom felt the need to hurry.

'Susan hasn't slept in her bed,' Rachel went on. 'I came home before her. Kyril said he would bring her home with Miss Rostron and Mrs Gibson. Of course, I didn't think anything of it. She is, after all, quite grown-up despite being only just eighteen. But I am responsible for her, you know, Countess Valkova. Her father is my brother. I cannot return to England without Susan.'

'Nor will you,' the Countess said firmly. She went across the room and, taking up the telephone, dialled a number looking, as she did so, over her shoulder at Rachel. 'You're sure there's no mistake?'

'Her case has gone.'

The Countess nodded and spoke rapidly into the telephone in Russian, nodding a few times as she paused to listen. Finally she replaced the receiver and came back across the room.

'That was Sergei Petrovsky. He will know what to do. He has all the resources to establish the truth at his command.'

'What does he do?' Curious as she had been, Rachel had never precisely understood the nature of Petrovsky's work.

'He is a senior official with the Cheka. You've heard of the Cheka, of course?' As Rachel nodded grimly, the Countess hurried on: 'People say all sorts of untrue things about the Cheka. In fact it is what it says: an Extraordinary Commission to protect the State from the counter-revolutionary elements among us. It is nothing like the Czar's secret police as some people allege; but it does have resources at its command that most ordinary people have not. Sergei too was a prince, you know, and is a devoted member of the Party; one of the early Bolsheviks like my brother. He would never associate with anything to do with terror. He said he will find out what he can and ring me back. Your niece may not be with my nephew. I hope she isn't for his sake. He is practically engaged to Anna Petrovsky.'

'I see.' Rachel slumped into the chair on whose arm she had been perching. 'That may explain the secrecy. I felt that Anna Petrovsky did not look too pleased that evening.'

'Indeed she did not. Your niece wears her heart on her sleeve, as I believe the English expression is. She made the attraction very obvious. Poor Anna; she is most attached to Kyril and very possessive. I was quite glad at the thought, if you will forgive me, that Miss Bolingbroke was leaving us. Though no beauty, she is young, has an appealing vitality, and is clearly interested in my nephew.'

'That's what I felt, too late I'm afraid.' Rachel dejectedly studied her foot.

The Countess took a cup from a dresser and, pouring thick black coffee into it, brought it over to Rachel. 'Kyril is a charmer to all the ladies, young and old. He is so like his father, who was a roué when he was young. I hoped that his devotion to the Party would stabilize him, but in that respect it hasn't. I was so glad when he appeared interested in Anna because she is a good, serious young woman and our families have always been close. We are united by birth as well as by common interests and allegiance to the Party. Petrovsky wasn't at all pleased to hear what I told him. Let's hope there *has* been a mistake.'

But there was no mistake. Told to remain all day in the Ferov Palace, Rachel was unable to say goodbye to other members of the delegation who were leaving Moscow in the afternoon. She did, however, send a message to Spencer, who arrived late in the morning to be told what had happened.

'It is *quite* certain that Kyril left on the train for Odessa, with the party of French and Italian Communist delegates to the Third International he was supposed to escort,' Rachel said. 'It is *not* certain whether Susan was with him; but as soon as the train stops he will be contacted through the Cheka and questioned.'

'Brought back to Moscow if necessary,' his aunt added angrily. 'Petrovsky is still hoping it will not be necessary to say anything about this to Anna.'

'I can't go today, Spencer.' In her extremity Rachel used his Christian name for the first time. She felt comforted in the presence of this solid Englishman, who was not only a staunch ally but a fellow countryman. The Countess obviously regarded Susan as a latter-day Jezebel, a spy sent to corrupt her nephew, loyal member of the Party that he was. Varvara Valkova was more concerned about what would happen to Kyril than the consequences for Susan.

'I would like you to contact my brother when you get back. You will find him either at the House of Commons or in his chambers. You may have heard of him, Adam Bolingbroke, the MP for Bisley in Yorkshire.'

'That's your brother, is it? He's not exactly one of us, is he?'

'He may not be a member of the Labour Party but he is a very good, caring Liberal who has fought many battles on behalf of the dispossessed, both in the Courts and in Parliament. You can tell him...'

'You'd better cable him, Rachel, or telephone him.' Spencer returned her use of his Christian name with a feeling of pleasure in the intimacy this crisis had established. 'I'm going to stop here with you.'

'But you can't!' She gazed at him, hope conflicting with despair – both clearly showing on her face.

'Yes, I can! I have another week's holiday, anyway. I won't leave you here with all these Russians.' He pronounced the word 'Roossians', and the Countess looked momentarily offended as if her countrymen and women were being slighted.

'I assure you, Mrs Askham will be *perfectly* safe with us. She is among friends. But I do think it would be nice for her to have a compatriot with her on whom she could lean. I'm sure you're very dependable, Mr Foster.'

In the anxious days that followed, Rachel had reason to be grateful for the dependable Spencer Foster, who went from government department to government department while Rachel stayed by the phone at the Ferov Palace. In order to travel anywhere in Russia it was necessary to have a *propusk*, a permit, and these were not easy to come by unless one had influence with an official in the appropriate department. In fact it was becoming increasingly necessary to have a *propusk* for almost anything in Russia; but certainly for a foreigner to leave Moscow without permission was unheard of. Susan Bolingbroke had applied for no such *propusk*, and nor had anyone on her behalf.

Despite their status as members of the British delegation and guests of the government, both Rachel and Spencer felt that their welcome was wearing thin. By now they should have gone and, with this attitude, was a certain hostility inspired by a suspicion of Susan's real motives for disappearing. In other words: where was she? Was she a spy?

Added to all this was the difficulty of knowing exactly what was going on in another part of Russia, owing to the poor communications. It was also a fact that the Cheka did not have an overall centralized control of the entire country; but had its own committees and departments, each autonomous, each bounded by definable borders. Each district, too, was governed by its own *Ispolkom*, or District Working Committee, which resented interference from Moscow. In 1921 the dream of the corporate, centralized state had not yet been realized.

So that once the delegation of French and Italian Communists had left Moscow, tracing the Odessa train on its route right across the country was not easy because of the many stops and diversions that was the lot of railway travel in those chaotic days.

Five days after Kyril and Susan had disappeared still nothing was heard of them except that the delegation was known to have arrived at Odessa, and steps were being made to trace Kyril and try and find news of Susan.

Rachel and Spencer found themselves isolated not only by the Moscow authorities but, to a certain extent, by the suppressed, and inevitable, hostility of the Countess and Sergei Petrovsky who had expected their respective relatives to marry.

'I think you should go to Odessa,' the Countess said one day, as Rachel paced up and down her pleasant room overlooking the gardens.

'I can't possibly go to Odessa,' Rachel replied, twisting her hands one into the other. 'I left home nearly a month ago. I must go back to London. Maybe my brother will come out and look for his daughter. Heaven knows what he and Susan's mother will say to me. It is a terrible situation to be in.'

'Terrible!' the Countess murmured, sitting down and taking up a box she had on the floor. As she opened it, she looked at

87

Rachel, her eyes gleaming with a sympathy that seemed not entirely genuine.

'I've really taken up too much of your time.' Rachel watched as the Countess, having unlocked the box on her knee, gazed lovingly at the contents, letting necklaces and rings run through her fingers. Rachel felt suddenly voyeuristic and turned away, but the Countess said, in a more friendly tone of voice than Rachel had heard for some days: 'Do look at these, dear Mrs Askham. They are some of the Valkov and Ferov family jewels. They're worth a great deal of money.'

Rachel stared into the box, or casket, where jewels gleamed and glittered like some fantastic projection from stories from the *Arabian Nights*.

'They are in trust for Kyril, and his brothers and sisters, of course,' the Countess went on. 'But I wondered if you would be interested in purchasing any item? Say, this fine emerald ring, which I could let you have for a fraction of its cost?'

The Countess held up a ring beautifully mounted in fine gold with a huge central emerald surrounded by diamonds.

'I don't think I could possibly afford it.' Rachel took the ring with amazement and gazed at it. 'It must be worth *thousands* of pounds.'

'It is. It is rumoured to have belonged to the Empress Elizabeth. See, here,' the Countess went on searching in the case, her long, claw-like fingers looking like talons. Then she held up an oval object, a small egg beautifully worked in diamonds, rubies and other precious stones. 'This egg Fabergé made for Alexander III, father of the last Czar. This I would let go for far less than it is worth, too.'

'Are you *really* trying to sell me these things?' Puzzled, Rachel gave the ring back. 'I have only a very few roubles, Countess, enough to get me out of the country.'

'I would trust you.' The Countess shut the box with an air of resignation and placed her hands along it. 'You could pay me something now and, maybe, send the rest with your brother. You have no idea how short I am of money. I am not *such* an idealist as Kyril, you know,' she gestured around her. 'He's young. I like pretty things. It was with reluctance that I gave up our beautiful home to this riff-raff...'

The Countess paused abruptly and Rachel, shocked despite herself, said: 'But I thought...'

'You thought I gave up my home *gladly*?' the Countess interrupted. 'To see all the beautiful pictures taken down and put up in some hideous offices of state? All our fine wines drunk by the peasants and soldiers? Like many people, when I planned for the Revolution I never thought it would be like this, go this far. It has gone much, much too far. I knew the Czar would go but, in his place, I wanted a President, maybe, a democratic republic such as France has. Now we are ruled by people far more autocratic than any Czar, I can tell you. We *dare* not offend ...' The Countess looked anxiously over her shoulder as though expecting the door to fly open. 'Sometimes, now, I wish that I had gone with my family to Paris.'

'Is it now too late?'

'Too late?' The Countess laughed. 'You think they would let me go? Do you not know that there are *thousands* of the former nobility who wish to leave Russia? I am only protected because of Kyril and ...' she looked at her scraggy, white hands mottled by brown liver spots, 'my relationship with Prince Petrovsky. As former nobles we are suspect. We have to be *very* careful. It is only because of our relationship with Lenin that we are spared, and he is not a well man. I tell you, I live in terror. That is why I fear so much for Kyril, if he has gone away with your niece. Most of the commissars and government officials are peasants. It is simply that Kyril and Sergei, myself and a few others like us are protected by the old Bolsheviks who surround Vladimir Ilich. But even he would sacrifice us if it suited him!' She snapped her fingers and Rachel, sitting opposite her, folded her hands over her knees.

'You are very bitter, Countess. I didn't realize how much you are suffering. I thought you were happy with what has happened to your country.'

'Who could be happy if they are honest?' The Countess's face crinkled in a sarcastic laugh. 'What sort of life do you think we lead? You don't know what Moscow and Petersburg were like before the Revolution – the balls, the parties, the dinners at the fabulous restaurant Yar on the Petersburg Chaussée; the receptions at Tsarskoe Selo and the Winter Palace. Of course there was a grim side of life and we saw it all around us, the beggars on the streets. Those of us who were progressives – and we were many – hated that. But is it any better now? If it were, then maybe, just maybe, it would be worthwhile; but I think now that there are more beggars, more prostitutes and more impoverishment. Now *no one* has enough to eat unless he or she is some high Party official like Sergei with his private apartment; or Radek who lives in luxury in the Kremlin and entertains lavishly. They are the new aristocracy and Lenin is the new Czar. Idealists like Kyril don't see this or, if they do, they pretend it will pass, that the new order is better than the old. My friend Sergei is governed by as much ambition to better himself as any former Imperial functionary.

'Meanwhile the lovely Ferov Palace which entertained all the high nobility, which was the scene of so many splendid parties and dinners, is a hostel for peasants who grew up in sties, and the children of the proletariat who don't know what culture means and never will. Now, I tell you, I would go if I could ... I would sell all these,' she opened the box and let the jewels, the strings of pearls, fall through her fingers again, 'in order to live in the West.'

'But can't Prince Petrovsky help you to leave?'

'Oh, I would never dare ask him! He would be shocked to know I felt like this. He thinks I am a genuine patriot, though I sometimes wonder if he is one. We dare not talk, you see ...' she broke off to look shyly at Rachel, 'even in intimate moments. *Then* one has to be more guarded than ever. No one trusts anyone any more! I tell you, if poor Kyril *has* done something wrong he will be arrested and sent to prison, or maybe shot or deported to Siberia. There will be no mercy for him. He will be declared an enemy of the people. It is a crime to fall in love with the wrong person, if that is what has happened. And then to run off with her without a permit is the highest form of folly. He will be doomed ... and if he is, I will be, too.'

Rachel clung to the railings as the little boat began to ease gently out of the Estonian harbour of Reval en route for Stockholm. For most of the thirty-hour journey it would sail in the shadow of the wooded coastline to avoid the thousands of mines said to have been planted in the sea between Estonia and Finland. It was really like a pleasure cruise, only this return home was no pleasure, lacking that almost insufferable sense of excitement that had possessed them all the way out to Russia.

Now she felt cold, but it was a cold born of dread. She had not dared to tell Susan's family what had happened. As she pressed against the rails, her hands in her pockets, the light sea breeze stirring her hair, Spencer Foster thought she looked like some beautiful Nordic goddess and, as he stood behind her, he allowed his arms to steal round her waist as he whispered into her ear: 'Try and relax on the journey. Forget about it.'

'How *can* I forget?' Rachel slowly turned towards him, surprised by his gesture of intimacy, but welcoming it at the same time. Quite naturally she leaned against him for reassurance, burying her face in his rough tweed coat while his arms slowly tightened round her.

It had taken this tragedy for her to see how much she needed him.

'I don't know what I'd have done without you, Spencer.' After a while she raised her head, searching his face, as usual strong and calm, smiling down at her. 'To say you've been a tower of strength seems inadequate. It was much more. After a while I began to think that everyone was plotting against us, that we had offended *them*.'

91

'Yes, they made me feel that. It was very clever. I wonder if they really thought she was a spy?'

In the end, getting out of Russia had needed all the skill and subterfuge that both of them could employ; the Russians were reluctant to let them go. At one time Rachel had thought they would be put in prison, as they were both taken to Lubianka Number Two, the Headquarters of the Cheka, and questioned by strangers for hours, together and separately.

Some said it had taken the intervention of Lenin himself to let them go. But Rachel's efforts to see Lenin who, after all, had personally invited her to visit Russia in the heyday of the Revolution, were in vain. He was too busy, it was said, too locked away, too powerful. Some also whispered that he was too ill.

'Of course they knew she wasn't a spy! A silly girl, that's all. I could kill her myself, the trouble she's caused. They really were so absurd to think I'd want to leave without finding Susan. The only reason I *want* to get home now is to get her father galvanized into action.'

Rachel gently freed herself from Spencer's firm clasp and leaned her back against the rails, looking at him.

'Do you want me to come with you?' he asked.

'Oh no!' Rachel shook her head quickly. Not the least of her problems in getting home was what to do with Spencer who, in the last month and especially the last weeks, had become something of a permanent presence in her life. Spencer, she knew, had to go back to Manchester; but he had talked of frequent visits to London, of the possibility of perhaps coming to work there permanently at Trades Union Headquarters. She couldn't throw him on one side now, as though he'd never existed. Besides, she didn't want to. She knew it would never be possible to feel for another man what she'd felt for Bosco, but there was something rather like Bosco in Spencer. There was certainly a similarity, hence the attraction. They were both firm, decisive, good-looking men, regardless of class. But Bosco had been the least class-conscious of aristocrats, and

Spencer didn't seem the type to be bothered much by class, either. But what would he say when he knew she was a countess? What would he say to her two homes, to the luxury of St James's Square and Askham Grange, when so many people were homeless and starving – not only in Russia, but in England?

How could she introduce Susan's mother as Lady Melanie – or, anyway, how could she do it so soon?

'Rachel!' Spencer spoke into her ear again, one hand on her arm. 'We're going to go on with this, aren't we? We're going to see each other?'

'Of course we are. But ...' she began, and then stopped.

She felt him trying to tilt her chin with his broad workman-like finger, but she pressed her head once more against his chest, her heart too full of remorse and foreboding.

CHAPTER 5

'How do you mean, "*left* her behind"?' Melanie demanded in tones strongly reminiscent of her mother. Rachel had hurried immediately to the house in St John's Wood, leaving her luggage in the care of Spencer, who had booked into the hotel next to King's Cross Station. She had rung Adam, asking him to pick her up and, on the brief journey to Cavendish Avenue, she had told him the story. Needless to say he had assimilated it at once, and without panic, as though his alert, incisive mind were already busy deciding what was best to be done.

'Susan appears to have eloped with a young man.' Adam kept his voice deliberately calm and low-keyed.

'Eloped?' Melanie's tone, on the contrary, seemed to rise by half an octave every time she opened her mouth. She put a heavily beringed hand to her head and Rachel, despite her grief and remorse, couldn't help but see the comic side of things and wondered if Melanie was about to tear her beautifully coiffured hair. The hand, however, stayed clasped on top of her head as if to prevent it from splitting and, carefully catching the arm of the chair, she sat down. The other hand was supported by Bobby, who had happened to be taking lunch with his mother, newly arrived from France, when Rachel and Adam arrived. Denton had been left behind in the new house.

'Susan was always impulsive,' Bobby murmured as though commenting on an amusing and predictable trait. 'I'm not the least surprised.'

'Not *surprised*?' Melanie's voice gathered strength again. 'Are you crazy, my dear boy? Your sister elopes with a Bolshevik and you're not surprised! Don't you know she's only eighteen? Really, Bobby!'

'We don't know he's a Bolshevik for sure.' Bobby looked at Rachel for support, but, ever honest, she shook her head. 'He must be. They all are in Russia.'

'He *is* a member of the Communist Party. I know that for sure, but he's also a prince, if that helps. The princely Ferov family now lives in France.'

'How can you be a prince *and* a Bolshevik?' Even Adam, as distraught as his ex-wife, though not quite so flamboyantly, smiled.

'The family, Ferov, were split in the Revolution. Prince Kyril Ferov was a revolutionary from his student days, and when his family fled he stayed behind with his aunt, Countess Valkova, his father's sister, so a Ferov too. Kyril is a very personable young man of twenty-five. He and Susan were obviously attracted from the beginning.'

'Then you should have come *straight* home.' Melanie dabbed her eyes with a lace handkerchief embroidered in one of the corners with an elaborate 'M'.

'Mother, don't be absurd,' Bobby yawned. 'Aunt Rachel could hardly come home just because Susan had her eyes on some young man. It was perfectly natural. She's a woman, even if you can't see it.'

'But she's so *plain*, I don't understand it,' Melanie wailed. Then she patted her knees with her hands, studying her jewels as if they could somehow speak to her and provide her with the answer. 'Well, what is to be done?'

'I am going to Russia,' Adam said. 'Straight away.'

'But what about your duties?' Melanie enquired apathetically.

'The House is not sitting and neither are the Courts.' Adam sounded firm.

'But you've a number of cases coming up,' his sister pointed out. 'You might be weeks, months in Russia. It's not like England, I can assure you. Getting an answer out of anyone, or even an appointment to see someone in the first place, is murder. We were nearly arrested.'

'*We?*' Melanie looked at her sharply. 'Who are "we", pray?'

'I was helped by a friend, a member of our delegation. His support was invaluable. His name is Spencer Foster.'

'Foster.' Melanie appeared mentally to be consulting *Debrett*, from whose pages came most of her friends. '*Spencer* Foster, you say? I don't know that I've ever heard of him.'

'It's not likely you would, Mel. He's a trade unionist.'

'How distressing.' Melanie got up and wandered over towards the open windows, fanning her face with the monogrammed handkerchief. 'Of course I suppose you *would* meet that kind of person on that kind of trip. I don't know how I can stand this heat,' she leaned against the French doors. 'I shall have to go straight back to France. At least we're near the sea, the mistral blowing every day. You must leave at once for Russia, Adam. You must see the Prime Minister before you go and...'

'I thought the Leader of the Labour Party ...' Rachel intervened. 'They are more in touch with the Russians than Lloyd George.'

'I *thought* Susan would do something silly.' Melanie seemed to be continuing her monologue as if she were alone in the room. 'There's always been something unstable about her...'

'Melanie, don't be so dramatic,' Adam said angrily. 'Susan isn't in the least unstable. She has had a very careful and sheltered upbringing. She...'

'She, of us all, has been most upset by you and Mother divorcing,' Bobby said sharply. 'I don't think anyone except Aunt Rachel really noticed how badly Susan took it. The boys absorbed it, but not her. It was because she was so distressed that Aunt took her to Russia.'

'That helped a lot, I must say ...' Melanie began, but Rachel rapidly said:

'She was terribly upset. She talked about it frequently on the trip. I felt she was seriously depressed and was worried about her. But once in Russia she brightened up. She changed,

96

literally, overnight. It was quite amazing. Kyril's family, too, had broken up. Maybe it helped draw them together.'

'Well, where is this person now? This "Kyril"?' When Melanie spoke his name it was as though it had inverted commas round it.

'He went to Odessa with a trade delegation the night before we were supposed to leave. I suppose he will go back with the delegation to Moscow ...' Rachel reached in her bag and drew out the note that she'd received several days after Susan had left, the post in Moscow, like everything else, being erratic.

'*Dearest Aunt. Don't worry. Isn't it lovely to be in love? I'm so happy. Susan.*'

She handed it to Melanie who, gazing at it with disgust, began to screw it up when Adam snatched it from her hand and smoothed it on the palm of his hand.

'Don't do that, Mel! Don't destroy it! At least we know she's alive and that she's gone off with this man. I will go straight to Moscow by the fastest train...'

'Why don't I come with you, Adam?' Bobby lit a cigarette in the insouciant manner in which he did everything. It was many years since Rachel had ever seen him moved by anything enough to lose his temper or burst into laughter, or tears. Even as a very small child he had had this quality of detachment. She had always supposed it was because, from infancy, everything he wanted he had, even love in the form of doting grandparents. They not only could deny him nothing but managed to be quite strict at the same time, so that he was not one of those wilful, bad-tempered, obviously spoiled boys whom nobody liked. People liked Bobby but they were a little in awe of him. No one really understood him.

'Better still,' Bobby waved his match into the air, extinguishing it. 'Why don't I go by myself? I would have the time to explore Russia. I'd enjoy that. I could travel the length and breadth of the country looking for Susan if necessary and maybe I could do business with them. Duncan Curtis says the

Russians are very keen to restore trade with the West. I could sell them some motor cars. Aunt Rachel already suggested it.'

'They don't have the money to pay for them.' Adam looked fondly at his stepson. They had always enjoyed a good, if distant, relationship, based on respect rather than love.

'We can give them credit,' Bobby brandished his cigarette loftily. 'That way we'll get them into our clutches.' He drew on his cigarette. 'Seriously, I could start at once and leave you to get things going in Whitehall. Presumably there are telephones in Russia, Aunt Rachel?'

'If they work, and it is very hard to get a line abroad. But I think it's a good idea, Adam, if you stay here and Bobby goes by himself. I should think that when he gets to Moscow Susan will have recovered her senses and will be glad to come home.'

'But will *we* be glad to have her? That is the point, is it not?' Melanie turned from the doors still fanning herself.

It had been one of the hottest summers on record, temperatures in London at one stage reaching 145° in the sun. Melanie had travelled to London in August to get her youngest son, Jordan, ready for school. Christopher was with his grandmother at Askham. Advancing into the room she was aware of three pairs of eyes staring at her. All three were used to Melanie's ways, but this possible rejection of her daughter seemed far-fetched for one who had done much, who had at times been quite ruthless, in the name of love.

'Well, will we?' she continued, ignoring them. 'I don't know that I shall. We are assuming that Susan has run off with this young man and has been to bed with him. In short, she is no longer a virgin. Who will want her now, a plain girl, sullied? Not a very nice proposition.'

'Oh, Mother, don't be so ridiculous.' Bobby stubbed out his cigarette in a gesture of irritation. 'All that sort of thing has changed from when you were Susan's age,'

'But has it, Bobby? Has it really? I think not. Everyone will know of Susan's escapade, that is, who matters, and what will they say to their sons, to their daughters? They will say . . .' here

Melanie dramatically stretched out her arm, her fingers spread in a warning gesture. 'They will say: "Keep away. Tarnished goods." I know of no young man who would seriously want an adventuress for a wife and that is what Susan has turned herself into: an adventuress. Maybe if she were astonishingly beautiful, it might make her more enticing, but she isn't. She is a plain girl who has gone with the first man to want her. Well, I shan't want her anyway. She has ceased to be my daughter. The way she has behaved is absolutely, in my view, unforgivable.

'You may have wondered that I did not seem more distressed about Susan left behind in Bolshevik Russia?' Melanie, glancing about her, sat down again, daintily crossing her legs. 'Because I am utterly disgusted by my own daughter and the way she has behaved. Years of boarding school and careful upbringing, to come to this! Certainly Bobby must go and see what has happened to Susan, and certainly he must try and bring her back. I can't imagine she will be able to survive for long in such a country. Of course she must be found or people will blame *us*! As far as I'm concerned she is Adam's responsibility from now on, certainly not mine.'

'I think you're a most unnatural woman.' Adam stepped towards her as though he wanted to hit her. 'An unnatural woman and an unnatural mother.'

'I wonder that it surprises you, Adam. You've never had a very high opinion of me.'

'It surprises me that Susan should behave like you!'

'And what do you mean by that, pray?'

Melanie drew herself up but her face went pale, and she looked at Bobby for support as Rachel hastily intervened.

'Don't let this develop into another family brawl, please! How about a little charity for once? I have come on a very long and tiring mission. I have been away a long time and not seen my own children for nearly six weeks. I am very distressed about Susan and I feel very guilty. Yet it seems that you and Adam, Melanie, cannot rise above your own petty differences to think of the consequence to your own daughter, who is just eighteen. I should imagine both of you did things at that age you would rather forget.'

'I did nothing I can think of,' Melanie said loftily. 'It is true I was in love at eighteen with Bobby's father . . .' her eyes rested meltingly for a moment on her eldest son. 'But I married him. I did nothing I was ashamed of before my marriage, I assure you. *I* was a virgin when I went to the altar . . .'

'Spare us the details, Mother,' Bobby said good-humouredly, bending to kiss her. 'Don't forget you're talking about the year 1898.'

'I'm not likely to forget it, dear one.' His mother reached up to stroke his cheek, her eyes filling with tears. 'It was the year I married your poor father, only weeks before he was killed at Omdurman. If he'd have lived, oh, how different my life would have been.'

And she looked witheringly at the man she had just divorced, wringing her hands, as if to show the world how much he had to answer for.

'Melanie has a very short memory,' Adam observed to Rachel in the cab taking them to King's Cross. 'She was never happy with Harry, was she?'

'Well, she was very young and it was a very brief time to be married,' Rachel said rather abstractedly, looking out of the taxi window as the buildings of Camden Town seemed to fly past. 'Before you meet him, Adam, I want to tell you about Spencer . . .'

'Ah, there *is* something.' Adam tucked her hand in his, patted it and smiled. 'I thought there might be.'

'No, there's absolutely nothing,' Rachel said quickly. 'Nothing, I assure you, except maybe an interest, a fondness. He has been so good to me that I can't forget it. He was someone to lean on, Adam, when, childishly, I felt so frightened and alone. Russia is a very frightening place. It is still in the throes of its Revolution. It has only just stopped fighting a civil war and, in many ways, it is still at war with itself. The officialdom and bureaucracy are quite stifling and there are few people in whom you can trust or believe. They actually seemed to think that Susan might be planted on Kyril as a spy. We were questioned for hours by the secret police.'

'I thought they had abolished the secret police!'

'Well, they haven't. The Cheka is much feared. It is certain that it kills people without trial. Some say many, many people, maybe thousands. The Bolsheviks excuse everything on the grounds that they are stamping out counter-revolution. In many ways I'm glad you're not going. I think you would be as bewildered by Russia as I was.

'I must confess I was disturbed; many illusions shattered. *Some* good things, but ...' Rachel's voice trailed off as she looked unhappily at her brother, whose face had grown solemn too.

'But do you think Bobby will be all right?'

'Bobby is very capable.' Rachel gave his hand a reassuring squeeze. 'I'm not a bit afraid for Bobby, but I would be for you. So you see Spencer Foster was indispensable because the Russians couldn't rattle him. He wasn't a bit afraid of them and, secretly, at the end I was and I'm afraid for Susan, despite her health and strength. I fear for her.'

'I fear for her, too,' Adam gripped Rachel's hand in a sudden spasm of anguish. 'But, like you, I feel that if anyone will get to the root of the matter, Bobby will. Like you, I trust him.'

'The thing that is worrying me for the moment,' Rachel said as the Gothic spires of King's Cross came into view, 'is that Spencer has no idea ... I was known as Mrs Askham all the time we were in Russia.'

'Well, you can't keep it from him for ever, can you?' Adam smiled.

'Apart from that, he's very nice but ...' she looked warily at her brother, 'not like you, even.'

'Working class?' Adam raised his eyebrows and Rachel nodded. 'But we believe in it, don't we? We believe in equality.'

'Of course we do! I don't mean that! I mean I wonder if *he'll* like *me* as much when he knows?'

'Are you very keen on him?' Adam enquired, his voice gentle.

'I like him. I respect him. He's a bit like Bosco, very direct and strong.'

'Then he won't mind about your shameful secret,' Adam said, half smiling. 'I'm dying to meet him.'

'But you won't tell him, will you? Not yet? Not about me?'

Adam looked at his sister in surprise, amazed at the note of pleading in her voice.

'You are worried, aren't you? You'll have to tell him sometime if you like him that much. You can't go on being "Mrs Askham" for ever.'

'It's not only that. It's the houses, the obvious wealth. Sometimes I feel ashamed of it all – particularly after what I've seen in Russia.'

'If he loves you a bit or even likes you a lot he won't mind, you can be sure of that.' Adam let go of her hand as he leaned forward to open the door.

They had coffee in the big lounge of the Great Northern Hotel and Adam and Spencer got on well immediately, as Rachel thought they would. She looked so happy and relaxed as she watched them, listened to them talk, that Adam thought he hadn't seen her so animated since Bosco's death, despite what had happened to Susan.

Yet for all his notions of equality, sincerely held, Spencer was a bit of a shock to him. He was a thick-set, rather surly man with thick brown hair brushed back without a parting and a large walrus moustache. He had a pronounced Lanca-shire accent and he sat with his cap resting on his knee, his legs apart, his manner very confident.

It was only after a while, after he had overcome this initial sense of shock, that Adam came to appreciate what Rachel meant by his resemblance to Bosco. For he didn't look in the least bit like that tall aristocrat who had been killed in the War, saving his, Adam's, life. What he did have was a quality of maleness, of sexuality that had made Bosco so attractive to women, that made them react and look at him in a way they never looked at Adam, with one devoted exception. In a sense he'd envied Bosco, much as he loved him. Was he going to feel the same about Spencer – this working man from the north?

Well, if Rachel married him she'd lose the title she so disliked. Marry? What was he thinking of? Rachel was a youthful and good-looking woman of forty-four, but Spencer was at least ten years younger, maybe more. He was a young man. Whatever had happened in Russia, that strange land, to turn Rachel's head?

In no time at all Spencer had clearly expounded the facts about Susan and suggested ways she could be quickly found and brought home.

'We've done the groundwork,' Spencer finished, twisting his cap on his knee. 'Rachel, Mrs Askham here, did all she could. She had no option but to return without Miss Bolingbroke.'

'I'm sure that's true,' Adam said warmly. 'And thank you for all you've done. How long will you be staying in London?'

'I have to make my report to the Trade Union Headquarters and then, if Rachel doesn't need anything...'

'I'd like you to meet Bobby before he goes,' Adam said suddenly. 'He's hoping to go tomorrow or the day after. Is dinner tonight possible?'

'I'll fit in with any of your plans,' Spencer smiled at Rachel, as the waiter came over to bring more coffee.

Massingham's in the Strand was a small restaurant, notable for its good food more than for the social standing of those who ate there. Adam used it a lot as it was near the Law Courts and his chambers in Gray's Inn which he still maintained, despite the house in Bedford Row which he'd shared with Flora since the spring.

There were just the four of them at dinner, and Rachel was glad to see that Bobby seemed to take to Spencer as quickly and unaffectedly as Adam had. As the evening advanced, with plans being discussed and preparations made, Adam grew more and more convinced that his sister was in love, or on the verge of love, with Spencer Foster. Whatever she might think, it was more advanced, maybe, than even she knew. Spencer Foster was a very nice man. He was decisive, firm, knowledge-able, obviously intelligent and with a quality of kindliness that emanated from him, so that Adam knew he would have helped someone who needed him whether that person attracted him or not.

Did he know Rachel's age? Did it matter? Was he exagger-ating the whole thing? Adam found himself beset that evening by problems other than the question of the disappearance of his daughter. Bobby seemed curious too, looking from one to the other in his quizzical, urbane way as he said how much he was looking forward to his visit and what plans he had after he had tracked down Susan.

'Supposing she wants to stay with Kyril?' Spencer lit a cigarette after their meal was finished and, sitting back, stuck his finger and thumb through the sleeve of his waistcoat, quite relaxed in their company.

'We'll have to consider that when I get there,' Bobby nodded. 'It's quite possible, but somehow I think it's just an adventure. Anyway, she must come home and the whole thing can be sorted out here. Even in Russia she's under age. Tell me, Spencer, did you like this Kyril fellow?'

'He was a very nice lad,' Spencer replied. 'In other circumstances he would have suited young Susan.'

'What "other circumstances"?'

'I don't think you really want her to live in Russia, do you? And he certainly doesn't want to come out. Your aunt and I had no idea what was going on or how serious it was.'

'I'm not Bobby's real aunt,' Rachel said suddenly, 'only by marriage.' Afterwards she didn't know why she said this.

'Bobby's my stepson,' Adam explained. 'My wife was married before to Bobby's father.'

'She must have been a young lass then,' Spencer smiled. 'About Susan's age?'

'She was only twenty when I was born,' Bobby continued. 'They were married in Egypt shortly before Omdurman where my father was killed. He was a great friend of my mother's brother, Lord Askham, who was killed in the last war.'

Rachel felt herself freezing as Bobby spoke the words, and this was followed by a rush of unnatural warmth and she knew she was blushing. Hopefully in the dimmish light her discomfiture would go unnoticed.

'Yes, Rachel has told me about her husband.' Spencer didn't look at her, after pausing just for a moment. 'How much I admire her for coping with five children after his death.'

'Did she tell you he was a hero?' Adam enquired. 'He died saving my life and was awarded the VC.'

'No, she didn't say that,' now Spencer turned to study her, for the first time since Bobby had spoken. 'She would be too modest to boast, but it doesn't surprise me. Anyone whom Rachel married would be the stuff of which heroes were made.'

It was then that Adam knew for sure that Spencer felt about Rachel the way she felt about him. Maybe Bobby noticed too, because he was not an insensitive young man, but he was very diplomatic and he continued talking as though nothing untoward had occurred, as though he hadn't noticed the warmth, almost passion, in Spencer's face; or seen his aunt blush. Indeed, from his point of view nothing had, since he had not been told about Rachel's deception. He thought it was to do with love, not deceit. And why not? Rachel had been alone for many years, her name never linked with another man's.

Afterwards, they stood on the pavement talking, Adam vaguely looking around for a cab.

'I'll take you home, Rachel, if Bobby will give Spencer a lift. I know his car is parked on the embankment.'

'Why don't I take Aunt Rachel, and you take Spencer, Adam? It is more your way. I want to talk some more with Rachel in case I don't see her again. I'm hoping to leave for Vienna tomorrow night.'

'Does anyone mind if *I* take Lady Askham home?' Spencer said pointedly, already hailing a cab in that commanding, practised manner Bosco would have used. 'I may have to say goodbye to her too.'

'What did you mean by that?' Rachel asked as the cab sped down the Strand. She was still looking behind her, waving at Adam and Bobby.

'Well, I don't know that you want me around, Lady Askham.'

'Don't be silly!' Rachel, feeling stronger now that the secret was out and more in command of the situation, leaned forward to pull down the window and let in the air. Even at night the London pavements still burned from the heat of the day.

'Why didn't you tell me?'

Rachel gazed at him for a second or two without speaking.

'What did you want me to say: "You know, Mr Foster, I am really the Countess of Askham, and don't you forget it"?'

'No, I don't mean that.' Despite himself Spencer smiled. 'But why did you hide it?'

'I didn't hide it; but I did think it was asking for trouble to go to Russia with a title. I thought things would be easier for me if I was known as "Mrs Askham" which I prefer, anyway. My brother and I were very ordinary people and I never wanted to be a countess. Bosco inherited the title by accident through the death of his elder brother. I assure you we aren't "lordly" people and like to live simply.'

'I can see that. St James's Square!'

For the first time the note of contempt that Rachel had been dreading crept into Spencer's voice. Just then they reached the house and, turning to him, she said: 'You'd better come in, Spencer, so that we can have this out. I'm glad you know. It's quite all right. My children are all in the country, but we will not be unchaperoned.'

'Lots of servants, I expect.' Spencer prepared to get out and pay the cabbie as Bromwich, Rachel's butler, opened the door and stood at the top of the steps smiling, waiting to greet them.

'Good evening, my lady,' he said, bowing deeply. 'Sir,' he added with only a subtle change of inflection in his voice.

'We'll have coffee in my sitting-room, Bromwich,' Rachel said, feeling self-conscious for the first time for many years. When she first became a peeress she was conscious of her title all the time but, gradually, as she grew used to it, she ceased completely to think about it. This was also the first time in six years she'd ever brought an unattached man into the house, and she wondered what her old family servant was thinking. As they went upstairs she was aware of Bromwich's eyes following her, Spencer's cloth cap still in his hand, which he had taken as he would any other hat, even a silk top hat, without servility and without comment.

As Rachel threw open the door of her sitting-room she said: 'Most of the house has been closed since the War. I just use a few rooms. Except for Hugo, my youngest son, all the others are at school.'

'These them?' Spencer went to the mantelpiece and started studying pictures, but Rachel could see his eyes were on the large head and shoulders portrait of Bosco.

'Yes,' she went over to stand beside him. 'That's my husband, Bosco, the one you're looking at. It was taken not long before the War so it is a good likeness, as he was ... when he died,' Rachel lowered her voice because, even after six years, it seemed odd to talk about Bosco in the past, even to imagine that vital presence being long dead.

'He was a good-looking man,' Spencer glanced at her. 'And this?' He stood in front of another photo.

'That's Ralph, our eldest son.'

'He'll be the Earl now.'

'Yes he is, and this is my youngest son, Hugo, with my daughter Charlotte who is now fourteen. That was taken in the garden of our country home shortly before she went to school. These two,' she paused before a large photo in a silver frame at the end, her confidence returning, 'are our twins Emmeline and Frederick, known as Freddie and Em. They are inseparable so we haven't sent them away to school yet though, as they are thirteen, they will probably have to be split up next year.'

'Why?' Spencer moved away from the mantelpiece and, his hands behind his back, started to circle the room rather like a dog sniffing for clues.

'Why what?'

'Why do they have to be split up?'

'Because it is difficult for me to look after them, and I know that my husband would have liked Freddie to go to his old school.'

'Public school, I suppose? Eton?'

'Yes. Freddie is down for Eton and Ralph is there now. There, I've confessed. Are you satisfied, Spencer?' Her voice was rather harsh, breathless, as Bromwich knocked on the door, entering with a tray. One of the maids followed him carrying a coffee pot and a large jug of hot milk. Rachel watched Spencer gazing at them as they put everything in its place. 'I'll pour, Bromwich, thank you,' Rachel smiled at him, then at the maid who looked rather curiously at the heavy man sitting in his late lordship's chair.

When they had both gone Spencer said: 'Confessed what?'

'That we are indubitably upper-class. That my husband was an earl, my son is an earl and all my sons go to Eton, that bastion of the landowning classes. Even my brother went to a public school, Rugby, and I was at a very good school for girls in Bath, where we lived. I speak Latin and understand the classics but...'

Suddenly Spencer rose and went to the door, but Rachel preceded him, standing with her back to it, her hand over the knob.

'Don't go, Spencer, because having heard that, you know all there is to know and I have no more secrets left. Now can't you stop being so bloody class-minded and accept me for what I am?'

Spencer stopped about a foot away from Rachel and stared at her. 'What did you say?'

'I said you were bloody class-minded. I'm not. I didn't marry him for a long time because his mother was so hidebound by class, just as you are, Spencer, that she couldn't stand the sight of me. I slept with Bosco for quite a few years before I married him, and I married him because I loved him, not because he was the son of an earl.

'I am a Socialist, an editor and I run a newspaper. I live simply in the houses that belong to my son Ralph, Bosco's heir. All I have I've got from the Askhams because my brother and I were not wealthy; but wealth and the sort of snobbery that you are displaying tonight mean nothing to me. You said you might have to say goodbye to me because you know I am Lady Askham! Don't you see how ridiculous that is? The very idea?' As she paused, rather out of breath, Spencer said:

'If I may have the chance to speak ...'

'What do you want to say?'

Rachel's directness seemed to disconcert him and, crossing his arms, he turned and strolled back across the room, pausing before the window to look out on to the subdued lights of St James's Square.

'Well, I was put off. I was bit shocked. You know, I was born in Preston and my father worked in a mill. I left school at twelve and went into the mill, too. We lived in a tiny terraced cottage in a small mean back street and I hated the bosses. I hated the people who lived in Fulwood, which is the smart part of Preston, and drove around in fine carriages. I loathed the man who owned our factory. I still do.'

'I'd probably have loathed him, too.'

'I hate phoney Socialists who are upper-class yet pretend they know what goes on in the minds of the workers. But somehow you didn't seem to fit into all that, Rachel. I thought you were an ordinary middle-class woman, a widow who had maybe struggled to bring up five children.'

'I'm sorry if you thought that, Spencer; but we didn't become intimate really, did we, until Susan went off, and then it hardly seemed the time to start telling you the story of my life. We have become intimate, haven't we? Or is that over too?'

Spencer shook his head and nodded all at the same time, and the fact that he seemed so distressed nearly broke her heart. For now she realized that the tenderness, the expectation she felt about Spencer Foster had, finally, betrayed the memory of Bosco.

But instead of happiness or exultation the feeling she had as she walked over to the tray and started pouring the coffee into the cups was one of despair – maybe the sort of emotion that Susan, in a different part of the world, was feeling now.

'There's another thing I must tell you, Spencer.' She put one lump of sugar in his cup and brought it over to where he stood by the window. He took the cup from her, looking into her eyes with a similar sadness to the one she was feeling. 'I must tell you also that I am forty-four years old and I should imagine you are, what, thirty?'

'Thirty-two,' Spencer said.

'Well, a little older than I thought, but not much. What happened between us happened, Spencer, maybe because of the circumstances. But now that all is revealed, my title, my age, everything, there is nothing left to hide, nothing to conceal. We can be friends.'

'You know it's more than friendship,' Spencer's voice was

gruff as he took a sip of his coffee. 'This feeling I have for you is more than friendship, Rachel.'

'But did you know how old I was?'

'I guessed, forty or so,' Spencer nodded, sipping the hot, scalding coffee again, his eyes looking at her all the time. 'I'm not concerned about the age, whether it's ten years or twelve or twenty. I love you and I did from the very beginning. I was going to tell you that, however old you were, when we got home. But now you being . . .' he looked around, 'all this, your family changes everything. Can't you see? Your family would laugh at me. Your son, the Earl, would be ashamed of me if I paid court to you, as I want to. Your mother-in-law, the Dowager Countess, would say you'd let the side down. I *have* heard of you now that you come to mention it, only I never associated it, even though I knew you sent newspaper despatches. The two things never connected – Mrs Askham and Lady Askham, the suffragist who owns *The Sentinel*, who once broke the windows of her own house with stones. This house?' As Rachel nodded, too choked to speak, he grimly went on. 'I've read a lot about you; it never occurred to me in that context, Russia, when none of us were ourselves, that you and she were the same person. You're not only noble, you're important, consulted by statesmen and people of affairs. I'm absolutely no one, a local Manchester Trade Unionist, living in lodgings in Salford. I have one room at the top of a house.' Once again he looked about him, as though to emphasize their difference. Sadly he shook his head. 'We're worlds apart, Rachel, don't you see?'

111

CHAPTER 6

The sunlight falling through the slats of the closed shutters cast a pattern on the floor which rose at a sharp angle over the bed covering them in criss-cross fashion like lattice work; like prison bars. Susan sat bolt upright from her half-slumber, staring in front of her, aware of the rapid pounding of her heart. Looking down, she saw Kyril still asleep beside her, his broad brown back turned to her slightly curved, his legs comfortably drawn up foetal fashion, his head resting on his hands.

Susan leaned back on her pillow with a deep sigh and put out her fingers to touch him. By running her hand up and down his skin she was comforted, because such intimacy was a sign of possession, of belonging and being wanted. Susan realized that she had never really felt wanted in her life until she met Kyril. She had been tolerated, but not loved; not really wanted. People like her father, Bobby and Aunt Rachel were kind to her, but had they loved her, really, as Kyril did? Her mother, the lovely Melanie, had certainly shown she didn't want her ugly duckling. But Kyril had not only shown that he wanted her; he made her feel beautiful and no one, not even her precious nanny binding her hair in rags to produce long ringlets when she was small, had made her feel that, hard though she tried. When one had a mother like Melanie Bolingbroke, a grandmother like Dulcie Askham, a girl felt very out of things if she didn't share this rare, legendary family beauty, and people always made it a lot worse by saying how unlike the Askham family she was.

The touch of Susan's hand woke Kyril, who lay for a few moments blinking rapidly. Then he turned and gazed at her anxious face, her tilted chin – a face that, at times, like now, reminded him that she was scarcely out of her childhood. It was rounded, snub-nosed; not beautiful, but warm and trusting; a face one wanted to cherish and protect from the ravages of her own loveless childhood. Kyril, who was always so self-confident, had met a woman, a girl, who was not, and this aspect of Susan – vulnerable, appealing – drew him to her as nothing else had.

'What's the matter?'

'I dreamt we were in prison. Then I woke to see these patterns that looked like bars. I think I screamed.'

'I think you woke me up.' He let a hand lie on her flat stomach. Her entire body was wet, drenched in sweat. 'That's the second time you've dreamed about prison.' Kyril touched her face. 'Why? We're not going to prison. We're going to live happily ever after, like the story book. The new Russia is made for young people like us. It is full of promises, of good things to come.'

'Yes, but I'm worried.' Susan slid down on the bed beside him, clasping the hand that lay on her stomach, thrilled by the touch, as she always was, of his long strong fingers.

'What are you worried about, Susan?' He brought their entwined hands up to his mouth and kissed the back of hers. 'There is nothing to worry about.'

'I think we have a lot to worry about, Kyril, really.' He could see her concern by the crease of her brow. 'In the first place you have denied any knowledge of my existence to the authorities.'

'Oh, but that's just a game. I'll own up when the time comes.' He chuckled.

'Won't they be very strict?'

'No!' He laughed outright now. 'They have too many really important things to worry about. You could see what a state Odessa was still in, even though the blockade is over. It is absolute chaos in Odessa and they are far too busy to think about a disappearing English girl.'

'But what about Moscow?'

113

Kyril's laugh was even more hearty. 'You think Moscow cares about *us*? Two tiny people tucked away in the Caucasus? I assure you we are of no importance whatever. As far as my immediate superiors know I am on holiday and not due back in Moscow until October. Russia is a free country, you know, Susan. That's why we got rid of the Czar, so that we could lead our own lives without all those controls.'

'I'm worried about what my mother and father will do. Aunt Rachel must have been home for at least two weeks now.'

'You sent her the note. She knew you were with me. There is no need to worry. She's a nice person – I liked her. In a way I wish we'd confided in her.'

'Oh, but she'd never have let us go! You did try, by asking if I could stay on. Besides, you don't know my mother. She's not like Aunt Rachel.'

'Oh? Is she so very stern?'

'She's very *correct* and conventional. She wouldn't approve of you and me ...' Susan looked down at their naked bodies lying side by side. 'Like this ...' Susan faltered.

'But your mother is of the old bourgeoisie.'

'The *nobility*,' Susan corrected, as if forgetful of her revolutionary principles. 'My grandfather was the Earl of Askham.'

'Oh? So?' Kyril looked at her with interest. 'You never told me that before.'

'It wasn't necessary. Was it?' Smiling, she gazed at him, almost too afraid to show her love.

'I suppose not. And your father?'

'He *is* bourgeois. He is Aunt Rachel's brother and is a Liberal Member of Parliament and a lawyer. Aunt Rachel, of course, is a Socialist.'

'And who was her husband?'

'Oh!' Susan leaned back against the pillows again, more relaxed now, and thought. 'He, too, was the Earl of Askham, succeeding my grandfather. He was my mother's brother and was killed in the War.'

'So a brother and sister married a brother and sister?'

'Yes; but my mother and father are divorced, as you know.'

He knew, and he knew how upset she was about it too, girlishly upset. This yearning to confide had first awakened his sympathy, slowly his love. But how much she had left unsaid! As a man from a noble Russian family he appreciated this link with the old nobility of England, even though, theoretically, he didn't approve of it. It made sense that he and Susan had so much in common; the establishment of a rapport had been instantaneous even though he had known many other girls, not always as lovers, from all walks of life since the Revolution.

He put his arm round her and squeezed her. 'You're not to worry about anything as long as we're here.'

'But what happens when we leave?' He realized she'd started to tremble.

'Then we'll see. Still we'll be together, never fear.'

Susan looked up at his strong, kind face and felt like weeping.

The Ferov country house, Esenelli, was an imposing two-storeyed building standing on a lake high in the mountains, within sight of the snowclad Main Caucasian Range, between the luxurious semi-tropical vegetation of Cape Zeleny and the oil port of Batum on the Black Sea. Not far away was the border with Turkey and this proximity to the orient seemed reflected in the style and way of life of the people who were swarthy and friendly, favouring loose, bright-coloured clothes and the soft Caucasian leather bootees, the *chuvyaki*, an ensemble which, in general, gave them a swashbuckling air.

The Soviet regime had hardly yet had time to colonize the Caucasus and this showed in the relative freedom of the people, their contempt for authority. A small train plied between Batum and Cape Zeleny which had toy-like open carriages crowded with the local population and frequently their animals and goods and chattels as well. The balmy climate, the rare bird life, the singing of the *sazandari* at sunset,

115

the exotic plants and shrubs, helped to convince Susan that she had left the ordinary planet for another, intensely emotional and sensual kind of life far removed from London and even Moscow.

The lake near the house was full of beautiful pink, fat trout which Kyril and Susan fished for every day during that autumnal idyll, when they had travelled from Odessa on a tiny tramp steamer to Batum, the last Russian port on the Black Sea. This they found just as chaotic as Odessa in the aftermath of the evacuation of the Allied troops: the Greeks, French and English, who had occupied it only a year before.

It had been Kyril's idea to take Susan to his home in the Caucasian mountains, scarcely touched by the Revolution and where the people still lived as they had for many, maybe hundreds, of years past. In Odessa Susan had been hidden in a room in the suburbs while Kyril showed his delegation around, and then said goodbye to them when they sailed away to Italy.

Susan had spent most of her time in Odessa feeling tired and frightened to death, bitterly regretting her action because the streets were full of brigands, petty thieves and gangs of White Russian soldiers, left behind by General Denikin, who roamed about preying for food and killing without qualm. She never left her small room in Black Sea Street, but spent her time gazing fearfully out of the window, like some latter-day Butterfly waiting for her Pinkerton to return.

Finally, this particular scenario had a happy ending and Pinkerton did return, not to bring news of a new love but to tell her that he wanted to take her to the family home in the mountains where he had spent so many happy, carefree childish days. The journey by boat to Batum, hugging the wooded coastline, via Yalta, Novorossiysk, Sukhumi and Poti, had taken nearly a week. Then the interior was breached by the tiny train and, finally, a cart hitched to a heavy slow-moving bullock to toil up the mountain roads.

Susan still didn't know how Kyril had achieved his release or what he had told his superiors because, despite what he said, he was a member of the Party and expected to be disciplined, dedicated, obedient and to do as he was told. Better, she decided, not to ask, thus learning the first virtue of adult women: discretion.

Later that day, as the sun began to hide behind the mountains, they fished again in the still clear waters of the lake. As soon as the sun disappeared a chill wind would sweep from behind, and the nights were frosty. The lights would appear in the house and the great iron stove, the *bourzhouika*, would be stoked by the two servants Peter and Nikolai, who had remained there with the old *nyanya*, Katia, who had looked after Kyril, his brothers and sisters and his father and *his* brothers and sisters before them.

After they had fished that night it was cooler than usual and Peter moved the table near to the *bourzhouika* in which a great fire made of dry twigs and logs blazed, while old Katia pattered in and out with trays and plates of food and Nikolai cooked the fish for them all that had been freshly caught. The servants, however, refused to eat with the Prince – they always referred, directly and indirectly, to him as *kniaz*, prince, as if they, or he, had never heard of Comrade Lenin – and his lady whom Kyril, out of respect for their sensibilities, had introduced as his wife.

Finally, the meal was set and Katia, smiling and bobbing, talked to Kyril as she made sure that everything on the table was as good as she could make it.

'Not like the old days!' he translated for Susan, explaining the smile on Katia's gnarled old face and, as Katia seemed to understand what he was doing, she stretched her hand in the direction of the next room and he went on: 'There we would sit down with my father and mother and, maybe, twenty relations and friends. There would be six or seven servants to serve the meal and . . .' he smiled and nodded at Katia, again to show he understood her nostalgia, 'and afterwards dancing in this room to which many people, including everyone from the village, would come.'

Katia started to clap and pretend to dance, her face still wreathed with smiles and Kyril, watching her, suddenly seized her by the arm and began twirling her about the floor while at the door stood Peter and Nikolai, in their aprons, smiling and clapping too.

Entering into the spirit, Susan held out her arms to Peter, inviting him to dance, but he shook his head and stepped back deprecatingly and later, when they had gone and Susan asked Kyril why this was, he said:

'He would never dance with the wife – the *kniaginia* – of the prince. For that is how they think of me, whatever has happened in Moscow abolishing titles. They always will. Nothing has changed here.' He paused for a moment, looking a little sad, then continued: 'The Revolution has hardly affected them at all and, in some ways, I'm glad because people here were never as badly off or as badly treated as peasants in other parts of Russia. Each has his little smallholding which he cultivates and they lead happy lives. I know that. My parents were very good to their servants, who hope that one day they will return.'

'But who pays the wages of Peter and Nikolai and Katia?'

'Oh, we have arrangements made in Batum to pay them and to look after the house and property which, one day, may no longer belong to us, when all private property is abolished, as it already is in Moscow.'

Susan looked round at the shadows dancing on the walls in the light of the oil lamps, at the friendly fire coming from the stove. In the parts that were not covered by local, beautifully woven rugs the bare floors gleamed, and the faces of generations of Ferov princes and princesses gazed upon them from portraits on the walls. Susan thought of Askham and Askham House, of Lighterman House and her mother's splendid home in St John's Wood; of the family portraits of generations of Askhams from the first Baron Askham in the sixteenth century, and she felt a strange kinship with Kyril that had nothing to do either with this newly-formed sexual bond, or the one created by their mutual adherence to the ideal of the Revolution. As if divining her thoughts he reached over and took her hand.

'Still worried?'

'No.' Susan brushed her hair back from her forehead with a hand. Even her hair seemed to have a life and lustre it had not had before. She had let it grow and it hung straight, falling over her face like a swath of soft French silk gleaming with highlights. 'I was thinking of Askham ancestors which, too, stare at us from portraits on the walls, and I wonder if the Askhams and Ferovs ever met? You were close to the Czars, and we have always been associated with our Royal Family. My grand-mother waited upon Queen Alexandra.'

'Who knows? They have met now,' Kyril's hand tightened on hers. 'I feel they should stay bound for good. If I take you back to Moscow as my wife, no one will dare separate us. Besides,' he said lightly, pretending not to notice her surprise, 'I think it is what Katia would like. Your mother too, perhaps.'

'My mother and Katia! What a contrasting pair, you have no idea.' Susan joined in his laughter, almost breathless with excitement. 'Marry? Are you serious?'

'Perfectly. It is now only necessary to register the marriage in a simple ceremony at the Department of Marriage Registra-tion, which we could do in Moscow when we return. But I feel we should ask our local priest to marry us quietly because he has known me since I was a tiny child; in fact, I think he baptized me. You see, you have no papers and the Department of Marriage Registration would be sure to ask questions. Father John won't ask any. Would you like that?'

'Marry?' Susan echoed, still astonished at the unfamiliar sound of the word – unfamiliar as it applied to her, anyway. 'If I marry you I shall be even younger than Mamma when she married Bobby's father. I never thought I would marry so young. I would like a career.'

'But you will have a career as a Soviet citizen; there will be many things for you to do.' Kyril poured fresh wine in their glasses and then, standing, raised his glass. 'In the south it is the custom to have a person called a *tomade*, someone in charge of making toasts. Every time one of the guests is toasted it is necessary to drain your glass. I am the *tomade* and you are my chief guest, my beloved.' He entwined his arm through hers and, drawing her up, kissed her gently before they raised their glasses to their lips, sealing their troth by draining the golden Caucasian wine to the last drop.

Although the room was quite small its walls were hung with red velvet and the huge mahogany desk at which the Czar Nicholas had worked was now occupied by a slight, bald, rather shabbily dressed man in a woollen shirt and a well-worn coat. His short red beard and moustache seemed to accentuate the pallor of his face caused by years and, since the Revolution, days and nights of overwork.

Bobby Lighterman, despite his customary *sang froid*, was rather nonplussed to be in the presence of the virtual ruler of Russia, whom even his Aunt Rachel had been unable to see on her visit. He didn't know whether to bow or shake hands as he approached the presence, whose head was still bent over his desk writing, as though time were too precious, until an assistant whispered something to him. Lenin cocked his head on one side to listen, his eyes still on the page before him and, as he raised them, Bobby saw that he had a slight squint which, however, did not diminish the magnetism of his red-brown eyes. These actually seemed to crinkle with pleasure as he rose to shake Bobby's hand, murmuring something which was translated by the interpreter, who was already in the room, as: 'How do you do? Please sit down.'

Lenin then apologized for the fact that he spoke no English, although he had lived in England for a short time and knew many English people. In fact he spoke only in Russian because his command of all foreign languages was so poor. He said he was sorry for keeping Bobby waiting, but it was his custom to see, first, all the peasants who wanted a word with him. That was the importance of the Revolution, that the last should be first; the poor placed above the rich. On the word 'rich' he paused and looked keenly at Bobby, waiting for his interpreter to finish.

Lenin spoke rapidly, and was as rapidly translated. Bobby smiled and lifted a hand in his customary deprecatory manner, assuring Comrade Lenin that it was a matter of no importance. He had enjoyed his visit to the Kremlin and the experience such a unique event gave to a foreigner like himself. Lenin then bent forward and consulted some notes which his assistant had placed in front of him.

'I understand that you have a very important proposition to make to us, Mr Lighterman?'

Bobby cleared his throat and moved his chair nearer the beautifully carved desk, to the Seat of Power in all Russia – Lenin.

'My family has for many years been developing a motor car which incorporates some new and quite exciting techniques. We also have developed a hardy engine and, in conjunction with a special sort of tyre, being made by associates of ours, this should make the motor car ideal for conditions such as you have in Russia: very low temperatures and icy roads. The motor car is called The Askham and a model we are currently developing would be very suitable, not only for country use, but for all conditions in Russia.'

'But England is not willing to trade with Russia, Mr Lighterman.' Despite his ignorance of the language Bobby could detect the sarcasm in Lenin's voice. 'Until only recently you have been blockading us.'

Bobby crossed one leg over the other and casually readjusted the cuffs of his grey barathea suit so that the correct two inches of white shirt showed. He had found himself an object of intense interest ever since he had been in Russia both, he knew, for his languid, casual approach to everything, including the search for his sister; and his carefully chosen, inevitably varied and obviously expensive wardrobe of clothes. In Russia, where everyone was shabby, or almost everyone, Comrade Petrovsky being a notable exception, and most visitors tried to conform to this universal stereotype, Bobby Lighterman stood out for his almost flagrant and, certainly, deliberate disregard of convention. He was an elegant man. He travelled elegantly and he expected elegance around him. In fact his suite at the Luxe Hotel was fully up to pre-war standards.

'I am sure you know that state of affairs won't continue, Comrade Lenin. No one wants it to. The British are pragmatic. They were the first to decide to recommend to the Supreme Army Council that the struggle against Bolshevism should be discontinued. We have enough on our own plates at home with over a million unemployed and industrial unrest. I assure you, Comrade Lenin, that England is anxious to have peace; peace to put its own house in order to recover from the dreadful cost of war. I think there will be no difficulty in arranging for quantities of my motor car to be exported to Russia.'

'But we cannot pay for them,' Lenin said, after Bobby's speech had been translated.

'We can arrange credit through our banking connections. I can offer you not only cars, Comrade Lenin, but a variety of goods and machinery which I know are in short supply in Russia.'

Lenin did not reply at once but stared at Sergei Petrovsky, who had accompanied Bobby and was acting as his interpreter. Then he said: 'Comrade Petrovsky spent an hour with me last night telling me about your visit and its purpose, Comrade Lighterman. He said that, although so young, you are the head of a great business empire created by your grandfather who was a poor working-class boy.'

'He was, sir,' Bobby said proudly. 'He had very little schooling and was a grocer's boy who finally bought the store he'd started at. My grandmother, his wife, was one of the first nurses to be trained by Florence Nightingale. They were, as

122

you say, ordinary working-class people who became rich, but not through inherited wealth. Then they did a lot for people worse off than themselves.'

Lenin seemed to approve of this. Although it was not up to the exacting Russian standards of fair shares for everybody, it was the best that could be expected in capitalist England. He took up his pen, scratched at a piece of paper for a few minutes, peering at it myopically as if his sight were troubling him. It was obvious to Bobby that Lenin was not a well man. Petrovsky had told him that he had never seemed fully to recover from the near-fatal attempt on his life by Fanny Kaplan in 1918. Although he was only in his early fifties the leader of Soviet Russia seemed quite old, with the bowed shoulders and air of a semi-invalid. But Petrovsky had also assured Bobby that this was deceptive because Comrade Lenin fully controlled the reins of government, and wrote an astonishing number of directives, pamphlets and speeches.

'Now,' Lenin sat back and gazed at what he had written. 'I have noted all this, Comrade Lighterman, and Comrade Sverdlov, the Commissar for Ways and Communications, or someone acting on his behalf will be in touch with you. I thank you for coming all this way to see me. Please give your aunt my kind regards and apologize for my not finding time to see her. On her next visit I hope I shall.' Lenin passed a hand wearily over his brow as if to indicate the meeting was at an end. He half-rose to his feet, but Bobby sat where he was, gazing with patrician unconcern at one of the most powerful men in the world, the awe-inspiring successor to the Czar whom people said had even more absolute power than the man he had replaced.

'There is just one more thing, Comrade Lenin, and I do apologize for troubling you with it.' Bobby paused while Petrovsky translated for him, and Lenin looked up at him, those rather shifty eyes fully alert.

'My sister has disappeared on her recent visit to Russia and

123

I want to take her home with me. All attempts to find her have proved fruitless and I am getting rather angry.'

As his words were translated, Lenin was given another sheet of paper by his assistant, running his eyes rapidly over it and nodding as Petrovsky finished.

'I have the details here, Comrade Lighterman. It is thought your sister was a spy.'

'I assure you she is not. She has gone off with a young man and I want her back. My Aunt Rachel, with whom she came, is, as you know, a bulwark of the British Labour Party, and the Labour movement is fully informed about what happened here. My sister is a foolish young girl just out of school who has run off with a young man, a Communist. She must be returned to us so that I can take her back to her family.'

'I see.' Lenin appeared to study Bobby, his face inscrutable. Then he held up his pen and sat with it poised in the air, his face raised in interrogation: 'The young man's name, please, Comrade Lighterman.' 'Ferov,' Bobby said firmly. 'Kyril Ferov. A member, I understand, of the once noble Ferov family.'

As Lenin wrote down the name neither he, nor Bobby, watching him closely, saw the expression on the face of Sergei Petrovsky, just behind him. It was as though he was seeing his own death sentence being written.

Batum was of unusual, semi-tropical beauty, an almost eastern-style city overlooking a deep calm bay. Behind were evergreen mountain slopes with, scattered here and there, the vine-covered houses of those rich people who had fled the previous year with the Allies. They were now occupied, as in Odessa and other cities deserted by the county nobility – the 'Gubernskoye Dvoriansto', the well-to-do – by an assortment of people: there were peasants who had come down from the mountains to the city, hoping for pickings from their former masters, bringing their animals, their sheep and their goats with them, which now nibbled in the apple orchards, the groves of tangerines and oranges. There were sailors who had abandoned their ships for the life of the lotus-eaters in this new democracy of the proletariat. There were former dwellers of the dingy shacks in the cramped areas of the port who desired more spacious accommodation, and there was an assortment of the riff-raff, the thieves, prostitutes and ne'er-do-wells such as proliferate in any large town or city.

Between the white pebbled shore and the town ran the Primorsky Boulevard lined with magnolias and, along the smaller roads and alleys, were palms and eucalyptus trees, Australian dragon trees, Japanese cunninghami and pungent mimosa. The gardens were full of exotic shrubs: gardenias, begonias, Japanese cryptomerias, and many different kinds of bamboo.

This profusion of trees, shrubs and plants gave parts of Batum a delicious all-pervading, but sometimes almost cloying, smell that continued along the coast road with its dusty, prickly hedges to the botanical gardens of Cape Zeleny, where many of the species now found in the town had originated, or the beautiful parks and gardens of the Makhanjauri valley.

The narrow streets of the town were full of old buildings covered with awnings to protect the inhabitants from the sun, which shone continually for most of the year. In July and August there was the danger of fever from the nearby marshes. Bathing in the sea was possible from May until November but even early spring, February and March, was full of sunny, halcyon days.

The town and port of Batum seemed very curious, strange and yet disturbingly exciting to someone like Susan with her western ideas. Most of the vehicles were still horse-drawn and in the open bazaars much commerce and bartering went on in a way that was no longer seen in Moscow, though Lenin's New Economic Policy would allow a certain amount of pre-Revolution type commerce. The most extraordinary sights for the stranger to Batum were the newly-made carpets laid across the thoroughfares on which all and sundry were invited to walk, the purpose being to have the bloom of newness trampled out of them, the bright oriental colours mellowed.

The horses that tramped the streets – sometimes pulling carts of black Isabella grapes – had garlands of bells round their necks which tinkled in a multiplicity of sound mingling with the cries of the street vendors, those going to and coming from the bazaars, the bleating of sheep which were moved slowly in droves from one place to another, regardless of traffic, and the cries of the maize sellers offering their wares. 'Hot maize, hot maize,' they called.

To the confusion were added the voice of the *muezzin* calling the faithful to worship in the Mosque, and the hooting of ships from the harbour.

Combined with all this were the smells of Batum: the rancid odour of roasting mutton which almost overpowered the fragrant smell of freshly-brewed coffee that had been ground in Turkish coffee mills, the fresh acrid tang of tangerines and oranges brought by the feluccas from Rizeh and Trebizond in nearby Turkey, and the smoke from Batumi kebabs roasted in charcoal on spits and then sprinkled with cinnamon and berberis powder. Eaten with fresh *lavash* – crisp, flat bread made of coarse wheat flour – and white Caucasian wine they made a feast of gourmand proportions that seemed strange to Susan, but stranger still to Kyril used, for so long, to the deprivations of life in Moscow.

They had come to Batum in the car that still remained in the Ferov garages – which had once housed several – driven by Peter, who wanted fresh provisions from the city. The iron fist of Bolshevik control had scarcely touched Batum, Baku and other ports on the Black and Caspian seas. Trade seemed to be what the population of Batum thrived upon. It was difficult to think of it ever changing, of the life and colour being removed from the streets as it had in Petrograd, Moscow, Kharkov, Kiev and many more cities.

Batum, one of the most southerly towns in Russia backed by the high mountains of the Caucasus and topped by a sky of intense cerulean blue, seemed not merely many hundreds of miles away from Moscow, but thousands, as Kyril attempted somewhat half-heartedly to establish communications once more with his life as a member of the Party.

It was nearly October and soon the streets of Batum would be swept by the autumn and winter rains which, when they came, fell continually so that the daylight was like a perpetually moist, warm dusk. Then all the carpets were hurriedly rolled up and removed from the streets, and the stalls and kebab stands taken into shelters. The horses, goats and sheep on their way to market tramped through the muddy streets resembling river beds with little channels of fast-flowing water, pebbles and the flotsam and jetsam of rubbish that city people threw away. Then Batum began to smell, an unwholesome smell that made visitors from more civilized places afraid of disease and anxious to move away.

But Susan didn't want to leave Batum as she hadn't wanted to leave the white building of the Ferov country home that rose up on the banks of the beautiful lake. She had pleaded with Kyril not to return but to make his life in his former home.

'What as?' Kyril had laughed at her surprising yet obvious sincerity.

'As a farmer. Say that you have property you want to develop.'

'But private property will soon be abolished all over Russia. We will have no more right to this than the peasants who live in the village.'

'But someone will have to live here. Why not you? Us?' And Susan had hurled herself against him as though she would tie him down. Besides, now that the time had come to return, she was afraid. She was afraid of all the things that she had put out of her mind since the idyll had begun. She was afraid of what people would say, of what had happened to her Aunt Rachel and, above all, of her parents' reaction to her disappearance – now of several weeks' duration.

127

But Kyril wouldn't listen to her fears. He said that, one day, they would return to Batum and the Ferov house, but now they had work before them: work for the Party.

Somehow, strangely, it was of the Party that Susan was most afraid.

The feluccas bobbing about on the turbulent, green waters of Batum harbour were painted in such vibrant colours that, massed together, they presented an atmosphere of festivity, of carnival. They were all gaily decorated, some embellished with brass, the sterns individually painted in bright, abstract patterns resembling the symmetrical hieroglyphics of the oriental carpets.

To the western eye the little feluccas were like gondolas drifting on the waters of a Venetian lagoon and, as on that lagoon, they wove in and out among much larger boats, sometimes ocean liners, skipping around like bright little fireflies. Great oil tankers came into Batum harbour, and so did fishing trawlers, smacks of all sizes and small cruise boats like the *Dimitry*, on which they had come from Odessa and which now again lay anchored against a jetty ready for departure.

Kyril had found obtaining a passage for two – one of whom had no papers – less easy than it had been in the chaos of Odessa. Though Batum was relatively free from restrictions a sizeable contingent of the Red Army had been based there after the evacuation of the Allies, and bureaucracy was gradually taking over the reins of government of that happy-go-lucky little port.

Kyril went on board to see the Captain of the *Dimitry* who recognized him and, over a bottle of vodka smuggled in from Tuapse, they did a deal. Only Kyril would be registered as a passenger on the schooner, but there would be room for his wife as well, whose situation would surely be regularized once they were back in Odessa or Moscow. Most of the port area was a slum made picturesque by the tall ships of many nationalities, some freshly painted, some berthed by the peeling *dukhans*, by the motley shacks and warehouses leaning drunkenly together, some half-dismembered, whose rotting timbers looked like severed limbs. A variety of lodging houses offered a poor standard of accommodation – some relatively clean, some infested by bugs and rats. The rats of Batum were well known, especially in the rainy season.

The boarding-house, however, in which Susan and Kyril lodged had been recommended by Peter, who was a Batumi, with a brother working in thé docks. Their tiny room overlooked the harbour, tucked between the coffee houses and *dukhans* which proliferated in the dock area of the port. The boarding-house was mostly occupied by sailors who had got drunk in one of the noisy *dukhans* and had missed their boats, and one or two officials who had recently arrived in the town. Except to visit the *Dimitry* and buy some food, Kyril stayed in the room with Susan, who scarcely moved out at all.

'Are you sure it will be all right when we reach Odessa?' she enquired anxiously after he told her of his conversation with the Captain and showed her the ticket for the trip.

'Sure, sure.' Kyril, beside her on the narrow bed they shared, blew smoke from his cigarette into the air, but he looked thoughtful. Now, at last, he was beginning to share some of her doubts. Caught up in the heady fervour of love what they'd done hadn't seemed so very bad, two or three weeks ago. Now it took on a more serious aspect as he considered exactly what he was going to say and how to explain what had happened to Susan. What, after all, did await them in Moscow and how would his standing within the Party be affected by this escapade? How much had he sacrificed his reputation as a loyal, dedicated member by running off with the granddaughter of an English lord? Maybe if he had known that he'd have thought twice – having overcome, with difficulty, the handicap of his own dishonourable, in Party eyes, origins.

But Kyril was not a man to brood. His nature was simple, idealistic and uncomplicated. He was at peace with himself and in love with the future of Russia and the Party. He believed in the Revolution. He knew that, in the best possible sense, all would be well and so, that night, they stole confidently out of the boarding-house towards the schooner anchored opposite.

There were a few sailors staggering around who had spent all day drinking and were now blindly trying to find their way to shelter. Kyril, however, pushed past them, his arm shielding Susan from the stares she received, because she certainly didn't look like the usual kind of woman found in the docks at twilight.

The gangway leading up from the jetty was lit by a solitary light under which stood the Captain watching them as they crossed the cobblestones and clambered aboard. He held out a hand to welcome them and, with an arm on Kyril's shoulder, pointed along the companionway to a door which was partly open.

'I've given you the best cabin,' he said but, as Susan tried to shake hands with him, he hurried away and she followed Kyril along the deck to the door.

She remembered that, as Kyril was about to go inside, he stopped for a moment to stare at her. Only later did she wonder whether he had a premonition that something was wrong, or whether he had already seen the men waiting for them inside, and tried to warn her.

Whatever it was he didn't turn away but stepped inside and, as Susan behind him looked over his shoulder and saw the two men rising to greet them dressed in the leather jackets of the Cheka with revolvers in their belts, she gave a cry, and tried to grab Kyril by his embroidered Russian blouse which hung over his trousers. Kyril didn't even glance at her as they began rapidly to speak to him in Russian and he only replied: 'Da, da. Yes, I understand.'

Turning to look at her, he clasped her hand and by its pressure she knew now, for the first time, how much he was afraid.

'They have been instructed by Comrade Lenin personally to find me,' he said. 'And I am to go straight back to Moscow by train.'

'You? Us, you mean?' Susan cried but, before Kyril could reply, they were bundled out of the cabin and back along the deck the way they had come a few moments before, their few possessions still in their hands.

The Captain had reappeared and stood to one side of the gangway watching them, his face in the shadows cast by the light. As they passed he shrugged and whispered in broken English so that only Susan could hear:

'I had to do it, or they said they would suspend my licence. I hope you understand.'

He watched them, rather sadly, from the safety of his ship, being hurried across the harbour towards the waiting car that had brought the two men only half an hour before.

An hour later Kyril and Susan would have been gone, safe on the waters of the Black Sea.

PART 2

Whom God Hath Joined ...
1922–1926

CHAPTER 7

Susan put her arms round her father's neck and leaned her cheek against his.

'It doesn't really matter,' she said. 'You'll have more time to do all the things you've wanted to do. You can write books, concentrate on the law.'

Adam reached up and stroked her cheek.

'I don't mind so much about myself as about the Party. It is such a shattering defeat. The Liberals are completely annihilated.'

'They'll come back, Daddy. They have been in power for too long. They are associated with the War and the Depression.'

'But to lose sixty seats! It's a shocking defeat. And for the Labour Party to reach second place! Who would have thought they would command 138 seats – twice the number we polled – in such a short time?'

'Aunt Rachel, at least, will be pleased.'

Susan left her father's side and wandered to the table by the window on which there was a selection of books and pamphlets. In Bedford Row the trees now were almost bare, their brown, discarded leaves thickly carpeting the pavement.

Susan looked at the deserted street with its piles of sodden leaves, which seemed to echo her own sadness.

'It's almost a year to the day since I returned from Russia.' Susan's voice was hardly above a whisper. 'And still no news from Kyril. To think he doesn't even know about the baby!'

'Well, we are doing all we can, and now that Labour has more power maybe Ramsay MacDonald will influence the Bolsheviks. I'm sure he's not allowed to write, wherever he is,'

Adam said gently, rising and going over to her, his own grief taking second place to his daughter's.

'They told Bobby Kyril would be allowed to write; that he had been sent somewhere for his own good. I think he's in prison. I always feared that would happen. I used to dream about prison bars.'

'Darling, you know that I say and Rachel says it's most unlikely. He did nothing criminal. He's probably in some far-off corner of Russia with his own job to do.'

'If he could write he would.'

'But would he know where to write if he hasn't received your letters?'

'Oh, don't!' Susan put her head in her hands; but, on that sad day of 15 November 1922, when her father had lost his seat in Parliament, the Unionists under Bonar Law having been swept to power, she would not let herself break down. 'I wish we hadn't behaved so foolishly. How ridiculous it all seems now to think that Kyril wouldn't be punished. If only Bobby ...' She spun round on her father, her normally pale face mottled with angry red patches. 'If only Bobby hadn't interfered. Fancy telling *Lenin*!'

'Bobby only did his best, my dear.' Adam, feeling inadequate, put a comforting arm round her. 'He said that he got nowhere until he saw Lenin; everyone had been stonewalling him. They were very angry indeed with Kyril. I think he would have been punished, whether Lenin had personally interfered or not.'

'Yes, but the Head of State to be concerned about us! It was ridiculous...'

'I believe Comrade Lenin calls himself merely the Chairman of the Central Committee of the Communist Party,' Adam said dryly, 'not Head of State.'

'It's the same thing.'

'Well, they say he's very ill now after his stroke. Perhaps someone milder will be in charge or, in view of the Russians' economic difficulties, perhaps, as Lloyd George said, "Bolshevism is just a passing phase". Somehow or other I never agreed with him.' Adam paused as there was a knock on the door and Flora popped her head round, a bundle of papers in her hand.

'Want to see them?' she said, advancing into the room. Her cheeks were red as though she'd been running and her usually neat hair was windblown.

'Not if it's bad news, Flora dear,' Adam said. 'This seems to be a house of gloom today. Susan reminds me it is the anniversary of her return from Russia.'

'Oh, my dear,' Flora put an arm round her niece and kissed her cheek. 'Still no news from Kyril, I suppose?'

'You'd be the first to hear, Aunt Flora, bless you. You and Daddy have been pillars of strength to me. I don't know what I'd have done without you.'

Adam and Flora exchanged glances and smiled, joined together in secret affinity.

'Well, we love you, and we love Alexander. He is the dearest little baby one could have wished for. He is so good and so adorable. Good does come out of bad, you know, my darling, and one day you and Kyril and your son will be united.'

'I can't understand why Bobby can't do more,' Susan angrily thumped the table with her bare fist. 'All he thinks of is trade.'

'He can't jeopardize his position with the Russians, I do realize that.' Flora lit a cigarette, exhaling the smoke. 'I think he's done all he can and is as upset as you are. It's an awful pity you and Kyril couldn't have got married properly without doing it in that secretive fashion; a marriage by a priest not recognized by the Party.'

'We were going to register it in Moscow when all my papers were in order. We felt if we were married by the priest they would have to accept it.'

'The Party have to accept nothing,' Adam spoke bitterly. 'We've learnt that.'

'Well, in our eyes you're married, darling.' Flora hugged Susan again. 'And even if you weren't it wouldn't matter. We

137

love you and we love Alexander and when we meet Kyril, and I'm sure it will be soon, we'll love him too.'

At the mention of his name Susan at last broke down and wept, pressing her head against Flora's bosom, while Flora looked distractedly at Adam.

'Why don't you go and rest?' she asked. 'Come on, you're tired with all the emotion, staying up half the night. I'll see you upstairs and take a peek at the baby.'

Chubby little Alexander, who had been born in July, lay in his crib under the watchful eyes of the new nanny, whom Rachel's more experienced nanny had engaged after interviewing many applicants. With unemployment nudging two million there was no lack of applicants for the post. Although there was very little of it, Alexander seemed to have Kyril's sandy hair and the blue eyes which were a legacy from his mother and father. He was a robust, sturdy child over eight pounds at birth and had, moreover, a temperament that was at once sunny and docile, causing little trouble either to his mother or his nurse.

The birth of Alexander had marked the climax of a momentous year for a girl of just nineteen, whose status as a wife was equivocal and questioned by some and who, in many ways, had once seemed so immature. But since her return from Russia Susan had grown up very quickly.

Even to come back, as she had, the previous November in the custody of her brother, having been practically booted out of Russia, was a humiliation that had been hard to overcome. She had to announce not only that she had secretly married, but she was also pregnant by the husband from whom she had been separated that day in October at Batum and had never seen again.

The Russians had refused to acknowledge the validity of a marriage in front of a priest. By the new Russian Marriage Laws of 1917 any woman of sixteen could be married to any man of eighteen or over, provided they were not already married, insane or closely related. But the wedding had to be legalized by a simple ceremony at the Department of Marriages. Such an option was not given to Susan or Kyril, nor were they allowed to meet again, owing to Lenin's displeasure that a Communist, a son of Russia, had offended an influential English family, some of whom were Socialist, but the more important part willing and able to supply much-needed goods to Russia.

Lying on her bed after she and Flora had spent several minutes in the company of Alexander, nursing her throbbing head, Susan tried not to think about the past; about that unhappy year, with the baby growing daily inside her, the sympathy of her father, aunts and cousins failing to compensate for the loss of her husband, the man she loved. It had been a difficult year, during which she learned to cultivate, as Bobby had, a distance from the world that had already hurt her so much. In three months she had left school, become a mistress, a wife, and almost immediately a widow of sorts. In many ways she was emulating her mother's experience, yet her mother was not the person to help and comfort her. That role was taken by Flora as soon as Melanie returned to France immediately after Susan's arrival home, clucking with indignation, the rift between them complete.

But, most of all, Susan had felt alone, cut off from Kyril in body and spirit, and no amount of family consolation had been able to help her. This solitary, grieving person had matured beyond girlhood, beyond even young womanhood, and those who loved her grieved too.

Yet, despite her determination not to dwell on the past it came too vividly before her, penetrating the deep reserves of memory: the little ceremony in the white-painted wooden church near the Ferov house conducted in secret by Father John, who had baptized Kyril and only married them because of that, being fully aware of the law and the consequences of flouting it. The two servants Peter and Nikolai and the old *nyanya* Katia as witnesses – finally being told the truth – holding the crowns over their heads as Father John went through the elaborate ceremonial of the Orthodox Church dressed in his splendid robes, taken out of mothballs, perhaps for the last time.

It had been a day full of sunshine, full of hope and promise and, as they journeyed back to the house in the bullock cart for the hastily organized wedding feast, there had seemed nothing at all to cloud the future which looked as bright and as clear as the sky above them – that rich Caucasian blue which was like nothing she had ever seen before or since. However much she tried to avoid thinking about it, the memory was so precious, mostly because Kyril, their love and the place seemed inseparable, and she knew with certainty that she would never go back there again.

Finally Susan fell asleep and, in her dreams, she did return, the dream so vivid that she could almost smell the pines, laurels and cypress trees which covered the mountain slopes, and feel her husband lying in her arms satiated, satisfied.

Rachel listened for some minutes to the voice speaking rapidly over the phone. She nodded her head several times, tried to interrupt, shrugged her shoulders, accompanying the gesture with a comical expression to the man sitting opposite her and finally, with a word of thanks, replaced the receiver on its hook.

'Hugo again,' she said, raising her eyes to heaven, and Rathbone Collier crossed his legs, put his hands in his pockets and tipped the chair back on its legs.

'What's it this time?'

'He's not at school. They think he's somewhere in the park.'

'But did he go to school?'

'Oh, he went to school all right. Nanny always takes him there in the car. Apparently he skipped out at break. It is the third time he's done it in the past two weeks and the Headmistress wants to see me.'

'What does he do in the park?'

Rachel resumed her seat, arms folded, her head thoughtfully bent.

'He looks for things to save – animals, birds, people ... anything lost, down and out or ill is of interest to Hugo.'

Rathbone Collier was a big man and he shifted uncomfortably in the narrow chair that he always thought was provided by Rachel so that no one would stay too long. Looking around he thought that her room hadn't changed since she first moved into it, after Bosco bought the paper in about 1911. The same furniture was there, the same pictures on the wall and, perhaps, the same dusty files in the cupboards and on the shelves. Even the wallpaper looked the same. The room had an air of orderly mustiness, the habitat of a busy person with little time for trivialities.

'But that is a very commendable aim. Very laudable.'

'Not in a ten-year-old boy who is meant to be in class, dear Rath.' Rachel got up, her arms still folded, still apparently deep in thought. 'I shall have to send Hugo to boarding-school.'

'I don't know why you haven't before. Ralph went at eight. Is it because Hugo is so ... special?' He gazed at Rachel, who avoided looking directly at him.

'Special? All my children are special.'

'But Hugo is special special, because he isn't yours.'

Rachel raised her head at last and smiled at him with that direct, honest smile that always seemed to make his heart lurch. He had never loved Rachel; but his admiration for her amounted to a kind of love, a veneration. Since Bosco's death his attitude had been one almost of hero-worship, because she had carried the paper on her own, as well as running her life and the lives of those dependent on her, with such calm and fortitude. He thought he was probably her best friend, yet even he didn't know how she did it. It was true she did not lack for money and had plenty of help; but even people so assisted broke down. In a way it was easier for them to break down. Rachel never had. Not only had she not broken down, she had,

141

by her help and example, been of assistance to many others like her – women widowed by the War but who had nowhere else to turn and no idea how to cope. He knew that, as well as looking after her own brood, Rachel gave much of her time to tireless charity, helping the less well off in a caring, practical way.

'That's perceptive of you, Rath,' she said. 'Maybe I do love him in a different way from the others. I always think there is a parallel with my attitude and his love for friendless creatures, unwanted animals, abandoned strays. Hugo doesn't know this, of course; but it's there. It's instinctive.'

'What does he know?'

'Well, he knows he's Bosco's son by another woman. That's all he knows, not whether they were married or not. He's too young to realize the meaning of titles, the fact that the others have the prefix Hon, Lord or Lady and he is plain Mister. He doesn't mind. Hugo is a natural radical.'

'And Ralph is a natural aristocrat?'

Rachel laughed, clasping her hands. 'Ralph is certainly very lordly, but not in a horrible way, I don't think. Do you?'

'I think he has a certain arrogance, but this is disguised by his charm. He is very, very like his father, who would have delighted in him.'

'The way Ralph has behaved in the last seven years has certainly been remarkable. He seemed to shed his childhood when his father died and has been like a companion to me, a young man. I think he will be a splendid adult. But Ralph is no problem, Hugo is. You see, he is the only child left at home and I fear so much I'll miss him.'

'You're lonely, Rachel?' Rathbone got thankfully off the chair and lumbered over to where she stood by the window thoughtfully looking out on to Ludgate Circus with the busy streams of traffic going eastward to the City, westward to Central London and south over the river. Sometimes she thought Ludgate Circus, bridging, as it did, Fleet Street and the City, was like the very heart of London and she was its pulse.

'Well, after having so many people about me, yes, I do feel a bit lonely in a house empty except for a few old faithful servants. I try to make up to Hugo for ... well being what he is, an unwanted child though, so far as I can tell, he has no memory of being abandoned by his mother. He was not quite three at the time. But Hugo knows he is different. He's not like the others. The trouble is that he's also not like the others in temperament. He is very vulnerable, tender-hearted. I don't know how he will react to boarding-school. I don't think I should send him to the same prep school as Ralph and Freddie, where Bosco went in preparation for Eton. I don't think he'll go to Eton either, though I have him down for it.'

'You don't want to make him out to be something odd.'

'Not odd, but different.' Rachel looked slightly worried as she turned to him. 'I'm afraid it might be his mother's blood, though I know that's a hopeless, prejudiced thing to say. What I meant to say is this mixture of genes – English, Egyptian ... after all we didn't know too much about Nimet.'

'But if he's compassionate that, surely, is the last thing she was, abandoning him?'

'Yes, but there's the wildness, lack of concern for authority, wilfulness, determination to have his own way. Hugo in many ways is a handful, which is why I'm anxious to keep him with me. Anyway, I must go now and see Miss Firkettle. She sounded very cross.'

'Shall I come with you?'

'There's no need, Rath. I'll take a cab. Did you know that Flora's somewhere in the building?'

'Is she?' Rathbone looked at Rachel with interest, his eyes, above his bearded face, gleaming with interest. 'Is she very put out by Adam losing his seat?'

'Well, she's disappointed, as I am, we all are. But Adam won't leave politics, that's for sure, and he is even more committed to so many causes like the League of Nations and the Reparations question. He says that if the Allies sting Germany too hard, and they are, the country will collapse entirely and some new Kaiser will arise out of the ashes, a kind of German Lenin. He says the break-up of the Reparations Commission and the collapse of the Mark will have unforeseen consequences. By the way,' Rachel looked in the small mirror on the wall, straightening her hat, 'did you know Susan is going to France?'

'Really? Why?'

'To look for Kyril's relations. They don't even know they have a grandson.'

'But will they be pleased?'

'I don't see why not.' Rachel took her gloves and bag from her desk and looked at her watch. 'After all they were married according to the Church, whatever the Communist government says. You'd think they'd like that. I don't know why she didn't think of it before. Now I must fly.'

Rachel pecked Rathbone on the cheek and hurried out of the room. He followed her slowly, thinking over their conversation, her concern about Hugo, her admission that she was lonely.

Somehow Rathbone always thought of Rachel as being too self-contained to be lonely, with her causes, her paper, her devotion to her family, including Bosco's mother, whom she made a point of visiting as often as she could despite their past differences. If anyone was lonely it was Dulcie Askham, who had always had a busy life surrounded by admirers and friends from Court. The War had changed all that. Dulcie was now seventy and going a little deaf and absent-minded. She was not the friend of Queen Mary that she had been of Queen Alexandra, who was now seventy-eight and living completely in retirement. The Queen was too frail to travel and, very occasionally, Dulcie visited her at Sandringham, but Alexandra's total deafness and near-senility made such visits very hard.

Rathbone ambled down the stairs, greeting one or two writers or sub-editors hurrying past him with copy. Since the war *The Sentinel* had become one of the great national newspapers, of a leftish inclination, but well to the right of the official Labour Party. A bastion of Liberalism, in the sense that it took a 'liberal' attitude to most things, a steady centre-of-the-road policy on important issues, which surprised people who knew Rachel's personal views. She was able to put her duty to the nation above those, and her leader writers were given a free hand to write dispassionately about events as they saw them. The paper examined everything carefully before taking sides and was particularly charitable to the Russia of the Soviets, despite what had happened to Susan. Maybe Rachel exerted more of an influence here.

Rathbone found Flora in the library delving into past issues of *The Sentinel*, her gold-rimmed spectacles, which her mother had always so deplored, on the tip of her nose. Flora at forty-seven was youthfully middle-aged, her lovely Askham auburn hair greying at the sides, her fine eyes concealed, as they always had been, by increasingly thick spectacles. Many years ago Rathbone, then the Editor of *The Sentinel* when Bosco was alive, had been in love with Flora and had asked her to marry him. But the love of her life was, and remained, her brother-in-law Adam. Rathbone hadn't seen Flora since the divorce had come through. He leaned over her as she studied the yellowing back issues going back to the 1870s and even then she didn't notice him, so intense was her concentration.

'Can I take you to lunch?' he whispered.

'Rath!' Flora's hand shot up to her spectacles, which almost fell off her nose, registering first alarm, now pleasure. 'I haven't seen you for ages.'

'That's just what I was saying to Rachel.'

'Is she lunching too?'

'Alas, no. She's gone to look for Hugo in Hyde Park; apparently he prefers the wilds of nature to being at school. But I would like to talk to you.'

Flora's expression turned from pleasure to one of doubt, as though she knew she was about to be pumped and wished to avoid it.

'Well,' she scratched her head, 'I've a mountain to get through. Adam is making a speech on the very early days of feminism, Elizabeth Garrett Anderson and all that. I said I'd help him.'

'Come on. Just a snack. You've got to eat, anyway.'

'I don't, actually,' Flora said, smiling, removing her spectacles to clean them. Once again Rathbone had the chance to admire the clear green-blue of her eyes which, with her fine bone structure, would have allowed her to be almost as beautiful as her mother and her sister if she'd allowed it. But Flora had never been one to compromise. She was accustomed to say that she was as she was, and nothing and no one would change it. Rathbone suspected that it was because of the competition of mother and sister, of the natural grace of her sister-in-law Rachel, that she decided to remain as she was: uncompromisingly Flora; some would say, uncompromisingly dowdy.

She put her glasses back on her nose, pushed them up and marked her place in the bound volume of the newspaper she was studying.

'I knew Mrs Garrett Anderson slightly, you know. I met her on several of the marches. I think she was even at Emily Dickinson's funeral, do you remember, in 1912, or was it 1913? But she never did as much for the feminist cause as she might have done. She was too conventional, too authoritarian. For all that, she was a very brave, dedicated woman though not a patch on her sister, Millicent Fawcett.'

'Or on Flora Down.' Rathbone affectionately took her arm and steered her out of the library, continuing to chat as they left the building, and walked up Fleet Street past Temple Bar. 'I thought the pub where we ate during the Askham trial? Does it distress you?'

'Of course not!' Flora looked at him in astonishment. 'I've eaten there often since. Anyway, it was ten years ago. Like everything else those memories have been obliterated by the War.'

146

The pub was an old one standing in a narrow alley between Temple Bar and the Law Courts. They were early so easily got a table in the old-fashioned dining-room with polished floorboards and deal-topped tables whose iron legs were screwed to the floor. A waiter in a white apron, pencil behind his ear, took their order without ceremony, and soon brought the bowls of steaming soup they'd ordered as a first course.

'Drink, sir?' Skilfully the waiter placed them in front of his customers without a drop spilling, rather like a clever conjuring trick he'd practised to perfection.

'Would you like a drink, Flora?' As she shook her head Rathbone said: 'A pint of bitter for me, please, and a jug of water.' Then he tucked his white napkin into his top waistcoat button, adjusted his glasses and started his soup.

'H'm, good,' he said, glancing up at her. 'I think you've lost weight, young woman.'

'Well?' She crumbled her bread and stared at him.

'It's not a good thing. You're thin enough. Is there anything worrying you?'

'What should worry me?' Flora bent her head. 'I'm fine.'

'But now that Adam's free ... '

'Rathbone!' Flora looked at him severely. 'You know that I have always said I would never marry Adam, could never marry him. How could I marry my sister's husband, the father of my nieces and nephews, to whom I am devoted? It would be like incest. I love Adam, but I am content – as I always have been – with the warm friendship, the love, if you like, that exists between us.'

'It may be all right for you, Flora. But is it all right for Adam? He is a relatively young man. Would he not wish for ...'

'Adam feels as I do.' Flora's glance was steely. Decidedly lofty, and Askham-like.

'But how would you feel if he didn't? If he married again?'

'He won't. He's assured me of that.'

Rathbone thought he detected a change in Flora's expression so he pursued his questioning undaunted. 'But how would *you* feel?'

Flora put down her spoon, pushed her glasses up her nose, a gesture which was a habit rather than a necessity.

'I would hate it, if you wish to know. I'm part of Adam's life. He needs me. We have a very intense interior life which we share. We enjoy the same things: walking, reading, foreign travel. Every minute of the day I can I spend in his company. We share a house. I am devoted to him and his children; poor, dear Susan, like a widow, and his little grandson Alexander. If he married another woman I would be lost. To change the subject, did you know that Susan was going to try and find Kyril's relations in France?'

'Rachel mentioned it just before she rushed out.'

'I didn't think she was serious at first, but she is. She doesn't know where they live but Adam is trying to trace them. She is becoming more Russian than the Russians, adopting Kyril's name and learning the language.'

'But she has his name already. Aren't they married?'

Flora carefully spooned the rest of her soup and shrugged, her eyes on her plate.

'Sometimes I wonder if they are, indeed, legally married. In the eyes of God, yes; but apparently not in Russian eyes – although marriage customs there are very strange – and probably not in ours. She was under age, anyway. Besides, who knows the status of the priest, or what happened in that tiny little village in the Caucasian mountains, miles from anywhere? She hasn't any documents either of a marriage. Kyril kept those, if there were any. Sometimes I wonder if he went through a form of marriage to please her because she felt very guilty about what she was doing, having an affair, as any well-brought-up young girl of eighteen naturally would. Especially someone as sheltered and protected as Susan was, immature and undeveloped emotionally. Sometimes I feel I hate that Kyril for what he did to Susan.'

'But isn't she happy with her baby?'

'Happy with her baby?' Flora looked at him in astonishment. 'She adores him. But she is merely nineteen. At that age I was on the threshold of life. Sometimes she seems to me to behave as though hers were over. You've no idea what Susan is now, compared to what she was. She seems to have passed the years in between altogether, and gone from being a young girl to a middle-aged woman. Where is her youth? Her young womanhood? I pray God she may yet know both. I bitterly regret that Rachel didn't stop what happened.'

'Not more than Rachel does,' Rathbone said sombrely. 'I think she is still racked by needless guilt.'

'Did you know Rachel had some sort of a relationship with a man in Russia?' As Rathbone looked immediately interested Flora hurried on. 'I only mention it because I saw his name in the papers today.'

'Is he Russian?'

'Good heavens, no! Rachel, at least, has a little sense. He was an Englishman who went on the same delegation. He was very helpful in looking for Susan after she disappeared ... '

'Oh, I did hear. Spencer someone ... '

'Spencer Foster. Well, he has become an MP. He is one of the new Labour members for some constituency in Lancashire. I wonder if Rachel knows.'

'And they had a relationship? You interest me.' Rathbone, who enjoyed gossip almost as much as his food, sat back, rubbing his hands with anticipation as the waiter set the main course of roast meat and vegetables in front of them.

Flora smiled. 'I thought I would. You like a good gossip, don't you, Rathbone?'

'No more than the next person.' Rathbone heartily poured sauce over his plate. 'I don't think you miss a lot, Flora dear.'

'Well, Adam told me that this Spencer Foster was very interested in Rachel, but when he found out she was a countess he would have nothing more to do with her. He thought there was too wide a gap between them socially. Also he lived in the

149

north of England. I wonder if things will change, now that he is to be at Westminster?'

'I wonder if she knows he's there?' Rathbone said. 'Maybe you should tell her? Rachel is a very lonely woman, you know. A man would make a lot of difference.'

'She wouldn't like to hear you say that! It goes against her feminist principles, as it does mine. I think she's right. But how can you possibly say she's *lonely*, Rath? She has all of us, she has you and a host of friends.'

'She'll be lonelier than ever if she sends Hugo to boarding-school.' Thoughtfully Rathbone Collier applied himself to his food – loving the Askham family and only envying those who were part of it.

Hugo sat on Rachel's knee, his arm tightly round her neck, so tight that his nails dug into her flesh, causing her quite considerable pain. In the other arm was the teddy that Rachel had given him as one of his first toys when she had first brought him to Askham House, and which he always had in bed at night, or rushed for when out of sorts or in trouble. He squeezed teddy and he squeezed Rachel, and it seemed that there was no end to the tears that streamed inexhaustibly down his face. The other children gazed at him with some interest as though he were a phenomenon, not to be missed. They were supposed to be cheering him up, adding encouragement to Rachel's, but now all of them, including Em, who hardly ever stopped talking, were bereft of words, silenced by the far from mute misery of the turbulent Hugo.

'School is quite a lot of fun.' Em was the first to speak after the pause, as she had been the last before it. She was a cheerful, attractive, rather tomboyish girl on whom the cares of the world sat easily, if they sat at all. In the summer she had been fourteen and was a popular, games-loving member of her school who had many friends and was always making more. 'I don't know what you're carrying on for, Hugo. I can hardly wait to get back.'

For answer Hugo glared at her and squeezed teddy and Rachel's neck in equal proportions even harder.

Young Ralph Askham stood by the window of his mother's sitting-room at Askham Grange where he and his brother and sisters had all been born. In the Hall across the lake, just visible from the corner of the window, lived his grandmother. This was the stability and order of home as he had always known it, except for the interruption of his father's death which he remembered vividly, recalling the memorial service at Askham Parish Church when, as a boy of nine, he had carried his father's war medals on a purple cushion.

From that day Ralph had resolved to take his father's place and look after his mother, his brother and his sisters. At that time he, like the others, hadn't known about Hugo, who joined the family several months later. It was only gradually he learned he was his father's child and, in a way, it diminished his father a little in his eyes because he knew he must have hurt his mother by having a child with another woman.

Even today, when he was a young man of sixteen, Ralph didn't know the whole story. He trusted his mother to tell him when she thought he was old enough. But although Ralph tried hard he had always found it difficult to love Hugo, to think of him as one of the family, a proper brother like Freddie. It was not only that Hugo didn't look like them – he had a dark skin and black hair rather like a gypsy – but he didn't act like them, either. Hugo was always different, liking different things, behaving in different ways and getting a lot more of their mother's attention than any of the children of her blood. It made him envious of Hugo's place in his beloved mother's life.

Rachel knew of this jealousy on the part of Ralph – the others didn't seem to share it to the same extent – and she did her best to diminish its impact. Hugo was different, she explained, because he had been unloved and, yes, even though she loved him and had since he was three, those early first years of little or no affection were very important in introducing a

151

child to close family ties, which he hadn't had. His mother didn't want him and had abandoned him, leaving him with a woman who was about to put him in an orphanage when Rachel found him six months after Bosco was killed.

Ralph, because he venerated his mother, did what he could to love Hugo, because he knew it would please her, but it was so difficult. It was difficult now as they were all on the point of going off to school, but Hugo was making more fuss than the rest of them put together.

Askhams were expected to go to boarding-school. He had been at Eton three years and Freddie had just joined in the last term. Charlotte and Em were at the same exclusive girls' school in Berkshire, which their cousin Susan had only left the year before and which was now startled to its seams by her marriage to a Bolshevik, her subsequent acquisition of a baby, and all in the space of a single year. From being a bit of a nonentity while she was there – someone rather colourless and not deemed particularly bright – her exotic adventures, her truly momentous experience, had transformed Susan into a heroine whom everyone now wished they had known better.

Hugo was not to go to the same prep school for Eton that his half-brothers had attended. There had been a lot of care in choosing a school, not too far from home, where his unusual personality would be absorbed rather than stifled. Green Bank Preparatory School for Boys in Wiltshire was very near the family home at Askham, and Rachel had promised that she would go and see him every week.

Ralph thought Hugo was being pampered and he showed it in the manner with which he behaved at this ceremony of departure before Hugo was taken off to school, in ignoring him as best as he could, turning his back on his childish tantrums.

Rachel finally pacified Hugo, who was persuaded to put teddy on the floor while they all had tea, which had been brought in by the usual procession of maids, the ceremonial with which all Askham meals in town or country were inevitably served. Rachel had always tried to keep the Grange as a family home, preferring to live there with her five children while her mother-in-law stayed at her own preferred home: Askham Hall. There Dulcie was frequently visited by friends, mostly rich aristocrats, who enjoyed the informality of the style of gracious living which the bereaved Dulcie had adopted since the death of her younger son.

If Ralph kept his distance from Hugo, it was the friendly distance maintained by many elder brothers on the ground of seniority. But fair-haired, blue-eyed Ralph, taking after his mother in looks and colouring rather than the Askham side of the family, seemed the antithesis of Hugo in many other ways. Perhaps because of his position as the eldest, Ralph had always been a good, steadying influence on the others, even though only two years lay between him and the twins. He had always seemed a lot older than his years; yet he wasn't a dull, ponderous sort of boy but a lively, charming member of one of England's most aristocratic and gifted families.

Charlotte, on the other hand, always felt protective about Hugo and watched fondly as he quickly recovered from his tears. He had two slices of cake and two glasses of milk. When he'd finished he picked up teddy, squeezed him to his chest and looked as though he were going to start crying again.

'Don't, darling!' Charlotte rushed over to his side and took him in her arms. 'I'm coming with you to school, aren't I, Mummy?'

'Yes, if you like,' Rachel said, startled, as she'd thought she was taking Hugo on his own. 'What a good idea.'

'What about Lenin?' Hugo looked wanly at the cat fast asleep in the middle of the most comfortable chair in the room.

'Lenin?' Ralph glanced up, and then burst out laughing. 'Oh, *your* Lenin. I thought you meant the revolutionary who keeps Susan's husband in prison.'

'We don't even know he's in prison.' Rachel began to clear up the things, signing to Em to help her.

'Of course we know he's in prison, Mummy,' Ralph retorted. 'Or else why doesn't she hear from him?'

'I can't think the Communists would imprison a man solely for getting married by a priest, for that is his only sin. Not even they would do a thing like that. There may have been something else we don't know about. I think you're very prejudiced against the Russian government, Ralph. Bobby likes the people he deals with a lot. Something very big happened there, you know, and they had to settle down.'

'Then where is Kyril?'

'That we don't know; but I'm sure we will in time. Aunt Flora said,' Rachel chose her words carefully, so as not to betray any reaction of her own that would reveal her feelings to her family, 'that the man who was so helpful to me in Russia has just been elected a Labour MP. He was very close to the Communists and is a champion of England recognizing Russia, which all sane people regard as inevitable.'

'Why must they be "sane"?' Ralph seldom argued with his mother and here she detected the influence of Susan, who felt very bitter about her treatment in Russia.

'Because the Bolsheviks have been in power five years. Whether we like it or not they're here to stay. Spencer Foster, for that's the new MP's name, will, I'm sure, be going over there very soon and will be able to find out more from the people in power. I must get in touch with him when we return to London.'

Hugo was displaying towards Lenin, the cat, an excessive degree of affection even by his standards. The cat, now a big tabby, though used to being petted and fondled, was draped round Hugo's neck like a fur boa, and bore an expression of panic on its normally smug, self-satisfied face induced by years of care, good feeding, grooming and complete forgetfulness of the fact that he had once been rescued from a dustbin in Mayfair.

'You can't take Lenin, darling.' Rachel smiled as two maids

came in in response to her ring on the bell and started to clear the tea things.

'Then I'm not going.' Hugo clasped Lenin's well-fed stomach between two sturdy hands and the cat gave an agonized shriek.

'Don't be a bully, Hugo.' Ralph went over to free the cat.

'I'm not a bully!'

'He's not a bully!' Charlotte put a protective arm around his shoulders. 'What an awful thing to say.'

'The poor cat can hardly breathe.'

'There's Freddie,' Em said, looking at the horses and riders passing the window. 'He and Aunt Flora have come back from their ride. I was worried. It's getting so dark.'

Em, though normally ebullient by nature, was a bit of a worrier, especially about her twin, whom she adored. She now tore out to welcome Freddie and Flora. The maids finished clearing the tea things. Lenin, restored by Ralph to his place of comfort on the chair, began to smooth his ruffled fur with his long harsh tongue, and Rachel asked Charlotte if she was really serious about coming with them. Charlotte said she was, to which Ralph had said he might as well come along too.

'Then let's get going.' Rachel looked at the clock on the mantelpiece. 'We have to be there by six, although it's only ten miles.'

Hugo, clutching teddy, looked on the point of tears again, which made Charlotte kneel and kiss his cheek.

'Teddy's excited,' she said.

'Is he?' Diverted, Hugo looked at teddy with interest.

'Yes, you can see he is.'

'But what will Lenin do without me, and parrot, and pidge and Carlos and Coker and ... '

Charlotte interrupted the recitation of the names of all his pets: the parrot, the hamster, his pony, his dog Coker and doubtless many more.

'You'll see. They'll cope. You'll like school so much you won't want to come home.'

'That will never happen.' Hugo managed at last to squeeze out the tears he'd been working on so hard. Sadly they trickled down his face. 'You can be sure I shan't be happy until I'm home again.'

CHAPTER 8

Now that the time had come Susan Bolingbroke wished that she had brought Bobby, who remained behind at the hotel. Instead, for some reason she didn't quite know, she had wanted to visit Kyril's relations, his mother and father, brothers and sisters, for the first time, alone. Yet, for all that, she stood now on the unheated staircase trembling. Her courage had fled, and she nearly fled too.

The large apartment house in the unfashionable district of Clichy had been hard to find. Even the cabbie got lost, meandering through the uniform streets of suburban Paris on a wet February day in 1923. The Ferov house was hard to find as had been the Ferov family because Paris in the twenties was full of Russian exiles of all kinds, from the most exalted noble to the meanest member of the stricken bourgeoisie.

It was the Polish Misia Sert, who had an apartment in the same hotel they were staying in, the Meurice, who put them on to the trail of the Ferovs, through Russian cousins of hers in a similar predicament. Her husband, the fashionable painter José-Maria Sert, was doing some murals in Bobby's Mayfair house. The Ferovs had obviously not come to Paris with all the family jewels, like the Youssopovs, or else she would have known their whereabouts. In fact didn't know of the Ferovs, which meant they had probably come very far down in the world indeed. She advised them to give the whole thing a miss, but Susan wouldn't hear of it. Nor would she hear of Bobby, in Paris partly to accompany her and partly on business, making the first overtures.

For this important visit to meet her new family, which she was tackling in a very adult way, by herself, Susan had carefully chosen what she was to wear so as to present the right initial image. She was not yet twenty but it was necessary, she felt, to look very grown-up. She had, therefore, selected a tailored coat and skirt, the former with a deep V and wide lapels. The long skirt had inverted pleats at the sides, a fashionable touch that was yet quite decorous, suitable for a mother-in-law one had never met.

Because it was cold she wore a fox fur round the shoulders of her grey gabardine suit, under which was a high pearl-buttoned blouse made of écru silk, a shade darker than the suit. Her cloche hat was trimmed with flat-pleated satin, fitting snugly on her cropped hair, a style that suited her as it got rid of that gauche, stringy look she had as an adolescent girl. Deliberately, she wore no jewellery, not even her wedding ring.

Indeed, Kyril Ferov might hardly have recognized in this tall, poised woman the girlish bride of eighteen months before. Time, and bitterness, had changed Susan, who now dressed in *couture* clothes, frequently visited her hairdresser and, as they suited her, adopted the latest styles and fashions including, today, on her feet, high-heeled shoes in grey morocco with pointed toes and patent leather straps. Her pale face had the benefit of judicious, lightly applied make-up which enhanced the indifferent colour of her eyes, her firm lips set more and more in a determined line. The duckling had changed dramatically into a gracious swan; almost a venerable, timeless sort of swan, since Susan could easily have added a decade to her age and no one would have known. For many years to come she was to remain like that: a type gracefully groomed, impeccably dressed and made up, whose age no one could fathom.

The Ferov apartment house was indistinguishable from a number of others that lined both sides of the broad, treeless road. It was not a mean or dingy street but a curiously characterless one for a city like Paris, famous for its beauty, for its tree-lined boulevards. The houses, all uniform, had been built in the middle of the nineteenth century for the bourgeois family man who had come from the provinces to make his fortune and raise his family in Paris. Gradually, as the families had prospered and moved to a more fashionable area, or failed completely and gone back to the provincial towns from which they had come, the area had declined. The houses had been turned into flats, many of which now served the exile population, from Germany and Italy, Turkey and Armenia, as well as Russia, who had fled to that most hospitable of nations, France, to escape persecution in their own countries.

Paris was indiscriminate about political beliefs. It had sheltered the Bolsheviks, the Social Revolutionaries, Mensheviks and Anarchists who had been driven into exile by the Czar, many of whom now ruled Russia in his place. In the nineteenth century it had given hospitality to the very Father of the Revolution, Karl Marx, until he had gone to an even more tolerant country where he had settled down and written his masterful work to formulate his doctrine of class warfare which would transform the world: England.

The Ferov apartment was on the second floor at the top of an uncarpeted flight of stairs which led from a large unwelcoming hall with peeling, stucco walls and cracked floor tiles reminiscent of a kind of past gentility. The banisters on the way up at times lurched rather dangerously to one side, as though indicating that it would be unwise to cling to them for support. Once at the top Susan paused to calm the rapid beating of her heart, then firmly pressed the doorbell of Number 6. After a moment, during which there was the sound of shuffling, the door opened and a tiny little woman with a creased face, a shawl wrapped tightly around her shoulders, the ends of which were clutched in her gnarled hands, peered out.

'Is Princess Ferova in?' Susan enquired, emboldened by the kind glance of the old servant, who reminded her of the *nyanya* Katia and those happy, far-off days.

The woman looked at her not unkindly, shaking her head, so Susan repeated her question in her faltering, schoolgirl French. The woman smiled even more broadly, then seemed as though she was about to shut the door when, from out of a room Susan was unable to see, stepped a much younger woman. She was a tall, rather striking-looking girl with ash-blond hair, who gazed imperiously over the head of the diminutive servant, speaking to her sharply in Russian and then addressing Susan in French.

It was a rather bad beginning in her attempt to get to know her in-laws. However, she replied in French, asking for Prince or Princess Ferov, whereas the young girl replied that she was Princess Ferova and was she English or American?

'English,' Susan said, thankfully reverting to her native language. '*You* are Princess Ferova?'

'Princess Hélène Ferova. What is it you wish?'

The Princess now began to look as unwelcoming, as inhospitable as the place in which she lived. More than that, she looked suspicious and widened the gap between herself and Susan by half-closing the door. Perhaps she thought she was an agent of the Cheka; so Susan smiled gently and placed a hand firmly on the door to prevent it shutting completely.

'Do you think I could speak to you?'

The Princess looked a little hesitant and then, gazing at the servant, spoke to her in Russian again as though asking her not to go too far away. The old woman stepped back and the Princess, in a gentler tone, said:

'Please do come in.' Leading the way along the gloomy corridor to a door at the end, which she opened, she said: 'I'm afraid it's very cold in here; but it's cold everywhere, isn't it?' She had on a cardigan as well as a scarf and, rubbing her hands, went over to the fire to rake over the few dispirited embers which remained.

The room was over-furnished in the manner of the mid-nineteenth century, with a number of uncomfortable-looking chairs with spindly legs, and a large horsehair sofa propped up at one end by a block of wood. There were several small tables with potted palms and a mantelpiece still draped with a red velvet cloth which, from its tattered appearance, had clearly seen better days. Parts of it were stained by candle grease, and parts had a tatty, decrepit look as though they had been nibbled at by hungry mice. On top of the mantelpiece were several sepia photographs, presumably of the Ferov family when they had enjoyed happier and more affluent times. On the tables there were one or two personal memorabilia: a large mosaic box, a cold pipe in an ashtray and, in a silver frame, a portrait of the late Czar and Czarina of Russia in state robes with someone standing behind who may have been the father of the family, Prince Ferov, in court dress. The heavy flock wallpaper had hung on it depressing winter scenes of some indeterminate Balkan country and, in the corner lit by tiny red lamps, were the family icons – the Virgin Mary with the Christus, St Helen, St Constantine being baptized, and Saint Kyril.

'Do sit down,' the Princess said graciously, pointing vaguely around the room. 'I apologize for this. It is just temporary accommodation.'

'It's perfectly all right.' Susan felt nervous again. 'And I apologize for calling on you like this.'

In another corner was an open bureau with some papers indicating, perhaps, that the Princess had been writing when she was disturbed.

'My name is Susan Bolingbroke.' Susan held out a hand.

'How do you do?' the Princess smiled, taking her hand and shaking it in a firm clasp.

'I came across your aunt and brother on a visit to Moscow and . . . ' Susan, who had never stammered in her life, began to do so now.

The Princess, stooping to poke the fire again, stopped before she had touched the grate with the long iron poker and straightened up.

'You've come about *that*?'

'I thought it might interest you.'

'It has no interest to me, or my family at all. Please don't think we are rude, but as far as our father is concerned neither his eldest son, nor his sister, any longer exists for him.'

161

'I am very sorry to hear that.' Susan, in the act of sitting down, decided to remain standing.

'We all feel the same. Thank you, however, for calling.'

The Princess politely pointed the way to the door when a noise in the street made her run to the window and Susan, curious, went with her just in time to see a rather battered Peugeot drive up and the driver spring out as soon as it had stopped and open the back door.

'Oh, my mother and father have returned. Please don't tell them what you've just told me.'

'Then what can I say?' Susan began to feel angry and also embarrassed.

'Say that ... say that we met in London. I only returned from there a few weeks ago. What did you say your name was?'

Susan told her and, with a nod, the Princess sped to the door. Susan remained by the window, watching, as slowly and in a manner befitting persons of rank, the Prince and Princess Ferov emerged from the pre-war car which, when associated with them, became as incongruous as the 'temporary' accommodation in which they lived with their family, including the beautiful, yet decidedly languid, Princess, who had entertained Susan.

Susan was quite familiar with the nobility, the aristocracy in her own country and some continental ones as well, through her mother and grandmother – the legendary Askham family. She was equivocal about her family, about her feelings towards it, and the nobility altogether. Like her Aunt Rachel she had firm democratic principles; but she knew class when she beheld it, and there was unmistakable class about the two people who walked majestically towards the door of the house as though expecting to be met by the doorman of the Ritz. The Princess wore a full-length sable coat which she clutched together under her chin and which, alone, looked as though it could keep the family in luxury for several months. She had a swathed turban-style toque on her head with a rather jaunty little side feather, and her elegant, high-heeled fur boots disappeared beneath the bottom of her coat. Behind her walked the Prince, dressed in a black velour coat with an astrakhan collar matching the cap on his head, which was worn rather like a war-time forage cap. He was clutching a number of boxes and parcels, some of which he gave to the taxi driver who, having closed the doors of the cab, followed the couple until they disappeared out of sight.

After a few moments – leaving them time to climb the stairs – a babble of noise broke out in the direction of the hall, loud voices talking together in French and then there was a sudden hush as Princess Hélène relapsed into rapid Russian, obviously explaining to her parents about the curious visitor in the parlour.

Susan, suddenly overcome with nerves, drew herself up as the steps came near and – at last – she faced the prospect of meeting Alexander's grandparents, of revealing who she herself was.

Princess Hélène preceded them and then stood back to make the introductions, first the Prince then the Princess. Behind them was the taxi driver still clutching the parcels, who looked quite at home.

Princess Hélène introduced Susan to her parents and also, to her surprise, to the taxi driver who stood, grinning amiably, behind them.

'This is my brother Dima. My other brother, Yegor, is still at school and my sister Evgenia teaches at a Russian school for exile children in Paris.'

The older Princess, Irina, was, indeed, formidably handsome. She had high Slav cheekbones, hooded dark eyes and a mouth moulded in deepest magenta. The curl of carefully coiffured hair peeping beneath her fashionable toque was heavily tinted auburn, looking as though it had been lacquered to her forehead. The sable was indeed a sumptuous, natural fur owing nothing to repair or artifice. It must have been her most priceless possession. The Princess was a tall, elegant woman; but the prince was even taller with a beautifully trimmed moustache, short hair *en brosse* and a monocle screwed into his right eye, through which he stared, rather imperiously, at his visitor. He bore a slight resemblance, Susan thought, to the exiled Kaiser except that the moustache lacked a twirl at the ends – but he had the same sort of Germanic countenance and staring eyes.

'You met Hélène in London? How charming. I hope you've been offered tea?' He spoke English with hardly a trace of a Russian accent, or any accent.

'I was just about to, Papa. I told *nyanya* to heat the samovar.'

'I hope you explained to your young friend that this is merely temporary accommodation.' The Princess, her voice deep and throaty, her accent decidedly Russian, her expression one of tragi/comedy, looked around. 'We are expecting funds at any moment from Batum.'

Batum. Susan shivered at the name and felt that her face paled.

'It will soon be sorted out by the Bolsheviks.' The Prince had a note in his voice that sounded more like resignation than confidence. 'They cannot just confiscate huge sums of money that don't belong to them.'

Princess Ferova sat down, looking gloomily at the floor, as though even she had ceased to believe in this fiction. Although it was mid-afternoon she didn't remove her coat. Nor did her husband. Dima, who looked distinctly Bohemian in a jacket with a scarf tied round his neck, put all the parcels on the chair next to his mother and rubbed his hands. With his curly fair hair and open boyish face Susan thought how like Kyril he looked, and realized she was staring at him. When he stared hard at her, she looked away, abashed.

'I'm sorry, you remind me of someone I know,' Susan said and Dima smiled and said, in the perfect English all the family seemed to speak, that he wondered if he knew him.

'I'm delighted that Hélène met some nice friends in England. Where did you meet?' he added.

The Princess turned to Hélène who had entered with a tray on which there were glasses of hot tea, the samovar obviously having come to the boil while she was out of the room. Hélène looked so nonplussed that Susan, who had never had a gift for lying, came to the rescue.

'At the home of my Aunt Rachel, Lady Askham.'

'Oh, Lady Askham?' The Princess looked up, the momentary expression of utter despair that Susan had glimpsed on her face being replaced by one of pleasant anticipation. 'Do we know Lady Askham, Alexei?'

'Mmmm,' the Prince furrowed his brow, searching his memory and Hélène, her composure restored, intervened: 'A friend of Aunt Tania, Mama. My mother's sister,' she explained to Susan who felt they were both sinking deeper into murky, untruthful waters.

'My sister lives in Barons Court,' the Princess said helpfully. 'Do you know it?'

'Only vaguely.'

'There are many Russians in London but not as many as in Paris.' The elder Princess looked kindly at Susan. 'France, you know, for many of us is a second home. My family only spoke French to one another and we encouraged it among our own children. But my husband's mother, Princess Elizabeth Ferova, was very fond of London and I believe knew Queen Alexandra quite well. My husband has always been a great Anglophile.'

'I wonder if she knew my grandmother, Lady Askham? She was a great friend of the Queen's, too.' The suggestion seemed to establish a rapport between them.

Yet it seemed unlikely because in all the talk about Kyril since she'd returned to London from Russia, her grandmother had never referred at all to a Princess Ferova. On the other hand she may not have connected the name with Susan. Her memory was not what it had been and the 'a' on the end of Russian names to denote feminine gender may have distracted her.

165

'How nice that you're in Paris.' The Princess rubbed her hands, pressing them towards the meagre fire. 'When we have our new apartment you must come and stay.'

Susan and Hélène looked at Dima, who glanced at his own watch.

'I must go soon. Maybe I could give you a lift?'

Susan didn't know whether she was supposed to have seen that the taxi belonged apparently to him or not. She shook her head then changed her mind. This interview was already strained, and full of lies. She needed badly to consult Bobby.

'Oh, yes, please. Could you take me to the Meurice? I nearly lost my way getting here.'

'You're staying at the Meurice?' The Princess perked up at once. 'How I *loved* the Meurice before the war! It was so smart and fashionable. I daresay it still is ... '

'Would you, would you like to dine there with us?' The words came out before Susan could stop them. 'My brother is staying there with me and I'm sure he'd love to meet you!'

'Well, I ... ' The Princess's eyelashes fluttered and her husband caressed his moustache.

'*Pourquoi pas?*' he said. 'Providing, of course, that your brother ... '

'He will send a note round tonight.' Susan felt the pace of her heart quickening. 'Would the night after next be all right, at say, eight o'clock?'

The Prince consulted the ceiling while his wife carefully produced a diary from her handbag and flicked through the pages in a busy, professional way, as though she were trying to find a space in a crowded engagement book in pre-war Petersburg.

'That *seems* to be all right,' she said, peering at the empty page which she tried to obscure with her hand. 'Just my husband and I and Hélène ...' She looked questioningly at Susan.

'All of you,' Susan said. 'I'm sure he'd want all of you to dine.'

After elaborate farewells and even kisses Susan, accompanied by Dima, took her leave. On the way back to the centre of Paris Dima proved to be much more informative, not so defensive as his parents.

'My mother didn't want you to know I drove a taxi. She kept on giving me a sign I should go. In fact, half the taxi drivers in Paris are Russians and I am not the only Prince among them, I can tell you! My parents still live in the past, calling all the accommodation we move into "temporary" which only means that we then move on to somewhere just as bad, sometimes worse. You know, to dine at the Meurice means an awful lot of money for your brother. I don't have a tuxedo and I know my sisters have not got nice enough dresses.'

'You must come in what you have,' Susan said earnestly. 'We don't mind.'

'But we do. It would never do to be seen dining there in an ordinary suit or dress. My mother will send you a polite little note declining the invitation once she has had the chance to think about it; to realize the implications. But thank you, anyway.'

Dima turned and smiled and once more Susan caught that startling resemblance to Kyril and she realized that, more than anything in her life, she wanted to be part of this strange, fascinating family whose blood her son shared. Suddenly, it became the centre of her existence; her purpose, she knew, in life until she and Kyril were reunited.

'My brother will contrive something,' Susan said. 'A little restaurant maybe, not the Meurice. He will arrange it very tactfully.'

'You're *very* kind.' Dima drew up outside the Meurice and jumped out to open the cab door. 'I don't know why you're doing all this.' Slowly he bent his head and kissed her hand.

Entering immediately into Susan's excitement, Bobby, with his usual skill, instantly apprehended the situation and asked the Prince and Princess and their family to dine at a small bistro

167

not far from their apartment, where he happened to know the owner and that the food was good. To his many attainments Bobby also added that of gourmet. He was not one to be mesmerized by show and expense and he said the food at Chez André was every bit as good as that at the Meurice, in a different kind of way. His only fear was that the Ferovs would think they were being patronized, but he needn't have worried, for when they arrived at Chez André Princess Irina looked to be wearing everything except the Romanov jewels, short of the tiara.

Any money that the Ferovs still had obviously went on clothes for the Princess. It was not mere elegance. She possessed an indefinable chic, wearing a simple black and white dress which showed up so well the diamonds at her throat and wrists, the cluster of diamonds and pearls pinned to her bosom. Her lacquered hair was plastered down over her forehead and her heavily mascaraed eyes beamed alluringly as Bobby greeted them in the tiny vestibule, and then helped her to negotiate the coconut matting with her four-inch heels as she teetered over to the table he had reserved in the corner.

The girls were totally eclipsed by their glamorous parent. They were alike to look at and wore dresses with waists and high lace collars, much too young for them. Their blond hair was youthfully dressed with bows and, unlike their mother, they wore no make-up. There was inevitably a suspicion that the Princess wanted to maintain the illusion of youth in herself by keeping her daughters like children. Princess Evgenia, at eighteen, looked many years younger. She was retiring and shy, keeping her eyes for the most part downcast – as though someone had wrested her from a convent.

Princess Hélène, a year older than Susan, was a different proposition, much more controlled and self-composed. She also looked rebellious at her state of imposed immaturity. There was also an air about her of apprehension, as though any minute the gaffe would be blown: her and Susan's duplicity exposed. Sometimes she looked frankly wretched.

But Bobby had been fully apprised of the situation and did his best to put the entire family at ease. He spoke quite openly about his trip to Russia the year before and about his attempt to do business with the new regime. Of this the Prince, who like his son was dressed in a well-cut lounge suit, and throughout the meal smoked through a long cigarette holder, expressed instant disapproval.

'Any attempt to do business with the Bolsheviks will only keep the accursed regime going. It must be isolated and shunned by the Allied powers.'

'But, my dear Prince,' Bobby said smoothly, 'I don't think you can put back the clock so easily. If you ask me the Bolsheviks, having achieved so much, are in power for good. It is simply facing facts. You have to accept it.'

'I accept nothing.' The Prince went pale and banged on the table, looking in outrage at his wife. Susan thought for a moment that he was going to get up and leave, but the Princess was not going to forgo a good meal so lightly – maybe the best one she'd had in days – and shook her head very imperceptibly.

'Are you a supporter of the Bolsheviks, Mr Lighterman?' Princess Hélène turned her imperious gaze upon him, raising an eyebrow. Now she looked like a woman – her natural aristocratic bearing overcoming the juvenility of her hairstyle and dress. In a way she was remarkably attractive – pale skin, fair hair, large blue eyes of astonishing clarity, the colour of a dawn sky, very pale. These were fringed by dark lashes, and she had rather thick dark brows which emphasized her Slavic looks, like her mother. She was tall, too, with a small bust and slim hips, the boyish figure that was currently very much in fashion, popularized by Mademoiselle Chanel, the creator of the little black dress, the simple suit.

Susan could see that Bobby was quite taken by this girl/ woman – as though he knew quite well what her mother was up to – and gazed at her for some time before replying.

'I am not a Communist, Princess. I am a capitalist. But I am also a realist. Now, while we talk of realism I want to be honest with you ...'

The main part of the meal by now was over and Bobby ordered coffee, brandy and liqueurs – cigars for himself and his male guests. Then he looked round and Susan, who knew what was coming – for the whole evening had been planned between them – closed her eyes. She was simply but tastefully dressed in a tea gown of green satin-beauté, waistless and with a square neck. She had a black velvet band round her short hair, wore black court shoes and smoked a cigarette from a long ebony holder. Had anyone been told she was younger than Hélène they would have found it impossible to believe. As Bobby, after a pause, started to talk she opened her eyes and drew heavily on her cigarette.

'There is a reason for us being here tonight, my dear Princes and Princesses, and what I have to say, what my sister couldn't say to you the other day, makes it specially difficult.' As the members of the Ferov family began to look at one another Dima, refusing a cigar, lit a fresh cigarette, while his father and Bobby sat back and lit cigars. 'It would be difficult to say it at any time, especially as I know how you feel about the members of your family who remained in Russia.'

'We never speak of them,' Prince Ferov said frostily, with an expansive, dismissive wave of the hand. 'It is as though they were dead. They died in our hearts. Please don't refer to it again.'

Susan thought Princess Irina looked as though her elder son was still very much alive in her heart because she cast her eyes towards the table, surreptitiously applying a handkerchief to her carefully made-up eyes. Maybe her intention was not to betray her grief to her husband, or maybe it was so that her emotion would not disturb her make-up. It was very difficult to say exactly what her true feelings were, and Susan felt that the more she knew this family the less she would know about them. Already she could tell that they were far more complex and circumspect than any group of Askhams, Lightermans or Bolingbrokes put together.

'I must tell you that Susan and my Aunt Rachel, who were visiting Moscow in the summer of 1921, met Kyril Ferov and the Countess Valkova, your sister, I believe, Prince?'

The Prince's eyes flickered, a nerve twitched in his jaw; he didn't speak but continued smoking furiously as though the subject of the conversation were intensely distasteful to him.

'I said I preferred not to discuss it. You must forgive me. Please don't insist.' Once again he looked about to rise and once again his wife shook her head.

'Oh, but I must,' Bobby went on in a calm voice. 'I do insist, in fact. I was about to say that on this occasion my sister Susan formed an attachment for the young man who acted as courier to the group of visiting English, your son Kyril Ferov ... '

Hélène gave a loud exclamation, leaned forward and looked about to intervene, but Bobby hurried on.

'Please don't say anything yet, Princess. My sister and your brother, your son, Prince, eloped and underwent a form of marriage in the Caucasus, on your estate I believe, or what is left of it. I'm sure you'll regard their marriage as valid, as I and my family do. Although, as yet, there are no documents to prove it, for reasons I'll explain. However, it is important to regard it as valid because they have a baby, a son Alexander born in the summer of last year. It was because of the son, this grandchild of yours, that Susan wished to find you. It is very difficult for her and for me to say this and I hope you understand. With all my heart I do.'

Bobby sat back, his cigar long since extinguished. As he stopped talking the silence from the corner table was of such a positive character that the air of melodrama seemed to infect those near them in the restaurant. Some fell silent too, watching, as though waiting for the reaction of the Ferov family, although they couldn't possibly know about what.

Princess Irina was the first to recover and, rooting in her bag, withdrew a small box which she held out to her husband

and said: 'You must take one of your pills, Alexei.' She gave something to her husband who, rigid with shock, reached for a glass of water and put the pill into his mouth. 'He has high blood pressure,' the Princess explained. 'Shocks are bad for him.'

'I'm sorry,' Bobby said sincerely, 'but might it not be a pleasure, Prince, to know you have a grandson, a daughter-in-law who was so anxious to know you? She could have said nothing.'

'It *is* a great shock,' Prince Ferov replied woodenly. Yet the instinctive, patrician politeness of one who had served in the Preobrazhensky Guard did not desert him in this hour of trial. 'We have not thought of Kyril as a son for many years, more years than you know because he supported the Bolsheviks when he was a student. When our family fled for its life he offered our Palace to the revolutionaries, a Palace which, incidentally, was not his to give – and they held some of the first meetings of the Moscow Soviet there. He had no care for us at all ...'

'Kyril *did* care,' Princess Irina softly intervened. 'It was you who would not understand him, Alexei.'

'What was there to understand?' The Prince's look of indignation increased as his colour returned to normal, and he took a large gulp of wine. 'He betrayed his family, a family that preceded Peter the Great. The Ferovs, I should tell you, Mr Lighterman, are more noble than the Romanovs. They go back to the very first boyars who governed Russia in the twelfth century. Our name is therefore among the oldest in Russia, and our Palace in Moscow one of the first great homes built in the eighteenth century before Peter moved the capital to St Petersburg. You will not even see the Ferov Palace in St Petersburg because it was sacked by the mob in the very first days of the Revolution and burnt to the ground. And my son, my heir, connived in all this. Do you wonder we have obliterated his memory?'

172

'He may have paid for it, sir,' Bobby leaned over the table pouring fresh wine into his guest's glass. 'He has disappeared.'

'How do you mean, he has disappeared?' Princess Irina asked in her sonorous voice, dramatically clutching her bosom, the fake jewels round her neck.

'He was arrested by the Cheka in Batum where he went with Susan to return to Odessa and legalize their marriage. He has not been seen since, and contacts I have in Russia have not been able to trace him. So you see,' Bobby neatly joined his hands together and looked round, 'he might very well be dead. All you have now to remember him by is little Alexander, just over six months old and, if you are interested, through his grandmother – Susan's mother and mine – heir to quite a fortune in his own right. When he is twenty-one he will inherit a great deal of money through the will of his great-grandfather, the tenth Earl of Askham, who died a wealthy man. Since his death, however, the property and assets he left have multiplied tenfold thanks to the acumen of Susan's uncle, and mine, Bosco, the eleventh Lord Askham, who was killed in the War. Now, I am sure the money does not interest you in the *least* – I just mention it to assure you that neither Susan nor her child would ever be a drain on you – but the existence of your little grandson, the plight of Kyril's wife, perhaps his widow, might.'

At the word 'money', the explanation of the grandson's circumstances, the Ferov family appeared to undergo a change of heart as sudden as it was dramatic. The sullen, doubtful expressions vanished, especially on the face of the Princess Irina who, perhaps, saw an end to the perpetual pawning of the sable to provide funds for them to live – there were only a few days in the entire winter when it was in her wardrobe or on her; the substitution, one day, of the fake jewels by real ones, though the originals had been sold long ago.

Doubtless the thought of money, too, newfound wealth, meant to Prince Dima the chance to abandon his taxi and take the university course he had always set his heart on. Maybe to the young Princesses the very suggestion meant the fact that they could give up teaching lazy, ungrateful pupils and resume the life to which the circumstances of their birth had accustomed them.

Doubtless, above all, to Prince Alexei Ferov it meant the end to the endless worry and speculation, the constant pretence, the juggling of inadequate funds to make ends meet, the perpetual hope, perpetually dashed, that the Bolsheviks would honour debts, unfreeze the vast Ferov fortune frozen in Russian banks.

Surely it was worth paying as light a price as this to buy such freedom, to welcome a possibly bastard grandson and his mother, to take them to the collective bosom of a family betrayed by the father of one, the husband of the other? Without a word, scarcely without a glance, the family seemed, with one accord, to rise, to stretch out its collective arms in a fond embrace of Susan, née Bolingbroke, now Princess Kyril Ferova, the latest member of a noble house so much older than that of Romanov.

CHAPTER 9

The house was in a small street on the borders of Pimlico and
Westminster. It was a neat, rather pretty house made of brick
like all the others and tempered by the weather over the years
since they'd been built – possibly in the late eighteenth century.
Such houses had been allowed to run down during the War,
and had thus been available quite cheaply for those purchasers
willing to do them up. For those who could and did they were
an investment, being within easy reach of the Houses of
Parliament and the River Thames.

Adam had called for Rachel at St James's Square, and they
had a drink before setting off at seven-thirty. Adam was in a
ruminative, reflective mood, the news about Susan's reception
by her new relations having only just reached him. Rachel felt
reflective too and rather thoughtful, even sombre. Hugo had
made a bad impression almost as soon as he arrived at his new
school and there was already talk of Rachel being asked to take
him away.

'What exactly is the problem?' Adam asked as he'd pulled
his new Askham motor car, with its easy gear shift, from the
kerb.

'He won't settle. He keeps on running away. Oh, not far, a
field or two, or possibly the village; but once he got as far as
Askham and my mother-in-law had to ring up and say where
he was. Askham is ten miles from the school. They say it is
unsettling for the other children. It's not only that but he is ...
naughty.' Rachel paused as Adam smiled and turned into the
Mall.

'Well, aren't all children naughty?'

'Yes, but they say he's ... wicked, whatever that means.'

'I suppose it just means high-spirited.'

'I suppose it does.' Rachel gazed from the car window at the lights in Buckingham Palace as they drove past it towards Victoria. Once Buckingham Palace had seemed part of their lives. Dulcie Askham had always been chatting about it, gossiping on this and that, and indeed had a grace and favour apartment in St James's Palace. Now they seemed completely cut off from the Court. Not that Rachel minded. As a countess she had had to be presented, but it was one of the very few times she'd been inside those hallowed walls. It was funny how quickly, and finally, the family had been cut off from Palace life after the scandal in 1913 which, some thought, had cost Bosco his life.

'Penny for them?' Adam glanced at her before crossing Victoria Street.

'I was thinking how we have nothing to do with the Court now that Lady Askham is retired. I suppose it started with the libel trial and Bosco's ostracism by society.'

'Melanie's divorce hasn't helped. Queen Mary is notably sticky about that sort of thing.'

'It doesn't matter one little bit. Times have changed so much. Tell me more about the Ferovs.'

Adam was glad to enlarge upon the news he'd had from Bobby until they were in Pimlico.

Rachel took her compact out of her bag preparatory to powdering her nose while Adam drove slowly past the houses in a particular street, looking at the numbers.

'This is it.' Adam finally stopped the car, pulling on the handbrake. Then he sat for a while gazing at his hands in the light of the street lamp. 'What I didn't tell you was that Susan's thinking of going to live in Paris, to be near her in-laws. Bobby's quite willing to buy her a flat so that he has a base there too.'

'Oh, that's splendid! That will give her an interest, getting to know Kyril's family. Oh ...' she looked at Adam and put a hand on his arm. 'But shall you mind awfully? You're terribly fond of little Sasha...'

'Flora is too, and of Susan. With the boys at school it will seem terribly odd if she goes. Awkward for us, Flora and me ...'

'I know what you mean. The whole purpose was for her to look after the children. Well, let people think what they like.'

'Let them!' Adam appeared cheered by his sister's reaction and smiled. 'My reputation already cost me the election. Who cares what happens now? Anyway, Susan's what matters and the Ferovs are apparently awfully charming. They lost all their money in the Revolution, but that doesn't mean a thing these days. The son drives a taxi.'

'Good for him! That sort of thing one can only approve of.'

'He'd like to go to university, though, to study medicine. He missed out on all that because of the Revolution. I think Bobby is devising some way to help them financially, without hurting their feelings. He might use Prince Ferov, the father, as some sort of representative of Lighterman's in Paris. He and Duncan Curtis are going over next week to talk about it.'

'That sounds exciting and so lovely for Susan.' Rachel finished putting powder on her nose, and glanced at the front door just as it opened and Spencer Foster stepped into the porch looking to left and right down the road.

'Just why are we invited?' Adam whispered, as Rachel raised a hand and called out.

'I've an idea it may be to do with Russia, or maybe he just wants to show us his new home.' Rachel waved as Spencer, in dinner-jacket, came down the steps and opened the door. He put out a hand to help her and, as she stood on the pavement rather nervously, looking at him for the first time in nearly two years, he bent and kissed her hand.

'Welcome, Lady Askham.'

'You're awfully gallant.' Rachel felt embarrassed, not knowing whether he was joking or serious. He smiled at her and walked round the car to shake hands with Adam.

'Nice to see you again, Mr Foster,' Adam said. 'I know I have to congratulate you.'

'I only thought, later, you might think I was rubbing it in.'
Foster put an arm on Adam's shoulder and drew him into the
house as Rachel preceded them.

'Rubbing what in?' Adam looked at him in surprise.

'Well, that I'd been elected and you'd just lost your seat.'

'I assure you I never gave it a thought. I'd just been through
a divorce and the slur stuck. They don't like that sort of thing
in the traditional North of England. I'll be back again, don't
you worry. People's memories are short. Rachel says Labour's
here to stay, but I don't think so. You can't oust the traditional
poles of Liberalism versus Unionism in this country.'

'Oh, can't you? Just you wait and see.'

A somehow transformed Spencer Foster led them into a
small white hall where a young woman stood, looking rather
shy, in a short evening dress of black tulle over brocade.
Around her waist a red cummerbund relieved the stark
simplicity of the dress. It looked a bit old for her, because
Rachel thought she must be in her early twenties. Her dark hair
fell in deep waves over her brow, her face was fashionably pale,
and she wore no make-up except a little bit of colour on her
lips.

Rachel's first emotion was one of shock. She had assumed
Spencer was still unmarried. But then, somehow, this girl
didn't look like a wife; she didn't look settled or stolid enough.
She didn't look part of the furniture as so many wives manage
to do.

'This is my sister, Margaret,' Spencer drew her forward. 'I
should say my little sister for, as you can see, she's a good bit
younger than I am. She's come to keep house for me while she
finds a job. Margaret, this is Lady Askham and her brother,
Mr Bolingbroke.'

'How do you do?' Rachel warmly shook her hand, rather
relieved to know her status, she couldn't say why.

'This is the first dinner party we've given since we bought the
house.' There was a note of pride in Spencer's voice. 'You're
our first guests.'

'We feel very honoured.'

Spencer led the way through the small hall to a room at one side which was pleasantly furnished with undistinguished, modern pieces whose aim was comfort rather than elegance. Green curtains were drawn across the French windows, and the walls were painted that pinky-white colour known in the trade as 'magnolia'.

'It's all very new,' Margaret said in a low, apologetic voice. 'One of our brothers is a decorator and we had to wait until he could find the time to come and do the place up for us. You can still smell the paint, I'm afraid.'

Rachel smiled at her comfortingly, assuring her that it all looked beautiful, that a decorator in the family was a useful person to have.

As they entered the living-room another couple rose and were introduced as Mr and Mrs Ashby; Mr George Ashby also being a new Labour Member of Parliament for a neighbouring constituency bordering on Spencer's. At the same time, a maid appeared with a tray of drinks and Spencer said he hoped they didn't mind cocktails, he wasn't used to entertaining and had only learnt to mix one kind. Everyone laughed and the atmosphere relaxed a little.

George Ashby was a man of about fifty and his wife, Freda, the same age. George was a knowledgeable, rather tough-looking man, an ex-miner, and Freda's careworn face showed she was no stranger to hardship. She wore a long red dress which didn't suit her and George looked uncomfortable in his dinner-jacket. It was rather tight under the armpits and stretched over his stomach. Rachel thought of Russia and decided it was a pity that Labour politicians felt they had to ape the middle classes they despised when they came to town.

George Ashby told Rachel he always read her column in *The Sentinel* and felt as if he knew her. He said she was the cleverest woman in politics, cleverer than Margaret Bondfield or Lady Astor, and ought to be in Parliament.

179

Rachel said she had enough to do with her family and running the paper and, besides, she felt she could be more effective that way, as Mr Ashby seemed to confirm.

They had all started talking informally and naturally and were in full swing when the maid reappeared again to announce dinner. Adam, Rachel noticed, was getting on very well with his hostess, sitting beside her on a sofa, his long legs crossed, drink in one hand, cigarette in another, talking chattily to her. Margaret was an attractive girl and whatever Adam was saying amused her, made her quite animated.

She could see that Spencer wanted to talk to her, but it was difficult to disengage the attention of George Ashby, who was anxious to ascertain her views on everything from the question of protection to recognition of the Russian government.

'I do think it is here to stay.' Rachel took her seat at the dinner-table on the right of Spencer, next to George Ashby. She knew they were going to discuss politics all night because Ashby had been on about the government's treatment of the miners, whose wages had actually been *reduced*. Rachel agreed it was dreadful; she had said so in her paper.

Next to Ashby, opposite her brother, was Margaret and next to her Adam and then Freda Ashby who, evidently, liked a drink and whose motherly face was getting rather flushed. She swept a ringlet of artificially bright blond hair off her brow, and her wrist, heavy with bracelets, set up a kind of jangling that distracted the serious talkers at the dinner-table.

'Oh, the Bolsheviks are here to stay all right,' George Ashby opined, sticking his napkin into his collar so that it covered his neat black bow tie. Having won agreement on the miners there was nothing to argue about. 'Never doubt it, we shall recognize the government before the year is out. At any road the first Labour government we have will do it.'

'I wanted to talk to you about Russia,' Spencer said to Rachel, at the same time watching the maid who was skilfully serving a fishy *hors d'oeuvre* on to neat lettuce leaves already on the plate before each guest.

'I thought you might,' Rachel smiled at him and, as she did, she experienced the same wave of comradeship and affection she'd felt for him in Russia nearly two years before. 'Did you know we got my niece out at last?'

'I wondered what had happened. It's that I'm due to go again this summer and I thought I'd try and find out.'

Rachel told him about Bobby, about Susan and Kyril and, now, the baby. 'Kyril disappeared, however. There you could try and do something to help us.'

'How do you mean, "disappeared"?' George Ashby had been keenly following the conversation, and frowned. 'People don't "disappear" in Russia. It's a very free state.'

There was a brief pause as the maid, following her expertise with the salad, poured white wine into glasses by the side of each setting, before Rachel replied: 'I'm afraid you're wrong, Mr Ashby. From all I've seen and heard, Russia is far from free. My nephew tries to do business with the Soviets and finds it the most difficult thing in the world. Nor can we get any word about Kyril. Adam, you know, is Susan's father. Kyril doesn't even know *he's* a father.'

'I'll soon sort that out for you in the summer,' Spencer said authoritatively. 'They won't hide anything from a Labour MP. A capitalist's another thing altogether. Just you give me the details, Lady Askham, and I'll bring her husband back with me.'

'I wish you would.'

As Rachel caught his eye she imagined she could see in his a glimmer of the same interest in her he'd shown before.

After an excellent dinner they returned to the sitting-room where there was a large fire, because it was a cold March evening.

'The talk is that Bonar Law is ill and will resign.' George Ashby took a cigar from a box offered by Spencer. 'They say the losses in the Conservative by-elections last month sickened him even further. Will you return to politics, Mr Bolingbroke?'

'I hope so,' Adam said, also accepting a cigar, 'even if just to prove Spencer wrong that the Liberals have ceased to be the main opposition party. But I have a large family – Susan's not my only child – so I might not contest the next election, especially if it is soon, which everyone seems to think will be the case.'

'What family have you?' Margaret Foster looked up with interest as she poured coffee, the practice of leaving the men in the dining-room with their port having – happily, to Rachel's mind – been dispensed with.

'There's my daughter Susan who, however, has plans to live in Paris – I hope not permanently. I have two growing sons and another stepson, Bobby, who is completely out of my care. It's quite a handful.' Adam seemed to pause abruptly and Rachel wondered if he was on the edge of mentioning Flora. Why shouldn't he? But he didn't.

Vivacious Margaret, twenty years younger than Flora, was decidedly keen on Adam's company, and what man would not be flattered by her obvious admiration? This was something Rachel hadn't anticipated. A romance between her and Spencer possibly, yes – but Adam and Margaret?

She thought about Flora alone in Bedford Row and felt uncomfortable, almost wishing they hadn't come. It was like deceiving a wife.

Adam chatted inconsequentially to Margaret for most of the evening, clearly relaxed in her company – filling his pipe or lighting a cigarette, for he was a compulsive, habitual smoker.

Suddenly, what had promised to be a pleasant evening seemed to drag as Rachel did her best to satisfy George Ashby's insatiable quest for inside political information. She got very little chance to talk to Spencer, who seemed at a loss, disappointed too at having so little opportunity to talk to her.

'I'll call you again,' he said to Rachel as they said good night in the hall, well after midnight. 'Let me have all the details.'

'Thanks so much!' Dropping with fatigue, Rachel felt devoid

of emotion and looked round for Adam, but saw that he was already outside saying his own private farewells to Margaret.

'I hope you remembered Flora all evening.' Rachel's tone was acid as they moved into the mainstream of traffic on the embankment going towards Parliament Square.

'Why should I remember Flora?'

'Because you seemed to be making eyes at young Margaret.'

'She's not so young. She's twenty-five.'

'She's still much younger than you.'

'Oh, Rachel, don't be so silly,' Adam said crossly. 'Nothing like that ever entered my head. She is an awfully nice girl, and pretty, I think, don't you? She is intelligent and asked me if I knew of a job. She's a trained secretary. I said I'd ask around. I liked her.' Adam looked happy and hummed under his breath.

'I should hate you to be involved with another woman. It would kill Flora.'

To her surprise Adam stopped the car at the kerb just outside the Houses of Parliament in the shadow of Westminster Abbey and then looked at her gravely.

'Rachel, do you think I am a celibate?'

'I don't know,' Rachel felt a sense of shock and surprise and looked away. 'I am.'

'But you are faithful to the memory of the man you loved. My wife divorced me after years of a miserable, hateful mockery of a marriage. We had had no intercourse at all since before the War ...'

'*Really*, Adam ...'

'It must sound offensive, I know; but I don't consider myself a celibate man. Flora refuses to be my mistress or even to consider marriage. She's a virgin. Did you know that?'

'I always supposed she was.' Rachel took out her handkerchief and began to screw it up in her hand. 'Do drive on.'

'I don't want to get too emotional in the car because I sense that you are critical of me.' Adam put his hands on the wheel, grinding his teeth.

'Oh, no, Adam.' Rachel clasped his arm, looking into his eyes and seeing how sad, almost wounded he looked in the pale subdued street lighting. 'I am never critical of you. I admire, I respect and love you. But I love Flora, too.'

'Would you respect me still if you knew I slept with prostitutes?' Rachel put a hand to her mouth, but said nothing. 'The woman I was "set up" with for the divorce proved very congenial. She was a war widow who said she found this was the only way to earn a living. I did not sleep with her that night, but she gave me her phone number. I liked her. I see her quite frequently, and if she's not available I see one of her friends, professionally. It is just sex. We never go out to dine or go to a theatre. We go to bed and I pay them. That's the sort of life Flora and her high-minded celibacy has reduced me to. You know I no longer think of Flora in that way? I no longer desire her at all, yet I feel trapped by her. Yes, tonight, young Margaret Foster woke the same interest in me that the young Melanie did. I'll admit it. I am a very carnal man.'

'You must never see her again!' Rachel shuddered, feeling a chill steal through the open window that didn't only come from the cold night air. 'Flora has loved you for too long, sacrificed too much for you. Stay with your prostitute, Adam, and please leave Margaret Foster alone – for Flora's sake. Please.'

The new Askham was a lovely motor car. It had solid brass pistons, electric starting and four-wheel brakes which had been part of its revolutionary design from the beginning. There was a racing model as well as the heavy-duty model that was secretly transported to Russia via Scandinavia. The *de luxe* version of the Askham, which was due to be launched later in the year as a rival to the Rolls-Royce Silver Ghost, had a long, sleek, grey body, leather upholstery, soft Axminster carpets and concealed inside lights. There was also a convertible model which gave it the dashing appearance of a tourer.

The creation of the Askham was not just due to the encouragement of the late Lord Askham and Sir Robert Lighterman, or their heir Bobby Lighterman, or even the members of their families, but to the dedication and skills of one man: Duncan Curtis. Curtis had come from America at the outbreak of war to work for Bosco. As the factory had been involved in making cars for the Army his work was regarded as a reserved occupation and he was not subject to the conscription though he was a Scot born and bred. Cars, however, had been his life. He had worked with David Buick and, later, Henry Ford, in the development of their first successful models in the States.

Duncan Curtis was a large jolly man and the only time in his life he could record being really sad, apart from the early death of his wife, was when the news came that Bosco, his patron and friend, had been killed in action. Then he would have liked to volunteer for active duty but for the fact that he was well past forty and had a motherless daughter still at school.

Duncan was the Works Manager at Askham Motors but, as only a few men were employed on the hand-made cars, he was the chief mechanic as well. He invariably wore a pair of stained white overalls and his hands, and often his face, were black with grease.

He was wiping his hands on a cloth as Bobby inspected the new model which had just been driven on to the tarmac in front of the body shop, running his hands along the side as though it were the flank of a prized racehorse. The car was ready for its new owner and, like all cars emerging from the Askham works, it was already sold; there was a waiting list of over a year for each new model.

Only this car was special; it incorporated all kinds of new features and had the monogram R.H.L. on the outside panels, beside the Askham crest. Bobby had had the new car made for himself and intended to motor all over the Continent with it, showing it off to possible purchasers in France, Italy, Spain and Germany. The walnut panelling inside included a number of advanced gadgets linked to the electric starter. A device for lowering and raising the windows, a lighter for cigars and cigarettes and a switch that controlled the two front seats, making them fully reclinable so that, if necessary, the traveller could spend the night in his car in comfort.

'It's absolutely splendid, Duncan!' Bobby's eyes gleamed with pleasure and, jumping into the driving seat, he beckoned to his chief mechanic, saying: 'Come on, let's go for a spin.'

Duncan shook his head, continuing to wipe his mucky hands on the greasy cloth. 'I have'na the time, Mr Bobby. We spent so many days getting this just right I have neglected other work. Maybe another day.'

'Today, I insist!' Bobby thumped the wheel in that commanding, imperious way he had which made people afraid to disobey him: he who must be obeyed. Duncan reluctantly threw the rag on to a bench, went on wiping his hands on the sides of his dungarees and went around to the passenger seat. A few of the men had wandered into the yard to see their boss's reaction and now stood there, arms akimbo, smiles on their faces. One or two clapped as Bobby let in the heavy clutch and lightly touched the accelerator with the toe of his highly polished shoe.

'A week's extra wages all round as a bonus,' he called, waving his left hand, and the men raised a spontaneous cheer, some doffing their caps.

'Do you know most of those men were here in 1908 or so when my Uncle Bosco started the company? Sam Styles was his first recruit. They haven't changed, have they?'

'Sterling men,' Duncan agreed. 'But Arthur Westerham, who was killed on the Somme, was one of the best. Then there were Patrick and Ben who were wounded and Joe Scully who married a French girl and decided to stay in France.'

'That's only four.' Bobby carefully took a corner and drove into the lane adjacent to the works. 'I like the old traditions, the old ways. I never want to get too big because I don't want to let the unions in; but I do want to expand, Duncan. I'm

186

trying to buy the land on either side of the works so that we can enlarge the body shop and the spraying shed. We could increase the workforce two- or threefold and improve our quality and quantity. Any day now England is going to recognize Russia and I will be able to export my models direct. All the top men in the Kremlin are buying them after I sent one for the personal use of Chairman Lenin. Unfortunately I don't think he's ever used it, owing to his illness. I am angling now to go and talk to them about building a factory there to assemble our cars, rather on the lines of the Putilov works which build tractors rather than import them from the US.

'It's not only Russia that interests me but the Continent. Why shouldn't we compete with the Italians and the Germans? Racing cars are the thing, Duncan, mark my words.'

'You're very ambitious, Mr Bobby,' Duncan glanced at him sideways, 'and I've no doubt you have the means to do as you say; but go cautiously, that's my advice.'

'My stepfather is going to be Chairman of our reconstituted Board,' Bobby said, half to himself, his eyes narrowed on the road. 'Now that he's not an MP he has the time. He'll keep an eye on things in England while I go selling abroad. There'll be a big future for you, Duncan, in charge of a much enlarged works. Works Manager with additional added responsibilities.'

Duncan blushed and studied his grimy hands. 'As we're passing my house soon, Mr Bobby, would you like to stop and take a wee bit of lunch? My daughter Aileen is home and will fix us a snack. I could also get washed and change my clothes.'

'That's a splendid idea,' Bobby glanced at the speedometer. 'Do you know we're doing thirty? There's a hint there'll be a speed limit on all these roads. Well, I don't think we want that sort of government interference and control. They say people will be killed. Well, people always are killed; they were killed when they walked in front of the car with lamps to show them the way. Over-enthusiastic drivers ran over them!'

187

Duncan looked curiously at Bobby. Duncan liked and admired Bobby, but there was still an element of doubt about what sort of person he really was. He was so charming and affable that it was difficult to detect anything wrong; but something was wrong and Duncan wasn't sure what it was. Now he thought he knew: there was a streak of ruthlessness in Bobby Lighterman, which wasn't only apparent in his approach to business. It obviously affected the way he felt about people too, as though he found it difficult to form close relationships either with men or women.

Duncan wondered how much Bobby was really touched by elemental things, things that reduced other people to tears? Did he ever cry? Had he ever cried? Had he cried when, as a boy of sixteen, he had attended the memorial service to his uncle at which he, Duncan, and all the men left at the works were present? On that day he could recall a lot of grief, but he couldn't recall Bobby's tears at all.

Bobby was immensely wealthy. He was also an attractive young man, walking with a self-confident swagger that went well with his clothes bought in Bond Street, Jermyn Street or Savile Row; all his clothes custom-made, like his cars. His hats came from Lock's, his shoes from Lobb. He was one of the greatest swells in London except for the fact that he hadn't got a title, and his grandfather had done his very best to rectify that by tipping, it was said, large sums into the pocket of Lloyd George before he died. But the Premier had procrastinated and the old man hadn't lived long enough to benefit from his generosity. How he must have cursed him. But for that slip-up the young, carefree man next to him would now be Baron Lighterman.

Perhaps he still would one day. He had plenty of energy, plenty of drive. He was not one of the idle rich at all, and it was for this reason if no other that Duncan admired him.

'Here we are.' Bobby interrupted Duncan's ruminations by stopping at a neat country cottage surrounded by an acre or two of well-cultivated garden. 'Sorry to interrupt your reverie.

What was it about?' He braked and glanced at the man in the seat beside him and Duncan felt embarrassed and rubbed his cheek with a grimy hand.

'I was thinking of this and that, Mr Bobby, how well you've done and that sort of thing. You're not one to sit on your fortune and do nothing.'

'I most certainly am not!' Bobby jumped out and preceded his host up the garden, pausing to comment on a fine patch of daffodils which covered most of the upper part of the lawn, clustering at the base of an oak tree. 'I bet that tree could tell a tale or two,' Bobby glanced up to where its tight little leaves were beginning to unfurl in the spring sunshine. 'Do you know how old the cottage is, Duncan?'

'I think it's about two hundred years, sir.' Duncan joined Bobby under the tree, hands behind his back, gazing up through the tree. 'This cottage, of course, belongs to the estate. I suppose it really belongs to your cousin, Lord Askham, though I always like to associate that title with his lordship who was killed in the War.'

'So do we all, Duncan.' Bobby shook his head and Duncan looked for the signs of sadness on his face; but they weren't there. Bobby was going through the perfunctory emotions of grief: head-shaking, down-turn of the mouth, but no real suffering, real sorrow. He had been sixteen at the time and now he was twenty-four. Maybe it was too long a time to mourn a dead uncle, even remember him very well.

'I suppose his lordship, Ralph that is, will come into the business too when he is of age?'

'No one quite knows what young Ralph will do,' Bobby said with apparent indifference. 'I've heard it said he will go into the Army, like his father. The businessman could be Mr Frederick – or maybe the little bastard Hugo. What fun that would be!'

Duncan almost winced. The appearance at Askham Grange of the little Hugo had caused a lot of gossip, too, and no one knew the truth about that. Some said it was Lady Askham's

189

own child, but few believed this. She was just not the kind of woman one associated with infidelity.

'You look shocked, Duncan!' Bobby gazed at him with amusement. 'Does the word "bastard" shock you so much? Did you not know Hugo was my Uncle Bosco's son by a prostitute he met in Cairo? Perhaps you won't admire him so much now.' He looked keenly at Duncan, who went very red indeed, stamping his feet on the ground like a pawing horse.

'I didn't know, Mr Bobby. Not my business ...'

'Nonsense, man, you must have wondered. He met her in Cairo and she followed him here. It was her appearance in court in the famous Askham libel case that stopped the whole thing. That mysterious woman in the box was the woman who had already borne him a son.'

'People did wonder about the lady ... so I hear.'

'Of course they wondered! My uncle might have been a hero physically, but morally he was a coward. He left his wife to face the music without saying a word. A lot of people even to this day think it's her child. She's behaved like an angel.'

'I'd rather not comment, Mr Bobby, but we all admire your aunt, that's for sure.' Duncan looked up with relief as the front door opened and a pretty young woman stood there shading her eyes against the glare of the sun.

'Is it you, Dad?'

'Aye, dear, with Mr Bobby. He's just showing off in his new car.'

'Oh, Mr Bobby!' Awkwardly the woman began to untie her apron. 'You should have let us know you were coming.'

'I didn't mean to, Aileen. I mean I didn't mean to come. It was such a lovely day, I said to your father, "Let's go for a spin in the beautiful new Askham, just out of the spraying shed." He suggested we should pop in for a snack or a drink because he wants to change.'

'I should think so, Dad!' Aileen looked with horror at her father, who slunk past her with a shamefaced grin.

190

'It's perfectly all right, Aileen.' Immaculate Bobby, creases intact, not a hair out of place, went up to her and shook her hand. 'This is quite an informal visit. I didn't even know you were home. Just a glass of beer, a piece of pie, whatever you have. Your dad has been crawling round my engine trying to get it right. He's the best mechanic in England, you know?'

'Oh, I know that!' Aileen laughed, and her rather pale face was transformed as twin spots of pink appeared on her cheeks, a mischievous sparkle came into her black eyes. Bobby looked more closely at her.

'I don't think I've seen you for years, Aileen. Possibly not since my twenty-first.'

Bobby was not referring to the splendid party in Manchester Square, but to the party for estate workers and employees of various Askham and Lighterman concerns held in the estate hall at Askham Hall. That was a much simpler affair, even though best clothes were worn and most of the family attended. The fare was plain but plentiful, and beer and cider were drunk rather than the best vintage wines.

'I went to Edinburgh after that, Mr Bobby.' Having divested herself of her apron and tucked it hurriedly away behind a chair, as though she had never had it on, Aileen led the way into the sitting-room. This was a pretty, simple, comfortable room with deep cretonned chairs and a long, low sofa. The sunlight beamed in through the small lattice windows and, instead of a fire in the grate, there was a huge urn of flowers: daffodils, narcissus and branches of sticky oak buds.

'Why Edinburgh?' Bobby glanced around and then, choosing the most comfortable chair, sat himself down as if he owned the place which, in an indirect way, he did.

'After my husband died I wanted to get a job. London didn't appeal to me much and I thought the opportunities would be better in Edinburgh, where my mother and father came from. I have a lot of relations there still. Anyway, prospects weren't what I thought. I've decided to come home for a while and look after Dad. He missed me.'

'I'm sure he did.' Bobby's tone was kind. 'But you should have come to me if you were looking for a job. I could have offered you something here, or in town.'

'That's very good of you, Mr Bobby, but …' Aileen was flustered.

'You didn't like to ask, I bet. Just like your father.' Bobby wagged a finger at her. 'Too proud. Well, I tell you now that we are looking for young women in our London office to answer the telephone or … can you type?'

'I can type and do Pitman's shorthand, Mr Bobby. I learned while I was looking after my husband.'

'Then that's excellent and you are, let me see, how old?' Bobby looked at her with the speculative interest of a prospective employer, but maybe there was something else.

'I'm twenty-six, Mr Bobby.'

'Too young to be a widow. Another victim of the War we forgot, eh, Duncan?' Bobby looked up as Duncan, hands and face washed, and dressed in a clean pair of white dungarees, came into the room sleeking back the few hairs on his practically bald dome.

'What's that, Mr Bobby? Didn't Aileen give you a drink?'

As Bobby shook his head Duncan looked reproachfully at his daughter, who said:

'We have only just got in, Dad! Mr Bobby has been talking about some work for me.'

'Ah, I see. A drop of whisky, Mr Bobby?' and as Bobby nodded Duncan tipped a generous measure in a glass and held it out to him. 'Which victim did we forget, sir? You were saying …'

'Aileen's husband, Fred. He was a victim of the War.'

'Oh yes, sir, gas. Terrible attack when the Germans first used it in 1916. In a way it's a pity Fred didn't die there and then because his sufferings, and Aileen's, were terrible.'

'Mine nothing like his, Dad.' The colour had gone from Aileen's bonny cheeks and, for a moment, the sadness in her eyes was haunting. 'Fred's mind was turned, too, by the gas and he was never himself after they invalided him out.'

'But he spent his last days in a home?'

'He was in and out of hospital for three years, Mr Bobby. He wanted so much to lead a normal life, but he couldn't. One lung was destroyed completely. Lady Askham, your Aunt Rachel, was ever so good to him . . . and us. She would visit him in the hospital.'

Bobby composed his expression into one that was suitably sympathetic, and nodded gravely. 'She was very good to a lot of people and so, I must say it because others tend to forget it, was my mother. She *and* my grandmother, Lady Lighterman, nursed in France during the War, even though my grandmother was over seventy. My other grandmother, Lady Askham, was too griefstricken by the death of my uncle, and indeed has seldom appeared in public since. Which reminds me, I was meant to be lunching with her. May I telephone, Duncan?'

'In the hall, Mr Bobby.' Duncan pointed to the door and started whispering to his daughter who got her apron from its hiding place, tied it rapidly round her waist and disappeared through a door in the opposite direction to the one taken by Bobby.

Angry at her father for bringing this august guest so unexpectedly to lunch, Aileen nevertheless managed, in a relatively short time, to produce an excellent meal of cold meat, salads, fresh bread and butter and Double Gloucester cheese, together with bottled beer. Bobby could be very easy and charming with his social inferiors and was, on this occasion, entertaining them with anecdotes about London life and tales of his sister's newly-found relations in France.

'They were about to reject her until they discovered she had money. They had buried their son in their hearts because he had become a Bolshevik, and they didn't want to know his wife or baby until I came along, gave them a good meal – which, incidentally, it didn't look as though they'd eaten for years – and announced that their grandson, young Alexander, was heir to his mother's fortune. They pricked up their ears at once at that and drew Susan into their arms.' Bobby chuckled, sat back and lit a cigarette. 'I know their type. They can't get used to not having what they had such a lot of. I daresay we wouldn't be any different, if the same thing had happened to us; if Askham Hall and Lighterman House were seized by a Communist mob and turned into homes for the so-called "people". I only hope we'd be a bit more dignified, not so obvious about it. Still ...' he played with his lighter on the table, 'the main thing is not to be too cynical. Susan is very happy with her new in-laws and is looking for a flat in Paris to be near them. That will suit me because I could do with a base, too.

'The Ferovs are utterly charming, don't misunderstand me, and completely genuine. I mean, there are a lot of phoney aristocrats around, but they're not among them.

'If Susan has her own establishment it will compensate her for the loss of her husband, a little, anyway. She won't be so dependent on her father and Aunt Flora. She needs to develop more confidence.'

Bobby looked at his watch and rose from the table, his eyes on Aileen. She was certainly a most attractive woman, earthy but none the worse for that. The fact that she'd been married and was older than him seemed, somehow, to make her more interesting.

'We must get back to work, Aileen. We're going to expand and I want to show your father some plans, but you ...' he stabbed a finger at her, leaning forward, 'come and see me whenever you want to, just as soon as you're ready to work. I mean that. I really do.'

'Thank you, Mr Bobby,' Aileen said, looking straight into his eyes without flinching.

CHAPTER 10

Before the War the Askham Summer Party was an event that was always noted in the social columns of *The Times*. In those days it was usually graced by one or two members of the Royal Family, sometimes more, as well as by various dignitaries of Church and State, including the current Prime Minister who was invariably a close family friend. But Stanley Baldwin, who had succeeded the ailing Bonar Law in May and now led the Conservative and Unionist Party, was totally different from those Prime Ministers the Askhams had known. In Dulcie, Lady Askham's, opinion he was a very ordinary, rather common little man not fit to occupy the same office as dear Hubert Asquith, cherished Arthur Balfour, or even poor Bonar Law with his troublesome health. One could shut an eye to the humble origins of that parvenu, Lloyd George, because he had grown with the office which, incidentally, he had held for such a long time. It had thus really been quite a shock when the Liberal Coalition was defeated, and Lloyd George was out and the Unionists returned to power. But there was Bonar Law, a family friend, and no one much minded.

The current Prime Minister might well have been invited to this first post-war summer party had he not been such an upstart as Stanley Baldwin, whom no one had heard of until six months before. The pencil had gone right through his name, in the still strong grasp that Dulcie Askham was able to wield, as she temporarily deserted the couch of the professional invalid to oversee the party.

Dulcie had decided to revive it in this summer of 1923 because it was the first time since the War that one began to feel the country was on its way to recovery. Also, there were some family events to celebrate: Melanie and Denton had at last thought it safe to return to England together. Now that they had been married for two years it would no longer be an item of gossip in the gutter press. Granddaughter Susan was happily established in Paris surrounded by new relations, and there was the *Askham de Luxe* which had been launched simultaneously in London and Paris in June to be favourably reported on by the motoring press.

Yes, it was a good time to revive an event which was a *sine qua non* of the social calendar in pre-war years.

In fact, at seventy years of age, Dulcie Askham possessed far more vigour than she liked others to see, nor was she as deaf as she liked to pretend, nor nearly so blind. The days before the party at Askham Hall not a speck of dust escaped the vigilant eyes of the Dowager Countess, nor the less than sparkling polish on the button of a footman. She was positively galvanic as, brandishing her stick, she hurried from room to room pointing out this deficiency and that, or stood in the middle of the marquee on the lawn peering towards the top for signs of wear. It was a marquee that had been used for many such occasions, pre-dating even Dulcie's long reign as mistress of Askham.

The sun streamed through the trees, glistening on the lake, up and down which swam the swans, many of whom had been cygnets when last there had been a party on such a scale in the grounds of Askham Hall. The laburnums leaning over the lake were past their bloom now, but the profusion of leaves was thick, not only on these low, hanging trees with their bent trunks, but elsewhere in the park: on chestnuts, elders, sycamores, elms and the famous Askham oaks which were rumoured to be older than any house which had ever stood there, though some thought this unlikely.

The sun was reflected in the windows of that long, stately, neo-classical mansion, with its colonnaded central block constructed by James Wyatt in the heyday of Palladianism in the eighteenth century, that stood on a hill rising up from the lake. Once the land between the house and the lake had been meadowland, scrub grass on which the family horses had grazed. When, however, it was thought that Bosco and Rachel would take over the house from Dulcie just before the outbreak of war, it had been dug up and returfed. Now its fine lawn, after nine years of care by the score or so of Askham gardeners, looked as green and as inviting as the turf of a well-kept cricket ground, freshly watered by the rains before the beginning of the cricket season.

The marquee was on a central plateau that the younger Askhams did indeed use for bat and ball when Grandma wasn't looking but sometimes, even if she was, it didn't matter because her eldest grandson was her favourite and she refused him nothing, or very little.

Ralph, tall and strong, recently turned seventeen, escorted his grandmother slowly through the grounds, pausing with her to greet this person or that, chat to this favoured retainer or family friend. Dulcie walked slowly, enjoying the crowds, leaning on Ralph's arm. Finally they paused in the shade of an oak, not far from the terrace where she would finally settle for the afternoon's celebrations, its position offering a panoramic view of the proceedings. A comfortable chair was hastily brought for her by one of the footmen and quickly a host of people gathered round her. The younger members of the extended Askham family crouched at her feet, though they did not intend to stay there for very long. Their excited eyes roamed over the concourse in search of diversion; past the Kittos – hundreds of them, it seemed – who were related to Dulcie and had numerous offspring too; past the Ffinches, the MacHughes, the Alderton-Warboys, the Cuthbertsons, the Savages, the Trents, the Duchess of Quex, who never missed a party even though she was in her eighties, past the younger friends of Bobby, Susan and the older grandchildren, who had been given *carte blanche* by their grandmother to ask whom they liked (providing they were respectable, of course), to the new arrivals not only at Askham Hall, but to this country. They were people who had accompanied Susan and her son by ferry from France to Southampton, where they had been met by two crested Askham limousines and driven across country to Askham Hall. They were people who were new to everyone and everything around them and thus were objects of special interest: Prince Alexei Ferov, the Princess Irina and their children Hélène, Dima and Evgenia. The youngest, Yegor, had stayed in France.

It was quite a number to accommodate even in the vastness of Askham Hall, because many of the Kittos, who came from Scotland, were staying, too, and one or two Crewes who thought the journey back to Crewe Castle or London too tedious after a party. Lady Frances Crewe, who now lived in Australia, had been married to Arthur, so the Crewes were still officially listed as 'family' and entitled to special privileges, like staying the night at the Hall and being on familiar terms with Dulcie. But Dulcie, having heard such interesting things about her beloved granddaughter's newly-acquired in-laws, had insisted that, even if it were a squeeze, then squeezed in they must be. Rachel offered to take two of the children at the Grange and so was hostess to Dima and Evgenia – Hélène preferring the magnificence and lavish comfort of the Hall.

Dulcie Askham was thought by many not to have looked so well for years as she sat under the oak surrounded by small relatives and numerous admiring adults. She was soon joined by Princess Irina who sat next to her in the place of honour, also on a crested, upholstered chair provided by a footman summoned from the house. The Dowager Countess had taken an immediate liking to the Russian Princess. Not only was she a beautiful and elegant woman of impeccably noble ancestry – if anything her side of the family, the Orloffs, went even further back than the Ferovs – but her great friend, Countess Welenska, had been an intimate of Queen Alexandra when she was Princess of Wales and had sailed into exile with the Empress Marie, mother of the last Czar. The connection between the Danish Princess of Wales and the Russian throne was a close one as the then Princess and the Empress were sisters. Thus any friend of Princess Alexandra's was a friend of Dulcie's or any friend *of* a friend of Princess Alexandra's was almost equally acceptable.

The harrowing tale the Princess Irina had to tell of the family's escape from Russia, the loss of vast estates, and an even vaster fortune, touched Dulcie's kind heart, not least because it made one realize how fortunate one was to live in a country where stability, respect for law and monarch, reigned. The Princess was a woman who had just turned fifty when she first met the Countess of Askham, who was nearly a generation older, but there was an immediate and mutual attraction and, since her arrival, the two had scarcely been separated except for a few hours. Now Dulcie's hand lightly rested on the Princess's arm as she introduced her to the many friends, relations and acquaintances strolling about the lawns and extensive grounds of Askham Hall on that propitious day, or admiring the gleaming silver-grey body of the *Askham de Luxe* which stood upon a plinth on the gravel in the drive. The Countess was looking over the heads of the throng for Melanie, who had not yet met Susan's parents-in-law, and finally she sent little Kelsoe Kitto, her grand-nephew, to look for her.

'The Kittos, of course, are *my* family,' Dulcie explained to her new friend who, despite her poverty, looked stunning in navy moiré silk with a hat from Caroline Reboux, in the Rue de la Paix, with a wide brim and trailing ribbons. The sable coat was once again in pawn but, as it was not needed in the summer months, it was thought that it might as well be stored in a pawnbroker's shop as taking up space in the Ferov household. They could certainly do with the additional cash. Besides, there was every hope that things would soon change; brighter, more prosperous times were just round the corner, thanks to Susan and her brother Bobby.

Dulcie continued after pausing to greet an acquaintance of even greater antiquity than the Duchess of Quex, who had hobbled up to pay her respects: 'I had three brothers and five sisters, so there are quite a lot of them. One brother was killed in the Ashanti campaign, so I named my younger son, Bosco, after him.' The Countess's face assumed a griefstricken expression, her hand tightening on Princess Irina's arm. 'Oh, I wish you had known my Bosco, a man the like of which we shall not see again.'

Princess Irina sighed deeply, too, and her hand slid into Dulcie's, comforting her.

'My dear, sad as the memory is for you, at least you know that others have suffered too. The fates of many of my family are unknown, and one brother, several cousins and nephews, also perished in the War. At least you know where Bosco and dearest Arthur lie. We have no knowledge of the final resting places of many, many of our friends and family.'

'You comfort me, dearest Princess,' Dulcie said. 'But we must not be gloomy on this day but save our sorrows for another time. Let me introduce you to my great friend Lady Claude Ware, whose husband knew my...'

Her voice was lost in the excited clamour as the crowds gathered round Melanie and Denton, who were progressing across the lawn, rather like the Royal Family at a royal reception in the grounds of Buckingham Palace or Windsor Castle. A path was made for them and friends, relatives of all kinds and all ages pressed forward to clasp their hands, most people not having seen Lady Melanie since her wedding.

Due to the vast numbers expected there had been only a brief, formal greeting of the main guests in the house beforehand. The rest, *hoi-polloi*, drifted in through the gates of Askham Hall, closely scrutinized by the village constable in his smart dress uniform and white gloves. As well as the nobility, the gentry, the eminent, titled, well-to-do and famous, senior staff and estate workers had also been invited, as was the pre-war custom – so that the occasion resembled a fête. There was, however, a clear division between workers and gentry, if only in that the former hung back to make way for the latter and the frequency with which they gave little bobs if they were female and doffed their hats if male, as some notable passed by.

'I think I see Melanie now,' Dulcie said, pointing towards the crowd who had gathered round the Rigbys. 'I am so anxious for you to meet her. Yes, Susan's bringing her over . . .'

'Most attractive man,' the Princess, ever susceptible to male charms, said *sotto voce* as the languid Denton brought up the rearguard of what was quite a party headed by Bobby, who had escorted his mother and stepfather, newly arrived from France, from the house.

Melanie looked absolutely exquisite in something fetchingly simple picked up from Cheruit on her way through Paris. It was a chemise style dress in tussore silk of a dazzling blue that enhanced the colour of the celebrated Askham eyes. The starkness of the square-necked dress was offset by rows of beads which hung to her waist, and the effect of a flowered waistband which sat, fashionably, just above her hips. She wore a small cloche hat with turned-up front brim trimmed with silk aigrettes. Bobby performed the introductions and his mother clasped Princess Irina's hand and, in the manner of royalty, they briefly touched cheeks.

'I'm sorry we haven't met before,' she said. 'I know such a lot about you from Susan.'

'And I *you*, Lady Melanie. Susan is very proud of her beautiful mother, as she has every reason to be.'

Susan's smile remained fixed, her eyes cold as Melanie introduced Denton, a spruce and immaculate figure in white suit and spats. It appeared that Denton's brother had once met Alexei Ferov in St Petersburg before the War and this was considered an ideal talking point as memories and reminiscences were exchanged and polite enquiries made.

The company then agreed to troop up to the terrace because the sun was beginning to invade the patch of shade beneath the tree. Besides, Melanie was afraid all the best seats would be taken and they might be induced to take tea in the marquee 'with all sorts of people one doesn't necessarily wish to converse with. Mamma?'

Dulcie agreed. Not, she hastily added, that one didn't want to talk to *everyone*, but there simply wasn't time. Also she wanted to find the rest of the delightful Ferov family for Melanie and Denton's inspection. Ralph and Susan were despatched to find them, so Denton gave his arm to his mother-in-law and a stately progress was made back across the lawn to the terrace. There, seats were rapidly being occupied at the tables laid out for tea for those chosen few who were considered a little too grand for the camaraderie of the large communal marquee.

Bobby was making sure that his grandmother and mother were comfortable when Rachel arrived, greeted Melanie and Denton, then flopped down in a chair, fanning herself with a handkerchief because of the heat.

'Has anyone seen Hugo?'

'Hugo?' Dulcie vaguely looked around. 'Is he lost?'

'Is Hugo lost *again*?' Bobby's tone was mocking.

'I didn't say he was lost,' Rachel felt tetchy. 'I merely asked if anyone had *seen* him.'

'He's by the lake, Aunt.'

Susan, overhearing, arrived at that moment with Hélène and Evgenia who had been boating on the lake, and who were now introduced to Melanie. Rachel was relieved to have everyone's attention deflected from Hugo. She knew they thought she fussed too much.

'Perfectly delightful girls,' Melanie said with approval, gazing at Bobby who sat with one leg languidly crossed, gazing around him with a quiet, proprietorial air. Bobby smiled and nodded and, for a moment, his eyes remained fastened on Hélène, who had been considerably transformed from the rather gauche creature of the previous winter by her intimacy with Susan, who had invited her to share her apartment on the Quai Voltaire.

Evgenia, like her brother Dima, was to go to university, but Hélène had been the member of the family least inclined to adapt herself to its changed circumstances, even though she was only fifteen when the Revolution had forced them from their home in Moscow to the life of wandering exiles abroad.

Unlike Evgenia, who was adaptable and grateful for charity or opportunities that came her way, Hélène had not taken kindly to the idea of work, to humdrum plebeian occupations such as learning to type or teaching the children of the dispossessed, like herself.

Of all the Ferovs, even her mother, she was the most aloof, the most instinctively regal by nature. There was something about Hélène that belonged to a much older age, when princesses were not supposed to do anything but look their parts and make good marriages. Instinctively, too, she modelled herself on the arrogant daughters of the old Russian nobility; on the four Grand Duchesses, children of the last Czar, of whom her mother still spoke with love, awe and grief ... Olga, Marie, Tatania and Anastasia, those imperious young women who had yet died a dreadful death they did not deserve.

It seemed like a gift from God when Susan, of all unlikely people, arrived on the doorstep of the depressing Clichy apartment house, soon to be revealed as a relation, a sister-in-law, mother of Kyril's child. No matter that no one talked of Kyril any more; no matter that even to think of him was forbidden. He was hundreds of miles away, well out of sight; and impulsive, restless Susan, eager for love, willing to share her life, her possessions, found an affinity with her elder sister-in-law that immediately drew the two together, young women who felt out of place in modern society.

Susan had the money, Hélène had the instinctive know-how, the expensive tastes, the flair for decoration, the sure instinct for a valuable object or work of art. In the last few months both young women had found in each other comfort that their families had hitherto been unable to give them. They became inseparable and, as Susan grew and developed, Hélène developed too, only with much more natural beauty to build on.

This day in August 1923 Hélène looked perfectly stunning in a tea frock of silk georgette with a matching underslip; the skirt had deep, picot-edged flounces which swirled around her knees as she shimmied past on her very high-heeled shoes, causing many an eye to turn and stare. The neck of her frock was perfectly round, and twin strings of pearls fell to her waist, which was beltless except for a single, huge artificial rose.

The modern style suited Hélène; her small bust and narrow boyish hips were ideal for this schoolboy type, and her thick fair hair, naturally waved and cropped at the back, curved over her high Slav cheekbones nearly meeting her thick, dark eyebrows. The amazing light-blue eyes, very lightly ringed with kohl, seemed to look appraisingly at everyone with only a trace of amusement.

Evgenia, on the other hand, bookish and bright, had shed all her aristocratic pretensions and was to study philosophy at the Sorbonne. She was three years younger than Hélène and her manner resembled that of Susan when she first went to Russia, gauche and schoolgirlish, though she had a practical nature and a well-developed humanitarian streak. She wore a simple cotton chemise that made no pretensions to *haute couture* and her hair, still curly, was caught up in a band, regardless of fashion. She was anxious to get back to the lake where her brother was boating, having been joined by Ralph to find them.

From the meadow Charlotte was waving to her. 'Come on,' she cried, 'the others are waiting,' and Evgenia looked at her mother, who gave her permission to leave, and she ran down the path, arms flying.

'Of course, she's very young.' Princess Irina gazed critically after her younger daughter. 'Hardly out of the schoolroom though, thanks to Bobby, we have been able to send her to the Sorbonne.'

'We have a lot to thank Bobby for,' at last Hélène returned his appraising look.

'No, it's Susan you should thank,' Bobby insisted. 'She's the one who wanted to find you in the first place.'

'I don't think anyone needs to be thanked.' Susan, next to Hélène, crossed her legs and shaded her eyes with her hands. 'I'm just grateful I found Kyril's relations. I love them like my own.'

Melanie looked at her mother, who fleetingly raised her eyes to heaven. Susan's move to Paris, attributed to the influence of Bobby, was interpreted as a gesture of defiance as well as independence. Susan, in her mother's opinion, had been a difficult adolescent and this tendency continued. She seemed to find less in common with her daughter than ever. They tried never to be left alone together because, since the almighty row when Susan returned from Russia, an attitude of mutual unforgiveness prevailed. They had nothing to say to each other.

'I'd love to meet that Kyril,' Melanie said as kindly as she could. Somehow she wanted to bridge the gap. 'One day I hope I will.'

Kyril's name was not supposed to be spoken in public; it was as though he'd died and a shadow always seemed to pass over Irina's face at the mention of his name. One had, however, to be nice about Kyril to Susan and her family; it was judged to be politic and expedient.

'Oh you *will*, Mummy,' Susan said firmly. 'Bobby's going to get him out.'

'Bobby *hopes* to get him out,' Bobby laughed. 'It depends how my rating is with the new Russian leadership now that Lenin's so ill. I don't think you've had a good look at the new Askham, Mamma. Do you care to come and inspect it now?'

'Not until after tea if you don't mind, darling.' Melanie sighed. 'It's much hotter here than France. Darling, have you a gasper?' She held out a hand to her husband, who reached for his cigarette case in his pocket.

'Denton?'

'Not at the moment, old man. Like your mother I'd love to, after tea.'

'I'd love to see the new car now,' Hélène turned invitingly to Bobby, 'and have it all explained to me.'

'It will be done this very moment.' Bobby jumped up and held out his hand. 'Susan?'

'I'm joining the tea party. I'll come with Mummy and Denton afterwards.'

As Bobby and Hélène walked casually off, chatting, Irina looked after them with a satisfied smile.

'I see you're thinking what I'm thinking,' Dulcie leaned over and whispered to her. 'They *do* make a very nice couple. My grandson is good-looking, don't you think?'

Irina smiled again and nodded.

'I would so like to see Bobby settled.' Dulcie continued. 'He's very clever, you know, and sure of a great future. Nothing would make me happier ...'

'Mamma, don't match-make,' Melanie yawned. 'I can hear everything you say. You know you love doing it.'

'Well, I was never very successful with you,' Dulcie snapped. 'I couldn't stop *you* making mistakes, and that is no disrespect to you, Denton.'

'None taken, Lady Askham.' Lord Denton was unperturbed. He was so unflappable that people couldn't decide whether he was stoical or stupid. In many ways he was ideal for Melanie, being so lacking in emotion.

'Where's Adam, by the way?' Melanie said, looking round. 'My last mistake.' She gave her mother a supercilious smile.

'Mummy, that's a horrible thing to say!' Susan jumped up, her pale face flaming.

'I'm sure your mother didn't mean it.' Rachel, half dozing in the heat, looked up.

'I *did* mean it, as a matter of fact,' Melanie said coolly, smoking her cigarette with care. 'Adam *was* a mistake. It doesn't mean I love Susan or the boys any the less...'

'It's still a tactless thing to say, darling,' Denton began but, quelled by the look in Melanie's eyes, he stopped abruptly.

'Mummy *implied* I wasn't good at marriage. I wasn't, until now.' She smiled reassuringly at him. 'It's no insult to Susan.'

'Well, I think it is, and a horrid thing to say...'

Susan started off impulsively down the path to the lake where all the fun seemed to be going on, her brothers Christopher and Jordan, cousins and the Russians bumping one another in boats.

'She's still a child really,' Melanie sighed, watching her. 'A child bride and mother. Much I blame you for, Rachel dear.'

'Oh, please, not *today*. Not again.'

'Now, if you're all going to quarrel I really can't stand it,' Dulcie said. 'In fact it is hotter on the terrace than I thought. Shall we go inside, Irina dear, and get one of the footmen to bring us a nice cup of tea ...'

'How lovely.' Irina rose immediately, turning to Dulcie. 'As you say, it *is* hot ...'

'I can't stand people quarrelling.' Dulcie looked reproachfully at Rachel and Melanie. 'Unfortunately my family always do. Do yours? Anyway, there's something I want to ask you.'

She tucked her arm intimately through Irina's and drew her towards the door leading into the house, her head leaning conspiratorially close to hers.

'I'm terribly lonely here, you know, in this large house with the children gone. I asked Rachel to come and live with me here, but she is so fond of the Grange. I banished her there in the first place, many years ago when she was first married, and how I regret it now.' Dulcie, whose hairstyle was as it had been in the days of Queen Victoria, piled elegantly on top of her head, removed a tiny wisp which had strayed across her face. 'I wondered,' she went on, 'if there was anyone you knew who would like to come to me as a companion? Anyone at all you can recommend? She would have to be a lady of refinement, of course, preferably noble; someone suitable who understands our ways, who is used to the kind of style in which we live.'

Dulcie paused, as if taking measure of her guest's reaction, her mood, even her temperature. 'One has everything one wants here, you know. One lacks for nothing. I wondered ... I hardly dare ask, but *you*, perhaps, dearest Irina? We have known each other such a short time, but already I feel we're like sisters, and you, with your background and breeding, would be ideal. I don't suppose for a moment that you'd consider it, even if your family could spare you just for a while ...' The emotions registering on Dulcie's mobile features ran the whole gamut, from hope to despair.

'Lady Askham!' Irina tightly grasped Dulcie's arm. 'It would be just like being back in Russia before the Revolution.'

'That's exactly what I thought,' Dulcie said, smiling to herself. 'I thought – but I didn't dare to hope – it might suit you very well. You would be free to come and go as you liked, of course. But it is so, how shall I put it ...?' Dulcie freed her arm, which she waved about in a gesture that was both suggestive and inviting. 'It is so gracious and spacious here. Just like St Petersburg in the days of the poor, dear Czar.'

The features of The Askham motor car were remarkable, everyone agreed. It was possibly the finest car in styling, design and performance on the market, even including the Rolls-Royce. Hélène was impressed, and so was her father, who had appeared late, having gone into the house to shower and change after a brisk game of tennis. The life at Askham Hall certainly suited him. It was just like the good times in old Russia.

'I didn't know you were an engineer, Bobby,' Hélène said admiringly from the driver's seat where he'd put her, thinking how well she and the car went together; they both had class.

'I'm not,' Bobby said. 'But it's something I know a lot about. I like cars and I want this to be the best. I'm going into racing motors too. They are one of the most successful forms of advertisement.'

'I see you're going to be a very famous man.' Alexei ran a tapered finger appreciatively along the grey bonnet, careful not to smudge it. 'Another Henry Ford.'

'I'd rather be an Enrico Bugatti. I admire him most. I'm going to fight him on the race tracks of Europe and this is the man who's going to help me.' Bobby held out an arm and gracefully drew Duncan Curtis from the back of a group of admirers who had been standing around the car. 'The car is as much his as mine. Duncan, this is Prince Alexei Ferov and his daughter, Princess Hélène, and this,' Bobby beckoned and Aileen modestly stepped forward, 'is his daughter. I'm hoping she's going to come and work for me too.'

Duncan shook hands, but he was a shy man with little to say to a worldly Russian prince who was extravagant in his praise of the car.

At the wheel of the car Hélène, listening, watching, stared at Aileen, her fingers tightening on the column. Maybe it was her imagination, but she thought there was something rather bold about the way Aileen looked at Bobby, and more than a suggestion of sensuality in the way he looked at her. Yet she was an ordinary enough girl, not common but not distinguished in any way. It was only a little thing and lasted less than a minute but, in that time, she seemed to Hélène to challenge the possibility that had suddenly opened of a future with Bobby. A future that had hitherto seemed remote; of security for the rest of her life and of almost incalculable riches.

'Hello,' Aileen said, looking up at Hélène in the raised driver's seat. She was neat and pretty with none of the flamboyance or the deviousness of the Russian. Bobby seemed mentally to be comparing them for a minute, then he said to Alexei:

'By the way, Spencer Foster has returned from Russia. He found no trace of Kyril, nor of your sister Countess Valkova. At the Ferov Palace no one could say where she was. Petrovsky, too, has disappeared. The Russians simply clammed up.'

'It was inevitable.' Alexei showed his indifference with a careless shrug of his shoulders. 'My sister was always a foolish woman, and Sergei threw in his luck with Lenin from the beginning. All those who betrayed their class betrayed not only their country but themselves. I am not sorry for them.'

'Nor Kyril, your son?'

'Kyril least of all. I brought him up. I warned him so often about the consequences of what he was doing.'

'Well,' Bobby continued to draw him some distance away from the car where Aileen and Hélène were engaged in polite conversation. 'That means that it is, indeed, very unlikely you will *ever* reclaim your property and fortune. I thought that while your sister lived there, and was friendly with the authorities, you had some chance, I don't know why. I can't offer you any hope at all, now.'

'I didn't have much,' Alexei said stiffly, 'but, thank you.'

'I could use you, though,' Bobby went on. 'You might be very helpful to me.'

'Me? Useful? Helpful? How?' The Prince, immaculately dressed in grey flannels and a blazer, looked quintessentially English, his resemblance, previously noted, to the Kaiser, first cousin to the present King, quite marked. He bent his head to light a cigarette and blew smoke into the air, his fine patrician eyes narrowing.

'I thought you might like to be my representative in Paris. I'd pay very well.'

'What *sort* of representative?' Alexei sounded unenthusiastic.

'Of my companies Askham Lighterman Limited. Mainly to do with cars, but other things as well.'

'I don't know the first thing about cars,' Alexei expostulated, gazing at his long white fingers.

'Oh, you won't have to soil your hands. Just be yourself. It's the image I'm interested in: aloof, aristocratic. You can be that all right. I'd be prepared, of course, to give you a salary commensurate with your position, an apartment in a better part of Paris. Maybe a house.'

'I'd have to think about it,' Alexei said offhandedly.

Bobby, amused, nodded and turned away, back to the car. Even impoverished aristocrats couldn't be bought so easily, it seemed. But he liked Alexei, or what that nonchalant image could do for the company and one day, he decided, he would come after Hélène too. But not just yet.

'Aileen,' he called, 'can we have a little chat about that job? I think I've just the very thing for you.'

Eagerly, willingly, with none of the hard-to-get reluctance of the Russians, Aileen came over to him. He took her arm and led her towards the marquee, making sure that Hélène saw the familiarity of the gesture; not knowing quite why he wanted to make her jealous.

When he did glance back, the Princess and her father weren't looking at them at all, but at each other as though in an attitude of mutual congratulation. Then, linking arms, without a glance, they nonchalantly turned their backs on the couple disappearing down the hill, and walked slowly back to the terrace.

Bobby liked that. He liked everything about the Ferovs. They had style.

Meanwhile, down on the lake, the younger element of the party, abandoning care for their best clothes, were having a very good time. The very young members of the various families, those who had clustered round Dulcie under the oak, had now been shepherded by their nursemaids to various safe pursuits where they could keep a watchful eye on them: the lake, needless to say, had been strictly out of bounds.

But the teenagers, led by Freddie, Em and Charlotte, had commandeered all the available boats and were busily engaged in a mock warfare with the use of paddles, oars and every conceivable, possibly lethal, implement they could find. One boat was commanded by Ralph who, having gone to find

Dima and Evgenia, had stayed to join in the fun. The other was in the charge of Dima who had as crew Charlotte, Em and Jordan, Melanie's boy staying for the holiday with his grandmother in the company of his brother, Christopher Bolingbroke who, with Evgenia and Hugo, was with Ralph. Freddie, always independent-minded, and having captured a one-man skiff, was propelling himself over the lake as fast as he could, causing all kinds of mischief. Jeremy Crewe, Frances's nephew and Paul Kitto, Dulcie's great-nephew, were younger, and alternately taken on or dropped as the games progressed. They were lucky they hadn't been despatched with their nannies.

But between Ralph and Hugo there was an enmity born of many years of close association. Hugo, who was naturally commanding and domineering despite the fact that he was a good deal younger than Ralph, only eleven at the time, though he was tall and strong, was literally rocking the boat, which he enjoyed doing. All of them had been soaked to the skin and Evgenia had once nearly been tipped into the water.

Finally Ralph had had enough. He called for a truce and, rowing his boat to the water's edge, lifted his hand threatingly and said to Hugo:

'Out!'

'What do you mean "Out"?' Hugo said, face flushed, his best clothes hanging skimpily from his body.

'Out of the boat, you heard me.'

'Why?'

'Because I said so, you know quite well why.' Ralph's voice took on a dangerous tone while Evgenia pleaded, in her soft accented English:

'Give him another chance.'

'He's had all the chances he's getting. If he tilts the boat again it will sink to the bottom of the lake and then Mother will be *very* cross.'

'Just because you're a lord,' Hugo said bitterly, 'you think you can boss me any way you like.'

'It's nothing to do with that,' Ralph shook his fist at him again angrily, 'and you know it. Now, you get out because I say so, and stay out.'

Hugo looked towards the other boat which had drawn up beside them, its occupants gawping at him with expressions of sympathy which, strictly speaking, Hugo did not deserve.

'Give him a chance, Ralph.' Charlotte, who always had a tender spot for the trouble-prone Hugo, came to his rescue yet again.

'I've given him several chances. He's spoiling our game. Last time he tipped the boat and nearly gave Evgenia a ducking. I said that if he did it again he wouldn't be allowed to play. I mean it. OUT!'

Hugo threw his paddle into the water and stormily, close to tears, stood up in the boat, again contriving to rock it dangerously, and jumped out. Then he ran up to the bank, cannoning into Jeremy Crewe who, perceiving his chance, flew out from behind a tree to take Hugo's place, leaving Paul, who hadn't been so quick, sulking.

Slowly the boats were rowed out on to the lake again and Freddie came from behind a bend to spiritedly try and attack; but the crews were quieter after the row; some of their former spirit had gone.

'I think you were a bit hard with him,' Christopher said.

'He doesn't mean it, you know,' Em added, moodily staring into the bottom of the boat. She wasn't as fond of, nor as understanding about, her half-brother as Charlotte. She thought that, most of the time, he was a pest.

'I think he *does* mean it.' Ralph knew that he had already been cast in the role of Fletcher Christian. 'Remember, I know Hugo much better than you, Chris. He's a real little trouble-maker, always misbehaving and always getting the limelight because Mother won't be stern enough with him. She spoils him.'

Evgenia listened in silence, thinking what a contrast there was between the brothers and wondering if tall, good-looking,

213

blue eyed, blond Ralph – every foreigner's idea of the typical Englishman – was aware of it. Of how much his looks, aristocratic bearing, titles and claim to the huge family fortune might grate on one who, from what she had heard, had no claim to anything at all except the love of that good woman who was not even his mother. Silently she let her hand dabble in the water while on the bank Hugo, contriving to look his most pathetic, sat disconsolately on a stone, kneading his fists into his eyes.

'Let him cry,' Ralph said. 'It will do him good,' and turning his back on Hugo he violently propelled the boat away, using the long pole with the skill of a Venetian gondolier.

For some time Hugo sat alone on the bank, a fist in one eye, a finger in his mouth, like a baby, unwanted, unloved, watching them all trying, without much success, to recapture the former fun of the game.

It was difficult to know when Hugo first realized that in some ways he was different from his brothers and sisters. It was a subtle, indefinable way that a young boy such as Hugo was couldn't comprehend. He couldn't remember joining the Askham household, when he was only three, and yet in some ways he could. He could remember a time before he was part of that large, friendly family; a time when he was very alone except for the company of a stray cat which used to come into the garden where he played and which he tried desperately hard to keep, to make it love him.

After that it was all animals and people and fun; moving in comfort, some splendour, from one large house to another. He was part of them yet, all the time, he knew he was different.

Then, when Rachel sent Hugo away, the rejection he felt was so terrible that he spent all his time trying to devise ways of getting back to her, a way that would please and not annoy her. But she was annoyed. The school had told her that if he ran away again it would be for good.

Now, once more, he was rejected. No wonder he wept.

Hugo watched Paul Kitto, despairing of another turn in the boat, climb up the bank towards the house. He wondered if he should go with him and see what fun there was going on there. But, suddenly, he saw the boat propelled by Dima, with Charlotte in the stern, coming towards him and Charlotte hissed:

'Get in quick!' She reached out a hand and Hugo, joyously clasping it, fell into the boat, his heart beating, his face triumphant as he looked over the gunwale at Ralph.

'I told you ...' Ralph shouted at her menacingly.

'Let him be, Ralph,' Dima said. 'We took a vote on it and agreed to have him.'

'But you've got too many people.'

'We'll be all right. Hugo will have to work twice as hard.'

Hugo seized the short paddle in the bottom of the boat as Dima steered it so that it came drunkenly across Ralph's bows. Then, with a blood-curdling cry to try and drum up the former competitive spirit, Dima jabbed his pole against the boat which tilted quite dangerously while Evgenia and Christopher cried out in alarm, and Jeremy and Em started baling water out frantically.

'Sink him! Sink him!' Hugo chanted with relish, and, standing up, lifted his paddle just as Ralph's tilted boat passed by them, and Ralph's head and shoulders were well within reach. The paddle held high, Hugo struck Ralph with all the force he could muster, quite deliberately, and Ralph, staggering, a look of surprise on his face, fell straight into the water and, for a few seconds, disappeared from sight. Charlotte rose in the boat and Evgenia, terrified, put both hands to her cheeks, looking down into the murky waters as though dreading what she would see. Suddenly Ralph's head appeared and he clasped the side of Dima's boat with both hands. Dima knelt down to help him while Christopher paddled the boat as strongly as he could to the bank, taking Ralph with it. Hugo stood in the bows, paddle still in his hand, as if waiting his chance to have another whack, when Em seized it and gave him a good cuff on the side of his face.

'That was very, very naughty,' she said. 'You did it deliberately.'

'He asked for it.'

'He only put you off the boat. He didn't try to kill you. Ralph, Ralph, are you all right?' Soaking wet herself now, Hugo's normal ally Charlotte leaned over and put her hand on Ralph's face, but by now his feet could touch the bottom and he was treading upright, helping to beach the boat.

'Wait until I get that little ...' he said but, as Hugo felt solid ground slide under the boat, he leapt out of it and started clambering up the bank towards the house, hotly pursued by a dripping Ralph.

Hugo thought it was half in fun; yet he was terrified as he heard the heavy footsteps of the much bigger boy behind him.

Up on the terrace Rachel leaned forward and said to Hélène next to her:

'Is *that* Hugo?'

'I can't tell,' Hélène shaded her eyes. 'He's very wet, whoever he is.'

'It *is* Hugo. My goodness!' Rachel cried out in alarm, jumping to her feet, 'and Ralph is running after him. *Whatever* can have happened?'

'He's wet, too,' Hélène said, giggling. 'I think there must have been a fracas on the water.' From where they sat half the lake was out of sight, obscured by the marquee on the field. Suddenly from the marquee Bobby appeared, a drink in his hand, chatting to Aileen Younghusband, Duncan's daughter. Then they both stopped talking, turned and watched the scene on the meadow, as Ralph caught up with Hugo.

'My God, he's *beating* him!' Rachel screamed, then, flying off the terrace, she ran as fast as she could towards the by now recumbent Hugo who, having been neatly tackled by Ralph, a practised rugby player, was getting the hiding of his life.

'Stop him! Stop him!' Rachel implored loudly as she reached Bobby who, previously undecided whether it was in fun or not, immediately gave his glass to Aileen and ran down the meadow, taking off his jacket.

Hugo lay on the grass trying to shield his head with his hands as Ralph, his face contorted, laid into him with all the strength, and more of the venom, of a professional pugilist.

'I say ...' Bobby called while Rachel, immediately behind him, shouted, her mouth cupped in her hands:

'Ralph, stop it!'

'He's getting the hiding he deserves,' Ralph grunted, pounding at his younger brother who had now tried desperately to curl himself into a protective ball.

'But what on *earth* has happened ...?'

By this time Dima's crew had left the boat and were standing awkwardly on the edge of the meadow while Charlotte ran fearlessly up to Ralph and, ducking beneath his blows, tried to rescue Hugo.

'Stop this *at once*,' Bobby thundered and, throwing his jacket on to the grass, hurled himself at Ralph, nearly knocking him over. 'Do you want to kill him?'

'*He* wanted to kill *me*,' Ralph said, and then Rachel saw that, on his neck, there was an ugly, bloody contusion that was rapidly swelling. 'The little bastard took aim at me with an oar, trying to brain me.'

'Ralph, I *forbid* you to use that word!' Rachel cried angrily, while Charlotte lay on the grass beside Hugo and began stroking his head, his tear-stained, muddy face.

'Bastard!' Ralph cried, baring his teeth. 'Bastard, bastard, bastard.'

Bobby hit him sharply across the face, which so surprised Ralph that his whole body jerked as he gazed at him, stupefied.

'Sorry about that, old chap.' Nonchalantly Bobby reached down on the grass for his jacket. 'But you heard your mother. Besides, I don't like to see a boy getting such a pasting, whatever he did. He's six years younger than you.'

217

'You *should* be ashamed of yourself, Ralph.' Rachel, pale-faced, sat on the ground beside Charlotte, taking Hugo's head protectively in her lap. 'Kindly go up to your room and don't let us see you again today.'

'Mother, I'm not a child . . .' Ralph shook himself like a dog, his face bemused, the blood oozing from the wound in his neck.

'You heard what I said.' Rachel's head bent tenderly towards Hugo, her eyes signalling Ralph's banishment.

Slowly Aileen came up to him and held out a hand. 'Come on up to the house,' she said kindly, 'and I'll look after that nasty cut. You may need a doctor.'

Ralph looked at her gratefully. Turning his back on the scene on the lawn he slowly followed her up the meadow, past the marquee which, happily, had prevented most of the crowd from seeing what was going on, to the house.

From the corner of his eye Hugo, who'd not been hurt half as badly as he pretended, watched him, his heart light with happiness.

'Oh Mummy, Mummy,' he moaned and Rachel rocked him protectively against her bosom, her hand tenderly touching his dark, curly head, crooning softly to him:

'There, there, darling. Mummy's here.'

PART 3

Accident of Birth
1926-1932

CHAPTER 11

Paris in the twenties was a place of dazzling gaiety, of artistic and intellectual excitement, as the country tried to recover from the rigours of the War. It succeeded only too well, its population swelled by numbers of refugees who came to enhance the life of the capital, not the least Stravinsky, Nijinsky, Diaghilev and the Ballet Russe. Diaghilev had been a cosmopolitan even before the Revolution, but after it he never went back. Like the Ferovs and thousands of others, he sought his home in a land far away from the one where he'd been born.

It was thus singular that a young woman who was not a refugee adopted a Russian name, and became even more Russian than the Russians. Susan Bolingbroke found in her new in-laws her *raison d'être*. Encouraged by them, she used the name of Princess Ferova, which they said she was entitled to, and embraced the Orthodox Faith, being received into the church in Rue Darue by the Patriarch of France.

The Russian liturgy had never reformed itself. It was as old and unbending as the church – beautiful, majestic, solemn. Princess Hélène stood as her sponsor when she was baptized, taking as her name Tatiana, after the second daughter of the Czar.

Susan knew that when Kyril was free he would feel as his family did about the Bolshevik regime, and would return to the faith of his ancestors. It was he, after all, who had wanted a religious wedding. Susan went on learning the Russian language, and furnished her flat on the Quai Voltaire with furniture and memorabilia that would make all the Russian exiles visiting her feel at home. In each room there was an icon with a burning lamp in front of it. But the huge apartment, overlooking the Seine, was not old-fashioned, heavy on the eye or depressing to the spirit as so many havens of exiles seemed to be – those who'd managed to transport their goods, furniture and chattels with them; very few. It was furnished with a remarkable degree of flair and imagination, from antique shops and dealers who went far afield to Austria and to Italy, where many of those fleeing Russians, who had managed to take precious items of furniture, bibelots and *objets d'art* with them, had then to dispose of them due to the currency regulations in various European countries.

With the help of the more cultivated and knowledgeable Hélène, Susan developed an interest in antiques that, as the months and then the years passed, grew into an obsession. She became an expert, a connoisseur. Her speciality was eighteenth-century Russian furniture, silver and bronzes and the ancient icons whose paintings went back to the beginnings of Russian orthodoxy, a religion with Byzantine origins, and the mystery of the East.

The reforms of Peter the Great, who reigned from 1696 to 1725, not only dragged Russia out of its backwardness but gave an impetus to all forms of culture including music, architecture, painting and the decorative arts. Men of talent hurried from all over Europe to the Petrine court which was established in the newly built St Petersburg, and among them were a number of gifted craftsmen and cabinet-makers. The popular European fashions were not slavishly copied, however, but adapted to suit the Russian character and temperament so that a recognizable style evolved.

Around Peter's palaces sprang up huge mansions for the nobles who followed the Imperial Court and they, too, attracted their own craftsmen, providing the impetus for Russian furniture-making. Carpenters imported by the Czar to build his ships on the banks of the Neva stayed to become woodcarvers, cabinet-makers and talented gilders, developing a unique style of their own that bridged the gap between the

'Chinese' taste of the late seventeenth century and the later development of the Baroque.

It became fashionable to paint woodwork in white or light colours to form an ideal background for the carved flowers and ornate scrolls with which the furniture was decorated. Chairs, sofas and settees had embroidered covers in cross stitch worked in crewel, or upholstery made of damask.

A unique range of eighteenth-century furniture was represented in Susan's apartment, though, with the help of Hélène's good taste, she favoured the less elaborate styles of the 1760s and 1780s when Catherine the Great was on the throne. Lines became smoother, carvings less intricate and techniques on inlaying were perfected by craftsmen such as Meyer, who had executed a beautiful inlaid corner cupboard, a rare example of his work, which Susan had in her drawing-room. There was a card table by Heinrich Gambs, cabinet-maker to the Court; a delicate kidney table by Vasily Bobkov, and a sofa of Karelian birch carved with gilt decorations and upholstered in damask by Andrey Tour, a prominent St Petersburg master.

Scattered here and there on painted and gilt tables in green and gold were small ivories made by the celebrated Kholmogory ivory carvers from North Russia – caskets, snuff boxes, statuettes and trinkets of rare beauty. In her library was an ivory inlaid bookcase by Meyer and a magnificent table of bronze made by the metalworkers of the Tula Armaments Factory in 1740, a very popular and uniquely Russian form of furniture-making. Along one wall was a set of tapestries designed by Rusca and made by the celebrated Petersburg Tapestry Works, and one of her most priceless pieces was an armchair – also quintessentially Russian – *en gondole* made in one piece in the early nineteenth century, its carved openwork brilliantly polished inside and out.

Thus in her beautiful, tastefully and, eventually, pricelessly furnished home Susan, at a very youthful age, found herself not only a mother, possibly a widow, but a young woman of wealth whose breeding, taste and position in society began to make her sought after by those in Paris who were tired of the effete, precious, world-weary circles surrounding such leaders of society as the Comtesse Greffulhe, Etienne de Beaumont, Marie Laure de Noailles, the Marquise de Ludre, the Duchesse de la Rochefoucauld or the Princesse de Polignac. The latter, whose friends of both sexes were almost exclusively homosexual, remained, in her late fifties, the leading patron of the musical arts, friend of Satie, Poulenc and Stravinsky. The extent of her generous purse, her fortune based on the Singer sewing-machine empire, seemed virtually limitless.

Not that the new star on the social scene, the Princess Tatiana Ferova, as she came to be known, attempted at a jump to rival all these notable socialites. For one thing, she wasn't interested in social life for its own sake. She liked elegant living, beautiful furniture and paintings, nice clothes for the pleasure they gave, not because they were enviable or fashionable. Incongruous as it might seem, she came in time to resemble that woman she detested, her mother Melanie, who had aspired to a similar position in society in gay, pre-war London. Similar positions, maybe, but very different types. Melanie was unashamedly sybaritic; Susan sincerely, but unselfconsciously, artistic and intellectual.

Gradually, as the years of the twenties passed and the regime in Russia cemented its grip on the country, she thought more and more about Kyril and how he could be found and restored to her.

Susan had always been close to Bobby. The Bolingbroke children had passed a great deal of time with the Lightermans because Melanie had spent so much of her life pursuing a good time. Susan had always loved and admired her half-brother, now a talented though enigmatic man, a man of almost unbelievable wealth and the ability to make more. He was someone, moreover, who approved of Susan's attempts to establish a home in Paris; to furnish it in a beautiful, unique way and to encourage leading musicians to perform there, and painters and writers to visit. Bobby loved popping over to

Paris for a concert, or to escort Susan to the opera or to preside as host at a dinner party. He gave generously of his time, money and talent to support her in her new and surprising role as arbiter of fashion, taste and discrimination.

And always, of course, never far away were the Ferovs who, thanks to him and his grandmother, had finally achieved some measure of financial independence.

Prince Alexei Ferov knew nothing of business. He had enjoyed an exalted, if largely meaningless, position in the household of the late Czar, which involved standing about a good deal in elaborate court dress. It was the sort of idle, useless occupation that led to idle, useless pastimes like eyeing pretty ladies, also in the service of the Imperial Family, most of whom were too virtuous to return his flirtatious glances, the odd insidious invitation to an illicit assignation.

The years before 1914 had passed pleasantly enough, if sometimes rather frustratingly, at the Czar's various homes in the north of Russia and the Crimea. In the War, Prince Ferov was not called upon to perform heroic deeds at the front, but he did accompany the Emperor on manoeuvres and on his weekly trips to Mogilev. But for the accidental fact that he happened to be on his Caucasian estates when the Czar abdicated in March 1917 he might have been among those who perished with him. He never saw him again.

His years in exile had depressed Prince Ferov, but they had not dimmed his spirit. A few years older than his wife, he remained vigorous, alert and strong. As a young man he had loved sport and this enthusiasm for exercise had not deserted him. When he couldn't ride, he walked, and during the years in Paris without private transport, when his son was busy with his taxi, he walked a very great deal.

By 1926 Prince Ferov had been installed for two years in a fine office in the Askham Lighterman business enterprise in Paris, consisting of a large house in the Rue Scribe. The two tops storeys had been converted into a home for the Ferovs. They considered themselves very fortunate, very happy. They had plenty of food, money to enjoy little extravagances and the Prince travelled a lot, promoting the aristocratic image of the Askham Motor. He enjoyed travel. As Bobby had said, he merely had to be himself, the little he did was considered to reap dividends. He always stayed at the best hotels in any city he visited, and spent lavishly on his expense account to entertain potential customers, which he enjoyed too.

Then Princess Irina, passing frequently between Paris and Askham, where she continued as beloved companion to Dulcie Askham, was able to indulge her passion for clothes, particularly from the salons of Chanel and her rivals, the Italian Elsa Schiaparelli and Monsieur Molyneux. In fact, when the Princess was in Paris that was, inevitably, where she was to be found: viewing collections, dresses, fur coats or hats by the celebrated milliner Caroline Reboux.

On the other hand, when she was at Askham in Wiltshire she scarcely ever left the side of her friend and patroness, Lady Askham, whose old age made her increasingly dependent on the Princess – nervous when she was away, anxious for her company. This put the much younger Irina in a very strong position indeed: it made her practically indispensable.

In 1925, to everyone's surprise, the intellectual Princess Evgenia, still a student at the Sorbonne, had fallen in love with and married a fellow emigré, a Russian without a title called Boris Kogan, who had taken over Dima's taxi when the latter went to the Sorbonne to study medicine. The Ferovs were a mite distressed by her marriage to a man even more impecunious than they had been. One, moreover, of a depressive tendency who was seventeen years older than Evgenia who, however, continued with her studies and was happy with her husband in a tiny one-room apartment off the Rue Jacob. She had never liked being a princess, but she wanted to be a writer and translator. She was the most sensible and, probably, the most unambitious of the Ferov family, the one who least missed money or their former status in life. It was certain, since often Boris couldn't work for weeks because of his depression, that she would have need of all those qualities of fortitude her exile and deprivation had developed.

The most discontented of the Ferov family was Hélène, who neither wanted to go to university nor marry a taxi driver. She continued as Susan's constant companion, accompanying her everywhere in her search for treasures with which to furnish the Quai Voltaire apartment.

By 1926 Susan was an elegant, good-looking young woman who seemed much older than her twenty-three years. She had almost as much charm as her mother, nearly as much self-confidence and that asset that made them both equal: money.

One morning Susan opened a letter which she perused in silence for a few moments, before bursting out excitedly to Hélène, who was sharing the breakfast table, that Kyril had been traced, at last. He was in exile near Marinsk in Siberia where he was serving a ten-year sentence for betraying the Revolution.

'Ten years! If he went in 1922 he has only six years to do.'

'Six years sounds like a lifetime to me,' Hélène said, greeting the news without enthusiasm.

'Yes!' Susan started to count excitedly on her fingers. 'But I'll only be twenty-nine if he comes out in 1932. We'll still have a lifetime in front of us.'

Hélène put a cigarette into a long holder, examining it thoughtfully, like a man a cigar, before lighting it and carefully drawing on it. Officially she now lived at the family house in the Rue Scribe, a fashionably furnished, large apartment very different from their former abode in Clichy even if it was, as it were, over the shop. But she had spent the night at Susan's, who liked her company in a flat which was big enough to accommodate her, Alexander, his nanny, her two maids and a cook, as well as several guests.

'How do you know Kyril will still feel the same, Susan, about you?'

227

'Why shouldn't he?' Susan looked up, startled, from the letter she'd resumed reading, which came from Bobby, who had received the news directly from Russia, now under the leadership of Stalin. 'In prison he would surely have no other distractions?'

'But being sent to Siberia is not exactly prison. It is a large, open, labour camp which no one can escape from because of the huge distances involved. Kyril will have some kind of work ...' Hélène shrugged. 'Who knows if he will come back at all? Many don't.'

'I can't think why you're being so cruel.' Susan sadly dropped the letter. 'Or maybe I can. None of your family can forgive your brother for fraternizing with the enemy.'

'Would you?' Hélène got up from the table and, taking her coffee cup, went over to a low suede-covered settee which was modern yet blended perfectly with so much of Susan's antique furniture. 'Would *you* forgive *your* brother, Bobby say, if there were a revolution in England and he gave the beautiful house in Manchester Square to the rabble that supplanted your King and Queen who, maybe, had been taken away with their family and shot like dogs in a cellar ... Don't forget we, my family, knew these people who were shot to death: the little Czarevich, Alexei, played with Yegor. The Grand Duchess Elizabeth, who was such a close friend of my grandmother's, was thrown alive down a mine shaft. She was a nun, a holy woman only doing good from her convent in Moscow. Why do you think we should forgive Kyril, one of *us*, who condoned these horrors? Do you think we want to see him? Do you think we can forgive him? No!'

'Even though the Bolsheviks have turned on him?' Susan looked thoughtful.

'No, we don't want to see him, even then. If he walked in that door this minute I would walk out by that –' Hélène pointed a finger at entrance and exit.

'Then why did you have anything to do with me, or his child?'

'Because we liked you. We were sorry for you, the way he had treated you, left you ...'

'It wasn't his fault ...'

'Your loyalty was something we admired.'

'And our money was attractive, too ...'

Susan didn't know what had made her suddenly voice a thought she seldom acknowledged, and despised herself for when she did. It was only when she was angry with the Ferovs that she allowed herself to entertain such despicable, low-class ideas. But it was true the Ferovs had latched on. Their association with the Askhams had transformed their lives.

'I'm sorry. I didn't mean to say that.' Susan bent her head, biting her lip.

Hélène flicked her ash into a wide onyx ashtray with an insouciant smile.

'I know what you think. Don't imagine I'm offended. Certainly it's true that your arrival changed our lives. But we were not poor before and, if we ever get our estates and money back that we left in Russia, maybe it is *you* who will be the poor relation. I am telling you, Susan, my father was one of the most wealthy men in Russia. It was not easy for him to adjust to poverty and he was never nobler than when he did. Frankly, if we hadn't liked you, loved Sasha, and taken you both to our hearts, we shouldn't have cared that!' – Hélène imperiously flicked her fingers together – 'for your money.'

'Well spoken!' Bobby, pausing by the door into the lobby, walked in, gently clapping his hands. 'I'm glad to hear you ticking off my sister, Hélène.' He bent and kissed her hand, dropping his briefcase on the sofa. Then he straightened and removed his camel-hair coat with its loose tie-belt. 'My dear Susan,' Bobby kissed her cheek and, going round, sat opposite her. 'I see you just got my letter.'

'I was just telling Hélène the news. When did you arrive?'

'I came over on the night ferry. I need a bath, a shave, a change of clothes and ...' he glanced at his watch, 'then a day of meetings, including one with Alexei. He is being awfully clever selling my motor car. I believe Mademoiselle Chanel is going to buy one to go with her new Rolls-Royce. She is apparently a great friend of your mamma, Hélène. It was she, too, who talked her lover, the Duke of Westminster, into ordering the special custom-built Askham he drove to Biarritz with Coco this summer.'

'You see, we Ferovs *do* pay our way,' the Princess smiled slyly at Susan, aware of Bobby's admiring glance. Yet he never paid court to her, despite his lavish compliments.

'You Ferovs *certainly* pay your way. I should object very much if it was suggested that you didn't.' Bobby looked at Susan and frowned. Much as he loved her she could be very tactless.

'Susan didn't suggest that,' Hélène murmured, comfortably tucking her ankles under her and lighting a fresh cigarette. 'She was angry with me because I said we never wanted to see Kyril again. Your efforts to find him get no gratitude from us.'

'But you would want to see Kyril, surely, if he turned up? You'd say, at least, "Hello"?' Bobby glanced at her, also lighting his own cigarette.

'I doubt it.'

'How very embarrassing then, if he does.'

'Is it a possibility?' Susan looked excited again.

Bobby shook his head. 'I can't promise, but I do have one or two feelers out, now that we know where he is. Stalin is keen to do business. I can supply him with machine tools for the huge Putilov tractor works, with hydraulic equipment for a massive dam project at the Dnieper. He despises our methods, he says, but admires our products. Only with Socialism, apparently, one can produce them better. Ha!'

'I can't understand how you can have anything to do with these people!' Hélène impatiently stubbed out her cigarette and got up. 'It really makes me angry.'

Without looking at them she left the room. Bobby gazed after her for a moment, then he shrugged, stroking the night's growth of beard on his chin.

'She's very stormy, isn't she? I would never have thought it when we first met.'

'I hoped you'd like her,' Susan said, after a pause.

'Oh, I do. I like her very much.'

'Yes, but ...' Susan was stuck for words.

'You're thinking of something permanent? A wife? Maybe I'll get round to it one day.'

'Maybe you'll leave it too late.' Susan realized how little she knew about Bobby's private, emotional life.

'That's too bad.' Bobby tilted his chin and his expression was enigmatic. 'To change the subject ... Do you remember our cousin, Jamie Kitto?'

'Didn't he get some medal in the War?'

'Yes, the Military Cross.'

'I haven't seen him for years.'

'Neither have I. After the War he went to India to plant tea, but things didn't work out. He was on the boat train and I invited him to have dinner with us tonight, if that's all right by you.'

'It's fine by me. Do you want to eat here?'

'I thought it would be nice.' Bobby stroked his chin again. 'Maybe we could ask Hélène to make up the four.'

The Honourable James Kitto was Dulcie Askham's great-nephew, the son of her nephew Charles. Always known as Jamie, he was a member of the large Kitto family which inhabited the Scottish Borders. Jamie was one of ten brothers and sisters, among whom he had rather got lost. In addition, he had the disadvantage of having been born in 1896, which made him exactly the right age to enlist in 1914. He had served in the Guards and been wounded four times. Jamie was awarded the MC, loved the War and wanted to make soldiering his career. But his wounds had left him less than completely fit and, disappointed as well as hard up, he was one of the half a million unemployed soldiers whom his cousin by marriage, Adam Bolingbroke, had stormed and ranted about in Parliament.

In 1919 Jamie went to India to stay with an uncle, a Pukkah Sahib who loved the country and hardly ever came home. He had bought a large plantation in Assam which he wanted to train Jamie to manage; but Jamie didn't take to the life. Despite having spent his childhood and youth in the beautiful Scottish border country he was a city dweller by inclination. The War had given him a taste for fast, dangerous living and he hated India.

He married the pretty daughter of a member of the Indian Civil Service, who thought that he had money and a title and quickly tired of him when she found he had neither. He would never be anything but an 'Honourable' because he had three elder brothers with first claim to his father's title: Baron Kitto of Kelsoe.

The marriage produced two children, a boy and a girl, both of whom remained with their mother in India. Jamie was waiting for a divorce and was also job hunting when he met Bobby on the night ferry to Paris.

Jamie was an extremely personable man, rather rakish and used with a tired, battered-looking face, as though he lived life to the full. As a boy he'd had a bad skin, but at thirty the deep pock marks that remained only made him look interesting. He had boxed in the Army and twice broke his nose, which had never been properly set; his eyes were blue, his hair very curly and brown. Needless to say, being a relation of Dulcie Askham and Melanie, he had a great deal of charm. Women fell for him in droves.

'This is a frightfully nice place you've got here, Susan.' Jamie pulled on his cigarette and appreciatively sipped his drink, looking out of the window across to the Seine. 'This brings back memories. My goodness, how I remember Paris during the War! It never changed really.' Smiling nostalgically, he turned his back to the view and raised his glass. 'Chin-chin! Good times.'

'Were they really good times, Jamie? You had a good war?' Susan thought him amusing, so far.

'I had a wonderful war. I'd still be in the Army if it weren't for this.' He gestured ruefully to his leg which, due to a bullet fracture and bad setting on the field, was slightly shorter than the other. He walked with a limp.

Cocktails were the thing those days. Hardly anyone drank straight spirits, unless it was American whiskey and water. When Susan had a dinner party she employed an out-of-work émigré Russian count who worked as a waiter in a *boit de nuit* and made extremely good cocktails. He was called Josef and knew the Ferovs well socially; but when at work he was punctilious, deferential and correct. It didn't bother him at all. Josef happily slung his shaker above his shoulder and refreshed Jamie's glass.

'Cheers again,' Jamie said. He could certainly drink.

'You know, Jamie, I can remember you in 1915 at Uncle Bosco's Memorial Service. I must have been twelve, but I remember you stood out from all the Kittos charging around.'

'Did I, Sue? Thanks, darling.' Jamie spoke rather slangily, like an Australian, took his cousin's hand and kissed the tips of her fingers, not elegantly, like a Frenchman might have done, but in a hearty, masculine way. 'You can say "all those Kittos" again. I never saw so many.'

'You've a family yourself, I understand?'

Bobby, perching on a Rusca-designed painted and gilt chair in the drawing-room, had his glass in one hand, the inevitable cigarette in the other. He was smaller and neater than Jamie and there was no discernible family resemblance. He could only recall meeting him two or three times in his life. The Kittos hardly ever came to London except for family events like weddings and funerals.

'Yes, I married a girl called Sally Menzies. Alas, it didn't work out, quite. I have two youngsters who are in India with her and her father. I don't expect I'll ever see them again.'

'You sound as if you don't much care.' Hélène had spoken very little since arriving late, half an hour before. She wore a long, straight, black strapless Schiaparelli gown, with a single concealed pleat of gold lamé which caught the light whenever she moved her legs, sparkling rather enticingly. Her ash-blond hair with golden highlights swept silkily across her cheeks, concealing half her face, and her use of make-up was much more lavish than either her mother's or Susan's, but skilful too. She wore no jewels except a diamond eagle pin on her bosom which, she said, had been given to her as a christening present by the last Czar.

'But what can I do? There is no point crying about it. My wife and I are getting divorced and the children are staying with her. I'm looking for work.' Jamie gazed keenly, flatteringly at Hélène, who kept on crossing and uncrossing her legs, the golden pleat catching the soft, subdued light in the room.

'I can probably offer you a job,' Bobby said, 'if you're interested. We'll talk about it at dinner.'

The dinner-table was of glass and the candles on it made it seem like a flashing mirror. Jamie took in everything, but was apparently unimpressed, which Susan liked. She thought her rugged, rough-diamond of a cousin rather interesting and they spent a pleasant hour reminiscing about various amusing or salutary aspects of family history. Compared to the Askhams the Kittos were very poor relations indeed – impoverished upper class – but had never shown the slightest jealousy or envy of them. Another eccentric cousin, Constance Kitto, had been in and out of prison several times as a suffragette and was now looking for other worthy causes to support. Her brother, Malcolm Kitto, had died a heroic death at Gallipoli.

All the time Hélène listened, pecking her way among caviare, stuffed quail and plover's eggs, goose, pre-war Chambertin, and a dessert of quinces and fresh strawberries, heaven knows from where in February – probably from some hothouse in the South of France, specially sent up by train.

234

In this free, emancipated post-war society there was no question of the women leaving the men to port and brandy, and the four continued to sit round the table as coffee and liqueurs were offered and Bobby talked about the business.

'I can offer you any number of jobs, really. It depends what you're interested in.'

'Tell me what you've got.' Jamie lazily half-closed his eyes.

'Well, we have one large organization called, simply, Askham Lighterman Limited. This was set up after my grandfather's death, that is Sir Robert Lighterman. He was running the joint business of Lighterman Limited and Askham Developments after my Uncle Bosco was killed. By that time I was twenty and being groomed for the business. I studied Law at Oxford, didn't take my degree. My uncle's love was the development of the Askham motor car, which is my chief hobby too – our *de luxe* tourer and a more workaday model, the Askham Elite. During the War Sir Robert turned numbers of factories that had been making machine tools into manufacturing ammunition and several of these still operate.

'In addition we make parts for cars, tyres and all kinds of machinery: Lighterman Diecasting and Tools is a colossal works in Coventry. We are mainly now into engineering and motor cars. A number of things that didn't fit into our portfolio we got rid of: some farms in the West Country and a sprinkling of service industries, laundries and so on.'

'Thanks all the same, but I'm not really interested in anything like that.' Jamie emptied his brandy glass, swilling the fine Napoleon cognac round his mouth. 'I want to work on my own, anyway.'

'Doing what?' Bobby looked nonplussed. In these hard post-war times he had only to mention work to anybody and they came running, except, of course, the Ferovs. He expected a hard-up, distant cousin to be glad of work.

'I want to look around,' said Jamie.

'Is that why you came to Paris?' Susan gently kicked Bobby under the table.

'Partly. I made a little money in India, you know. I'm not quite as poverty-stricken as you seem to think. I don't need charity.'

'It's not *charity*,' Bobby's expression turned to indignation.

'Oh, yes, it is. You thought I was the poor relation, Bobby, hand out, eager for work. I thought you'd a bit of a nerve, assuming I wanted to work for you as a salesman or something, I suppose?' He had all Dulcie's arrogance, all right.

'I thought ...' Bobby began, and stopped.

'Bobby only meant well, Jamie,' Susan said, faintly embarrassed.

'I am being frank so that we don't get our wires crossed.' Jamie pushed his chair back from the table. Susan thought that he'd had too much to drink, as Jamie continued, 'I'm rather sick of the bloody patronizing types like Bobby, who never fought in the War and think they own the world. The Askhams always did give me the pip, if you want to know. I began my army service in the ranks. I got to know the common man and I would rather have him and his kind any day than a whole barrel load of bloody Askhams. Present company excepted, of course.' Jamie kissed his fingers and blew in Susan's direction. 'Now, I don't suppose you'll be sorry if I go.'

'Could you give me a lift?' Hélène rose silently from the table, as if the sense of what Jamie had said had gone over her head. 'I really must be getting home, too.'

A few weeks later, when Prince Ferov returned from a successful business trip to South America, he found only his two sons at home and was told that Hélène had moved out and was living with a man near the Trocadero.

The Prince was only a little mollified when he heard the man in question was related to the Askhams.

'But "un type" if you ask me,' Yegor, the younger son, said. 'I didn't take to him.'

'How do you mean "un type"?'

'Not very nice. Rough.'

'But how could he be if he's an "Honourable"?' Alexei expostulated. 'You're *sure* he's an honourable?'

'I'm not sure,' Yegor wasn't very interested. He was hard at work for his Baccalaureate exams.

'Then how do you know he is?' Prince Ferov moved to the door of his son's room.

'It's what I was told. His father is a nephew of Lady Askham, the old one.'

'He's a Kitto then?'

'A Kitto? I don't know. Yes, I think it is Kitto. The address is on the sideboard.'

Yegor put his head in his hands, trying to get on with his work.

Prince Ferov walked downstairs, staring for a long time at the card, an address and phone number written on it in Hélène's strangely schoolgirlish hand. He dialled a number but he got no reply so he went out, leaving his bags unpacked, to hail a cab in the road. He drove straight round to Susan, who was entertaining someone to lunch.

Susan had rather lost interest in the artistic Paris, represented by many leftovers of the belle époque like Lady Mendl and Natalie Clifford Barney; the ageing, wheezing Diaghilev with his coterie of young male dancers and his breathless admirers, like Chanel and the Serts who, in turn, had adopted a young *soi-disant* Georgian Princess called Roussy who went with them everywhere.

A younger group of artists, writers and musicians had come to Paris, were painting interesting things in ateliers never visited by José-Maria Sert and reading their books to one another in Sylvia Beach's bookshop in the Rue de l'Odéon.

There, Susan had already met Ezra Pound, the young Hemingway, T.S. Eliot, an American poet who lived in London, John dos Passos. She preferred the music of George Antheil and Vladimir Golschmann to the more established Poulenc, Satie and Georges Auric, and her salon now was

237

peopled by young men and women who, like her, had been too young to serve in the War or to be much affected by it.

Susan's guest was an American writer called Josh Baker who had been in Miss Beach's shop one day when Susan was ordering some books. Miss Beach's English bookshop was one of the most famous of Parisian literary establishments, and it was through her influence that Susan became more interested in younger talent than established names.

'Alexei!' Susan jumped up when her father-in-law was shown in, and introduced him to the polite, well-dressed young American. 'Will you have lunch with us?'

The Prince waved his hand agitatedly, asking to talk to her alone.

'I suppose it's about Hélène,' Susan said when they had gone to the drawing-room, leaving the American with his cheese.

'Yegor says he's a relation of yours.'

'I'm afraid he is. What is more, she met him here. I can't tell you how sorry I am.'

'But is there something wrong with him?'

Alarmed, the Prince sat down, his hand still grasping the silver top of his cane.

'Not exactly *wrong*,' Susan screwed up her nose. 'But not right, either. He was extremely rude to Bobby, who had been awfully nice to him, and he has no money. He is also married. But that is the debit side.' Susan, who was fond of her father-in-law, groped for words to allay Alexei's fears. 'On the credit side he is a cousin, a Kitto, well brought up. They're one of the best families in Scotland and he had a distinguished War record. He can't be all bad. He's proud, too. When Bobby offered him a job he took umbrage, called it charity.'

Alexei studied his fingernails, as though applying some of this message to himself, as Susan went on: 'Although he had no car, Hélène asked for a lift when he left abruptly, and very early. It was quite obvious to me, by her behaviour all evening, that she was interested in him. This is a pity because Bobby rather likes Hélène, I think. I was trying to put the notion into his head that she'd make him a good wife. Don't you think so, Alexei?'

'She would certainly be very *decorative*,' the Prince said cautiously. 'As for a good wife ... she knows absolutely nothing about housekeeping. What little she learned in the years we were wandering she's forgotten.'

'Oh, Bobby doesn't need a housekeeper!' Susan looked appalled at the idea. 'He needs a figurehead; someone he can be proud of, who dresses beautifully and looks elegant. The Lighterman fortune is quite vast, I assure you, and Hélène would have had everything she needed...'

'I've no doubt of that,' Alexei said bitterly, nervously lighting one of his Turkish cigarettes. 'But I notice you use the past tense?'

'Well,' Susan shrugged her shoulders in the Gallic mannerism she had taken to very quickly. 'Soiled goods, don't you know ... I doubt if he'd want her now.'

CHAPTER 12

Rachel heard the noise of people running up the stairs and knew at once who it was even before the door of her office burst open and they stood, laughing, on the threshold. The sight of Freddie and Em always lifted her heart however depressed she felt and, just now, she was very depressed indeed. Em's impulsive nature was supercharged whenever the irrepressible Freddie was with her. In a way it was just as well they went to separate boarding-schools, or else their lives together would be like one explosive impact on others, difficult to live with for too long.

Rachel often felt that Bosco's nature had been shared by his sons except, perhaps, for Hugo. She could see very little of him in Hugo; but in Ralph she saw his dignity, honesty, integrity and statesman-like qualities, also his temper; and in Freddie she saw the fun, the ebullience of the days when, as the younger son who didn't expect to inherit, he enjoyed a hell-raising reputation in his cavalry regiment, the 21st Lancers.

Freddie had always been fun, never took anything seriously. He had a freckled face and dark carroty hair, brilliant blue eyes and a wide mouth that always had permanent laughter creases at each corner. His looks were odd, but not unattractive; he hadn't the classical, conventional style of Ralph and it was difficult to tell they were brothers.

Rather to everyone's surprise the tomboy Em had grown into rather a lovely girl. She was like Freddie to look at, but her hair was long and curled about her shoulders, pure auburn, Askham hair. Her cheekbones were more pronounced and with her wide mouth and flared nostrils, one had the impression that she possibly came from the Balkans. She was tall but, unlike Charlotte who was slight and willowy, Em was a sturdy, well-built girl who looked as though she excelled at games, which she did.

'What a lovely surprise,' Rachel said, putting her pen down and getting up to greet them. 'What brings you here?'

'Bobby has given *two* motors to help beat the strike, Mummy. Freddie is driving one of them and Tony Tancred the other. I'm looking after the depot.'

'Which is where?' Rachel's pleasure evaporated and she returned almost wearily to her desk.

'In Manchester Square, Mummy. Mabel has put her car in the pool as well, and...'

'If you can't sympathize with the strike I'd rather you stayed out of it. Apart from anything else you're embarrassing me.' Rachel threw her pen down on the table on top of the article she was writing, attacking Baldwin. 'If men who work in the conditions the miners do are asked to take reduced wages and accept a longer working week, what else can we expect but that their fellow workers, and we, must support them? In this dispute *we* are at one with the strikers...'

'But, Mummy, it's such a lot of fun.' Em pulled a face, looking over her shoulder at her twin. 'I knew she'd be cross.'

'I'm absolutely furious,' Rachel said. 'It's not as though you're particularly anonymous, and my support for the miners is well known.' She pointed to her article. 'I've written *reams* about it. The next thing will be an article in the *Daily Mail* about *you*.'

Freddie, abashed, hung his head, but Em tossed hers defiantly.

'Fiona says that if the workers win we'll have Bolshevism. We don't want *that* after what happened to Susan.'

'That is nonsense. You can't compare Britain and Russia. The miners are badly paid, their conditions are so awful that even some of the mine owners like Lord Henry Bendinck and Lord Londonderry say they have a case. The court of enquiry into the dispute was based almost entirely on the evidence of the owners. It was very one-sided.'

'Mummy, the miners are one thing.' Em moved towards her mother placatingly, her hands outstretched, 'bringing the whole nation to a halt is another. Anyway, I'm not a Socialist.'

'That has been obvious to me for some time,' Rachel smiled at this much beloved, rather wilful girl. She supposed it was her fault for sending her to an exclusive girls' boarding-school where all her friends were titled or well off, or both. It was very difficult to meet any ordinary members of the human race in circumstances like this. Rachel, as well educated as her children, had always had a Radical streak which Em, at one time, had seemed to share. As quite a small girl, she had jettisoned her baptismal first name Augusta in favour of her second after the suffragette leader Emmeline Pankhurst, an old friend of her mother's. For Em there had been something too imperious about Augusta and, later, something too long-winded about Emmeline, which she had shortened to Em.

And Em had stuck. It suited her. A Socialist she might not have been but she was a warm-hearted, compassionate girl who got on well with everyone. At her age it was perhaps inevitable that she was influenced by her school friends, that she reacted away from her mother's political views. She seemed to be aware of that now as she said:

'It's not that I don't *care*, Mummy, I do. I know there are many people very badly off, but I can't help thinking of what happened to poor Susan's husband.'

'He was a declared Bolshevik. It's not the same being an English Socialist. Our ideas are based firmly on democracy and freedom.'

'I suppose that's what they say in Russia. Anyway, the Russians are supporting this strike. They've given millions of pounds to the miners.'

'That doesn't mean they're trying to overthrow our own institutions. They are simply showing solidarity with the workers.'

'Some people think they are.' Em sat on the edge of her mother's desk, untying the silk scarf she'd wound round her

242 -

hair to keep it out of her eyes. Rachel stared at her – loving her, proud of her, wishing so much that Bosco could see her, could see all his children now. 'People call you the "Red Countess", Mummy, because they think you'd like to overthrow our society too!'

'That is such rubbish ...' Rachel sat back and sighed, pressing her hands to her brow, feeling tired.

'Besides, look at the effect on our personal life. Askham House is full to overflowing with strikers from the north ...'

'Only for a day or two while they organize a march ...'

'Freddie couldn't get into his own room last night ...'

'That was a mistake ...'

'But, Mummy, don't you *see*, we find it intolerable to have our home invaded by strangers, our mother insulted in the newspapers ...'

'Your mother's a very brave woman.' Spencer Foster came into the room, slipping quietly through the open door, his hat in his hand. He, too, looked tired and careworn. Most of the people in Rachel's house were from his constituency and his own house was overflowing too.

Em jumped to her feet as Spencer came in. Freddie righted himself from his perch by the door where he'd slumped, and brother and sister moved closer together as though against a foe. They didn't like Spencer's interest in their mother. They resented it.

'I'm sorry, I didn't know you were here.' Spencer looked as though, aware of the sudden chill in the atmosphere, he was about to put on his hat again, but Rachel held out a hand.

'No, don't go! I have to see you, anyway ...' She shrugged her shoulders and looked at her children, aware of their instinctive jealousy. Since she could no longer belong to their father they didn't want her to have anyone.

'I was saying, Rachel is very brave,' Spencer went on, twirling the brim of his hat in his hands, which emphasized his nervousness, 'because she stands up for her principles; she's fearless ...'

243

'Is it so brave then to have your home invaded by strangers?'

'Not invaded ...' Rachel began but Freddie cleared his throat, speaking out at last.

'We all feel you should keep that life apart from us, Mother, in your office, here ... but not at home. Friends and people we know we don't mind ...'

'During the War it was used as a convalescent home for soldiers.' Rachel's tone was sarcastic. 'I don't suppose you'd have liked them either. They were strangers, too.'

'That was different.'

'Not to me. These people are also fighters; fighting against injustice and oppression. If people call me the "Red Countess" for that reason, then I am proud to be so called. I am proud to be on the side of the working people.'

Spencer put his arm round her and Em looked away as though the sight upset her. 'Your mother and I ...' he began, but Rachel looked at him sharply and shook her head, a gesture not missed by Freddie, who impulsively tugged at Em's hand.

'Come on, to the barricades ...'

'They'll be gone by tomorrow or the next day,' Rachel said.

'Thanks, Mother, but we're staying tonight with Mabel.'

Em, face strained, blew her mother a kiss. As they shut the door Rachel was sadly aware how quietly they descended compared to the happy and exuberant way they had come up.

'They really dislike me,' Spencer said, dejectedly sitting down.

'What were you going to say?' Rachel perched on the desk as Em had, and began to massage his shoulder.

'That we wanted to get married.'

'Hardly the time, today.'

'When, Rachel, then?'

Rachel got up and began to pace the room.

'Certainly not now, Spencer, whatever the children think. What's more important is our work; we want to keep publicity for that, not ourselves. RED COUNTESS WEDS SOCIAL-

IST MP. I can just see it.' Rachel ran imaginary headlines across the room with her hands.

'Well?'

'People are prurient. If a woman marries a much younger man they think it must only be for sex.'

'I can't see that at all. Surely they will know how much else we have in common? Anyway, do we care what they think? You're just making excuses, aren't you, Rachel? You have, ever since I first told you I loved you.'

'Spencer!' Angrily Rachel removed her hand and sat with her arms akimbo, her head bent. 'We've been together for three years. Aren't we happy?'

'Very happy,' tenderly he reached out for her hand, 'but not in the way I want to be. I want to be with you permanently, not just snatching moments when no one is around.'

'Nevertheless, we have a lot of those.'

'I think your children would like me better if things were legitimate. Suspicion makes matters worse. I want us to be asked everywhere together, to be a couple. Like the Webbs.'

'Like the Webbs!' Rachel threw back her head and laughed until tears unexpectedly sprang to her eyes. 'That is the funniest thing I've heard all day. God forbid we should ever be like the Webbs.'

'I don't mean like *them*, but a couple as they are, united by principle as well as love.'

Rachel's hostility to the Webbs was well known. She found Beatrice arrogant and fanatical, unwilling to tolerate anyone who disagreed with her. Sidney resented anyone who didn't like Beatrice so, although they had to mix a great deal politically, socially they kept their distance.

'Why do you want to bring all this up just now?' Rachel again ran her hands over her head as though trying to stifle a headache, and looked at her unfinished article. 'The copy boy is waiting for this; we have a meeting to attend tonight, several tomorrow and the next day. There is work to be done, Spencer. Plenty of time to consider personal matters after we've won.'

245

'We shan't win,' Spencer shook his head sadly. 'The strike is already crumbling. The government is in complete control. I expect it not to last the week. But I do want to marry you. I am not just content to be your lover.'

Rachel looked past him to the dome of St Paul's gleaming in the spring sunshine, an act she did many times in the course of the day in her functional office, scarcely changed since Bosco had first bought the paper. Once again years seemed to slip away, many years, and she heard the echo of that other voice, also loved, saying he was tired of their relationship and wanted to marry. Then she had not been wrong to marry Bosco. Too many good things had come out of it to regret it: her children, his love. But also there was the excruciating pain of his death; a pain which never entirely left one, and the position she had to keep up as his widow. Her mother-in-law was always accusing her of debasing the family name with the publicity she got for her activities. Maybe it would be rather nice not to be Lady Askham, to be Mrs Foster instead.

Mrs Foster ... Lady Askham. Rachel suddenly looked at her lover and somehow 'Mrs Foster' didn't seem right. It seemed like a denial of Bosco, of her children and their name. Maybe this was why she held back and, as if divining her thoughts Spencer, who was not a fool, suddenly added:

'I don't believe you want to give up your title.'

'That's a stupid thing to say. You know, I'm rather tired of attacks on me today. First my children, and now you.'

Rachel threw herself at her desk and, seizing her pen, scored through what she had written and began again.

'Please leave me alone, Spencer, there's a dear. I'm not throwing you out but ...'

She looked up, smiling, meaning to soothe him, but all she saw was his back angrily going through the door.

It was true that the Russians were mischievous. Relations between Russia and England were strained. The supposed letter from Zinoviev, Head of the Third International in

Moscow, allegedly sent to the Communist Party of Great Britain, urging them to work for the violent overthrow of British institutions, had led to the fall of the first Labour Government, after only nine months in office, in 1924. In the subsequent election the Unionists were swept to power because of the fear of the Bolshevik menace, and it was hard to get anyone to say a good word for the Russian government. The Liberals were almost annihilated in this election, and Adam's chances of returning to Parliament seemed to have gone for ever.

Rachel, the 'Red Countess', found it wise to keep a low profile; but this did not prevent her espousing those causes in her paper which had always been dear to her: justice, equality, the franchise for women.

Once again the House of Commons had voted against admitting all women over twenty-one. It was still restricted to those over thirty. There were many similar inequities that occupied Rachel, beside the vexed question of Russia and the risk of being called a Communist if one voiced approval of the Soviet regime which had been recognized by Ramsay MacDonald, the first Labour Prime Minister, as *de jure* rulers of Russia, in January 1924.

In the course of the week of the General Strike in May 1926, offices were opened by the government for the enrolment of voluntary workers, and the bright young things of the twenties, including her twin son and daughter, thought it all a tremendous lark. Rachel and Spencer, together with other like-minded people, were trying hard to bring justice to the working-class people of Britain, Rachel in her paper, Spencer in the House of Commons, of which he was still a member and, as he represented a Lancashire mining community, he found himself in the thick of the fight, subject to much abuse.

As Rachel expected, the dailies soon took up the chance of a good story with pictures of Freddie and Em, in one of Bobby's cars, pulling out of the huge house in Manchester Square. Perched on the bonnet Em didn't look as though she were doing much to ease the hardship of those allegedly deprived by the strike.

'CHILDREN OF "RED" LADY ASKHAM HELPING TO PUT AN END TO THE STRIKE!' screamed the papers, and then there were accounts of what they were doing with money from the Askham and Lighterman fortunes:

Lady Askham, one of the richest women in the country, who is active on behalf of the strikers, and has also visited Russia, has not managed to convert her two younger, attractive and level-headed children, the Honourable Freddie Down and his sister Lady Emmeline, both of whom hope to go to Oxford in the autumn.

Together with some young contemporaries on half-term holiday from school, they are working twelve hours a day, offering transport to those affected by the strike in two of the luxurious Askham motor cars made by the family. 'Lady Em', as she is known, admits it's a bit of a lark and says Mummy isn't very pleased.

We should think she isn't. Maybe Lady A. would be better off in Russia where most people don't even own a motor car and strikes are forbidden. There she could really see Socialism at work ... Why doesn't she go where she belongs? Meanwhile carry on with the good work, sensible Lady Emmeline and the Honourable Freddie. The country needs you, but not your mother.

By the time this offensive item appeared in one of *The Sentinel*'s main rivals, the strike was over. It was ended not by the solidarity of the workers, but the alliance between the ruling classes and the bourgeoisie: by a united, determined front; by people who regarded it as vital for national survival and others, like Rachel's younger children and their friends, who regarded it as 'fun'.

Lady Charlotte Down was completely unaffected one way or the other by national events on her life given, as it was, purely and solely to her own satisfaction and pleasure. She celebrated her nineteenth birthday in the week after the strike. Her only relief in the fact that it was finished was that it would not affect the celebrations, and that the ghastly people her mother had allowed into the house would all be gone.

Charlotte's attitude was equivocal, however. Her charm and friendliness always seemed so genuine that even the striking miners of Lancashire were convinced she was on their side. She managed to be all things to all people, everything to everyone. In many ways she was genuine. She didn't lack compassion but, above all, she needed to be loved; and hated people to be angry with her.

The day after the piece about her mother appeared in the paper Charlotte, rising late as usual, was still poring over it when Rachel came into the breakfast-room, having taken the last of the strikers to Euston Station.

'All gone, Mummy?' Charlotte said brightly, moving up to let her mother sit next to her. 'Coffee, darling? You look all in.'

'Of course I'm all in! The General Strike may be over, but the miners are not going to go back.'

'Why ever not, Mummy? I thought they'd lost.' Charlotte, ever polite, was always willing to learn.

'The strike may have failed, but *we* have not lost.' Rachel, frowning, pulled her coffee cup towards her, sipped. 'This is good.' As she smiled the colour flowed back into her face.

'Mummy darling, why do you always say "we"? You are not a miner.'

'But I'm on their side.'

'Yes, but you're not a miner, Mummy. You're the Countess of Askham, the "Red Countess", as this paper informs me.' Charlotte made a pretence of studying it intently. 'Apparently you're one of the richest women in the country. I suppose you've seen this rag?'

'Yes, I saw it last night.' Suddenly she looked at her daughter, saying impulsively, 'Would you like me *not* to be Lady Askham, Charlotte?'

'How do you mean? Of course you're Lady Askham.' Charlotte, mystified, pushed a lock of thick, curly hair away from her eyes.

'If I married Spencer I'd be Mrs Foster.'

249

Abruptly Charlotte bent over as though her subsequent laughter gave her a pain in the stomach. It was rather a theatrical gesture, but Charlotte was theatre-mad. 'Mrs Fo…ster,' Charlotte rocked backwards and forwards. 'Mummy darling, on those grounds alone you could never marry Spencer, unless he changes his name.'

'I don't think Foster's too bad,' Rachel looked nonplussed. 'Why is it bad?'

'It's *awful*. Whatever would Daddy have said?'

'If Daddy were here it wouldn't come up.'

They both fell silent, gazing at each other. Charlotte put a hand over her mother's.

'You still miss him, Mummy, don't you?'

'Of course I miss him.' Restlessly Rachel got up and walked round the table. 'I will miss him all my life even if I did marry Spencer. You know you may not think so but Spencer is very like your father. He is a strong man, a kind man … he's a terrific support to me.'

'I know,' Charlotte's eyes filled with tears. 'I *know* how you feel. But I don't know how you can *think* of marrying him when there was Daddy.'

'*Was* Daddy,' Rachel cried. 'Isn't that the point? My darling Bosco died eleven years ago. Spencer is *very* nice, a good man. I wish …' Rachel paused. 'I wish you could all be nicer to him, try and like him …'

'Oh but, Mummy, I have never …' Charlotte began protestingly, but Rachel shook her head.

'I know you don't like him, none of you do. Is it really because of Daddy? Or because he's a Socialist MP? Because he's working-class?'

'Oh, Mummy, who can say?' Charlotte crossed her legs, her gown falling aside to reveal that she had nothing on underneath. Rachel felt rather shocked. Did her daughter sleep in the nude? What would happen if one of the footmen walked in? Come to that, what did she know about Charlotte's private life? Very little. She had a score of young friends, men and women, and never gave her mother any trouble, seldom had. She was sunny, friendly and, apparently, thoroughly well balanced. Everyone liked her.

Yet Rachel always felt a little sad that none of her children had any intellectual pretensions. Rachel knew that Charlotte would marry soon; she was too sought after, also too idle to want to work when there was no need to do so for money. Next year, the year after, there would be a big wedding at Askham or St Margaret's, Westminster. Who would it be who would take care of her darling, emotionally, because financially she would always be independent? Who would cherish and protect her for the rest of her life? What lucky man?

'What I want to know is, would anyone actually mind?' she said, breaking the silence.

'I think we would actually hate it, Mummy. I think it would split our family but, having said that, I feel you must do as you like.'

'Thanks very much.' Rachel's tone was bitter. 'Now, effectively, I *am* tied for life ...'

'But, Mummy, you *do* sleep with him, don't you? What's the point of marrying?' At the look of polite enquiry on Charlotte's face, Rachel slowly turned pink. 'I'm sorry, I shouldn't have ... but you know your room *is* near mine.'

'Do you think it's awfully sordid?' Rachel felt like a miscreant schoolgirl being interrogated.

'Not at *all*, Mummy! Everyone is doing it these days.'

'Are you?' Rachel looked at the bare thighs, but Charlotte was giving nothing away. She wouldn't reveal herself, whatever her mother did. She didn't even blush.

'Mummy, you are an old married woman! I'm a young girl. I think you have a perfect right to sleep with him if you want to. In fact, I think it's very modern.'

'Do the others know?'

'I've never told them, or discussed it with them, but I think ... they may guess.'

'Maybe that's why none of you like him.'

'Maybe.' Charlotte looked wise, nodding her head. Then, as if the intimacy of the occasion gave them a special bond, she leaned forward, tightly clutching her gown across her legs. 'Mummy, could we talk about *me* for a minute?'

'Of course, darling!' Hastily Rachel went over to Charlotte, wrapping a hand protectively in hers.

'Oh, Mummy, it's nothing like that ... not about sex or anything. It's about my ... life.'

'Are you in love with someone, darling?'

'Now you're at it again.' Charlotte looked at her reprovingly.

'I can't think what you want to say.'

'Would you mind most awfully if I became an actress?'

Rachel wondered if she'd be more shocked if her elder daughter had said she was going to work in a brothel. 'An *actress*?' she boomed.

'Yes, you know, on the stage.' Charlotte, impulsively freeing her hand from her mother's, got up and did a little pirouette ending in a neat curtsy, hands extended on either side. 'Like Edna Best or Lilian Braithwaite. I'd like to go and study drama, become a real actress.'

'But you never said ... I know you love the theatre.'

'I love it and I think I'd be good at it. There *is* a man.' Charlotte looked at her from beneath thick lashes, 'Oh, nothing like that, emotional or anything. His name is Philip Pride, we call him PP. But he's a theatrical producer and he says he thinks I have talent ...'

'Have you acted for him?' Rachel began to feel terribly alarmed, as though she'd been seriously neglecting her maternal duties. 'I mean, in front of him?'

'I think it's my looks, Mummy,' Charlotte tried to sound modest. 'He's always on about them, and about me going on the stage. He says with sound coming to the cinema there will be a huge expansion in motion pictures.' Charlotte stretched her arms very wide. 'Do you think it would matter *very* much if the daughter of an earl were an actress?'

'Well, as you say, these are modern, democratic times. Enough actresses have, in the past, married earls, but you must give me a chance to think about it. I would also like to meet Mr Pride.' She gave Charlotte a searching look, trying not to sound censorious. In a way she felt as concerned as any Victorian parent. At a time like this she wished that Bosco was still alive.

There was a tap on the door and Peter, the footman, entered with a tray.

'Come to clear away, Peter? We shan't be a minute.'

Peter bowed. 'It's the telephone, my lady. It's young Master Hugo's school – I'm afraid.'

Charlotte and Rachel looked at each other and Rachel ran.

Hugo did, in fact, look abjectly sorry; he also looked frightened. In all his escapades before none had ever involved the police. Yet here he now was with two policemen, his headmaster and his mother, all looking very grave, in his headmaster's study.

'I hope you realize, Lady Askham,' the chief policeman with buttons on his shoulder was saying, 'that normally a child caught stealing would be prosecuted.'

'Yes, I know ...' Rachel's heart seemed hardly to have stopped its fast, unnatural beating since Peter had summoned her to the phone. 'But he is very young ...'

'We have many delinquents younger than Master Hugo. He *is* fourteen.'

Hugo looked older. He was a tall child and dark down covered his upper lip.

'Yes, I know.' Rachel lowered her head.

'However, Lady Askham, we know what this would mean to you if it got into the paper. The name of a juvenile would not, of course, be revealed; but there might be repercussions that would identify you. The press know everything. A person of your stature would suffer more than a normal person.'

'That's very kind of you, Inspector. I assure you he will never, ever ...'

'Well, if he does do anything like this again I'm afraid his chances of avoiding the juvenile court would be remote.'

'Are you *quite* sure there's ... no mistake?' Rachel looked at Hugo, to whom she had not yet had the chance to speak alone. Her eyes pleaded with him to tell her he was innocent. Instead, as he studied the floor, she knew he was guilty.

'Hugo broke into the village store in the early hours of yesterday evening after it had shut. He was heard by the owner who had not yet left the shop and caught red-handed. He had fifty pounds on him.'

'Fifty pounds!' Rachel looked at him, horrified. 'He has no need of money.'

'All boys are the same, Lady Askham. He may have no need of it, but taking it is the object.'

The Inspector rose, took up his hat and nodded to the constable with him. 'We'll leave this matter now in Mr Frewin's hands. I think he has something to say to you. Good-day.'

'Thank you very much,' Rachel said, putting out a hand.

The Inspector either didn't see it or didn't want to take it and, for one of the very few times in her life, she felt belittled and humiliated; the mother of a petty criminal.

Bobby lay with one arm under his head, the other round Aileen's waist. From the windows of her flat in Battersea he could see the tower of Big Ben at Westminster. They seemed very isolated here from life – cocooned from the world. How long could it go on? For how long would she put up with it?

'Penny for them?' she said, as if she knew what was in his mind.

'I'm just thinking I must go,' Bobby lied, looking at her and smiling. Anyway, she was used to his lies, his evasions, his reluctance to discuss them or their future. She now seemed to expect it. Was it because she knew, in her heart, that with him she didn't have one? No chance at all of a legal union with the fifth richest man in England, as a recent survey had showed?

'When will you be back?'

'In a few days.' He leaned over and kissed her, his cheek lingering against hers. Like this he always felt a heel, a coward, a man in the presence of a woman who was too good for him, though some might think it was the other way around. He was extremely attached to Aileen and he knew that if she were not who she was, the daughter of his works manager, she would be perfect. Because she was accomplished. In the years she'd been with the business she had proved herself in many ways. Naturally, being a woman she'd been kept in a relatively lowly position: telephonist, clerk, typist, now secretary to one of the group managers, Dennis Altmark.

When he got up to dress she usually got up with him and made him coffee, but today she didn't. She lay where she was looking at him and, feeling uncomfortable, as though his naked body revealed his mind, he turned his back. Several times she seemed about to say something but changed her mind, the atmosphere between them charged with unspoken thoughts and utterances.

'Rachel is in a devil of a mess with that Hugo.' Bobby, tying his tie in the mirror, looked past his reflection at her. How often had she seen that imperious face in the boardroom, the smooth dark cheeks giving him a rather swarthy appearance – an untypical Askham – the brilliant intelligent eyes alert; the captain in command. Yet he was her lover, too, a man gentle and tender in bed, who needed her. But he only needed her there; nowhere else. She was not part of his life.

'What's happened now with Hugo?' Aileen sat up and shook a cigarette out of the packet.

'He's been caught stealing from the Post Office near his school. Rachel has been asked to take him away.'

'And has she?' Aileen lit her cigarette and coughed.

'She had no option. The police apparently would have prosecuted him. It was all hushed up because of who he was or, rather, who Rachel was. The Headmaster said that Hugo has been nothing but a trial since he joined the school. Many times they thought he'd pinched something but lacked proof. Personally, I think he's wicked; bad blood. Do you remember when Ralph gave him that beating! He's hated him ever since. Although we know his father was Bosco Askham we don't know anything about his mother except that she was a tart.'

Bobby didn't notice the flush that stole up Aileen's cheek.

'A tart?'

'She was a prostitute, didn't you know?'

'I know nothing about Hugo's mother.'

'She was someone Bosco met in Cairo after Omdurman and then he met her again in England years later. She operated from a brothel in Streatham, but he was hooked on her and bought her a house in Hampstead. It was she who caused his downfall at the libel trial, and after that he never saw her again. She went back to Cairo when the War began and in the first year of the War he was killed.'

'But how did his wife know about Hugo?'

'He left her a note. Nasty way to find out.'

'Awful, I should think.'

'Yes, but Rachel is an exceptional woman. She took it in her stride and found Hugo, who was just on the point of being sent to an orphanage. The irony is that she's always seemed to love him best of her children.'

'The prodigal son,' Aileen murmured as Bobby put on his jacket. 'The one who was lost, and came home.'

'I see what you mean,' Bobby bent down to kiss her. 'Are you all right? You look tired.'

'I'm fine.' Aileen smiled a reassurance she didn't feel.

Afterwards, when he'd gone, she thought that Battersea was not so far from Streatham.

CHAPTER 13

In many ways Spencer Foster had reason to be well pleased with life. At the age of thirty-seven he found himself in a position of some importance, not only as a man of the world, but as one who had moved well beyond the humble class into which he had been born. Not that Spencer was a social climber. He didn't consider himself anything other than a member of that working class which he still fought for, in Parliament and out. His family was linked with poverty and the class struggle; his father and grandfather, both mill workers in Preston, had fought for the establishment and success of the trades unions for their industry.

Spencer still strongly identified with his family, who lived in the house where he was born, a terraced house facing on to a cobbled street, with a yard at the back in which there was a double washing line and a dustbin. The street sloped steeply towards the park and Spencer used to daydream in his top room as a boy, looking over the hundreds of identical sloping roofs and chimneys beneath him, each with wispy spirals of grey smoke twirling into the sky. At twilight it gave that dour landscape an air almost of enchantment, hinting at mysterious, unknown realms beyond the skyline. Spencer had always aspired to escape and, with that aspiration, had gone a peculiar sense of poetry, of wonder that had never left him.

In a large family Spencer was the only one ever to go to grammar school. His proud parents had hoped he would be a doctor or a lawyer. He was such a bookish lad, always dreaming and studying, never like the others. Their dismay can be imagined, therefore, when Spencer decided to ally himself with the industrial, rather than the new middle, class and went into the office of the local trade union branch when he left school with excellent grades in his Higher School Certificate.

Unlike many of his fellows and friends, Spencer had survived the War spent in the ranks, in the trenches, seeing men he knew, and didn't know, perish in the same ghastly way: blown to bits or shot in the head, or simply disappear for ever under the Flanders mud. He was probably not far away when Bosco Askham was killed and he emerged from the War not only angry at the bloodletting and waste, but at the ruling classes who had allowed it to happen.

When he heard of the Revolution in Russia he tried to get out there to fight with the Reds; but there was not a lot of scope for a young idealist without skills or a knowledge of the language, and he was unacceptable. Instead, he was demobbed and went back to Preston until an opening occurred in Manchester where the trades unions combined all the Lancashire cotton industry, then in a very depressed state. Shortly after that he finally achieved his ambition and went to Russia, but as a tourist, not a fighter.

This was a turning point in Spencer Foster's life, too. Instead of marrying a girl of his sort, settling in a small terraced house like his folks and raising a family, he fell in love with a widow who happened to be a peeress of the realm, a woman twelve years his senior. It was because of Rachel he stood for Parliament, and because of her he consciously set out to better himself, to familiarize himself more than before with culture and the arts.

But when he became Rachel's lover Spencer's difficulties in a sense only began. He had thought marriage would naturally follow and it didn't; there were so many obstacles: her status, her age, not least her family. All these obstacles were created by her. He would have taken them all lock, stock and barrel, and ignored them. It was only gradually that he saw, because he was really quite a simple, straightforward man, that these obstacles were not contrived by Rachel as excuses: they were real. From being the Countess of Askham with two main homes to being plain Mrs Foster, with a share of one small house in Pimlico, was quite a leap, even for a Radical like Rachel.

She had a family of five children, none of whom, except Hugo, had ever taken to him. He suspected this was jealousy of their mother rather than a consciousness of his class. They had revered their father so much and didn't want him to be supplanted. But, for Spencer, it had created difficulties and it was thus with the youngest, the unwanted, with whom he built an affinity that gave strength both to Hugo and himself. It was specially important to Hugo when he was expelled from school and had to be tutored at home.

It was Spencer who had spent hours with Hugo, talking to him, getting to understand him, introducing him to the House of Commons, taking him to exhibitions and museums, so that in time he felt, in truth, like his father: that Rachel had, indeed, given him the son he would like to have had by her.

In a sense this made the jealousy of the older children worse. Spencer felt that, in their opinion, he and Hugo deserved each other: they were outsiders.

However, there were compensations. Life with Margaret in his house in Pimlico was very comfortable. He had a study on the top floor, and a view over roofs that reminded him of his home town, Preston. They led a regular, full, orderly life and the curious thing was how their destinies had become involved with a brother and sister, rather as Bosco and Melanie, another brother and sister, had before them. For Spencer knew that, however much she tried to conceal it, Margaret was involved with Adam. He knew that she loved him and the only possible obstruction to their ultimate happiness was another member of the Askham family: Lady Flora.

The summer of 1926, following the General Strike, was a very busy one for Spencer. There was a continuing state of emergency over the miners' strike which continued, and Ramsay MacDonald had derisively described the Baldwin government as a very efficient, faithful and loyal sub-committee of the mine owners.

The Trades Unions Congress at Bournemouth, in one of the hottest months of the year, was to have been addressed by a Soviet representative, Mr Romsky, but the government refused him permission to enter the country. He sent a long telegram instead, attacking both the Conservative government and the Unions, which annoyed everyone, even the Labour Party, and further set back the cause of improving relations with Soviet Russia.

Rachel had gone with the twins and Hugo to stay with Melanie and Denton in Cannes where their young cousins Christopher and Jordan also were, as well as a number of Rigby relations and smart friends from the social set. Bobby would go too, sometime, and so would Charlotte and Ralph, who were spending much of the summer going from one large country house to the other in search of diversion: parties, all kinds of amusement, sport.

It was a very different life from his and Margaret's, Spencer thought, walking through Westminster to his appointment with Adam at his club in Whitehall. He had just got back from Bournemouth and was still mulling over events, rather than the subject of the meeting, when he arrived at the club and found Adam waiting for him in the hall.

Adam greeted him in his usual friendly fashion and led him to a corner of the lounge, ordering Scotch and soda for them both. Adam sat himself comfortably in the broad leather chair, stretching his legs out before him. He was a good-looking man, Spencer decided, gazing at him while Adam's attention was still caught by the waiter; not handsome, but with rather bland, distinguished features that age had, if anything, improved. He knew a lot about him: that he was the same age as Rachel's dead husband, which made him fifty; that he was a King's Counsel, a former Liberal MP and now Chairman of the mighty Askham Lighterman empire, a fact which had, at a very late stage in his life, made him a wealthy man. The Bolingbrokes had no fortune of their own.

In Spencer's opinion this helped explain Rachel's Socialism and the failure of Adam's marriage to the vain, spoilt and very wealthy Lady Melanie. In his middle age Adam had money, prosperity, respectability and position. It was a wonder that, with all these things, he was not made a peer and elevated to the House of Lords. The Liberals had very little hope of ever gaining power again, their numbers in the Commons reduced to around forty.

'Have you political ambitions?' Spencer asked him, when Adam settled back in his chair again, joining his hands and gazing at Spencer over the tips, as if he had already been elevated to the Bench of judges.

'Is that what you've come to talk to me about?' He smiled.

'Good Lord, no!' Spencer felt flustered. This cosy, leather atmosphere of clubland was alien to him, although, in some respects, it resembled the House of Commons.

'I thought it wasn't. No, I have finished with politics, Spencer, though, of course, I will always remain a Liberal. I would never espouse Socialism because I think it is too much in danger of following the Bolsheviks, and I believe in the essential liberty of the individual.'

A portly man advancing slowly through the lounge, clutching his copy of *The Times* to his chest, bowed solemnly at Adam, who inclined his head and waved. Adam clearly knew, and was known by, everyone in the club. He was an establishment figure, which made what Spencer was about to say more difficult.

'I came about Margaret.'

'I thought that might be it.' Adam sat up, taking his drink from the waiter, and took a sip. 'That's good. I'm hoping to go to the country at the end of the week and I feel I need it. One needs a break. Did you have a break?'

'I went to the Trades Unions Conference at Bournemouth.'

Adam grimaced as if in sympathy.

'That doesn't sound like much of a break. I'm going to visit my ex mother-in-law. I'm glad to say that Lady Askham and I have remained good friends since the divorce. In fact *better* friends since the divorce. She never liked me marrying her daughter, and is glad now that we are apart.' Adam laughed good-humouredly.

'Why didn't she like it?' Spencer sipped his Scotch.

'We were middle-class, Rachel and I. But it was all so long ago. Do you know it was the turn of the century?' Adam gazed around him with amazement. 'No, it was *before* the turn of the century when we first met Lady Askham, Melanie and Flora in Cairo. It was before Omdurman. My goodness, what things one forgets.' Adam passed his hand across his face as if he were an old, tired man and, indeed, well-preserved though he was, he did look older than fifty. He would be an adornment on the benches of the House of Lords. 'I'm avoiding the point, aren't I? You want to know what my intentions are towards Margaret?'

'I'm not her father.'

'I understand that, my good chap. You're her brother and you're rightly concerned about her.'

'She doesn't know I'm seeing you.' Spencer moved to the edge of his chair, nervously sipping his drink.

'I'm quite sure about that. She'd be here if she did.' Adam chuckled. 'No, you know how I feel about her. But there is Flora ...' Adam closed his eyes momentarily. 'Ah, poor Flora.'

'I never quite understood the situation with Lady Flora,' Spencer said testily.

'It's quite simple, my dear boy,' Adam opened his large blue eyes again. 'Flora and I loved each other a long time ago. Bosco used to say that I should marry Flora; and so I should have.

'But I was dazzled by her beautiful sister. I soon found out my mistake. I married Melanie in 1901, would you believe it, twenty-five years ago, and for most of that time I've loved another woman ... and I love yet another woman now.' He stared at Spencer.

'That's Margaret?'

'Yes, I love Margaret. I would have married Margaret at once if she'd have had me, but Flora ...'

'Have you ever lived with Lady Flora, in the biblical sense?' Spencer shifted uncomfortably. 'I don't mean to pry.'

'It's not prying. All the world knows that our relationship is platonic. The fact that I'd married her sister made me forbidden as a lover to Flora. Yet she has found her life in this kind of spiritual love for me, looking after me. I can't be ungrateful for that. She kept me sane in all those years of marriage to a monumentally selfish woman. Flora *did* buy the house we're in. It was a great mistake, of course, I realize that now; but, at the time, we thought we'd have Susan and her baby, see more of the boys. All that turned out very differently indeed. Flora and I live like old friends who are fond of each other. Nothing more. When I was in politics she used to help me with my work, but now there's not so much for her to do.'

'Can it go on indefinitely like this?'

'I suppose so. She thinks so. I can't be cruel to her, can I?'

Spencer cleared this throat and said firmly: 'Then I don't think you're fair to Margaret. She's nearly thirty.'

'I know that.' Adam inspected the backs of his hands.

'She, too, would like children.'

'I dare say, although the thought of becoming a father again at fifty plus is not very appealing to me, I must say.'

'Then I think you should tell Margaret all this and release her. I think she still hopes.'

'You think she does?' Now Adam looked embarrassed.

'I know she does. She doesn't talk about it much, of course, but I know how she feels about you and I don't think that she'll hang on for ever if there's nothing to hang on for. It sounds very mercenary to say this: but a woman in her position has no status – no husband, no child. Technically, you are both free to

263

marry and, if you know that you will never marry Margaret, then you must tell her.'

'But what will she do?' Adam looked genuinely distressed.

'I think she'll probably go back home and find a man of her own kind there.'

Spencer felt angry. Instead of a benevolent, rather avuncular figure, he now saw Adam as a self-absorbed, middle-aged man playing off two good, virtuous women one against the other. Maybe his years with Lady Melanie had made him selfish, too.

Princess Irina Ferova found Askham Hall and the society of its chatelaine most agreeable, so much so that she had practically removed herself from France to stay permanently at the Hall. She knew that Alexei strayed a bit and, apart from this, which she didn't mind too much, they quarrelled a lot. They had quarrelled over Kyril and now they quarrelled bitterly over Hélène and the man she was living with. In Irina's opinion her father should have horsewhipped him and brought her home. That's what would have happened in Russia in her girlhood – maybe even a duel. In vain did Alexei try to explain how difficult, if not impossible, it was physically to abuse a woman of twenty-four who, in this modern age, felt entitled to a life of her own, however foolish.

The fact that Hélène's lover was Dulcie Askham's great-nephew gave the two women a bond. They tutted a good deal together over it, and talked about it incessantly. The Kittos had never done as well for themselves as they might have, in Dulcie's opinion, and Jamie was typical; brave, but silly.

But Princess Irina was furious. She had not only lost a daughter but, potentially, an affluent son-in-law as well; one who would have ensured a return of the family fortunes for good. Whereas now, he had only to tire of Alexei, who was a lazy man, and who knew? What then? It was all most unsatisfactory.

At Askham Hall Irina had her own suite, her own maid. It was very like pre-revolutionary times at Esenelli, the house in the Caucasus. It recalled a life of simple luxury and muted grandeur; breakfast in bed, afternoon tea on the lawn in white tea dresses and large hats, and changing for dinner. Even when she and Dulcie were alone they behaved as though they had a houseful of guests. They both loved it. It was a style that suited them ... a long-ago, old-fashioned, forgotten style, but one that was part of them and would be part of Dulcie, Dowager Countess of Askham, until she died.

Her old friend Queen Alexandra had died in November 1925 and she had gone to the interment at Frognal, when it was such a delight to see her old friends among the Royal Family again, young Georgie, looking very old now, and Mary of Teck, who had been meant to marry his brother. She was able to introduce Irina to the King and Queen, members of the Court, and Irina felt transported to St Petersburg in the days of the last Czar, and wept when she saw how much he resembled his cousin, George V.

Now it was early September, the following year, and once again there were guests for the weekend. Lord and Lady Press-Barker, contemporaries of Dulcie; Lord and Lady Duplessis who had been with Dulcie and her family years ago in Egypt; Sir Arnold and Lady Plumb-Daventry, rather boring *nouveaux-riches* friends of Bobby, and dearest Bobby himself, as well as Ralph, Flora and Adam.

It was such a happy family weekend. Such a happy family. Dulcie loved a large party. The weather was fine and there was tennis, croquet on the lawn, and hunting with the Askham Hounds, of which Dulcie's husband, and then her son Bosco, had been Master. They were now waiting for young Ralph to come into his inheritance to be invited to be Master, too.

Dulcie thought Ralph restless that weekend and told him so one evening, at that pleasant time of day after tea but before drinks and dinner at eight-thirty. The Princess and most of their guests, including Adam and Flora, were playing croquet

265

and the air was redolent with the gentle end of summer, the smell of cut grass and the hum of drowsy bees. She put a hand on his arm and, looking gently into his eyes, saw Bosco again. They were both strong men – tall, vigorous, very English. Why, then, this restlessness on the part of Ralph, soon to be twenty-one and a subaltern in the Blues and Royals?

Ralph was silent after his grandmother's question, sitting back in his chair, still in his riding breeches, though he had removed his pink coat. The sleeves of his white shirt were rolled up.

'I don't think you look happy, Ralph. Is it some girl?'

Ralph snorted. 'I'm not Charlotte, you know, Gran, a new love every month.'

'Oh, *has* she a new love every month?' Dulcie's eyes twinkled, though she pretended concern. 'That is *very* naughty. I can see, though, how she must drive the men wild. She is lovely.'

'It's nothing, Gran,' but Ralph continued to brood as his eyes roamed over the lawn, fastening first on this player and then that.

Dulcie touched his arm. 'You know I'm your old gran, Ralph, and I love you very much. Do tell.'

Maybe it was the insistent, comforting pressure of her hand on his arm; the feeling that, in this indomitable, determined old woman, he could really place his trust. Impulsively he looked at her and then grasped the thin hand on his arm, enclosing it in his.

'It's not that Mother doesn't understand or sympathize, Gran. I think she does, but I also think she wants me to be like Father.'

'How do you mean, darling?' Dulcie drew her chair closer to his in order to hear him better, hoping that the game wouldn't break up.

'I don't really like the Army, Gran. I feel I should, but I don't. I want to get out.'

'Oh!' Instinctively, Dulcie knew how Rachel felt. It was the sort of thing that she now wanted Ralph to do, too; to be a soldier, a hero like Bosco. They were such very similar types.

Ralph gazed at her anxiously. 'I see you feel like Mother.'

'We thought you so *suited* to the Army, Ralph. And you've such a fine regiment, the Blues and Royals. What is it about it you don't like?'

'I don't like any of it. I don't like the discipline, the formality, the endless ceremonials, the stiffness, the pomposity of most of the officers ... Above all, during the strike I hated their attitude to the workers. We were always ready to go in if required and most of the men *wanted* to go in. They were dying to have a go. I hated that.'

'Yes, that is your mother in you,' Dulcie said reprovingly, 'the Socialist streak. I wish she had never joined that awful Labour Party. It gave the family such a bad name. It's bound to have influenced you. I only hope none of the other children suffer, that it doesn't affect your chances of good marriages.

'I love Rachel,' Dulcie said quietly, pausing to sigh. 'I never thought I'd say it but I do. She has been a wonderful mother, since Bosco died, to you all, a friend to me. I had never been nice to her, yet night after night she sat with me when I couldn't sleep, just so I could talk about him. The memories hurt her as much as me. Rachel always had character, too much of it; but she came into her own in those sad, dark days. Oh, I do hope she doesn't marry that Foster man! He's not our sort at all!' She looked anxiously at Ralph. 'Is he? Do you think she will, Ralph?'

'Not unless we give her permission, Gran,' Ralph's smile was also tense. 'There's a lot that's admirable in him, but we don't feel he's right for Mother. It's not a class thing. He has no money and if he loses his seat he'd go back to Manchester as a Trade Union official. What life for Mother would that be?'

'But do you think she *thinks* of that?' Dulcie's tone was horrified at the thought of a life of such potential deprivations.

'She thinks of us, of Father. My guess is that she won't marry Spencer Foster because she realizes all these things, even though she calls herself a Socialist.'

'But she is a Socialist!'

Ralph smiled. 'Well, not really. We had all these people staying in the house during the strike and they were so in awe of her. They didn't for a moment consider her as one of them. "Lady Askham this" and "Lady Askham that". It was comical. Mother can never be other than what she is, what she has become: a member of the upper classes, a wealthy woman with a social conscience. She's *not* a Socialist.'

'Oh, I'm *very* glad to hear that. I'm comforted by it.' Dulcie patted his arm, her formerly strong voice now thin and reedy with age but still bearing that echo of authority Ralph remembered from so long ago. 'Then I will support you if you want to leave the Army. You stop your mother marrying Mr Foster, and I'll support *you*.'

'You will, Gran? Oh, thank you. I thought you'd be the most adamant of the lot.' He sprang up and kissed her, looking into her faded blue eyes. She had been a great beauty in the eighties and nineties, the toast of London. To him she was beautiful now.

And as for Ralph, Dulcie thought he was perfect, too. 'I can see the folly of expecting young people to do things they don't want to do. Naturally we would like you to have been happy in the Guards and made a career of it, at least until you married and, perhaps, I died and you came into the Hall. Your father did love the Army, the Lancers, and had he not inherited would have made it his life. Maybe he wouldn't have been killed if he had because his Regiment of Lancers – the 21st – went to India during the War and missed all the fighting.' Dulcie's eyes suddenly brimmed with tears. 'But that is another story, what might have been.

'I have never thought you very like Bosco, Ralph, only in some ways, some dear ways – your courtliness, your sense of responsibility, your niceness.' Despite his blushes she gazed into his eyes. 'Yes, you are *very* nice. Perhaps you are too nice, too kind for the Army. I must say I never felt a moment's sympathy for those frightful strikers, trying to bring the country to its knees, and you did.'

'Maybe it was just part of my discontent, Gran.'

'No, Freddie is more like your father in many ways than you; especially like your father when young. And you see, Ralph, you don't *have* to be like him, do you? You're your own man. What would you like to do instead of the Army?'

'I thought I'd like to go to South Africa and farm, just for a while, you know, not for ever.'

'Oh, I do hope it's not for ever,' Dulcie sounded panic-stricken. 'I couldn't *bear* you to go for ever. I'd rather you were unhappy in the Army than lost to us for good.'

'I do want to get away, Gran, be my own man, as you say. Now I feel a bit like the Prince of Wales in the reign of Queen Victoria. You live here, Mother lives in London, Bobby runs the business. There's no room for me. I want to stretch my wings, Gran. Learn to fly.'

That warm September of 1926 Askham was seen particularly at its best. The white Palladian mansion seemed to preside with a timeless, beneficial eye over the lush foliage and lawns, the flower gardens surrounding it, the lake sparkling with pristine, diamond brightness in the middle. Flora thought it was like a honeymoon for herself and Adam, in the platonic sense in which they had always lived; the perfect scene for a perfect happiness, a perfect union untrammelled by carnal yearnings. They were too old now, anyway. She was a year older than Adam who had, she knew, for years led a celibate life with Melanie.

But that week, settled and happier than at any point for some time, she felt young again. She played tennis, croquet. She rowed, and walked long distances with her two nephews, Ralph and Bobby. She ate hearty meals in the company of her beloved mother and old family friends. She even found herself growing fond of Princess Irina, something she thought would never happen. She had suspected her of being a parasite, fawning on the family for what she could get out of them. Now she felt she had been unjust and that this noble, still beautiful and once wealthy woman of the world reminded her mother of her own gilded youth, and was thus a welcome and dear addition to the circle of intimates round her.

That evening she went into Adam's room to see if he was ready for dinner and found him sitting by the window gazing out of it, unheeding as she came in.

'Is all well, dearest?' she asked in her gentlest tones, tenderly kneading his neck muscles in an intimate gesture, to provide that welcome massage that eased his tension after a day in the Courts or the office.

'Perfectly well, my dear.' He reached for her hand and kissed it.

'You seemed so thoughtful, almost sad.' She bent round to gaze at his face, the pressure of her hands continuing.

'I feel peaceful. I was just thinking there can't be a spot in all the world as beautiful as Askham with its park is today. Do you ever think it will end?'

'Ah, then you *are* sad.' She pressed her cheek against his, drew up a chair and sat by his side, taking his hand in hers.

'Well, I don't suppose it can go on for ever. The War has changed so many things. Look at the Ferovs, once one of the richest families in Russia. Rachel only saw one of their houses, which was magnificent. Now they are more or less completely dependent on us, or rather on Susan and Bobby. What happens when your mother dies? Will Ralph want this huge house with its upkeep, the huge number of servants it requires? You may think he will always have the money, but financial empires have crashed before.'

'You're very pessimistic, dear. Have you any reason for saying all this?'

'None at all.' Adam patted her hand and got up, fastening his dinner-jacket. He had got just a trifle paunchy, Flora thought. Lack of exercise due to his War wounds. 'But we can't expect everything to remain the same, can we?' She imagined he looked rather wistfully down at her, and this impression, which made her uneasy, remained with her during dinner, which was served with the customary formality that guests would have expected before the War, except that the men wore dinner-jackets rather than tails. The ladies wore evening dresses and pearls. Princess Irina was particularly resplendent and vivacious in a low-cut gown of black fulgurante with the fake Ferov jewels round throat and wrist. She was entertaining them with an account of some anecdote concerning the late Imperial family, which Dulcie always loved to hear. Irina managed to make even the simplest tale sound amusing and this concerned a practical joke played by the Grand Duchess Olga, a favourite of hers, on the little Czarevitch and his father when staying at their palace in Yalta on the Crimea.

'What far off, happy days they were.' The laughter had scarcely subsided when Dulcie produced a handkerchief and dabbed at her eyes, rather as if stories of those days of innocence had brought much sadder memories she couldn't bear to recall. 'Do you remember, dearest Sophie, that time we were in Egypt ...' Her voice trailed away as though the vision of twenty-eight years ago were but yesterday.

'That perfectly frightful picnic in the desert ...' Sophie Duplessis began, until a warning look by her portly husband sitting opposite her made her stop.

'Oh, pray don't go on!' Dulcie held up a hand. 'That awful Madame, whatever her name was, and ... oh, no, *don't* remind me.'

Flora burst out laughing and then, just as suddenly, she stopped and looked round.

'Do you know, five of us are here tonight, twenty-eight years later? Your mamma was one, Bobby, and your father. Adam was there too and our beloved Bosco,' she paused for a moment, then hurried on, 'Bosco, and Rachel, too, of course.'

'Tell us about the picnic in the desert.' Bobby, affluent and handsome in his well-cut dinner-jacket, sipped at the Burgundy personally selected by him and shipped over from France by a firm of shippers he had just bought in Beaune.

'Well, there were many sad things about it as well as funny ones,' Flora searched Adam's face. 'There was a misunderstanding between your grandmother and ... well eventually, in a strange way, it all led up to the 1913 Court case that you know about.'

Bobby assumed a wise expression. 'No *wonder* you don't want to talk about it.'

'But it was part of life,' Dulcie said, her eyes now quite dry. 'We learn from experience, and to think that we had Harry with us then, and darling Bosco ... I would almost have those days back again just to see those dear men alive, those darling faces.'

Later they split up into the usual bridge four – bridge had been played on the desert picnic too, Adam recalled – and those who wanted to read or smoke. Adam and Flora always took a post-prandial walk, and no one ever thought of joining them. They had been doing it for years, at various times, for various parties and occasions since they had first been thought of as a couple, well before the War. People knew they valued this little moment of being alone together, near to each other in the comforting enclosure of the familiar dark.

'Bobby is so talented, isn't he?' Flora slipped her arm through Adam's, having first allowed him to put a shawl protectively round her shoulders. This was routine, too.

'What makes you say that now, dear?'

'Oh, he takes the bite away from anything, turns a disadvantageous moment to an advantageous one. No wonder he has done so much for the business. He is so gifted, talented. I wish he'd marry.'

'He's young enough. Isn't he?'

'Mamma would have liked him to marry one of the Ferov

272

girls. Too late for that now, I'm afraid. One's married, and the other ...'

'But I thought Jamie Kitto wasn't divorced?'

'Nor likely to be, from what I hear. His wife has flatly refused.'

'Well, then, there's a chance?'

'Oh, no.' Flora indignantly shook her head. 'Not to someone like *that* ... you know what I mean.'

'Living in sin?' Adam's tone was gently mocking as he turned his head to look at her profile, much softer than in the day, against the background of the lighted house.

'Well, yes. What nice woman would do a thing like that?'

'Don't we know a few?'

'Oh, Adam, I suppose we know a lot. Morals have gone to pieces since the War. But I, for one, am glad I was brought up with standards I never lost. I repent of nothing in my life.'

'Nothing?'

'Nothing. I've got you.' She pressed his arm again and Adam, who was about to speak what was on his mind, faltered. 'I do regret a little,' she went on, 'the fact that your work in the Commons is over. We have almost won what we wanted for the women's vote, and there don't seem so many things to work for. I'm sorry that Susan didn't settle with us. I'd have loved to help bring up Alexander. Do you know, my nieces and nephews have been such sources of satisfaction to me that I really don't regret not having had children? I feel I have shared in them all, yours, Bosco's, in a special way.'

If he put it off now, when would another opportunity arise? But Adam faltered again, too cowardly to do what he had to do. Maybe he'd put it off for good, and he took some comfort at the thought.

Flora stopped suddenly and looked at the house.

'Do you know, I remember standing here years ago with Rachel, just on this spot, looking at the house and talking about the family. It was before Bosco had declared himself to her, the day you had that awful fall from the horse. Do you remember?'

'I remember,' Adam began to laugh, 'and I so annoyed your father. "Can't hunt?" he bellowed. "If you can ride you can hunt." Well, I couldn't and never did again. Flora …' He stopped suddenly, the tension having been broken. 'There *is* something I want to tell you tonight, something special. I want you to take it in the right way and listen until I've finished.'

'Oh, go on, then.' Flora resumed their walk, a fond smile playing on her lips. 'What is it this time?'

'I want to marry Margaret Foster.' Adam's voice sounded mechanical even to him, something he'd rehearsed again and again since his talk with Spencer, his subsequent proposal to Margaret, all the careful planning that had gone into what he would say and when. 'When she is relaxed at home with her family,' Adam had said to Margaret, 'that would be best. I don't really think she'll mind when it comes to it.'

But Margaret hadn't been so sure. There had been no final demand, no ultimatum; but he knew that if he didn't speak she would go. She was that kind of woman and Spencer, in warning him, had been that kind of man.

'Foster?' He heard Flora faintly repeating the name. 'Do you mean Spencer's sister?'

'Yes.'

'But do you know her well?'

'Yes. She works in the chief whip's office.'

'I know that; but I mean "well"?'

'Yes, very well.'

'Is she your mistress?'

'Yes.'

'Oh, I see, another of "that" kind. How base.' Flora looked away.

'I was waiting for that, Flora. They're not all "that" kind of woman.'

'It *is* a way to get a man. It makes him feel so guilty, doing what is wrong for his own selfish ends, because I've never

274

believed women needed sex as men seem to do. I remember the shock we all felt about Rachel. Well, I still feel shock. As I've said, morals don't change for me, like fashions.'

'Margaret loves me and responded to my needs. You know I had needs, Flora. I told you. I never deceived you. You can call them base and carnal, anything you like ...'

'Oh, I know they exist,' Flora said airily. 'I thought our love had risen above them.'

'Mine hadn't, but I *do* love you. Margaret knows that.'

'Then what does Margaret propose to do about it?' Flora gazed into his face; the haughty Askham look he was familiar with which, he also knew, concealed hurt. 'Really, I can't believe this conversation is happening. Do say it isn't. You're a man of fifty, Adam. She's a young girl.'

'A woman. She's nearly thirty. She wants children, respectability, marriage.'

'Isn't there anyone else?'

'Apparently not.'

'And do you want *more* children at your age? You, a grandfather?' She looked at him scathingly, he thought, almost with pity.

'Well, not really, but I do want Margaret. I also want to do the right thing by her. I need her. I need you both. We have even talked about you continuing to live with us. If you don't, I'll buy the house from you; but you must stay very near, close to me, close to her ...'

'I can't be close to someone I don't know, and shan't know ...' Flora's face was very taut, tense.

'When you know her you'll like her.'

'Those Fosters have come into our family like parasites.' Flora now was every inch the daughter of an earl; the taunting, derisive, clever woman with a Cambridge degree. 'They're a bit like the Ferovs, only they offer less. They're destructive. Spencer has practically broken up Rachel's family. Mother tells me Ralph wants to leave the Army and go and live abroad! Imagine that! It's terrible, I think.'

'Do you know for *sure* that's Spencer's fault?'

'Whose is it, then?'

'I know he wasn't happy in the Army. He was pushed into it, unwittingly maybe, by Rachel, to be like Bosco.'

'Well, it's nice to hear you criticizing your sister for once. You might criticize her a little more. I love Rachel, don't misunderstand me, I do; but I can't understand her relationship with that man Spencer, or her uncritical love for Hugo that alienates her own children.'

'I think Rachel is to be commended for her devotion to Bosco's son. Who knows what damage a childhood like the one he had does to a young child? Since he left school and had those tutors he's been much, much better.'

'Oh, Adam, don't be so naive! It's his way of getting her exclusive affection. As soon as he is sent away he'll start misbehaving again. I don't think Hugo will ever amount to much.'

'That's not like you, Flora,' Adam chided, trying to put his arm round her; but she moved away. He knew, now, how much he'd upset her.

'No, nothing's like me tonight, or ever will be again. I have given my life to you and now you are casting me off for someone else. Something you said you'd never do. It's too banal.'

'I am *not* casting you off, but I want to marry. You never did. You'd never even consider it. It was *you* who cast me into this unnatural, celibate role. I am only fifty. I might have twenty or thirty more years of active life. Margaret has been a good, discreet companion to me and I want to legalize the position. She is willing to meet you, to like you, to live with you in the same house. If we have children, you...'

'How *can* you talk to me like that!'

Adam felt almost personally abused by the contempt in Flora's voice, contempt and rage. It was almost as if she'd hit him and he backed away.

'Do you think I can share you so easily with another woman? Is that all I meant to you – a sort of glorified nanny? What kind of fool do you think I am? Am I to be bridesmaid at the wedding? Is it not really a nurse you want for your children, a companion for your new wife? Is not that all you want from me, after all these years? Yet have I not loved you, supported you, comforted you...'

'Yes, all these things Flora, please...' Adam tried to take her hand. 'Please understand; show your generosity. You will always have my love, whatever you do. Please believe...'

But she was no longer listening, running along the path by the lake into the forest, into the dark.

CHAPTER 14

Few could recall such an occasion; such a gathering of notables not only from the motoring and industrial worlds but from those of *haute couture*, finance, the arts and politics – as well as society people who like to be seen indiscriminately on any occasion, no matter what.

Bobby had been planning for years to break into Grand Prix racing and the first Askham built for that purpose was unveiled in the Askham showrooms on the Champs Elysées, with great splendour, in the spring of 1927 just after Ralph's twenty-first birthday.

For those who remembered the party at Lighterman House in 1920 when Bobby reached his majority, Ralph's twenty-first at Askham House had been a very quiet affair. For Rachel it had almost been like a wake to say goodbye to her beloved son before he left for South Africa. For her, the chance to go to Paris and try and forget her misery had seemed irresistible.

When Rachel opposed Ralph's leaving the Army she knew she was being awkward; yet again she felt she had inherited the mantle of her mother-in-law who, in the old days, had disapproved of everything she and Bosco did. The fact that Ralph had stuck Army life for three years before telling her how much he hated it had shocked her. It seemed an indication of a lack of trust and intimacy between them. When it came it was a case of everyone knowing but her. Even Dulcie knew. Was she, his mother, so frightening, she had demanded? It was a family row of classic Askham proportions, whose reverberations had echoed for weeks as Ralph went through the motions, aided by Adam, of buying himself out of the Army, a process which, at the time, seemed like a disgrace, an admission of defeat.

Rachel had known that it was irrational to feel that, by his action, Ralph was betraying the memory of his father. In the end Bosco had not been a professional soldier; but he had died a soldier, a hero, and there had seemed something very right about Ralph following the path he had taken. Bosco would have been proud of him. Rachel realized that she was demonstrating old-fashioned, even Victorian, attitudes she didn't know she had; ones she should be ashamed of. It was silly to want her son to be a soldier, no matter what.

But as Ralph quietly and doggedly stuck to his determination to detach himself from the colours it made her look at herself; at the woman she now was, compared to the idealist at the turn of the century who had not wanted to marry a man because he had a title. Was she, in truth, reluctant to marry again because she would have to give it up? Had she been corrupted by those things she had once professed to despise: wealth, position, influence?

It was in a very unhappy, self-critical mood that Rachel went with Hugo and Charlotte to Paris to stay with Susan. It offered a complete break – a break, too, from the memory of waving goodbye to Ralph as he left Tilbury, bound for Cape Town.

But on this day Ralph had been gone two months and Paris seemed to sparkle in the May sunshine – or was it that the new Askham, with its white and burgundy racing colours, sparkled most of all? Rachel knew absolutely nothing about racing cars and, herself, preferred the elegant brown streamlined Askham Coupé which, as a director of the family firm, she kept in the Mews behind Askham House in St James's Square. Spencer, too, had come over with her, but was staying at a hotel. Adam was there with his fiancée – they were due to be married in June – but not Flora, who was planning a trip to Egypt, or Melanie, who was recovering from the flu in the South of France. Some said she was too lazy to make the journey.

The twins were in the third term of their first year at Oxford and Rachel saw very little of them. It was Charlotte and Hugo, especially darling Hugo, who comforted her for the loss of

Ralph; who made up to her for the mistake she felt she'd made about her eldest son, who never blamed her.

Jamie Kitto kissed Rachel on the cheek almost before she knew who he was. She started back, then smiled.

'Hello, Aunt. You look very lovely.'

'Am I your aunt?' Rachel screwed up her nose. 'In a very tenuous way, I suppose. I'd rather you called me Rachel as you usually do. "Aunt" makes me feel old.'

'That's why I said you looked so lovely; elegant, I'd say. Did Mademoiselle Chanel design your costume?' He stepped back to admire the new creation that Rachel's slim figure did, indeed, show off to advantage. Rachel, who didn't know Jamie very well, could see his attraction but, although she couldn't say why, she was glad neither of her daughters was involved with him.

'No, I haven't time for *haute couture* clothes,' she said. 'I bought it at a little shop in Bond Street.'

'The hat's stylish, too.' The hat was wide-brimmed, partly concealing her face. Now, in its shadow, she smiled.

'Why all these compliments, Jamie? Do you want something? If so, there's very little I have to give.'

'A word in the ear of Great Aunt Dulcie might not come amiss, Rachel. She won't even have me at Askham Hall, and I'd like to go and stay there with Hélène when she visits her Mamma. I'm *persona non grata*.'

'You're not allowed to visit? I am surprised. Maybe you should talk to Hélène's mother, who is Dulcie's confidante.' Rachel peered through the crowds that gathered round the car, finding it difficult, amid the clamour, to hear everything Jamie was saying.

'Oh, *please*, angel.' Jamie grabbed her arm. 'If the Princess sees me, she will go. I am absolutely beyond the pale as far as she's concerned, and the Russians know because they invented the term.'

'Then where is Hélène?'

'Oh, she's around.' Jamie looked vaguely about him.

'And what are you doing, Jamie?' Charlotte disengaged herself from an over-friendly newspaper reporter holding a bottle of champagne, and joined her mother and cousin. 'I haven't seen you ...' she was going to say since the War but that wasn't quite true. Once or twice she made a discreet little visit to Paris with a boyfriend and she'd bumped into Jamie. But she didn't want her mother to know that. She and Jamie exchanged conspiratorial smiles. Rachel, however, was paying little attention, her eyes anxiously on Hugo weaving in and out of the crowd, trying to get a better view of the car. The anxiety she felt about Hugo never left her; she always worried about him, either that he should get into trouble or trouble should come to him. Hugo was now talking animatedly to a young man who towered over him, even though Hugo was tall.

'Excuse me,' she said, leaving Jamie and Charlotte to continue their reminiscences, brushing past the Minister who had come instead of the President of France, past notables and celebrities some of whom she knew and some she didn't.

'Hugo, darling,' she began as Hugo, face alight, seized her arm.

'Mummy, look who I found. This is Paolo Verdi who is to drive the Askham in its first race at Monte Carlo.'

Rachel knew little about racing, but everyone had heard of the Italian driver and his many successes as well as his remarkable escapes as he crashed, time and time again, in his efforts to achieve world records. Despite this he looked very fit; his handsome, interesting face like that of a Renaissance prince, only scarred in one or two places. He wore a dark, double-breasted suit and his straight black hair was plastered back from his high, intelligent forehead.

'I'm Rachel Askham, Bobby's aunt. How do you do?' With the ease that had come from so many years of meeting strangers, celebrated and unknown, Rachel gave him her hand, which he grasped and kissed most elegantly.

'Lady Askham, wife of the heroic Bosco. I am *very* pleased to meet you.'

'Surely you're too young to have known my husband?' Rachel stepped back in surprise.

'I am, alas, but Bobby talks about him whenever the question of courage comes up. I know that Bosco saved his stepfather's life. But don't let's spoil the day with sad, if cherished memories. Besides, I want to meet your beautiful daughter.' Paolo Verdi pointed in Charlotte's direction. 'I had been asking Hugo who she was, and imagine my delight when he told me she was his sister! I see a family resemblance. I hear she's an actress.'

'Not a very successful one yet,' Rachel said guardedly. Charlotte was sensitive on the subject of her career. 'She would like to be but, so far, only one or two smallish walk-on parts.'

Another thing that Rachel didn't like, apart from Ralph leaving the Army, was Charlotte going on the stage, where professionally she was known as Charlotte Askham. So far the name hadn't helped her get very far. What worried Rachel was how Charlotte got the parts she did; and the number of older, rather raffish men friends she was inclined to bring home for after-theatre supper parties. It was a wonder that Philip Pride, the impresario, wasn't here with her now. Rachel could never recall twenty-year-old Charlotte being in the least attracted to a man who was anywhere near her in age. She preferred the father figure.

Now, as she looked at her, Charlotte caught her eye and she beckoned. After a minute or two she saw Charlotte kiss Jamie on the cheek and begin to edge her way through the crowd. Everyone instinctively turned to gaze at this beautiful young woman whose black suit, with its striking white blouse, *was* by Chanel and not from the little shop in Bond Street, just round the corner from home. Charlotte wore no hat and her hair, fashionably waved, was short at the back, tapering at her neckline, and flopping over her face in front. She used plenty of make-up, which suited her; her deep carmine lips adding years to her age without making her lose her allure.

'This is Paolo Verdi, the racing driver,' Rachel said as Charlotte arrived. 'He wanted to meet you.' As their eyes met it seemed to encapsulate a moment, a *coup de foudre*, that she would remember for all time, as well as the fact that it was she who introduced them.

But, meanwhile, *le tout Paris*, it seemed, was talking about the Askham 'Bosco', as it was called, running hands along it and admiring its sleek lines. Anyone who knew anything about cars wanted to inspect its inside, and have details of all the things they couldn't discover merely·by touching it. Some took turns to sit behind the heavy steering wheel with all the complex gear in the driver's cockpit.

As Paolo Verdi and Charlotte smiled at each other, merely touching hands, Rachel slipped away once again to look for Hugo who she found chattering excitedly to Spencer about the car and the famous driver who had promised him a run on the track. Hugo was nearly as tall as Spencer, a dark-eyed, black-haired, gypsy-looking boy who would be fifteen in the autumn. Since he had been at home everyone said he had improved, was not so excitable, unpredictable. But others thought it was simply the calming presence of his adoptive mother, his live-in tutor and the teachers who gave him his various lessons, who kept him on the rails.

In their opinion, Hugo would always be wild.

'I thought Henri's in the Place Gallan tonight.' Spencer held his hand out to her as she came up to him.

'What's that?'

'Lady Askham! It is supposed to be one of the best restaurants in Paris.'

'How would I know that?' She smiled at Hugo and touched his nose. 'Happy, darling?'

'Mummy, Paolo Verdi! He is *the* greatest racing driver in the world. Do you think he'll take Charlotte in his car, too?'

'I imagine so.' Rachel turned to look at them once more, finding them engaged in conversation as though there was no one else in the room. Beyond them she saw another familiar figure and grasped Hugo's hand.

'There's Susan. I think she's looking for Bobby. Will you go and …'

'Bobby's here and I can see Susan!' Bobby – appearing from nowhere – kissed his aunt, shook hands with Spencer and his young cousin. 'When did you arrive?'

'Late last night on the Golden Arrow. You've been here for days, I expect.'

'Weeks,' Bobby replied. He looked tired but excited, with that slightly frenetic air of a man who could never stand or sit still, eyes darting everywhere, his hand describing arcs in the air like some peripatetic magician. 'I'm going down to Mother's after this is all over. I'm just going to collapse.'

'It's a great triumph,' Spencer said. 'I do congratulate you, even if it *is* capitalism at its worst.'

'Oh, Spencer, with all the trouble the Russians are giving you do you really mean that? I must say I find them almost impossible at the moment to do business with. Even the machinery is reduced to a trickle. They seem to have a hate against England. It's that Arthur Cook stirring up trouble, fresh from his visit to Moscow.'

'It's the exhaustion of the miners' strike,' Spencer said gloomily. 'Everyone's tired. Both right and left get more entrenched, more fanatical. Baldwin says he's lost faith in the democratic instincts of the people. I ask you! What sort of Prime Minister is that?'

'Russians are bloody difficult,' Bobby said, amiably. 'For instance, I can never find Alexei when I need him and most of the time I don't even know where he is. As now, for instance.'

As he looked around Rachel saw Hélène come through the wide doors of the salon, pause and take in the scene. Bobby caught her eye.

'Ah, Hélène. I'll ask her about her father.' Bobby was about to make for the door when Hélène began to steer a course in their direction. She seemed to be heading towards Jamie then, seeing him earnestly in conversation with an attractive woman, came straight towards them. Bobby stood and watched her, the smoke from his half-smoked cigarette staining his fingers.

'Bobby,' Hélène said in soft, almost purring tones, and held up her cheek for his kiss. 'It is *such* a long time since I've seen you. Lady Askham, Hugo,' she smiled and made as if to pat Hugo's head, then changed her mind. 'Ah, you're growing too tall for me. What a handsome boy you are.'

'Do you know where your father is?' Bobby enquired brusquely.

'He said he would be here at one to take us all to lunch.'

'But he is supposed to be here taking orders!' Bobby snapped. 'That's why I pay him.'

'Oh, Bobby,' Rachel glanced at him, 'not a very nice thing to say.'

'Nevertheless it's true. I'm sorry, Hélène, I'm a bit cross with Alexei.'

'Oh, I don't mind.' Hélène laughed and, as Jamie looked towards them, she clasped Bobby's arm and drew him apart, whispering something in his ear which seemed to please him. Jamie frowned and turned away.

Susan was making regal progress through the room arm in arm with Princess Irina, who had forsaken Dulcie for the week of the show. Rachel thought that Susan grew almost imperceptibly into her role as a Russian princess. It was hard to believe she was merely twenty-four, because she had the stately mien of a much older matron whose choice of clothes was bizarre as well as elegant; stylish, expensive but dramatic. Her salon was achieving a formidable reputation, and she was always in the company of some budding poet or fashionable novelist. Now she was explaining something to Irina, hands gesticulating, in the fluent Russian she had now mastered.

It must be nice to be twenty-four with money and, despite an early tragedy, to have found oneself, as Susan appeared to have. Rachel knew that Susan would never forget Kyril but she had done the next best thing: become reconciled to his loss while always hoping to see him again. Rachel was thinking of the contrast between the happy, secure Susan and restless Hélène, and the confused signals she'd caught between her and Jamie ... and Bobby.

She was still thinking about it that night when, instead of eating out as Spencer had suggested, they were all in Susan's apartment where she'd organized a supper party. The day seemed to have been non-stop eating, drinking and chattering with the same people and Rachel, who had managed only to snatch ten minutes' rest and to change, was beginning to regret that she hadn't stayed at a hotel as Spencer had suggested. The talk at the party was interminable, too: about the car, the economy and the strength of the German Mark now that the Allied forces had moved out of Germany and left it to the League of Nations. Had anyone heard of a man called Adolf Hitler, someone demanded; he was stirring up trouble in Bavaria. Someone else replied that he was too insignificant to be worth anyone's attention. No one in Germany took any notice of him except a few fanatics.

Hélène was there, but not Jamie. Rachel didn't know why, and it didn't seem the right thing to ask until Charlotte volunteered the information that he never appeared when Irina was about. The Princess had threatened to kill him for dishonouring her daughter. If anyone thought such a threat in 1927 amusing, they didn't dare say so.

Prince Ferov had appeared, unchastened by a reprimand from Bobby, accompanied by an Austrian baroness who was rumoured to have connections in the motor trade.

When the music started from a gramophone the couple who immediately took to the floor were Charlotte and the prince of racing drivers: Paolo Verdi.

'No one else seems to want to dance.' Charlotte felt self-conscious.

'No matter.' Paolo expertly enfolded her in his arms and leaned his cheek against hers.

286

'Careful,' Charlotte pulled back. 'My mother's looking.'

'Are you so frightened of your mother? I thought she was delightful.' Paolo drew her closer. 'A magnificent woman. Brave, yes?' He held her away again, his smouldering Italian eyes extraordinarily fascinating.

'Brave?' Charlotte screwed up her nose.

'All these years without your father.'

'Yes, but the man with her has been her lover for ages; so she's not quite alone.'

'Ah!' Paolo thought this news most interesting and steered Charlotte round so that he could examine Spencer, who was trying to persuade Rachel to follow her daughter's example and dance on the tiny strip of floor that had been cleared in the middle of the drawing-room. 'You sounded a little disapproving. Should your mother not have a lover?'

'I'd rather she had a nice, settled husband who was the sort of person we are. This one is a Socialist Member of Parliament.'

Paolo laughed, showing his beautiful teeth. Charlotte thought him the most handsome man she'd ever met.

'My dear Lady Charlotte, I can see you are a little snob. You would like her to marry another earl?'

'Preferably a duke.'

'I see you've a sense of humour, too. Do you like motor racing?'

'I feel it could sweep me off my feet,' Charlotte said, thinking that, at twenty and for the very first time, she was unexpectedly deeply in love.

'Charlotte seems to be getting on awfully well with Paolo.' Bobby, more formal with Hélène, kept a respectable distance between them.

'He's certainly attractive.' Hélène nodded her head.

'Do you find him so?'

Hélène nodded again, her eyes glinting provocatively.

'Jamie not here tonight?'

'He's frightened of my mother.'

287

'Do I detect disapproval?'

'Of me, or Jamie, or my mother?'

'Of Jamie being frightened of her?'

'Well, he has a lot to be frightened of.' Hélène sounded contemptuous.

'I wonder if you'd like to lunch with me tomorrow?' Bobby murmured. 'I thought afterwards we could drive out to Long-champs and look at a horse I'm interested in.'

Susan, who didn't like dancing, had a small intellectual coterie in her study off the lounge. They were discussing the latest news on the left bank and Evgenia's husband's brother, who was a poet, read them a poem he'd just written about Stenka Razin, the seventeenth-century Cossack patriot.

In the company of Spencer Rachel found the evening congenial, the people agreeable, the coterie of exiles – mostly Russian or from the Balkans – entertaining. She went from the dance floor to the study, a glass in her hand, feeling, for the first time for many months, relaxed. Hugo was safely, she hoped, in bed and asleep at the end of the corridor and really she had nothing to do but enjoy herself, guilty thoughts about Ralph, now far away, temporarily banished.

But Charlotte, now Charlotte ... here was a fresh worry. Whatever would she do if Charlotte fell in love with a racing driver?

She wasn't left in suspense for long. At the end of the week, before Rachel had time to pack her bags for London, Charlotte and Paolo announced their intention of marrying. They were in love, no doubt about it, for ever.

'But you're only twenty!' Rachel vividly recalled the moment they'd met, wondered if it could have been avoided? Bosco had always believed in fate though, oddly enough, she thought that he had never believed he would be killed. This much, this premonition, had been spared him.

Paolo and Charlotte had decided to confront her with the news together. Rachel hadn't seen much of either of them during the week; she and Spencer had been too busy enjoying themselves and showing Hugo Paris to take much notice of her whereabouts. Charlotte was always a flitter, not a mysterious person, but one who came and went as she pleased.

Now here they were, breaking this momentous news at three in the afternoon when she had just begun packing for the boat train that night.

'But, Mummy,' Charlotte protested, her mother's reaction not a total surprise, 'Aunt Melanie had *had* Bobby by the time she was twenty.'

'Yes, but Aunt Melanie had known Harry Lighterman for much longer than you've known Paolo. It's only a *week*, scarcely that.' Rachel, fully the Victorian parent at that moment, looked outraged. 'I'm sure, Paolo, that you don't think you really know my daughter well enough to marry her?'

'Not as well as you, but I know her well enough to marry her. I loved her, Lady Askham, from the moment I saw her.'

He was twenty-seven, he had a soft melodious voice, but he was firm. One felt he was a decisive man, one who took quick decisions on the race track involving life, and death.

'We don't see any point in waiting, Mummy, as we both feel the same. Please.'

Charlotte dramatically wrung her hands as if trying to wring the heart of Rachel who said, almost in despair:

'What about your career? Next year you'll be twenty-one, Charlotte. I think you should wait and decide then. It will also give you more time to get to know Paolo. I know, darling, how hard these things seem but, believe me, marriage is a *very* serious thing. It is for life, and think what fun it will be to get to know each other over the ensuing year?'

'We shan't see each other a lot, Lady Askham. That's why we don't want to be parted. I have racing commitments all over the world, six months in America and South America. I should hardly be in England at all.'

'And you want Charlotte to lead that kind of life?' Rachel appeared amused. 'When she's trying to establish a career on the stage? She has had a very settled home and upbringing. How do you think she will react to all that?'

'I'd love it, Mummy, really I would. My career doesn't matter at all. You don't want me to travel around with Paolo unmarried, do you?'

'I wouldn't allow it.'

'I don't know how you could stop me.'

'Easily ... I would have you made a ward of court.'

When Rachel and Charlotte rowed it was always quick; a flare-up, things said in the heat of the moment, retorts made that one repented of for weeks. By implying she was still a child she could hardly have chosen a worse thing to say to a young, sophisticated woman only a year away from her majority. Charlotte seized her bag, tugged Paolo's arm and was about to walk off; but he gently put his arm round her shoulder and held her, still smiling at Rachel.

'You see, I know her well, Lady Askham. I think I know you both, mother and daughter. I would not marry Charlotte without your consent; nor would I take her round the world with me as an unmarried woman. I know how much that would hurt you. What I want – come, sit down – is for us all to discuss this rationally and quietly together.'

He pulled Rachel gently towards the sofa, at the same time depositing Charlotte on his other side so that he eventually sat in the middle.

'Now,' he put a hand on the arm of each woman as if to draw them together.

Paolo Verdi should have been a diplomat. By six that evening Rachel had agreed that he and Charlotte should be engaged and that if, after three months, they felt the same they should be married. Meanwhile she would take instruction in the Roman Catholic faith.

It was a tremendous decision to make alone; but Rachel felt stronger for making it. She also felt bamboozled and a little dazed as, leaving the lovers in Paris, Susan to chaperone

Charlotte, she sat with Hugo and Spencer in the carriage of the Golden Arrow taking them back to London.

'I think you were wise,' Spencer nodded approvingly.

'He's really an awfully nice man. I think I didn't want to lose him as a possible son-in-law. He's so strong. So right for Charlotte.'

'I liked him too, the little I saw of him.'

'Besides,' Rachel smiled wanly, 'I didn't feel I had much choice. He's that kind of man.'

'Perhaps he could give me a few tips,' Spencer's smile, too, was wan. 'He obviously knows how to manoeuvre Askham women.'

Hugo was ecstatic. He imagined himself travelling the world as Paolo's mechanic.

Spencer smiled at the boy he always felt was a son to him; not like the others. They were strangers, but he and Hugo were very close. In loving Rachel he loved the child who wasn't even hers.

'Do you know anything about machines?'

'I'm going to learn,' Hugo gave a wide smile, 'and then I can be a racing driver, too!'

Flora read about the unveiling of the Askham Bosco in *The Times* as she sat at her desk, alternately sorting through her papers, consulting her exacting schedule for Egypt and then taking up the newspaper again, mesmerized by the group picture round the car in the Paris showroom: Bobby, Rachel, Charlotte, the racing driver Paolo Verdi and Adam Bolingbroke, chairman of the company, with his fiancée Miss Margaret Foster, sister of the Labour MP. Adam had his hand round Margaret's shoulder and, even in the poor print of the picture, sent over by wire from Paris, one could see how happy he was, so fondly looking at Margaret, not the new motor car. To Flora it still didn't seem possible, despite the formal engagement.

Accompanying the picture was an article about the development of the car, its many new features designed to enhance its speed, Bobby's climb to the top as a car manufacturer, his obsession with motor racing, the price he was probably paying Paolo Verdi to drive for him. Flora had always objected to the car being called 'The Bosco'. She didn't think it showed any reverence for Bosco, or his name, but the family didn't see it like that. Even Dulcie, who probably had mourned Bosco more deeply than any of them, even Rachel, thought 'The Bosco' seemed a fine, flamboyant name for a racing car; but it made Flora sad every time she heard it or saw it in print. Also, for some reason she clearly couldn't define, she thought it unlucky.

But Flora's general mood was melancholic anyway, no matter how much she tried to fool others. There had been general admiration for the way Flora had taken Adam's engagement, as well as a good deal of surprise. But this was to misunderstand Flora, who was a lady, and ladies didn't make scenes. She even had tea with Margaret at the Ritz to have her officially introduced to her as Adam's intended, both of them wearing hats and fixed smiles.

That was six months ago and during that time Flora had continued as before: the fixed smile, the gracious nod, the careless shrug of the shoulders when the wedding date was mentioned. Maybe Rachel guessed, because they had always been close, but no one knew how much she really suffered. Her reason for existing for all these years had gone. Slowly all the real reasons for living were disappearing – Egyptology, Liberalism, the suffrage – very soon the government would introduce the vote for all women over twenty-one. Votes for flappers, someone had called it. And when they had it Flora wondered if a girl like Charlotte, say, would know what she was doing. Were she and her friends ready for the vote? She didn't think so.

A lifetime wasted, when you came to think of it. Better not think. Flora got up from her desk and looked at the packing cases on the floor. She was moving out before Adam got married in June and, for a while, she would stay at Askham with her mother. Now she was perfectly free to go where she liked, do what she liked. No one really cared, and no one would miss her. No one would miss Flora in the whole world.

Later that week Flora went down to Askham to see her mother, to make arrangements for moving her luggage until she'd made up her mind where to go. Adam was not yet back from Paris, but Rachel had returned with the staggering news that Charlotte was engaged to a man she had known for a week.

'*And* becoming a Roman Catholic. My granddaughter, Bosco's daughter, marrying a racing driver *and* becoming a Roman Catholic. I can't think which is worse.' Dulcie was appalled.

'Charlotte was always a law to herself, Mamma.' Flora didn't feel very strongly about either her niece's marriage or conversion. It was very strange how little she seemed to care about anything; how dull and apathetic she felt towards life. Every morning she seemed to have to force herself to get out of bed, and when she did all she could think of was the time when she would be able to get back again and go to sleep.

'Somehow I think the family's breaking up. Ralph in Africa, Charlotte marrying this frightful Italian. Sometimes I wonder if Rachel really knows what she's doing. She seems to have lost control over a family she so carefully brought up.' Dulcie furiously fanned her face with her handkerchief as Flora poured fresh tea from the silver pot. They were sitting on the terrace, in a sheltered spot because it wasn't really warm enough. The park below them looked so beautiful in the late spring sunshine, tiny fronds bursting from the trees, about to give birth, give life.

Maybe this time next year Adam would be a father again. There would be sickening pictures of him gazing at some dreadful baby's face, he and Margaret wreathed in the habitual smiles of the new parents, as if they had done something no one had thought of before. Every time she looked anywhere she seemed to see Adam's face; Adam and Margaret as they had looked out of the pages of *The Times* on their engagement: 'Former MP and Chairman of the huge Askham Lighterman empire to marry again.' There they were, hugging and smiling yet she, Flora, had considered herself married to him for nearly twenty years.

How could a man, any man, *do* such a thing?

'Is there anything wrong, Flora dear?' Lady Askham looked up at her with the irritation of one forced to consider the feelings of others. She was a self-centred woman and her own needs were and always had been paramount.

'Nothing, Mother.'

'You've been so frightfully gloomy all week. I suppose it's Adam?'

'Why on earth *should* it be Adam, Mother?' The carefully rehearsed look of surprise, the clenched fist out of sight, the awareness of a slight invisible tic by the side of her right eye; the control; Lady Flora Down carefully in control, as always.

'Well, everyone knows how you felt about Adam. How I thought *he* felt about you. It can't have been very pleasant for you, this getting engaged to a much younger woman.' Dulcie gave a slightly salacious laugh. 'For him I don't doubt it's very pleasant indeed.'

'Mother, Adam and I have only *ever* been friends, you know that. Naturally, being no longer married to Mel he was free to marry whom he liked.' Flora glanced at her watch. 'I think I'll go for a walk.'

'You can't deceive me, you know, darling. I think your heart bleeds for Adam, I really do. And all the time you go about concealing it.' Dulcie, her expression unusually compassionate, reached for her, arms extended, as though to embrace her; but Flora sidestepped, twisting her belt about her waist, eyes gleaming behind her thin gold spectacles; the tight, fixed smile.

'You're so frightfully dramatic, Mother,' she said and went quietly down towards the lake.

Always peace by the water.

CHAPTER 15

As soon as Rachel saw her she knew who she was, even though she had changed over the years, but not much. It was the same woman who had appeared in the witness box and made Bosco drop the case in the year 1913. It was Hugo's mother.

'You know who I am, don't you?' the woman said, rising as Rachel entered the room and walking towards her, smiling in a rather insolent kind of way, her hand outstretched. But Rachel didn't take it. Instead she reached for the support of the chair in front of her and abruptly sat down. The shock was so great as to make her forget her manners, and her unwanted guest remained standing.

'Yes, I know who you are,' she said. 'I remember you quite clearly.'

Nimet smoothed her skirt with the rejected hand and sat down opposite Rachel.

'He's like me. I've seen him once or twice. He's a nice-looking boy.'

'Spying, I suppose, watching ...' Rachel tried to keep the emotion out of her voice. 'What do you want?'

'Is it unnatural for a mother to want to see her own son; to see how he is?'

'In your case, yes. You dumped him as a baby of eighteen months and have never seen him since, or been in touch. We tried to trace you but couldn't; but for the chance that Bosco, even after his death, remembered his son and I found Hugo with Madame Hassim, he would have been in an orphanage these past twelve years.'

'Poor Hugo.' Nimet sadly shook her head. She was a beautiful woman; jet black hair and eyes, and pale skin, whose proportions were of classical dimensions. 'He had an unhappy

295

start in life. Your husband wasn't good to me, you know. He stopped the money.'

'*You* weren't good to him! You helped to kill him.'

'Oh, how could you possibly say that?'

'Because,' Rachel rose, indignation now overcoming her shock, and jabbed a finger at her, 'because *you* ruined him in court. I don't think he would ever have joined up but for that. He was too old; it wasn't necessary.'

'Bosco was always impetuous.'

Rachel hated the familiarity, the use of his Christian name, as if Nimet had known him well. In a way she had, whether Rachel liked it or not.

'Well, now that you know he's well you may go.' Rachel walked pointedly towards the door, but Nimet said:

'Not so quickly, Lady Askham. I have rights, you know.'

'What rights?' Rachel spun round.

'The rights of a mother. Hugo is mine. You never adopted him.'

'I never could because of the circumstances. We even had lawyers searching for you in Cairo. Someone thought you were dead.'

'Oh, no, not dead. Maybe someone wished me dead, but that is another thing.'

Rachel thought that Nimet certainly had style, poise, allure. It was not difficult to see why Bosco, or any other man, would have fallen for her – even over this long span of time, twenty-eight years since Cairo in 1899 when Bosco first met Nimet. She was also beautifully and elegantly dressed in an aquamarine silk dress with a box-pleated skirt, a fox fur round her shoulders, a large picture hat on her smooth head.

'I'm now married,' Nimet went on, 'to a man of great wealth. Maybe you noticed my car outside your door?'

Rachel shook her head. She'd noticed nothing, only the look of concern on Bromwich's face after he'd told her an unknown woman had almost forced her way in, demanding to see her.

'A friend she said, my lady.' Rachel had hurried upstairs, dreading she knew not what; but not Nimet, after all these years.

In 1913 Bosco's Egyptian mistress had appeared in the witness box to give evidence against him in a libel trial. Few knew of her existence, certainly not Rachel. He had stopped the case and from that day on everyone presumed him guilty of infidelity, if nothing else.

In the event of his death he had asked Rachel to look for his son by Nimet, to make sure he was all right. She had eventually found the little boy playing in the garden of a run-down house that had once been a brothel. She had loved him at once, taken him to her heart: Bosco's last child.

So much was history.

'I would like to have my son back,' Nimet said casually, 'now that I can offer him a good home, a settled home. My husband has properties in many countries: France, Switzerland, America. He himself is Turkish.'

'I'm afraid all this is of no interest to me at all,' Rachel said. 'Your having Hugo is absolutely out of the question. Even if he did wish to go with you, which I doubt, I wouldn't let him. I would fight you tooth and nail. I regard Hugo as my son and I love him.'

'Very touching I'm sure, Lady Askham.' Nimet took a gold cigarette lighter out of her bag and lit a black Sobranie, blowing smoke in the air with that same insolent manner.

Rachel realized, to her shame, that she felt afraid of her. Finally the past had caught up with her.

'I intend to accuse you of kidnapping if you do not restore my son to me,' Nimet continued. 'I'm sure you wouldn't like that.'

'You would be laughed out of court, if court is what you have in mind.' Rachel found she was shaking. 'I would fight you and I would win. A prostitute who abandoned her son to the mercies of a brothel keeper ... do you think any English judge would give custody to you?'

'Nevertheless, my husband thinks we have a good case.' Nimet's disturbing coolness seemed rooted in an unshakeable confidence. 'He is prepared to try, anyway. He has ample means. Surely you wouldn't like to go through the courts *again*, Lady Askham, maybe to be ruined once more?'

'How do you mean?'

'I mean I would ask if you were a fit person to look after my son ... a woman who has a *lover* I understand, someone to whom she is not married. What an example!'

Rachel came close to striking her. The whole terrible evil force of the Egyptian connection, which went back to 1898, seemed to possess her; bringing death, tragedy, lies and deceit in its wake. First Achmed Asher, then Madame Hassim, now, twenty-eight years later, Nemesis itself in the person of this Nimet whom Bosco had loved.

'You've clearly been doing a lot of work, Madame ... I don't know what your name is.'

'You may call me Nimet, I think you know me best by that name. Yes, my husband has employed a detective to look into your circumstances. It was he who found out that Hugo has been expelled from school and has tutors at home, and that you have a lover who is a Member of Parliament. A Mr Foster, I believe?

'My husband then employed a lawyer who thinks we would have a good case in trying to prove you have not brought Hugo up well. Why, for instance, was he expelled from school? Also that your present way of life makes you unfit to keep him. If you give him up gracefully there will be no trouble.'

'If it were only money you were after,' Rachel said bitterly, 'I would pay you. Pay you anything to keep you out of my life.'

'Money is of no interest to me now at all.' Nimet smiled and rose to her feet, stubbing out the cigarette on the parquet floor. 'It is revenge I am after.'

'But revenge for *what*?' Rachel demanded.

'Revenge for the slight on me all those years ago. The way he treated me, regarding me as a plaything, a person of no

298

consequence at all. He never even said goodbye to me or wanted to see our son again. *You*, his widow, are paying for it now.'

A minute or two later Rachel watched her drive away in a large maroon chauffeur-driven limousine that had been parked right outside the house. And she hadn't even noticed it.

It was soon established that the former Nimet El-Said was indeed married to a wealthy Turkish businessman who had houses in half a dozen countries, and a yacht based in Cannes. He was forty-five years old, about the same age as Nimet, who was his third wife. A Moslem Turk was allowed to have several, but Mr Igolopuscu had only one at a time and he appeared very much in love with Nimet, to whom he had been married for a year.

All this was discovered in a short time after Adam, back from honeymoon, and Spencer had been quickly called in to help Rachel, still suffering from the shock of the encounter, the fresh assault on her security after Ralph's departure for Africa, and Charlotte's forthcoming marriage. But to lose Hugo, the beloved ...

'It is quite out of the question,' Adam agreed. He looked well and relaxed after his holiday in the Aegean, but distressed now on account of Rachel. 'We should win the case without any doubt, but ...'

'But what?' Rachel played with the tie of her shantung blouse as if wishing she could strangle someone.

'But, of course, it could be very ugly, lots of personal details, publicity of the kind no one wants; not even Mr Igolopuscu, I should think.'

'But isn't this sort of thing respected by the courts? The fact that Hugo has lived with me for twelve years, as my son. That *she* disappeared off the face of the earth?'

Adam shrugged. 'Once the papers get hold of a case they respect nothing. You should know that.'

Rachel knew it only too well, the slinking into Askham House by a back entrance during the 1913 trial, the insinuations, the ceaseless lies and speculation.

'It can't come to court,' Spencer said at last. 'There must be another way.'

'What way?' Adam looked at him. They were in his chambers at Gray's Inn where they'd gone to be away from prying ears and servants' gossip.

'Rachel and I could be married.'

'You needn't think that would stop Nimet,' Rachel said. 'You didn't see the look in her eyes.'

'Nevertheless, it would help,' Adam agreed. 'It's on the cards anyway, isn't it?'

'Not yet,' Rachel said quickly. 'Anyway, I wouldn't just to . . . well, be frightened into it by Nimet of all people. There must be a limit to *some* things she can say in court.'

'No one yet knows what charges she's going to make.' Adam thoughtfully tapped his pencil on his desk. 'Kidnapping . . . that's very rare. Certainly she's crazy. Maybe I should go and see her husband?'

Adam seemed rather to relish the case that had been thrust upon him so soon after his marriage, even though it involved the possible humiliation of his sister. He felt a resurgence of youth and energy in the company of the delightful companion who had become his wife, who was to him everything he had wished; like Flora, though more so because there was her body, too.

It was generally agreed by the family that Flora had been a brick about the whole thing, a perfect sport. She'd sold him the house, moved out of it after filling it with flowers and having her room redecorated, and even sent a congratulatory telegram to the reception when she was *en route* for Cairo. Her behaviour was just what one would have expected of her; perfectly correct, perfectly Askham. He anticipated that, in no time at all after her return, they'd resume their warm friendship again, if not in quite the same way as before, because Margaret mightn't like that.

But now this challenge, this business with Rachel ... He wished she would marry Spencer, though it was quite bizarre that once again a brother and sister would marry a brother and sister – he marrying a much younger woman, she a much younger man. Not that Spencer looked young. In fact he looked quite old, older, some said, than Adam, because his hair was heavily flecked with grey and his face was lined with the marks of frustration and tension, the burdens of social and political responsibility.

There was no sign of Nimet when Adam was admitted to Mr Igolopuscu's suite in The Ritz, just round the corner from Askham House. Mr Igolopuscu greeted Adam cordially, offered him cigars, a drink. Adam refused both but accepted coffee. Yes, Turkish coffee. Mr Igolopuscu was delighted.

They exchanged pleasantries before Adam got down to business, trying to explain what it was that Rachel had done for Hugo; how unreasonable to expect her to give him up after she had looked after him for twelve years.

'It *is* reasonable for a mother to want her child.' Mr Igolopuscu was a large, cheery Turk who looked as though he enjoyed life and lived well. Clearly, too, he had a lot of money which would attract someone like Nimet, regardless of looks. Those wouldn't come into the important business of marriage at all.

'After twelve years?' Adam had hesitated before replying.

'She was not able to provide for him before. It broke her heart.' Momentarily the cheerful oriental managed to look sad.

'She left him with the keeper of a brothel! You know she was a prostitute herself?'

Mr Igolopuscu lowered the lashes over his fine, twinkling brown eyes. He held up a deprecatory hand: 'One hears so many stories. My wife has told me that she was never one in the

301

proper sense. She was a woman of good birth but no fortune. Lord Askham had promised to keep her for life.'

'He left her a house, some money for the child. She sold the former and squandered the latter. She kept the money he left her for the child.'

'But it was not enough to keep up the position he had led her to expect ...' Mr Igolopuscu frowned. 'Not very nice behaviour, really, for an English gentleman.'

'But is it right to take it out now, twelve years later, on Lady Askham?'

Mr Igolopuscu looked at him sharply. 'I hear she is not a very nice woman. She has a lover. What kind of behaviour is *that* for an English lady, may I ask?'

It was true that even in this modern day it was not regarded as proper for a woman to sleep with a man to whom she was not married, though a lot of people did it, as they always had. As for Mr Igolopuscu, Adam was quite sure his own emotional life was not above reproach; but then he was an oriental, and a man.

'This is really quite ridiculous.' Adam looked at his watch. He was due to pick Margaret up and take her to the theatre; Marie Tempest in Noel Coward's new play *The Marquise*. 'I am sure we can reach some compromise. Neither you, nor your wife, would wish to have many unpleasant things on both sides dragged through the courts?'

Mr Igolopuscu shrugged. 'All my wife wants is her son. Is it not understandable, Mr Bolingbroke? I can see you're a clever, reasonable man. Please think of a reasonable way out of this. I'm sure you will.'

Mr Igolopuscu patted Adam affably on the shoulder as he led him to the door of his suite.

It was a very wet summer in England, one of the wettest for years, and it was a good place to be out of, though France, just over the Channel, was not much better. For people who were in love, however, the state of the weather was a matter of minor importance, the warmth from their hearts making up for the lack of sun.

Susan, who regarded herself as a cynic in matters of love – in many ways it was a defence against a fresh commitment on the part of one who told herself she had never ceased to love her husband – thought that there was no doubt that Paolo Verdi loved her cousin Charlotte very much. For one as old and worldly-wise as he she thought this surprising. She imagined that all older men, especially the dynamic, successful kind like Paolo, who travelled the world and knew their way around, must inevitably have slept with a lot of women, would be accustomed to adulation and getting their own way. Inevitably they would be very vain. But Paolo didn't seem to conform to this image. He may well have slept with a number of women – if he had he certainly wouldn't tell Susan – but he was gentle, courteous, not in the least bit vain, and he pursued Charlotte with an old-fashioned courtliness that both women found charming. There were flowers, invitations to lunch, to dine, trips to the country, to the châteaux of people both he and Charlotte knew, trips to the races which both he and Bobby adored.

Inevitably Bobby needed a companion; inevitably, more and more, Hélène was invited to join them, but she had to come alone.

Hélène and Jamie had been lovers for more than a year and, now that the initial excitement was over, Hélène was forced to accept the fact that she shared a small, cramped left-bank apartment at the top of a very long flight of stairs with an unreliable man who gambled, drank too much and had little to offer her. She was not even sure what he did for a living except that there was always just enough money, never too much; but almost always too little for a young woman who belonged to one of the oldest and richest families in Russia. She found herself almost as poor as she had been after the Revolution, before that golden day when Susan Ferova stepped into the lives of her family and herself. For a while it had been enough

303

to live on the excitement of her first love, and Jamie when sober, and even sometimes when he wasn't, was an exciting and amusing companion, a skilled and tender lover. He was also wild and unconventional. They did lots of unusual, interesting things; exploring the low-life districts of Paris or making unexpected forays to the country homes of the well-heeled or aristocratic French who Jamie seemed to know too, for he knew everyone and all types of people; she didn't know how.

Altogether the Honourable James Kitto was a poor proposition for a Princess who was twenty-five years old and ambitious, even if his family did go back to Robert the Bruce. There is no doubt that Hélène's passion for him remained undimmed, but there were so many other things that were less appealing – the penny pinching, the drinking, the feeling that Jamie neglected her.

It was not very difficult, as time went on, for Hélène to compare Jamie with his distant cousin Bobby and to find the former wanting. For though Bobby didn't have Jamie's sex appeal – didn't attract her at all, in fact – he had everything else: availability, desire for her company, unlimited money, and a certain charm, even if it left her cold. She found something reptilian in his small stature, and saturnine looks, something faintly sinister after the warm, spontaneous, frankly attractive Jamie. Time spent in his company, however, especially if it included Charlotte and Paolo, could be very good indeed. It was exotic, lavish and always very expensive; no low dives there except artificial ones patronized by the rich.

One night that summer, when Hélène came home at her usual hour of three in the morning after dining and dancing with Charlotte, Paolo, Bobby and friends, Jamie was not in his usual nocturnal position of torpor, either dead drunk or unpleasantly on the verge. He was sitting up alertly waiting for her. His eyes were red-rimmed and looked ugly, and he was certainly not drunk, if not completely sober.

'Where have you been?' He got to his feet as she quietly let herself in, turning with surprise to see him.

'With Susan.'

'And who else?'

'Charlotte was there, Paolo, Bobby, an American named ...'

'Why am I never asked?'

'Perhaps they think you can't afford to pay.'

Hélène languidly began to draw off her elbow-length evening gloves and wandered round the flat, noting the peeling wallpaper on the walls, the cheap furniture, the empty bottles on the floor. 'All this is unbelievably sordid,' she added. 'I don't know why I stick it.'

'Then why do you?'

'Maybe because I love you.' As she turned to look at him she wondered suddenly if she did. She felt in a curious mood, a mixture of elation, disappointment and discontent. Even drunk he attracted her, but the life they led ... always borrowing from Father, little gifts from Susan, knowing that Bobby regarded her as some sort of charity, a family relative who had to be watered and fed, to whom he had an obligation. She wanted more from life.

'You're not to go out again with him, do you hear?' Jamie, advancing towards her, shook a finger at her, a gesture which she found rather comical, so she reached out and tried to flick it over, a little bit drunk herself. Jamie, inflamed by her gesture, the sulk on her face, grabbed her by the neck and flung her violently on the bed.

'Jamie ...'

'You're a little tart,' Jamie said, bending over her. 'You were a tart when I met you and you haven't changed. If you go near Bobby again I'll beat the daylights out of you. And just to show you ...'

Jamie reached for the hem of her dress and, drawing it up violently over her buttocks so that it tore, turned her on her side and began to slap her bare flesh hard.

The couple who slept in the flat next door often heard many curious sounds, sighs, laughter and noises coming from their neighbours, but never anything quite as violent and prolonged as they heard that night. It was a long time before they were able to go to sleep.

'There's nothing I can do about Hélène if she won't come,' Susan said, 'do stop pacing up and down.'

'But did you ask her?'

'Of course I asked her. I've asked her several times.'

'She loves horses. Tell her it's Longchamps.'

'I have.'

'What does she say?'

'She says she's busy.'

'Do you believe her?'

'I don't know.'

Susan gazed at Bobby, her plucked eyebrows quizzically raised. 'Are you in *love* with Hélène, Bobby, finally? I wish you'd tell me.'

Bobby stopped pacing and then started again. 'I like her very much. She's really quite extraordinarily attractive.'

'Doesn't Jamie put you off?'

'Not at all. I don't consider him in my league. I don't regard him as a rival.'

'She's crazy about him.'

'Are you sure?'

'The reason she won't, or can't come is that he's jealous. It isn't that she doesn't want to.'

'Ah, now I see. And you didn't tell me.' Bobby looked alert and interested. He studied himself in the mirror, sleeking back his perfectly smooth hair. He wore a cream suit and two-tone brown and cream shoes. 'That gives me something to go on,' he said. 'I wish you'd told me before. Be ready by two-thirty.'

Taking his hat, he ran out of the flat, down the stairs instead of taking the lift and out into the road where he hailed a cab.

* * *

306

Even in these sordid surroundings she looked dignified. He realized then that he probably did love her. In so far as he was perfectly self-contained he could do without anyone – he could do without Aileen and without Hélène. With the former he had got himself into a mess. He had started something quite ephemeral, a brief affair, he'd thought, with a pretty woman that had got out of control.

But Hélène was different. He regarded her as a valuable object, something to be acquired, more like a business asset than a person. Whatever her faults of personality, her family's title was almost prehistoric, and the value, the authenticity of that no one could take away from her.

Bobby needed a titled bride because, despite the plethora of titles on his mother's side of the family and the knighthood of his paternal grandfather, he himself was untitled, and it rankled. No amount of wealth could make up for that – but Princess Ferova could: Mr Bobby Lighterman with his wife Aileen was unthinkable. Many times he'd visualized the headlines: MARRIAGE OF BOBBY LIGHTERMAN, MIL-LIONAIRE BUSINESSMAN AND SOCIALITE, TO THE PRINCESS HÉLÈNE FEROVA. He saw the picture of them leaving St Margaret's, maybe members of the Royal Family close behind. Hélène, on his arm, in a dress of centuries-old Brussels lace, himself attired immaculately, as usual, in morning-dress, everyone saying what a handsome couple they made. If Bobby had a dream it was that and, inevitably, they drove off into the sunset in an Askham *de luxe* motor car down to Estoril or the Riviera. It was unlike Bobby to be so fanciful but about this particular subject, he was; quite foolishly so.

When Hélène abruptly went off with the bounder Jamie Kitto it was a rebuff but only that. It made her slightly more desirable to him, more attractive, as the fact that Aileen had been married had initially interested him. It was something to do with sexual experience that was exciting and slightly mystifying. 'Soiled goods', in Susan's phrase, would never have worried him in the slightest; on the contrary.

307

Bobby had had a busy year; he had a mistress and was not deprived of stimulation, or of sex. He knew that Hélène's affair with Jamie could not last because he knew the sort of person Hélène was, and he'd bided his time.

Now he knew, with that instinctive flair he had for a good business deal, that the time had come.

Hélène had let him in, disconcerted, surprised.

'Jamie's just gone out,' she said, looking anxiously past him through the door. 'I don't know when he'll be back.'

'I know. I saw him go. Now I want you to come with me.'

'I said I couldn't.'

'But you can and you will. This place ...' Bobby gestured round, grimacing, 'it's not for you at all. I don't know how you can live here.'

'Well, it's not a palace.' Hélène looked pale as though she hadn't slept. Through a half-open door Bobby could see a large, double unmade bed, with crumpled sheets.

'I can offer you something much, much better, Hélène.'

'What do you mean?'

'Marriage is what I mean,' Bobby said, surprising even himself, because this had not been part of the dream, not in the sordid room in sight of the bed where she slept with her lover; but in some more salubrious surroundings, like Susan's gracious apartment or his house in Mayfair, with low lights and roses. It just showed that one couldn't plan everything, even if the name was Lighterman.

It didn't occur to him that the rest of the dream might be not quite according to plan either.

Whereas Susan knew that Paolo loved Charlotte it was perfectly clear to her that Hélène was not in love with her new fiancé. It seemed so odd to her that Bobby, who was so perceptive, didn't realize it too, because Hélène made very little attempt to be anything but decorative, which came easier to her now with the money Bobby lavished on her. Sometimes she didn't even have to be pleasant. Bobby, equable and good-tempered, didn't seem to mind.

Hélène Ferova entered a world which even in pre-war Russia she hadn't known, because there was a lot that was primitive about Petrograd or Moscow before the Revolution. To be in Paris in the summer of 1927, engaged to a wealthy man who could open the door to everything, would be most women's idea of paradise. Not only the couturiers: Molyneux, Chanel, Schiaparelli, Cheruit; the boutiques, the *grands magasins*, but the restaurants, the night clubs, the whole world of a Paris which had not died with the *belle époque* but, if anything, surpassed it.

It seemed to be the end of Jamie who, unexpectedly, came when Bobby sent for him, seeing him in a small room in the office in the Champs Elysées and offering him a salary to keep out of his and Hélène's way; to be stopped if he appeared on the scene again.

'You could also sober up,' Bobby had added, witheringly with the kind of scorn of which only Bobby was capable, 'you look disgusting.'

The whole transaction, really, was about money. Hélène knew she had been bought, paid for and was being packaged to be Bobby's wife. Her mother, amazed at the turn of events, told her to look on the best side of things as she was getting a happiness she didn't deserve.

'You don't have to *love* your husband,' she said practically. 'Look at it like that, just do your duty ... and spend his money.'

'You sound like an eighteenth-century courtesan, Mother.'

'Beggars can't be choosers. Eighteenth, nineteenth, twentieth, what does it matter? Women are bought just the same, always have been and always will be. Not many marriages are made for love, even today. Look, you are a poor woman, a Russian Princess maybe – yes, with an old title, but poverty-stricken. Maybe he loves you, I don't know. It suits Bobby Lighterman to marry you, and it must suit you to marry him.

We could certainly do with the security. I must say I'm very pleased ... and surprised. Believe me, you're a lucky woman.'

Princess Irina, who had come over to Paris the moment the announcement was made, peered anxiously out of the window as if anyone passing four storeys down could hear her.

'Your father,' her voice sank to a whisper, 'is not exactly an asset. I know Bobby is getting sick of him. He makes so many mistakes, he is never here, can never be found. Bobby won't go on paying him for ever. He will go – "shoosh",' the Princess made a dismissive gesture with both her hands, her violet lips pursed as though she were kicking someone in the backside, '"out you go!" Bobby is not sentimental, I know that. He is too shrewd, too clever; but he wants you, and you must be to him everything that he wants. It shouldn't be difficult. You have no option.'

The Princess looked her daughter up and down, as though she were inspecting merchandise, and swept out of the room to keep an appointment with her milliner.

Bobby began to plan the wedding with the attention to detail with which he planned everything. The place: St Margaret's. The time: December, a winter wedding with the bride dressed in white velvet. The honeymoon: Africa, with a visit, perhaps, to Ralph. He would take six months off from business to enjoy the sun with his bride, or maybe they would cruise to India.

The only thing that was difficult to plan was breaking the news to Aileen, though this he also managed not to do because she read it in the newspapers first, just as he had dreamed:

SOCIALITE MILLIONAIRE TO WED RUSSIAN PRINCESS.
The fairytale engagement of Bobby Lighterman, millionaire heir to the massive fortune left by his grandfather Sir Robert Lighterman, and the Princess Hélène Ferova, daughter of Prince Alexei Ferov, who was a chamberlain to the late Czar, was announced...

310

Bobby tried to make it sound reasonable. 'Remember I *am* a member of the Askham family. I had to marry an equal.'

'Oh, I know you're a member of the Askham family, Bobby! How could I forget it?'

For a moment Bobby felt his façade crumble in the presence of someone who knew him as he really was – a humbug. He had been born to wealth, he had inherited a name, but he was rather an insecure individual, and it was sure that Aileen, who knew him better than most people, knew that.

He knelt on the floor and laid his head in her lap. At first she caressed it and then she ruffled it and, finally, she bent her head and kissed it.

'You know me, Aileen, better than anyone in the world. I never want to lose you. Is it possible?'

'I suppose so,' Aileen said. 'I knew you'd never marry me, anyway. I didn't expect it. I am the daughter of your works manager and I knew it would never do. I suppose I should be grateful.' She paused and looked at him, her pale face going pink. 'I don't suppose it's the time to tell it you, but any minute now and you'll notice. I'm going to have a baby.'

Bobby remained where he was, surprised and yet not quite surprised. She had been fatter lately, her belly rounder, and she had always been such a skinny little thing.

'I want to go ahead and have it because I may not have the chance to have another.' She sounded awfully practical – good, sensible girl that she was. 'I don't want to be a burden on you, Bobby; but after what you said today ...'

'I'll always look after you and the baby,' Bobby said, his normal matter-of-fact tone of voice returning, despite the undoubted shock of her announcement. 'I'll buy you a house and make sure you have everything you want. I'll come and see you, but there has to be one condition.'

Wearily Aileen met his eyes. 'Yes? I suppose it's that I must never ever let your new wife, or your family, know about us.'

'It's reasonable, don't you think?' Bobby said, rising from

the floor and dusting his knees. 'It's hardly a good way to start married life.'

He'd known it was a foregone conclusion she'd agree.

Charlotte and Paolo were married in September, three months and a bit after they had first met. It was a society wedding at the Jesuit Church in Farm Street, where Charlotte had been instructed in the Roman Catholic faith and then received by the urbane priest who subsequently married them. Charlotte looked beautiful, Paolo handsome and accomplished. It was just as everyone would have wished, and everyone was there.

There was a reception for two hundred at Askham House, which reminded many people of the similar occasions that had taken place before the War: weddings, funerals, baptisms, Queen Victoria's funeral and the Coronation of two Kings – Edward VII and his son George V. Charlotte was the first of the new generation of Askhams to marry and, as well as all her new friends, there were the usual sprinkling of old family friends who never missed a party, an occasion to mourn or celebrate.

It was rumoured that it was all right, really, because the groom was related to the Italian composer Giuseppe Verdi, but everyone thought it a shame he was not at least a count. Melanie came with Denton, combining the happy occasion with a fresh inspection of Bobby's fiancée and a closer look at the shops. She stayed with Rachel in St James's Square and managed to sprinkle most of her conversation with criticisms of this or that. Mostly, this time, they seemed aimed, directly or indirectly, at her husband.

'He has no money, of course,' Melanie said one night when, for once, they were dining alone after the bridal pair had left on honeymoon. 'I'm keeping him. It's just like Adam, after all.'

Rachel flushed, but ignored the barb because she thought foolish, selfish Melanie didn't intend, in this instance, to be malicious.

'But didn't you know that?'

'I thought he had a *bit*. He is also a gambler and too fond of the Casino for my money, and my money it is.'

'I did so hope you'd be happy,' Rachel sighed. 'That *at last* you'd be happy.'

'Happiness is relative, isn't it?' Melanie said sadly. 'Are you happy?'

'I'm relatively unhappy at the moment.' Rachel was cautious. 'Adam is trying to do something about Nimet. She seems quite determined to go to court, though I suspect she doesn't really want Hugo because she's told me she only wanted revenge.'

'She's the most appalling woman,' Melanie shuddered and reached for Rachel's hand. 'You must avoid a court case at all costs. It will break you. I've always been terribly fond of you, Rachel, you know that?'

'I know that.'

'And poor dear Flora, wherever she is now. What a *beast* Adam was to her.'

Flora had not returned for her niece's wedding. She had only just reached Egypt when she heard of the engagement, and she did want to lose herself in the study of ancient things, the perfect way to forget present unhappiness. She'd drifted, irresistibly, to Shepheard's Hotel, where they'd all foregathered nearly thirty years before for Melanie's wedding to Harry. It seemed so incredible how much the atmosphere of Cairo had changed, even though the British still maintained a presence there. Gone were all the red and blue coats of the militia. Of course, there had been another, more terrible war since Omdurman. Really, it seemed like a lifetime away.

Soon she moved from Shepheard's to a flat in the old quarter where she and Rachel had once lived, in sight of the Citadel. But then, everything in Cairo was in sight of the Citadel, built by Mohammed Ali to defy the Turks. It towered over one as it had in the days when the British guns had raked the streets in case of insurrection by the rebellious *fellaheen*.

313

But Flora was restless and, as Charlotte's wedding came and went, it made her more fretful as she realized that no one would really care if she wasn't there; no one would miss her – probably her name was hardly mentioned – just one of a crowd, not an important person at all – not even a lynchpin of the family like Rachel ... or Adam. Her family surely loved her. She knew her mother did; but her nieces and nephews would hardly regard the absence of middle-aged Aunt Flora as a catastrophe. Melanie, Rachel, and Adam had focal points in their lives: children, husbands, wives, lovers. She, Flora, had nothing.

In September when it got cooler Flora booked a passage up the Nile on one of the Cook's steamers which had carried most of the supplies, and many of the troops, towards Omdurman. Many of these had been replaced now by more modern vessels, but some of them had not and still lay low in the water, heavy, cumbrous boats built for sight-seeing and comfort rather than speed.

As the boat left Cairo Flora sat on the deck watching the scenery. But when they passed Bedrayshin, where Madame Hassim's fatal party had gone to meet Melanie and Harry returning from honeymoon, she experienced such an acute melancholy, a feeling of time irretrievably lost, that she had to go to her cabin and lie down. There she watched the reflection of light and water on the ceiling until night fell and it was time to change for dinner.

On the boat during the voyage to Aswan, Lady Flora was a celebrity. Not only was she the daughter of an earl, though this was a factor; but she had extensively studied Egyptology, was an authority on the tombs and the pyramids. Each day a little doting crowd collected round her, her company sought for enlightenment about the ruins they were going to see. People clung to her, deferred to her. She was flattered, fawned upon and given the best places and seats on every excursion. Confidently sure of her facts, guide book in hand, she would advance down the valley of the Kings, or the catacombs behind the statues at Abu Simbel and lecture her audience with the authority of one who was not only an accomplished Egyptologist, but had visited Egypt many times, after that first time in 1898.

Eighteen ninety-eight! It was a lifetime away, a forgotten epoch.

'Tell me, Lady Flora, I heard your brother was a hero at Omdurman?'

Mrs Ffitch-Nightingale was one of Flora's most devoted followers. She made sure that her chair was out on deck every morning in the position she liked it, shaded from the sun, or that her favourite place in the dining-salon was always kept ready for her. Mrs Ffitch-Nightingale claimed some remote ancestry with the celebrated Florence and clearly felt that she and Flora had much in common, being elevated from the rest of the company by their good connections.

'My brother *was* at Omdurman, yes, but I don't think he considered himself a hero. We were very proud of him, though.'

'Wasn't there a *court case* ...' Mr Bradley screwed up his eyes behind gold-rimmed glasses and the woman next to him nudged him while Mrs Ffitch-Nightingale looked perplexed. Then, realizing he had committed some gaffe, he slowly reddened.

'I hope I haven't ...'

'My brother died in the Great War,' Flora said sadly. 'He was killed in 1915.'

'Ah, *that* Lord Askham! He was a hero, then,' Mr Bradley, anxious to make up for his lapse, interjected hurriedly. 'Didn't he receive the VC?'

'Yes, that Lord Askham.'

'So many men lost in the War,' Miss Carruthers, a lady of about the same age as Flora, leaned over sympathetically. 'A whole generation sacrificed ...'

'I saw something about an Askham in the newspaper

recently.' Mrs Ffitch-Nightingale was determined to impress everyone else with the status of their fellow traveller.

'My sister-in-law writes for a newspaper.'

'That's it!' Delighted, Mrs Ffitch-Nightingale snapped her fingers. 'Didn't her daughter get married? To a *racing* driver, I believe.'

'That's my niece Charlotte. The family are delighted about the marriage. Now, if you'll excuse me, I think I'll retire. The sun seems to have given me a headache.' There were times when to be an object of interest, of adulation, only made her feel more lonely.

As Flora rose, the whole table rose to its feet except Mrs Barker-Stewart, who didn't quite reverence Flora the way everyone else did. Mr Bradley escorted her to the door of the salon, opening it for her and, nodding her thanks, Flora set off along the gangway, back to her comfortable cabin on the boat deck.

Yes, she did have a headache. She dipped a handkerchief in the jug of water standing on the antique tallboy and, lying down, placed it on her brow.

Why did everyone always talk about Omdurman, of Bosco? Why did they all remember the Askham case, even though it happened fifteen years ago, and a major war had intervened to divide those far-off days from these?

Eighteen ninety-eight. She had been twenty-four and Adam a year younger. Then he was free, Melanie married to another, who no one guessed would die so soon. Flora had immediately been attracted by his grave, quiet demeanour, so unlike the other rowdy officers among Bosco's friends. Adam was even an unusual choice for Bosco. Yet what good friends they became! She, Flora, had liked his sister, too, Rachel. She'd been drawn to her as she had to Adam. What fun they'd had that year in Cairo before the tragedy struck – Harry's death and Bosco gravely wounded. Everyone knew how well suited they were, except Adam, who had been seduced by Melanie's beauty, trapped by her selfishness.

But even then, the years with him, working with him, sharing interests had been worthwhile, until now ...

Sacrifice. People talked about sacrifice. She, Flora, had sacrificed her life for a man who hadn't really valued it, or, perhaps, deserved it. If he had he wouldn't have been *able* to marry Margaret; to appear to look forward to a whole new life without his devoted companion of so many years.

The years came flooding back, episodes etched in her mind as though they had happened yesterday: Arthur's death in America, the marriage of Rachel and Bosco, the births of Susan and Christopher, the death of her father, the death of the King in 1910. They all became jumbled up, fragmented in her mind, so that she wasn't quite sure if she were awake or dreaming.

The sense of isolation with which she had started the voyage had persisted, grown deeper every day. Now it seemed like an all-enveloping cocoon, separating her not only from her family but from those who would be her friends. In life she was alone, bitterly alone. There was no place left for her; no home. She would become a wanderer. No one would really care if she lived or died.

It was probably after midnight, as the steamer lay anchored quietly for the night, that Flora rose from her bed and carefully placed the cloth that had been covering her brow on the table beside her. For a while she sat on the side of the bunk, her hands joined, perfectly tranquil – almost as if in prayer.

Then she got up, glanced round the cabin, put out the light and went out on to the deserted boat-deck, carefully closing the door behind her, locking it.

It was a beautiful night, one to remember. The water was only a few feet below her and she imagined how easily, almost joyfully, one would sink beneath its cool embrace; the only lasting, loving embrace she would ever know.

Gracefully she slid over the side of the boat, dropping into the water with hardly a sound. Then she began to swim quite strongly, unhampered by her thin dress, against the swift current of the Nile.

No one saw her go and for quite some time, late into the next day, no one worried about her, thinking that she had slept late because of her headache; even Mrs Ffitch-Nightingale, who sat for an hour in the sun on the deck beside the shaded chair, waiting for Flora.

Only the waters of the Nile that flowed down from its source past Omdurman, past Khartoum and the Atbara, where the British had camped on their way to the war, past Bedrayshin where the Askhams had embarked on that fateful picnic so many years ago, past Cairo towards the Delta and the sea, knew her secret.

And for many days they kept it.

CHAPTER 16

The Château de la Forêt, where Bobby kept his horses, was fifteen kilometres from Longchamps, his trainer one of the best in France. The Askhams had never gone in much for horse racing as a family. Unlike the Royal Family, they had never bred horses; and it was when studying the best attributes of a man of the world that Bobby decided horse racing went very well with wealth, in the same way that he was to decide that he needed a bride with an old princely title, partly to make up for the fact that his paternal grandfather's colossal wealth was based on trade.

Bobby was not wholly hypocritical in his attachment to horses; he had kept a book at Eton and regretted the fact that his grandfather had a polo ground, but only the most perfunctory stable.

Now Bobby's stable of racehorses was one of the most outstanding in England, closely rivalling that of the Aga Khan in France. Horses were a sign of the kind of limitless wealth Bobby possessed. It made him happy that people could see how truly rich he was.

Hélène also loved horses with the true passion of the Russian aristocrat who numbered Cossacks among the forebears on her mother's side, and whose family had bred some notable trotters on the Caucasian estate. Hélène was never happier than when inspecting Bobby's stables in France and England, or watching the racing at Ascot, Kempton Park, Goodwood or Longchamps.

In September Bobby and Hélène travelled to France after Charlotte's wedding, he to do business, buy new horses and, later on, to watch trials of the Askham 'Bosco' round the racing circuit at Strasbourg, where Charlotte and Paolo would go after their honeymoon. Bobby and Hélène were considered by the world's press to be an elegant, sophisticated couple suitably matched, if not too obviously in love. Wherever they went there were photographs. They were seen everywhere at the smartest clubs and occasions in capitals all over Europe, and at all the best house parties on both sides of the Channel. The fact that Hélène had openly lived with another man gave her a sort of notoriety that the gossip-writers enjoyed, which went rather well with the dissolute atmosphere of the post-war, well-heeled generation who were able to whoop it up in the twenties while everywhere there was massive unemployment, widespread poverty and an ex-corporal in the Kaiser's Army slowly clawing his way to power in Germany.

But this day in September Hélène and Bobby were strolling round the stables in the company of Etienne Dumont, who trained horses for a number of other wealthy men, including the Aga Khan. It was a mellow autumn day, a touch of chill in the air and, as the horses were paraded before them by the stable boys, their breaths became vaporized, expelling clouds into the air. Etienne was explaining the merits of a newly-acquired foal when a man who had been inspecting a fine roan that had just completed its canter nearly cannoned into them.

'Pardon.' The man turned, removed his hat and then stared at Bobby, blinking his eyes.

'Mr Lighterman!'

Bobby's frown of annoyance changed into a smile.

'Mr Igolopuscu! I didn't know you were a breeder.'

'I am about to become one, sir. My new wife is extremely interested in racing.'

Bobby held out his hand. 'I congratulate you, Mr Igolopuscu. I didn't know you had married recently.'

'A year ago, Mr Lighterman, just after I had the pleasure of first meeting you in Istanbul.'

'Then I'm happy to introduce my fiancée, the Princess Hélène Ferova.'

'How do you do?' Mr Igolopuscu bowed.

320

'Delighted,' Hélène said graciously, shaking hands.

'Mr Igolopuscu and I had business dealings, my dear,' Bobby said, 'and hope to have more.'

'Yes, indeed, Mr Lighterman.' Mr Igolopuscu looked extremely happy. 'We are more than pleased with the consignment of motor engines produced by your firm.'

'Ah, then you must come and see my car while you're in Paris. I might be able to persuade you to buy one for your wife.'

'That would be charming,' Mr Igolopuscu nodded and smiled, producing a card from his wallet.

'I am staying at the Georges Cinque. My wife is still in London where we hope to purchase a property, but I would be delighted if you and the Princess would dine with me.'

Mr Igolopuscu looked obviously impressed by the status of Bobby's future wife. Bobby knew immediately that his hunch that she would be good for business was right. He looked at her proudly. Everyone then shook hands and a tentative date was made for the following week.

But it was finally arranged that Bobby and the Turk should meet at the showrooms near the Étoile, and follow it by a lunch at Lapérouse at which Hélène would join them.

On the appointed day Mr Igolopuscu appeared in a grey barathea business suit with a faint white stripe, looking rich and prosperous, his bare dome shining as though newly polished. He was a pleasant urbane man and he and Bobby got on well. He walked round the gleaming car, stroking it as he had the thoroughbred mare the day they had met at Longchamps.

'The Prince of Wales has an Askham,' Bobby said, thinking to administer the *coup de grâce*. 'You could have your initials on the side like him; a crest too, if you have one.' He glanced at Mr Igolopuscu as though such a symbol of status would help clinch the deal, surprised to see an expression of astonishment on his guest's face.

'I beg your pardon?'

'Your initials on the side. It's quite simple. I ...'

'No, what *name* did you say?' Igolopusco patted the car. 'The Prince of Wales has an ...'

'An Askham,' Bobby said, 'that's the name of the car. I'm sorry, I thought I mentioned it.'

'Why is the car called an Askham?' The Turk, looking agitated, produced a gold cigarette case from which he extracted a Sobranie and lit it, fanning the smoke away from Bobby.

'It's a name,' Bobby looked puzzled, 'a family name. The business was started by my uncle who was called Askham, Bosco Askham. This is named in his memory.'

'Oh, I see.' Mr Igolopuscu studied the motor, ran his hands over the trim, but appeared preoccupied. 'Was it *Lord* Askham, by any chance?'

'Yes, it was. Why do you ask?'

Mr Igolopuscu sighed heavily, his hands expressive of despair.

'Alas, I'm afraid we have something else to talk about.'

When Hélène later found them at the restaurant they were deep in conversation over an aperitif.

'What studied concentration,' she said as they stood up to greet her. 'You look rather gloomy for a successful business deal.'

'Do sit down, my dear,' Bobby beckoned for the waiter. 'I have quite an extraordinary story to tell you.'

Rachel and Adam had kept very quiet about Nimet Igolopuscu's claim on Hugo. Not even Margaret, Adam's new wife, knew. It was not the sort of thing one wanted to get out, even in the family. Adam had been trying to arrange a settlement while briefing lawyers, because Rachel was quite determined to hang on to Hugo. It had also been important for Hugo not to get wind of what was happening, so the fewer who did know the better.

As she listened, Hélène's carefully made-up face registered various emotions: outrage, bewilderment then amusement.

'It *is* nice to think you, too, have skeletons in the family cupboard, Bobby. I thought it was *sans peur et sans reproche.*'

'It is the most extraordinary coincidence,' Mr Igolopuscu nodded. 'It is unfortunate yet, maybe, fortunate too. I have tried to dissuade my wife from this action, but as she is very bitter there was little I could do because I love her and, naturally, moved by her sad story, want to please her. Indeed, I had no idea Lord Askham was related to you, your mother's brother. Good heavens!'

'I wonder your detectives didn't discover the connection,' Bobby murmured. 'They can't have been very good. The Askhams are a large and powerful family, though perhaps not quite as they were in the time of my uncle. His son, the present Lord Askham, is in Africa looking for a farm.'

'But the Askham business is connected with yours?'

'It is integrally part of it. We are amalgamated and have a joint chairman. It would be very, very distressing for my family to have this matter aired in court. Yet my aunt is devoted to Hugo. If I know her she will not give up lightly.'

'Nor my wife, I fear,' Mr Igolopuscu grimaced. 'She is a *very* determined lady, slighted by this family.' Mr Igolopuscu looked suddenly tormented, bursting out: 'It is not exactly true to suggest she was a prostitute. She lived a hard life and, as was not unusual in those days and sometimes in these, was protected by men. She felt herself very badly done by Lord Askham who, I believe, promised marriage.'

'I can't believe that. He was always very much in love with Rachel, his wife.' Then, seeing Mr Igolopuscu's obvious embarrassment and displeasure, Bobby leaned towards him, saying earnestly, 'We can't let this happen, Theo. It would do no one *any* good at all. You must see that. It would involve credibility, all kinds of things. Scandal is very bad for business. I assure you this case would make the headlines as a similar case did in 1913. Perhaps you don't know about that?'

Mr Igolopuscu expressed further ignorance and Bobby realized that, although he personally had never met Nimet and knew very little about her, she was undoubtedly a schemer who had grossly deceived her husband about her past.

When he had finished the tale the first course was complete. Even Hélène's boredom had vanished and she became riveted by the tale of the English aristocrat who had fallen in love with a beautiful young woman in Cairo, the year after Omdurman. The fact that she had borne him a son, and was still intimately linked with the family after twenty-eight years, sounded like a romantic fiction. She could hardly drag herself away to keep an appointment with her hairdresser, leaving Bobby and the bewildered Turk to try and reach a compromise in the interests of maintaining integrity in the market place.

'Just as well we met,' Bobby said as they toasted each other with brandy. 'I can't tell you what a disaster this would have been for us both, socially and commercially. To say nothing of the effect it would have had on my marriage. Members of the Royal Family are expected to be present ... and you, too,' he added, raising his glass.

In a way, he thought, it clinched the deal.

Some people are sceptical about coincidence, others can vouch for the part it has played in their lives. Rachel was a believer in coincidence because she knew how often it had affected her own life. It was coincidental that she and Adam should have bumped into the Askham family on the terrace of Shepheard's Hotel in Cairo in 1898; if they hadn't, it is unlikely she and Bosco would ever have met. It was coincidental that, when they did visit the Askhams again in the winter of 1899, Adam should break his leg at the same time that Bosco was an invalid, thus allowing her and Bosco to get to know each other better. If they had just stayed for the brief visit planned it was doubtful if they would ever have seen each other again. In that case Adam and Melanie would not have married and thus a

324

whole generation of children – hers and Adam's – would not have existed.

Yes, life was peppered with coincidences, Rachel thought, her arms hugging Hugo, not the least being that Bosco should bump into Nimet again at Quaglino's twelve years after his romance with her in Cairo and that the whole affair should start up again. She hugged Hugo tighter. Pain it might have brought her, but it was worth it: just for this.

Hugo had his head against Rachel's breast like a baby, instead of a fifteen-year-old boy. At his feet, inseparably as always, was Lenin, rather a grand old cat by now, who had already survived his namesake by three years. Lenin sat with that inscrutable expression, eyes narrowed, occasionally blinking, that has given the cat its reputation for mystery, sorcery, enchantment. They had sat like that, the three of them, for some time, in the companionable silence they habitually enjoyed like three old friends: Lenin blinking, Hugo clinging and Rachel stroking his head.

It had taken Rachel a long time, and much courage, to explain to Hugo about his mother and why, years after she had abandoned him, apparently to an English orphanage, she wanted to see him. Rachel who, if she hated anyone, hated Nimet, had had to be kind. A person's natural mother is, after all, important. Some people spent years trying to find a lost parent. Hugo had not yet seemed to realize the strength of the bond he might feel for Nimet, and his attitude now was one of resentment.

'I don't have to see her if I don't want.'

'I'm afraid you have, darling. In order to avoid a court case, solicitors acting for us have had to draw up a legal document. Your mother, Madame Igolopuscu, does have legal access to you, whether you or I like it or not. It is out of our hands – Bobby's arranged it all.'

'You can't love me to let me go.'

'Oh, my precious!' Rachel squeezed him even tighter and Lenin blinked rapidly several times, maybe with jealousy. 'Of *course* I love you.' She brushed the thick black hair away from his forehead. 'Hugo, I think you have always known I loved you best of all. Better than Ralph and Charlotte, Em and Freddie. I don't know why and I'm ashamed of it in a way – I think it drove Ralph to Africa – but it is a fact. Your daddy, before he died, wanted another baby which I was unable to give him. When I saw you playing in the yard of that dreadful house, alone and abandoned, I thought that God had given me the child Bosco wanted, Bosco's own child, and I have always loved you just that little bit more.'

Tears began to steal down her face and Hugo gazed at her with concern, timidly touching her cheeks.

'You're crying,' he said, inspecting the tips of his fingers as if to be sure they were real. 'Oh, Mummy.' He pressed against her, clutching her even tighter. 'You *are* my Mummy, the only one I have or want. I will not see this woman!'

It was very hard for Rachel. Sometimes she wondered whether it might not have been better to go to court except that, once the whole family was in the secret, they were quite adamant. Newly-married Charlotte was distraught at the idea. Melanie, socializing in the South of France, was appalled. She reminded Rachel in very strong terms how much they'd all been ostracized in 1913, 'struck off the lists of all the best people, my dear'. Only the advent of war had concentrated people's minds on more important things.

But most of all it was Bobby who minded. He wanted to start his married life on the crest of a wave that would surge forward, continuing onwards and upwards, not impeded by a nasty trough of scandal.

'No one would win, Aunt,' he had said quite sternly with Adam, nodding, behind him. 'No one could possibly win, but the real loser would be you.'

It had taken Bobby and Adam weeks to draw up the compromise with the helt of the best lawyers dealing with custody cases. Nimet would waive custody in exchange for reasonable access which included holidays, if her son wished.

'Reasonable access' was to incur further wrangling and the legal bill amounted to thousands of pounds, but still far less than a court case.

All in all, Rachel felt that Nimet had won. She had her revenge. Even the thought that she was living nearby, in a house in Chesterfield Street, was enough to make the flesh creep. It was much, much too near.

Yet Rachel, who had endured so much, had to endure this. Worse, she had to face the thought that Hugo might prefer his mother to her, that all those years of love, care, and often torment, would be lost.

Now Adam stood at the door, stooping a little, his kind face creased with pity.

'Time to go, Hugo.'

But Hugo clung to Rachel and the cat, disturbed, got up, circling several times, as though with concern, before settling down again, his tail neatly tucked round the contours of his body. He, too, was restless, he seemed to say.

'It's not as though you're not coming back, old chap,' Adam said comfortingly. 'I shall be there all the time. I will deliver you back to your mother, I mean this mother, Rachel.'

It was an embarrassing moment. Adam glanced away as, gently, Rachel pushed Hugo towards him, wiping the remaining tears from her eyes.

'Uncle's quite right, Hugo. We're being terribly emotional and silly; you will only be gone an hour or so and I'll be here when you come back.

'It's not as though it were for ever.'

But in a way it was for ever because from the day Hugo met his natural mother he changed. Certainly the relationship between Rachel and himself was never the same again. When, much later, they did resume their old rapport it was in a different way.

It was quite obvious that Nimet would go out of her way to charm, but not so obvious that she would succeed. But it was not only this – her looks, her personality, her gentleness with him, her grace – but the fact that she was all his. He didn't have to share her with grown-up brothers and sisters with whom he had never completely got on, who had a right to Rachel's care, her time. Hugo found it very nice to be the sole object of Nimet's affections because he was; it was obvious that Theo Igolopuscu, though extremely kind, enjoyed henceforth a subsidiary role in her life. Nimet lavished on Hugo not only love and beautiful gifts, but a priceless quality that Rachel couldn't give him: exclusivity. He was exclusively hers and, in his way, this was what he had always longed for: not brothers or sisters, or many homes or animals, but a mother to himself.

Of course all this took time and started gradually. The first visit went all right, Hugo didn't say too much about it. The second was a success and lasted longer. Gradually he started to trot round to Chesterfield Street by himself; gradually he took to sleeping there in the room that Nimet had had expensively done up for him.

Rachel, always busy, found herself tormented when she was at the office, wondering where Hugo was and, as Bobby's wedding grew nearer and the facts about Hugo and Nimet clearer, she began at times to feel quite ill, the worry and anxiety dragging her down, debilitating her as nothing had before.

'I'm going to take you for a holiday,' Spencer said, as Christmas approached. 'Why don't we go and see Ralph after the wedding? A trip to Africa would do you, and me, the world of good.'

As Rachel shook her head he added: 'Don't tell me you can't leave Hugo.'

'Well, I can't.'

Spencer, standing in front of her, seized her by both shoulders and made as if to shake her.

'Rachel, you *must* come to your senses or you'll be ill, really ill. Do you hear me? It is no use grieving for Hugo. He is a boy of fifteen and he will lead his own life. You've had his best years.'

'She's stolen him from me.'

'He's fascinated by her.'

'She wants to take him to *Cairo*.'

'Let her. Rachel, you must realize that from now on you are sharing Hugo with Nimet.'

'I wish to God I'd obeyed my instinct and we'd gone to court. Then he would never have seen her. I was sure I'd win. How could I have lost? This was your advice, yours and Adam's. All my family were against me, even my brother!'

'Darling Rachel,' Spencer tried to put an arm round her, but she wriggled free. 'Please listen to me. What has happened has happened. It *is* unfortunate and I know how unhappy you are. Maybe we gave you wrong advice, but I don't think so. That case could have destroyed you and who is to say you really would have won? No lawyer could say so with certainty. A judge would look very sympathetically on a hard-luck story about a poor woman forced to abandon her child and now trying to reclaim him. Nimet, poised and beautiful, would have looked very pitiful in the witness box. It was wartime, she was poor. Bosco did treat her badly, or so it seems in retrospect. It was not only that we didn't want the case for the sake of its publicity, but we couldn't be sure you'd win. Nimet, with a rich husband behind her, had a very powerful case indeed. Even our lawyers thought so. It's a pity you couldn't find her at the time to sign adoption papers.'

'You've just said it was war.' Rachel still didn't look at him. 'You try and find a prostitute in Cairo in wartime. It was impossible. Some people said she was dead. We've never even been able to find Madame Hassim again. But why she should come now and steal my child ... through hate!'

Spencer reached for her again, but she moved swiftly out of his way, turning on him. 'Oh, leave me alone, Spencer! You irritate me, you know. If you had a bit more to you than trying to be nice all the time I might have married you. Now I wish to heaven you'd leave me alone!'

At her words Spencer's face turned alarmingly grey and, after hovering a minute or two indecisively, he left the room, bumping into Em as he rushed down the stairs.

Em glanced at him, shrugged and continued slowly up the stairs, changing her mind about her destination when she got to the top and turning into her mother's sitting-room. Rachel sat in a corner by the window, also pale with shock, and with an exclamation Em closed the door and ran over to her.

'Mummy, what is it? What happened with Spencer?'

Rachel shook her head, kneading her handkerchief in her hands, incapable of speech. In all her life Em had never seen her mother like this and she felt seriously alarmed.

'Did he say something beastly? He … Oh, I could kill him!' Em peered out of the window as if she would rush after him.

'It's not Spencer …' Rachel spoke slowly. 'He was only trying to be nice.'

'Nice?' Em's freckled face looked indignant and perplexed, and she tossed back her hair, running her hands through it. '*Nice?*'

'Yes, he was nice. I was horrible to him. I said he got on my nerves.'

'Well, maybe he does …'

'Oh, I know you've never had very much time for Spencer, you children …' Rachel gazed down at her handkerchief, smoothing it over her knee, then blew her nose.

'That's not true, Mother. When we were younger we were perhaps a bit jealous, very loyal to Daddy even though we didn't remember him much. But I think we all see now that Spencer has been an anchor to you, especially this year with Ralph gone, and now Hugo …' She stopped as Rachel's lower lip trembled. 'Is *that* what the row was about?'

Rachel nodded, and Em, arms akimbo, leaned against the windowsill.

'Poor Mummy, you've had an awfully bad year. Charlotte gets married and goes off for ever, Ralph goes to Africa, maybe for ever, and Hugo . . . well, I don't know what to say. Who would have thought he would think so much of that awful mother of his?'

'She's not awful,' Rachel blew her nose. 'I mean, to be fair. I absolutely hate her, but she does have a feeling of grievance against this family and maybe, in her heart, she does love Hugo. I don't know why she'd do this otherwise. I'd hate to have given up a child. But, yes, I am upset because I hardly ever see him. By "access", I didn't quite mean that. But you see, at fifteen he is nearly an adult. A person with a mind of his own. I could no more restrain him than I could Charlotte or Ralph, or you...'

'Three babies gone in a year.' Em tenderly bent over her mother and put an arm round her. 'You've got me and Freddie, we'll never leave you!'

Rachel made a determined effort to be brave and, raising her head, smiled at last. 'You'll go off and get married like the rest.'

'I'm never going to marry,' Em said solemnly. 'I don't like men very much.'

'Really?' Rachel looked at her in surprise. 'Not Freddie, not Ralph?'

'Yes, they're brothers, but men ... as men, you know. Not in *that* way. At Oxford they're for the most part frightfully silly. I find women more interesting, women like Aunt Flora...'

Em blinked her eyes and for a moment Rachel thought she was going to cry. They talked about loss; but Flora's puzzling death was the tragedy of the year for the family. It wasn't a personal loss, it was true, in the sense that Ralph, Charlotte and Hugo were losses. Nevertheless they had all mourned Flora, her body found wedged in a cleft of the bank of the Nile several days after she was first missed. Her death remained a mystery because everyone in her party affirmed how much she had seemed to be enjoying herself; how clever she was, how many new friends she had made. Happy; yes. Lady Flora had seemed happy, they all said. She had left the dining-salon early and gone to bed with a headache. It was thought that she had subsequently gone on to the deck to take the air and had, maybe, slipped. It was certainly nicer for all concerned to think that, rather than that she had deliberately lowered herself over the side of the ship to sink beneath the swift brown waters of the Nile, seeking annihilation.

Flora had been buried in Cairo, her funeral attended only by members of the British community. None of her family had time to be present.

Adam was her executor. He'd organized a memorial service for her shortly after Charlotte's wedding. She'd left him the bulk of her fortune with a few bequests for her nephews and nieces. It had made him quite rich, that share of the Askham money.

Rachel had worn black for a long time for Flora because she loved her and she missed her. Knowing Flora better than most, she was never quite sure that the death was an accident.

'We're both awfully morbid today,' Rachel said after a pause during which they'd both been reliving their own memories of Flora. 'I must cheer up. I really must. As for men, darling, there is plenty of time. I don't want you rushing off to be married. It isn't wise, however suitable the man might be.'

'Do you think Charlotte and Paolo will be all right?'

'It's a risk; but he's so awfully nice that I think he'll be the understanding husband she needs.'

'Why *don't* you marry Spencer, Mummy?'

Rachel looked amused at her youngest daughter. 'Oh, you want me to be looked after now, do you?'

'I think it might be a good thing after all. He is nice and it is true you are on your own now. You need someone for your old age. When I leave Oxford I may not marry, but I want to travel.'

'Any plans?' Rachel put an arm round Em. Yes, she was companionable, and sensible, this calm, level-headed, interesting daughter of hers.

'I'd like to be a journalist, like you. Only more so. I'd like to be a reporter, at the centre of world events. So much is happening.'

She looked at her mother who stared, rather fearfully, back.

As was intended, the wedding of Bobby Lighterman and Hélène Ferova at St Margaret's Westminster was the wedding of the year. It took place in December and, although the Prince of Wales couldn't be present, many other members of the Royal Family were, as well as exiled members of the Imperial Russian Family, of whom there seemed to be hundreds. The bride's side of the church was packed.

Dulcie made the effort to attend, because it was such a special occasion, but really she would have preferred the quiet of the Wiltshire countryside in the company of the bride's mother, Irina. Mabel Lighterman, still dressed in the tasteless style that seemed to have its origins in the last days of the Old Queen, was there with her daughters, the growing number of relations on the Lighterman side pushed well well to the back. Not all of them had done as well as Sir Robert.

The huge reception at Lighterman House was, if anything, on an even grander scale than the party for Bobby's twenty-first birthday; no expense spared to obtain the finest wines and out-of-season delicacies from far-away places.

Dulcie and Mabel held their respective courts at opposite ends of the room. All the titles of the old aristocracy were up at Dulcie's end, and the wives of self-made men and the *nouveaux riches* at Mabel's. After receiving their guests, Bobby and Hélène moved through the three reception rooms, the bride gracious and resplendent in white velvet with the Ferov tiara – now, hopefully, permanently redeemed from the pawnbroker – on her head, holding down yards of borrowed Brussels lace that Dulcie had worn at her wedding to Bobby's grandfather in 1873. Blue was provided by the huge sapphire and diamond ring that was Bobby's engagement present, and to this was now added a platinum band, the rarest precious metal that could be found.

It was Rachel who first saw Nimet arriving late at the door of the grand reception room. With her was a man she judged to be her husband. Her first thought was outrage that she should have been asked and her first reaction was to leave, but dignity made her change her mind.

Melanie, also eyeing Nimet with interest, said that Bobby had invited them months ago when he was first discussing ways of avoiding a legal case.

'I must say she's kept her looks,' Melanie observed to Denton. 'I saw her when Bosco first met her again in 1911. I'll never forget the night at Quags. I've often recalled it since.'

Melanie immediately seemed to forget about Nimet, who was greeting Bobby. Although she was happy that day to see her son married at last, she had few illusions about his bride.

'Well-bred but a tramp,' she confided to her cousin Agnes Kitto who also enjoyed a gossip, which led them to Jamie, who was thought to have gone to America.

The Ferovs circulated among the numerous Russian exiles, most of whom considered that Princess Hélène should have been married in the Russian Orthodox Church. But it was *much* too small.

'They're going there for a blessing by the Patriarch,' Princess Irina assured them, so happy at last to feel that Hélène was safely married and the family fortunes secure, that she felt she could withstand any criticism. She was delighted with the day, everything had gone so well and Royalty, as promised, had turned up, too, if only to stay a short while. Prince Ferov, not the most punctual of men, had managed to arrive on time with the bride, for which everyone was thankful, but Evgenia had not troubled to dress up and her husband, feeling depressed, didn't come at all. Susan, elegant and soignée, speaking fluent Russian to the exiles, had little Alexander in tow, who as the only page had worn a replica of the uniform of the élite

Preobrajensky Guard in which his grandfather had once served.

Bobby was due to go to Russia the following year and had promised to try and find out more about Kyril, and what the chances were of getting him out. Hope for Kyril, even if it was illusory, kept Susan going emotionally. Yet, socially and intellectually, she had a very good life and was just completing the purchase of an elegant small palazzo in Venice near the Rialto bridge.

Susan had a good life and this was a good day, seeing her sister-in-law married to her half-brother. She had never lost her affection for Hélène, despite what had happened, and was relieved to have her restored to the fold. She shared with the Askhams a belief in dynastic affiliations and she thought Bobby had done well for himself, made the right choice, while Hélène could scarcely have done better.

Even one who cynically marries for gain is rather caught up on a wedding-day. It is rather special and, in retrospect, the bride was to remember very little of it; the ceremony, the reception, the presence of so many eminent guests. Her mother kept on nodding to her as though with approval. 'Well done, my daughter,' she seemed to be saying, not 'good luck, my dearest, may you be happy ever after.'

But maybe she was wrong, and her mother meant that after all.

CHAPTER 17

Joseph Stalin, the soft-spoken Georgian who was now the indisputable successor to Lenin as Leader of Russia, gazed benignly at Bobby Lighterman across the desk of his simply furnished office in the Kremlin. He was the only one of the English delegation to be received in this manner and Bobby felt duly honoured. This was his first visit to Russia since 1921 when he had brought Susan back with him, and there had been many changes. Not the least was the complete reconstruction of the Party hierarchy, brought about by Lenin's death in 1924, the subsequent fight for the leadership culminating in the expulsion from the Party of Trotsky and others who had opposed Stalin.

The name Stalin meant 'steel' and Bobby knew it was not his real name. Yet his dark face, with its high cheekbones and his curly hair, seemed to belie the formidable reputation he had acquired of one whose path it would be foolish to cross. Bobby had been one of the few Englishmen who had consistently contrived to trade with Russia, that great backward country of some 150 million people, of whom 80 per cent had been peasants, and which was now being developed into one of the great industrial nations of the world.

'It is the people that matter, Mr Lighterman, not individuals.' Stalin finished his speech, delivered in a quiet, even voice that had the quality of a lullaby. But Bobby had not missed a word of the interpretation delivered in a low voice by the man at Stalin's side. Stalin had been expounding the virtues of Soviet ideology, its achievements and triumphs, and the formulation of the *pyatiletka*, a five-year plan which would boost production of oil, coal and grain.

336

From what Bobby had been able to gather in private conversation during his week in Moscow the *pyatiletka* was sorely in need of boosting because much of the Russian population was starving. Stalin had also spoken of his regret that relations with England had not been easy, and looked forward to the speedy return of a Labour government. Bobby politely replied that that was the wish of his aunt, Lady Askham, who had visited Russia in 1921 and was a great admirer not only of the Soviet system but of Comrade Stalin himself.

All this might or might not have been true. It was many months since Bobby had discussed politics with his aunt, a subject on which at any rate they always disagreed. But he needed this support for the very delicate subject he was about to introduce which, for all he knew, might result in his immediate expulsion from the Republic. Stalin, however, was nodding agreeably, as the interpreter translated Bobby's words and made some congratulatory remarks about Lady Askham and also Mr and Mrs Webb, who were well-known Soviet sympathizers.

As Stalin seemed to indicate that the interview was about to end Bobby hurriedly went on:

'Comrade Stalin, I had the good fortune to marry a Russian lady in December and thus have acquired a renewed interest in this great country. The family of my wife are, alas, in exile but they have every intention one day of visiting, if not returning to, the Soviet Union.'

As Bobby's words were translated Stalin's brow puckered in a deep frown and, before he had even mentioned it, Bobby heard the name Ferov. His heart sank.

However, undaunted, he went on: 'My brother-in-law, Kyril Ferov, who remained an ardent Communist, was sent to Siberia when his marriage to my sister was discovered. He had disobeyed Party rules and was sentenced to ten years in a labour camp. I understand this was his only crime. My purpose today, Comrade Stalin, as well as to thank you for your hospitality, to tell you of my admiration for your wonderful country – and to assure you of my wish to continue to do business with it – is to ask if Comrade Ferov may be released and allowed to return to his wife in Paris. They have a son whom he has never seen.'

Stalin's heavy brows remained knitted together in the middle of his forehead and, still gazing at Bobby, he spoke quickly to his secretary sitting behind him.

'We will look into it.' Stalin stood up and, leaning over his desk, firmly shook hands with Bobby. 'We are grateful to you, Mr Lighterman, for your firm support of the Soviet system, when so many in your country have condemned it. I thank you also for your personal gift to me of a splendid Askham motor car. I have seen it. It is very fine. I shall treasure it.' Suddenly those formidable eyes seemed to twinkle.

'Thank you, sir.' Bobby bowed deeply as he shook hands and turned towards the door.

'Do not hurry away, Mr Lighterman,' Stalin called. 'There is much for you to see in our country and, besides, who knows, someone may be waiting to travel home with you at the end of it?' He held up his hands. 'I promise nothing.'

Bobby felt overjoyed. He had not, after all, gone too far, though he had strayed beyond his brief. He had, it is true, promised to supply the Soviets with huge and expensive pieces of machinery which they were as yet unable to pay for because of the difficult circumstances of trade between England and Russia; but it was a risk he had to take. For Susan's sake he wanted her husband restored to her again.

Kyril Ferov had spent the past years in exile in Siberia on a *sovkhoz*, a State farm. During that time he had risen to the position of *nachalnik*, or man in charge of the field workers. Kyril spent half the day in the fields and half working in the office. He had three good meals a day, slept in a warm bunk at night and was on good terms with the GPU, successors to the Cheka, who ran the camp.

It had not always been like this. The first two years of the sentence had been full of terrible hardship which included a spell on the notorious Solovetsky Islands from which many people never returned.

After his arrest he had been imprisoned and interrogated in the Lubianka prison in Moscow and the Shpalkers prison in Leningrad before being handed his sentence for consorting with the enemy and attempting to spy on the Soviet Republic. His elopement with Susan was never referred to. He had been sent to Solovetsky in the White Sea, which contained the main camp of the GPU. There had been no trial, no chance to defend himself, except verbally to an unbelieving interrogator; simply a sentence. In the end he came to believe that he had committed a crime and deserved to be punished.

Abruptly and, again, without explanation he had been taken from Solovetsky back to Leningrad and then sent to Siberia, where he had passed through a number of camps, all with their share of bugs, bed lice and inedible food, before he found himself on the Shulavsky farm which was mainly devoted to crops and pig breeding. It was an immediate improvement.

Now, after four years, it was like home and he felt, in many ways, that he had known no other. The vast Siberian wastes had a quality of timelessness that sometimes suspended the past, if it didn't block it out altogether. Many fellow detainees had lived in Siberia since the Revolution and had no wish to leave.

Kyril finished his paperwork, sat back and rolled a cigarette from the Makhorka, chopped up stems of the dried tobacco plant which smelt awful; but one got used to it as one got used to anything. Outside, the winter snows were giving way to spring, and over the flat landscape he could just see the beginnings of the cedar forest which stretched for miles towards Tomsk. In the spring the countryside was lush and green, and the narrow streams which had run through the snow-covered landscape all winter suddenly seemed to bubble and burst with a superabundant energy over the glistening rocks. In the distance he could hear the call of the capercaillies, a sure sign that spring was in the air.

Kyril had given much thought to his life in the years he had spent in exile, and his conclusion was that his attitude towards Communism had not changed so very much. If the system was unfair it had been more unfair before, and, if people suffered, some upheaval was to be expected in a revolution on this scale. He had studied and he had thought and his conclusion was that Communism represented a great leap forward for mankind. Its only weakness was in some of its adherents. He had thus accepted his fate philosophically, not blaming the great men of the Party – Lenin, Zinoviev, Trotsky (he had yet to hear of the disgrace of Trotsky) or Stalin – but the bureaucratic officials of the Cheka and the GPU with their petty ambitions and peasant-like attitudes of envy and ignorance. If the leaders knew how the lower echelons of the Party operated he was sure they would act to stop the injustices perpetrated in their names; but it would all take time. When he was eventually released he would do his best to right these wrongs, convinced that Comrade Stalin would listen. He finished rolling his cigarette, took a deep breath of stale tobacco and coughed.

The door opened and the head of his section came in, a piece of paper in his hands which he waved about like a fan as though to rid the air of the stench of tobacco. Comrade Golkov sat at the desk vacated by Kyril and studied the paper, a smile on his face.

'Now you will be able to do all those things you want to do.'

'What's that?' Kyril turned round, peering at the paper on the desk.

'Tell the Party bosses all the things you want to tell them.' Golkov made a gesture of strength with his elbow, bending it to show the muscle. 'You are to be released.'

'But I have another four years ...'

'Friends in high places, apparently.' Golkov looked at him meaningfully. 'Someone said Comrade Stalin himself. It is to be immediate. You are to proceed to Tomsk and take the train to Moscow. There is a droshky waiting for you outside.' Golkov pointed towards the window and linked his arm through Kyril's as they made their way to the bunk room. 'We shall miss you. It hasn't been so bad here, has it? Tell Comrade Stalin you were not too badly treated!'

Kyril didn't reply but quickly got together his few possessions – the spare shirt, jumper and trousers that were the only clothes he possessed other than what he had on. He put them in a paper bag and shakily wrote his name on it in large characters: Ferov. As he walked towards the waiting droshky – realizing that his gaint was a little unsteady – the horse champing at the bit in the cold air of late afternoon, a few who had heard the news gathered round to wish him well. He only had time to shake a few hands, clasp a few shoulders.

Yes, when he was in Moscow he would do what he could . . . He smiled, shrugged as the driver flicked the horse with his whip and the cart drew away – away from people who were comrades but not friends, a cabin that was not a home yet the only one he had known for years.

As they approached the shelter of the sweet-smelling cedar forest he looked back until the farm, his home, was a tiny dot on the horizon.

He knew that he would never see it again and, also, that he would miss it. For what did the future hold? It might be worse than the past.

The Hotel Bristol on the Tverskaya had not, to his knowledge, existed when Bobby had been in Moscow in 1921. Now it had been beautifully restored as a comfortable tourist hotel and he had a suite on the second floor. He had heard on his return from the Caucasus and the Crimea that Kyril would be brought to the hotel and allowed to leave with him the following day.

341

Bobby found his journey through the Socialist Federative Soviet Republic at once instructively inspiring yet also depressing. It was obvious that great inroads had been made in educating and informing the masses, but the absence of personal freedom was obvious and the rumours of large-scale famine among the people persisted. Of course, on his escorted Intourist trips to some of the great industrial sites in Russia he saw nothing of the suffering of the people; but there were many beggars in the streets of all the towns he visited, and the absence of shops, of any sense of gaiety, was monotonous.

He was anxious to be gone because his visit had not been unaccompanied by a sense of anxiety, now that his relationship to the Ferov family was known. He had actually married one of them – an enemy of the people. He never expected for a moment on his return to the Hotel Bristol to receive a courteous note that his brother-in-law would accompany him out of the country. He wrote an immediate letter of thanks to Comrade Stalin, and praised again every aspect of the Socialist Republic. As he finished there was a knock on the door and a man whom he had never met, but recognized at once, stood on the threshold, dressed in a new-looking suit, a shining leather suitcase in his hand.

'You must be Kyril.' Bobby held out his hand, which Kyril took with an expression of bewilderment. 'You don't know who I am?' Bobby drew him into the beautifully furnished room, which Kyril surveyed with even more of a sense of astonishment. 'Your brother-in-law, Susan's brother.'

Kyril seemed nonplussed by the name of Susan as though he didn't know who Bobby was talking about. He looked rapidly at Bobby and round the room again, like one of the startled Siberian hares he was so used to gazing at from his room at the farm.

'It must be a shock,' Bobby said sympathetically, handing him a glass half filled with vodka from a bottle on the sideboard. 'Did they tell you anything?'

'That I was to be released.' Kyril's English was not fluent, and he spoke slowly. Bobby guessed it was many years since he had used the language in which his father had been reared.

'You are to be allowed to visit Susan, to leave the country with me. We are leaving tomorrow. I understand you are to sleep in the hotel tonight. It's all arranged, personally, by Comrade Stalin.'

Bobby smiled encouragingly, but he felt depressed at the sight of this timorous man of medium height and gaunt appearance, who had been in a labour camp for so long, who betrayed no recognition of the name of Susan, no light of welcome in his eyes that he would be seeing her again after such a long time. He could see the resemblance to the Ferov men, but he already seemed worlds apart from their lives, particularly the life of Susan and his own wife, Hélène. Bobby sighed.

'I have a lot to tell you,' he said, pushing him towards a chair. 'Do sit down.'

Kyril sat. He suddenly thought of the long, low buildings of the farm as he had seen them on that beautiful spring evening of his departure from Siberia, and he wished, most fervently, that he was back.

Nearly four thousand miles away from the place where his cousin Bobby was rescuing the reluctant Kyril Ferov in order to transport him from a life of hardship to one of ease, Ralph Askham was also starting a new life.

It was a year since he had left home and arrived at Cape Town. After visiting family friends there and in Johannesburg he had gone to work on a farm in the Transvaal as stable lad to Jimmie Farthingale, an old family friend. Unlike all the other stable lads, however, he lived with the family, who treated him with an exaggerated respect they might not have adopted towards a young man who was not an earl.

But Ralph soon knew that this life wasn't what he wanted and, also, he was tired of the family connection. Everyone he stayed with, everyone he met, knew or was known by a member of the family. He felt he was being passed from one to the other to be looked after. Besides, cattle farming wasn't really what he had in mind by farming; he wanted to dig in the soil, to plant and to grow. He felt an intense need to work with his bare hands and smell the bood, rich soil falling through his fingers.

Altogether he stayed with Jimmie Farthingale six months and then left, with mutual expressions of goodwill on both sides. He gave Farthingale the impression he was going home, but in fact he sailed from Durban for Mombasa, arriving unknown, and knowing no one, in January 1928. He had missed his sister's wedding and Bobby's wedding, the memorial service for Aunt Flora, the reunion of Hugo with his real mother. There was plenty of news in letters from home. Never mind. At last, alone in Kenya, Ralph Askham felt he was his own man, responsible to no one, unknown by anyone, and free.

He made his way from Mombasa to Nairobi and soon he learned that the farming country was in the White Highlands, where coffee and flax, jute, wheat and maize were grown. The land there was very rich and the fertile soil used for all kinds of experimentation by the settlers to grow crops and exotic fruits: Japanese plums, October Purple and Sultan; strawberries; quinces; sub-tropical peaches, especially Angel and Peen-To; loquats, loganberries, apricots and figs. Using the family name of Down, but not his title, Ralph put it about that he was a young man looking for work. Soon he was chatting to farmers in the bar of the Norfolk and Victoria hotels, confessing his ignorance of farming matters but saying how willing he was to learn.

There was no shortage of takers for this young Englishman, six foot two inches in height, with a strong, handsome face, his straight blond hair bleached by the sun. He was the type the colonials loved and, in fact, he looked like one of them. There would be no problems about fitting in.

344

In the end, though, he went to work for a man called Lars Strindberg, a Norwegian from Lapland who had lived in Kenya since the turn of the century, and farmed twelve thousand acres of arable land on the slopes of the Aberdare mountains. Lars had an English wife called Maisie who was a brusque, hard-working woman not given to socializing in Nairobi or with the white settlers who formed a large part of the farming community. Many of them had been given land by the government as an inducement to settle, some of whom neglected it shamefully. Lars and Maisie had a son and a daughter in their twenties, both had been to school in England and both were living there now. Apart from them, the Somali servants, and the large camp of squatting Masai on the periphery of the estate who worked for Lars, Ralph was alone. It suited him perfectly.

He only had a large rucksack with him, he'd travelled light on purpose and, once the deal was made, hands shaken, he climbed into Lars's truck to be driven the thirty miles to his farm where he lived. Ralph was shown a large, clean room overlooking the foothills of the Aberdares and, not for the first time, he was able to admire the brilliant landscape of Kenya illuminated by its own peculiar quality of light.

Ralph settled down well with the Strindbergs, who were kind, taciturn people believing in those fundamental virtues of thrift and hard work. They saved, and what they saved they spent on their farm, investing in crops and fruits and new machinery for the coffee factory down by the river. Here the Masai took the fresh coffee beans to be dried out in big spinning drums before being hulled, graded and sorted into sacks for transportation to Nairobi and then to the sea.

The Strindbergs were intrigued by this young Englishman who worked hard but had little to say. They saw that, like them, he eschewed the social life; that he preferred working, riding, shooting and reading by the oil lamps at night to the fast life of the social set in Nairobi, or those who haunted the Muthaiga Club on the road to the Swahili township.

Ralph went into Nairobi once a week to collect his mail, do some shopping and have a few drinks in the bar of the Norfolk. He drove there in the Strindbergs' truck so that he could pick up any goods or bits of machinery that had been ordered and, after a meal, he drove himself back.

The pattern of his life was fairly steady by the time that summer came. He loved the country and he thought he might begin to look for a smallholding for himself which he could develop in the way the Strindbergs had developed their farm, which was called Newlands. Newlands had a low colonial structure built of brick and wood, rather like a Norwegian farmhouse. It had a thatched roof and a balcony running round it which the main bedrooms led on to. Ralph would wake at dawn when the natives woke, and he could see the smoke curling up in front of their dukas as they prepared an elementary meal before they began the day's work. This was when Kenya was seen at its best; the lower foothills of the Aberdares still clouded in the early morning mist, the air keen and sharp and shrill with the sound of exotic birds: francolins, harlequins, the helmeted guinea-fowl, tiny namaqua doves, golden orioles and the greedy Egyptian kites.

Ralph told Lars of his plan one day as they sat on the balcony at nightfall, drinking whisky before the evening meal, while inside Maisie sewed in the light of the oil lamp.

'Have you got a little money put by, then?'

'A bit.'

'Pity, I'll miss you. I was thinking of asking you to be my manager, but if you've got your own money...'

'I could manage a few acres, build on them like you have.'

'They say the Arkwright property over by Njoro is for sale. Arkwright grows wheat though, not coffee, but he's got a nice place, a good few acres of land. Might be too much for you though, the price he's asking.'

'Maybe I could squeeze the family at home,' Ralph began to look excited. 'Do you know why he's selling?'

'He wants to go home. He's tired. His wife died last year and he has no family. Wants to go back and live in Devon!' Lars, a big, plain man with a deeply pock-marked face, chuckled and rekindled his pipe. 'I think the social life there got him down. Too many parties, too much drinking. They say drink killed his wife.'

Lars looked at Ralph and rubbed the tobacco between his fingers and thumb. 'Can't emphasize too much how people kill themselves out here by the kind of life they lead. It would be very tempting for a young, good-looking fellow like you to get involved with women, the wrong sort, that kind of thing. Lonely here as a bachelor.'

Ralph smiled and sat deeper in his low cane chair, his hands behind his head.

'I'm not tempted by that kind of life at all, Lars. You should know me by now.'

'Thought I did, thought I did.' Lars finally lit his pipe and went on gazing at Ralph through the smoke. 'Wonder now if I do. You're a mysterious chap, keep yourself to yourself, which I admire, but sometimes I do wonder ...'

Ralph shifted in his chair. He had always tried to avoid personal conversation.

'I wonder if there's something you're running away from ...' As Ralph looked startled, Lars held up a hand. 'Oh, I don't mean to pry, and I'm sure it's nothing you're ashamed of, but ... life is slipping by. You need a wife.'

'Ah, is that what you're saying?' Ralph relaxed. 'Well, I have no guilty secrets, no skeletons in the cupboard, I assure you, Lars. I told you I was in the Army and didn't like the life. That's all there is to it.'

'Sorry I asked,' Lars said. 'I'll get on to Arkwright tomorrow.'

'Boss Arkwright' was a Northerner whose family had made its fortune in cotton and who had lived in Kenya since the 1890s, before the country was taken over as the East African

Protectorate by the British to prevent German expansion in East Africa. By 1899, when Nairobi was established as the capital, between the Masai and the Kikuyu tribes, Arkwright was well settled before the first settlers arrived, induced by grants of land. Not far from Arkwright was the estate of Lord Delamere who had been the leader of the settlers since 1901.

From the turn of the century Kenya had been a fashionable place in which to settle. It had its sprinkling of English peers as well as American millionaires, adventurers, drifters, idlers and fugitives from justice. Maybe it was because of the profusion of the latter that Lars had wondered about Ralph and his reasons for keeping such a low profile. When he announced that he liked Arkwright's property and was prepared to buy it Lars began to wonder even more about the young man who had walked into the Norfolk one day with a pack on his back. Maisie was aghast at the doubts about Ralph this purchase had brought into Lars's mind. In the time he had been with them she had become as fond of him as her own son.

'But, Lars, he's been with us for nearly nine months. How can you *say* you don't trust him?'

'I don't say I don't trust him!' her husband protested indignantly. 'I just say we don't *know* anything about him. Arkwright wants thousands for the house and all that land. How can a young man, with a rucksack on his back, afford that much? Besides,' he grumbled, 'what *do* we know about him? He never gets letters here, but goes to collect them. Why? He doesn't seem to want to mix with other people. I like Ralph, like him as much as you; but I'm beginning to wonder who he really is.'

By the time he'd finished even the devoted Maisie wondered, too.

In the part of the White Highlands known as Happy Valley were a number of beautiful farms and homesteads, many – some said too many – of them occupied by the fast set, who were rapidly ruining the reputation of the white settler colony.

The legend 'are you married or do you live in Kenya?' had many a matron from home gossiping about her visits to the Colony, with some justification.

Ralph was well aware of the reputation of the inhabitants of Happy Valley: the Errolls, the de Janzes, the Reptons, the Soameses and he was quite determined to avoid them as he tramped round the property with Gerald 'Boss' Arkwright. The large, well-cultivated garden was a mass of colour, carefully coordinated with the seasons: banks of bougainvillaea lined the drive and around the spacious lawns, beneath the shadow of the white colonial-style house, were blue jacaranda, hibiscus, silver-leaved dudleya, bright red geraniums, mauve and purple verbena, white philadelphus, yellow cassia, pink and red roses, figridias, echiums, pink oleanders, and red begonias. The brilliant blue ipomoea leari trees abounded, either in clumps, or surrounding the house to protect it from the scorching sun. The silver-stemmed Albizzia tree mingled with pyramid cypresses, cape chestnuts, blue gums, tall lean cedar trees, mountain bamboo and the indigenous croton or makinduri tree. The vast acres of fertile land beyond the house were devoted to wheat, flax and maize. There were apple orchards, chicken runs and, grazing in the distance, the horses which Ralph loved.

'I'd like to develop the stables,' he said enthusiastically. 'My cousin, who's helping me in this project, breeds them in Europe.'

'Oh, you've got plenty of capital behind you then?' Arkwright looked at him curiously. All negotiations had been between lawyers in Nairobi and London and even then, though certainly nothing was amiss, little was revealed about Ralph Down that no one knew already; he was a mystery, a loner, a young man with a past.

This reputation about the mysterious stranger grew as it became apparent that no one knew anything positive about him; but that he was young, attractive and apparently rich. 'Down' was such an ordinary name; there could be thousands of Downs. People began to go out of their way to stop him at the Norfolk or the Victoria and invite him to dinner; but he always politely declined, saying he was too busy, and asked them for a drink instead. He wasn't at all unfriendly. On the contrary.

By the spring of 1929 the purchase of the Arkwright place was completed. Arkwright moved out and sailed back to England and Ralph had the decorators in at the Arkwright house and prepared to say goodbye to Lars and Maisie Strindberg, who insisted on giving a dinner party for him at Newlands the night before he left.

Ralph didn't realize that the Strindbergs knew so many people as the cars drew up in the drive and the host of African servants swarmed out to open doors for them. Ralph had been in the fields all day and the party had been a surprise. The large table in the dining-room was laid for twenty places, with many more expected for dancing to the gramophone afterwards. The ladies were in dinner dresses, the men white jackets and black ties, and Ralph was only the possessor of such an outfit because he had been to a dinner at the Muthaiga Club for the Prince of Wales who had been on safari in Kenya in November. Ralph had carefully avoided meeting His Royal Highness in case he was recognized by this friend of his family's, though he had not in fact seen the heir to the throne since he was quite a small boy.

Ralph took the gesture of Lars and Maisie in good part, shaved, showered and changed into his evening clothes just as the last of the cars arrived and a crowd had gathered in the lounge, the open doors leading on to the veranda.

As soon as Ralph entered heads turned because, although much had now been heard about him, few had met him apart from those hard-working farmers who pronounced him a 'good chap'. The music from the gramophone playing a contemporary tune could hardly be heard above the babble of voices, and the white-coated native waiters circulated with trays of cocktails and gin and tonics. As soon as she saw him

Maisie took Ralph in hand, introducing him to all her guests. She had been very careful about the list, the fast set rigidly excluded, though it is doubtful if they would have come as they tended to patronize one another to the exclusion of the Colony 'bores', the serious farmers, government officials and businessmen, usually visitors from abroad.

Maisie had been sure, however, to invite some young girls, bearing in mind Lars's doubts about the wisdom of a young man living by himself on the Arkwright place. They were all nice young girls, well brought up and educated in England, and Ralph dutifully bowed and shook hands, aware of a creeping *ennui* as the evening progressed and the atmosphere resembled one of the stuffier evenings at Askham House.

Near him stood George Lee, an American who had been farming in Kenya for seven years. He and his wife Cheryl lived not far from the Arkwright house and Maisie decided to put Ralph next to the Lees so that he could get to know his neighbours, who would introduce him to other sober, hard-working farmers like George. Cheryl Lee was always known as Cherry. She was a farming girl from Wyoming, the mother of two young children, but she had been well educated and was thirty when Ralph met her at the Strindbergs'. As soon as he saw her he knew that, clearly, she was the most fascinating woman in the room, far eclipsing anyone else he had met that night, the well-spoken young women from home, the dutiful daughters of the hard-working settler community. He was more than pleased to sit next to her and at once engaged her in animated conversation that to Lars, watching him from the head of the table, seemed most unusual. He wondered to himself if they'd done the right thing by selecting the Lees as his companions at dinner.

George Lee was a slow-spoken, slow-moving cattleman from Chicago who had become bored with the life of luxury as the younger son of a meat importer. He'd met Cheryl in Wyoming where he wanted to farm; but for their honeymoon they'd gone to Kenya and had fallen in love with the place, returning home only to sell up and settle on the side of the Aberdares that overlooks the Rift Valley.

Cheryl was known to the fast set, whose numbers she would have liked to swell; but George abhorred socializing and knew that there was a reckless, slightly dangerous side to his young wife and that she should be kept safely at home away from temptation. Cheryl was petite and dark, with an oval face like a ballerina. She had deep eyes of a most startling violet colour and high Slavic cheekbones, which made Ralph think at first that she might be of Russian extraction, which was a starter for conversation.

'Russian?' Cheryl gave him an amused smile, observing in her soft, instantly appealing American accent: 'Good heavens, no! I'm a gal from Wyoming, though my family originally came from England, years back.'

'I just asked because my cousin is married to a Russian and, although you don't look a bit like her, I thought … I'm sorry,' Ralph blushed. He was so fair that the colour on his face was appealing. Suddenly, out of her boredom at the thought of another dreary evening with the farming community, Cheryl raised her eyes and looked at him with interest.

'Do go on,' she said, 'about the Russians.'

People say that when the innocent fall they fall hard, and for a man of twenty-three Ralph was extraordinarily innocent. He had never looked with any seriousness at a woman but, that evening, Cheryl Lee emanated for him everything that was desirable and sensuous about womankind and he could hardly take his eyes off her or get her out of his mind when they had gone.

By the time that Ralph had moved in and settled into the Arkwright place – which he had renamed Downside – everyone was talking about his romance with Cheryl and how unexpected it all was. Everyone, of course, except Cheryl's husband George, who continued to plough his acres and plant his crops in blissful ignorance.

Cheryl shared Ralph's passion for horses and encouraged him to develop his stables. They spent hours riding over the countryside together, as parts of their estates bordered on each other. Gradually, imperceptibly, they became more and more involved.

Cheryl was the first woman Ralph had ever slept with. He was enslaved and, after six months, he knew that he wanted to marry her. But Cheryl had other ideas. To begin with, Ralph was very young and, although this was exciting in a lover, it could be tiring in a husband. Also, although he appeared to be wealthy, one didn't know how wealthy or where his money came from. Also, truthfully, he was, she thought, just the teeniest bit dull – naughty enough to become her lover, but not really naughty like some of the well-known studs in Happy Valley. One could imagine Ralph settled, and rather a bore, like George.

Cheryl had had other affairs, not only in Kenya, but in America when she went home. She was thus a worldly woman of considerable experience when she met Ralph. But she thought he might be fun, for a while.

Ralph told her he wanted to marry her at the end of that year, just after George had had to rush home because his family fortune had practically vanished in the Wall Street crash. The lovers were able to spend not only days, but delicious nights together because Cheryl was not only alone but also considerably worried by what might happen to George. She was on edge.

'You mean you might have to go home?' Ralph, aghast, turned on his side, mesmerized, as always, by the beauty of his lover.

'We might.' She glanced at him and, groping for her case on the table by the side of the bed, lit a cigarette.

'But you know I can't lose you.' Ralph sat up, propping himself on an elbow. 'It would be the end of my life.'

'Ralphie.' Cherry lay down and drew an imaginary line

353

along his chest, the smoke from her cigarette in her other hand rising into the night air. 'You know this couldn't last, poppet.'

'But it *has* to last.' Ralph swung his legs over the bed and put on his dressing gown. 'I think I'm much more serious than you are, Cherry.'

'Maybe. You're also much younger.'

'Seven years. It's not that much.'

'It is between men and women, angel, this way round. The other way it's not so bad. George is six years older than me, but he's like a child, really.'

'But do you *love* George?'

Cheryl laughed, in that way that so fascinated Ralph.

'Well, of course, I'm *fond* of him. But love …'

'Do you love me?'

'Oh, Ralph, darling, you're being so serious tonight. Why, sweetie?' Anxiously she stroked his face.

'I have to be serious, Cherry.' Ralph sat down again and leaned across the bed, his arm over her body. 'I want to marry you.'

For a while Cheryl was silent and the cries of the night birds flitting through the trees were the only sounds to penetrate the room.

'Are you *quite* serious, Ralph?'

'*Quite* serious. I'm sure it's what I want. I wish it was what you wanted.'

'But I'm the first woman you've had an affair with! You told me that. You were a virgin!'

'It's true. You are, the first and the last.' Ralph lay on his back beside her, entwining his fingers through hers. 'My mother and father had a long passionate love affair, which continued to his death. Fidelity is in the family. Well, almost,' he added, thinking of Hugo.

Cheryl glanced at him, never having heard him speak of his family. 'Your father's dead, then?'

'He died in the War. My mother's an amazing woman. She met another man a few years ago and because we venerated the memory of my father we didn't want her to marry him. I've two brothers, two sisters, by the way. I feel bad about it now and I'm going to write to her and tell her that she should. Knowing you has changed how I feel. I also want to tell her that I want to marry you.'

Cheryl looked towards the dark corner where the portrait of Rachel stood, like a shrine. He never spoke about her, his father or his family. This mysterious side of him worried her, and she remembered the rumours that he was on the run from something, or someone. Maybe he'd escaped from an English prison, or been cashiered from the Army.

'I wonder what she'd say?'

'I'm sure she'd love you. My mother and I were always close, though I broke her heart coming away.'

'Why *did* you come?'

'Because I was in the Army and I hated it. She wanted me to be like my father, and I resented that, too. I was running away from myself, I suppose, growing up. Our family was very close. I needed to get away. I'm glad I did.' He gazed at her with the sort of veneration that, for a fraction of a second, made her feel almost humble. Was it really fair to induce such devotion? She seldom had moments of truth like this and, when she did, they soon passed.

George Lee had just returned when some new settlers to the Highlands – the Grants from Tunbridge Wells – gave a party in order to get to know their neighbours. As usual, there was dinner beforehand and George Lee and his wife had been invited, together with their neighbour Ralph Down. George had returned with a lot of worries; the prospect of financial ruin at home forcing him to face the possibility of selling up in Kenya. Cheryl was worried too, because it threatened her whole lifestyle; and Ralph was frantic in case it took her away from him, even though she had treated his offer of marriage as a joke.

'Much, *much* too young!' she kept on saying, whenever he raised the subject, playfully tapping him on some part of the body – an arm, a leg, his head – as though he were a child. 'Don't you know that women are much older than men, mentally? That's why men marry younger women. Besides,' she'd add with a sly smile, 'what do I know about *you*?'

Ralph knew a divorce would cost him a lot, especially if George was difficult. He'd spent a small fortune on the farm, and family finances worried him a bit. Yet it had been quite easy to persuade Bobby to release funds for the farm with the minimum of fuss. Bobby's only comment had been that there wasn't as much money as Ralph thought. A lot of the Askham money in America had been lost in the crash when its agent, Arped Vanderveld, in whose huge Cape Cod mansion Arthur had died, went broke. The house was now up for sale. Ralph didn't know how much Askham money there'd been in America and he didn't much care. From now on he intended to live a modest life in Kenya, and he was sure there would be plenty for that.

He kept on glancing across at Cheryl as the Grants' dinner party progressed, knowing how concerned she was about the news George had brought with him; but it never showed. Some people thought her stylish beauty was brittle and hard, but he knew better. He knew how tender and romantic she was, and he loved her.

So busy was he contemplating his beloved that he almost missed seeing the man, a complete stranger, who leaned rather rudely right across the woman beside him, saying to Ralph:

'I say, are you any relation to the Earl of Askham?'

There was a sudden pause at the round dinner-table and Ralph started, roused from his reverie.

'Why do you ask?' he managed to stammer.

'Because the Askham family name is Down. You bear a resemblance to my Army friend Bosco Askham who was killed in the War. My name is Pickles, Geoffrey Pickles, late Captain in the Middlesex Regiment in which Bosco also served. I hear you're called Ralph Down. I'm sure Bosco's young son was called Ralph. Noticed you immediately. Making enquiries about you all evening.'

Ralph swallowed, his eyes on the table. Now he knew his anonymity was gone for ever.

'I'm Bosco's son,' he said.

'Then *you're* the Earl of Askham?'

'Yes. I am.'

'Well, well, good lord! Lord Askham, *here*.' The stranger, the hated Pickles, leaned over and stretched out his hand. 'How do you do, sir? I know your dear mother, too. I was at Bosco's memorial service when you carried his VC on a purple cushion. Wouldn't recognize you now.'

A hum of excitement broke out as those who had missed this fascinating exchange were informed of its contents by those who had not.

'Well, well, who would have thought it, Lord Askham, here in Kenya,' Pickles repeated, and Ralph heard the word 'Askham', 'Askham', 'Askham' reverberate round the table.

Ralph, who had only confessed because he could not deny his beloved father, was still wrestling with the dilemma this revelation would bring when he raised his head to see Cheryl gazing searchingly at him as though she, too, were as shocked as he.

Slowly she sank back against her chair, eyes demurely cast speculatively towards the table, an expression that he, who knew her every mood, hadn't seen before. Then she raised her face to look at him and, as their eyes met, he saw that it was lit by a brilliant smile.

CHAPTER 18

'Ralph's getting married,' Rachel said, trying to sound pleased. As Em leaned over her shoulder she gave her the letter. 'She's older than he is!'

'Well, that doesn't matter, Mother.' Em started to read. 'I know you have a thing about it but most people don't.'

'I think most people do.' They were sitting at breakfast in Askham House reviewing the programme for the day when the post had arrived, including a letter from Ralph. Rachel poured herself a fresh cup of tea and buttered her already cold toast. 'She is also married, but they're getting a divorce.'

'I know, Mummy, I'm reading it.' Em turned the pages, her eyes glinting with excitement. 'It sounds terribly romantic. She has two young girls. They must be madly in love to go through all that.' Em put down the letter and clasped her hands.

'Or madly foolish.' Rachel reached for the marmalade. 'I feel rather upset about the whole thing. It sounds most unsuitable.'

'Oh, Mummy, don't be stuffy!' Em, the irrepressible, jumped up and came round to her mother's side. 'Don't you see this is a whole new chapter: Ralph married? You should be *happy* for him, not sad.'

'I'm not sad in general, of course not,' Rachel said hurriedly. 'Just sad that when Ralph came to marry it should be to a woman who had to get divorced to do it. It means they must have had ... an affair. How does her husband feel?' Rachel seemed to have difficulty in finding the right words, and Em began laughing again.

'You once told me that *you* and Daddy ...'

'I know I told you and it was foolish of me,' Rachel managed a half smile. 'I wanted to show you how much in love your

358

father and I were, and also that I did not want to marry him because he had a title. Besides, neither of us was married. That was the reason. An affair with a married woman with all the gossip, all the scandal, is not the start in life I wanted for Ralph. I had a good start in my married life, not based on the unhappiness of other people, like her husband and, i suppose, daughters. Ralph is probably wrecking their lives.'

'Mummy, you're surmising. The husband may be perfectly horrible – the children glad to get a new father – you just don't know.' Em swallowed her coffee and sat down, her eyes on *The Times*.

After leaving Oxford Emmeline had turned to journalism and, after serving an apprenticeship on two newspapers in the provinces, had come to *The Sentinel* as a reporter under the watchful eye of the editor Henry Robertson, a young man also newly appointed from a provincial paper. Rachel, as editor-in-chief, kept a watching brief on the whole paper but she was content to leave more and more to Henry in order to help him find his feet.

She realized that she and Spencer were out on a limb, away from the mainstream of the Labour Movement, and they were just about to go off to America for a working holiday when the Wall Street crash happened and they changed their plans.

The previous year Charlotte had had twin boys and was already expecting again. Rachel was worried because she didn't want her travelling the world racing circuits, as the couple had no permanent home.

She felt her brother needed her, too. Margaret had had a very difficult labour in producing their first child, a boy. Margaret had subsequently suffered from depression, which was quite a well-known post-natal phenomenon but which had not been at all expected from an apparently normal, healthy and extrovert young woman like her.

Adam seemed doomed to be unfortunate in his marriages; but if one could have predicted the outcome of his marriage to Melanie, his marriage to Margaret was a different matter.

Except for the nearly twenty years' difference in their ages, it had seemed a marriage of true minds. Yet Adam had been very affected by Flora's death. Blaming himself most of all the family, he was the one also most inclined to believe it had been deliberate. Some said that Adam had become depressed then and morose, and it had affected Margaret.

Charlotte had come home to have her next baby, so that Rachel could see a lot of her first grandchildren, playing now in the old nursery on the second floor with a newly-engaged nursemaid.

'I must go up and see Charlotte, tell her the news. Ralph may be married already.'

'I thought she had to get a divorce?'

'It's apparently nearly come through. There's never much trouble with adultery. Didn't you read what he said?'

'Ah, not properly, I'm too excited.' Em picked up the paper again and leaned forward to study it, waving to her mother as she went out of the room.

Bobby's son David was beginning to talk and, as he had been an early developer, had been walking well for over a year. He always ran to greet his father at the door of the house in Harrow which Bobby had bought for David and his mother Aileen, keeping his promise not to desert her and her child – born, by some irony, the day his father married Hélène. He paid regular visits because, despite his faults, he was a meticulous man, true to his word.

Hélène had produced a daughter in November 1928, and she also was pregnant again. The marriage, ostensibly happy, had several cracks to those in the know; and many bitter domestic quarrels behind the scenes about different things, but all traceable, again to those in the know, to their essential incompatibility.

He had also never stopped wanting Aileen and she him. But did he love her?

'I wonder if you love anyone,' Aileen said, passing him a cup of tea as David played around his feet. It was raining, and the sodden trees in the garden leaned towards the house, as if reproaching him for his misdeeds, Bobby thought. The peace that he had when he came to this house was such that it made him want to come often. No reproaches from Aileen, who had much to reproach him for. She also made a point of never criticizing Hélène, either. She was detached, amicable, loving, a perfect woman in fact. Just right for him, too. But for an accident of birth she would have made him a most suitable wife, he could see that now. Better than any princess.

Bobby had been telling Aileen of his latest quarrel with Hélène, saying how impossible his marriage was and, at the end, wondering if he had ever loved her. 'I love you,' Bobby had added, a shade bitterly.

Aileen smiled. It was the only thing to do, take it on the chin. He had no real idea what her life was like on her own, bringing up a small child. She had a good allowance and help in the house, but not a live-in maid because she didn't want one. Servants also gossiped. Her neighbours knew only that she was a widow and that David was the son of her husband who had died as a result of the War. Part true, part false. But it was a lonely life. She seldom saw her father. In many ways it was an unfulfilled life, walking the pavements and the local park first with the pram, then the pushchair, the same lonely route, nodding to a few acquaintances, the dog, Sneaker, on a lead. It was all very orderly; regular and dull.

'You say you love me because I make no demands. Well, you wanted a Russian princess and you got one.' A little barbed remark every now and then wouldn't hurt. She made very few – stifled them as soon as they came to mind.

'My sister and I made fools of ourselves with our marriages,' Bobby frowned into his teacup. 'I wish to God we had never met the Ferov family. That was fate, indeed.'

Aileen was a pretty, fresh-faced, natural-looking girl with brown eyes flecked with black. She was always neatly, conventionally dressed in a twinset and pearls, her brown hair falling over her face. Looking at Bobby, she thought that her entire life was her vicarious knowledge of his family; the Communist prince who had come to Paris, refusing to abjure his beliefs, had exercised the whole family for months. 'I can't understand how, after his experiences in the labour camp, he could *possibly* still believe in Bolshevism.' Aileen had discovered years ago that it was always wiser to agree with Bobby. This was one of the main reasons he fought so much with his wife. She never agreed with him about anything – on purpose, he said.

'Well, he does. He thinks it's necessary for world revolution and he wants to go back. He objects to Susan's money, yet he spends it as though it were a bottomless coffer. He's absolutely crazy. I wish to God now I'd left him in Russia. All those years to get him out, compromising myself with Stalin, and then he didn't want to come! He makes Susan very unhappy and yet, despite all, she loves the ungrateful blighter. I must say I can't stand him, which leads to more family rows.'

'Poor Bobby.' Aileen passed him a piece of the cake she'd made the day before. 'You make your life sound very hard, yet I don't think it is – all the time.'

'Most of the time it is – oh, something else, interesting,' Bobby bit into the cake. 'Ralph Askham is coming home. He's got himself a wife.'

'That *is* interesting.'

'What he doesn't know, though,' Bobby spoke almost with relish, 'is that if he's not very careful the Askhams are going to find themselves short of cash.'

'But I thought they were enormously wealthy?'

'They *were*. My grandfather, Sir Robert, canny old man, did his best for the Askhams, as he promised Bosco he would. But he looked after our side of the family first, as I do now. Who wouldn't? But there is an Askham Trust which has made some foolish investments – nothing to do with me, though I'm a trustee. In fact I've husbanded my uncle's company and

362

money to the best of my ability. Before he died he went out of coal and into oil, that was all right; but a substantial part of the Askham fortune was invested in America and, since the crash, there's not much of that left. Not one penny.' The crumbs fell into Bobby's lap.

'You sound almost pleased.'

'I'm not *pleased*,' Bobby protested, 'but the Askhams have always given me the pip. They can't help it, but they think they are inherently superior.'

'You're half an Askham yourself!'

'That's the superior bit, the bit that wanted to marry a princess. But the other bit, the hard-working me, is from the paternal grandfather, the grocer. And I think he would have done what I'm going to do, because he was a shrewd businessman.'

'What's that?' Aileen said, a watchful eye on David, who was playing with the laces on his father's shiny shoes.

'I'm going to offer to buy the Askham share of our joint business. I'm pretty sure he'll sell. He'll need the money.'

The Honourable Freddie, as he continued to be called, almost as a nickname, since the article in the paper during the General Strike in 1926, had never found a niche in life, unlike his twin sister whom he adored. He was, strictly speaking, a playboy and, as such, the despair of his hard-working mother. In the summer of 1930 while the family were awaiting Ralph's arrival he was twenty-two. People kindly said that there was plenty of time to develop, but in the year since they'd left Oxford – Em with a degree, Freddie without – he had done little but run through his allowance with such dexterity that he always had to come back to his mother for more. All Rachel's earlier talks did little to change Freddie, who could never be persuaded to take life seriously. His sense of responsibility remained completely undeveloped. Coming from a family with vast wealth and estates he didn't see the reason for work, and thought no more of his twin and mother, his elder brother and cousin Bobby because they did.

Freddie was a popular young man and had many friends, but his greatest friend was his cousin, Jordan Bolingbroke, who was a year younger than Freddie and had, too, an attitude to life very much like his. Jordan was a tall, extremely attractive boy – some still called him beautiful – who had always been considered old for his years. In a way, his childhood had passed him by.

He had never got on with his assumed father, Adam Bolingbroke, and thought even less of his supposed stepfather, Denton Rigby, who was an idler as Jordan wished to be. Jordan had never yet been told that his real father was Denton Rigby. When it came to the point, all those whose duty it was lacked the courage to tell him. In many ways Jordan was very like his natural father, and had inherited many of his less pleasing characteristics. There was nothing in him of the hard-working, abstemious ethics of the Bolingbrokes. In a real sense he belonged to the degenerate aristocracy of whom his mother and natural father were such shining examples.

Freddie and Jordan suited each other. They showed the same aimless, inconsequential elegance enjoyed by the English upper classes from time immemorial; but none more so than in the present frenetic age when, for many, life seemed to be lived on borrowed time and, as events were to show, frequently was.

When he was in London Jordan lived with Adam and Margaret, neither of whom enjoyed having him as their guest. Jordan was thoughtless, untidy, dissolute and, they feared, a bad influence on his brother Christopher, who took after his father and was already in practice at the Bar. They need not have worried. Christopher remained, as he always had, unsusceptible to Jordan's influence.

Christopher had recently become engaged to a nice, quiet girl with a personality like his own, who came from a middle-class family such as the Bolingbrokes. Her father was a solicitor. She had not been to university but she had travelled widely and was a good linguist. Her name was Sylvia and it was she who suggested taking Jordan Bolingbroke off his father's hands and to Germany in the autumn of 1930. Adam was only too anxious not to bar his way. Freddie, with nothing else to do, decided that it sounded like an awful lark and went, too.

That was the year that the National Socialists had captured a fifth of the German vote under their leader Adolf Hitler.

Freddie and Jordan, however, had no interest in politics. All they wanted was fun and they found plenty of that in the decadent atmosphere of Berlin in the twilight of the Weimar Republic – a last-ditch attempt to democratize itself after the War. One of the factors that had made the National Socialists so popular was their attitude to the Reparations question: they were going to refuse to pay their debts to the Allies who had conquered them, which won universal approval among a German people smarting from what it considered the outrageously unfair terms of the Treaty of Versailles which settled the 1914–18 War. In addition there were not only over five million unemployed, but vast numbers of the middle class and the disaffected intelligentsia who agreed with the extreme right-wing stand taken by Hitler.

Freddie and Jordan went along with the fervour that gripped so many people that year in Germany. In time they thought that the Nazis were a good thing too. They were doing so much for the country, making a defeated people hold up its head. They were so at home in Berlin that, on the pretence of learning German, they decided to rent an apartment and stay on there after Sylvia went back. Sylvia was not so enthusiastic about the Nazis as the boys; but then she came from the cautious, cultivated middle classes who were instinctively democratic and would have no truck with would-be dictators, which is what Hitler clearly had in mind to be.

In England Rachel was delighted that Freddie and his equally idle cousin had found something useful to do at last and was happy to increase Freddie's allowance. Even she had little real apprehension of the threat posed by Herr Hitler to the entire German nation.

By that time, anyway, Ralph and his bride of a few weeks had arrived and her mind was on other things.

Cheryl Askham was a beautiful woman, of that there was no doubt. She had looked exquisite, like a small, perfect jewel, standing beside tall, bulky Ralph on the boat. The life in Kenya had suited him and from being as lean as a giraffe his frame had filled out. She wore a coat almost down to her ankles, a plain felt hat pulled fashionably over one side of her face. All the family who were available had met them at Southampton: Charlotte, whose new baby was only a month old; Susan, who was visiting London to see her father; Adam, and Margaret who now felt well enough to come, and Em who was excited and intrigued about her new sister-in-law.

Cheryl impressed them all – for different reasons, and in different ways – immediately. Besides her beauty she was poised, sophisticated, obviously an asset to Ralph; in a way a perfect Countess of Askham. A beauty, an adornment, as Rachel had never been nor wanted to be. More in the mould of Dulcie or that legendary Phyllida, who was one of the great beauties, the great names, of the eighteen-seventies.

What was so appealing, too, was Cheryl's obvious affection for Ralph; she was a clinger, a toucher, she was always near him, but not in a way offensive to other people. Rachel soon realized that her initial reservation about a certain brittle quality in her new daughter-in-law was confined to herself. Everyone else was very taken by her indeed.

She had to be careful or else she would earn the tag of being a jealous mother-in-law, that most pathetic and despised of creatures.

But Charlotte's reaction was the most extreme, and the most enthusiastic: she found in Cheryl a fellow spirit, someone who liked parties, drinking and fast cars. For though Charlotte was a good wife and devoted mother, she hadn't lost her zest for life

– just her ambition to be a career girl. She was single-minded about her marriage, but could combine it with having a good time, too. Paolo shared her enthusiasm. In England for a brief visit he pronounced himself in love with Cheryl at first sight. Em thought she was a good sort and intelligent; she also admired the air of romantic intrigue that seemed part of the persona of her new sister-in-law, an air of mystery and apartness that managed to be beguiling and not off-putting. One wanted to get to know her better and then felt flattered by her friendship. Even Hélène, flitting between London and Paris, found her the perfect companion to take to fashion shows, with whom to spend hours in idle gossip over cocktails at the Ritz or lunch at Maxim's. Paris or London, it made no difference.

No one for a moment blamed Ralph for being so keen to marry her – except Rachel. Rachel was, and for a long time remained, the odd one out.

Ralph had been back for nearly a month when Bobby invited him to lunch at his club in St James's, an indication that something serious was afoot. For a while they talked about Kenya and the turn their lives had taken in recent years. As cousins they'd never been close. Besides being seven years Bobby's junior, there was something about Ralph that made Bobby not fully at ease in his company. He was too straightforward and uncomplicated. He was also very tall and Bobby had the small man's dislike of people who towered over him. He hated looking up to anyone.

'When do you hope to return to Kenya?' Bobby enquired after the amiable opening.

'Soon after Christmas. I wanted to see Mother and Gran and introduce Cheryl to everyone.'

'She's a beautiful girl, you're lucky.'

'She is.' Ralph glanced at him. 'I think you're lucky, too.'

Bobby, accepting the compliment with a graceful nod of his head, went on: 'Are you going to settle in Kenya for good?'

367

'I expect so.' Ralph pushed back his chair and crossed his legs, while Bobby indicated to the waiter they'd order. 'It's a wonderful country and I really love the life. I have acres and acres of wheat, maize, jute but, you know, the landscape's superb. I have never seen such life and colour, so many species of flowers. The smell of Kenya is delicious, like being surrounded by a perpetually lovely fragrance.'

Bobby, completely indifferent to the charms of the colony, looked as though he thought this a feminine remark and brusquely nodded his head, without smiling, as he ordered a light lunch of smoked salmon and beef. Ralph said he would have the same. Bobby had a cocktail but Ralph drank beer. This done, Bobby leaned over and began drawing a pattern on the white damask cloth with his fork.

'Ralph, I expect you know that more than half the Askham money vanished in the Wall Street crash?'

'That's how I got my wife,' Ralph said. 'Her husband was broke too. He wanted to go home and she didn't.'

'Well, that was one good thing, I agree.' Bobby smiled carefully. 'But I don't know if you're taking it seriously enough. The thing is that you are worth approximately half of what you were when you left England in 1927.'

'There's still plenty left, I thought?' Ralph wasn't very interested in money, except in so far as he had enough, and it pleased Cheryl to spend it. He could never conceive of there *not* being enough. He looked at his watch. He was due to meet Cheryl in Bond Street in an hour. He hated being apart from her even for a short time.

'There's plenty left, but it's going down fast. The farm was expensive and you've a lot invested out there. I hope it's worth it – these experimental schemes. You got through an awful lot of money in Kenya.' Bobby looked puzzled. 'I don't quite know how or why.'

'I had to buy out Cheryl's husband.' Ralph sounded quite cheerful. 'It was the only way I could get her. I paid off his debts out there, which were substantial, and settled a large sum on him. I also have to support her daughters, of whom their father has custody. They go to an exclusive private school in the States. Altogether it was rather an expensive business.'

'Very!' Bobby frowned. 'Ralph, I know you have never had any interest in the business and I take it you don't intend to?'

'Quite.' Ralph looked cheerfully unconcerned.

'Freddie has no head for business either.'

'Freddie hasn't a head for anything!' Ralph leaned forward confidentially. 'You know, Bobby, I always think we boys have failed our mother. The girls have done better. Anyway, Mother thinks Freddie is quite happy in Germany, and not costing too much either.'

'Your mother has no money of her own, you know.'

'Of course not, she never had.'

'All her money is Askham money, so the drain of money on Freddie, on you and the farm, Cheryl's matrimonial difficulties, goes on. You see, Ralph, let me make myself clear,' Bobby took a sip of the cool Chablis that had been served with the salmon. 'I am working bloody hard to keep this family ticking over. Your father left you individual amounts, I know, but the Askham men have never married money. The Kittos had none so Dulcie came without a dowry, and your mother had none, either. Neither have we men married money. Hélène has none, Cheryl has none. Your sister's husband, Paolo, as far as I can see, spends all he earns, and I know he gets a lot because I pay him.' Bobby looked indignant at the suggestion of a lack of frugality. 'So you see,' Bobby opened his arms as though between them lay a great chasm. 'Spending, spending, spending – all the time.'

'What about the Trust and all our investments?' Ralph began to look concerned as he divined what all this was leading to.

'The Trust was badly advised by its lawyers – Adam among them, I'm sorry to say. Still, others were fooled, too. All the American investments are practically worthless and getting less valuable all the time. Vanderveld was a millionaire several times over and now he has nothing. Had to sell the house where your uncle died, I hear. Beautiful place by the sea. Your family lost millions in America, literally millions.'

'My family lost them? Yours, too, I suppose?' Ralph leaned over the table, his interest in the good food before him gone.

'No, you, the Askhams, lost them. There was no Lighterman money in America.'

'But I thought that Sir Robert, as Father's executor, had everything tied up with you?'

'Oh, no! You don't understand a thing, do you? There was Lighterman Limited and Askham Developments. They are still separate companies. Askham Lighterman, the holding company, is quite separate. It assures minimum running costs, shared resources. Your grandfather's and father's Trust, administered by Trustees, was quite separate. My grandfather, Sir Robert, was really very good and astute – but even he couldn't see into the future.'

'Then what does Askham Developments consist of?'

Bobby twiddled with the fork. 'The newspaper, which has never made money. Askham Machine Tools, which did well, and the Askham Automobile Company. That has been helped by Paolo and his racing victories. The car has got a good image in the racing world. Askham Armaments, which did well in the War but not so well now, and a host of other companies have been hit by the slump, especially cotton in Lancashire and wool in Yorkshire. There is too much unemployment. Too many people on the dole. Hunger marches, even if exaggerated, are no good for the country. Things are very depressed indeed. On the other hand you do have assets, vast ones.' Bobby looked up cheerfully. 'Some of the prime property in London, in St James's Square, and our head office in Berkeley Square are yours as, of course, is Askham Hall, Askham Grange, Gore Hall in Yorkshire, and now the farm in Kenya which is yours outright, unmortgaged. What I am saying,' Bobby cleared his throat and poured himself more wine, 'is that you are by no means poor, but nor are you as rich as your family was in your father's time. It's a great pity that Uncle Arthur didn't live because, from what I've heard, he was a very astute businessman.'

'Even if he did put all our money in America?'

'True, that was lacking in foresight, compounded later by the Trustees.' Bobby pulled down his lower lip and played with it. 'Come on, let's go to the lounge. Now that you know the basic position, I want to make a proposition to you over coffee.'

As the two men rose and strolled out of the crowded dining-room quite a few of the eminent clubmen signalled to them as they passed.

Once ensconced in comfortable armchairs with a view over St James's Palace, Bobby ordered coffee, and brandy for himself, Ralph declining. Bobby outlined what he had in mind, emphasizing that it was not a sudden idea, but carefully thought out over a period of time. Ralph listened without interrupting him, occasionally nodding to show he under-stood. When Bobby finally had stopped Ralph looked at his watch and saw that he would be late for meeting his wife, but this was too important. He summed up.

'So, am I to understand, Bobby, that you want to buy *all* our side of the business outright and that will be the end of that?'

'Part cash and part shares in the newly constructed company. You will still be a shareholder in Askham Lighter-man but a minority one. You will no longer have any business interests except the newspaper, which I am going to offer your mother on favourable terms and, frankly, I think you will all be better off. I am family, you know. I do have your interests in mind.

'If you invest the cash wisely you will be very well off indeed. The depression isn't going to last for ever. You will still have your property, except for Berkeley Square, which I would like to include in the deal as it is our headquarters. Incidentally, I've talked about this to Adam. He was surprised, but basically wholeheartedly in favour.'

371

'I must go and meet my wife,' Ralph said, getting suddenly to his feet.

'Naturally,' Bobby smiled, rising to shake hands, scenting victory.

Ralph kept Bobby's proposal to himself, mainly because he knew what a potential storm it would create in the family, each of whom would have their own, maybe opposing, views. After all, as titular head of the family, it was up to him; his to sell. His father's inheritance was entirely his from the day he was twenty-one. The more he thought about Bobby's deal the more attractive it became. As Adam was his mother's brother, a trusted uncle and family friend, he talked to him about it and Adam convinced him that Bobby's proposal was a fair one, made with the Askham interests at heart.

'Whatever else Bobby is not, he is a first-class businessman and he is honest.'

'What do you mean, "whatever he is not"?' Ralph smiled, looking with affection at the uncle he had regarded as a second father for so many years.

'Well, he is ruthless, vain, terribly ambitious and not always popular. He has made a disastrous marriage by the sound of things, but that's not our affair.'

'Isn't three years rather short to call it disastrous?' Ralph felt rather prickly on the subject. Even though his family seemed to approve so much of Cheryl, he suspected his mother didn't. Anyone could make mistakes, even his mother.

'It was disastrous from before it started but, as I say, it isn't our affair. Bobby has a very clear vision of the future business-wise, and he is well thought of in the international community. They respect him and I do, too. You would do well, my dear boy, to sell out and live the life of ease in Kenya with that sweet little wife of yours.'

'Thank you, Uncle.' Ralph looked gratefully at him as Margaret popped her head round the door.

'More coffee?'

'My dear, do come in.' Adam rose, his arms outstretched in a welcoming gesture. 'You've never really got to know young Ralph, have you?'

As Margaret came into the room Ralph jumped up.

'I'm so sorry to hear your health hasn't been good.'

'Oh, but I'm fine now.' Margaret, blushing, sat down nervously next to Ralph, tucking her legs under her. Ralph remembered a strong, attractive, determined young woman and thought something about Margaret seemed to have shrunk. She looked ill-at-ease. He'd heard she'd been afflicted by depression, and felt slightly shocked.

'And the baby is fine, too?' he enquired.

'The baby is wonderful,' Adam replied with enthusiasm, getting to his feet to fetch a photograph down off the mantelpiece. There young Giles Bolingbroke, sitting between proud father and mother, smiled at them. 'He's in the country at the moment. At last I have been able to afford a place outside London, thanks to dear Flora ...' He seemed immediately to regret what he'd said because his eyes flew to Margaret, who gazed rather defiantly at him.

Ralph didn't remember Margaret as pretty, but certainly as an attractive woman with dark hair, brown eyes and a direct, rather pleasing, expression. He thought she looked like a shop girl, one of the newly emancipated working class – capable, independent, uncomplicated.

He felt, now, that there was something wrong in the juxtaposition of Adam and Margaret which had changed their personalities. His mother had told him that Flora's death had hit Adam particularly hard; that he had never seemed to recover from it as though daily bent down under a burden of guilt. And poor Margaret had suffered too. The competition from a dead woman was almost impossible to defeat. One merely succumbed to it; and she had.

Ralph felt a chill even when an hour or so later he said goodbye and left the house.

'Well, all that seems very satisfactory,' Adam said, closing the door. 'Ralph is a fine young man. I hope he hasn't made the same mistake about marriage as Bobby has ...'

Margaret, who had only met Cheryl once, looked sharply at him. 'Why, do you think he has?'

'Well, she's a lot older than he is and there was the scandal about her marriage. A bad beginning. Rachel is not happy about it, I know.'

'Mothers are always jealous.'

'Rachel isn't the type to be jealous. She just wanted Ralph to be happily married.'

'Something she apparently didn't want for herself.' Margaret's tone grew sharper as she preceded Adam into the drawing-room.

'What do you mean, my dear?' Adam frowned.

'She has kept poor Spencer on a string for nearly ten years.'

'I think you'd hardly call it a string. She was very conscious of her duties.'

'Then why didn't she let him go, so that he could marry someone else?'

Adam was startled by Margaret's hostility, worried by it.

'Margaret, please be reasonable. She never, as far as I know, tried to *keep* him. She told him quite clearly why she wouldn't marry him. It is his bed and he has chosen to lie on it.'

'Nonsense. Your sister has used Spencer; always there when she needed him. Spencer this, and Spencer that. She has always treated the poor man like a puppet and still does.'

'People used to say that about me.' Adam put his elbow on the mantelpiece and studied Giles's photograph. 'It all seems drearily familiar: that Melanie used me. Perhaps she did.'

'But perhaps it was that you used *her*, as Rachel uses my brother. Did you ever consider that, Adam? You've both done *very* well out of your relationships, I must say; an impoverished brother and sister without wealth of their own ...' Margaret stopped as though her own words shocked her, too.

She put her hands to her cheeks, and stared at Adam. 'I'm sorry.'

'No, you've said it,' Adam nodded sadly and slumped into a chair, his air of dejection almost overwhelming. 'Perhaps you're right if that's how it seems to you. All I can say is that we never wanted anything, in the sense of worldly possessions...'

'But you got them, didn't you, Adam? Very fortunate and very clever. You pretend they don't mean a lot to you, and yet they do. You've never earned a decent living at the Bar and hardly a penny in Parliament, yet you manage to live like your dead brother-in-law, the lord. You've easily acquired expensive habits and tastes, Adam ... thanks to Lady Flora!'

Adam put his hands over his ears, as though to block out the sound of her harsh, grating voice.

'Margaret! I don't know how you can *speak* like this! What you're saying is absolutely monstrous! Is it really what you feel? Have you been concealing it from me all these years?'

'I've been concealing nothing, Adam. Yet I've discovered much about you I didn't know. You're not as nice or as selfless as you like everyone to think. You're very *selfish*, really.

'And you're so hypocritical!' Margaret gave a shrill laugh that was so untypical that Adam decided she must be heading for a fresh nervous breakdown. 'You talk about *Bobby's* marriage and *Ralph's* marriage. Don't you see the beam in your own eye? Don't you? What about *ours*? When did you last look at that! You say Cheryl is "so much older than Ralph", but just look how *very* much older you are than me! By your standards I married an old man. And what did I get? Nothing but Flora, Flora, Flora.' Wildly Margaret gestured around. 'Everything in this house is a shrine to bloody Flora.'

'Don't speak about her like that!' Adam jumped up, eyes blazing. 'Don't you *dare* use that word again.'

'*Bloody* Flora,' Margaret shouted. 'Bloody, bloody, Flora. Bloody Flora who ruined our lives the minute we were married. She made damn sure that we wouldn't be happy when she sank beneath the murky waters of the Nile! Oh, no, Flora, you didn't drown, you made yourself immortal!'

As she rushed out of the room, face flaming, hair flying, Adam hesitated, undecided what to do about her. He could hear her running up the stairs, probably to fling herself on her bed, and the next moment her maid would come and they'd be telephoning for the doctor.

Before this happened he poured himself a large whisky, slumping again into the chair. It was true he felt guilty, but *doubly* guilty, not only on account of Flora, but Margaret as well.

He had married her out of a sense of duty as much as out of concupiscence, of lust. Having gone to bed with an unmarried woman he felt he had dishonoured her, and only marriage could put that right. He simply couldn't overcome the instincts of a lifetime. Flora knew how he had dissembled, what he was doing to himself, and her. He leaned his head against the chair as, slowly, the tears began to roll down his cheeks.

'Oh, Flora,' he said aloud. 'Flora, Flora, Flora, where are you now?'

CHAPTER 19

'All this furniture should be thrown out,' Cheryl announced, the smoke from her cigarette seeming a danger signal as she moved her arm about as though jettisoning this antique and that, this Chippendale chair or Louis Quinze escritoire. 'If I had my way it would.'

Rachel, startled, paused as she was about to open the door to lead Cheryl into her sitting-room. Her daughter-in-law had expressed a desire to take a detailed look at the house, for what reason Rachel didn't know as they were supposed to be going back to Kenya in a month's time. Maybe she wanted to imprint it on her memory. The pace of the social life they led in London meant that Cheryl and Ralph had seen very little of Askham House, besides their bedroom, and then that not until the small hours of the morning.

Rachel turned the handle of the door and looked back at Cheryl, who was running her hand along the polished rosewood of the Hepplewhite sideboard. Watching her, Rachel remembered that day in 1912 when Dulcie had so reluctantly handed the house over to her, recalling the days of Phyllida who had brought so many of the beautiful things into the house.

'Of course, the house *is* Ralph's.'

'Yes, but you live here, don't you? I could hardly start throwing all this junk out and filling it with new pieces. Don't you ever feel you want a change?'

'It isn't actually junk,' Rachel tried hard to keep her voice even. After all, this was Ralph's wife, whether she liked it or not. 'It's extremely valuable antique furniture, mostly bought by Ralph's great-grandmother who was a connoisseur.'

'That sort of thing's all right if you like it,' Cheryl smiled in the gracious, charming way she seemed to be able to manufacture with such ease. 'I hate it, personally. Thank God we'll have nothing like that in Kenya ... that is *if* we go back to Kenya.'

'*If?*' Rachel removed her hand from the door handle. 'You mean you might not return?'

'You don't sound too delighted, Lady Askham.' Cheryl and Rachel, awkward with each other, had not yet established the kind of bond that permitted intimacy, the use of a term of endearment like 'mother'. Rachel wondered if they ever would.

'I'd be delighted if you stayed here. I miss Ralph. This is his home and he can have it any time he wants. It's his inheritance.'

'Well, that's nice to know, anyway,' Cheryl sounded chatty. 'I guess we haven't made up our minds.'

'I thought Ralph's was very made up. He is even buying machinery to modernize the farm.'

'Well, he has *me* to consider now.' Cheryl looked speculatively out of the window. 'Did you say there was coffee somewhere? I have an appointment at the dressmaker.'

The thought that her son and daughter-in-law didn't see eye to eye about the future haunted Rachel all over Christmas which, as usual, was a traditional affair at Askham Hall where Dulcie, now seventy-eight, happily presided over the large house party for the family in honour of Ralph. In many ways it was a lovely occasion with frosty mornings and roaring fires giving it the atmosphere that the true celebration of Christmas requires.

The Ferovs came over from Paris except Susan, who had taken a reluctant Kyril to Venice to keep him apart from the rest of the family because of the intense friction that the presence of their long-lost son seemed to inspire.

Hélène and Bobby, who were there with their two daughters, were always very good in public, managing to keep their natural antipathy hidden from the rest of the family. Paolo and Charlotte were there with their three children, talking excitedly about a house they had just bought outside Paris, an old water mill they were turning into the family home.

Rachel had never seen Charlotte so relaxed and happy and thought that, in all the family alliances and misalliances so far formed, hers was, so far, the most successful. Paolo was a mature man, a caring father and husband and his promise to give up motor racing, though distressing Bobby, pleased the family, because of Charlotte's concern about the danger of the sport.

Freddie was in Germany but Em had come over with a young German newspaperman, Peter Klein, who was to work for six months for *The Sentinel*, improving his English. Peter was invited for Christmas at the Hall, though Rachel suspected his relationship with her daughter was strictly professional rather than romantic. She so longed for Em to have an emotional engagement which, as far as she knew, she had never had. But she and Peter, a serious young Jew worried by the emergence of the National Socialist movement, spent hours engaged in earnest discussions rather than amorous dalliance.

Melanie and Denton had travelled up from Cannes to be introduced to Cheryl, who immediately numbered her husband's aunt and uncle among her admirers. Cheryl and Melanie had much in common, Rachel thought, observing them one day; a certain superficiality that would always ensure them a place in the sun.

Adam and Margaret were supposed to come, but didn't because Margaret's depression had returned and she wanted to be with her son alone in their country house. Christopher was there with his wife Sylvia, who was expecting her first child, and Constance Kitto, who had been a suffragette with Rachel before the War and had just returned from China with dark tales of the threat posed by the Communists.

The number who sat down to traditional Christmas lunch filled the great round dining-table and that year, 1930, listening to the talk and watching the animated faces gathering about her, Rachel, for no particular reason, recalled Christmas 1914 and how she had had a premonition that it would be Bosco's last.

Rachel felt a little sad this Christmas, though she should have felt happy with Ralph at home, the first time for over three years. But Hugo was away, the first Christmas he'd missed at the Hall for sixteen years. He'd gone with Nimet and her husband to spend the holiday in their Swiss home. Spencer, too, was absent, in the North visiting his mother who was ill.

Dulcie seemed aware of her sadness and, from the top of the table, smiled at her benignly. Then, as the turkey was brought in above the heads of two footmen, she firmly banged her stick on the floor and, with difficulty, got to her feet, lifting her glass towards her grandson, head of the family, at the other end.

'My dears,' Dulcie said in a strong voice, 'I wanted to tell you how happy I am to have you all here together in my house for this festive occasion – the first year for many that we have been so united. To Ralph, the head of our family, and his lovely young wife, I raise my glass in loving welcome and blessing for their future happiness and that of their children.'

'Happiness and blessing ...' the company rose and, as Ralph delightedly reached over for the hand of his wife, they raised their glasses and drank. The lights reflected on the deep red wine, as they had so many years before and, suddenly, Rachel felt a tremor of apprehension recalling a similar sight when Bosco had drained his glass that last Christmas.

It was nice to be a matriarch and yet she wasn't really one, Rachel thought, as seats were resumed, the butler started to carve the turkey after putting it in front of Ralph for his inspection, and footmen took the plates round to the assembled guests. The matriarch was still Dulcie, the true head of the family. Now there was yet a third Lady Askham, Cheryl, and she had her sights firmly set on the top.

380

No, she, Rachel, would never be the matriarch Dulcie was. She felt that, somehow, the mantle would be transferred in time from Dulcie to Ralph's wife, but how soon that would be she didn't know.

It was then that she heard someone mention Omdurman. Bobby was recounting the exploits of the 21st Lancers, where his father had been killed and Ralph, listening with deep attention, kept on interrupting him to correct a point.

'I see you've made a great study of it,' Rachel said in a pause. 'I'm quite surprised. Why?'

'It's part of our heritage, Aunt, part of the family history.' Bobby looked at Hélène whose eyes, glazed with boredom, were staring straight ahead. 'We all have our heritages, haven't we, darling?'

'Indeed, *our* heritage is a fine one, too,' Alexei Ferov leaned forward. 'We always had senior members of the family in the Emperor's personal guard.'

'Fighting and dying.' Hélène turned her gaze towards her father. 'It all seems so pointless. I can never understand why Bobby goes on and on about Omdurman, as though it were yesterday instead of thirty years ago.'

'Thirty-two,' Rachel said quietly. 'I *do* remember it as though it were yesterday, and I vividly remember Bobby's father ...'

'Oh, darling, poor Harry. *Must* you?' Melanie produced a lace-edged handkerchief and shook it. Rachel was more astonished that, after thirty-two years, Melaine could still squeeze a tear for Harry, whom she had been unable to weep for when news of his death reached her.

'Family history *is* a very important part of the family.' Paolo spoke in his pleasant, deeply accented, voice. 'My family claims Italian patriots too: Garibaldi, as well as the composer Verdi. I feel it is necessary to have heroes to give a family identity, as nations are nurtured by the blood shed in wars.'

'I think that's rather ghoulish,' Charlotte shivered, rubbing her bare arms. 'Did you have anyone in the American War of Independence, Cheryl?'

'Oh, no, my family were nothing but farmers,' Cheryl replied matter-of-factly. 'Ralph knew when he married me that he could get no lower.'

'You mustn't deprecate yourself, Cheryl dear,' Dulcie said kindly. She had taken to her new granddaughter-in-law because she recognized a fellow spirit, born of rebellion and a sense of independence. 'The Askhams have *never* married for wealth or prestige but for love. I hadn't a penny, I can assure you, the Kittos being undoubtedly noble but impecunious. But love is the best basis for marriage, as Rachel will tell you.' She looked sweetly at Rachel who, trying to detect some note of sarcasm in her mother-in-law's voice, failed. It seemed that, in her old age, Dulcie really had forgiven her for marrying her son.

'That's absolutely true, Mother,' she said warmly.

'But some people *do* marry Askhams for other things.' Melanie put away her handkerchief and her tone of voice was waspish. 'Like money.' She glanced at Denton who always found Irina Ferov good company, and had spent the whole of dinner gossiping with her in a low voice.

Denton, aware of her gaze but not hearing her words, said: 'Beg pardon, dear?' but went on chatting just the same. Melanie said it didn't matter, she was only joking, while Bobby shot her an angry glance and Cheryl tried to hide a smile.

Ralph, sitting next to Hélène, was telling her about Kenya, a subject on which it was always difficult to stop him once he'd begun.

'I *do* envy you,' Hélène said. 'I like France, but Kenya sounds marvellous, like the Caucasus.'

'You must come and visit us,' Ralph replied enthusiastically. 'Bobby is going to come out in the spring. You must come with him.'

'Really?' Hélène looked sharply at Bobby. 'You didn't say anything.'

'It's not fixed yet, darling. Ralph and I have some business to complete.'

'What business?' Rachel looked up but Ralph avoided her eyes, saying, 'I'll tell you later, Mother.'

'You must go to Kenya even if we're not there,' Cheryl said with her shy, delightful smile. 'You can stay at our house. The servants will always look after you.'

'But we'll be there by Easter, darling!' Ralph expostulated.

'Will we?' Cheryl, looking vague, picked delicately at her food, being very conscious of her figure. 'Somehow I thought we might stay on.'

Walking briskly round the lake after lunch, hands tucked in each other's pockets, Charlotte said:

'I don't think Ralph and Cheryl see eye to eye about going back to Kenya.'

'Well, it's a big thing to disagree about,' Paolo replied. 'She doesn't look like the farming type to me.'

'But she's a farmer's daughter, yet she loves London and Paris. She adores that. Do you think she married Ralph for his money?'

'Do you?' Paolo looked at her and kissed her cheek.

'I think she has her eye on the main chance and that it happened to be Ralph. But I like her.'

'Your mother's dislike is quite obvious. It's a bit unfortunate.'

'It *is* a bit too obvious, isn't it? She adores Ralph so, and doesn't think Cherry is right for him. I do. I think she gives him glamour and poise. He was a bit youthful before.'

'He's very youthful now, compared to me. I'm an old man.'

'Yes, and you're too old to race.' Charlotte squeezed his arm tightly in hers. 'I wish you'd talk to Bobby about managing the motor company.'

As Paolo and Charlotte had furnished their house in Chantilly, laying out the garden on either side of the stream that flowed past the old water mill, they had thought how lucky they were to have it and each other, and how nice it would be to spend more time together with the children. Paolo had been racing since he was nineteen. He and Charlotte had agreed that this season would be his last.

Paolo squinted through the skeletal trees towards the lake where a solitary procession of dignified swans glided towards their nest at the end. A fire, lit from leaves by the gardeners that morning, even though it was Christmas Day, still smouldered, sending spirals of smoke towards the bare boughs, filling the air with that nostalgic pungent smell of winter. Paolo breathed in deeply, feeling very happy.

'I wonder what Bobby meant about going to see Ralph on business?'

'Must be something about the farm.'

'I heard he was selling all the Askham holdings to Bobby.'

'Who told you that?'

'A broker I know in the City.'

'But Ralph would have told us!'

'Not necessarily. He doesn't have to.'

'At *least* have consulted us.'

'Why should he? It's his.'

'I hate primogeniture,' Charlotte said, yawning. 'It's so unfair. That lunch has made me sleepy.'

'Let's go and rest then.' Paolo's eyes lit up at the suggestion and they raced up the hill towards the house.

'I didn't think it was your business,' Ralph said in the tone of voice his mother was unaccustomed to. Ralph had never been rude; firm, but not rude.

'Of course it's my business. It's my paper and I have shares in the firm, left me by your father. I'm shocked.'

'Yes, but I have control. Look, Mother, I wanted to spare you.'

'Spare me what, though?' Rachel now felt very angry indeed.

'You know all the fuss, the endless arguments. We have a very good deal. Uncle Adam says so.'

'I think my brother might have told me. I feel very put out. This is the twentieth century, you know, not the eighteenth. Women do have the right, in matters concerning them, to be consulted.'

'Mother's right,' Charlotte put in her oar. 'We should have been consulted. We are all involved. Even Paolo thinks Bobby has no right to behave the way he did.'

Bobby, sitting at the back, had anticipated a family brawl and said little during the stormy meeting Rachel had requested with her son after breakfast. Em had said she found business boring and had taken Peter for a long walk in the wintry sunshine.

'Anyway, it's too late,' he said. 'It's all signed and sealed.'

'You mean we can do *nothing*?'

'Nothing. It was all completed two days before Christmas at our lawyers' in the City. Adam was there, too.'

'I find it *quite* monstrous.'

'But, Mother, the paper is yours, and for a very good price. I thought you would be pleased and congratulate me on my good sense.'

'Good sense nothing! You have been swindled.' Rachel glared at Bobby.

'I object to that, Aunt Rachel. I did it in the very best interests of everyone, Mother too.' Bobby glanced at Melanie who, taking no part in the proceedings, had sat gazing out of the window.

'How I love this country in the winter. It reminds me ...' She smiled and her voice trailed away. 'Oh, there I go, nostalgia again, but it does remind me of when Bosco was so ill and you and Adam, Rachel ... That was when Bobby was born.' Melanie looked at her eldest son almost with surprise. 'How vividly now it all comes back, and Mother so angry that you and Bosco spent so much time alone together. But Flora ... poor Flora.'

'Mother, we *are* talking business,' Bobby said patiently. 'Nostalgia is all very well ...'

'Darling, Christmas *is* a time for nostalgia, not business. There's Denton on the roan and who's that with him?' Melanie squinted through the window. 'I didn't know the Princess rode.'

'Which Princess?' Bobby got up and hurried over to stand next to his mother.

'Irina, darling. I don't call Hélène "the Princess". I know she rides very well. Do you know I think Denton rather fancies Irina. She's rather superb, isn't she? They get on very well ... I must ask her to Cannes more often.'

'Aunt, you *are* an intriguer.' Ralph started to laugh.

'It keeps him off my hands and out of the casinos while I play bridge and entertain my friends.' Melanie smiled mischievously at Bobby and touched his cheek.

'You are really frightfully clever, darling, and I'm proud of you, little baby born here nearly thirty-one years ago. Rachel was such a beautiful girl, still is though she'd deny it, and Bosco ...' she pressed her hands together almost in an attitude of prayer ... 'I wish I could tell you how handsome he was and remained to the end. They were a wonderful couple. It was too cruel it had to end.'

Ralph was watching his mother, whose face underwent a number of changes as Melanie spoke as though she, too, were recalling those long-lost days. Suddenly he realized that his aunt was skilfully trying to defuse the situation and slid his hand into his mother's.

'Still *is* beautiful. Mother, we *have* done what we've done for the best. I didn't mean to deceive you. I honestly thought that you wouldn't much mind, be very interested. We have lost a lot of money and the offer Bobby has made is more than generous. Bobby *is* family, after all, he wouldn't do us down. Our independent lawyers, as well as Uncle Adam, agree on that and we still have a percentage in the combined business.'

'It's a *fait accompli*, I suppose,' Charlotte shrugged her shoulders. 'I thought you should know how we felt, Ralph, and I hope that one day you won't regret it.'

When finally the meeting broke up, still in some discord, and they all went their various ways, Charlotte asked if she and Paolo could talk to Bobby. When they opened the door they saw Paolo hovering in the hall outside, his arms crossed, admiring the family portraits gracing the walls.

'Come in, come in,' Bobby said genially, closing the door after Paolo and telling him to sit down. He still regarded him as an employee rather than a cousin by marriage and was gracious with him rather than familiar.

'I want Paolo to give up motor racing, Bobby.' Charlotte came straight to the point. 'He says next season, but I say this. You know that he just missed killing himself at Le Mans.'

'Yes,' Bobby frowned. 'That was nearly terrible publicity for us.'

'But it nearly killed Paolo, that's the important thing!' Charlotte said indignantly, and Paolo put his arm tightly round her waist.

'He *is* thinking of the image rather than me. It's understandable.'

'But it wasn't your fault.'

'It was a bad mistake for Marcellini, but nearly fatal for me. If we had turned over it could have been disastrous for us both – me, and the reputation of the car.'

'Everyone knows it wasn't your fault,' Bobby intervened. 'The Bugatti overtook too quickly. But I'm sorry you mean to give up, Paolo. You will be irreplaceable. Your prestige alone is worth a lot to me.'

'There are younger men coming up. Franco Roma is one of them ...'

'I wouldn't mind signing Roma to replace you eventually, but not now. Not for a year or two.'

'Oh, please, Bobby! We love our house and our little family. We want to be together all the time. It's that ... Paolo did get wind of what was happening with Ralph and wondered if he could manage the Askham car company, develop the racing side.'

'Oh *that's* how the family heard, is it? Through you? I wondered.' Bobby, who didn't like mysteries, looked momentarily relieved, then a rather ugly expression came into his face that his business competitors knew only too well. 'I can't release you, Paolo. You have a contract and you must keep to its terms.'

'That's spite,' Charlotte said heatedly. 'Just because ...'

'It has nothing to do with what you just told me. The family had to know some time, anyway. I'm only glad that it was all signed and sealed days ago. Because the fuss this morning is spoiling my Christmas, incidentally, which I hoped to spend peacefully in the bosom of my family.'

'Then *why* are you going to Kenya?'

'I said I'd put some money into breeding horses out there if I liked what I saw. But, if you ask me, and Cheryl gets her way, Ralph won't be going back. He'll be staying here.'

'What makes you say that?'

'Cheryl makes me say that. I saw her roving around the house this morning making a very careful inspection of everything, taking notes. And when I asked her what she was doing she smiled in the beautiful way she has – rather like a cat – and said she was making a list of all the pieces she wanted to chuck out. Most of it is old rubbish, according to her. I must say I had to laugh quietly to myself, but of course I said nothing. Maybe they never heard of Chippendale in Wyoming.'

Little David greeted his father at the edge of the wood and held up his face for a kiss. Aileen stood shyly to one side, as though reluctant to intrude on this precious moment between father and son. Aileen was spending Christmas with her own father, and this meeting in the wood had been hurriedly arranged by a note sent round to the house. The sight of David always filled

Bobby with deep joy. He truly loved him and he raised him in his arms, holding him close to his cheek, his face pressed to his.

'Sorry,' he said to Aileen, arms still round David. He leaned across and kissed her, savouring, as he always did, the wholesome smell of this undemanding woman who had been his mistress for so long, the mother of his only son. Hélène always had a marvellous fragrance of some very expensive French perfume, but Aileen smelt of fresh air and soap, a good English smell that went with her natural complexion. 'Sorry this had to be hastily arranged, but I missed you. You and David.'

David, who was an alert, inquisitive boy of three, looked round with interest, then up at the big house from which Bobby had come.

'House,' David said. 'Up there. Daddy's house?'

'No, it's not Daddy's house,' Bobby said with a sad smile. 'It belongs to friends of Daddy's.'

'And Davy's,' David insisted. 'Davy, too.'

'Friends of Daddy's and Davy's, of course, that goes without saying.' Bobby lowered David reluctantly to the ground holding tightly on to his small hand. The other arm he put round Aileen's shoulders.

'All right?'

'All right.' Momentarily she leaned her head against the warmth of his cashmere coat. 'Missed you.'

'I missed you, too; but I have had an awful lot of business lately. I am taking over the Askham half of the business as I said I would.'

'Lord Askham agreed?' Lively and interested, she looked at him.

'He did. I wanted to do it quickly before the family started to object, as I knew they would.'

'Lord Askham didn't tell them?'

'I made it a condition of acceptance that it had to be done quickly. Any queries or delays from the family and I'd forget it. As he is anxious to be gone back to Kenya before his wife

389

gets too happy here he was ready to do a deal. Yesterday, though, we had a frightful row with the rest of the family, particularly my Aunt Rachel, and now no one is talking to anyone else. I shall be glad to go back tomorrow. It will all blow over once Ralph returns.'

'But *why* did you want to do it so quickly?' She linked her arm through his, delighted when he wanted to discuss family or business matters with her. It made her feel important.

'Because I got a very good price,' Bobby said tersely. 'I bought it for about a third of what it was worth.'

'Isn't that dishonest?'

'Aileen.' Bobby looked affronted and moved his arm from hers. 'It's good business. I'm in this to make money, not to be a philanthropist.'

'But it's family, isn't it? I'm surprised Lord Askham didn't make enquiries.'

'He did. But not from businessmen, from his uncle, who knows as little about it as he does. Adam is a lawyer, a politician *manqué*, not a businessman.'

'But he's chairman of your company.'

'In name only. It looks good to have a King's Counsel as titular head. It gives us prestige and if, one day, he is knighted or ennobled in some way it will look even better. A KC and a prince on the letterhead never did any business any harm, especially if it has my brains behind it.'

'You're a great one for show, aren't you, Bobby? Marrying a princess who doesn't make you happy is all part of the show.'

'We're very critical today, aren't we, Aileen?' he said crossly. 'Feeling discontented, are we? Marriage to Hélène, on the contrary, *does* make me happy. It achieves what I intended; to have a beautiful and aristocratic wife who is seen in all the best places disporting her wealth, a sign of my money, as everyone knows she isn't rich on her own account. I have two pretty daughters who are delightful, or will be when they get older, and if I have a son I can leave her alone and we can get on with our separate lives.'

'You have a son.' Sadly Aileen looked at David wandering along by his father, kicking the damp leaves on the ground.

'Yes, but you know ... a son who can inherit. I shall always see that David is very well provided for, never fear, but I need a legitimate heir, Aileen. That's all that Hélène has to do now.'

'It sounds like the life of some medieval monarch.'

'It's not so very different. Dynasties are just as important today among people of wealth and possessions as ever they were. I know this must seem hurtful to you, dear, but you knew what you were doing when you started this affair.'

'Yes, I knew.'

Aileen also knew that wealth and ambition had made Bobby not exactly ruthless, but very hard. He got what he wanted, whatever the cost, and he seemed to enjoy doing it. She saw that Hélène fitted into the apparently more intimate institution of marriage because he saw her not as someone to love and cherish but as an asset. Strictly business.

'I must go back now,' Bobby said when he had walked them up the path back the way they had come through Askham woods.

'When shall I see you again?'

'Soon.'

Bobby always said 'soon'; but 'soon' meant any time from a few days to weeks and weeks. Her money came regularly, but not his love. She had no rights such as Hélène, surrounded by nannies and servants. The lives they led were very different.

Now they stood on the brow of the hill and quite clearly they could see the house opposite them, the late afternoon sun casting a deep yellow glow on its white walls. Bobby picked up David again and hugged him.

With a wave of his hand he went back down the hill without even saying goodbye.

Opposite, in the house Hélène, looking out of the window towards the lake, saw the couple with the small child standing between them. Then she saw the man run down the hill and around the lake and walk quickly up the path on the other side.

Thoughtfully she turned away from the window and lit a cigarette.

Cheryl was terribly bored with the country, the house party, being nice to Ralph's numerous relations, the lack of excitement, the smallness of it all – even though Askham Hall was one of the glories of the heritage of the English country house and her husband owned it; even though the guests had included one of the richest men in England, Bobby Lighterman, and more titled people than she had ever met in one place in her life, always excepting the Muthaiga Club on gala night.

Above all she was bored by the frequent attentions of her uxorious young husband. He also kept on talking about children which didn't please her at all; the last thing she wanted was to be encumbered by another baby, even if it might be a future Earl of Askham.

On the second day of January 1931 Cheryl lay next to the sleeping body of her spouse, and gazed out of the window at the seemingly endless stretch of the white English wintry sky.

Ralph stirred and she quickly got out of bed, put on her silk dressing gown and, lighting a cigarette, rang for her maid to draw her bath. Kenya had made Cheryl quite used to servants and this aura of luxury, though initially strange to the democratically-reared daughter of a farmer from Wyoming, seemed by now perfectly natural to her. Later, as she lay in the bath soaping herself the door opened and Ralph, attired in a dressing gown, came in and sat on the edge of the bath, gazing at her.

'You're a bit *rude*,' Cheryl said, attempting to cover herself with a cloth.

'You're my wife.'

'Still, I do have rights, like the right to privacy when I'm taking a bath.'

Ralph looked taken aback, as though not sure whether she was serious or not. His tone had been bantering, but hers wasn't.

'I'm sorry. I'll go out again, knock and come back.' Half smiling he got up and she said:

'Don't be silly! What is it you want?'

'Merely to look at you, I told you. I'm still excited by your body, even in the bath.'

Cheryl felt ill at ease, irritated, and swiftly turned her face to the wall, her back to him. Moments later she heard the door close behind him again.

She dressed in her dressing-room, with her usual care, choosing a lambswool dress in pale mauve that had been modelled for her by Captain Molyneux in the autumn. It was cold in the huge house, despite the presence of central heating and large fires, and she took a cardigan to carry over her arm. As she finished dressing there was a tap on the door and Ralph said:

'Am I allowed to come in?' Then he poked his head round the door, smiling. 'I know you have your rights.'

'I wish you wouldn't be so childish,' Cheryl said sharply, fastening her pearls round her neck, adjusting the gold bracelet on her wrist. Then she dabbed powder on her nose again, subjected herself to a critical inspection, rubbing her lips together before blotting them with a tissue.

'What's the matter with you this morning?' Ralph, dressed in jodhpurs, yellow polo-neck sweater and a hacking jacket, sat on a stool next to her, gazing lovingly at her. 'You're very cross, darling.' He reached out a hand towards her and she stepped back with a muttered exclamation about her make-up.

'I'm not cross, Ralph, I'm just a bit bored.' Cheryl shook her bangle and looked at it critically before glancing sharply at him. 'When are we going to leave here?'

'But we've only just arrived.' He looked surprised. 'I love the place. Don't you?'

'Ralph, we've been here over a week. We've had Christmas, we've had New Year. Bobby and his family have gone, his mother and stepfather leave today, Charlotte and Paolo have

393

gone. The Prince has gone. There's just us, Em, your mother and Princess Irina, who seems to live here.'

'She's my grandmother's companion, in a manner of speaking. This is my home, yours too. I thought we could stay here until it was time to go back.'

'Go back. Where?'

'Kenya, of course.' Ralph looked at her in surprise, got up, crossed the room and leaned against the window, looking out. 'I love this place *next* to Downside. I never thought I'd love anywhere else more, but I do. I want to get back to our farm, the horses, the garden. In fact, I will go up to town, if you like, in the next day or two because I want to order some new lightweight suits. But otherwise I thought we could stay here until it was time to sail.'

'*I* think otherwise.' Cheryl opened the case on her dressing-table and rummaged for a fresh cigarette which she lit with a heavy onyx lighter. Blowing away the smoke, the cigarette remained in her mouth, tilted at an angle.

'But I thought you liked Askham?'

'I love it, darling, but not for ever! And another thing, Ralph, I'm not so keen on Kenya. Have you ever thought that it really is your duty to stay in England and look after your estates here? We could go to Kenya maybe every other year or so, just for a holiday. We could do the most wonderful things with Askham House, at least I could. And darling,' she jumped up, her tone warm, her face animated, 'I *would* like to do it over completely with Neil Asherson, that smart interior decorator. I already let him have a little peep at it and he has the most marvellous schemes. He's working on them now. As for this mausoleum, in a year or so Neil could have the whole thing transformed into a most beautiful, modern country house. You see ...' She touched his arm but Ralph moved away. Seeing his face, she decided to change her tactics. 'In time ... not all at once ... darling?' The wheedling, little girl tone was one she usually adopted with success but not this time. Ralph looked angry.

394

'Am I hearing right, Cheryl?' He only called her by her proper name when he was upset, otherwise it was always 'Cherry', more usually 'darling'. 'This is my grandmother's home and will be until she dies. My mother has Askham House for as long as she wants it.'

'Then where are *we* to live?'

'In Downside, in Kenya.'

'But I've told you how I feel.'

'And I've told you how *I* feel.'

'Oh, Ralphie, don't be so cross.' Cheryl went up to him, cigarette still smoking between her fingers, making little mewing sounds. 'You know I love England, and being so close to Paris. Remember I'm just a poor little American girl from Wyoming to whom the great big city is so exciting. I'm absolutely entranced by Paris and London and the chance to travel to Rome, Spain, Austria, winter sports in Switzerland. Darling it's like a dream, paradise . . .' she flung her arms round his neck, trying to kiss him, but for once he held his face back.

'I'm going back to Kenya, Cheryl. That is my home. I have sold my family share of the business so that I can invest more in the farm. I want to have the greatest stud in Kenya, in the world. I've left England for good. That is my life and you knew it when you married me.'

'I did not.' Cheryl withdrew her arms and petulantly stubbed out her cigarette. 'You *never* said you wanted to make a *life* in Kenya. Good God! I assumed that one day you would want to go back to your own country and reclaim your birthright.'

'Yes, but not now, not with my grandmother alive and living in this house, and my mother having every right to St James's Square.'

'Darling, they'd hardly be homeless. Isn't the Grange big enough for both of them? And we could find your mother some little house in Mayfair.'

'My mother doesn't want "some little house in Mayfair" thank you. Askham House is our family home. We all share it.'

'Well, I don't want to live with her, or your grandmother. I might as well make that clear. Your mother doesn't particularly like me, and the feeling's mutual.'

'That's not fair.'

'It's true, though. Anyway, I don't want to live with her.'

'You won't have to!' Ralph shouted, 'because we're not going to be here.'

'That's what *you* think!' Cheryl grabbed her handbag and swept out of the room.

No one had heard the row between Ralph and Cheryl, but its effects were very apparent to all who remained at the house. Even the servants noticed the coolness between their master and his bride. Cheryl had a way with servants and they all loved her. She managed to combine firmness and dignity with a friendliness that was not patronizing, as Dulcie's was, or a bit too familiar like Rachel, the Radical who believed that all people were equal. Cheryl's attitude was just right.

The day after the row Ralph announced they were going up to London and Em asked for a lift, Peter having gone back before New Year. Em was surprised to see all the cases that went into the boot of the Askham.

'I thought you were staying here until the end of the month?' she enquired, as a footman tucked a rug around her in the back seat, while Dulcie and Rachel watched from the steps.

'We're undecided about our plans.' Ralph's reply was short and, waving to his mother and grandmother, he got into the driving seat while the footman cranked the car because it was so cold.

As the engine sprang to life he reversed the Askham until their back was to the house, turned for a final farewell wave and drove at a stately pace down the drive.

'Well, Gran thinks you're coming back.'

'Oh, we'll be back,' Cheryl pulled her fur firmly around her face and shivered, 'but we don't know when. We've a lot of shopping to do.'

'For Kenya,' Ralph said firmly.

'I just want to shop, anyway.' Cheryl glanced over her shoulder and smiled at Em. 'What a nice man that Peter is. I saw you having a good many nice intimate chats. Is he Jewish?'

'Yes, why do you ask?'

'Well he *looks* so Jewish, doesn't he? I always think one can tell.'

'Do you mind if he's Jewish?'

'Good lord, not at all!' Cheryl's laugh was just a little false as she groped in her bag for a cigarette. 'Good heavens, I know *plenty* of Jews, though not very well socially. They're not allowed at the Muthaiga Club.'

'Why ever not?' Em's tone was furious.

'Well, dear, they're not really socially acceptable, are they? I mean, be honest. Do you really have many close Jewish friends?'

'Yes I do. My best friend at Oxford was a Jewish girl.'

'How interesting. Well, I've nothing against them, I assure you. Please don't misunderstand me, but I always think that the Russians had the right idea, putting them in the Pale of Settlement, was it called? I expect your Russian relations could tell you all about that.'

'I find this conversation hateful,' Em said, 'and surprising. I have never ever met someone so blatantly anti-Semitic before.'

'Haven't you?' Cheryl laughed again. 'Then you obviously haven't talked to your cousin's wife, Hélène. She knew immediately that Peter was Jewish and kept well out of his way. She says the Jews are always after something and it was they, more than anyone else, who caused the Russian Revolution.'

'But a lot of Gentiles are Communists, too.' Discomforted, but trying to remain detached, Ralph, who hated an argument, concentrated on his driving.

'The worst Communists are Jews,' Cheryl corrected. 'That Trotsky was a Jew, and he got his just deserts.'

'Well, you will be pleased to know then,' Em said silkily, 'that in Germany the Jews are under attack from the Nazi

397

Party. There have been several assaults on Jews since their success in the September elections.'

'I'm not pleased at all, please don't misunderstand me, Emmeline ...'

'Peter, in fact, has gone back to Germany because he's afraid for his family.'

'Dear me, has it come to that?' Cheryl pulled at her cigarette and gazed out of the window. 'Well, I suppose, in a way, they deserve it. The Jews are too greedy; they control the banks and all the business. No wonder they're hated! Has Bobby got any Jewish blood in him, by the way?'

She glanced at Ralph who, momentarily, seemed to lose control of the car before hastily correcting his mistake.

'Cheryl, I think you're going too far.' Ralph looked apologetically behind him at Em. 'Sorry, did you get a jolt?'

'Well, he's sort of Jewish-looking, I think,' Cheryl went on, 'being so dark, and so crafty – making off with the family fortune like that.'

'He *hasn't* made off with the family fortune,' Ralph said stiffly.

'Oh, hasn't he? Just you wait and see, my boy. Just you wait and see.'

Christmas really broke the end of the happy time Ralph had with his bride of a few months. The honeymoon period was over. The deterioration in their relationship became obvious for all to see, especially Rachel, aware of the uneasy atmosphere as soon as she returned to Askham House.

It was some time before she could get out of Ralph what was amiss, though she noticed him moping round the house alone more than usual while Cheryl flitted back and forth to Paris, regarding the Flèche d'Or rather as an extension of her home, or came back from the London shops and the *haute couture* collections, the chauffeur behind her laden with parcels.

Ralph found it difficult to tell his mother that the bride of his dreams was in reality less than dream-like.

'I suppose she's right, really,' he said, 'Kenya *is* pretty dull for her.'

'But she liked it before, didn't she?'

'Well, I didn't know her very well I suppose. As soon as she was free we got married. There was such a lot to do. I think we just had a misunderstanding. Apparently when we came back she thought it was for good.'

'I find that *very* hard to believe.' They were in the library where Rachel was busy cataloguing the Askham archives which had been brought up to date by one of the historical-minded journalists on her staff. Ralph had wandered in, hands in his pockets, and sat opposite her, his long legs stretched out, chin slumped on his breast. Like that, reflective, adorable, he reminded her of Bosco and in manner he was like Bosco and seemed to become more like him the older he got. Like her late husband, it was Ralph's kindness that dominated his personality more than anything else; his gentlemanliness, his concern for others and, because he was like this, she had seen over Christmas how his wife was able to twist him round her little finger, and had once again.

Much as she adored Ralph and wanted to have him home, the thought of having to share the house with him and Cheryl was depressing and she told him that if they did, indeed, decide to stay in England she would wish to live elsewhere.

'But this is your home, Mother.' Ralph looked distressed. 'I know that in his will Father wanted you to have it for as long as you wished, and Gran to remain in the Hall.'

'Darling,' she replied, 'the Hall has always been too big for your grandmother. I always think, in a way, she insisted on living there to spite me. One woman in that vast house, with all those servants, is the kind of thing that starts revolutions. I can quite see how, if you stay in this country, your wife will want her own establishments and Askham House and Askham Hall are, whatever you say, yours. Your grandmother and I only live in them out of courtesy. Charlotte is married, and I don't think Freddie will ever settle down to one place. Hugo is lost to me now, I feel, and Em and I will be quite happy in a much smaller house. I shall gladly give up all this to your wife. I only wish, however, that before you decided all this you hadn't signed the business interests away, because what will you do now?'

'I'll farm. I'll develop the home farm at Askham and raise a stud there. I'll do exactly as I would have done in Kenya.'

'And will Cheryl like that any better?'

'She'll bloody well have to.' Ralph's mouth was grim. 'She can't have it *all* her own way, can she? I'm not flinging Gran out of the home she's had for nearly sixty years, and Cheryl will just have to fit in there.'

'You can have the Grange, I don't really need it.'

'No, we shall not have the Grange. That, at least, is yours and you love it. You've made it your own, the garden and so on. Askham is plenty big enough for us to share with Gran, and Princess Irina if she chooses to stay. Cheryl will have to settle down to being a country wife and raising a family.'

Rachel looked at him and smiled, as if concurring. But there was doubt in her mind, as she knew there was in his.

Suddenly a cloud seemed to have emerged, hovering over them all – a large big black cloud created by Cheryl.

CHAPTER 20

By the early spring of 1931 it was quite clear to everyone that
Ralph and Cheryl would not be going back to Kenya.
Moreover, Ralph seemed also to have had a change of heart,
and to so concur with his wife's wishes as to give the
impression that the idea had originally been his. He found it
hard to criticize her, either to his family or in the depths of his
own heart. Such was her influence over him that he seemed to
feel that, automatically, she must be right. He never stayed
angry with her for long.

Not that they always agreed. In fact mostly they disagreed;
but in the sense that Cheryl got her own way and Ralph
concurred deciding that, after all, he had been wrong, or it
wasn't worth arguing about. If Rachel was prepared to move
why not have Askham House and, if his grandmother would
accept them, and in a way she had to, why not move in with
her? The place was big enough. There were so many easy
answers, after all.

So while Rachel looked around for a house and Em went to
Germany to report on the political situation for her mother's
paper, and Spencer spoke bitterly in the House about
alleviating the economic plight of so many in England, Cheryl
was busy feathering her own nest with not a thought for any
other person, anything that went on around her except her
own gratification.

On that last morning before Rachel moved out of Askham
House into a house she'd rented in Hill Street, until she found
something suitable, she remarked to her daughter-in-law, 'I
remember going round this house with *my* mother-in-law the
day she decided to settle in the country. We didn't get on very
well and she waited for me here in this room,' Rachel gazed

around her cosy sitting-room, 'and then she told me about all the work that had been done by *her* mother-in-law, Phyllida Askham, who was a connoisseur of antique furniture. She asked me not to make too many changes.'

'That was about a hundred years ago, I suppose.' Cheryl looked impatiently about her as though she couldn't wait for Rachel to be gone. 'I mean to make plenty. I must tell you, Lady Askham, this furniture is not to my taste and I'm going to make a good many changes. Ralph knows this and agrees with me.'

'I'm glad to hear that.' If surprised, Rachel's tone was inscrutably polite. 'You see, Ralph has always been very fond of this house, and he likes old furniture. Many of these pieces are priceless, but styles today are very different and, of course, it's your home.'

Cheryl turned and gazed at Ralph's mother with an expression that few people saw other than when Cheryl was herself, which was seldom. It was a frank, unfriendly, rather malicious expression which was very well known by those people who had ever offended her; by the native servants in Kenya, the Jewish and Asian shopkeepers in Nairobi. Rachel wondered how many times Ralph had seen it. Herself, she felt satisfied to see Cheryl as she really was.

Cheryl sat down, crossing her legs and lighting a cigarette. As she leaned forward towards the light, her elegant profile sharply outlined, Rachel thought that she was indeed a very beautiful woman and it was easy to see what captivated Ralph about her. She had exquisite taste and dressed well, though Rachel wondered if she knew how much the Askham fortunes had contracted recently. She didn't think she'd cope too well with adversity.

'I do hope you'll come and visit us often.' Cheryl raised her head, extinguishing the light and placing the golden lighter, a present from Ralph, back into her bag. 'I know you must feel that your family are all drifting away.'

402

'Well, you're drifting back.' Rachel made a show of being cheerful and looked up as a maid brought in a tray with morning coffee. 'Yes, Em and Freddie are in Germany and Charlotte is in France. However, I have Ralph home with me again. And you,' she added carefully.

To tell the truth she was not sorry to leave Askham House. It had never been a home in the way The Grange had. It was the scene of her long alienation from Bosco and, since his death, it had always seemed empty despite the number of youthful bodies filling it. It really should be turned into a club, an institution, or offices – a number of them were now filling the Square: some library or learned body where portly old men wandered in to read their papers and take a snooze in the huge easy chairs.

All the rooms were too large. It had been built at a time when people had bigger families and lots of leisure. Sadly those times were changing. Sadly? Rachel wasn't sure.

'Ralph was telling me about his half-brother Hugo. I must say it's a fascinating story,' Cheryl said chattily, taking the cup which the maid had offered her first, as though assuming that now she was the senior Lady Askham. In a sense she was. Then, waiting for the girl to withdraw, she went on: 'About the circumstances of his birth, how fond you had been of him and how he had returned to his mother. That must make you very sad, such ingratitude!'

'It wasn't ingratitude.' Rachel resented Ralph passing on this gossip. 'He enjoys the company of his real mother. She was able to give him her exclusive affection and Hugo needed lots of affection. He needed to be the only one. He comes to see me, and his cat.' Rachel looked over at Lenin, who followed her round the house now, apparently resigned to losing his master. He sat in the embrasure of the window washing his face with his customary equanimity.

'That old thing!' Cheryl looked at it in disgust. 'That will have to be put down.'

'Oh, no, he won't! He will come with me. He's a much loved family pet.' Rachel looked at her strangely. 'I hope you don't make *too* much of a clean sweep of everything, Cheryl. You might find you've bitten off more than you can chew.'

'Oh, no, I shan't, Lady Askham!' Cheryl gave that knowing smile, a row of perfect white teeth just catching the top of her lower lip. 'I know *perfectly* well what I'm doing. You can be sure of that.'

Although it was a warm spring day a chill seemed to hover round Rachel's shoulders and she shivered, wishing to be gone.

'You can come and live with me,' Spencer said in the drawing-room of the house he had lived in since coming to London. 'It's a forlorn hope, I suppose.'

They were no longer lovers, passion having yielded to affection and the feeling that their best years together were over. Rachel had been strongly affected by Margaret's anger, relayed by Adam, and the charge that she had ruined Spencer's life. It was shortly after that that she told Spencer the physical side of their relationship, diminishing in intensity over the years, anyway, must finish.

They were discussing a speech he was to make in the House on the unemployment problem. His friend Oswald Mosley had left the Labour Party to form a new party which he'd wanted Spencer to join, but Rachel had strongly advised him against it and had attacked Mosley in *The Sentinel*.

Spencer felt frustrated by what was going on around him, the inability of the government to get to grips with the problems that were, in his opinion, ruining the country. The fact that he had also lost the physical comforts of the woman he loved was an added aggravation. Sometimes Spencer Foster, only forty-two years old, yet looking ten years older, felt a very bitter, disappointed man.

'Spencer dear, you know we can never go back.' Rachel affectionately gripped his arm. 'My family has dwindled and I have no children living at home. My great comfort is dear old

404

Lenin, Hugo's cat. That woman – of whom I scarcely have a good word to say – my daughter-in-law suggested he should be put down.'

'She's a hard nut.' A smile illuminated Spencer's tired face. 'But I can see why she fascinated Ralph.'

'I can't.'

'You're a woman. She is very sexually attractive, witty and clever. Whether she'll give him an easy life is another thing. Was that the doorbell?'

They were already in evening clothes waiting to dine with Margaret and Adam. Margaret spent a lot of her time in the country and had not seen her sister-in-law since Christmas. Margaret, from being a healthy, vital young woman, had turned into an introverted hypochondriac and it was not an evening Rachel was looking forward to. In a way she knew that Adam's marriage to his sister had complicated, probably finished, her relationship with Spencer. Yet she had no rancour against Margaret.

But that evening the couple looked transformed; Margaret robust and healthy, Adam sharp and witty, in good form.

'You look as though you're bursting with news,' Rachel said over cocktails in the drawing-room.

'We are.' Adam smiled at his wife. 'I am to be made a High Court Judge.'

'At last! He feels he's recognized, at last!' Margaret grasped the hand Adam held out to her, swinging it tightly. 'I'm also expecting a baby.'

'Oh, my goodness.' Rachel took Margaret's free hand and pulling her towards her, kissed her. 'I do congratulate you both.' She looked searchingly at Margaret. 'Are you really pleased?'

'Yes, I am. The doctor has allayed all my misgivings about having another.'

'But he thinks this should be the last. I do, too. A boy and a girl, that's what we hope for.' Adam seemed to glow.

'This is *really* good news.' Spencer rang the bell and when the maid appeared asked her to find a bottle of champagne in the cellar. 'I don't know which has done you the most good – elevation to the bench or becoming parents again. However, it is splendid on both accounts. When's the baby due?'

'In the autumn.' Margaret glanced down at her trim figure. 'In five months' time. Hard to tell, I know, but I didn't want to say anything until we were sure it would be all right. I can't tell you how happy we are, Rachel, but I wish you were happy too.'

'Who says I'm not happy?' Rachel looked indignant as the maid returned to announce dinner.

'Being chucked out of your home by your daughter-in-law?'

'But I'm not "chucked out",' Rachel protested. 'I offered to leave and I *want* to, as Cheryl plans to throw out all the rubbishy furniture we have and put in nice modern stuff.' She shivered. 'I have found a dear little house in Hill Street, and Lenin and I are very happy there until something more suitable and permanent occurs. In a way I feel very happy, believe me.

'I worry about Freddie and Em in Germany but they assure me it's an exciting place to be, and Em sends the most marvellous reports for the paper. I tell her if she goes on reporting Hitler like this she'll be thrown out, but I'm proud of her. She travels all over the country and we at *The Sentinel* print news that *The Times* fights shy of. Do you know,' Rachel continued, as they sat down to dinner, impelled by a feeling of excitement, 'I feel, in many ways, that I'm entering the best part of my life; I've brought up my family to the best of my ability, given succour to Bosco's son as he would have wished me to do. I speak the truth fearlessly in my paper and try to influence events. I am living in a house that is much more suitable for a single, middle-aged woman than that huge place in St James's Square and I am happy.' She looked around. 'Yes, I'm very happy.'

'What a splendid evening it is, then,' Adam said, raising his glass. 'We have much to celebrate.'

The echo of happiness might have been heard in France where Paolo and Charlotte were putting the finishing touches to their water mill, damming the river so that it was like a moat on one side. From the windows they could fish straight into the water. It was a beautiful place and Susan liked to spend time there with Kyril, her new baby Anna, who had been born the previous September, and Alexander, now known as Sasha, who was nearly ten years old, and at school in England.

Kyril was a complicated, withdrawn man very different from the one who, ten years before, had wooed Susan with such passion and verve in Moscow and at the family home in the Caucasus. Physically he hadn't changed a lot, but mentally and emotionally it was as though he'd undergone a complete transformation. He seldom talked about his experiences, and what had happened to him in Siberia was largely guesswork. Susan thought it was because he didn't want to betray the Party, in which he said he still believed.

He was a poor conversationalist, with no time at all for small talk, and he spent his days reading and writing in the luxury which his wife's money had provided for him. His life was spent almost exclusively in the company of fellow exiles – speaking Russian, arguing, forming various groups whose complexions and loyalties changed from day to day.

Why Susan liked going to Charlotte's was because Kyril, the introvert, got on so well with Paolo the extrovert and Charlotte, with her newly-discovered passion for housekeeping and domesticity, was always a pleasure to be with.

Susan was slow to recognize that Kyril was a problem, that their love wasn't as it had once been. For so long she'd lived an illusion that it was hard to abandon it. Yet if he'd changed, so had she; and in her maturity, her composure and her artistic interests she found a satisfaction now lacking in her marriage.

Yet she remained true to Kyril and supposed she still loved him. It would never do for him to feel himself betrayed twice.

Before the motor racing season began the Ferovs and Verdis spent some days together at the water mill near Paris, the two women gossiping and working – mainly in the garden – the two men taking long walks together through the leafy spring lanes.

Kyril, because of his secretive nature, had few close male confidants, and yet as they walked that day Paolo was keenly aware that Kyril wished to unburden himself about something that seemed to be tormenting him.

'I'd like to go back to Russia,' Kyril said, after a fair amount of prompting, a few false starts.

'You're not happy here?'

'I don't fit in.'

'Maybe you haven't given it long enough?'

'Don't you think three years is long enough?'

'Would you go with Susan?'

'Do you think Susan would want to go? The "Princess Tatiana Ferova"?' Kyril laughed unkindly. 'She'd have to give all that up in Russia.'

'You don't sound too happy with Susan?'

'When I've been kidnapped, why should I be? I never wanted to leave Russia in the first place. I was captured – spirited abroad despite myself.'

'Even after being in prison?'

'I wasn't in prison. I was doing useful work on a farm in Siberia, where I'd been sent, quite rightly, for disobeying Party rules. You don't understand, Paolo, what the Revolution means to us who believe. It *is* a new ideal, a new way of life.'

'I think I do understand,' Paolo said after a while, 'even if I don't agree with you. But Susan has waited all these years for you to come back …'

'Living on a memory of something which happened, very briefly, when she was so young, not yet twenty. I can understand her loyalty and appreciate it, especially with Sasha. But I have no sympathy for the way she has developed, the princely airs and graces she assumes, the lavish entertaining, the palazzo in Venice. She betrays the Revolution in which I thought she also believed. I don't want to be a White Russian. I want to be a Red Russian.'

Susan, on her knees in the garden, looked up when she saw the men appear and rubbed her blackened hands on a smock.

'Everything all right?' she said anxiously, always anxious. Ever since Kyril returned she had done nothing but worry: that he was happy, that he didn't want to leave her again.

'Everything's fine,' Paolo said but, as he was a man used to taking decisions, he brought the matter up again at dinner after all the excited children had been put to bed, and the grown-ups could relax round the large table in the kitchen where they had home-made pâté and Boeuf Bourgignon, with lots of strong country wine.

Kyril drank a good deal and his tongue loosened from its effects.

'Kyril spoke to me today about going back to Russia.' Paolo looked instinctively at Susan who leaned back, closing her eyes as though at last she were hearing the bad news she'd dreaded for so long. Now, at last, it had happened.

Charlotte, one ear cocked for a baby's cry, helped herself to more salad. She had blossomed in her state of happiness, and the extent of her contentment showed in her ample maternal figure, one that few of her friends of a few years before would have recognized. Seeing that she spent all her time in the country now with the children, while Paolo travelled on the Grand Prix circuit, she wore her hair unfashionably long, wore no make-up, favouring loose comfortable clothes. She looked like a contented peasant girl rather than the sprig of an ancient English aristocratic line.

'For a visit, of course?' she said, putting down her serving fork and spoon.

'For a long visit. Maybe for good.'

Kyril always smoked between courses and lit another cigarette. His fingers were yellow with nicotine and so was his upper lip, while his eyes had the rather bright, opaque gaze of the heavy smoker. Maybe, also, he took drugs.

'I knew this was in his mind,' Susan said at last in a bright, rather false-sounding voice, as though she were talking about a stranger. 'You can see he's not happy in Paris.'

'But I *am* happy in Paris, that's where you misunderstand.' Kyril always spoke impatiently to Susan as if he were explaining something complicated to a rather dim child. 'I just don't want to live there all my life.'

'I understand why you want to change.' Paolo poured more wine for everyone. 'I'm dying for a change, too, but Bobby won't release me. Not for another year. I'm too old for motor racing and too tired. Every Grand Prix race now takes its toll.'

'Bobby should release you if you wish it.' Susan was glad of the change of topic. 'I'll speak to him.'

'You won't change him,' Charlotte spoke bitterly. 'Sometimes I can't believe he's a relation, he's so hard. There is so much competition with Bugatti and Alfa Romeo on the racing circuit, and in the commercial field he's so busy trying to outsmart André Citroën that he says he wants Paolo's prestige, even if it kills him!'

'It will never kill me,' Paolo winked at her, stretching over the table to take her hand. 'You can be sure about that. I am much too careful, my darling.'

'I'd like to know how many other racing drivers said that. There were ...' Charlotte raised her fingers as if to count the number of fatalities, but Susan held up her hand.

'Don't be so morbid, please, dear, not now when you're so happy. I do think if Paolo wants to stop, it's time to stop, and I'll tell Bobby so. Don't worry, I'm not afraid of him. He's not a hard man. He is just ambitious and ...' she glanced at Kyril ... 'not very happy at the moment, personally.'

'I'm afraid the Ferovs do not make for happy marriages,' Kyril said equably, as though making an interesting philosophical point, cutting himself a large slice of cheese. 'My sister appears to be going through Bobby's money like a knife through this cheese. But she does not give good value. She does not have male babies. Mr Lighterman is displeased with her.

And you see, like Susan, he's always used to getting his own way.' He finished cutting his slice and put it on his plate, looking at it with the satisfaction of a man who remembered the many years he never had enough to eat. He shrugged, cutting into the cheese before popping a sliver in his mouth. 'I do not make Susan happy either, so she's displeased with me.'

'I didn't *ever* say you made me unhappy,' Susan cried. 'Besides, why bring it up now?'

'Well we're talking about change, aren't we? Paolo wants to give up racing and I want to go back to my homeland. I know you are too in love with your possessions to want to come with me.'

'I am not in love with my possessions! I like comfort and nice things, but is that a crime?'

'While millions are starving, yes.'

'But if I give up what I have I can't help the needy millions. That is nothing to do with me; it is to do with governments. It is too big a problem for individuals. Your system has created millions of unhappy, starving people and you refuse to acknowledge it.'

'I acknowledge the problem is there, but not that Communism is to blame. It is her enemies who are to blame.'

'That's what you think,' Susan sneered. 'It's not what *I* hear.'

'From my family, of course,' Kyril was sneering back, while Charlotte looked on, horrified.

'*And* a lot of others. Em went briefly to Moscow from Germany and said it was frightfully depressing, everyone looked half-starved. The Revolution was thirteen years ago and the population – what's left of it – is starving. What I can't understand about you, Kyril, is that you're so self-satisfied, so blind, so sure you know all the answers when you don't. You'd think that if anyone could see sense you would, after what happened to you.'

'The problems of people in Russia are caused by the climate, not the government,' Kyril said calmly, ignoring her as if she hadn't spoken. 'There are vast, bleak, uncultivated acres and if you knew the number of schemes the government had you would realize what a task they have on their hands. At least we haven't the huge gaps between rich and poor that I see in France and England. Your family live like the Royal Family and have no idea what is going on.'

'That's not true. My Aunt Rachel campaigns against poverty all the time.'

'Your Aunt Rachel is as remote from reality as you are yourself. Lady Askham, with her money and possessions, what can she *possibly* know about poverty?'

'My mother does know a lot, actually,' Charlotte spoke quietly, pained, on Susan's behalf, at the extent of their disagreement. 'She certainly does all she can. She hammers the government from the columns of her newspaper. She has never been a conspicuous spender, and she has now moved into a much smaller house where she lives very frugally. I think even *you* would approve, Kyril.'

Not for the first time on that unhappy visit Kyril threw his napkin on the table and stumped out of the room.

Later, in the intimacy of their bedroom, Charlotte snuggled up to Paolo, glad of the comfort and love of his strong body.

'They don't get on, do they?'

'Not a bit.'

'She says they quarrel like that at home all the time, only worse. Tonight was quite mild. Maybe it would be better if he did go back to Russia?'

'And leave her and the two children?'

'Sasha hardly knows him, anyway. If he went now little Anna would miss nothing. Personally Kyril rather frightens me. He's a fanatic, you know, irrational.'

'Fanatics are irrational by definition.' Paolo stubbed out the cigarette he had been smoking in the dark. 'Seeing them together one can't imagine how they ever became attracted in the first place. They're so different.'

'But Susan was different ten years ago. In 1921 she was only eighteen. I can remember her very well, though I was four years younger. She was terribly shy and withdrawn – not a bit as she is now. She doesn't let him get away with a thing.'

'She should let him go,' Paolo said, turning towards her, embracing her. 'If she tries to keep him here, I can only see trouble.'

It was true that Susan may have been better off without Kyril, but that was not how she saw it. She hadn't waited for him all these years to lose him again. Despite their differences, the difficulty of his moods and silences, the many rows, she felt she would rather have him than not have him.

After the Easter visit to the Verdis she was more careful not to offend him, and one of the best ways to please him was to entertain his friends to lavish suppers and lunches, with plenty of drink, while she stayed discreetly out of the way as the country women did back home, in Mother Russia. She realized that Kyril liked using her as a kind of servant, that he did it on purpose to humiliate her, to teach her a lesson. But, at that time, she was prepared to suffer his contempt in order to keep him near her, to prevent him from returning for good to his native land.

As the spring days lengthened into summer Bobby came to Paris to go over the racing programme with Paolo and continue his battle with André Citroën, who illuminated the whole of the Eiffel Tower to advertise his cars. Hélène asked herself to lunch with Susan too, to keep her company while the men talked shop.

'I want to ask you something,' she said, patting the seat beside her, sipping her pre-lunch cocktail while, on the other side of the room, Bobby and Paolo consulted schedules. 'You must keep it very confidential,' she lowered her voice, 'it's about Bobby.'

'Bobby?' Susan seemed surprised and couldn't help herself looking across at her brother.

'Do you know if he has a mistress?'

'Bobby?' Susan looked amazed.

'Seriously, I wondered.'

'What made you wonder?'

'I saw him at Christmas with a woman in the woods by Askham Hall. I've seen her before, years ago. She had a small child whom Bobby took into his arms and kissed. He kissed her, too.'

'But the idea of Bobby having a mistress is absurd,' Susan whispered, 'anyway, why should he meet her secretly like that? It was probably some employee.'

'That's what he said because, naturally, I asked him about this meeting, which seemed to me to occur by pre-arrangement rather than by chance. She is the daughter of his works manager, he said, and he is godfather to her child.'

'Well, that's that, then.'

'Yes, but still, I wonder.'

'Why?'

'I was in his study one day. The study at home where he does a lot of private business, and saw something on his desk about the upkeep of a house in Harrow. I wasn't prying. It was there for anyone to see. When he saw me looking he slipped it under something else. But why should he lie?'

'I'm sure Bobby hasn't got a mistress,' Susan said firmly. 'He hasn't got the time. He's not the sort, either.'

'Don't misunderstand me,' Hélène said. 'I shan't mind at all if he has. I'd just like to know.'

'But why?'

'Well, wouldn't you? It's something to have up one's sleeve.' Hélène smiled mysteriously at her sister-in-law twice over, and shook fresh cocktails expertly in the shaker.

The excitement was absolutely enormous as the crowd gathered for the start of the first big race of the 1931 season: the

Italian Grand Prix at Monza, and the racing cars lined up for the start.

Bobby had spent a fortune redesigning the 'Bosco' so that it could keep pace with its main rivals – Alfa Romeo and Bugatti, who had a beautiful new model, the Type 51. There had been a lot of publicity about the 'Bosco', its chief driver Paolo Verdi and his connection with the Askham family, their links with the saloon car. In fact the news cameras paid more attention to the huge gleaming white and burgundy Bosco, when it was wheeled out, than Alfa Romeo's new 3½ litre twin-six-cylinder *monoposto*, which Tazio Nuvolari was hoping to do great things with at the race. Masarati could not make the team in time having had two cars wrecked in the Sicilian Targa Florio, run in terrible weather conditions two weeks before.

Alfa had experienced a setback when Arcangeli had a fatal accident in practice, and the works team was subdued and would like to have pulled out. But a telegram from Mussolini ordered them to 'start-and-win'.

Charlotte, as usual, was not there; increasingly she had a thing about watching her husband race, and Paolo posed before the race with an arm round the necks of the two princesses, Susan and Hélène, which the press also made much of – Bobby standing smiling in the background.

Susan looked smart dressed in a flecked tweed costume with a pleated skirt, a shantung *café-au-lait* blouse underneath, a felt hat with a round crown and small brim pulled low over her forehead. Hélène wore a cardigan suit, her tunic blouse underneath nipped in the waist by a wide leather belt. Over her shoulders, because it had been fresh in the early May morning, she had slung a Burberry weatherproof overcoat. She was hatless, a fact which made her stunning looks, her straight blond hair and dark brows, all the more newsworthy because many of the pictures in the world's press about the event were of her by herself – smiling, confident, just a shade arrogant – 'Princess Hélène Lighterman photographed at Monza where her husband, millionaire sportsman Mr Bobby Lighterman ...' Bobby loved that kind of thing.

After four hours' racing Varzi's Type 51 Bugatti dropped out with back axle failure, and Nuvolari retired after only managing to reach third place. The crowd got to its feet cheering as Paolo raced ahead. Suddenly the car swerved to one side, slowed down and Paolo drove it into the pit.

Hélène, Bobby and Susan raced down from the stands to see what the trouble was and to see Paolo, who was drinking coffee, his face black with oil as two of the mechanics were working under the raised bonnet of the car.

'What's wrong?' Bobby said, peering over their shoulders.

'They're looking at the steering,' Paolo said, 'she seems to pull to the right.'

'I noticed that. I thought you did it on purpose to get a better position.'

'I have a damned difficult task getting it to steer to the left.' Paolo wiped his mouth and lit a cigarette, looking anxiously towards the car, then at his watch. 'I was making damn good time, too.' Grand Prix races had recently been fixed to be *de facto formulae libre* of ten-hour duration, starting at eight in the morning until six in the evening. They were tests of endurance as well as skill. Paolo preferred to drive himself for as long as he could. It was now eleven in the morning and already he looked tired.

'I think you should rest and let Rafael take the next few laps,' Bobby said, but Paolo shook his head. Rafael was the skilled Anglo-Argentinian co-driver.

'This is my race, all ten hours of it. If the car wins I want it to be with me.'

He clasped Bobby on the shoulder and went into the pit to talk to the chief engineer. Two minutes later he was off again.

By the time Bobby, Susan and Hélène got back to their seats in the stand, Paolo was racing to overtake the lead, the expensive new supercharger recently fitted to the car justifying its cost.

Suddenly Hélène craned forward, nudging Susan in the ribs. 'See who I see?' Her eyes were not on the track, but looking lower down in the stand.

'Who?' Susan shaded her eyes. There were so many well-known people at this important event.

'Jamie Kitto.'

'Oh, not that bad news!'

'I think he's quite good news.' Hélène glanced at Bobby who was studying his programme and, in the general din around them, had not been listening. He was still worrying about the car's performance.

Jamie appeared to be on his own, sauntering elegantly along, one hand in his pocket. He saw them at the same time they saw him and it was difficult to avoid meeting. Not that he seemed to want to, but deliberately came up to them.

'Why, hello!'

'Hello, Jamie,' Hélène shook his hand, smiling warily.

'Bygones are bygones, Bobby?' Jamie held out a hand.

'I hope so,' Bobby, looking angry, shook it briefly, and resumed his study of the programme.

'I hear you're a family man now?'

'Yes.' Bobby's monosyllabic reply didn't discourage Jamie, who bestowed on them his charming smile saying:

'Congratulations Bobby – and Hélène.'

Hélène pretended to ignore him too, her eyes fixed on the track.

Susan patted the place next to her. 'What brings you to Monza?' she asked.

'Oh, seeing old friends. I've a bob or two on the race.'

'Are you living in Italy?'

'Just about to return to Paris, as a matter of fact.'

'You must look me up, no need to lose touch. You *are* family,' Susan said and, as she did, she noticed his eyes stray past her and settle on Hélène.

'How *are* all the family? I feel awfully out of touch.' Jamie

417

settled in his seat and folded his arms. He looked tanned and had lost weight.

'Ralph Askham is home for good. He's married. Em and Freddie are in Germany. Charlotte, you know, is married to Paolo Verdi.'

'I like the new Askham, I must say. "The Bosco". It's a fine car, Bobby. If it wins the race you'll be made.'

'I'm made already, thank you,' Bobby said, getting up, his programme under his arm. 'Hélène, let's go down again and have another word with the chief mechanic. Hopefully when we get back this creature will have gone.'

Susan saw Jamie flush and look away, and for a moment she thought Hélène was going to say something, but Bobby pulled her up and, linking his arm through hers, firmly led her away.

''Bye ...' Hélène raised a hand but Jamie ignored her.

'I'm terribly sorry about that,' Susan looked angrily at Bobby's back. 'He had no right ...'

'He's a shit anyway, isn't he? That girl doesn't look at all happy.'

'I don't think I ever did see Hélène look really happy,' Susan murmured. 'Certainly not with you. Don't think I approve of what happened between you and Hélène, Jamie. But you are my cousin and I don't intend to ignore you, however much it annoys Bobby.'

'You always were the decent type, Susan.' Jamie gave his winning smile. 'But I really loved Hélène, you know. I was very cut up when she left as she did. She humiliated me. She'd have married me, you know, if I'd had any money. I've been desolate since she left me. I'd do anything to have her back.'

'I don't think you've a chance,' Susan turned her eye back to the track. 'She's too much to lose.'

For several laps Paolo comfortably held on to the lead, his chief rival the Alfa Romeo 2.3 litre 'Monza' driven by Campari with help, now, from Nuvolari who had earlier retired.

'I thought Verdi looked tired,' Jamie said. 'Is he quite well?'

'Very well.' Susan paused and got out her binoculars, focusing on the Bosco. 'He wanted to retire, but Bobby can't afford to lose him.'

Jamie nodded agreement. 'I'm surprised Paolo wants to retire.'

'Charlotte doesn't like him racing. She wants him to manage the Askham Motor Company which has got a lot of competition from the big names, Ford, Citroën, Renault and so on. That's why this race, this year, is important to Bobby.'

'Were you serious about me looking you up in Paris?'

'Of course,' Susan glanced at him with surprise.

'That's good, because I'd like to keep in touch. Sometimes I feel very lonely and cut off.' Jamie got up and put out his hand. 'Bobby and Hélène are coming back. "That creature" had better be gone.'

Susan put up her cheek to be kissed. 'Do look me up, and good luck.'

She thought he looked rather pathetic as he turned to go. Hélène and Bobby said nothing about Jamie as they resumed their seats, but Susan thought Hélène looked more detached than usual – more remote, keeping herself tightly in control.

Paolo had been in the driving seat for seven hours. He'd kept the lead but with increasing difficulty as the Alfa Romeo gained on him and correcting the thrust leftwards, quite obvious at times, became harder. He knew that if he could stick it just three more hours he was there, but the steering was heavier and he began to think little of his chances. In his mirror he could already see the Alfa *monoposto* gaining, and as he took another bend he put his foot right down on the accelerator, feeling the car surge forward under him as the supercharger did its work. The crowd were roaring him on. Paolo began to feel new confidence.

Suddenly, with no warning, the steering became unnaturally light, the wheel swung and, whichever way he tried to turn it, nothing happened. Paolo gently let in the clutch to change gear and try and prevent a skid, but the heavy vehicle continued out of control, veering now towards the barrier at the side of the road. Paolo was aware of the roar from the crowd abruptly ending, of the body of spectators rising solidly, in awful silence, to its feet. Desperately he braked hard and what he had dreaded happened: the car went into a furious skid on spilled oil and leapt upwards before crashing down hard on the surface of the track and overturning.

He didn't even have the chance to call her name: Charlotte.

CHAPTER 21

Cheryl looked with satisfaction at the gleaming chrome and mirrored surfaces in the drawing-room of Askham House, the lacquered bureau which had replaced a Louis XV escritoire which, like the rest of the furniture, had been banished to the sale rooms. Much of the furniture, the *art deco* motifs, were inspired by the best craftsmen of the period and a sideboard of Caucasian burr walnut had been designed by the master himself, Emile-Jacques Ruhlmann, and made at his workshops in Paris.

One wall was entirely covered with lacquer panels lit by subdued lighting and inspired by the Japanese lacquerer Katsu Hamanaka. A set of *bergère* brocade-upholstered chairs was by the English designer Alistair Maynard, whose creations were mostly bought only by the very rich.

The walls were pale green and various other items of furniture, hand-made in macasser ebony, white pine or glass had decorations in silvered bronze and shagreen. In one corner a large tubular lamp had many branches, like a tree from which the bulbs on the extremities resembled pineapples.

In a way, the effect throughout the house was very remarkable, a monument of modernism and good taste, but it was all very, very different from the style preferred by great-grandmother Phyllida and her immediate successors.

The polished blocks of parquet which had been trodden on for centuries, graced here and there by a priceless Persian rug, by so many distinguished feet, were covered with wall-to-wall carpet with an abstract motif which had been specially woven for Cheryl in Axminster, regardless of expense. No expense had in fact been spared on anything and the refurbishing and refurnishing of the house had cost a fortune, only a fraction of which, in this depressed market, was recovered by the sale of the antiques.

'Now I feel it's my own place,' Cheryl said to her new friend Fiona Ashdown. 'Mine at last!'

'It really *is* lovely,' Fiona enthused. She was a colonial, born in South Africa, and had as little regard for antiques as her American friend. 'I can't understand how people could have lived in that mausoleum for so long.'

'My mother-in-law has no taste and no concern for style,' Cheryl confided maliciously. 'You should see how she dresses!'

'I can see you don't like each other.' Fiona sat down on the chaise-longue – a copy of a piece by Le Corbusier – with its suede and leather upholstery on a chrome and steel frame.

'We hate each other. It's quite open,' Cheryl sounded gleeful. 'War was finally declared a few weeks ago when she came to see what we had done. She said she thought it simply dreadful, and walked straight out again. She had come to collect that mangy old cat which keeps on coming back here, and I told her that if I found it once again I would get one of the footmen to take it straight round to the vet and have it destroyed. I can't have it on my new furniture!'

'I should say not! But what does Ralph think of the war between you?'

'Well, he takes my side, of course.' Cheryl sat carefully down on one of her new Maynard chairs, straightening her skirt as she did. 'I'm *very* careful about what I say to his mother in front of him. He says, anyway, he expected us not to get on because it seems to be a family tradition. Rachel didn't get on with Dulcie who never made it with old Phyllida. These noble families are quite absurd, don't you think?'

'Charming though,' Fiona crossed her elegant legs. 'I wonder how you'd get on with *your* daughter-in-law?' Archly she gazed at her new friend. Cheryl never seemed to keep friends for very long, changing them frequently.

'Well, that's a long time off, if it happens at all.'

'Surely Ralph wants children?'

'Oh, Ralph wants children, but if that's what he wanted most he shouldn't have married me. I never promised him an heir. I hate having babies, anyway. I left my husband and two daughters for him. Don't you think that's enough?'

'It depends what you want,' Fiona said carefully, not wishing to offend this person of title and distinction she had met at a bridge party in Mayfair one afternoon. Cheryl played good contract bridge and belonged to several clubs, which made her reluctant to abandon London for too long while Ralph continued his search for the right farm in the country. 'I suppose the Earldom has to go on.'

'Personally, I don't care what happens to it,' Cheryl said casually. 'I have no sense of history. I shan't be there to see it, I don't suppose, and Ralph does have a brother who can inherit the title for all I care, as his father did. I think I've done my bit marrying him. I'm not going to spend the best years of my life having more children. No thank you! He had an uncle whose wife only had girls and it nearly broke up the marriage. Well, I seem to produce girls too, and I don't want that to happen to me, as it is also happening to his cousin Bobby.'

'Excuse me, my lady,' the footman, Herbert, stood inside the partially-opened door. 'Lady Bolingbroke is here to see you.'

'Oh, yes, I'd forgotten. Do show her in.' Cheryl jumped up, running her hands down her slim hips. 'Ralph's aunt-by-marriage said she was dying to see the house. I'd forgotten I'd invited her to tea.'

Cheryl went to the door just as Margaret reached the top of the stairs, and stood there for a moment puffing.

'Dear me,' Cheryl said, alarmed. 'Are you all right?'

'They're not very steep, are they?' Margaret looked apologetic. 'It's my condition I'm afraid.' She tried to laugh it off.

'Take all the time you want,' Cheryl linked her arm through Margaret's and drew her into the room, waiting for Margaret's astonished exclamation, which duly came.

'But do you *like* it?'

'Like it?' Margaret tactfully put her head on one side. 'It is *very* different. I can see why you and Rachel wouldn't agree over it. She's so traditional.'

'Stuffy, I'd call it,' Cheryl laughed and lit a cigarette, introducing Fiona to Margaret.

'So you heard about that row, did you? I thought it would stir things up a bit. Feathers flew, as they say.' Cheryl looked pleased.

Fiona shook Margaret's hand and said she must be going.

'Do stay,' Cheryl insisted. 'Then I'll show you and Margaret over the whole house. That's if you're able.' She stared at Margaret who, having collapsed into a chair, shook her head and smiled.

'I'd better stay here, I think. I don't want another miscarriage.'

'Oh, you poor dear.' Cheryl went to the fireplace and tugged sharply on the bell to order tea. 'Do you have that tendency? I do, too. I had two miscarriages and two live births and Fiona here is lecturing me about my duties. Wait until *you* have to go through it, Fiona, then you'll know.'

'You don't intend to have children?' Margaret enquired.

'Not at the moment, anyway.'

'You surprise me,' Margaret looked embarrassed. 'The Askhams are very keen on the proper succession. No one would think Freddie very suitable to succeed.'

'But Ralph won't die for a long time.'

'You never know. Look what happened to Arthur. Bosco was the younger son.'

'Well, I am keeping the Askhams on a string,' Cheryl said firmly. 'That's typically Weldon, by the way, which was *my* maiden name. We Weldons, hard farming stock from Wyoming, won't be pushed about, I can tell you! I showed my mother-in-law that. She needs keeping in her place and, now that I'm Lady Askham, I intend to do it.'

Ralph, pausing outside the door before he went in, heard Cheryl's raised voice and hesitated.

'You'll find it very hard to keep Rachel Askham in her place,' Margaret said. 'That cool, pleasant exterior conceals a heart of steel. Everyone thinks she's soft, but she's not. She's quite ruthless. She manipulates everyone and everything, and the classic example is the way she tried to keep Bosco Askham's bastard bound to her before he was able to break free and be with his real mother.'

Ralph pushed open the door, and the three women, wholly engrossed in slander, looked at him in astonishment.

'I'm sorry.' Ralph entered the room, hands in his pockets. 'I couldn't help hearing your remarks about my mother, Margaret. I must say I'm *very* surprised at you. And you, darling,' he turned to his wife with an expression on his face she had never seen before. 'The last thing my mother is is ruthless. She is the kindest, warmest, gentlest person alive. You and she have just got on to the wrong foot. As for you, Margaret, I think Mother would be quite shocked. She's very fond of you. Besides, she is your sister-in-law ...'

'You don't necessarily have to like your sister-in-law,' Margaret said nervously, 'although I'm sorry you heard me. I feel I should go now.'

A small figure in a rather shapeless coat and a beige felt hat, Margaret stood up, her face pale.

'Please don't go,' Ralph sat awkwardly in the *bergère* chair with chrome handles. 'I realize I was eavesdropping; but I happen to admire my mother very much, as well as love her. It's hard for me to hear something about her which I know isn't true. It was *Hugo* who behaved ungratefully to her and now, with Paolo's death, she is very sorely put upon by Charlotte's grief. It's a very bad time for the family.'

'Oh, I know it is,' Margaret suddenly sat down again, her hands on the handle of her bag. 'Everyone liked Paolo, and his death was the most awful tragedy. Believe me, I mean no real harm to your mother, who I know has many good qualities. But she is rather a formidable lady. I'm thinking of my brother, whom she used like a lackey.'

'Your brother had free will,' Ralph said, eyes narrowing. 'Let's forget it, anyway.' He accepted a cup of tea from Cheryl. 'I have good news, darling.'

'What's that, sweetie?' Cheryl smiled brightly, rather put out by the contretemps. She didn't like rows in public.

'I have found a wonderful farm not too far from Askham, so we shall be able to live in the house.'

'Which house?' Cheryl looked at him sharply.

'Askham Hall.'

'But I'm quite happy here, darling. I've told you several times.' Her tone hardened. 'I shouldn't, anyway, want for one moment to kick your poor old grandmother out.'

'Darling, you can't live *here* if we're farming in Wiltshire...'

'But *I* don't want to farm in Wiltshire, dearest...'

'Cheryl, I ...'

'I really think I should go.' Margaret Bolingbroke got up quickly, nearly spilling the half-full cup of tea in her hand.

'I must go, too.' Fiona Ashdown produced a diary from her pocket and flicked through it. 'See, we're meeting at Gertie's for bridge on Tuesday, darling. 'Bye-bye, Ralph.' Kissing Cheryl on the cheek and nodding at Ralph she beckoned to Margaret, who hurried after her.

'Throwing my friends out!' Cheryl stormed, going to the window to wave to them as they went down the steps of Askham House, 'God knows what they'll say about us.'

'Cherry darling,' Ralph stole up to her putting both hands round her shoulders. Angrily she shook him off.

'Oh, please stop mauling me, Ralph. It's more than I can stand. It's time you got over that youthful pawing. I can't bear it.' She shuddered and clasped her arms, an expression of revulsion on her face.

Ralph dropped his hands, opened them again as if to touch her and then moved away. He saw her mouth 'Goodbye' to her friends. Then, to him: 'I'm sorry, darling, but really ...' she brushed a piece of hair away from her forehead, walked over to the deep chair she'd recently vacated and lit a cigarette.

426

Ralph anxiously watched every move like a small boy who'd gone too far, wanting to be taken in her arms again and shown he was forgiven.

'I'm sorry too, darling,' he said placatingly. 'I mean this wasn't a row or anything, and I didn't mean them to leave.'

'But it was embarrassing, going on about farming in Wiltshire. What nonsense! If I'd wanted to be a farmer's wife we could have stayed in Kenya. You must drop this silly idea at once.'

'But you knew I was looking for a place.'

'I didn't take it seriously. I thought it would stop you thinking about Kenya.'

'Where we'd have been happier,' he said, adding, 'I think.'

'What do you mean "you think"? Don't you think we're happy here? I am.' Cheryl looked about her with satisfaction. 'I have created something really beautiful out of this appalling mausoleum to the dead – your great-grandmother and so on. Now it must be one of the loveliest houses in London and *Vanity Fair* wants to photograph it and do an article on us.'

'What about?'

'Well, the house, us, everything. I said, of course, that it wasn't nearly finished and when it was I'd think about it. "The Countess of Askham, photographed in the beautiful setting of Askham House..." just think of it, Ralph!' Cheryl sketched an imaginary portrait of herself in the air. Ralph ignored her.

'What do you mean it's not *nearly* finished? It's cost a fortune!'

'My dear, it will cost another fortune before I'm through. He's hardly started.' She gestured again with those mobile, expressive hands. 'You don't call *this* finished, do you?'

'Well, this room is surely finished?'

'It has to have lots of little touches here and there and then Neil will go through the rest of the house. My goodness, you can't transform a place from a museum for dinosaurs into a modern dwelling in five months. Incidentally, I don't want to go to your grandmother's again for Christmas. I'd like to go to Paris. Last year was stifling!'

'But it's a tradition that we go to Gran's.' Ralph looked dismayed. 'Except when I was in Kenya every Christmas of my life has been spent there.'

'Well, from now on it won't be, darling. That is if you want me to go with you.'

'Of course I want you to go with me!'

Ralph got up and started pacing the room while Cheryl lay back in her chair, staring at him.

'Ralph, please stop doing that, it's giving me a headache. Look, my sweet, my precious, I think it's time you grew up. Yes,' as he stopped and looked at her, 'grew up, became a man rather than a big boy: Mummy's boy and Granny's boy. What you have "always" done is no excuse for continuing to do it. You are now married to a woman of the world, and I'm not going to be bound by what you did in the nursery. Please understand that. I would like to go and stay in a hotel in Paris, or Susan says she may go to Venice and...'

Ralph drew in a deep breath. '*I'm* going to Askham,' he declared. 'I'm quite sure about that and you, my dear, are going with me. I have just about had enough of these gibes about my youth, Cheryl. I am twenty-five, which is older than my father was when he fought at Omdurman. I am old enough to make my own decisions, to do what I please, to be a husband, and a father...' as he stared at her she lowered her eyes, momentarily unprepared, taken off her guard. He hurried on:

'When we married I told you I wanted children and whenever I bring up the subject you talk about something else. All right, you wanted to settle down and so on. All that I understand. Well, we have been in England now for over a year, you have flung out my mother and transformed this place into a gin palace and I've said nothing. When I married you I thought our life would be in Kenya. You never told me you didn't want to live there...'

'I never *dreamed* I'd like England so much!'

'Well, you never considered me, did you? Because I thought we were going to live in Kenya I sold the Askham share of the family business to Bobby. As it happens – because of the hurry I was in at the time as I thought we were going back to Kenya – I sold it for less than it was worth. In fact Bobby, family or no, pulled a fast one. I find out now that, in fact, we are really not nearly as rich as I thought.'

'What do you mean, we're not as rich as you thought?' Cheryl, her face aghast, interrupted him.

'Just that we haven't as much as we had. Like your ex-husband we lost a packet in America...'

'B...but...' Lost for words, for once, Cherly looked around her. 'All this, the house ...'

'I'm talking about cash. We've plenty of assets, but if we get rid of these, soon we'll have nothing. You'll just have to face that and control your expenditure. Apart from all this, incidentally, I don't want to wait idly about carrying your parcels instead of doing a useful job.

'I have found a beautiful farm, not far from Askham, which has recently come on to the market. If I buy it I can make it a really paying proposition. I can have a stud which I've always wanted, and Bobby wants, too. Happily, because it's only twenty miles or so from Askham, we don't need to live on the farm but can live in the house. And I want *you* there as my wife, not in London, not in Paris, but there. Do you understand that, Cheryl?'

Without waiting for a reply Ralph walked out of the door, closing it behind him. Then he leaned against it for several moments, desperately trying to regain his composure.

If Cheryl Askham thought she saw the writing on the wall that day in December when, for the first time since she'd known him, Ralph had attempted to put her in her place, she may have been right. It was the first time in their relationship that Ralph had really shown any displeasure, and it was not a pleasant occasion. For the first time she thought she saw in him something of the considerable presence and capacity for authority that everyone said his father Bosco had and, from that day, she began to feel just a little in awe of him. It was not a pleasant experience.

Cheryl Askham was not a woman who liked masterful men. In her first husband she certainly hadn't had a master, and she didn't want one in her second, either. On the other hand there was more to Ralph than there had been to poor old George Lee, and if he had indulged her whims and given in to her for the past eighteen months, she could sense that time was over now.

At twenty-five Ralph had decided to be what his father had effortlessly been before him, and to assert himself.

Was Cheryl like his mother? Some people thought so, which was why they didn't like each other. Both were strong and uncompromising; both, these people said, had come from nowhere to become Countesses of Askham. Rachel would have been quite horrified to have been compared with Cheryl. But those who compared them, standing on the sidelines; those who saw similarities, were not very far from the truth. His mother had gracefully given in, relinquished Askham House and retired from the fight; but Cheryl soon found herself deeply engaged in a battle for supremacy.

In the first place, Ralph gave her an allowance for her personal use, and introduced a budget for her expenditure on the house in St James's Square. The new farm was costing him a lot of money and he still hadn't sold the Kenyan farm because Bobby thought it a good financial investment. They'd put in a manager.

Cheryl and Ralph were given a suite at Askham Hall and Ralph forbade her to touch its contents or decoration as long as his grandmother was alive.

Consequently, soon after Christmas, which they spent in the usual family house party, much more sombre this year because they were still in mourning for Paolo, Cheryl found herself in a different role: not flitting between London and Paris, playing bridge most afternoons, lunching at the Ritz, Lapérouse or Maxims, but trailing after her husband admiring acres of farmland freshly turned over for the spring sowing. In the evenings there was dinner with Dulcie and Princess Irina and usually a game of bezique or backgammon afterwards, never bridge. The sameness of the routine nearly drove her mad.

But Cheryl, wise to the ways of the world and affairs of men, knew she had to bide her time and be careful. She had been through a divorce once and she saw that, with this new and determined Ralph perhaps, at last, over the first flush of love, it could happen again.

There was some consolation, though, for Cheryl as the year advanced and the spring followed the dreary winter. Hélène, expecting a third child, had come over to be with her mother, and the two younger women became good friends, discovering that they had much in common besides the fact that they were both married to wealthy men.

They were both discontented and, in this sublime discontent, they found a source of mutual comfort and harmony, endlessly complaining about their lot and the husbands who had reduced them to mere chattels.

Chatteldom, however, was far from the case for both of them; but it provided much consolation and companionship as they grumbled endlessly about their lot.

Berlin 6 August 1932
In the Reichstag elections held two days ago the National Socialist Party led by Herr Hitler polled nearly 14 million votes, or 37 per cent of the votes cast. He can thus command 230 seats out of 608 and, though many people say he will never get any more, your correspondent, who has consistently warned you of the dangers of this man and his policies, begs leave to doubt.

During the campaign I travelled round with Herr Hitler hearing him speak throughout the length and breadth of Germany – in Mecklenburg, Lotzen, Konigsberg, Hanover, Dresden, Aachen, Frankfurt and Munich – and I can testify to the power of his oratory and the enormous influence he has on the masses who flock to hear him.

For Hitler represents for the average German triumph over defeat, a resurrection of pride after the humiliation of the Treaty of Versailles. He has said that he will not continue to pay the reparations demanded by the Allies and that he will make Germany mighty again and many – not only the poor and dispossessed but a large proportion of the bourgeois – believe him.

I ...

Em stopped to consult a statistic in one of the many notebooks she had made during her tour with Hitler and on looking up found Freddie regarding her with his customary air of amusement.

'Writing again, sis?'

'Freddie! When did you tiptoe in?'

'Frau Marx let me in. Incidentally, she said she is no relation to Karl. I asked her. I think it upset her a bit because of the implication she was Jewish. She looked quite nervous.'

'I could have told you that!' Em put her arm round his neck and kissed his cheek. 'Freddie, it's very good to see you. What have you been up to?'

'It's very hard to get up to anything in the fever that's taking hold of Germany at the moment.'

Freddie, who had taken to wearing a German student cap, tipped it on the back of his head. 'Jordan is beside himself with happiness.'

'Mmm ...' Em frowned and shook a cigarette from a pack on the table. 'I'm very worried about Jordan. He is constantly trailing round after Hitler and the Nazi thugs who follow him about.'

'He says he wants to take out German nationality, that Hitler is the best thing that has happened to this or any country since the defeat of France in the Franco–Prussian war. I never saw Jordan so excited as when he heard the result of the elections.'

'Don't you find it disturbing, Freddie, seriously?'

As he perched on the arm of the sofa opposite her she offered him a cigarette.

'Oh, no, Jordan doesn't worry me. He's a lot of fun and, in a way, I think Hitler does have something.'

'But what about the Jews? They're terrified of him. Think of poor Frau Marx and her reaction that you might think her Jewish?'

'I'm not happy about it,' Freddie agreed, 'but his anti-Semitism is well known. I mean, he won't actually *harm* them or anything ...'

'But he *does* harm them already, Freddie. That's what I can't get into your thick head.' Em got up and tapped the top of his curly head lightly with a book. 'The SA are forever *beating up* the Jews. Please believe it, because it's true. If Hitler does get into power God knows what will happen to them. The Kleins are extremely apprehensive.'

'Yes, but we know Hitler won't have complete power. The Nazis are too busy quarrelling among themselves. The German people will never let him take over the state.'

'I wish I shared your certainty. Anyway, the Kleins want you and me to go to dinner next week.'

'Not Jordan?'

'Not Jordan, definitely not I'm afraid. They don't like him at all.'

'Well he doesn't like them much, anyway, and not just because they're Jewish.'

'Sometimes I think Jordan isn't a good influence on you, Freddie. It worries me. I wish you'd move in with me.'

'Dear old sis,' Freddie looked at her lovingly, protectively. 'Whatever can happen to me? Jordan is our cousin and I find him a good chap, good fun. His politics don't bother, or interest, me at all.'

'But they *must*, Freddie! They're sinister. How can you call it fun trailing the Nazis around?'

'Well, you trail them around.'

'Yes, but it's my job.'

'Oh, by the way,' Freddie blew smoke casually into the air. 'Jordan told me to warn you that some of the people he knows in the Party are talking about you. They say you'd better watch out.'

Not for the first time in the past few weeks Em felt a prickle of fear. She was aware of the glances, not only of members of the Party, but of fellow journalists who supported Hitler, of whom there were many. Her chief ally was the American newspaperman Edgar Mowrer, who also wrote the truth about Hitler and had recently been elected President of the International Press Association in Berlin.

'How do you mean?' Em lit a fresh cigarette from the stub of the old one.

'They know about these critical reports in *The Sentinel* because, on the whole, the British press is favourable to them, including *The Times*. You know, Em, just for once you might try seeing things from the German point of view. If most of the nation approves of Hitler, why should they be wrong? But, please, take care. We don't want you beaten up in an alley on a dark night.'

It was true there was the possibility of violence, which Em was well aware of as, daily, she toiled seeking out the truth. Her German was good, and no bar to her digging out the facts, or following the harangues made by Hitler, who had declined the Vice-Chancellorship following the elections because he regarded it as an insult. It was the Chancellorship he was after.

Peter Klein and his family continued the warnings when she and Freddie went to dine in their apartment in the pretty suburb of Berlin Dahlem about ten days after the Reichstag elections. Peter tried to ram home his point.

'Especially as a woman, it is difficult for you to protect yourself. Your mother should send a male correspondent and you should go home, Em. Berlin is no place at the moment for a critic of Hitler whose work is printed in a national paper.'

Em stared round the table, noting the grave faces of his doctor father, Hans, and mother, Trudi, who was Austrian and worked in his children's clinic. Also there was his sister Marian Klein, whose frailty and pallor seemed only too indicative of the disease Em heard she was suffering from: a serious lung disorder, if not tuberculosis itself. She was a student at Berlin University. Peter now worked on an anti-Fascist newspaper, published in Hamburg, as their Berlin correspondent.

'I find what you are saying utterly incredible,' Em said at last, 'even with all I know. Are you *quite* serious?'

'Quite, *meine liebe* Emmeline, brave lady that you are.' Hans Klein had studied medicine in London and, like all his family, spoke English perfectly. He was the director of a government paediatric clinic which dealt largely with poor children in Berlin. 'I tell you if I could get out of Germany I would. I have not the optimism that some people have that Adolf Hitler will be stopped or broken by the divisions in his own party. Do you realize this man,' Hans leaned over the table, shaking a finger at her, 'with *no* education, from the lower middle classes and without even a commission in the War, has created a huge political party from one political group, The German Workers' Party, which he joined in 1919? From his earliest days he has written against the Jews advocating the *Entfernung*, their complete removal. I know a man who has made a study of every piece of anti-Semitic writing produced, and every remark made by Hitler, and he has no doubt about its seriousness. If Hitler does get what he wants, that is complete power, the Jews will be finished.'

Across the table from her father Marian started coughing and her mother looked at her with concern.

'Is it the smoke? I'm sorry,' Em promptly extinguished her cigarette but Trudi shook her head, passing a glass of water to her daughter, the expression on her face anxious.

'No, it is not the smoke, Emmeline. Marian has not been well. It has been a bad winter for her chest. She should go to the

435

mountains but, because of her exams, she wants to stay here working in the library.'

'I am perfectly all right, Mamma.' Marian took a sip of the water and, looking up, smiled. 'There is absolutely nothing wrong with my chest except a little weakness. As you say, the mountain air is good and, maybe, at Christmas...'

'Why don't we all go to the mountains at Christmas,' Peter said excitedly, 'and ski?'

'Em and I feel we should go home at Christmas.' Freddie's normal, cheerful expression was replaced by one of concern as he looked at Marian. 'We have not seen our family for over a year and Mother is too busy to come and see us. Political issues at home take up so much of her time. Naturally she disapproves of Ramsay MacDonald and the National Government, because she thinks MacDonald has sold out to the Conservatives.'

'But is it not really the best thing for your country?' Hans shrugged. 'As for us. We are still, all of us, fragmented by the War. The only thing to do is unite and better under a benign Labour Prime Minister, than a National Socialist driven by fanaticism and hatred.'

Marian started to cough again and Freddie rose from his chair and took her arm.

'This smoky atmosphere *is* no good for you. Let's go outside and get some fresh air in the garden.'

Smiling at him, Marian rose from her chair and allowed herself to be led away, anxiously watched by the rest of the family.

'Freddie is so good with Marian,' Trudi smiled at Em. 'I think she is a little in love with him.'

'And I'm sure he has a soft spot for her.'

'He is such a lovable boy,' Trudi sighed and cracked a nut in her hand. It had been airless in the room but, suddenly, a little breeze stirred the curtains and she said: 'I think sometimes Freddie has been protected too much from the

436

harsh things of life. He is always good, always smiling. He sees the best in everyone. Even Hitler!'

'Some people think he's irresponsible,' Em took a nut, too, 'but I agree with you. Everyone says he is like my father when he was young, and the word they always use is "lovable". Ralph is kind and compassionate – and ridiculously soft with his wife – but he's not tender, like Freddie. Sometimes I worry about Freddie, wondering what will become of him. He *is* very idle.'

'But he is an aristocrat, is he not?' Hans leaned towards her and smiled. 'I think we forget that. Is it not allowed for rich young men to do nothing?'

'My mother wouldn't approve of you saying that,' Em replied. 'She's tried to bring us all up to remember we have to contribute to life.'

'It is not really necessary to have to earn one's living if one has money and a title. We still have many young men in Germany like that.'

'Besides, Freddie hasn't got a lot of money. We lost quite a bit in the Wall Street crash. Freddie should, in fact, think a bit more about earning a living and less about enjoying himself; but at times I do despair for him.'

'I don't,' Trudi replied. 'I think there is much more to Freddie, much that we don't know about.'

In the garden outside Freddie leaned back in his cane chair so that he could see Marian's grave profile beside him. Although it was much cooler in the garden she still seemed to find breathing difficult and he felt concerned for her.

'You know, I don't think you're as well as you would like us to believe. You can't seem to get your breath.'

'Please, Freddie,' Marian put a hand on his arm. 'I am quite well; but it has been a very hot day, a hot night. I have been working hard and I'm tired.'

'I don't know why you work so hard. I don't.' Freddie looked puzzled and a smile illuminated Marian's gentle face.

437

'That's what is so nice about you. Your frankness, your refusal to be anything you're not.'

'I'm bone idle.' Freddie's face was grave for once. 'Believe me, I know it now. I put up this pretence of finding life a joke but in Berlin, in England, in the world at large, it is becoming less funny all the time. I am utterly untrained for anything. I depend entirely on the small income I have from the money left me by my father, and if I'd been in Germany in the twenties that would by now have been worth nothing. I make my mother anxious. I left Oxford without a degree and all I've done since is learn the German language. Don't be deceived by me, Marian,' he looked at her with unaccustomed gravity. 'In a family like mine I am considered a disgrace.'

'What do you want to do about it, then?' Marian said teasingly.

'I would like to do something, but I don't know what. Sometimes, you know, I feel I'd like to be a soldier, as my father was when he was young. He got a medal when he was younger than I am now. I bet he'd find me useless. I hate myself at times.'

'I don't find you useless,' Marian tentatively put her hand over his. 'I like you very much, Freddie, as you are.'

While the problems of Germany continued to preoccupy some members of the Askham family, and those of the political situation in England others, Rachel's brother Adam was solely concerned with the health of his wife Margaret, who seemed to get thinner and more frail as she awaited the birth of her baby that hot month of August 1932 at their country house.

She was not only frail, she was fretful and apprehensive, with nothing of the calm euphoria she had as she awaited the birth of their son Giles.

Adam blamed himself for allowing the pregnancy at all, even though they had both wished it and the doctors had allowed it. Margaret was fully recovered, they said, mentally, and physically quite capable of bearing another child.

But, too late, Adam wondered if they'd taken everything they should have into account, not least the tension between them aggravated by the death of Flora, the treasured memories he still had of her. Flora kept him and Margaret apart, and he knew that part of her wish to have another baby was to try and close this gap.

But it was useless. Flora dwelt in him, her presence constantly making itself felt in moments when he was alone, in the calm tranquillity of Darley Manor, his country home. Sometimes the air seemed full of Flora as though she had never left him. Once she'd promised she never would, and he felt she'd kept that promise. It was he who had left her.

Besides, he thought, he was too old and Margaret's health too unstable to have a baby in the house once more. He was an old goat. He bitterly regretted what they'd done and seemed as full of forebodings as she, unable to comfort her. Frequently he wished for the calm, sanctifying presence of Flora and knew he was being punished for the brutal way he'd let her go.

'I know what you're thinking of – Flora,' Margaret said to him one day as they sat in the garden under the willow which bent down to the ornamental pool. In every way their little country house was a gem, a minor architectural miracle, perfect in every way. Flora would have loved it.

Adam started guiltily.

'You were thinking of her then, weren't you?'

'It's only natural, dear. She gave so many years of her life to me.'

'And all her money.'

Adam wriggled awkwardly in his chair as though it were he who was carrying the burden of pregnancy. 'Margaret, that is a very unworthy thing to say.'

'But it did make a difference. This ...' she looked around.

'Yes, it did. I'll admit it; but without it I would have been quite happy.'

'With me? You made a mistake marrying me, Adam.'

Margaret gazed stonily in front of her. 'I don't regret it, but I know you do.'

'Of course I don't! The number of times you say that and the number of times I deny it.'

'Yet it's true. Flora obsesses you, even after all these years.'

'That's not true.'

'It is. Flora, by keeping you at arm's length, tormented you. She ingratiated herself with you, made herself a part of you. I see it all now. Poor Adam, if you'd have been a less scrupulous, less honest man you would have kept Flora and had a mistress. You'd have been a lot happier.'

Adam lumbered to his feet and, coming over to her, sat on the ground by her feet.

'Margaret, there is no need for you to torment yourself like this. Most of what you say is untrue. Now, you have not had a good pregnancy and your health worries me; your attitude also worries me. You must keep strong for the baby. I want you to know that I loved you and I still do. I loved Flora in another way and I miss her; but you are my wife. Please realize that.'

'If the baby's a girl,' Margaret said abruptly, as if speaking from far away, 'I'd like her to be called Flora.'

Adam, looking at her in alarm, didn't reply, wondering if she herself knew the implication of what she was saying: after the baby's birth, she would not be there.

Later on, recalling that summer's day in the garden, Adam thought there was an inevitability about the whole thing: that Margaret should die because she meant to die. No one knew why. It was true she was not strong, that her labour was difficult and prolonged, but there was something else.

'It seems your wife does not wish to live, Sir Adam. I don't know what we can do.' The doctor in the hospital to which Margaret had been rushed, not long after the conversation under the willow, looked puzzled. He had been summoned from Winchester and still wore his consulting room clothes of cut-away jacket, winged collar and black tie. He looked rather like an undertaker, Adam thought, with his hair sparse on top and thick at the sides.

'Lady Bolingbroke was very depressed,' Adam said. 'She felt that she shouldn't have had the child.'

'But it is a fine baby, perfectly formed and of a good weight. Yet your wife continues to decline.'

Spencer was sent for and Rachel came by the first train from London, and they all gathered round Margaret's bed as though the wake had already begun. The thin, wraith-like figure lying in the white counterpaned bed seemed to bear little resemblance to the hearty, happy, country girl Adam had married only five years before. Rachel thought she had never seen anyone deteriorate more dramatically than Margaret in these five years; even her character had changed. She glanced at Spencer, wondering if he too was thinking the same thing and how much Adam was to blame for it. Or was it really Flora? Was she the one who had cast the spell?

As Rachel's eyes roamed from Margaret to the window she had a moment of enlightenment, almost of hallucination, the implications of which were deeply shocking to her. It was as if someone had entered the room to claim the woman who had taken Adam from her.

Naturally, they called Adam's infant daughter after her: Flora.

PART 4
Viper in the Nest
1932–1934

CHAPTER 22

Hugo came regularly to see Rachel after he moved in with his mother, Nimet. It was always rather an awkward occasion as though the intimacy they'd shared for so many years, to the exclusion of her own children, had been lost for good. It was the blood tie that mattered, Rachel used to think sadly; nothing could replace it, except that she had loved Hugo dearly, and he was Bosco's blood – not hers. Perhaps that was why. She had been more of a mother to Hugo than Nimet ever had – loving him, shielding him, encouraging him, bearing the brunt of her own children's jealousy for his sake; yet when his natural mother appeared to claim him it had all counted for nothing.

On his visits, Hugo would sit there stroking Lenin, not saying much, not like the days when he would be happy in her company. It was really as though the only one he came to see was the cat.

But this day in December, two months after Margaret's death, Rachel was preoccupied and Hugo followed her around the house asking questions. It seemed as though he were rather indignant at what she was going to do, that he still felt some concern about what happened to her.

'But you can't take care of your brother's children!' He seemed quite annoyed at the whole idea.

'Why not?' Rachel paused from folding some freshly laundered sheets to gaze at him with surprise.

'Because . . .'

'There is no one else to do it. I am a widow and all my children have fled the nest. Adam, poor man, newly appointed to the Bench, can't cope by himself.'

'But there are nurses, housekeepers, servants . . .'

'Yes, Hugo,' Rachel sighed patiently. 'But it isn't the same with two very young children. Giles is only four and baby Flora newly born.'

'But you don't want ...'

'Yes, I do, as a matter of fact.' Rachel smiled, anticipating what he was going to say, and, folding the last sheet, put the pile into the airing cupboard. Always busy, she even liked to do the work that was normally reserved for the domestic staff. As a girl she had grown up with hardly any servants and this independence never left her, this desire to do things for herself. After all, she thought, she did them best.

She put an arm round Hugo and led him down the stairs into the drawing-room. He was so tall that he towered over her: tall, strong and handsome. The older he got the more he resembled his father, more than any of his other children, although there was a lot of Nimet in him too, a strong Semitic streak. It was very ironic, Rachel always thought, that Bosco's natural son favoured him most.

But it was not only in looks that Hugo had changed. Now twenty, he had become a young man. He had matured. It was hard to think of the naughty child of pre-adolescent years. For Rachel was forced to admit to herself that Hugo's adoption by his natural mother had done him good. Never a scholar, he had refused to go to university; but he had travelled with Nimet and her husband, and now he had all the self-assurance of a man of the world, being trained by his stepfather to take his place in his extensive business. One day she would lose him altogether.

Hugo had become a grave young man; grave and thoughtful. He didn't smile a lot, but he didn't seem unhappy. He appeared still to have, as he had when he was a child, his own private world where few were admitted.

'When will you leave, then?' Hugo looked round.

'Probably after Christmas. Actually it's all worked out very well. This house was only rented, as you know, and I did want somewhere permanent. Adam's house is in a nice quiet part of

446

London and is certainly large enough and near Fleet Street. Then he has his house in the country and I will gladly give up the Grange. Your grandmother's disagreements with Ralph's wife are threatening to break up the family, and I'm hoping to persuade her to move there. Now that she doesn't have to share it with me perhaps she will.' Rachel smiled grimly.

'Unlikely,' Hugo too smiled, as if at the memory of his grandmother's stubbornness. 'I don't see it, Mother ...' He stopped abruptly, staring at her, and Rachel stared back, frozen. He hadn't called her 'mother' once after he had left Askham House and all his things, his treasures and mementoes, as well as his clothes, had gradually been taken to Nimet's sumptuous, double-fronted mansion in Chesterfield Street. What a triumph for Nimet that had been. Revenge, at last.

All the precious things had been taken, that is with one exception: Nimet refused to allow Hugo to bring Lenin – on the pretence that they were away a lot – and Rachel, who loved the cat almost as much as Hugo, agreed to keep him. It was, anyway, she hoped, an excuse for Hugo to come round and see her.

Hugo had paused, too, realizing what he'd said. Rachel held out her hands to him.

'I'm glad that sometimes you can still call me "Mother". I do feel I am your mother, Hugo. I didn't stop loving you when Madame Igolopuscu came on the scene. Of course, I am not your mother in the sense that she is, and I never could be, nor would I wish it. But I do love you just as much, still.'

'Mother, Mummy ...' Hugo, big man that he was, leant down and put his head on Rachel's breast. 'I've behaved so badly, haven't I?' Looking up and searching her eyes he saw only love and forgiveness. 'I can't think how you can stand having me around after the way I treated you.'

'I can understand a lot, Hugo, my darling.' Rachel, grateful for the moment, sat down and tenderly drew him towards her. 'I know that life has not always been easy for you. You had a very insecure childhood and then, even when you came to me,

447

you had the rivalry and jealousy of your brothers and sisters. Because they are *all* your brothers and sisters, your father's children, like you. They were jealous too of you and as they were older they showed it more. You were the stranger.'

She reached out and stroked his thick wiry hair, identical in texture to Bosco's, springing in curls from the fingers.

'I think you felt a stranger all your life, my dear Hugo, and I tried to shield you from the children and overprotected you. When Nimet, your mother, came, you realized that here was someone of your very own, someone you didn't have to share. And I am glad for her too, because to want you the way she did means that she did care.'

'She did, she does,' Hugo nodded. 'I was so mesmerized by her at first, by everything about her that, as you say, it did seem the perfect life, the perfect world. I think for a little while I was in love with my mother. I thought she was so beautiful, I followed her everywhere. Now my love is more normal, the kind of love I have for you. I didn't really love you less, but I was glad to be away from the others, though at times I missed Charlotte.'

'Who missed you, too, and needs people now that she is alone. You should go and see her, Hugo. She would love it.'

'I will,' Hugo said, straightening up. 'I'm so *glad* I came today and yet, you see, I felt jealous immediately you told me you were going to look after Adam's children. I really resented it. I think I still want your love as well as Nimet's.'

'But you have my love. It has never lessened and never will. I still have enough for Adam's poor motherless little children.'

'But why can't someone else help with them. Susan, for instance!'

'Susan!' Rachel laughed. 'Poor Susan has enough on her plate with two children of her own and a husband who is exactly like a child, needing her attention all the time. He's such a petty man, I really feel I dislike him,' for a moment pain showed in Rachel's eyes, 'which is a pity because he wasn't like that ten years ago. He was strong and admirable then. His experiences certainly haven't improved Kyril.' Rachel wearily passed her hand over her face. 'How much I have regretted that visit to Russia all those years ago. How would I not love to have spared Susan from Kyril. But then how much he's changed ...' She looked wistful. 'I suppose all those years in Siberia must do something to a person; but they certainly didn't bring out nobility of character. I have never known anyone so selfish, self-centred or spoilt. And, of course, she gives in to every whim because he's always talking about going back to Russia, and she's afraid of losing him.'

'Why doesn't she let him go if he's like that? He sounds awful.'

'Because she loves him, I suppose,' Rachel looked puzzled too. 'I can't understand it, yet in a way I can. She waited for him all those years, she invested in their love, and she doesn't want to lose him. Nor does she wish to go back to Russia herself, understandably. Susan likes the good things of life and can indulge them ... anyway, now you know why she can't look after Giles and Flora. She's much, much too busy.'

'What about their uncle?' Hugo lay idly back on the sofa and looked at her.

'Oh, Spencer? Poor Spencer. Spencer couldn't cope with two young children. He is a bachelor and he is too busy in Parliament worried, as I am, by events both in this country and in Germany. Em is very full of foreboding about the situation there. She is convinced Hitler is on the point of seizing power and, frankly, I fear for her safety. I want her to come home, and she has promised that for Christmas she will.'

'We are going to Istanbul for Christmas.' Hugo got up and, putting his hands in his pockets, strolled to the window, looking out into the street. 'Where's Lenin?'

'Do you know, I haven't seen him today.' Rachel looked round as though expecting him to appear. 'I don't think I saw him last night, either. Dear, dear, I'm getting too absent-minded. He'll be all right. I'll ask one of the servants ...' She rang the bell to summon a maid, who reported that no one in the staff hall knew where Lenin was or had seen him since the day before.

'His dinner has not been ate, my lady.'

Hugo began to look worried but, thanking the maid, Rachel said:

'There's no need to be worried at all, Hugo. Lenin often pops over to Askham House, just for old times' sake, I think. I suppose he sees some of his friends in the Square there.'

'But it's very dangerous – all the traffic, Piccadilly...'

'Poor Lenin. I think he's been as upset as you by all the changes. I shall take him with me to the new house and make sure he stays there. Don't worry, darling... May I still call you darling?'

'Of course you may, Mother. And I ...'

'Hugo dearest,' Rachel went over to him and put an arm round his waist. 'You have been calling me "Rachel" for the last few years and I think you should continue to do that. Continue to call me Rachel, lots of children do when they get older and I think your mother will not be pleased if she hears you refer to me in the old way.'

A look of such anguish came into Hugo's eyes that, for a moment, Rachel thought he was going to cry and memories of the tearful, insecure little boy came flooding back. Hugo was a very sensitive young man, she realized, as vulnerable and sensitive still as he had ever been. She also suspected that, although for the moment he was too loyal to admit it, there was something wrong between him and Nimet or, maybe, between him and her husband.

But Rachel was too wise to probe. She knew that now that their intimacy was re-established any personal revelations would come later.

'I think I'll stroll over and look for Lenin,' Hugo said. 'I don't like him to be missing for so long. Anyway, I haven't seen the old place for ages.'

'You'd better be careful.' Rachel, her arm still round his

waist, strolled with him to the door. 'There's now a viper in the family nest who might bite.'

'A viper ...!' For a moment Hugo stared at her and then burst out laughing. 'I see you still don't like Cheryl.'

'Cheryl and I can't stand each other. It is almost openly admitted. I had a much better relationship with your grandmother than I have ever had with my daughter-in-law. This causes me much pain, because it also alienates me from Ralph, who can see nothing wrong with her, or very little – though I think he has moments of enlightenment.

'Apart from anything else she is busy turning Askham House, with all its beautiful hangings and furniture, into a temple of modern art: all chrome, glass, lacquer, statues of naked ladies and bright lights. I suppose I can't hold that against her, as many people think as she does; but I am fearful of what will happen when she gets her hands on that lovely Palladian mansion in the country which has some of the finest pictures and furniture in England.

'I wouldn't mind if she consulted Ralph in all this but she doesn't. She makes a fool of him, and spends an awful lot of *his* money.' Rachel sighed and, reaching up, kissed Hugo on the cheek. 'Ignore me. I'm just a jealous mother. I'm so glad you came, Hugo darling. I think this marks a new stage in our relationship, a more adult one. Now off you go and find old Lenin and send him back home. The trouble is, I think, he is too old to change his ways. Sometimes I think I am, too.'

It was true that the thought of being a mother again to a baby and a young child was very daunting to one of Rachel's temperament. Yet, clearly, it was her duty to go and help the stricken Adam who, since Margaret's death, had tried two housekeepers and a number of nurses. He was now at the end of his tether caring for two children he had never really wanted, and Rachel, whose devotion to her only brother had always been strong, herself made the suggestion that they should once more have a home as they had thirty years before.

Thirty years. Rachel raised a hand as Hugo, crossing the street, turned to look at her and, in that gesture, she saw his father once again, dear familiar figure to the life, and her eyes filled with tears.

Also, in her heart, she murmured a little prayer of thankfulness for the return of the prodigal son.

Hugo wandered into Askham House by the back way as he had when he was a child. He looked round the yard for signs of his beloved cat, but it was deserted. Then he peered round the door of the kitchen, but that was empty too.

A fancy took him to steal into the house which had once been his home and inspect all those new monstrosities that Rachel had warned him about. Certainly no signs of modernity were apparent in the huge kitchen with its big stove and grates. No sign, either, of cat food on the kitchen floor. Under the new regime all animals had been banished to the country, Cheryl considering them unhygienic.

Hugo, warm with renewed pleasure at the encounter with the woman he still thought of as his real mother, got an added pleasure through stealing along the corridor towards the steps and the green baize door that led into 'the house', as it was always called. He could see the back of one of the maids polishing the brass by the door and, as she bent down, he went swiftly up the stairs to the first floor where were the main drawing-room, the reception rooms and the room that used to be his father's study.

Hugo peered through the door of the drawing-room and then drew back, startled and dazzled by the change that had come over it since he had last been there. It was almost impossible to recognize the same room with its profusion of chrome, lacquered-topped tables and mirrors on the wall, an ornamental bamboo screen in one corner with a large vase full of waving ostrich plumes standing in front of it. No sign of Lenin there, of course and, as he opened the door of the room that Rachel had used as her sitting-room, Bosco's study, he dwelt nostalgically on memories of the past; many happy days spent there working with Rachel at her desk or reading with her beside the fire. Now it was impossible to recognize, having been transformed into a smaller drawing-room with the same, to him, tasteless furniture and modern pictures on the wall. No sign of Lenin there, no obscure comfortable corners as of old, where a lazy cat could lurk unseen. Maybe this was the viper's actual nest.

Smiling to himself, he shut the door. Then he had an idea. Lenin had always slept with him in his bedroom on the third floor, so he went up another flight of stairs, then another; along the corridor and up a small passage to the room overlooking the back of the house. He tiptoed up to the door and gently opened it, gazing into the room where he had spent so many mixed-up, emotional years; years trying to find himself, to prove himself an Askham worthy of his father, yet always seeming to fail.

The room hadn't changed. No modern furniture or hangings here; just the same dear old room, stark, rather bare, always a little untidy when he had it, overlooking the buildings and roofs at the back, an aspect he always loved, preferring it to the pleasant view of the Square itself.

His room. His bed, his furniture. The marks on the wall where he had his trophies; his mementoes of a not always very happy youth. It seemed desolate now. No one slept here at all; unlived in, unloved.

Dear room. Hugo ran his hands over the dressing-table with its cigarette marks when he had started furtively to smoke, the bed still with its tartan cover that one of the Kitto family had given him for his birthday.

The room was full of ghosts, full of memories but there was no Lenin curled up under the bed, pretending to hide. No Lenin outside on the windowsill from which he used to try and jump on to the roof next door. Once he had nearly succeeded, almost at the cost of his life! He'd hung on to the sill with his paws until his pitiful miaow sounds had drawn the attention of a servant working in another room in the same part of the house. How Hugo had loved Lenin that night, taking him in his arms and covering him with the bedclothes, warning him not to dare to be such a naughty pussy again.

Nostalgically he looked once more round the room, then he turned the door handle and slipped into the corridor to find himself face to face with a woman who, with a startled, frightened expression, put her hands to her face as though she was about to scream.

'It's all right,' Hugo hissed urgently. 'I'm not a burglar.'

'Then who are you? Clearly you're not a servant!' Imperiously she ran her eyes up and down his long, lithe form.

'I used to live here. I just came to see. Sorry.' He smiled at her with his engaging charm, but she seemed unmoved.

'You'd better come and explain yourself, young man, or I'll call the police. It had better be a good explanation, too. I've never seen you in my life before.'

No, he'd never met Cheryl, the viper, because he assumed, by her proprietorial air, her hauteur, that she it was. She was very beautiful, though with a steely expression that was definitely daunting. She made him go down the stairs before her, as if afraid he might attack her from behind, and then she marched him into the drawing-room, switching on all the lights so that she could look at him in their full glare. He blinked. She peered at him, noting his well-cut Oxford bags and Fair-Isle sweater, his shirt casually opened at the neck despite the cold, his tweed jacket, obviously of good cut.

'Who are you?'

'I'm Hugo Down.'

'Hugo who?'

'Down. Ralph's half-brother. I believe you must be Cheryl.' He extended a friendly hand but she declined it, turning, instead, to a glass-topped table. She took a cigarette from a box on it and lit it, a sarcastic smile on her face.

'Oh,' she said. 'I've *heard* of you.' Hugo flushed and conceived, in that instant, a dislike for his sister-in-law that would, in time, surpass even that of Rachel. 'I'd still like to know what you're doing here,' Cheryl went on, gazing unkindly at him. 'As far as I'm concerned, it's trespass.'

'I am sorry,' Hugo said quietly. 'I was looking for my cat.'

'Your what?'

'My cat, a tabby called Lenin. He used to live here too and my mother, Rachel, Lady Askham, said he often comes back.'

'And I told her if he came back again I'd have him destroyed.'

'You *what*?' Hugo was about to seize her by the scruff of her pretty V-necked jumper when he remembered who she was and where he was.

'I said to Lady Askham I would *not* have that fat, filthy thing in my house, sitting on all my beautiful new furniture, scratching the chairs. It has been found here several times in this very room, sitting on one of my priceless *bergère* chairs, if you please, and this time I had enough. I told one of the footmen to take it to the vet and have it destroyed.'

'How *could* you do such a dreadful thing?' Hugo lurched forward and Cheryl nervously took a few steps back and sat down.

'I had every right.'

'You had *no* right at all! I've had that cat since it was a tiny kitten and I was a small boy and found it wandering around here, and it has lived here all its life. That's why it kept coming back. Have you no heart?'

'Well, it's gone now,' Cheryl expelled smoke like a dragon, to give her confidence. 'And good riddance. Now could *you* take yourself off, please, and don't dare trespass again.'

'Willingly. I'm going.' Hugo felt himself close to tears, but he didn't want to break down in front of the snake. 'And now I know everything I've heard about you is true.'

'And I know everything I've heard about *you* is true,' Cheryl said with a cruel smile. 'Violent, undisciplined ... everything. A proper bastard.'

Hugo backed to the door, fearful of the very real violence he felt towards her and, once out of the room, ran down the stairs right into the arms of Ralph who, with the aid of the butler, was taking his coat off in the hall. For a moment the two men stared at each other, then Ralph held out his hand.

'Hugo! It *is* good to see you.'

'Well, it's not good to see you,' Hugo shouted. 'Your wife has killed my cat.'

'My wife has *what*?'

'Lenin,' Hugo continued to shout, 'kept on straying back here and she's had it destroyed.'

'Oh, Cheryl wouldn't do a thing like that.' Anxiously Ralph looked upstairs but Hugo, still beside himself, said:

'Cheryl would, from what I've heard of her, and Cheryl has. She said she told Rachel that's what would happen if he came back again and he has. I came over here looking for Lenin because your mother hadn't seen him for some time. There was no one around so I came upstairs...'

'As you've every right to,' Ralph took his arm and led him towards the stairs. 'This is the family home. You've never met Cheryl before, have you, Hugo? Always been away when there have been any family events. You must let me introduce you properly now.'

'I have met your wife, thank you,' Hugo said, beginning to tremble, 'and once was quite enough. Killing my cat.'

'I assure you Cheryl is an animal lover. She doesn't like animals here because she has recently done a lot to the house, but she would never *harm* an animal, of that I'm sure.'

'I'm afraid I *have* had him destroyed, darling.' Cheryl, one hand on the balustrade, came with dainty model-like steps down the broad staircase. 'He was a most horrible cat, and I saw no way of keeping him out of my house. I've asked your mother repeatedly, but she seemed to enjoy letting him wander over here. I think she did it on purpose, you know.'

'Cheryl, I can't believe this.' Ralph looked at her with

bewilderment as she reached the hall, a cigarette still in one hand, her air of unconcern clearly quite real.

'Naturally, I'm sorry to have caused your – er – half-brother distress,' momentarily she glanced at Hugo, as if thinking him no better than the cat, then she looked appealingly at her husband. 'But I thought that your mother did not care sufficiently about the cat, who was very old, and it was the kindest thing to do.'

'But we *all* loved Lenin,' Ralph sounded very angry. 'I think it was an overhasty act, if I may say so, darling. You should have asked me. Anyway, it's done now and I'm sorry this was the occasion for you to meet my younger brother Hugo...'

'I have already met him, thank you, darling, and I found him intemperate and rude. I thought at one moment he was going to attack me and remembered all the things you told me he did as a child. Now that I've met him it doesn't surprise me in the least. I don't think we've anything more to say to each other.'

'Oh, please, Cheryl, you're going too far. This cat business has got you both off on the wrong foot. Hugo, I can't say how sorry I am...'

'Please don't apologize, Ralph. All *I* can say is that I'm sorry for you.'

With a withering look at Cheryl, Hugo walked quickly towards the front door and Bromwich was only just in time to open it for him and bow him out.

'Good day, Mr Hugo. Nice to see you again, sir.'

Hugo, his eyes now filling with scalding tears, went round the side of the house to King Street and was walking quickly towards St James's Street when he heard footsteps running after him and someone calling his name.

'Mr Hugo, sir. Stop.'

He turned round and saw Alfred, one of the under-footmen in his time, now promoted to footman. He was dressed in an ordinary suit and his overcoat was open, but closed round something bulky which he clutched to his chest.

'Mr Hugo, sir,' Alfred panted, 'I heard what happened with her Ladyship, but I didn't dare let on.' At that moment there was a sound of feline indignation from under Alfred's coat and the ruffled head of Lenin appeared, apparently not in the least grateful that he had been saved from the vet's lethal ministrations. 'Her Ladyship asked me to have Lenin destroyed, sir. She found him yesterday in the room that used to be your mother's on her best chair.' Alfred seemed to enjoy the thought. 'She said "take him straight to the vet, Alfred, and have him put down" and I says "yes, my Lady, of course", but I knew I couldn't. I took him to my room, sir, and kept him there and I was going to take him to her Ladyship's, your mother's, this afternoon when I had my off duty time. Yesterday I didn't have none.'

'Oh, Alfred!' Hugo clasped the footman round the shoulders, close to kissing him. 'Oh, you heroic fellow. I can't ever thank you enough.'

'I would never have done nothing to Lenin, Mr Hugo,' Alfred said, gazing foolishly at the cat with the uncritical expression of the besotted cat lover. 'But her Ladyship wasn't arf cross and you must *never* let him come near here again. She is ever so proud of what she's done to the house.'

'Don't worry. Lady Askham, my mother, is moving to Bloomsbury and there is a very high wall there that Lenin will not be able to get over. Thank you a thousand times, Alfred.' Hugo reached in his pocket for a pound but the servant vigorously shook his head.

'Thank you, no, Mr Hugo. I am that fond of this cat and her Ladyship sir, your mother, that I would never take any money for anything I did. It was a privilege. I only hope, sir, that, one day, Lord Askham's wife will turn out as nice as his Ma. But I has my doubts.'

Alfred regarded him gravely for a moment. Then, after carefully handing Lenin into Hugo's care, they parted while Lenin snuggled up against his master, first looking at him reproachfully before he started to purr.

Ralph said: 'That was a bit of a mean thing to do about the cat.'

Cheryl, turning to him in bed, rubbed her face on his shoulder, feline herself.

'Oh, Ralphie, I feel *awful* about it. If only I'd have known the cat meant so much to you all.'

'It was a family pet. Even I was only fifteen when we got him.'

'But I thought he was a stray?'

'Well, he was found as a tiny kitten by Hugo in the back yard. He was only a few weeks old. He was really Hugo's cat, but we all loved him.'

Cheryl ran her fingers along his bare chest, causing him to tremble with suggestive thoughts – the mighty power of sex to assuage all anguish, sufferings, doubts and misunderstandings.

'Why didn't Hugo take him with him?'

'Because Nimet, his mother, wouldn't have him. She didn't like cats or something. Anyway, Lenin really belonged to Mother. She looked after him. She called him Lenin because that was her terrific pro-Russian phase. Lenin has, in fact, always been a very capitalistic cat, liking the good things of life: comfort, good food and so on. Well, I suppose talking about him won't bring him back.'

'I was so horrid to Hugo, too,' Cheryl confessed in the appealing little-girl voice she saved for when she wanted to get something out of Ralph. It might well be imagined that such obvious hypocrisy would have put him off, it was so different from what she was normally; but, in fact, he seemed to like it. Maybe it made him feel powerful. 'Of course, I didn't know who he was and I got such a shock seeing a perfect stranger come out of a disused room. I had no idea it used to be his room. None of you really liked Hugo though, did you? Honestly?'

'It was a very difficult situation,' Ralph's arm round her tightened. 'I was only nine when Mother brought him home.

Father had just been killed, and our whole family life disrupted. We needed her and, instead, she brought this tiny, rather foreign-looking creature home and promptly seemed to lavish all her love on him. Of course, he needed it because of the circumstances, but I didn't know that. I think it's why, as children, we have always been rather self-contained, a little detached. I know people think that and I think it's because of Hugo coming into our lives when we were quite small, and never really fitting in. I mean, he never seemed to be *like* an Askham, though now everyone says – and from the pictures and my memory of Father I agree – that he resembles him more than any of us. It really is all very odd.'

Cheryl thought for a few moments, not wishing to provoke a fresh storm because, after Hugo had gone, Ralph had disappeared into his study until dinner time without speaking to her, and had very little to say over dinner. Cheryl didn't like these remove, thoughtful moods of Ralph's. She was discomfited by them because then she felt him slipping away from her.

Cheryl was very conscious of her power over her husband. She knew that, in a way, it did emasculate him in her eyes. She didn't want a booby as a husband but, in order for her to keep her command over him, he had to be, as it were, squeezed dry like a well sucked orange. She knew that to other people Ralph didn't present this image at all; he seemed strong and in control. But with her he was weak, and Cheryl needed this weakness to maintain her position. It was the way she had dealt with her first husband, the only way she knew how to deal with men.

Using her beauty and her natural talent for attracting men, her allure, she had got further than anyone would ever have expected, and she had set her sights quite high.

But George Lee was nothing compared to an English earl, an Askham ... and Mrs Lee was nothing to being the Countess of Askham, with all that that implied.

When Ralph seemed nearly asleep Cheryl said: 'Wasn't it a

strange thing for your mother to do? Bringing up your father's bastard child?'

'It might seem strange to you, but it was very like my mother. She's the noblest woman I have ever known, terribly selfless and without side. Imagine, she's now, at her age, going to look after Uncle Adam's two young children.'

'Yes, but there are lots of servants and things. I mean, she's not doing it all on her own.'

'But Cheryl,' Ralph withdrew his arm. 'She has the responsibility. They are in her charge. She also abandons the idea of her own home with its privacy to share one with Uncle. She is leaving the Grange for us. I can't think why it is that you and Mother don't like each other – the two women I love most. It grieves me all the time. I can't help thinking you had Lenin destroyed because you knew it would most hurt my mother.'

'Ralph, that is a horrible thing to say!' Cheryl sat up, the folds of her crêpe de chine nightie falling on the bedclothes, and lay back against the pillows.

'I do *not* wish to hurt your mother.'

'But you knew the cat was hers ...'

'I *told* her if it came around I'd have to do something. I did warn her.'

'Yes, but this is her home.'

'It's *my* home.'

'It's *our* home,' Ralph insisted, his voice getting stronger. 'It's the family home – Mother's home and Hugo's home; the home of Charlotte and her children; Em and Freddie. It is *not* exclusively yours. Mother's cat has as much right to wander round here as yours – if you had one. In fact the more I think about it the more annoyed I get.'

'I think you're quite determined to push me out, you Askhams,' Cheryl said sulkily. 'I sometimes wonder what rights I have.'

'You sometimes wonder!' Ralph stared at her. 'You amaze me, Cheryl darling, you really do. You have taken this house over in its entirety, thrown out all the pictures and furniture,

461

much of it quite valuable, and completely redone the place to your own taste. Not, in all its history, has Askham House seen such a revolution. There was something timeless about it. Now how long will all this last? Five years, three? How long do modern fashions last? Will we then have to go to the enormous expense of doing it all over again?'

'Oh, Ralph, you're being petty.' Cheryl slipped out of the bed into her gown which lay on the foot, and walked over to the window, peering out into the Square, the only bedroom in the house to command such a view. 'I don't know what's got into you tonight. You seem to be spoiling for a fight. For what? All over a cat. Now *you're* accusing *me* of extravagance! This house was almost unfit for human habitation, in my view, with all that moth-eaten junk. It fetched a very small price in the sale rooms, didn't it?'

'That's because the market is very depressed. Europe is full of aristocrats hit by the War and the slump, selling off their country estates in order to raise cash. It was a very bad time to sell, and people who bought our furniture and pictures bought bargains. I don't know if you fully realize, Cheryl, that the Askham fortune is nothing like it was. I can't afford to spend thousands on doing up a house.'

'Then it was your fault to let the business go. You can't blame anyone but yourself.'

'But I thought ...' he began.

'Oh you "thought" we were going back to Kenya,' Cheryl flounced across the room to grope in her cigarette pack again. 'Please don't tell me that all over again. I can't bear it.'

'It's true.'

'Well, even if it is true you should have announced something as important as the sale of the family business to your family, at least to your wife.'

'I thought we wouldn't be in this country for years. I realize now it was very silly, but ... I am going ahead with the farm, you know that, and with that and raising bloodstock I hope, in a few years, to make up for what we've lost.'

'You want to keep Bobby Lighterman out of your life if that's the case.' Cheryl's thin lips moulded into an invisible straight line.

'Oh? Why?'

'Because he's a crook. Anyone can see that.'

'If you don't mind, you're talking about my first cousin.'

'Cousin he may be,' Cheryl retorted, sitting down on a chair and crossing her legs. 'But you're as unlike as chalk is to cheese. Bobby is a ruthless, ambitious man and he doesn't give a damn whether the rest of his family sinks or swims. He thought you were a ninny and, frankly, I think you were! He pulled a very fast one over you about that business, and if you have any sense you will steer very clear of him in the future. You're not in his league.' Cheryl rose and took a few paces across the room, then walked slowly back and sat down again, enunciating slowly. 'As for something you said a few moments ago, I must say I'm mystified.'

'What was that?'

'You said – if I'm right and correct me if I'm not – that your mother was moving out to leave the Grange for *us*! You mean, of course, for your grandmother?'

'No, for us,' Ralph said, a note of defiance in his voice. 'She is a woman who has just had her eightieth birthday, and I wouldn't *dream* of moving her out of the house she has lived in since she came there as a bride sixty years ago.'

'But what about me?' Cheryl said shrilly. 'I'm *your* bride. Don't I count?'

'Of course you count, darling,' Ralph stretched his arms out to her, 'but can't you understand? It is Gran's home. Even Mother has never lived there. My father didn't move her out, and neither will I.'

'Then you can't expect me to live in the country,' Cheryl said, folding her arms. 'For I'm damned if I'm going to live in that pokey little Grange when enormous Askham Hall is just waiting to be remodelled and refurnished by me. Why, I could restore it to its former glory. Think of the marvellous parties

463

we could have there, the social life? It would quite rival Fort Belvedere, I assure you.'

As Em, along with many others, had forecast, Hitler became Chancellor of Germany in January 1933, and in February the Reichstag was burnt down, an act for which the Communists were blamed. Many were inclined, however, to lay it at the door of the Nazis themselves in their efforts to discredit the Communists and establish power.

In March elections were held at which the Nazis gained power – over 17 million votes, but only a third of the seats they needed to obtain a majority. There was widespread lawlessness in Germany, which Hitler condemned publicly while privately condoning it. In March also his Enabling Bill gave him full powers to act without consulting the President.

To her domestic worries Rachel had the added anxiety of Em, whose reports from Germany, revealing aspects of the new regime which the Germans would rather have kept secret and which the British public found hard to believe, were becoming world famous. Rachel was dividing her time between country and town, sitting in her office until all hours of the night while requests poured in from newspapers world-wide to syndicate Em's column.

She was, however, far more worried about her daughter's personal safety than the success of her reports, though she was proud of them as well. Whereas *The Sentinel* carried the reports on the front page, under a byline 'from our special correspondent', the American and Continental papers weren't so reticent: Emmeline Down reports from Germany.

When Rachel printed an allegation that there were concentration camps in Germany to which opponents of Nazism were being sent Ramsay MacDonald asked her to lunch and begged her to tone down Em's reports. Rachel refused, but she returned to the country that weekend a very worried woman and resolved to consult Ralph and Adam on the matter, to have a family conference.

To her delight when she arrived it was to find Hugo ensconced in a seat by the window stroking Lenin who, busy cleaning himself behind the ears, nevertheless was reluctantly emitting a deep-throated purr at seeing his master.

'Hugo.' Rachel threw down her parcels and rushed over to the window to embrace him. 'How *lovely* to see you, though I know it is only him you've come to see.' She pointed to Lenin, who paused in his ablutions to wink at her.

'It was awfully good of you to give him a home here, Rachel. It's safer than town. I feel much better about him now. I just came to tell you that we're off on our travels again.'

'Oh, where?'

'France, Spain, Italy. We may go to Germany.'

'In that case you must look up Em and Freddie.'

'I will if you give me their address.'

'And ... oh Hugo, I am awfully worried about Em. I was really thinking of recalling her to London. Her reports are very controversial.'

'Isn't that what sells papers?'

'Yes, but she's my daughter. If half of what she says about Germany is correct, and I'm sure it is, I am getting very concerned indeed. There's no doubt it's becoming a one-party police state.

'I have asked Ralph to dinner tomorrow and ... oh,' she looked anxiously at Lenin, 'Cheryl, too, of course. I hope you can stay.'

'Well, it will be very interesting to meet her again,' Hugo said dryly. 'I'd be terribly intrigued to know what she thinks about Lenin, too.'

The advent of Rachel into his home had given Adam a serenity and sense of security he felt had been missing in his life for some time. He enjoyed entertaining, and received the evening's guests with Rachel by his side – happy because they were all family, related to him one way or another. Spencer had also been invited for the weekend to visit his niece and nephew and give his own assessment of what should be done about Em. Bobby and Hélène were staying at Askham Hall to visit Princess Irina and Bobby's grandmother, and they were invited for dinner too, driving over with Ralph and Cheryl.

The two young women, poised and beautiful, the presence of an eminent High Court judge, the men in dinner-jackets, gave to the proceedings a splendour that Rachel hadn't anticipated, as eight of them sat down to a table lit with candles and the fine silver that Adam had inherited from Flora.

Spencer had refused to join the National Government with Ramsay MacDonald, whom he regarded as a traitor to the Labour Party, and at first the talk was about English politics and then, inevitably, about Germany and appeasement.

'There is no question of appeasement,' Spencer said indignantly. 'Some people think, and I agree with them, that Hitler has shot his bolt. Such extremism can't possibly last.'

'I wish I agreed with you.' Adam sat back and judicially joined his hands. Gazing that night at Sir Adam, expounding on the evils of the Third Reich, Rachel was hard put to remember those far-off days when her self-effacing brother, completely eclipsed by his flamboyant wife Melanie, had stayed up night after night working in his shirt sleeves on briefs for his law practice, usually in defence of the suffragettes, and his first speeches to the House of Commons.

Now Adam was about a stone heavier and well into middle age. Although clearly an establishment figure, he was not a pompous man. His love for his children, his concern for them, his gratitude to Rachel, kept him human, if no longer quite as humble. Rachel supposed that Adam would never find love again and nor would she. She looked over at Spencer who was arguing, rather alarmingly, that he thought Hitler merely a passing phase – which she recalled was what Baldwin once, memorably and wrongly, had said about Bolshevism. People had short memories.

Bobby looked grave this evening, quiet and reflective, while Hélène sparkled with her usual vivacity, not letting the men monopolize the conversation, but joining in. If anything Hélène seemed to admire Hitler as many virulent opponents of Communism, like the Ferovs, often appeared to do. Finally Rachel burst out:

'You actually seem to be *approving* of Hitler!'

Hélène gave her a rather superior smile.

'There's certainly something about him, don't you agree? I think Germany needs a strong man and, in a way, they're lucky.'

'How can a country possibly be lucky with Hitler?' Rachel expostulated. 'You obviously haven't read Em's reports.'

'Oh, but I *have*, Lady Askham.' Hélène had such a polite, friendly way of speaking that it was hard to be offended by her. 'But it is simply *her* point of view. Others think differently. She seems singular, don't you think? Even *The Times* praises Chancellor Hitler. You, if I remember, admired the Communists. Yet we, for our part, thought of them just as you and Emmeline apparently think of Hitler. Only in Germany there is still democracy. In Russia there was none.'

'There won't be democracy in Germany for much longer,' Rachel replied, asking for Vance, the butler, to clear the table and serve the sweet. 'And more wine, Vance, for anyone who wants it.' Vance nodded and, signalling to the maids to remove the dishes, began solemnly to move round the table, the Burgundy wrapped in a white napkin in his hand. 'I'm afraid that the Nazis and the Communists have too much in common.'

'Yes, but which do you prefer?' Hugo had been watching everyone without having much to say on his own initiative, clearly willing to listen before reaching a conclusion. Maybe, just a little amused by it all. Did not his Turkish stepfather approve of Hitler, too?

Rachel, glancing at him, took a deep breath. 'Well, if *I* had to make a choice I think I would prefer Communism to Fascism. It is more equitable.'

'After all, you once called a cat after Lenin,' Cheryl's voice lacked any trace of amusement. 'And look what happened to poor Lenin.' Hugo stared at Cheryl who, on greeting him that evening earlier on, appeared diplomatically to have had difficulty recalling their last encounter.

'Do you mean the cat or the man?'

'Both.'

At that moment through the door, which had been left open by the maids clearing the table, his head held high, his tail high too and curling slightly at the end, walked Lenin, rather as if he owned the place and had come in late for dinner.

Cheryl, who had been about to answer Hugo, gazed wide-eyed towards the door and then, inelegantly stuffing her hand in her mouth, stood up and uttered a curious moan, as if someone were trying to throttle her.

Everyone turned to see what had happened and the butler, having replaced the wine, rapidly advanced to scoop up the cat. Ralph rose to his feet and went anxiously over to Cheryl. Rachel and Hugo exchanged glances which were not devoid of carefully concealed mirth, as the whole exercise had been strategically planned to teach Cheryl a lesson – the cat having been pushed through the door by a well-briefed maid.

Cheryl took her hand out of her mouth and abruptly sat down again, patting her chest as if she had choked on something she'd eaten.

'I'm frightfully sorry to make such a fool of myself. I thought it was the cat.'

'It is.'

'Yes, I know it's a cat but it looks just like ...'

'It looks remarkably like Lenin,' Ralph said affably, attempting to stroke the creature as Vance quickly bore it, protesting, past him.

'Perhaps he's come to haunt you.' Hugo was staring at Cheryl from under lowered brows and, with a pang, Rachel thought once again how like Bosco he was and how much Bosco would have enjoyed this practical joke. But would he have approved of her taking part in it? The planning had amused herself and Hugo all day – getting the cat in at just the right time, the secrecy and so on. How close together it had brought them again! She leaned over and touched Hugo's arm.

'Don't be naughty, Hugo. It *is* Lenin, Cheryl. He was saved by one of the servants, who brought him home to me.'

Cheryl, from terror to fretfulness, now wore an expression of outrage as she looked from her husband to her mother-in-law.

'Kindly give me the name of the servant and I'll have him dismissed.'

'Oh, *darling*!' Ralph, who had resumed his seat, threw down his napkin.

'I'm perfectly serious, Ralph.' Cheryl was positively smouldering. 'I *ordered* that cat to be destroyed ...'

'Yes, but after you said ...'

'*After* I said I was sorry, but that doesn't mean that the servant who disobeyed my orders shouldn't be dismissed. Was it Alfred, the footman?' she demanded of Hugo, who was still puce with merriment.

'I'm not likely to tell you that, *Lady Askham*!' His particular emphasis on her name seemed to render it intentionally insulting.

'And I think this is an awful fuss over nothing. May I?' Ralph consulted Rachel who nodded; then he lit a cigarette. 'I'm very glad Alfred, or whoever, saved the cat. I know that Cheryl was sorry about it and said she'd acted hastily. And now I feel we should forget about the whole thing. It was quite amusing, really.'

Cheryl stood up, reaching for the silver brocade bag that matched her evening dress, and turned to her husband. 'I'm afraid *I* cannot forget it, Ralph. And it did not amuse me. I feel I've been made a deliberate fool of and I'd like to be taken home.'

'Oh, I say!' Now Adam rose and motioned to Vance to leave the room. 'It wasn't done on purpose.'

'No, please, Sir Adam,' Cheryl glanced gratefully at him. 'I think it *was* done on purpose, judging by the expression on Hugo's face. He's enjoyed the whole thing. You've no idea what it's like to marry into the Askham family, to have your decisions repeatedly questioned, to be continually made a fool of...'

'My dear Cheryl, you're mistaken. Both Rachel and I married into the Askham family. I assure you ...'

'Well, now I think of you all as Askhams,' Cheryl looked pointedly at Hugo, 'whatever your origins and, believe me, it's a pretty awful thing to come among you for the first time. It is like meeting with a high wall with KEEP OUT written on it. To bring in that wretched cat tonight, deliberately, was the worst insult I think I have ever received. In Kenya we'd have a boy whipped if he'd disobeyed his mistress's instructions. Here it seems I can't even sack the offending servant. They work for me now, you know, not Ralph's mother. Well, I'm going to dismiss whoever is responsible, because I want you all to know that in my own home I will not be mocked and I insist that my orders are obeyed.'

Cheryl firmly tucked her bag under her arm, straightened the long string of pearls that had become entangled on her corsage of hot-house orchids and swept towards the door, saying over her shoulder, 'The car, please, Ralph.'

Rachel got up and went over to Cheryl, putting a restraining hand on her arm.

'I am most awfully sorry, Cheryl. I do beseech you not to spoil the evening.'

'*I* spoil it?' The look of outrage returned to Cheryl's face again. '*You* have utterly spoiled it with your cheap joke...'

'It was just meant as harmless fun. We were all upset about Lenin. One gets very fond of a household pet. You can understand that servant, who knew us and how important Lenin was in our lives, would disobey your orders. We didn't mean to make you feel so wretched, and I apologize. Do now let's forget the matter. We wanted Ralph here tonight to discuss family matters. It is about my daughter in Germany, whom I'm worried about. Please, Cheryl...'

'Kindly take your hands off me, Lady Askham!' Cheryl forcibly removed Rachel's hand and continued on her way out of the room. Ralph remained where he was, staring at the table. For a few moments no one spoke and then the sound could be heard of the car starting and sweeping up the drive towards the gate.

'You can't let her go!' Bobby suddenly got up, gazing guiltily at them as the beams of the headlights reached the road. But Ralph remained where he was, slumped in his chair, hands in his pockets, chin on his chest, looking quite indifferent to the fate of his wife.

Everyone looked towards Ralph, hesitating, until Adam said:

'You can't stop her now.' He began to take the band off a fine Havana he had produced from his cigar case. 'She's gone. I must say it was very unfortunate, this. A practical joke that went wrong. Can someone explain to me, please, about the cat?'

As they drifted back into the lounge, Rachel ordering coffee on the way, Hugo filled in for Adam, Spencer, Bobby and Hélène what they didn't know about the Lenin saga.

Even Bobby seemed rather shocked that Cheryl would think of killing the family pet. Hélène looked detached and amused, Spencer thoughtful.

After that it was very difficult to enjoy the evening, even though the discussion about Em was hardly meant to be enjoyable. It was Bobby who said that she should be brought home and that, as he was going to Germany soon, he would try and persuade her.

'I do hope you're not going to do business with the Nazis,' Adam said sharply.

'Why not? They do business with us.'

'Well, be very careful.'

'I've done business with the Communists and I'll do business with the Nazis. As it is, Germany is one of the main importers of my car. I don't want that to stop.'

Bobby could hardly mention his beloved Askham motor car without pausing, as if to reflect on the past. The level of his voice changed, as though he'd been bereaved. In a sense he had been. He missed the racing car more than its driver, because he thought Paolo had committed the cardinal sin of carelessness on the race track. There had been tell-tale marks of how hard he had braked.

The disastrous crash of the Askham 'Bosco' at La Monza two years before had put paid to Bobby's racing ambitions once and for all, not only because of the tragic death of Paolo Verdi but because the inquiry also showed that the racing car had a major steering fault. The consequent publicity given to the whole affair was nothing short of disastrous as firms like Fiat, Alfa Romeo, Renault and Citroën went from strength to strength, some of them relying on successes in Grand Prix racing to advertise their makes.

Instead of trying to rebuild his reputation Bobby had closed down the whole racing car works. No more Boscos were made. The Askham saloon was still built, but something of the fire had gone out of Bobby and his enthusiasm for cars. He had deflected this passion to racehorses instead, and it was to this that he now tried to change the conversation. He asked Ralph how the farm and stud were coming along, and Ralph enthusiastically began to outline his plans, while Rachel, Spencer, Hélène and Adam sat in another corner, still discussing politics.

Hugo sat with Ralph and Bobby listening carefully, an unrepentant Lenin on his lap purring as he stroked it, as if he, too, had enjoyed the joke.

At this moment of his life Hugo believed himself to be an unhappy young man standing at some crossroads or the other. He no longer enjoyed trailing round Europe with his mother and stepfather, good though they were to him, staying in luxurious hotels, visiting expensive restaurants and chatting inanities with the *beau monde*. Hugo knew how much Nimet loved him and how much she disliked him seeing Rachel. His visits to her made his mother uneasy. She had opposed this weekend in the country, even though he said it was to see the cat. In two days' time they would set off for Europe, travelling as usual in style. It was difficult to see life permanently from a first-class carriage, a chauffeur-driven limousine. Hugo envied Freddie, Jordan and Em their independence. Nimet had made him her prisoner.

Hugo had discovered, however, that he shared something very fundamental with Ralph. They were both close to the land, close to animals, and as he listened now to his half-brother outlining his plans for the farm something stirred in Hugo's blood, a fire that had been absent for many years.

Separation had meant that the rivalry between them was now long past, and Ralph had been very decent the time he found him at Askham House after the first meeting with Cheryl. He had been decent to him this evening about the cat, apologizing for his wife's exaggerated reaction to a bit of fun; seeming to disown her. He'd singled Hugo out to talk to, and then drew him into the conversation with Bobby.

It seemed, though, that Ralph had an object in life and he didn't. He leaned forward, following Ralph's words, interjecting now and then until his speech became a torrent; a torrent of praise for the land, enthusiasm for the basic laws of life: insemination, birth and growth.

After a while he saw Ralph looking at him with interest and he said:

'You sound very keen on all this, Hugo?'

'I am. I envy you.'

'You envy just what, exactly?'

'The farm, the animals.' Hugo's hand rested on Lenin. 'You know I love animals.'

'I know that.' Ralph smiled conspiratorially. 'You mean, you might be interested...'

At this point Rachel, who had had one ear cocked to what was going on in their part of the room, excused herself. The *rapprochement* between Hugo and Ralph was very sweet to hear. It was years since Ralph had thrashed Hugo, but it had taken years for the bitterness to go. There had always been a wariness between the brothers, but now that seemed on the wane. How splendid it would be if they could be friends.

Getting up, she left Spencer, Adam and Hélène to the political discussion and went over to the group on the other side of the room.

'Spencer and Adam will never agree, I'm afraid. I think if I go on listening to them it will affect my judgement.' She sat down next to Ralph and placed a hand on his arm. 'What's this I hear?'

'Hugo seems awfully interested in the farm.' Ralph turned with enthusiasm to his mother. 'I can do with a right-hand man.'

'You're not serious, are you?' Rachel looked at Hugo with raised eyebrows.

'To tell you the truth I never thought about it until just a moment ago, but why not? I've no plans, no career. I love horses and livestock. If Ralph really needs me to help him I could think of nothing I'd like better.'

'I don't know what your mother will say,' Rachel sounded doubtful. 'She won't be pleased. She'll think I've taken you away again.'

Hugo nodded understandingly.

'But you haven't, have you? It was Ralph's suggestion, my decision. I can't let them put me off if it's something I want to do. I really think it is. Up until today I have lacked any idea of what I wanted to do, but this really does appeal to me, whereas business doesn't. Never has. It upsets my stepfather, but he knows it. I don't want to be his heir.'

Bobby raised his eyes to heaven and got up.

'I don't know what it is about the Askhams that makes them so anti-business. I suppose I should be thankful as I have no rivals; but seriously, Ralph, I'm willing, as you know, to be your partner in the stud and I can put a lot of work your way. If Hugo, who is a member of the family after all, wants to join in too, personally I'd be delighted. Now I think we should all go home and help you make your peace with Cheryl.'

Ralph stubbornly leaned back and put his hands in his pockets.

'Or let her make her peace with me.' A gleam came into his eyes. 'I consider she is the one who has behaved badly tonight, not me. She went overboard. A joke, after all, is a joke.'

Rachel, about to turn and lead the way out of the room, raised both her hands in a silent handclap. But no one, other than Adam, seemed to see her as they all got up to follow her to the door.

CHAPTER 23

Jordan Bolingbroke was quite familiar with all the bars, casinos, strip joints, beer cellars, clubs of dubious propriety, as well as the better class ones, that proliferated on the main streets of Berlin: the Kurfurstendamm and Friedrichstrasse, the Jägerstrasse and Behrensstrasse, the Unter den Linden and the Munzstrasse. Jordan was a man of many parts, many lives; a young man, only just twenty-four, but older, far older, than his years.

In the time he had been in Germany Jordan had lived a crowded life, cramming into it many things that most people would never experience and would never want to. He was also a man of many places; he even had two homes, and several different personalities: the down-and-out; the man-about-town; the student; the affluent English aristocrat. He was a heterosexual who also liked men; he could move from the gutter to the opulent comfort of the Kaiserhof with practised ease.

Anyone who presumed that Sir Adam Bolingbroke, Judge of the High Court, was his father would have been astonished at the manner in which Jordan, from the best of families and educated in the best schools, took to a life of dissipation, which is perhaps what had attracted him to Berlin in the first place.

Yet in fact much of Jordan's tendency to what was then known as loose living was inherited from his natural father, Lord Denton Rigby. He, in his day, had been an acknowledged roué, from whom mothers of nicely brought up, yet nubile, young girls steered well clear, instructing their daughters – without notable success had they but known it – to do the same. This tendency would not have been diminished by Jordan's kinship with his mother, Lady Melanie, who had

476

enjoyed the plaudits of those who, before the War, were gentlemen in name only.

Jordan had led a pampered, sheltered life in surroundings of elegance and ease. Yet as a child he was comparatively unloved, rejoicing in many relations – aunts, uncles, cousins, friends and so on – but little real affection. He had managed to counteract this by pretended indifference, a remoteness that remained with him and probably added to his charm, his mystique among both sexes.

Admired in his childhood for his looks Jordan had, in fact, been a strikingly beautiful boy. As a man his looks were not merely handsome; they were beautiful, too. Jordan was extremely thin, immensely tall, and this width and height seemed to give him a satanic air which he exaggerated by a flamboyant style of dress, usually in black. On his head he always wore a round, black matador's hat, the brim lined with red silk, or occasionally he sported a red cardinal's hat when the mood took him.

Such an apparition was not considered strange, even in better class Berlin, when it presented itself at the Grand Hotel de Rome et Du Nord at the corner of the Charlottenstrasse and the Unter den Linden, and asked to speak to Mr Lighterman.

Bobby was waiting for him in the foyer of the hotel, as it was eleven in the morning and Hélène was still asleep. After greeting his half-brother reluctantly – for he did not approve of Jordan – he took him into the small room off the reception where there were two or three people asleep already over the *Berliner Tagblatt* or the *Morgenpost*. Bobby ordered coffee but Jordan airily waved a hand enquiring if there was champagne at the hotel.

'There *is* champagne,' Bobby said sharply, 'but you're not drinking it, not at this hour, anyway. Mother is very concerned about you, and your father too, and they have asked me to find out what you're up to.'

'Oh, Bobby, don't be a *bore*,' Jordan gave a huge, artificial yawn and fell to a contemplation of his well-manicured hands.

477

'You know I can behave myself, and do. At the moment I am the darling of the Nazis and what can be a better guarantee of behaviour, or, if it comes to it, safety than that?'

'That's what we heard and what worries us. In England the Nazis are not known for good behaviour.'

'That's because you read all that bilge that Em writes about them. She only knows half the story. In fact most Nazis are a very dedicated, well-disciplined body of men. I am almost on the verge of being introduced to Ernst Röhm,' Jordan rolled his eyes, 'he's so divine.'

'I think you should go back to England, or go to see Mother at least, for a few weeks. She worries about you terribly.'

'And does *Father* worry about me, too?' Jordan looked archly at Bobby.

'Your father is preoccupied by domestic cares and his duties on the bench; but I think he does worry. The whole family would like to see you all out of Germany and I'm here to see Em and Freddie too, and try and get them to leave as well. You will all have your fares paid, and I can get my representative who deals with my business affairs here to pick you up at your lodgings, or wherever you like.' Bobby looked at him sternly. 'You know, Jordan, you have never done much in life to justify your existence, but I do think you owe it to our mother not to worry her.'

'You think I owe *anything* to my mother?' Jordan gave a most impolite noise that sounded like a snort. 'What do I owe to Lady Melanie but a childhood full of insecurity and doubt? You know she's a *most* unnatural mother. When did I ever see her? Did you?'

'My case was different because I had a different father and my grandparents ... come on, Jordan,' Bobby swallowed his coffee in a gulp, 'you didn't do too badly.'

'*You* didn't do too badly, you mean.' Jordan looked at Bobby from under the brim of his black hat which he had kept on. '*You're* the one with the fortune. I would consider I hadn't been very badly done to either if I had your money.'

Two soldiers in uniform passed and Jordan glanced at them, eyeing them up and down; they were handsome in a blond, Nordic way, walking with the swagger of the Reichswehr, the German Army. The sight seemed to inspire Jordan and, drawing his chair towards Bobby, he leaned forward conspiratorially.

'Stop preaching at me in this brotherly way, Bobby. I know it's well meant, and you always were too bloody self-righteous for your own good, but if you have a proposition for me, which I can't accept, I have one for you which I hope you will. It's a business deal and I'll expect a commission. Such a good one, in fact, that if you co-operate I'll be able to stay in comfort in Germany for the rest of my life.'

'Really? As good as that?' Bobby looked amused and bent his head to Jordan's ear. 'I'm listening.'

'It is said that the divine Röhm is in need of arms.'

'Arms – you mean guns?' Bobby looked up in alarm.

'Guns, bombs, bullets, you know. Now that Hitler is Chancellor the Reichswehr, the official German Army, is trying to get rid of the SA, the Sturmabteilung, who brought Hitler to power. Hitler is proving as ungrateful to them as to everyone else who helped him on the way to the top. One day I think the divine Röhm who, after all, has known Hitler since the early days in Munich just after the War when Hitler was still a corporal in the Army and Röhm was a captain, will want to put the little NCO in his place.' Even though he was speaking in a voice scarcely above a whisper Jordan looked round and drew his chair even closer. 'I know that you have sole control, now, over Askham Armaments. Röhm is willing to pay whatever is asked for a consistent source of supply.'

'Are you mad?' Bobby moved his chair well back from Jordan, as though from fear of contagion. 'I wouldn't even supply the official German Army with armaments, never mind some little Hitlerite group of thugs. That's what I've heard Röhm is. Why do you keep on referring to him as "divine" for God's sake?' Bobby's voice was harsh with irritation.

'Because he's so handsome. He has such thrilling presence, not that I know him well, but one day I hope to. With your help I could. Surely you can wangle a little something, Bobby, for your brother?'

'I can do nothing of the kind.' Bobby rose as Hélène came to the door, looking in to see if they were there. Jordan stood up too, letting out a gasp of admiration.

'I say, I *say*!'

Hélène smiled as she shimmied towards them in a tight silk dress swathed at the hips to emphasize her bust. The dress came down to her calves and over one shoulder was a fox fur. A large hat, the brim pulled well over her eyes, was of the same material as the dress.

'It must have cost a fortune.' Jordan bent gallantly to kiss her hand.

'So must yours,' Hélène returned his admiring glance, nodding at his own outfit – black suit, silk shirt, shoes, black hat with its red lining, no tie. 'Are you a blackshirt?'

'By inclination, certainly. The Fascists wear brown shirts here, though.' Jordan sat down, drawing her with him, keeping her hand in his. 'Do you disapprove?'

'Not as much as Bobby,' Hélène glanced offhandedly at her husband. 'Of course we anti-Communists are all on the same side.'

'I thought you might say that.' Bobby returned her casual glance.

'And we're anti-Semitic too,' Jordan went on in a mono-other places since the War. Do you know they say that thirty they were in Russia. The Jewish conspiracy is at the root of all the bad things that have happened in Germany and many other places since the war. Do you know they say that thirty Jewish bankers divided the world between them after the War, and...'

'Oh, for God's sake!' Bobby got up and looked at his watch. 'Not even in fun, please. If Em or Freddie heard you talking like this they'd think you were raving mad.'

Jordan looked alarmed.

'Don't say the dreaded Lady Emmeline is about to join us?'

'She is, *and* the Honourable Freddie. I thought I'd take you all to lunch.'

'Not me, thank you.' Jordan patted his hat. 'I must make myself scarce. Freddie, of course, I adore even if we do differ. We still share a flat, you know, or sometimes we share a flat. I have many abodes where I park myself. But Em is quite beyond the pale,' Jordan stopped, amused at his own wit. 'Ha, ha! See the joke?' Then he turned to Hélène and kissed her cheek. 'You're divinely beautiful, chère Hélène. You're the best of all the women of the Askham family, loosely speaking.'

'What do you mean "loosely speaking"?' Hélène looked curiously at him through the smoke of the cigarette she'd just lit.

'Well, Charlotte, Cheryl, Mother ... all the acknowledged beauties. Not poor old Em, of course, no beauty she, or Susan. Aunt Rachel ...' Jordan made a gesture with his hand, '*comme ci, comme ça*. Handsome, I think, is the word. But seriously, belle Hélène, I think you can help me.'

'Me help you? How?' Hélène, amused, looked from Jordan to the back of Bobby, who was disappearing in the direction of the foyer to look for Em.

Jordan leaned close to her and whispered in her ear.

'I am trying to get Bobby to sell arms to the Sturmabteilung, the stormtroopers. One day they might, just might, unseat Hitler.'

'But do you want Hitler to be unseated?'

'I want to be Ernst Röhm's lover.'

As Hélène pulled away in some alarm, Jordan cried: 'Oh, I see I've shocked you. I didn't mean to. I thought you knew? I like women too, of course; but Röhm sends me to heaven – so brutal, *so* sensuous. I'm quite serious, though, Hélène. I always feel your hold on Bobby is stronger than people say.'

'I have no influence on Bobby, that I can assure you,' Hélène glanced towards the door. 'Since I can produce only girl children he's less interested in me than ever. But, seriously, if you want guns ...' for a moment she paused and looked at him, 'why not ask my father? He knows all about Askham Armaments. He'd do almost anything for money.'

'Quite, quite serious?' Jordan stared at her, his limpid eyes alight with speculation.

'Quite serious. But you mustn't say a word to Bobby, because he really has got this thing about Germany rearming. He's frightened of trouble. It *is* illegal to supply them, you know. Cars and machine tools are in, but guns are definitely out. If you like, I'll try and have a word with Father for you to prepare the ground.'

'I do adore you, Hélène. If I can ever return the favour,' Jordan lightly kissed her on the lips then rose, adjusting his hat. 'I must fly before the dreaded Em appears. I think she is trying to have me shot. Now *she* does frighten me to death!'

Em dismissed the news that she'd just missed Jordan with a wave of her hand.

'He's not dangerous, but irresponsible. He associates with the riff-raff at all the Nazi *lokals* and is notorious for the company he keeps, and the way he dresses, even in Berlin where, these days, almost anything goes. Or that was the case. Once Hitler became Chancellor it was possible to see a change, and things are not as easy as they were. He is supposed to want to clean up the city, so we shall see. What I hate about Jordan is his blind and irrational anti-Semitism. Personally I'll have nothing to do with him, but I am ashamed of him as he's a relative, and I wish he would take your offer and go.'

'Jordan is a puzzle to me.' Freddie agreed with his sister. 'The company he keeps, not only Nazis but with the minor criminal fraternity in Berlin, is deplorable. He says he wants to be a writer, but I have yet to see him putting pen to paper.'

'The thing is that we do want you to leave Berlin.' They were lunching at the Horfleys, a restaurant known for its variety as well as its high prices. 'Your mother is very worried about you, Em. Have you been threatened in any way?'

'One or two interviews at Big Red Alex, the Police Headquarters; but I'm not afraid of them. I am much more afraid for Peter Klein who has been arrested twice since Hitler became Chancellor. He edits a small journal called *Die Wahrheit* which is German for The Truth. I want him to come and edit *The Truth* in London but, like many Jews who think of themselves as first and foremost German, he refuses. He says that Hitler will never dare hurt the Jews on a large scale, but I say that Hitler has sworn to do just that and will. His father is like Peter; devoted to his clinic for children on the Büschingplatz which is the really poor area. The Kleins think nothing can touch them. I only hope they're right.'

'If that's the way they think then you must leave them. I'm concerned for you, not them. Through me your mother *begs* you to come home. Freddie?'

Freddie screwed up his nose.

'I'll stay with Em. She needs someone to look after her. I really agree with the Kleins. A few nasty things go on, but not to those who don't provoke the regime. After all, technically it is still a democracy even though Em thinks Germany has had its last free elections. She takes too gloomy a view of things. I'm staying, but thanks all the same.'

'Well, I have done what I can,' Bobby drained his wine glass and looked at his wife. 'Some more sightseeing? Tonight we're going to the Metropol. Anyone want to come?'

'Then where, after Berlin?' Em leaned her chin on her elbows and smiled interestedly at Hélène, who was touching up her face. She was a little in awe of Bobby's wife, whose sophistication made her feel like a gauche schoolgirl.

'Then Rome, thank heaven,' Hélène said, peering at herself. 'There's something really very unsettling at the moment about Berlin.'

*　　*　　*

483

In truth, Hélène Lighterman found most things in life unsettling, whether she was on the move or staying put. Basic to her was her discontent despite the fact that she was married to one of the richest men in England, and wealth and its power meant much to her, more than love.

At the age of thirty-one, married to Bobby for nearly six years and now the mother of three daughters, Hélène, despite her beauty, habitually wore a peevish look as though something was not quite right. It made people uneasy just to look at her.

Hélène travelled around with Bobby because it gave her something to do, and they did it in style. The places they visited – Paris, Vienna, Berlin – were somewhere else to spend more money. But by the autumn of 1933 all was not well in Berlin; it had an air of frenzy, as if the population were preparing itself for even more cataclysmic events – if that were possible – than the ones it had undergone since the War.

Bobby was easily persuaded to leave Berlin, where he had arranged with his agent to draw out of a number of German business undertakings, and leave for Rome. He had failed in the family task of persuading his half-brother and cousins to leave; but none of them mattered enough to him for him really to care. Very little about other people was of concern to Bobby Lighterman.

But in Rome the Lightermans were restless, too. Under Mussolini Italy was rapidly becoming a copy of Nazi Germany. Bobby wanted to return to England, but Hélène wished to stop over in Paris because of the promise she had given Jordan to talk to her father. There were few things Hélène enjoyed more to liven up a boring life than intrigue, whether in her own personal life or that of others. Guns sounded quite fun.

Bobby went on to London after leaving Hélène in Paris. Rather than go to a hotel for a few days she decided to stay with Susan, despite the presence of her brother with whom, like the rest of the family, she was not on conversational terms.

But it was easy to get out of speaking to him, because Kyril was hardly ever at home – rose late and stayed out until the small hours.

'If he is as difficult as you say he is – and I believe you – surely you'd be happy to have him back in Russia?'

Hélène and Susan, who'd always got on well, had spent the morning shopping and gossiping before meeting Charlotte, and then going on to Mademoiselle Chanel's boutique in the rue Cambon. For Hélène it was a perfect kind of day, a day spent in congenial company, no Bobby, free to do as she liked and spend money.

But no, Susan was reluctant to admit she would be happy to have her husband back in Russia, although they had little in common.

'People *do* get divorced, you know.' Hélène thoughtfully gazed at the passers-by in the rue Royale where they were drinking coffee at a bar, packages stacked round them on the floor; more to come. In a few moments Susan's chauffeur would arrive to pick them up and take them back to her flat, and then they could begin all over again.

'Oh, I know; it may surprise you, but I do love Kyril. I think he loves me too – inasmuch as he can love anyone. He'd never admit it.'

'Funny things, men. In a way I think they're all alike. Did you, for instance, ever think Bobby loved me?'

Susan was disconcerted by the question, and concentrated on sipping her hot coffee. Like Hélène she was smart, but favoured clothes with a severe cut, which was why she liked the boyish, tailored lines of Chanel. There was an autumnal nip in the air and both women wore costumes with fox furs, and hats – Susan's a little pillbox, also designed by Chanel, and Hélène the broad-brimmed hat she favoured because huge brims set off her Slav good looks.

'I'm sure Bobby loved you and still does,' she murmured after a long pause. 'Bobby is a very reserved man, slow to show

485

his feelings. In his way I know he loves you and is faithful to you.'

'Hmmm!' Hélène grunted, gazing at her cup as though the answer lay there. At that moment the chauffeur came in, scooped up the parcels and took Susan and Hélène to their rendezvous at La Coupole with Charlotte, who had come up to Paris for the day.

It was nearly two years since Paolo's death, difficult years for his widow left with three young children, a large house not yet completed, and a pile of debts left by her husband. Secondary only to the shock of his death was the revelation that Paolo had been almost penniless, having no private means and having spent his earnings as fast as Charlotte had spent her inheritance.

It was about this time that the Askham children were beginning to realize that they had not the resources enjoyed by their father and mother before the War. This was largely due to the fundamental error of Ralph's in parting so hastily with the Askham share of the family business to Bobby; but it was also due to other factors: the Wall Street crash, and the economic situation in European countries which had still not recovered from the War. There was widespread inflation – in Germany, before Hitler, people had had to carry their money round in suitcases – and many other unstable currencies beside the Mark.

It didn't help if there were large houses demanding upkeep and women like Cheryl and Hélène, who were totally unconcerned about spending, convinced that there was always more at the bottom of the barrel. In Hélène's case there was, but in Cheryl's there was not, only she wouldn't believe it.

For Charlotte that bottom had been scraped increasingly over the past two years, and now she felt that there was no one to whom she could turn. Nor did she particularly want to. Her pride prevented her asking Bobby for help, and she knew that her mother and Ralph were unable to put their hands on spare cash. Ralph had the expense of his new farm and Rachel had the paper which had never paid its way, always preferring news to advertisement, the truth to commercial good sense.

The two years of grief had left their mark on Charlotte, who was only twenty-four when she was widowed. Yet it was a woman of extraordinary charm and beauty who stood up to greet her cousins as they entered La Coupole, deposited there by the chauffeur on his way home. Charlotte had lost the weight she had put on during those contented years of marriage and childbearing. Her tall, slender figure was thought, by some, to verge on the malnourished, while her face could be considered cavernous were it not for the brilliance of her aquamarine eyes, the curve of her well moulded lips and the deep auburn gloss of her swept-back hair. Everyone in Paris wore hats these days but Charlotte had preferred a velvet bandeau which hit just the right note of stylish elegance, despite the simplicity of her tailored costume over a plain tie blouse.

The women had not met together for some time, and over the inevitable cocktails were details of trips to Venice and London by Susan, and a quick résumé of all the capitals of Europe by Hélène.

'I came especially to see you,' Hélène clasped Charlotte's hand. 'I really have missed you.'

'You must come and stay, although how long I can keep the house I don't know.'

'But you can't sell that beautiful place by the water!' Susan, looking aghast, signalled to the *maître d'hôtel* that they were ready to order.

'If I can get a buyer I will, though I don't want to live in Paris. I prefer the suburbs.'

'Why stay in France at all? Did you ever think of returning to England?'

'No, I never did,' Charlotte said slowly, accepting the menu and studying it. 'It feels like a defeat to go home, back to Mummy. Besides, where can I go?'

'Well, back to Mummy; or Cheryl, I'm sure she'd love to have you.' Hélène ordered snails and *filet* steak and handed her menu back.

'Cheryl! Oh, I couldn't go there! There is war enough already.'

'War?' Susan would have *salade de tomates* followed by roast quail, and returned her menu with a smile. 'War with whom?'

'Well, war, generally speaking. Cheryl has offended most members of our family including my grandmother, whom she is trying to eject from her house.'

'I do see Cheryl's point of view.' Susan was asked to taste the wine. 'She has had an awful job trying to establish her right to her own home and life, as Ralph's wife. She didn't like this communal way the Askhams seem to want to do everything.'

'I like Cheryl well enough, though I must say I scarcely know her.' Charlotte, despite rumours, decided to be magnanimous. 'As long as she makes Ralph happy what do we care? But she *has* ruffled a few feathers, not least my mother's. I could *never* go back and beg for room at Askham House, even if it does belong to my brother.'

'Are things as bad as that?' Susan, cushioned not only by her own inheritance but Bobby's, looked concerned.

'They're bad,' Charlotte shrugged, 'but I can cope.'

These were brave words, however, spoken in the presence of two women she knew to have almost unlimited wealth. Askhams did not advertise misfortune, or beg for money though, later, in Chanel's salon, where they were received by the head vendeuse, she was careful not to show too much interest in any of the gowns or frocks especially modelled for Princesses Hélène and Tatiana, well-known patrons of that establishment.

The private showing was halfway through when the curtains parted and the great woman herself entered, arms outstretched in welcome as she embraced first Hélène, then Susan.

'I heard you were here and I *had* to see you.' Gabrielle Chanel spoke excellent English because of her long liaison with the Duke of Westminster, now over. Because of her passion for secrecy her age was a matter of some speculation, but in the year in question it was supposed that she was around forty-five, maybe fifty. She no longer had the beauty of her youth, when she had numbered among her lovers most of the military garrison at Saumur, but she was incomparably chic in the black dress known round the world for its style and simplicity. Mademoiselle was also extremely wealthy, due to the success of her perfume, Chanel No. 5, which, legend alleged, was based on a fragrance originating from a Russian émigré and was supposed to be the best-selling perfume in the world. The previous year she'd held an exhibition of jewellery designed by herself in her own inimitable style, which had aroused the envy of professional jewellers.

Since her liaison with Westminster she was received by the best society in Paris, and counted innumerable people of wealth and position among her friends. She was particularly fond of Hélène and attended all the Lighterman parties, entertaining them in return in her beautiful house in the Faubourg St Honoré.

'And who have we here?' Mademoiselle Chanel turned to Charlotte, standing behind her cousins.

'This is my cousin, Gabrielle. May I present Lady Charlotte Verdi.'

'Ah! Lady Charlotte,' the diminutive Chanel, her face creased with sympathy, reached up and embraced the woman she had never met before and drew her cheek against hers. 'Now I know who you are. That terrible accident to your husband, and you are so young …' She stepped back and gazed at Charlotte, bird-like head first on one side then the other, clicking her tongue, 'and so beautiful. Did anyone ever suggest to you that you should model?'

'*I*, a mannequin?' Charlotte laughed aloud. 'Mademoiselle, I am not even very interested in clothes.'

'I can tell that,' Chanel said, regarding her critically from head to foot, shaking her head, 'but we can soon change it. You would be a sensation.'

'Are you serious, Gabrielle?' Susan looked excited. 'Would you really think of employing Charlotte?'

'I am sure that Lady Charlotte does not need the money, but the prestige of modelling for me would be considerable. I am asked, you know, by Mr Goldwyn to design clothes for his films. It could change her life which, if I properly divine, is not happy.'

'A widow, with young children ...' Hélène began and Chanel nodded.

'How I can imagine! To lose such a famous husband, one so handsome.'

'And loving,' Charlotte said quietly. 'That was the most important thing. It is his love I miss more than anything else.'

'And you are lonely too, I expect?' Chanel nodded her head wisely, looking at the bored mannequins who, still draped in their poses as if fixed for all time, gazed at her with vacant expressions. She clapped her hands.

'The next garments, please, girls, for the Princesses and Lady Charlotte. *Dépêchez-vous!*' She clapped her hands, sweeping them before her with a little flurry like a flock of geese. Then she sat next to Charlotte, tucking her long slender hand in hers.

'I promise you, I can transform your life: LADY CHAR-LOTTE VERDI MODELS FOR CHANEL.' Mademoiselle sketched imaginary banner headlines on the air. 'You have wonderful bones, and you're so thin! I like my girls to be like birds, wraith-like. Don't put on an ounce of fat! Then you will be a sensation.'

While his wife dined at one of the best restaurants in Paris and then viewed the latest models of Mademoiselle Chanel, Kyril sat on a bench in the Tuileries gardens, his hands in his pockets, a paper stuck in one of them, his legs stretched before him. He didn't look like a tramp, but nor did he look like a Russian prince, married to an extremely wealthy woman. He looked like a member of the proletariat which is what he considered himself to be, the only description he would really appreciate.

The years had aged Kyril so that, although he was not yet forty, he looked about fifty with thinning, fairish hair – thick at the sides and almost bald on top – and a crumpled careworn face. He was a man constantly at war with himself and his ideals; passionately opposed to Fascism and committed to Communism without seeing, like many other people, how related the two were. In France there was a considerable body of right-wing opinion which supported such movements as the Francists, Croix de Feu and the French equivalent of the SA, the stormtroopers of the Cagoule. All these were approved of, if not actually supported by, the exiles from Communism like the Ferovs and their friends. It was no wonder that Kyril, daily running from one meeting to another, embracing various left-wing factions and Communist calls, didn't speak to his family, nor they to him. He despised them.

The leaves fluttered down from the sparse trees to join more damp, trodden leaves on the ground and Kyril shivered. Looking up at the sound of footsteps along the even path of the Tuileries gardens, he saw a man dressed like him in a raincoat with the same newspaper sticking out of his pocket. The man sat down next to him, without greeting, and proceeded to search his pockets until he produced a pack of cigarettes. One of these he extracted before stuffing the packet back again.

'*Du feu?*' he asked, turning to Kyril, who took out a box of matches, lit the man's cigarette, replying in Russian: 'Certainly.'

The man nodded, inhaled and appeared to regard the pleasant, tranquil scene with some satisfaction. The cold did not seem to bother him.

'It was not wise for us to meet at the Embassy,' he said at length, in Russian. 'We don't want your name on our files.'

'But you received my application to go home?'

'We received it,' the man nodded, glancing briefly at Kyril, 'and, since then, we have done a lot of work on your case, made many enquiries. We wonder why you should want to return to a country which kept you in exile for eight years, deprived you of the company of your wife and child.'

'Because I love it. I love Russia.'

'But do you love Communism? Still?'

'Yes, I do.' Kyril's voice was firm. He knew he would be cross-examined.

'But how can you, when you were so badly treated?'

'Because the Revolution meant that there were some injustices, inevitably, everywhere. It had to be. You cannot sweep away a complete way of life without making mistakes. I believe fervently in the Revolution. I repent of my errors, and I wish to serve Russia.'

The man nodded, as if satisfied.

'It appears that you are known to several of our Communist cells in Paris and Berlin, and yet you are married to the sister of the notorious capitalist Robert Lighterman.'

'That is not my fault. When I married her – an act done in a moment of folly for which I have paid dearly – I didn't even know he existed.'

'True. I have checked on that, too. But Prince Ferov, your father ...'

'I never speak to him, nor he to me. I assure you, comrade, that when I go back I will divorce my wife and have nothing to do with my family again.'

'But how do we know we can trust *you*, comrade Ferov?' The man threw his smouldering cigarette on to the leaves. 'These may all be fine words in order to gain an entry into Russia to spy for our enemies.'

Kyril's answer was a bitter laugh.

'You think I want to spy for them, these friends of Hitler who have killed hundreds of our colleagues in Germany? I detest them. I detest my life here and never wished to come.

Had I been consulted I would never have agreed to go to the West with Bobby Lighterman. Comrade Stalin didn't know how I felt. He thought he was doing me a favour, for my wife's brother. Yet life here is a torment. I am not free. I am willing to give up everything I have – my wife, my children, any claims to any money and, incidentally, I have none of my own, for the motherland. I would even go to Siberia again, and resume my detention there in order to return home. But it is my humble hope that I may eventually be of service to the Party.'

The man leaned back and stared thoughtfully in front of him, fumbling once more in his pockets for a cigarette. Once again Kyril went through the ritual of lighting it and, briefly, their eyes met through the flame. Kyril saw a man of about fifty with close-cropped black-grey hair and a lined face like his own, also marked with scars, one of which went right across his left eye. Kyril then saw that the eye didn't move like its fellow and guessed that it was made of glass, giving rise to a hard, staring look that gave his companion a sinister expression. Kyril shivered and, drawing his coat more firmly round him, extinguished the match.

'You can be of service to the Party,' the man said at last, 'but not in the way you think. I'm afraid I am here to dash your hopes though, in the long run, you may gain more than you expected – the thanks and admiration of our leader Stalin.'

'How can I do that?' Kyril shuffled on the bench, aware of the cold penetrating his bones.

'You are of more use to us in the West, where you are. Gradually you will stop attending Party meetings and announce your conversion to Fascism. Not too quickly: it must be done gradually. It is our belief that a right-wing coup is intended to topple the government in Spain, rather as has happened in Germany and Italy, and we wish to have advance knowledge of it. In your position, with your record, your family opposed to Communism, people will believe you.'

'But everyone knows I want to return to Russia.'

'You will have a change of heart.' The man shrugged. 'Slowly, not too obviously, you will confess your mistakes, see the error of your ways. Did you know your father, for instance, Prince Ferov, was heavily involved with right-wing groups? No?' He looked quizzically at Kyril. 'Your father is already doing your work for you. Mr Lighterman has recently visited Berlin. What did he do there? Your wife's half-brother is a notorious Nazi supporter, a homosexual and a degenerate, a friend of Röhm. Why don't you go and visit him? You might get on. You are too well placed, comrade, for us to want to lose your services. If you love Russia you have the chance to make up for your error in defying the Party in 1921, and becoming a hero of the people in the process. Will you do it?'

'I must think about it.' In his heart Kyril was weeping. 'Please, give me time.'

'Time is what we don't have.' The man looked at his watch. 'I am giving you the chance to be recruited, now, into the forces of Soviet espionage, and I must return to the Embassy with an answer. Otherwise you will be cast into the wilderness.'

Kyril hunched his shoulders, staring at the ground. He was being asked to do everything he hated: to pretend to be a bourgeois, a supporter of the Fascists. But it did make sense. He *was* well placed, none better. Finally he stood up and held out his hand.

'Tell the comrades there was never any doubt of my answer,' he said. 'I await your further instructions.'

'Meet me here one week from today.' Unsmiling, the man began to button his raincoat. 'My name is Gregor.'

Without a word of thanks or farewell Gregor turned his back on Kyril and walked quickly back along the path, the wet leaves squelching beneath his feet.

CHAPTER 24

In the same way that the realization had come to members of the Askham family that they no longer could command the wealth of previous years, so did it slowly dawn on them that, instead of the bride they would all have wished for him, Ralph had, indeed, taken a viper to his bosom. Her dark, soft, beautiful looks became synonymous with witchery and even her most benign actions came, in time, to be called into question.

Maybe the truth came home to them all at last when the story about the cat became more widely known because, whatever one thought of the human species, animals in a family like the Askhams were sacred; especially an old, well-beloved cat like Lenin.

Lenin had unexpectedly united the family against Cheryl. The story of the night that he walked into the dining-room at Darley Manor spread like wildfire until there was hardly a member of the family, or a branch of the family, even remotely placed in Scotland like the Kittos, who hadn't heard of it. They heard, too, how the worm Ralph, for the first time since his marriage, finally turned and allowed his wife to drive herself home. They learned what happened when he got back to Askham Hall, that she refused to allow him into their bedroom and that Ralph had driven up to London the same night and stayed there for a week completing the purchase of his farm, out of touch with his wife altogether.

Ralph then travelled back to Askham Hall with an ultimatum: Cheryl did as he wished, behaved like his wife or they would get divorced. It was almost the last that Cheryl was to see of that soft side of Ralph which she despised; but she knew how to get her own back. She merely bided her time.

The awareness that her husband was, after all, a man of steel and not straw made her look carefully at what she was likely to lose if she disobeyed him, and she saw that it was too much – far, far too much.

So the Askham watchers, that spring and summer of 1933, saw a *rapprochement* between husband and wife, what some called a second honeymoon. Cheryl, dressed in casual cotton frocks or, occasionally, in tailored trousers, went about the farm admiring this and that, waxing lyrical about acres of golden gleaming wheat and the latest brood mare for the stud.

To Ralph – but to him only – she became docile, compliant, eager to please. If only Ralph would let her go up to London occasionally? Of course he would. Or just pop over to Paris for a day or two? Why, certainly. In that summer of 1933 Ralph thought he had reached the pinnacle of his happiness as a man and as a husband. There was only one thing he wanted to complete this contentment, this sense of fulfilment: a child.

But Cheryl said there was time; plenty of time. Wouldn't it be better to wait until the farm was really running well? Ralph, because he had never ceased to love his wife and trust her, believed her, and agreed.

Dulcie Askham had been born in 1852, the year after the Great Exhibition, the heyday of Victorianism. By Christmas 1933, when another large Askham gathering was being planned, she was an old, rather enfeebled lady of eighty-one. But her bright, alert mind was completely unimpaired, and she maintained a firm grip on everyone and everything about her with the energy of a much younger woman. It was now eighteen years since Bosco had been killed, incredible as it seemed, and memories of the Great War were being lost in a vague apprehension about future conflict as Hitler consolidated his power over Germany, and withdrew from the League of Nations and the disarmament conference. These actions led Ramsay MacDonald, who headed a coalition government in

Britain, to declare that 'the fabric of civilization could almost be heard breaking about our ears'.

England, however, had rallied under the National government and Rachel ceased to rail against it in her paper, concentrating, instead, on what was happening in Germany. She was increasingly fearful for her two children there and the fate of their friends, the Klein family. Peter, in particular, was in danger. He was afraid his paper would be suppressed and kept on moving its offices out of range of the stormtroopers who had twice attacked it and broken the furniture. Rachel would like to have got them all out of Germany, for good.

Princess Irina loved making lists and organizing people. Thus she frequently came into conflict with Cheryl who, while she was at the Hall, found herself with not enough to do. Accordingly she spent her time planning what changes she would make if, and when, she and Ralph ever had the place to themselves.

'I can't think why you have to invite the bastard,' Cheryl said, inspecting the latest list Irina had drawn up, together with the placement of rooms.

'Who?' Irina, knowing quite well who Cheryl meant, spoke coldly.

'Hugo, the late Lord Askham's illegitimate son.'

'I don't know why you have to refer to him like that.' Irina moved her pencil down the list. 'We all call him Hugo. As a matter of fact I like him very much. He is a young man of great charm and ability and has done an awful lot for Ralph.'

'Ralph would have managed to farm quite well without him.' Cheryl angrily lit one of the many cigarettes she smoked in the day. 'He was just being kind.'

'Ralph was not being kind,' Irina insisted. 'Hugo loves animals, as you know ...' her tone took on a malicious note and she looked meaningfully at Cheryl who, stung by the insinuation, replied:

'Oh, don't we know just how kind he is to animals! But not to humans. Breaks his mother's heart moving away from home. Just when she was so kind to him. He plays one off against the other – from Lady Askham to Mrs Igolopuscu, and back again. Like a flirt. I don't think he's quite normal.'

'Don't you? I do. It's clear to me he wanted to lead his own life. It's perfectly natural. He still sees a lot of his real mother, I understand.'

'I heard she was going to disinherit him. I hope not,' Cheryl added, 'we don't want him as an added burden on our hands.'

'Sometimes I can't understand you, Cheryl.' The Princess looked at her frankly. They had been standing in the small parlour, from which Irina directed the housekeeper and the staff, and Cheryl now crossed her arms and perched on the side of a chair. 'Why are *you* unpleasant about Hugo? Why are you always criticizing people? What's wrong with you? Are you *so* unhappy?'

'Maybe I would like to be alone in my own home,' Cheryl said, after appearing to give the matter careful thought. 'Maybe I don't like bastards, and poverty-stricken aliens who toady up to Ralph's grandmother ... for gain,' she added spitefully and then sprang back as Irina slapped her hard on the cheek.

'That is the very worst, nastiest thing you have ever said,' Irina spat at her.

'And that is the very worst thing *you* have ever done,' Cheryl said, leaping up, her hand on her face. 'Don't think, Madame Princess, that you won't live to regret it.'

She ran out of the house, jumped into her small car parked in the drive, and wept all the way to the farm twenty miles away where Ralph was showing some horsebreeders his collection of thoroughbreds.

As soon as he saw her running towards him Ralph excused himself and flew along the path catching her in his arms as though she was about to fall.

'Darling ...'

'I can't stand her a moment longer!' Cheryl clasped her cheek. 'She will have to go. She's the most evil, malevolent influence.'

'Darling ... who? Who?'

'Irina. She hit me.'

'She hit you?' Ralph's expression of concern turned to one of outrage. 'Where? Why?'

'I told her a few home truths. How bossy she is in the home, always toadying up to your grandmother. Have you ever thought that she probably steals things?'

'But she doesn't need to steal. She has plenty of money.'

'Thanks to your family. Not a single penny of her own.'

'Thanks to the Lightermans, not us.'

'Don't you see, Ralph? Are you blind?'

Cheryl brushed back the hair which had fallen over her face and, suddenly dry-eyed, linking her arm through his, strode away from the stables where Hugo had taken Ralph's place in the discussions.

'Blind about what, darling?'

'We are stifled, Ralph, you and I. You say you want us to be happy and me to be a wife to you and so on, and that you want children, and I do too; but how can we be happy and normal always living with other people in the house? It's hateful for me. Can't you see that?'

'Darling, we can move to the Grange ...'

'But I don't see why *we* should move to the Grange,' Cheryl stamped her feet petulantly. 'If *anyone* moves it should be your grandmother and her dreadful companion. If we had our own home, darling, if I could feel free and do what I liked there, why ...' she stopped and turned to entwine her arms round his neck, 'we could start the family that we both so much want.'

'Cheryl, we can do that anyway.' Puzzled, perplexed, unhappy, Ralph looked down at her, linking his arms around her waist.

'I might be able to stand your grandmother,' Cheryl said at

last, 'but that Ferov woman will have to go. Frankly, darling, it's her or me. Now, what do you say?'

And Cheryl, breaking away from him, tears completely forgotten, pursed her mouth in that familiar expression of defiance that Ralph, his heart sinking, knew so well.

It was put around that Princess Irina had gone back to Paris for a while to be with her family, but no one believed it. For one thing her husband was hardly ever there and her devotion to Dulcie, coupled with her love for Askham Hall, to which she had contributed a lot, was well known.

But Ralph, taking her aside, had told her that Cheryl refused to stay in the place while she was there. He begged for her understanding because it was his hope that she would soon conceive, and start their much longed for family. Cheryl was so tense. That was the matter with her. Once she had a baby things would be all right and Irina could return again. It was only temporary.

In exchange the Princess told Ralph what she considered were a few home truths about his wife, which alienated her from him even further so that he agreed with Cheryl she should go and, within days, Irina had packed everything she had and gone. Dulcie took to her bed, refusing to leave it, and the customary, traditional Christmas party was in jeopardy. Hélène refused, anyway, to speak to the woman who had virtually ordered the exile of her mother, and the whole family were thrust into a state of unease which was almost worse than before.

Because his wife wouldn't go, Bobby refused as well, and they went to Mabel Lighterman instead where his old aunts, his father's sisters, all of whom had married well, also foregathered with their respective spouses, children and grandchildren.

Because Bobby didn't go Susan wouldn't go, and she took a reborn Kyril and their children to Venice instead. Recently, for reasons no one quite knew, Kyril had undergone a profound change of heart and had broken with Communism. He said his years in Paris had made him so disillusioned with Russia, when he compared its isolation and deprivation with the freedom, the economic benefits of living in the West. He pleaded for forgiveness and reconciliation with his family, which was immediately, and gladly, given – for was there not joy in heaven for the one sinner who did penance? So his mother, father and brother Dima were included in the family party at Venice as well.

Em felt that if she left Germany she would never be allowed to go back. The fate of the Kleins was causing her and Freddie much anxiety. They had begged them to leave the country after the passing of Hitler's Aryan laws, forbidding Jews to hold offices of state; but Peter wanted to tell the truth in his journal and Dr Klein refused to leave his patients as long as he was allowed to stay with them.

No one had seen Jordan for some time. He had taken a flat in Munich to try and see more of Röhm, whom Hitler had appointed a Reich Minister together with Rudolf Hess. Hitler had a flat in the Prinzregenstrasse in Munich and spent a lot of time in the city which had seen the beginnings of his movement.

Charlotte, free now from the feeling that she was a parasite after her acceptance of Chanel's offer, was happy to go to the Hall for Christmas; but Hugo wanted to be with Nimet, who was much more unhappy about his move to the country than he thought she would be.

So it was still a large, though much reduced party who gathered at the Hall on 23 December: Ralph, Cheryl, Rachel with Adam and the little children, Charlotte and her children and Christopher Bolingbroke and his wife Sylvia who now had two babies of their own.

Christopher Bolingbroke was a solid, worthy man who reminded everyone of his Uncle Arthur, who had died in America in 1904. Looking at Christopher across the table at traditional Christmas lunch, Rachel thought it was quite possible to see Arthur sitting there: stolid, industrious, hard-working and dull, even though she had not known him well because he died before she and Bosco were married. None of Melanie's children altogether lacked looks, and Christopher was handsome in a rather bovine way, with a lot of Adam about him – sparse hair, features it was difficult to imprint exactly on the memory.

But in all his twenty-eight years Christopher had never given anyone any trouble. He had been good at home, good at school, good at university, had gone into a safe career – law like his father – and married the pretty, unremarkable, unexceptional girl who now sat next to her father-in-law. Sylvia had been one of a number of girls just like her whom Christopher had been seeing when he decided it was time to get married. For Christopher Bolingbroke, indeed, there was, in the biblical sense, a time for everything under heaven and he stuck to it.

There was quite a lot more to Sylvia, however, than was at first apparent. The daughter of a prosperous solicitor from Leicester, she had been in London doing a secretarial course when Christopher had met her. She was fair with pale blue eyes and pink cheeks, rather tall and with a good figure.

But, unlike Christopher, Sylvia had sparkle, and she had a temper. She wasn't content to do the dreary housewifely things everyone expected her to do, and had engaged a nanny for the babies so that she could have plenty of free time of her own. Sylvia aspired; not to domestic chores like housework, flower arranging and gardening, though she was good at all these things, of course; but to leading a more exciting social life among the sort of people that the Askhams belonged to, and she enjoyed foreign travel. For instance, she was responsible for Freddie and Jordan going to live in Germany.

It was purely coincidental that Sylvia's fascination with Germany coincided with the rise of Adolf Hitler. To her now Germany was but a distant memory and the Führer a matter of complete indifference as she made her plans to mount the social scale of the ladder so conveniently provided by her husband's mother, once a *doyenne* of fashion and social kudos on the London scene.

Sylvia competently held her own at her end of the table, keeping her father-in-law interested in whatever they were talking about. She gestured a good deal and her rather high voice was audible above the rest. Clearly, she enjoyed a drink. Not that anyone could take exception to that but, Rachel thought, she grew more obtrusive every year from small, almost insidious beginnings.

Dulcie sat at the top of the table, a peerless and graceful matriarch who had been born at the time when women wore crinolines and England was the undisputed mistress of the world.

Rachel tried not to brood on Germany during this happy family party, but it was hard not to. Em was still there, and Freddie had become involved with a German girl and was staying with her family in the Bavarian Alps. According to Em it was quite serious. 'A pity,' Em had written in her letter, 'because Marian Klein is head over heels about Freddie and she is such a sweet, good girl who needs an emotional anchor in this very trying time the family are going through. I thought he liked her, too. The new girl is a blonde Aryan called Sophie Schmidt. Her father is a civil servant – one of the old *Junker* class and strongly in favour of Hitler. But he is not alone. So many of his fellow countrymen and women believe he is the only one who can save Germany from anarchy.'

Dulcie had tinkled her glass with a fork and the conversation stopped abruptly.

Then, smiling, she began her speech: 'I always feel a little sad at this time of the year because, as you know, it is a time when thoughts go to our loved ones, those who are dead and those who are absent, and this year there are so many in this last category. I hoped our dear Emmeline and Frederick would be home by now, as what is going on in Germany worries me, although Rachel tries to reassure me on this point.

'Alas, Melanie couldn't be here to join us and nor, for family reasons I understand, could Bobby. I must tell you how much I miss my friend Princess Irina and hope that her visit to Paris will only be of short duration. In my old age she has become almost indispensable to me.' Here she paused to get her breath and a riveting glance was cast at Cheryl, who had her chin propped on one hand on the table, her eyes on its shining surface, avoiding Dulcie's.

'This brings me to memories of the beloved dead, my husband Frederick; my sons Arthur and Bosco, always in our memories, so very, very dear; my beloved Flora, and also dearest Paolo, so cruelly taken from Charlotte. So I say: to absent ones, and the beloved dead.'

Dulcie's hand holding her glass trembled and, as the company rose, she remained sitting, raising her glass to quivering lips as the toast rang round the table: 'absent ones ... the beloved dead'.

Rachel looked anxiously at Dulcie, comparing her this year with last and wondering if she would see another Christmas. Her mental faculties were as acute as ever but she was frail. Some spark had left her since the departure of Irina which, everyone knew, would not be temporary if Cheryl Askham had her way. There was little gratification for Rachel in that the family as a whole were now beginning to see Cheryl in the light that she did. In a way she had hoped to be proved wrong. Instead she was increasingly proved right. It was difficult to see how two such strong-willed women as Dulcie and Cheryl, separated by generations, could coexist for long in the same house, however large.

Ralph made his customary gracious speech, welcoming relations and giving an account of the year's progress on the farm – his hopes for its expansion, the outlook for the stud. Ralph, with his straight blond hair greased back, his face alight with optimism, looked the exact embodiment of young, strong England; the hope for the future. Looking at him, Rachel felt that familiar spasm of fear as though she was seeing something too good, too noble to last . . . too like Bosco who had given his life for his country and his friend.

After lunch Ralph led his grandmother slowly into the big hall where the servants had their customary party, and distributed the prizes for the children's games while Rachel and the rest of the family stood around chatting to various members of the staff. One of them was Aileen Younghusband, whose father was works manager at the Askham works, now in danger of closing after the collapse of Bobby's racing dreams because the bad image of the smash had resulted in lower sales of the saloon version of the car. It was now no longer so smart to own an Askham, and Bobby cursed his bad judgement that had made him name the fated car after his unlucky uncle. But Bobby would rebound again. Would Aileen's father?

Aileen had a young child taking part in the races, a mysterious child she had somehow acquired in London and about whose father no one liked to ask. It was the first time that Rachel, who knew of the child's existence, had seen him because Aileen had never attended the Christmas staff party before.

'Hello, Aileen,' Rachel said, giving her her hand. 'How nice to see you here.'

'Thank you, Lady Askham,' Aileen gave her a rather frank stare that Rachel momentarily found disconcerting.

'Visiting your father, are you?'

'Yes. We always go at Christmas.'

'I hope he's well,' Rachel had her eyes on the attractive young boy sliding across the floor, in the lead in all the games.

'He's very well, thank you, Lady Askham, but worried about the future of the works.'

'I'm sure Bobby will be able to re-employ all the workers if it closes.'

'Then it *is* a probability?' Aileen did not mask her anxiety.

'Yes, I'm afraid it is.' Rachel sat on a vacant chair, inviting Aileen to sit on an empty one next to her. 'Bobby never really recovered from the shock of the crash or the harm it did to the name. As it was a mechanical failure rather than a collision it did untold harm and brought the whole reputation of the car into question. Besides, there is so much competition from the continent and America. I think Bobby is more interested in other, more profitable fields.'

'Bobby says ... I mean Mr Lighterman ...' Aileen's retrieval was not fast enough to prevent a deep blush and, in order to give her time to recover, Rachel looked away and began talking to the wife of the head gardener on the other side.

'Mr Lighterman *did* say to my father that he could be works manager at the armaments factory in Birmingham, but it would mean moving.'

'Yes? How sad.' Rachel looked at her questioningly, unable to solve the puzzle, the reason for Aileen's blushes, the startling solution that had suddenly presented itself to her as she looked at the energetic little boy, David – who was so like Bobby.

The house guests stayed on until after New Year with the usual round of parties, dances and hunts in the locality in all of which Sylvia Bolingbroke participated with enthusiasm. She could ride, she could dance, she could hunt. She was a woman of more parts than when Christopher had married her three years before. In that time she had produced two attractive children as well, a fact that Dulcie commented upon to Rachel as they sat in her sitting-room one day looking, as they customarily did, over the Askham lake clothed in the wintry mist of late afternoon.

Below them Sylvia was walking round the lake with Charlotte and their young children while Ralph, Cheryl and Christopher walked more slowly behind. It was a happy family scene, one that brought back many memories to Rachel who felt she knew every inch of that path, every stone, every plant, shrub and tree by the wayside. The bench on which Bosco had first proposed to her in 1899 was there still, a little in need of repair and a fresh coat of paint. The family walks round the lake were traditional at Christmastime and had become such a part of her memory that they seemed, too, a part of her mature life, as though she had always been an Askham and never a Bolingbroke. Indeed, she had been Lady Askham now for far longer than she had been Rachel Bolingbroke.

'What a dear girl that Sylvia is, don't you think?' Dulcie, in her uncanny way, seemed to be following her train of thought. 'So unexpected.'

'How, unexpected?' Rachel looked with amusement at her mother-in-law whose sharp, abrasive tongue had never lost its edge.

'She seemed such a little mouse. Just the sort of girl I would have expected dearest Christopher to marry. I don't mean that in any insulting way. But, you know, conforming. She isn't! She's blossomed. That's good because I like spirit in a woman.'

'I thought how like Arthur Christopher was at lunch yesterday. Did you notice it, Mother?'

That 'Mother' seemed so natural now. But, for many years, until the death of Bosco, Dulcie and Rachel had not got on and it was the formal 'Lady Askham' with which Cheryl now addressed them both. She sighed when she thought of Cheryl, and Dulcie interpreted that sigh, her gnarled, arthritic hands clasping her cane as she leaned forward.

'You don't like her, do you?'

'Mother, I am all at sixes and sevens with you. I don't like Sylvia?'

'No, not Sylvia, but that girl, that other one. Ralph's wife. I was taken in by her at first, but you weren't.'

'I'm sorry you don't like her, Mother. I hoped you did as you live in the same house with her.'

'Oh, she's going off to the Grange.' Dulcie airily waved her hand. 'I shan't have her about much longer. Do you know she was so rude to Irina that she left? Of course you know – but imagine the *nerve* of the girl. In my house, too. Why, even *you* never lived here, and you had far more right to it than she.'

507

'Not really, Mother. Ralph is the Earl of Askham just as Bosco was; but it was in your husband's will that you should live at the Hall, and Askham House, in fact, if you wished, in perpetuity. Bosco and I never wished to deprive you of that privilege, or ignore your husband's last wish.'

'Dear Rachel,' Dulcie touched her arm. 'How fond I am of you. But you were wilful in those days, weren't you, dear? Be honest? Mind you, not like *her*.' She jerked her head in the direction of the lake where, on the other side, surrounded by dogs and running children, the grown-ups had disappeared in the mist.

'There's something sneaky about Ralph's wife.' Rachel noticed how seldom Dulcie referred to her by her name. 'You were openly rude.'

'Oh, Mother, I *wasn't*!' Rachel, appalled at first, burst out laughing. '*You* are trying to provoke me, now.'

'You were rude, dear, open and honest about it. Do you remember the day you and I had that most frightful row, just before the twins were born ...'

'Oh, yes, and you said you'd never speak to me again and refused to receive me at the Hall!' Rachel convulsively clasped Dulcie's arm, as though what had once been a terrible family scene were the most amusing thing in the world.

'And to think *how* fond I am of you now, dearest Rachel!' Dulcie's eyes now seemed too bright with affection rather than mirth, and she entwined her fingers through Rachel's. 'You have been the most wonderful daughter-in-law, the best of mothers, grandmothers and, now, look how selflessly you are looking after poor dear Adam and his two babies.

'Do you think Bobby a rather brutal young man, dear?' Dulcie, eyes sparkling with mischief, glanced keenly at her daughter-in-law. Such rapid changes of subject were quite common with her, as though she enjoyed taking people unawares. 'Rather ruthless? I don't think he has made Hélène very happy. I was annoyed he didn't visit, as usual, this Christmas.'

'I think he and Hélène were not suited in the first place.'
Rachel sounded brisk. 'Hélène was in love with Jamie Kitto
and Bobby ...' Once again she thought of the young boy
sliding about on the polished floor of the big hall. No one knew
who David's father was, but she wondered now how many
people guessed. Aileen had used to work for Bobby and then
she suddenly left. About a year later she appeared with a baby.
'Well, I think Bobby had his reasons for marrying Hélène, and
they were not necessarily admirable ones.'

'Her title?'

'Bobby could have married any young woman, with a title
or not, and Hélène was very fascinating.' Rachel looked
doubtfully at Dulcie as if wondering how much she should
confide in her. 'The fact that she was in love with another man
might have interested Bobby. You see, he always has to have
what he wants. She was a challenge. Bobby *is* rather hard, but
he has much charm and, of course, as Bosco's nephew I'm very
fond of him. But he did make Paolo stick to his contract when
he was tired of driving, and when Paolo died he only settled the
tiniest allowance on Charlotte, saying that Paolo should have
saved more; he was too extravagant. One can't blame Bobby
for Paolo's death, but I think he might have been more
generous with Charlotte.'

'At least it would have spared her being ... a *mannequin*.'
Dulcie uttered the word with a rapid rush of breath. 'I think
that a most *frightful* thing to be, so common, though, of
course, in these modern days ...'

'Charlotte is a very unusual kind of mannequin,' Rachel said
reassuringly. "I mean, Mademoiselle doesn't treat her in any
ordinary way. She only models for the best clients. But lots of
well-brought-up girls work these days and Charlotte is happy
and independent, earning her own money. Chanel is one of the
most famous designers in the world.'

Dulcie sighed. 'I still can't quite get over it, I'm afraid. An
Askham modelling clothes! I only hope the dear Queen never
gets to hear about it.'

How innocent Dulcie was, Rachel thought, gazing at her fondly. The dear Queen, that practical daughter of the House of Teck, had probably known about it for months and, being an eminently level-headed and sensible woman, would not have minded in the least.

The party below appeared through the mist now, Charlotte strolling ahead with Cheryl and Sylvia, her arms folded in her warm wrap-around tweed coat. Rachel always regarded her elder daughter with the mixture of pleasure and surprise with which one greets a beautiful stranger. They had few intimate moments together, but their bond was deep and Charlotte had confided in Rachel her happiness at being independent, thanks to Chanel. She had sold her large country house and moved into an apartment in central Paris where she was able to employ a nursemaid, a housemaid and a cook.

'I don't suppose you'll ever marry now, will you, Rachel dear?' Dulcie broke the silence, gazing curiously at her daughter-in-law, who shook herself from her reverie.

'I don't suppose so, Mother.'

'That Spencer man was awfully nice, but ...' Dulcie frowned as if looking for a way to continue without giving offence, 'somehow not quite us. Do you know what I mean, dear?'

'I *think* I know what you mean,' Rachel eyed her doubtfully.

'You know I'm no snob,' Dulcie said reassuringly.

'Oh, I know that,' Rachel lied. 'What you mean is that he was middle-class, like me.'

'My dearest girl, if you were ever middle-class you are no longer and haven't been for many years. You are a countess and an aristocrat.'

'By marriage only,' Rachel said. 'At heart I am and always have been middle-class. You know that, Mother-in-Law, and you don't much like it. Spencer was middle-class ...'

'Working-class,' Dulcie interjected.

'Well, whatever he was, we were very close in our ideas. But, somehow,' Rachel's hands were expressive, 'he was not Bosco and, in my heart, I have always remained married to him, even though I can say that, in a different way, I did love Spencer and I miss him.'

Dulcie took her hand and pressed it, her eyes once again filling with tears.

'I'm glad you remained faithful to Bosco and his memory, that you remained an Askham. Something I didn't much care for about a "Mrs Foster",' Dulcie wrinkled her nose as if suddenly assailed by an unpleasant smell. 'Do you know what I mean?'

Cheryl gazed after the departing guests, wrapped in rugs as their cars took off down the drive, and turned towards Sylvia, who was staying on for a week or two because Christopher was going north with his father on legal business.

'You can see how dreary this place is on one's own, can't you?' She linked her arm companionably through Sylvia's and, together, they wandered across the vast entrance hall to the small parlour which, in the winter, was the warmest room in the house. 'You can see how futile it is to try and do anything with it so long as old Lady Askham lives here. She hardly moves from her room.' Cheryl lifted her arms expressively into the air and shook her fists at the high ceiling.

'But I don't see why you can't proceed without her?'

'Because my husband won't let me! Won't let me touch my own home. It would give me so much to do. I'm so *bored* here, so bored!' Cheryl put her knuckles on either side of her forehead as if the thought were driving her mad.

Sylvia nodded sympathetically. She was bored, too. Christopher gave her all the freedom she wanted but, like Cheryl, she didn't know what to do with it. She was not in society and she felt her life was circumscribed by this fact. She found other legal wives interminably middle-class and dreary. She had stayed behind on purpose to try and ingratiate herself with this exciting, alluring and rather unusual recruit to the ranks of those women of society who spent their days being entertained by bridge parties, fashion shows and endless cups of tea, coffee, or some stronger beverage at *thé-dansants* at fashionable hotels.

But Sylvia's plans for that January of the year 1934 didn't quite work out as she had anticipated. She wasn't quite Cheryl's type. Welcoming her company at first, she soon got bored with her too and left her a good deal on her own.

Each evening Sylvia, Cheryl, Ralph and Lady Askham dined together, and afterwards there was usually bridge or bezique or, sometimes, backgammon. But more often Ralph went to his study to work, Lady Askham went off to her room and Cheryl sat by the fire yawning, bored.

'How boring it is here,' was her refrain, day after day.

One day a smart car drew up outside the house and a man of great elegance emerged, dressed in a double-breasted striped suit under a pale camel-hair coat. The dark brown velvet trilby on his head was pulled at a jaunty angle over one eye.

Sylvia saw him arrive from the children's room, which overlooked the drive. Cheryl ran out to greet him, reached up to kiss him on the cheeks and, linking her arm through his, drew him into the house.

He didn't look like a lover, an intimate, but who was he? Sylvia could hardly wait until luncheon, but even then her curiosity wasn't satisfied because the table was laid for one person only. The footman explained that Lady Askham had gone out to lunch and the dowager countess was not well and lunching in her room.

The mystery deepened that night when nothing at all was said about the visitor during the day except that Cheryl was more than usually quiet and thoughtful, even to the extent that Ralph noticed it and commented upon it.

'Is there anything wrong, darling? You're awfully quiet.'

'Nothing wrong at all, dearest,' Cheryl reached out a reassuring hand and touched his.

'I hope you're not getting Granny's cold. Have you called the doctor?'

'It's just a chill, Ralph.'

'Yes, but she's eighty-one.'

'I'll do that tomorrow, if you wish, darling.'

They were a curiously polite couple, Sylvia thought, almost unnaturally polite to each other. She felt this all the time as though they were trying very hard to get on, but mainly to be *seen* to get on. That night she realized that she was not really happy at Askham Hall. It was cold and bleak and she would be better off at home. Her plans had fallen through. She had not got to know her cousin by marriage any better. Cheryl was a very hard nut to crack, an unusual person; someone, Sylvia felt, for all her charm, she didn't really like very much.

The following day, the 15th January, Sylvia was in the same place, with the babies at the same time, when the same car drew up in the drive, the same man got out to be greeted by Cheryl, as he had been the day before, and drawn into the house.

Later that day the mystery was revealed. He was Neil Asherson, the famous designer who had done up Askham House, and he was now doing a survey of the Hall to plan exactly what could be done with it. This time he had lunch with Cheryl and Sylvia, though his presence was still kept a close secret from Dulcie, who remained confined to her room with a chill.

Neil Asherson was an extremely charming, accomplished man of about forty who had brought Art Deco into all the best salons of London, though few of such elegance and antiquity as Askham House. His work was featured in *Vogue*, *Harper's*, and magazines in America and the continent, and he was extremely knowledgeable about everything to do with art, ancient and modern.

'And where do you live, may I ask, Mrs Bolingbroke?' His alert, intelligent eyes twinkled kindly over his wine glass.

'Oh, we only have a small house in Kensington. Nothing smart at all, I'm afraid.'

Sylvia was aware of the expression in Cheryl's eyes as she looked at her. Rather than making a friend of her Cheryl was beginning to despise her. Sylvia was, she seemed to be saying, unutterably middle-class. Sylvia hung her head, feeling ashamed and frustrated – also rather angry at the failure of her visit.

After lunch Cheryl and Neil disappeared and Sylvia didn't know when he left because her depression gave her a headache and she lay down until nightfall. There was no mention of him at dinner – even Ralph didn't know about him – and afterwards she rang up her husband to say she wanted to go home.

The following day there was no sign of Neil, and Sylvia went riding alone in the morning. In the afternoon she began to pack in her room which was on the same floor as the suite occupied by Dulcie Askham. It was around tea-time that Sylvia heard an unusually loud noise coming from Dulcie's apartments and popped her head through the door, looking towards that end of the corridor. Dulcie's sitting-room door was half open and Sylvia could see Dulcie sitting in a chair by the fire, beating the floor with her cane, while Cheryl sat on the arm of a chair gazing insolently at her mother-in-law. Sylvia could see them both quite clearly, yet remain unseen herself. It was a sight that remained etched on Sylvia's mental retina for many months, possibly years, to come.

'Decorator!' Dulcie exclaimed. 'Interior decorator?'

'Yes, Lady Askham.' Sylvia could see Cheryl's neat profile, the back of her head now turned to her. 'I'm going to have him do up the whole of this house.'

'*When*, may I ask?' Dulcie's tone was anything but calm.

'As soon as I can. As soon as he can begin.'

'That is over my dead body!'

Sylvia felt she should go back into her room and close the door, but some awful fascination, certainly the expectation of further melodrama, held her glued to her position of vantage.

'That's as maybe, Lady Askham!' Cheryl's voice was lowered now, making it a little hard to hear. Suddenly she looked up and seeing that the door was open, got up to close it. Sylvia ducked into her bedroom, then slowly came out again and stealthily moved nearer to the closed door until she could lean her ear against it.

'No right,' Dulcie was saying, 'no right at all to ask such a person to *my* house.'

'*My* house,' Cheryl replied. 'Ralph is the Earl of Askham and it is his house – his house and mine. It isn't yours.'

'It was the wish of my husband *and* of my son Bosco, Ralph's father, that I should stay in *both* houses for so long as I liked.'

'Yet you left Askham House.'

'I wanted to live in the country.' There was a sound as if Dulcie was standing up, followed by a noise as though her chair had fallen over. Then there was fresh stamping on the floor with her cane. 'This is my house and I shall stay here for as long as I live, make no mistake about that, my girl. And may I say at the same time, Cheryl,' Dulcie pronounced the name in a rich, rather plummy tone that exaggerated the 'i': Cheril. 'May I say what a disappointment you are to my daughter-in-law and me as a wife for our beloved Ralph. We were prepared to welcome you to our hearts, even though you were a divorced woman, one who had abandoned two small gals, because the fact that Ralph loved you was sufficient for us. However, further acquaintance has not improved the first impression we had of you.

'You do not share Ralph's interests or his life; you don't appear to want the children he wants, and you seem to have nothing in common at all. Even if you were a good wife one could forgive a lot of things but, apparently, you aren't even that. You squander money and lead, I'm told, a hectic life in London and Paris whenever you can sneak away. You're no companion to dear Ralph at all.'

Dulcie's voice faded slightly, and she appeared to be tiring. Both women were silent for a moment, but there were the sounds as of some kind of repositioning in the room. Sylvia gazed fearfully back along the corridor. She'd hate to be caught eavesdropping, yet she pressed her ear closer to the door.

'If that's what *you* think, Lady Askham,' Cheryl's brittle voice was rising again, 'it's a wonder you wish to be in the same house as me.'

'I don't, I assure you, I don't.' Dulcie's voice was now almost hoarse. 'Now, if you don't mind, I have not been very well and I am very tired...'

'I am going but I want us to understand each other once and for all,' Cheryl said firmly. 'I'm not leaving the Hall and I'm going ahead with the redecoration. The place will be in an upheaval for at least *two* years. There will be chaos and workmen all over the place. If I am to live in this hole, married to a man who is still a boy and at the beck and call of his interfering mother and grandmother, you can be sure I will have my house – *my* house, do you understand, Lady Askham – as I want it. Now, you ridiculous old woman, do you understand me? If you don't agree to go to the Grange, which has been vacated especially for you, I'll have you put in a wheelbarrow and transported there ... if I have to do it myself. Kick and scream about it all you like, but it will be done. I'll pack up and I'll...'

There was a sudden heavy sound as if something, or someone, had fallen and Cheryl's voice stopped abruptly.

After a minute Sylvia heard her say:

'Lady Askham ... are you all right?' Then, again, loudly: 'Lady Askham ...'

Sylvia scampered along the corridor to her room and had just closed the door when she heard the one at the far end of the corridor open and someone flew past her door. She lay back against it, her heart beating wildly. Then she heard Cheryl screaming at the top of the stairs:

'Will someone come quickly, please. Lady Askham is very unwell.'

Nimet stood at the door of the house in Bedford Row, beautifully dressed in an elegant costume of grey marocain with a short, double-breasted coat and large buttons. Underneath was a pure silk blouse also in grey with a pleated jabot. A fox fur draped over both her shoulders fastened across her breast, and the sealskin toque on her smooth head had the suggestion of a brim.

'I hope I may come in?' Nimet gazed past Rachel at the butler who had heard the doorbell too late.

'Please.' Rachel reluctantly inclined her head, stood back to make way for Nimet and then said:

'It's quite all right, Vance. I was passing the door. Would you bring us tea?' Then to Nimet as she led her into the drawing-room: 'We've just returned from the country so you'll find us a bit disordered.'

'I suppose you've been to see Hugo?' Nimet came straight to the point without taking the seat Rachel offered her.

'No. I haven't seen Hugo since before Christmas. Is he all right?'

'I wonder you don't know, Lady Askham,' Nimet's tone was menacing, 'seeing that you *lured* him back.'

Rachel took a deep breath and sat down.

'Madame Igolopuscu, I thought we had this matter settled once and for all? We have both shared Hugo but, whatever happened in the past, the fact is that he is now a young man of twenty-one. He celebrated his majority in your company, I think? Not ours, though we had a small celebration afterwards. Could we not, after all these years, let the matter rest?'

'How can it rest if you alienate my son from me, poison him against me and my poor husband, who has done nothing to him but good?'

'I assure you I have never ...'

'You *have* alienated him from me, deliberately, Lady Askham. I say so again. You have done it maliciously and intentionally. Was it not for the sake of Hugo that I took up residence in this country with its wretched weather?' Nimet shivered realistically and rubbed her arms, looking through the window, as she did, at the grey January street outside, the

517

skeletal trees, the leaves lying in damp mounds by the side of the road ready to be burned. 'I hate England, cold and gloomy place. Do you not know that on the Bosphorus my husband has a magnificent villa where I could live quite happily, the sun and the warmth on my poor rheumatic body, all the year round? Yet not only does Hugo *not* appreciate my sacrifice, he refuses to go into my husband's business which, in time, might have made him every bit as rich as Bobby Lighterman, if not richer. The Bey, my husband, feels very hurt and angry at the way Hugo has treated me and, whereas he intended making Hugo his heir, now he is not so sure. He has only daughters by his other marriages, which is a great disappointment to him. He doted on Hugo.'

'Is this not a matter you should discuss with Hugo, Madame?' Rachel felt ill-tempered and uneasy. As well as worry about Freddie and Em she had left baby Flora unwell in the country, and there was a vague apprehension about Dulcie's health. She didn't quite know why, except that she still hadn't shaken off the cold she'd had since Christmas. She intended to telephone her this evening. Should Dulcie perhaps see a specialist about her chest? Were they doing enough?

She turned her face from the window back to her guest, who was conducting a long peevish monologue in which the word 'gratitude', or its lack, seemed to occur frequently.

The maid came in with tea and there was silence while she fussed with the pot and cups, the jug of milk, the small cakes on their silver stand.

'Will that be all, my lady?'

'Thank you,' Rachel nodded and then turned her attention again to Nimet.

'I'm awfully sorry. I must appear to be not very attentive but I have many quite serious problems on my mind. My son and daughter are in Germany ...'

'Oh, don't I know!' Nimet held up her hand. 'The Bey always sees *The Sentinel*, as well as other newspapers, of course. He says your daughter has got it quite wrong about Hitler, who is the best thing to have happened to Germany since Bismarck. She is most mischievous.'

'Indeed?' Rachel lowered her head trying to control a display of anger.

'Hitler is a marvellous man, a saviour of his country. My husband knows him personally and has no doubt of his nobility of mind, the purity of his intentions, his goodwill towards England, his love for his own fatherland.'

'If you don't mind, Madame Igolopuscu, I am quite ready to have a difference of opinion with you or your husband about the motives and ability of Herr Hitler, but you have come here with a rather serious accusation that I have enticed Hugo from you and I wish we could stick to the matter in hand.

'My dear Madame ...' suddenly Rachel leaned forward in her chair and held out her hand as if in an appeal, 'we both love Hugo. He is very precious to you and to me. He is Bosco's son and I can say that I love him as one of my own children. But he is your son, too. I accept that and when he left Askham House to live with you I accepted that too, even though I nearly died. I'd brought Hugo up from a little boy, don't you see, and he meant so much to me. But now he is his own man, a tall, strong man, no longer a boy. He loves animals and wants to be a farmer. What better than that he should go into partnership with his half-brother? They never got on too well when they were younger and I am delighted that they should find so much in common now. Hugo never quite fitted in with his brothers and sisters, though we all tried. Be happy for him as, at last, he is such friends with Ralph. You should be delighted, too. From being a difficult, problem child, Hugo has developed into a most delightful man.'

'Thanks to you, I suppose.'

'You could say thanks to me he was a problem,' Rachel said generously. 'I spoiled him. You helped to give him the security and special love he needed because he was of your blood. He blossomed after that and I give you the credit for it.' Rachel glanced at her watch as Nimet showed her amazement by modifying her expression. 'But I would like you to realize, however,' Rachel began when there was a knock on the door. Without waiting for a reply Vance put his head round the door.

'There is a phone call for you, my lady.'

'Take a message and say I'll ring back.'

Vance looked distressed.

'It's from the Hall, my lady. I'm afraid it's about the dowager countess ... I'm afraid it is *not* good news, my lady.'

CHAPTER 25

As the cortège wound its way from Askham Hall to the church, just outside the walls, it was difficult not to believe that one was seeing a re-enactment of all Askham funerals since the family came into being. Like Royal occasions it seemed that each burial of an Askham had a precedent, a form, a ritual stretching back into ages past.

Dulcie was not the first Askham to die since the advent of the motor car but her coffin, like that of her husband, was borne on a carriage pulled by four black horses. The driver, postilions and attendants were dressed in deepest black with ribbons around their top hats. But when Frederick had died in 1911 mourners and guests travelled in carriages, a line that stretched for almost a quarter of a mile. This time black limousines took the chief mourners or more important guests, including a representative of the King and Queen, the King himself being in poor health. It was odd to think that 'young Georgie', whom Dulcie had known as a boy, had grown into an old man, shortly, perhaps, to follow her to her grave.

Askham funeral weather was usually good, so the records showed, and this January day was no exception. The sky was that peerless washed blue, the horizon tinged with pink. Sitting opposite Ralph, Rachel, as she looked out of the car window, was reminded of the exact time of year, thirty-five years before, when she had come as a guest to this house. It would be very difficult to think of it now without Dulcie.

Opposite her, next to Ralph, sat Cheryl, a veil covering her face. Yet it was difficult to believe that Cheryl mourned, not in the way Ralph mourned, or Freddie, next to her, mourned, or Hugo in the car following them mourned, or Melanie, last

521

surviving child of Frederick and Dulcie, and her children following behind mourned.

Dulcie had been a great matriarch, a woman whose life had spanned more changes than it would have been possible to envisage when she entered the world as the third daughter of Lord and Lady Kitto.

The Kittos, naturally, were there in force and so were representatives of the nobility, the local squirearchy and the municipality. Every estate worker who had ever worked on the estate, and could still walk, was there; representatives of the Askham and Lighterman interests all over England.

As her coffin was borne aloft by the bearers and entered the church, the choir, supplemented by boys from the cathedral, sang 'Praise My Soul the King of Heaven'. And it did seem at that moment, as their treble voices burst into song, as a sunbeam blazed through the stained glass windows behind the altar, that the heavens opened, welcoming Dulcie, Countess of Askham, to the company of angels and the sight of her loved ones.

The Askham vault occupied part of the apse of the church, divided from it by a grille. Only Ralph and Melanie and the Rector entered as, after the service, the coffin was placed on a slab next to Frederick, the last Askham to be buried there. It was sad to think that, of her four children, the three who had predeceased her were buried in different parts of the world: America, Egypt and France.

Melanie was supported by Denton on one side and Christopher on the other during the service. Susan was there with Sasha and Kyril and, behind them, a lonely, griefstricken figure: Jordan. However, he seemed to stand apart – with the family, but not of it; a loner. Many people noticed his aloofness and commented upon it between themselves. Today there was no trace of the long black locks falling almost shoulder length or the black outfit with the red silk-lined hat. Jordan had had his hair cut and plastered, with difficulty, to his head with brilliantine. He wore a morning suit of impeccable cut, and carried a grey top hat in his hand. He smiled politely and addressed himself courteously to the older family friends among his grandmother's mourners.

As the congregation emerged into the sunlight the Rector held Jordan back for a few words before allowing him to join his mother, sister and brothers who were talking to the Ferov family, who had come over from Paris, Irina's eyes still red from weeping.

'If I had known ...' she was saying.

'If any of us had known,' Melanie comforted her. 'We knew Mummy had a dicky chest, but not that she would go just like that.'

'The strain on the heart,' Irina said emotionally, 'for a woman of that age ...' She burst into uncontrollable tears again and Alexei Ferov put an arm round her shoulder. 'I cannot but think that if I had stayed with her she would be alive now,' Irina said between sobs and then, gazing fixedly at Cheryl who, with Ralph, was greeting tenants from the Yorkshire estates, said in a low voice: 'That woman killed her.'

Sylvia Bolingbroke, passing nearby, whose attention had been diverted by some acquaintance on the far side of the churchyard, jerked her head round at the Princess's words and said sharply: 'What makes you say that?'

'The strain of living with her. She wanted her to leave, you know, go and live in that little Grange. Imagine Lady Askham, who all her life had been used to the company of Kings, Queens, Princes and Princesses, members of the nobility, living in that pokey house. The present Lady Askham's nothing but ...'

'Shhh,' Melanie chided. 'The least said the better, for today anyway, Irina. Now Askham *is* indisputably hers, and I doubt if we'll have any more Christmas parties. I wish so much we had been at the last one, Denton dear.'

Denton was chatting to Jordan, whom he had scarcely seen for the last year or two, though it is doubtful if Denton Rigby even knew of the existence of a man called Adolf Hitler, so

523

intent was he on the mysteries of the baccarat and *chemin de fer* tables at the Casino in Monte Carlo. From there he would make his way to the English club where the variations on the French Bourse and the Stock Exchange were discussed and then, after dinner, a rubber of whist or bridge and home to bed. His routine hardly ever varied. It was a remarkably pleasant life.

Adam, looking rather forlorn, stood by himself, contemplating a stone in the graveyard, glancing at his wrist watch from time to time as though wondering when they were all going to move off.

'Sad business, Bolingbroke.'

'Very sad,' Adam tossed his head, thinking it was civil of his former wife's husband to seek him out, 'Very unexpected. She was not hale but quite hearty at Christmas. A sudden seizure.' Adam shook his head, tapping a tombstone with his stick. 'Could happen to anyone.'

Denton and Adam never had much to say to each other and, after a while, conversation lapsed and they watched Melanie, surrounded by friends, supported by her young grandson Sasha, maintaining a stiff upper lip, Askham style. No Askham should ever be seen to show grief in public, though when Melanie had bade farewell to her mother as the coffin was slotted into its place in the crypt she openly wept, though out of sight, for some time.

Susan, not far away, was greeting a number of people she hadn't seen for years, and beside her the Ferov family, grim-faced, hands in pockets, waited for the cars to draw up to take them to the house. Kyril had his arm through his mother's, sign of a *rapprochement* indeed, but as Kyril had always been her favourite child she'd had no difficulty in welcoming him back to the fold.

Jordan now wandered over to join the group as Melanie beckoned to Susan and the Ferov family to join the cars.

'I think I'll walk,' Alexei said, glancing at Kyril. 'Anyone join me?'

524

'I'll join you,' Jordan said as Kyril and the rest shook their heads, and Alexei looked at him with some surprise.

'Why not?' he said. 'You can probably show me the way.'

'It's a very pleasant saunter through the woods.' Jordan looked round to be sure no one would accompany them. 'Besides, I wanted a quiet word with you.'

'Ah, yes,' Alexei also looked round. Jordan, somehow, made him nervous. Trust him to buttonhole him at this point, when he couldn't escape. 'Sorry I couldn't get in touch with you before. I'm a very busy man.'

'What a pity,' Jordan said politely. They were now out of sight of the church and about to take the path through the woods, 'What I can offer you will make you, and me, a lot of money.'

'Guns, I understand,' Alexei whispered, though there wasn't even a squirrel in sight to overhear them. 'My daughter mentioned something.'

'Guns and more besides, all the equipment necessary for modern warfare.'

'I can't really do it,' Alexei continued to whisper. 'Bobby would go mad if he knew. He doesn't like Hitler and has always got on rather well with the Russians.'

'But Bobby won't know, he mustn't know. You must be able to arrange something without alerting Bobby?'

'The armaments side is a totally different sphere from the one I'm in. On the other hand I *may* have a change of job. You know he is closing the Askham motor works?'

'I heard it was a possibility.'

'Well, it's definite. Selling the name and goodwill to Ford who will absorb it, thus getting rid of another rival. The Askham car never survived La Monza, which was a pity. But Bobby doesn't really care. He has his fingers in too many pies.'

'Then he won't notice yours in the armaments. Someone told me Askham Armaments is actually expanding.'

'Well, it's these troubled times. He'd be a fool to abandon it altogether. Must say I rather admire Hitler. Do you know him at all?'

'Unfortunately no. I have seen him, of course, and listened to him countless times.'

'I would have thought he could get plenty of guns on his own initiative.' Alexei, puzzled, stared at the youth beside him. He was a man, no longer a boy, but there was something perennially juvenile about him. Something rather feminine – a full lower lip, sparseness of facial hair – that made him beautiful rather than handsome. And, as with a woman, his head of shining black curls was an eye-catching attraction.

Yet, to his surprise, Alexei, his senior by some thirty years, felt rather afraid of him as he tried to keep up with his long, sure strides. He was certainly an Askham, with his air of authority. Yet what would the family have thought of this conversation?

'My dear Prince,' Jordan said impatiently, 'this is frightfully secret. The arms are for the SA – the stormtroopers, who are forbidden to carry them. My source there will pay anything to get his hands on a quantity of weapons. Hitler, of course, can get guns … Röhm can't.'

'Your source is actually Röhm himself?' Alexei felt depressed. This wasn't simply chicanery, which he was used to, but something more sinister.

'Not *himself*,' Jordan sounded testy. 'He is almost as big a shot as Hitler since he was made Reich Minister. Röhm has ambitions to control the Reichswehr, the army, but the generals oppose him. Röhm has to be careful. It is very difficult for him to get arms for his men. They are not supposed to rearm, but Röhm fears the Army wants to cut them down and his force needs guns to defend itself.'

'You're very well informed,' Alexei said, treading carefully on the hard frosty earth. 'But is it wise to anger Hitler?'

'My dear sir we, you and I, are very small fry indeed. Hitler could never be angered by *us*, because he won't know about us!'

'But is it a plot to overthrow Hitler? If so I can't contemplate...'

'Don't be absurd,' Jordan's eyes were contemptuous. 'Röhm couldn't overthrow the Führer! He just wants to be prepared.'

'I couldn't possibly ...' But Alexei already knew it was hopeless. Somehow in a few minutes this young man had established a superiority over him. Plainly it was ridiculous. 'I'll do what I can,' he finished lamely.

'As quickly as you can,' Jordan said sharply. 'There is real urgency on the part of my friends.'

Alexei stopped, short of breath, and looked about him. In the heart of the Forest of Askham, deep in the English countryside, with the single church bell tolling its melancholy farewell to the once proud chatelaine of the house before them, the grim, sleazy ambience of Berlin seemed like another world.

Hélène, about to get carefully into the car after her mother and Charlotte, paused for a moment to look over at Bobby. Marshalling the guests in the churchyard, he had stopped to talk to a woman with a boy much younger than Sasha. It was a few years since she had seen the woman, and the boy had been smaller, but she recognized them both.

Hélène paused, as though wondering whether to get out or go on, but someone behind her suddenly gave her a gentle push and said: 'Hop in. Can I cadge a lift?' And, as she turned, a tall man doffed his hat and smiled round the interior of the car. 'Good morning ladies, Princess Ferova, Hélène ... my dear Charlotte, how *are* you?' Jamie Kitto edged himself in between his cousin and Irina so that Hélène sat on the seat facing them. The door closed and the car was waved on by Bobby, who didn't even glance into the interior of it.

Charlotte said: 'Jamie, it's ages since I saw you. We heard you were in the Argentine.'

'Well, I'm back here now. Here and Paris.' Jamie glanced at

527

Hélène, who looked away. 'Times have changed for Jamie. I am now a man of means.'

'Oh? That's good. What do you do?'

'Sell things.' Jamie spread his hands, regarding the fine black hairs on the backs of his knuckles.

'What things?'

'Things!' Jamie smiled that familiar smile of great charm. 'All sorts of things. You'd be surprised. And you, Charlotte, are one of Mademoiselle Chanel's celebrated mannequins. I see your picture frequently. Tell me, how does the life suit you?'

'It's exhausting,' Charlotte said, 'but it suits.'

'You're frightfully scraggy,' Jamie's appraising glance was embarrassing. 'Is that part of the act?'

'Mademoiselle likes us to be very thin. *Maigre* she calls it.' Charlotte lingered on the word, pronounced in a very good French accent.

'Well, *maigre* is right.' Jamie appeared suddenly to lose interest in his attractive cousin. 'And how are *you*, Hélène? Still blooming?'

'Yes, thank you.' Hélène met his eyes but her face was pale. Beside her Irina didn't trouble to conceal her annoyance by looking away from Jamie, out of the window.

Jamie looked at Irina, who kept the back of her head towards him, raised his eyes heavenwards, with a wink at Hélène, and tapped his fingers on his bulky knees. 'Poor old Dulcie, hey? How she loved this museum. Can't think why. Wonder what will happen now?'

As the car stopped Hélène put down the window to wave to a brace of Kittos who were disgorged from a companion limousine like picnickers from a charabanc. They looked anything but sad. In her hurry to get out of the car, Irina trod on Jamie's feet and didn't even apologize. Jamie didn't mind. Despite the death of Great Aunt Dulcie he felt in a sunny mood. He had money in his wallet, and a beautiful woman on his mind.

He glanced meaningfully at Hélène as he made way for her to leave the car. Then, slowly, he ambled after her.

Aileen said after the family cars had gone:

'We haven't seen you for weeks.' She pushed David towards her father, who'd kept his back to Bobby.

'I've been frightfully busy,' Bobby took off his hat to Sir Oliver Patchett, who had represented Queen Mary. 'I'll be busier than ever now. You get your money, don't you?'

'It's not only the money, Bobby. You always said you'd keep in touch with me and David.'

'I do. I will. I promise to see more of you. I'll phone you next week.' Unusually, for him, Bobby sounded strained. 'You know, Aileen, that I am a very, *very* busy man. I have many things, too many, to occupy my mind. The decision to discontinue the Askham hit me very hard.'

'And a lot of other people, too,' Aileen glanced over at her father, who was talking to a group of men and women he knew.

'I offered him another job. I hope he'll take it.'

'But he's settled here. He's lived here since the War. He doesn't want to go to Birmingham.'

'That's his hard luck then.'

'No, it's *your* hard luck, Bobby,' Aileen said spiritedly. 'My father has his pride. It seems to me that you've lost yours.'

And she turned on her heel and walked towards her father who, his arm now round David's neck, had been gazing at her and Bobby, while appearing to listen to his friends.

Bobby looked angrily after her, wondering who'd seen the scene, glad the family had gone. The main guests had made for the house and only those who wouldn't expect to attend the reception, tenants and lesser fry, were left. Bobby waved genially, like a seigneurial lord and, jumping into his car, drove himself back as fast as he could.

'That woman was there again.' Hélène greeted him in the hall like someone waiting to pounce. The hall was full of other people removing their outer coats and hats, but Hélène was hovering just inside the door.

'What woman?' Bobby hadn't worn an overcoat and glanced irritatedly at her. 'Have you seen Ralph?'

'The one with the little boy I asked you about.'

'I told you she was the daughter of an employee. I was merely greeting her.'

'Which employee?'

'Oh, for God's *sake*, Hélène, have you no sense of propriety? On this day of all days.'

Bobby hurried past her, upstairs to the reception room on the first floor where the mourners, talking in low voices, were drowning their sorrows in champagne.

After a while Hélène wandered up the stairs after Bobby and found herself face to face with Jamie coming from the library. They bumped into each other at the top of the stairs.

'Oh, Hélène! Just the very person I wanted to see.'

'Why?'

'Can't you guess?'

'Don't be silly. That was all over a long, long time ago.'

'Not for me. It's like it was yesterday.'

'Jamie!' Hélène hissed, 'I haven't the slightest intention of starting up again.'

'Why not? I still love you. And I can see you're not happy.'

Hélène looked quite startled at his unexpected declaration and tried to push him roughly out of the way, but now the guests coming up the stairs were more numerous than the minute before and one or two people were staring at them.

'I *must* talk to you,' Jamie whispered loudly. 'Let's find somewhere quiet.'

Rachel, standing in the doorway of the main reception room shaking hands with the guests next to Ralph, observed the encounter on the stairs and hoped that not too many other people had seen. Bobby had hurried in to join the receiving line, looking annoyed, and she was quite sure that he and Hélène had had words on the stairs. At Christmas she had learned that quite a lot of people knew that Bobby was the father of Aileen's little boy, and that she lived in some comfort in a house provided for her by him in Croydon. Her father, angered at the way Bobby had treated him as well as his daughter, had begun to talk about it. She wondered how long it could possibly be before Hélène knew, if she didn't already.

But that was just one of the many problems that troubled her on the day of Dulcie's funeral, not the least of which was her own overwhelming sense of grief, the need to mourn. Afterwards there would be a family dinner party and the talk would go on far into the night as the lady who had seen the best part of a century pass was mourned and missed.

Rachel wandered through the throng which occupied two of the rooms and was moving into the third where there was a buffet luncheon which some hungry guests had already begun.

Susan, her hand in Kyril's – whose first visit it was to Askham and its Hall – was introducing her husband to her many friends and numerous relations. Twelve-year-old Sasha followed them – completely at home in his surroundings.

What a transformation there had been in Kyril, Rachel thought, waving to them. From being a discontented Bolshevik he had become the arch-capitalist, with a leaning to Fascism. He was a frequent visitor to Germany and from Venice to Rome, where he had once been entertained by the Duce himself.

His conversion, while it puzzled, did not surprise her. She sensed a basic instability in him that would attract him to extremist philosophies. Meanwhile she hoped that, as a family, they were as happy as they looked – relaxed and urbane: Kyril charming everyone with his suave appearance, princely courtliness and affability.

There were many members of the Crewe and Kitto families, dispersed among all sorts of professions and industries with a large sprinkling in the Army. Arthur Crewe had gone into the Air Force and looked handsome and distinguished in blue – a tall, dark-haired man with a distinct look of his aunt Frances about him.

'Hello Aunt Rachel,' he said, stooping to kiss her. 'It was frightful news about Aunt Dulcie.'

'It was so unexpected,' Rachel replied, her hand still in his. 'We were all here at Christmas, a mere month ago. I can't believe she's dead and I don't think I will for some time.'

'I say, Aunt Rachel, would you do me a favour?' Arthur gave her an attractive smile.

'Anything I can.' Rachel smiled and looked up.

'Would you introduce me again to Charlotte? I don't think she remembers me. She's a smashing girl!'

Thereupon Arthur looked so overcome with embarrassment that Rachel stared at him for a moment or two, in surprise.

'Do you mean *my* Charlotte? Of course she remembers you. You used to play here together when you were small. You're about the same age.'

'Yes, but I don't think she remembers who I am. I've looked at her once or twice, but we haven't met for years and she walked right past me. I must say, Aunt Rachel, she's the most stunning woman in this room.'

'Do you know she's now a mannequin?'

'A what?' Arthur bent his head as Rachel repeated herself.

'A mannequin. She models clothes for Chanel.'

'Good lord!' Arthur looked astonished. 'Does she really? Did that racing driver fellow leave her badly off?'

'Very badly off. Isn't it splendid of her to go to work? She supports her three children herself. Doesn't want a penny from us.'

Arthur's eyes gleamed with admiration. 'She *is* a splendid girl, Aunt Rachel. Always was! Always liked her.'

'But she *does* live in Paris.' Rachel smiled.

'No trouble,' Arthur said in his clipped Air Force voice. 'I'm always buzzing over there in my plane.'

Rachel beckoned to Charlotte, who seemed to have inherited the ability to attract men of all kinds from all parts of the room that her Aunt Melanie had had in her day. Although, if the cluster of gentlemen, some portly now with grey moustaches, in the far corner of the drawing-room was anything to go by, she had it still.

Charlotte was glad to extricate herself from her admirers, and came as soon as her mother waved. She opened her eyes wide when she saw the man next to her.

'Arthur!'

'So you *do* remember me?' Arthur looked pleased.

'Of course I remember you. I didn't recognize you in that uniform. What are you, an Air Marshal or something?'

'Merely a Squadron-Leader, but if we ever get the chance to have a crack at Hitler an Air Marshal I might be.'

'Oh, please, *don't*,' Rachel shuddered. 'The last thing we want to think about on a day like this is the possibility of war.'

Freddie was almost as popular as Charlotte, being surrounded in the middle of the floor, next to his mother, by acquaintances of both sexes from his Oxford days and later. Even in funereal black Freddie managed to look festive. His tail coat and trousers were immaculate, as were his white shirt and grey waistcoat, the grey spats over his shining black shoes. His grey tie was loosely knotted, giving him a somewhat rakish look as his curly hair fell over his forehead, his cheeks already flushed with champagne.

He, too, had spotted Arthur and disengaged himself, coming up to the group which included Charlotte now as well as his mother just in time to hear the word: 'war'.

'War is definitely not a possibility, Mother.' Freddie shook his head vehemently after shaking hands with Arthur. 'Hitler has told everyone he wants peace. He's just trying to bring the German nation together.'

'Surely you don't believe that?' Rachel sounded indignant. 'When you think of what he's doing to our Jewish friends.'

Freddie's cheerful face lost its smile. 'The truth is, apparently, that he doesn't know what his men are doing. It's mainly the SA who cause the trouble, and he's trying to put a curb on them.'

'I think it's that girl you're seeing who has changed your mind about Hitler,' Rachel looked at him knowingly. 'It's a very rosy view you have of him, if I may say so.'

'A *girl*?' Charlotte raised her carefully plucked, arc-shaped eyebrows. 'Is she German?'

Freddie nodded. 'Her family are awfully nice people; her father's a civil servant from a good, bourgeois Bavarian family. He's on the staff of Hitler's Chancellery and has a high opinion of the man. I assure you, you couldn't find anyone nicer than Herr Schmidt. I respect enormously what he says.'

'And what does Em think of that?' Hugo, wandering round, had been standing on the edge of the group listening for a few moments.

'Em, of course, is crazily anti-Nazi. She's lost all sense of proportion. Herr Schmidt says if she isn't careful she'll be expelled.'

'You must have an awful dilemma with your girl friend and sister?' Arthur observed, his eyes still on Charlotte.

'Dilemma? Not at all. Sophie and I aren't in the *least* interested in politics. Not in the least, my dear chap. I must say I like her family and they're very level-headed; not fanatics at all. Like most of the Germans I've met they feel humiliated by the Allies and want Germany to be a great power again. But definitely, most definitely, they don't want war. Sophie's coming here in the summer. You'll meet her then.'

'Engaged?' Arthur murmured.

Freddie scoffed. 'Oh no, Arthur, nothing like that! She's studying at Berlin University. That's how we met. She's a very serious girl, I tell you, as I've told Mother. If she met Sophie and her family, and one day I hope she will, she'd quite change her mind about Hitler.'

Cheryl had had a headache since she'd opened her eyes that morning. She dreaded the funeral, the crowds, the awful family party that would follow afterwards. She wondered if she could use the headache to stay away, but how awful it would look and, to her, like an admission of guilt. Not that Cheryl felt herself responsible in any way for the old lady's death. The doctor said she could have gone at any time, and Cheryl had convinced herself that Dulcie would have dropped dead at that moment whether they'd been engaged in an argument or not. She'd looked pale and a bit trembly when Cheryl had gone into the room, Dulcie having sent for her because she had heard that the man who had been wandering round the house was an architect. Dulcie had really brought the whole thing on herself. She had already got into a state before she'd sent for Cheryl. She'd brought about her own death by being absurd and wanting to interfere in something that wasn't any of her business.

So it wasn't that Cheryl felt guilty. She merely felt irritated as the cortège had made its slow way to the church, by the interminable time the funeral seemed to take, all the people wallowing about afterwards in anticipation of a good feed. And the way the champagne flowed! She gazed around her now at the pink faces, feeling angrier than ever, as Ralph, who was on and on about money all the time, was paying for this beano. She put her hands to her head and pushed her hair back off her forehead.

'Are you all right?' Hugo, one of the last people she wanted to see, came over to her, looking at her solicitously.

'Of course I'm all right,' she snapped, about to move away when Hugo, clearing his throat, said:

'I *have* wanted to apologize, Cheryl. But lacked the nerve.'

'Whatever for?' Cheryl, curious, stopped in her tracks.

'About that day. The cat. I did ask someone to pop him in through the door to give you a shock. I hope you've forgiven me. I do wish you would. I'd like to be friends with Ralph's wife.'

'Oh, would you?' Far from feeling forgiveness Cheryl felt an overwhelming hatred for the upstart who was the cause of so much dissension between her and Ralph's family. She really felt she couldn't stand him. 'Well, *you've* certainly caused enough trouble in your life, and not only recently, from what I've heard. Always in trouble.'

'I didn't mean to start another argument,' Hugo flushed, 'I am genuinely sorry, and hoped to see you at the farm to apologize again, but you never seem to come.'

'I'm not interested, that's why,' Cheryl said heatedly. 'I couldn't give a damn about the pigs and the cows ...'

'It's awfully unfortunate you feel like that, because it's really going well. It's going to be a show place and Ralph should be proud. Maybe you could come over one day and we'll show you round. Bring a friend ... bring ...' Hugo spotted Sylvia, about to pass them, and said: 'Wouldn't you like to come over and see the farm, Sylvia?'

'The farm?' Sylvia, who had had, perhaps, one glass of champagne too many – or maybe two – stopped and looked at him as though she didn't quite know who he was.

'Ralph's farm. I'm Hugo ...'

'The hired boy,' Cheryl explained helpfully. 'Mucks in with Ralph on the farm.'

'But I thought ...' Sylvia blinked and looked up at him carefully.

'That's Cheryl's little joke,' Hugo said, his voice losing its pleasant timbre. 'I'm actually investing in the farm as part owner.'

'Of course, you're Hugo ... the ... er,' Sylvia looked at Cheryl for help. Clearly, in her inebriated state, she couldn't place him.

Appearing anxious to help, Cheryl said in a slow, controlled voice: 'Bosco's son by the Egyptian woman.'

Sylvia looked abashed and Hugo clenched and unclenched his hands as if he'd like to have them round Cheryl's slender neck. Instead he bowed to Sylvia, ignored Cheryl, and strode away, while Cheryl looked after him triumphantly, a finger on her cheek.

'Did I say something wrong?' Her eyes innocently gazed at Sylvia, who giggled.

'It wasn't really very nice, was it? Naughty.' She wagged a finger at Cheryl.

'But it's true. It helps to distinguish him from all these other awful relations of Ralph who sweep over one like a great all-engulfing tide.'

'I think he's rather a nice young man,' Sylvia enunciated with care.

'That's probably because you don't know him. You didn't even know who he was. He has a very vicious streak and is probably a criminal. When he was young, only the protection of Rachel Askham – and powerful that protection was – kept him from being sent to prison.'

'Really?' Sylvia looked interested.

'He kept stealing things, running away. Had to be kept at home for his own protection. Ralph couldn't stand him.'

'Then *why* has he gone into business with him?'

'As far as I know he hasn't. He employs him. That's probably another of Hugo's lies. People don't change, you know. Criminals don't. Ralph should take care of what Hugo gets up to on that farm or one day he'll find himself in trouble.'

'Anyway,' Sylvia said in a rather arch, ingratiating tone of voice, 'now this place is all yours. At last!' She smiled, showing well-kept, even teeth.

'Yes, at last,' Cheryl looked round in a proprietorial manner.

'*And* you didn't have to put the old lady into a wheelbarrow and take her over to the Grange to get it.' Sylvia laughed as if the absurd idea made an amusing joke.

Visibly Cheryl froze: 'I *beg* your pardon?'

'Oh dear!' Sylvia carefully put the half-glass of champagne in her hand down on a nearby table, thinking that, perhaps, she'd had enough. 'I've goofed, haven't I?'

'I'm sure I don't know what you're talking about.' Cheryl's dulcet American-accented voice managed to sound at the same time pleasant, yet menacing.

'You see,' Sylvia fixed her with her tipsy gaze, 'I was just on the *point* of coming to see your husband's grandmother ... shortly before she died, to see how she was.'

'And stayed listening at the door?'

Guiltily Sylvia hung her head. 'Awful, wasn't it? Of course I wouldn't *dream* of saying anything to a *soul*.'

Cheryl gazed at her thoughtfully. 'Did you mention anything to anyone already? To your husband?'

'Of course not. What was there to say?'

'The doctor said she would have died anyway,' Cheryl said calmly. 'I just don't want people, the family, to know we had ... words. Naturally it would upset them. I've enough to put up with from them as it is. It was her time.'

'Of *course* it was.' Sylvia felt emboldened to go nearer Cheryl and take her arm. 'Anyway, you can rely on me not to add fuel to the flames. I know what families are and, you see, I do *so* want to be your friend.'

'Why so pensive, darling?' Rachel patted Hugo's hand on her way to the buffet. She hadn't felt like eating, but now that the guests were drifting away and one could relax she felt a pang of hunger.

'She's poison, isn't she?'

'Who?' Rachel looked around her in alarm.

'That one.' Hugo pointed at Cheryl, now hunched together with Sylvia in an alcove, as if the pair of them were plotting the downfall of the Askhams.

538

Rachel sighed. 'What's she done now?'

'Drawn attention yet again to my origins.'

'I think it's her American sense of humour.' Rachel, angry, tried for Ralph's sake to be charitable. 'She finds embarrassing people amusing. But the term "poison" seems to suit her well. Just that, on its own. The viper in the nest, I call her, with a poisonous tongue. Come on, forget about her.'

Rachel linked her arm through Hugo's and walked slowly with him towards the buffet. 'You know that I talked to your mother on the day Gran died, so I've hardly had time to speak to you.'

'She told me,' Hugo said, adding with surprise, 'she said you were rather nice!'

'There.' Rachel looked surprised too. 'That's kind of her.'

'She said she was angry that I was living at the farm, but you were very reasonable and praised her for what she has done for me.'

'Well, she *has* done a lot for you. Given you a feeling of really belonging. Now you know you have a mother and a father, and everyone needs to know that.'

'And sisters and brothers ... and you,' Hugo pressed her arm. 'I always used to feel so out of things but I don't now. Ralph has been splendid to me. I only feel so worried for him that he's got her.' Hugo half turned his head to look back, but Rachel dragged him on.

'I think we all feel that,' she said, 'and Ralph is in a dilemma too, because he does know what she's like. Frankly, if there was a divorce I'd cry – with joy. Now isn't that an awful thing to say? But you've no idea how much I want to see Ralph happy, with the sort of woman he deserves.'

Cheryl lay in bed listening to the sound of voices that still came from downstairs.

'Do you think they'll *ever* go to bed?' she said to Ralph, who had just crept in beside her. 'What time is it?'

'It's nearly two o'clock.' Ralph lay on his back. 'God, I am whacked. They're the family who never see one another – they'll probably chatter away until dawn.'

'You shouldn't have *had* so many people!'

'My darling, how could I help that? So many people wanted to honour Gran.'

'Well, there were far too many. Anyway, it's over now … thank God.'

Ralph listened to her breathing in the silence that ensued, conscious only of her warm body beside him, guilty at feeling lust on the day of his grandmother's funeral.

'I really loved her, you know,' he said aloud, as if in expiation of the wicked thought.

'I know. She was a dear,' Cheryl's voice remained unemotional. 'I shall miss her too.'

'Really?' She felt Ralph turn his head and the fear she knew she would always have now, after that wretched Sylvia had said what she did, welled up in her heart. She knew that once and for all, for evermore as far as she could tell, her peace of mind was destroyed. Of course the woman was meant to die – but if the family knew the circumstances … she shuddered – why, she'd be a pariah. The thing about the wheelbarrow – oh awful! Sylvia, of all people, the little menace. The little hypocrite – *her* friend indeed. Some hopes. She raised her eyes to the ceiling in the dark and silently swore.

'I beg your pardon?' Ralph moved nearer to her.

'Of course I loved her, not as much as you and your family, naturally, but because of what you felt for her.'

'I'm glad about that,' Ralph said, 'I thought you hated her.'

'Whatever gave you *that* idea?'

Cheryl sat up leaning on one elbow and stared down at him, her heart pounding.

'Well, because of the house. She was stubborn. Anyway, good does come out of bad because that argument is over now. The house is ours.'

'Yes, ours,' Cheryl, relaxing, stretched luxuriously in the dark, all memories of tormenting, frightening things temporarily banished, 'all ours.'

PART 5

The Tangled Web
1934–1937

'Oh what a tangled web we weave,
When first we practise to deceive!'

Sir Walter Scott
Marmion can. VI, xvii

CHAPTER 26

Freddie had met Sophie Schmidt in the spring of the year Hitler became Chancellor, 1933. She was just one of a number of acquaintances, young men and women, from which he soon noticed the Jewish element was becoming rapidly excluded. He was a warm-hearted, good-natured man – apolitical, no flagwaver, but disturbed nevertheless by the situation with regarded to the Jews in Germany. However, because of his friendly, malleable nature, Freddie was not disturbed enough to do anything about it, or to court trouble. With his cheerful, optimistic nature he was convinced that this anti-Semitism would pass, resisted by the good sense of the German people, once their new social system had stabilized.

Yet the Kleins were a worry. Peter persisted in flouting the authorities who had tried to close his magazine by breaking into his office several times, taking away all the files, and throwing the broken furniture into the street. Now he was on the run while his father, asked to resign from his directorship of the State clinic after the laws passed against the Jews holding public offices the previous spring, was hanging on for dear life, making one appeal after another. They had moved out of their beautiful house in Dahlem into a large anonymous block of flats in a seedy quarter of the city, not far from the paediatric clinic, in order to try and achieve anonymity.

With them had gone Marian, whose health was giving increasing cause for concern as she struggled to keep up with her studies, even though she found it more and more dangerous to go to the university. Instead she stayed at home, breathing in the dank fumes of the large industrial city when what she really needed was clear mountain air. But those days when escape to the Alps could even be thought of were past; it was increasingly risky even to leave the house to cross Berlin.

After a while Freddie realized that to argue against Hitler or in favour of the Jews was foolhardy, so he held his peace proclaiming himself, like Sophie Schmidt, apolitical and spending more and more time in her company.

Herr Werner Schmidt lived with his family in a large comfortable house in the best quarter of Berlin; in one of the leafy groves at the end of the Unter den Linden. He had a pretty wife, Maria, and the two well-behaved children, Kurt and Sophie, nicely spaced two years apart and studying at the University of Berlin.

Werner Schmidt would, in any age, be considered a good, hard-working enlightened man who loved his family and his country and served both well. He had fought bravely in the War and returned to his government post determined to help build his country up again from the ruins of defeat. But it was a hard job and, in common with most of his fellow countrymen, Schmidt felt only bitterness for the terms of the Treaty of Versailles and the behaviour of the Allies who sought to grind Germany's face further in the mire by their attitude to the question of reparations.

At last here was a man who claimed he could undo all the harm that had been done in the last ten years: the loss of a national morale, the six million people unemployed, the rampant inflation, and the to-ing and fro-ing of heads of state as one Chancellor succeeded another: Bruning, Von Papen, Streicher, while the various parties sought vainly for a solution to the country's difficulties.

Now there was only one party, and Adolf Hitler led it.

When Herr Schmidt had seen the way the wind was blowing he had joined the Party, one of the many thousands known as *Marzgefallene* who had jumped on the Nazi bandwagon. Not that Herr Schmidt had any vulgar ideas of enhancing his position, he just didn't want to lose it. Kurt joined the Hitler

Youth, but Sophie, disclaiming an interest in politics and with a career as a teacher in mind, kept her own counsel. Her main aim was to get good grades in German Literature, which she wanted to teach.

When Freddie got back from his grandmother's funeral, which he did as soon as he was able, his first stop, after depositing his bags at the flat he still shared with Jordan, was the Schmidt house in the Tiergarten. There he was welcomed with great cordiality by the parents and unalloyed joy by Sophie.

'I thought you weren't coming back.' Her eyes shone with happiness as they sat in the lounge, hands touching, while Frau Schmidt prepared dinner.

'Of course I would come back! Whatever gave you that idea?' He looked at her tenderly and touched her pink cheek, remembering the conversation he'd had about her with his mother. Somehow he was more urgently aware of Sophie than before. He loved Germany and maybe he could find a job, maybe ...

'My father is *very* worried about your sister and her journalism,' Sophie whispered while they were still alone. 'He says it gives the family a bad name.'

'I thought they considered her a harmless eccentric?'

'No, not at all,' Sophie shook her head, large blue eyes solemn now. 'They think she is a danger, and *in* danger, maybe. There are things one can't control ...'

She stopped as her mother came into the room to announce dinner, where politics were rigidly eschewed and, instead, after some small talk there was suitable intellectual conversation about the merits of the great English dramatists Shakespeare and Marlowe versus their German counterparts, Goethe and Schiller. There was no doubt that Shakespeare won, hands down, but who was next ... a lot of fun and argument ensued until, after dinner, Herr Schmidt touched Freddie on the shoulder and invited him into his study where, after a few preliminaries, he offered him a cigar and asked him to sit down.

'Do make yourself comfortable, Freddie.' Herr Schmidt snipped off the end of his own cigar and, clasping it firmly between finger and thumb, twirled it round in the flame of his lighter before putting it to his mouth and drawing on it.

'Excellent cigar.'

'Excellent,' Freddie agreed, exhaling, wondering if Herr Schmidt thought the time had come to find out his intentions about his daughter.

'You know, for a time we couldn't get good Havanas,' Herr Schmidt said.

'Really?'

Herr Schmidt nodded gravely as if the news were of some earth-shattering importance. 'When the inflation was at its worst, no one could afford them, so no one imported them. Now, thank heaven, all that is changing.'

'So you really do approve of Hitler?' Freddie felt he didn't need to ask the question, but it was a way of making conversation.

'Yes,' Herr Schmidt nodded, 'I really do. And you?'

Freddie grimaced and shook his head. 'I'm not really interested in politics.'

Herr Schmidt was a large man with a creased, but benevolent face, a little blond-grey hair left on his head and a quantity of gold teeth in his mouth prominently on display when he smiled, which he did often. He wore a well-cut grey suit, a white shirt and blue tie with some sort of motif on it. In his lapel was the little emblem of a member of the Nazi Party, *de rigueur* now for all civil servants who valued their jobs.

'That surprises me, Freddie,' Herr Schmidt said, after a careful study of Freddie's mobile features, 'because your family are active in politics, are they not?'

'No.' Freddie looked surprised. 'My father sat in the House of Lords, but that was before the War and on the cross-benches, I believe. My brother Ralph has never taken his seat, though he may do so soon in order to discuss farming issues. My uncle was a Liberal MP, but is now a judge.'

'Was the Lady Askham who died the one who owns the paper?' Herr Schmidt appeared to choose his words carefully though Freddie felt that, in reality, he knew the answer.

'No, that was my grandmother, Dulcie. She was eighty-one and I doubt if she'd ever heard of Herr Hitler.'

'Then it is your *mother* who owns the newspaper?'

Seeing that Freddie knew that Herr Schmidt knew this quite well he began to feel rather annoyed, as well as a little alarmed. Why was Sophie's father playing games with him?

'My mother owns *The Sentinel*, yes. And my sister writes for it.'

'Ah!' Herr Schmidt touched his nose with his index finger and rubbed it vigorously. 'That is the point, isn't it, Freddie?'

'The point of what?' Freddie's smile was bland. 'I can't stop them. It's nothing to do with me.'

'But you see, in a way it *is*, Freddie, because – how can I put it?' Herr Schmidt carefully searched the ceiling, frowning, the smoke from his cigar weaving its way into the air. 'A *sort* of notoriety deflects from them to you – it's inevitable isn't it? – and from you to my daughter and from my daughter ...' Herr Schmidt pointed his finger at his own chest, 'to me. You do see that, don't you?'

'I can't see it. No. It seems a very tenuous connection. My cousin, Jordan, is also in Germany and no one tries to say anything to him.'

'I believe that is quite a different matter.' Herr Schmidt showed all his gold teeth in a silky smile. 'He openly supports the Führer's regime. Now, Freddie, if you ...'

'I'm afraid I can't, whatever it is you want me to do,' Freddie said mulishly. 'I have no politics and I intend to stay that way.'

'Then in that case, Freddie,' Herr Schmidt carefully placed his smoking cigar in the large ash tray on his desk and linked his hands in front of him like a schoolmaster delivering an unfavourable judgement, 'I must tell you that, although I like you personally very much, and consider you a man of great charm, I cannot allow you to continue to associate with my daughter, as long as you are connected with notorious anti-Nazis and, Freddie, with the Jews.'

'I am *not* connected with the Jews,' Freddie said indignantly and then the thought of the harassed Kleins flashed across his mind and he felt like Judas. 'At least, not much.'

'Yes, but a little, Freddie, and that's quite enough. Don't forget I now work in the Reich Chancellery and many things are known to me that were not known before. Peter Klein is wanted by the police for a vicious anti-Nazi propagandist magazine he edits, with support from the Bolsheviks. There is reason to think that your sister is hiding him. I tell you she is in terrible danger and so are you ... so are *we*, which is more to the point, if you continue to come here, without letting it publicly be known that, somehow, your views have changed. A good way would be to persuade your sister to leave Germany – voluntarily.' Somehow the word 'voluntarily' contained a hint of menace.

'I'm most terribly sorry.' Freddie got up, stubbing out his cigar, which he didn't like very much, anyway. He looked extremely boyish and robust in his Oxford flannels, tweed jacket, open-necked shirt – and very English, too. His eyes flashed. 'That seems to be all there is to say, sir. Good night.'

He was about to walk straight to the door, but Herr Schmidt, showing surprising alacrity despite his bulk, was there before him, leaning against it.

'I do *plead* with you, Freddie. For your own sake, for Sophie's who likes you very much. I say this with the best intentions – you see, you are not fair to Germany.'

'My dear sir,' Freddie said, summoning up his best Askham manner of injured arrogance, 'I assure you I can give no undertaking that goes against my conscience. What you have said to me tonight disturbs me very much, but not in the way you think. Hitherto I have loved Berlin and enjoyed my time here, preferring to regard politics as nothing to do with me.

Now I'm not so sure I was right, that I can keep out of them. I like and admire Sophie, you and your wife and Kurt and I hope that, one day, we can resume our friendship. I even spoke to my mother about the possibility of Sophie visiting us. She was delighted. In the meantime I find your insinuations about my sister and our friend Peter Klein offensive. I find myself more and more on their side, sir. Please let me pass.'

Sophie and her mother, waiting in the lounge, hearing raised voices in the study, silence again and then the opening and closing of doors, eyed each other in surmise, then in alarm, then, as the front door banged shut, despondency.

Freddie walked furiously through the Tiergarten along the Unter den Linden to his flat in a pleasant apartment block on the Kronenstrasse near the Post. Here and there, in the brightly lit streets, he saw sporadic gangs of stormtroopers entering houses or emerging from them. Once he thought he heard a shot. But in the cafés and bars of the Unter, the Behrenstrasse and the Friedrichstrasse, it was difficult to tell that anything was amiss, although there were more Nazi-uniformed men among the drinkers and revellers than a year before. With the official German Army, the Reichswehr, now sporting the Swastika it was almost impossible to know who were members of the Party and who were not.

He had loved his years in Berlin but now, as he turned into his road leaving the lights and revelry behind, he began to wonder how much longer he could remain there. How long could anyone remain who did not bend the knee to the new German God, Adolf Hitler? He had gravely offended Schmidt who might report him to the Chancellery, where his name was obviously known, anyway.

As he opened the door of the apartment he saw a light under the sitting-room door and, casually flinging his trilby on to the hall-stand, he called out, 'Are you there, Jordan?' At the same time he noticed that there was no sign of Jordan's flamboyant hat which he sported in the streets of Berlin, the black sombrero, or the red cardinal's. He and Jordan had travelled back together on the train from Boulogne, via Paris.

There was no reply and, thinking the light had been left on in error, he opened the door to find his sister sitting in an armchair, thumbing through a German magazine.

'Hello,' Freddie said cheerfully, 'am *I* glad to see *you*!' Em rose and he enveloped her in his arms.

'Whatever is the matter, Freddie? How was the funeral? Awful?'

'It was a rather noble family occasion.' Freddie wiped his brow, and taking an apple from a dish began crunching it. 'Everyone missed you, especially Mum who sent her love. Em ...' Freddie stopped and bit hard on the apple. 'I don't want to talk to you now, just now, about that but about a perfectly frightful talk I just had with Herr Schmidt. Of course, I went steaming round to see the lovely Sophie as soon as I got back and the old boy gave me a right lecture about you, which I didn't mind, but also about associating with Jews, and I did mind that very much. He asked me not to see Sophie unless I could give up my friends and, I gathered, give the Nazi Party the loud handclap as well. Oh, you should be booted out of Germany. Did you ever hear anything *like* it?'

'And what did you do?' Em looked from Freddie to the closed door of the kitchen which led directly off the room.

'I gave him the heave ho. My best Askham manner: "Don't *dare* to talk to me like that, my man, etc." ...'

'Oh, Freddie, thank God! I'm proud of you. It would have been *awful* if you'd given in.'

Just then the kitchen door opened and Peter Klein walked out, beaming, his hands together almost in an attitude of prayer or praise, possibly thanksgiving.

'Peter,' Freddie sprang warmly to his side and clasped his shoulder, 'what on earth are you doing here, old fellow?'

'They are looking for him to arrest him.'

Freddie noticed now that Em was very pale, with dark circles, betraying many sleepless nights, around her eyes. As for Peter, he wore the hunted look of a fugitive with two or three days' growth of beard, and real fear showed on his face.

'But this is absolutely intolerable. That's why Schmidt spoke to me, I suppose. It's all out in the open, now.'

'The SA have tried to hound Peter without success,' Em spoke rapidly. 'Now there's a warrant out for his arrest and *The Truth* is proscribed.'

'Em is in terrible danger, too,' Peter said.

'Then you must both leave.' Freddie suddenly felt confident and in command. 'We must get you over the frontier into France or Switzerland.'

'I can't leave my family or my magazine,' Peter's voice was stubborn. '*The Truth* will be published, no matter what. I am *not* going to leave Germany or let that Bohemian corporal defeat me!'

'You can't win, Peter.' Freddie shook his head. 'Now I regard Werner Schmidt as a very decent chap – a rational, logical, well-ordered, clear-thinking man. But when he starts that Nazi bilge with me I know that the end is nigh. Can't see his daughter unless I retract my views! The bloody nerve.'

'But how can you retract views you haven't got?' Em lit a cigarette with an unsteady hand. 'Didn't you tell him you didn't give a fig for politics?'

'I did, my dear sis. He laughed at me. I think I'm finished with Germany. I think I'm off. But what about your father and mother, Peter? Marian? They can't stay here. Out of the question. They must all go to Askham.'

'That is what *I* say,' Peter replied, 'but my father says that as long as his patients need him he will remain, and there are very many seriously ill children. My mother won't go as long as he stays. Now also, for them, it is almost impossible to get a permit to leave – because of me. They have no lever over me if my parents are free. You've no real idea what the Nazis will do to persecute people they consider their enemies. There *is*, however, Marian ...'

'But Marian is sick, too. When I last saw her she looked terrible.' Freddie's face showed his concern.

'We *do* want to get Marian out, Freddie. If Peter is arrested and his father too, we don't know what will happen to Marian ... Frau Klein couldn't cope.'

'She'll die,' Peter's voice was matter-of-fact. 'She needs treatment that she can no longer get in Germany.'

'Then she must go to England. We'll wire Mother ...'

Em shook her head, and sat on the arm of the chair as though she were carrying a very heavy weight.

'Peter thinks that if Marian tries to leave the country as she is she might be arrested, to spite Peter, and sent to a concentration camp. She would be an ideal ploy to get him. He'd do anything for Marian, and if she were arrested he'd give himself up – with no assurance that she'd be released, of course. She *would* surely die in prison. Just one more tragic statistic.'

'But she has done *nothing*! It's preposterous.'

'It will be to get at Peter. But there is one way we think Marian *can* leave the country without fear or conditions.'

'Tell me and we'll do it.'

'With a British passport.'

'Capital,' Freddie snapped his fingers. 'How do we get one?'

'Through marriage, Freddie ...'

In the corner of the large living-room with its heavy, cheap German furniture was a grandfather clock that surely came from Switzerland in the last century. Apart from a distant hum of traffic the only sound then that Freddie was aware of was the heavy, ominous ticking of the clock.

'Marriage?' He saw the hopeless look in Peter's eyes.

'If she married an Englishman she would automatically be provided with a British passport and no one would be able to prevent her leaving Germany. She would have the protection of the Foreign Secretary and would and could begin immediate treatment in England, or even Switzerland, which might save her life.'

'Yes, but *who* could she marry?' Freddie put his head on one side as though giving the matter serious thought. Then as neither his sister nor Peter said anything but continued to stare at him the penny suddenly dropped. 'Me?' Freddie gasped.

'There's no one else, and it must be done quickly,' Em spoke urgently. 'There is really no time to lose.'

'It would only be a marriage of convenience,' Peter said hastily. 'No obligations, I swear to that. As soon as you get to England you will annul it on the grounds of non-consummation.'

'It's an *awfully* serious thing to do though, marry someone,' Freddie said, scratching his head fretfully.

'It *is* the only way . . .' Em's voice was appealing, but her tone somehow commanding.

'I'll do it,' Freddie said without another moment's hesitation. 'Tell me, do I get on one knee to propose?'

As he spoke a vision of fresh-faced, pink-cheeked, golden-haired Sophie flashed before his eyes and he bade farewell to it without a qualm.

All at once gloom yielded place to excitement and they fell to discussing plans with a vigour that reminded Freddie of boyish pranks at school in the dorm to outwit the Housemaster.

'First we'll . . .'

They stopped, frozen, as the sitting-room door opened and Jordan, with his red hat on, a cigarette dangling from the corner of his mouth, leaned against the portal looking at them.

'Jordan!' Freddie jumped up. 'I didn't hear the key.'

Jordan didn't answer, remaining where he was and staring at Peter. His expressive features registered various emotions from indignation to outright rage.

'What's that Jew doing in my flat?' he barked at last. 'Get him out at once, for God's sake, or you'll ruin my reputation.'

'Jordan,' Freddie began, 'it's my flat, too . . .'

'Get him out, do you hear me?' Jordan, his voice hysterical, looked around as if any moment he expected the SA to burst

555

in. 'Don't you know there's a warrant out for his arrest? If they find him here they'll think *I'm* involved too. And I want nothing to do with it, or you or *her*,' he looked at Em, 'do you hear? Get out.'

Then he pointed towards the door. But before anyone could stop her Em had walked quickly across the room and, raising her hand, slapped Jordan hard across the cheek.

'You filthy little beast,' she said, 'speaking to *us* like that! You contemptible little Nazi follower; you bring shame upon the house of Askham!'

'*The* house of Askham!' Jordan said with a sneer, his hand stroking his cheek. 'Please don't link me with that. *I'm* not an Askham, thank God, and want nothing to do with the family or the name – a name that is reviled in Germany, thanks to you and your mother. I spend my time denying I have anything to do with you, and if Dulcie had not been my grandmother – of whom I was truly fond – one of the few people who showed me genuine love as a boy – I would not have gone for anything.'

Jordan didn't think it necessary to say that, loving his grandmother or not, he wouldn't have gone home in any case, were it not for the chance of nailing Alexei Ferov. His real reason for attending his grandmother's funeral was business. It was heaven-sent.

Em went back into the room and, picking up her coat, flung it over her arm.

'You're a disgrace, Jordan, and *I'm* ashamed to be related to you ...'

'Get him out of here,' Jordan shouted, ignoring Em, his face now very frightened indeed. 'Get him out and don't let *anyone* see you going.'

Peter went quickly to the door as Em opened it and, as Freddie began to follow them, Jordan put out a hand to stop him.

'*You* don't have to go, too. I just don't want that Jew in my flat.'

'From today I am a Jew; please consider me one,' Freddie said loftily, flicking Jordan's hat off his head as he passed him.

The following day at noon Freddie and Marian Klein were married by special licence at the British Embassy; only Em and a puzzled Embassy official were witnesses. Two days later they crossed the frontier into Belgium, travelling first-class on the train as the Honourable Mr and Mrs Frederick Down. There had been no attempt to stop them and nothing but a casual glance at their passports, either on the station or at the frontier. Maybe, because they acted with such speed, they had foxed the authorities. Maybe in bureaucratic Berlin even news like that didn't travel fast enough. They left Berlin without any fuss and very little luggage, no goodbyes. There was no one at the station to see them off.

They went straight to Paris, to Susan's, where that first night they slept in separate bedrooms, Marian going straight to bed as soon as she arrived.

'She's clearly *very* tired,' Susan said over dinner, which they ate in her apartment.

'She's very ill,' Freddie replied. 'She has to have treatment for her lungs.'

'What a frightful thing. She's awfully pretty.' Susan gazed at Freddie and then looked away.

'It's purely a marriage of convenience, you know,' Freddie said. 'I like her a lot, but not as a wife.'

'I know. What a pity. It's tragic, really, to be separated from her family like that. Who knows when she will see them again? You were a terrific brick to do what you did, Freddie old thing.'

Kyril had said very little since the unexpected arrival of Freddie and his bride. Freddie scarcely knew him. He saw now a quiet, well-dressed man of around forty who smiled gravely, nodding sympathetically, all through the meal.

'Things are really not so bad in Germany as you make out,'

Kyril murmured politely. 'This policy towards the Jews is really aimed at the Communists.'

'Who are *not* synonymous,' Freddie said drily. 'Most of the Jews I know are not Bolsheviks.'

'Still, in the Nazi's mind they are and I must say I do sympathize with that point of view, though it may seem paranoid. So many of the leading Russian and European Communists *are* Jews. It does *seem* like a conspiracy.'

'I'm rather sorry I came. I can see I might have upset you.' Freddie, feeling close to exhaustion himself, got up from the table. 'We should have gone to Charlotte, or a hotel.'

'No, you were right to come here,' Susan frowned at Kyril. 'It's just that Kyril is very anti-Communist and these are his considered views. He's very knowledgeable; he really is.'

'The last thing *I* heard Kyril wanted to go back to the Soviet Union,' Freddie's expression was sarcastic. 'What caused the conversion, or shouldn't one ask?'

'Common sense,' Kyril smiled blandly. 'And, believe me, I do not wish to seem inhospitable, but welcome you here, with Susan. I underwent a change of heart with many other people when, like them, I realized just what was going on under Stalin. I have to thank my dear wife for her trust and fidelity ...' Kyril reached out and took Susan's hand. 'I can only say that Hitler's stand against Communism should command the enthusiasm of *all* right-thinking people. It is the only way.'

'You'd better not let my sister hear that. She is currently being pursued by the SA.'

'Em was always terribly impulsive,' Susan murmured, happy and expansive in the tranquillity of her husband's renewed love.

Freddie rose, banging the table. 'Em was not always "terribly impulsive", Susan. What's got into *you*? Don't you know that in Germany terrible things are being done; people hounded, imprisoned, disappearing without trace? Does that happen in France, in England? No. But it does happen in

Russia and it happens now in Germany, too. If you ask me there is little to choose between them.'

'Oh, Freddie, how *can* you possibly say that?' Susan, her hand still entwined in Kyril's, looked at her cousin reproachfully. 'How *can* you compare Hitler with Stalin? Why, Germany is a civilized country and, although I do think they're mistaken about the Jews, I'm quite sure everything will be straightened out when things calm down, when they defeat the Communist menace.'

'Susan,' Freddie lowered his head to within an inch of her face. 'Until a few days ago I thought that, too. I said I wasn't interested in politics. Well, believe me, now I am for, in the short space of time since I returned from Gran's funeral, I have seen a man hounded for his views, a good and clever doctor sacked from his post just because he is a Jew, a sick woman forced to marry a man she doesn't love just to get out of the country, and an honest German burgher, with a long and honourable family tradition of public service, talking the same kind of bilge as you.'

The next day the newly-married Downs left early on the boat train for London. Neither Prince nor Princess Kyril Ferov were at all sorry to see them go.

April in England and, with the beginnings of spring, there was a general feeling that the policies of the National Government had started to work. Baldwin, working in harmony with the Prime Minister Ramsay MacDonald, was of the opinion that the prospects before the nation were better than for any country in the world. In the budget the Chancellor said that England had finished the story of *Bleak House* and seemed to be sitting down to the first chapter of *Great Expectations*.

Germany continued to be a thorn in the side, however, even though Anthony Eden had visited Hitler in February and received a promise that the SA would be reduced in power and not be rearmed. The two men reportedly got on well. Nevertheless the British government was asked to ban the

Fascist Party, which was causing disturbances on the streets in England, and there was worry about the lack of progress towards general disarmament. France felt in danger of attack by Germany and was supported by Winston Churchill in her efforts not to disarm completely. Hitler went on consolidating his position, trying to convince the world at large of his trustworthiness, his kinship with the common man.

In April, at Adam's house in Bedford Row, Marian Down was finally told by doctors that her health was out of danger and she should take some time in the country to recuperate. For two months there had been tests, treatment, periods in hospital. But no doctor had been able to give a prognosis as to her future – either could not, or didn't want to. Her English improved every day and she began to talk about going back to university to resume her studies.

'But not to Germany,' Rachel said.

'But they did not find Peter. Perhaps he is in Switzerland.'

Rachel turned over the pages of the latest article from Em, which was a clever analysis of Hitler's attempts to fool the West. In particular Em criticized the British government and Anthony Eden for their blindness.

'If Peter was in Switzerland we should have heard. He is still in Germany and still in danger and your father now has lost his post at the clinic. I wish we could get them out; all of them out safely.'

'But they have no money abroad, Lady Askham. Jews, who cannot support themselves, cannot be given visas.'

'As they are now related to us by marriage we should consider ourselves obliged, and pleased, to support them.' Rachel smiled comfortingly at a girl of whom she had become very fond. She wished she was a real daughter-in-law, that this curious, anomalous marriage of Freddie's could be consummated. Freddie was very tender towards Marian, obviously concerned about her. But his attitude was that of a brother rather than a spouse. He was even talking about legal steps to end it.

'I think a little time in the country,' Rachel said cheerily. 'How about the Grange? It's empty and, technically, it's still mine as Cheryl and Ralph never used it.'

'But we can't go there alone, Mother ...'

'Why not?' Rachel began studying Em's article again, her brow furrowed: 'I don't really know that I should risk publishing this. Heaven knows what Eden will say.'

Freddie was looking at Marian. 'If we want to get an annulment, Mother, we can't compromise ourselves.'

'I see. In that case you had better go to Darley Manor,' Rachel said. 'I'll be able to chaperone you both next week. There are plenty of servants about, anyway.'

And so it was agreed. A day or two later Marian and Freddie were packed into the train by Rachel, who promised to follow as soon as she could.

Marian immediately loved the small Tudor manor house, the slowly burgeoning countryside of Wiltshire. She adored the children and proved a wonderful playmate for them. Adam, coming down at the weekend, declared to Rachel that he found her more and more appealing, 'now that she has lost that pinched, gamine look and filled out a little.'

'I think she would be very good for Freddie, too,' Rachel said, watching her on the lawn with Giles and little Flora, throwing them a ball and watching them laugh delightedly when she failed to catch the one they returned, falling over herself in pretence. Freddie was practising in the nets he had constructed for himself at the far end of the garden in preparation for the cricket season, one of the gardener's boys bowling for him.

'But is she really Freddie's type?'

'What *is* Freddie's type?' Rachel wondered.

'Well, someone blue-eyed and blonde, I would have thought, I don't know why. Like you, I suppose.' Adam turned to Rachel and smiled, content, with his pipe in his mouth, his half-moon spectacles on his nose, *The Times* on his lap. 'I think it's going to be a lovely summer.'

'Perfect.' Rachel leaned back in her chair in the summer-house which protected them from the rather keen wind. 'If only Em were home I would be happy. As for a blonde, blue-eyed girl, apparently Sophie Schmidt was like that and Freddie did like the girl, whatever he thought of her father. Maybe he still does. Because he and Marian seem to mean to go ahead with the annulment, which I think a pity.' She gazed at Adam, who nodded sagaciously, his pipe still in his mouth. 'Yes, he's asked me to start the process when I get back next week.'

After Adam returned to London, as usual, the following Monday, Rachel decided to stay down for a few days because she had a longish article to work on, on the general theme of world disarmament, and she felt peaceful and happy at the manor. One day, to her surprise, Freddie came to her early in the morning and asked if he and Marian could have a key to the Grange and a picnic and motor over there for the day.

'Of course,' Rachel said, pleased. 'What a good idea. Do you want me to come with you?'

'Don't be absurd, Mother. We don't need chaperoning *all* the time. We intend to go on being good friends. We like each other very much, you know.'

'I'm happy to hear it,' Rachel said. 'Marian will always be a very dear friend of mine. She's a lovely girl.'

Freddie gave her a bored look and held out his hand peremptorily for the key, as though afraid that she'd go on – he divined very well how his mother felt about Marian.

'Give my regards to Cheryl if you should pop in,' Rachel said as an afterthought, to which Freddie replied:

'Don't worry, we won't. We want a *nice* day.'

It was indeed a lovely day. It was warm, an English spring day at its best and the Grange, nestling in the valley formed by the hill on which the Forest of Askham began its rise, and the lake below the main house, looked particularly charming with the wisteria and clematis coming into thick, elongated buds on the old walls of the house, the tiny rose creepers beginning to form.

Freddie showed it to Marian from top to bottom, exclaiming as they went first into this room and then that, explaining to her who had slept where and done what in which room. It was obvious he loved it, that it meant a lot to him, and she began to share his sense of excitement.

A lot had happened to Marian Klein in the space of a year. From terror and fear she had known the loss of her family, then the acquisition of a new one, of their love and acceptance as well.

The admiration that Marian had felt for him the day Freddie had first come into her life had very soon deepened into love on her part. But, philosophically, she knew that it wasn't reciprocal. Freddie was the sort of person that everyone loved, blessed from birth with a warm, outgoing personality.

She'd known she wasn't Freddie's type – she'd guessed what that would be, blonde, Nordic, outgoing. Whereas she, Marian, a small, dark, introverted Jewish girl who liked to study, would never interest him except as a friend.

And then, unexpectedly, there'd come marriage to Freddie, and illness, and now fear and terror were returning again with the thought of separating from him, his wonderful protective family; above all, his mother. Tightly she clasped his hand as he helped her up some steps to a landing where there was yet another, very large room. Immediately she was attracted by it.

'This was my parents' room where they last slept together before my father was killed,' Freddie whispered, as if in awe. They gazed around it, then walked to the huge window which gave a view of Askham Hall on the hill, and the lake below. The long lawn gently inclined to the lake – a scene of serenity that had remained unchanged, perhaps, for centuries, like the room itself.

'It *is* a lovely room,' Marian whispered. 'And your father was killed by the Germans and yet,' she looked timidly up at him, and her big, dark eyes suddenly filled with tears, 'you are so good to me.'

Immediately he was all concern, and put his arm around her.

'My dear girl, *you* didn't kill my father, nor did the German people, the good people. Father was killed by those dreadful forces which seem to govern our lives for the worst; inexplicable and sad. Mass folly, mass hatred. I don't blame the German people; especially I don't blame you, dear Marian ...'

He looked down at her, aware of her fragile shoulders beneath his strong arm, and suddenly, in that room where his parents had last slept together, he wanted to take her in his arms and kiss her.

It wasn't a new sensation. It had come upon him increasingly in the last few weeks as Marian's health improved, something of her old vivacity returned, the colour to her previously wan cheeks, the sparkle to her formerly dull eyes. He felt that an entirely new person had been created, and that this was partly due to him. It was so rewarding, it was like love. The better she got, the more his she became, the more he felt responsible for her. *Was* it love?

As though divining his thoughts Marian suddenly shivered and said:

'Let's go into the sun again. It's like a ghost ...'

As she turned towards the door Freddie hesitated, knew a moment lost might never be recaptured, and drew her back to him. He was going to kiss her; and then he didn't. He saw the tears beginning again.

'Don't distress yourself, Marian,' he said tenderly. 'I'm here.'

'Yes, but ...' as they walked down the stairs and out on to the lawn, his arm still about her, her own small hand cautiously fumbled round his waist.

'But what?' Freddie stopped and gently drew her down on to the lawn with him, near the place where they'd left the picnic basket.

'Well, you've been very good to me, Freddie. I will never forget what you've done. Never, never.'

'But Marian, we're not splitting up or anything,' Freddie felt a sense of desperation, of frustration, at his failure to kiss her, his failure to find the right words moments before. He felt totally and terribly unsure of himself in the face of this emotion, almost afraid. He wrenched the lids off the boxes, feeling clumsy, indifferent to the good things that cook had prepared for them. 'We don't have to split up at all, if you don't want to.'

As Marian looked at him the breeze blew a lock of hair across her eyes. It was almost a mystical moment in which he knew that they shared infinity – that Fate, not chance, had drawn them together. He knew, then, that it was love, after all. He swallowed.

But Marian's question sounded almost prosaic. 'How do you *mean*, we don't have to split up?'

'Well, we like each other. We get on.' Freddie's mouth was dry. 'We can remain married ... if you like.'

'That's a funny thing to say,' Marian laughed unaffectedly. 'It's as though you were proposing again. The first time was very funny, too. You made it sound so nice.'

'Yes, but then I didn't mean it.' Freddie put the piece of bread he was buttering down. 'Now I do.'

Marian held out her hand for a slice of meat, but Freddie put his bread down, took her hand instead and placed it in his own.

'I know I'm talking like an ass, not used to this sort of thing; but I've become terribly fond of you, Marian. We all have. Mother has too. I know she would like us to marry ... I mean remain married.'

'I know you do this as a kindness,' Marian said, quite calmly. 'You think the future is very bleak and you're sorry for me. I assure you that, now that I'm so much better, and stronger, thanks to you, I am not afraid of the future. And I know that in you and your family I'll always have friends.'

565

'Friends be blowed!' Freddie cried, regaining his composure, not so lost, so tongue-tied, humour and a bantering tone entering his voice again. 'You don't seem to understand at all, you silly girl. I'm a lazy fellow and I simply can't be bothered to find someone else and go through all that business of getting married again.'

'But we ...'

'What?'

Marian shrugged. He wondered if she really understood, or were her feelings quite different from his? He felt afraid again.

'In a way,' she said, 'we're so unsuitable. I'm Jewish ...'

'As long as you don't ask me to be Jewish, I don't mind.'

'I'd *never* ask you to be Jewish ...'

'Mother said would we like to say hello to Cheryl,' Freddie, feeling awkward, sharply interrupted her, 'but I thought not.' He looked towards the house.

'Why not? She's your sister-in-law, no? It's a lovely house.'

'We'll see it another time, but not now. She's like a bad omen. I'll take you down to the bench where my father first proposed. My mother refused him, too.'

'But I haven't refused you, Freddie.' Nervously she put her hand in his as he led her down the steep pebbly path.

'Well, you didn't accept me.'

'I don't know what to think. Is it that you're trying to be kind?'

'Well, I'm not being kind.' Freddie looked at her, her pale cheeks now tinged with colour; her fine, dark intelligent eyes mystified. 'A person can become extremely fond of someone without knowing it. I mean, if you left, if we split, I'd miss you. I'd miss you terribly, old girl.'

But the logical mind of Marian remained uncertain, unswayed. She was too proud not to want to be sure. 'If we were to go ahead with the annulment,' she said carefully, 'don't you think that would be better? Then we could see how we felt?'

'I know how I feel.' As they began to walk round the lake he roughly put his arm tightly round her, pressing her to his side. Was it possible he might lose her, after all? Had he left it too long? He felt at home here, at this spot between the Hall and the Grange where he'd been born. How many times had he played on this very lake as a boy? Sat on the bench? Climbed the surrounding trees? Now he saw it all with new eyes – sharing it with this dear person he so unexpectedly found he loved: tough, courageous, resilient yet frail. What, indeed, was her future without him?

'This is the bench,' he said, stopping at last. 'This is *the* original bench. They were always going to mend it but they never did. They first sat on it in 1899, thirty-five years ago, and Dad proposed to Mother. But she thought he couldn't mean it because he was recovering from an injury received at Omdurman. She thought he must be out of his head. Like you think I am.'

'I don't think you're out of your head!' Marian laughed a little shakily. 'I think you're very sweet and emotional and ...'

'What?' Freddie tenderly took her hand as she lowered her face.

'And I do love you. Only ...'

'Only you daren't admit it, as Mother daren't. Oh, my God, how history is repeating itself, here on this very spot. *She* thought she and Father were too unalike. She thought of herself as rather a serious-minded girl and he was a bit of a lad in those days, considered quite irresponsible: the younger son. You think we're too unalike too ... a bit like Mother and Dad.'

'Yes, that's what I do think. Very different from me. We could hardly be more unalike.'

'Or more attracted to each other,' Freddie whispered, bending to kiss her at last as, once, many years ago, his father did to the woman who became his mother. 'My parents were very happy,' Freddie murmured into her ear. 'We will be, too.'

* * *

When later Rachel heard that the couple were spending several days alone at the Grange and didn't want to be chaperoned she was glad. She sent them a hamper of food, some champagne, and a large bunch of flowers and told them not to hurry back, but to put the central heating on in case Marian got cold. Then she went happily back to London – a dream fulfilled.

CHAPTER 27

Rachel leaned her head back in the darkened carriage, unable to sleep. Booking her seat at the last minute she'd been unable to get a couchette and, as the train tore through the French countryside, she thought back to that dreadful moment two days before when she'd had a cable to say that Em had been arrested on charges of spying against the Reich. The cable coincided with a call from the Press Association who rang her up, and then Reuters, with both of whom she pleaded to put an embargo on the news until she'd had a chance to go to Germany herself.

'If my daughter's case is made a *cause célèbre* the Germans might really turn nasty. They hate bad publicity. It makes them vicious.'

Her friends who ran the powerful news agencies agreed, wishing her, at the same time, Godspeed, and any help she wanted from their representatives in Berlin.

Rachel had tried to speak to Ramsay MacDonald and Eden, but without success. She was popular with neither of them. Spencer had been telephoned at the House and had promised to do all he could through parliamentary and diplomatic channels.

When the train stopped at the German border Rachel's passport was inspected with great care, and then taken away for a few moments before being returned to her. Her fellow passengers were curious, but little was said during the night-time journey. Most of them slept.

Soon after dawn the train from Paris arrived in Berlin and, with very little luggage, Rachel was one of the first off the train. She took a *Droschke*, a cab, to the Kaiserhof Hotel where her London office had arranged for a room, and after a bath, a change of clothes, and breakfast she started telephoning to see what arrangements had been made for her to see Em, where she was being held.

She had somehow expected the bureaucracy, the difficulty of getting a straight answer to a straight question, but not the length of time it would take to learn nothing at all. Finally she jumped into another *Droschke* and asked to be taken to the British Embassy in the Wilhelmstrasse, near to the hotel, where she was received by an official who had notice of her coming. He was a pale young man who viewed her with some disfavour as he glanced at the scanty papers pertaining to the case.

'Spying is a very serious charge, Lady Askham. Apparently Lady Emmeline has been under surveillance by the authorities for some time and was frequently warned by them.'

'She was a newspaper correspondent. She had a job to do. My daughter was certainly *not* a spy.'

'Well, she obviously found out things she shouldn't or the authorities wouldn't have arrested her. They're very careful with foreign nationals.'

'You evidently have a greater trust of the bureaucratic mind than I have,' Rachel said. 'Well, what are you going to do about it?'

'We have made representations, of course, and an appointment for you to see someone at the Foreign Ministry, a Herr...' Mr Spence consulted his papers again, 'Schreider, unfortunately not until tomorrow.'

'I can't hang about all day,' Rachel said. 'They might be torturing my daughter.'

'Oh, I don't think they'd go as far as that, Lady Askham!' Mr Spence appeared all cheerfulness. 'Not the daughter of a British peer!'

Rachel returned to the hotel in the early afternoon and lay down. It was thirty-six hours since she'd had any sleep, and very little then. As she lay on the bed she remembered, as a sort of last hope, Herr Schmidt who Freddie had advised her to see as soon as she got to Berlin, because he worked at the Reich Chancellery. He was sure that Sophie's father was too much of a gentleman to decline to help her for reasons of petty spite.

Rachel rang the Schmidt home, but the maid who answered said none of the family were in, and declined to give her her employer's office number during the day. She asked Rachel to ring back at seven.

Finally, having done all she could, Rachel slept and when she woke it was dark. Outside the lights from the brightly furnished cafés and restaurants in the Zieten Platz, the sounds of laughter and accordion music, the general air of bustle and gaiety, made it very difficult for one to believe that this was a city in the grip of sinister forces, and that somewhere in it her daughter was imprisoned against her will.

Just after seven she phoned the Schmidt residence again. Her German was limited and she once again spoke with difficulty to the woman who answered the phone who finally said: 'Ein Moment' and then, after hurried whispering, a man came to the phone and said cautiously, in English:

'Yes?'

'Is that Herr Schmidt?'

'Yes, who is that, please?'

'It is Rachel Askham, Freddie's mother. You remember ...'

'I remember Freddie very well, Lady Askham,' the voice was polite but chilly. 'What can I do for you?'

'It's about my daughter. She has been arrested.' There was a sharp intake of breath and she thought for a moment that Herr Schmidt was going to hang up on her, so she said quickly, 'Please don't ring off. I am very desperate, Herr Schmidt. Is it possible to see you?'

'I never met your daughter. I want nothing to do with her. Besides, there's nothing I can do. I assure you, nothing.'

'It would help me, very much, just to talk, to get some advice. I'd be grateful all my life. I'll be very discreet. Could I come to your house?'

571

'Oh, no! Please don't!' Herr Schmidt sounded seriously alarmed. 'Where are you staying?'

'At the Kaiserhof.'

'It is too public for me to come there.'

'I can't understand why you're so frightened.'

'Lady Askham ...' The voice sounded tired, exasperated, afraid ... 'I will explain when I see you. Yes, I will meet you, briefly. If you leave your hotel and cross the Zieten Platz to the Wilhelm Platz you come to a broad street called the Vosstrasse. You walk up this, or take a cab, and I will meet you on the corner of the Vosstrasse and the street it runs into, past the Tiergarten, called Koniggratzerstrasse. I have a blue Volkswagen car. I will see you there in one hour's time. Goodbye.'

Before Rachel had time to reply he put the phone down and she began rapidly to dress, having removed most of her things to lie down. She'd bought two light summer dresses for the month of July, and a light woollen grey coat which seemed just the sort of anonymous garb she needed for her strange rendezvous. Then, her feeling of excitement, of conspiracy, tempered by fear, she set out to walk, stopping once or twice to ask her way.

This was the area of vast, imposing buildings, of government departments, which was why she'd chosen the Kaiserhof. The area lacked the gaiety of the Unter den Linden, although Rachel had never been to Berlin before and hoped on this occasion that she wouldn't be staying long.

After a while she saw the dark shadows and open spaces of the famous Tiergarten; the huge park, formerly belonging to the Crown, which stretched from the Brandenburg Gate to Charlottenburg. Already there, parked on the corner of the broad avenue running alongside it, was a dark blue Volkswagen car with its lights off. Looking to right and left and behind her, she lowered her head as the kerb door opened and a voice urged her to get in. As soon as she had, the car drove off, turning into the Tiergarten itself and stopping in a quiet, unlit cul-de-sac. Rachel and the man next to her had not exchanged a word and, for a moment, she felt real fear, such was the all-pervasive atmosphere of suspicion. Supposing this was a trap? Then he spoke.

'I apologize for the caution, Lady Askham. Really, I shouldn't have come to see you. It is a real risk for me.'

'Then I appreciate it,' Rachel held out her hand. 'How do you do?'

Herr Schmidt reluctantly shook her hand and then let it fall abruptly.

'You know, in Germany we have just had a series of terrible arrests and peremptory executions without trial. Everyone goes in fear of their lives, including good law-abiding citizens like myself. Hitler has completely wiped out the leadership of the SA and has settled a few other scores as well. No one is safe.'

'When did this happen?' Rachel, aghast, was now terribly afraid for Em. The nightmare was turning into reality.

'A few days ago. News is trickling through and it will soon be in all the newspapers. I'm afraid it also coincided with the arrest of your daughter.'

'Then I do have real reason to be afraid?' Rachel's voice, quiet, apprehensive, was yet controlled.

'I don't know, truly,' Herr Schmidt wiped his shining face. 'I told Freddie, tried to warn him for his own good and hers. He didn't treat me very well, I'm afraid, and broke my daughter's heart. But I do not bear a grudge. The Jew, Peter Klein, has been on the run for months and the Nazis believed she helped him bring out his paper.'

'Well, that's not spying!'

'No, but they couldn't accuse her of treason. She is not a German subject so they chose spying instead.'

'Did they get Peter Klein, too?'

'Since you telephoned me I made discreet enquiries – a colleague also in the Chancellery. They arrested them together in a little room in a very bad part of Berlin, near the Büschingplatz. I think the Nazis will also try and make out they were lovers, because they do not like Jews and Aryans to have any sexual relations.'

'I'm sure that was not the case!' Rachel expostulated. 'There was never any hint of it from my daughter. Their relationship is purely platonic.'

'It is *very* unfortunate that your son married that Jewess, a daughter of the Kleins, I believe? The deception angered the Nazis. It's a wonder they didn't try and prevent you coming.' Schmidt wiped his face again and glanced anxiously behind him.

Rachel found her mouth was dry. 'In these circumstances it really is very good of you to see me. I didn't understand things were quite so bad.'

'If I were you, Lady Askham, for your own safety I would leave Berlin as soon as I could and hope that diplomatic channels will restore your daughter to you. That is the best chance, believe me. I work in the Chancellery and I know what the atmosphere at the moment is like. No one knows a thing, or pretends not to know. It isn't Hitler, you understand, who is responsible for all this, but the underlings who work in his name, without his knowledge, settling old scores. For many years, since the War, the Jews have been hated in Germany... they control all the wealth, you see, while the people have not enough to eat. Now Hitler – a truly great man – is changing all that, but it will take time. Meanwhile, there will be many injustices. It is the price of social change.'

Herr Schmidt put his hands on the wheel of his car and regarded her gravely, she thought with an air of despair.

'You know, Lady Askham, I have lived through the War and the terrible aftermath of war, when we nearly saw the breakdown of the German state. We really feared a Communist conspiracy organized by the Spartacists who were supported by the Bolsheviks. Karl Leibnecht and Rosa Luxemburg were personal friends of Lenin, you know. In the intervening years, although the threat of Communism has receded, the Weimar Republic was in a perpetual state of disorganization. We Germans could scarcely bear to live with ourselves.

'In the time he has been in power Hitler has given us a sense of pride. The President, Hindenberg, is very ill and everyone imagines that when he dies Hitler will succeed him. Personally I hope he does, because I think he will restore Germany's greatness, though many unpleasant things will happen on the way to normality. But people like you who attack Hitler and the Nazis do not help Germany.'

'I wonder if you realize, Herr Schmidt, if you have ever considered the fact that, if you Germans had not sent Lenin back to Russia in a sealed train, had not supported the insurgents with vast sums of money, there might never have been a Bolshevik revolution? If you feel as you do, and I don't doubt your sincerity, Germany has a lot to answer for, too. But, believe me, Hitlerite fanaticism is not the answer.'

Herr Schmidt's voice began to sound more and more dispirited, as though he didn't really believe his own words. 'All we want is peace and to live in harmony with our neighbours.'

'And the Jews?'

Schmidt shrugged. 'Unfortunately the Jews cannot keep out of other people's business. They are here, there and everywhere and Hitler did hear of an international conspiracy.'

'But not involving the common Jew in the street?'

'They are always up to something, Lady Askham. They can't help it. Have they not helped to ruin your family – the common Jew in the street, like the Kleins?'

'Certainly not. The Kleins have by no stretch of the imagination "ruined" our family. Freddie is very much in love with his wife – as a matter of fact she is now expecting a child. We're quite delighted.'

'Then I'm very sorry for you,' Herr Schmidt lifted his wrist to try and see his watch in the dim light, squinting closely at the dial, 'if having a Jew as a grandchild makes you happy.'

'I realize, Herr Schmidt, that what happened between your daughter and Freddie must have embittered you.'

'Embittered *me*?' Herr Schmidt smiled. 'Not a bit. I liked Freddie, but he was not what I'd call a steady young man though my daughter was rather smitten by him. But I wish you and him, and your family, no harm. I'll drive you back now to where I picked you up and, please, don't contact me ever again. Get the first train or plane out of Berlin, if you can.'

After Herr Schmidt put her off, Rachel walked slowly back along the broad Vosstrasse, pondering over what she had heard, more depressed than ever. She was now really frightened on Em's behalf and resolved the next day to storm the doors of Hitler's Chancellery if she had to, to get her daughter's freedom.

She was walking across the Wilhelm Platz, within sight of the hotel, when she felt a tug on her arm and jerked herself away, raising her voice to cry out for help.

'Aunt Rachel!' the voice hissed. 'Don't shout. It's me. Jordan.'

'Jordan, why ...' Rachel hardly recognized the unkempt creature who stood before her with haunted, frightened eyes and three or four days' growth of beard. 'What on *earth* has happened to you, Jordan?'

'I'm on the run, Aunt Rachel. I'm in danger of my life ... It's all been terrible, I can tell you. *Please*, please help me.'

The arrogant Jordan looked at her so piteously, as if he were an actor in some absurd theatrical, that, for a moment, Rachel was tempted to laugh, had the circumstances not been what they were. Clearly she was in danger of becoming hysterical.

'You look like a tramp,' she said instead, her voice sounding practical, reassuring. 'I can't take you into the hotel like that.'

'There is a back way in. I just wanted you to know that I was here. If you can get me a razor and some soap ...'

'How did you know where I was?'

'I rang Mother who told me to get help from you. You really *are* my last chance. It's miraculous you're here. Please ...'

He began plucking pathetically at her arm, and Rachel, looking carefully around her, made a rapid decision. 'Give me an hour while I find a chemist and get a razor. Tomorrow I'll get you some clothes. Try and get to my room in an hour.'

She gave him her room number and watched him scuttle across the square in the direction of the back entrance to the Kaiserhof, an ungainly, unkempt figure. Difficult to visualize the urbane Jordan now. Then she hailed another cab and asked it to take her to a chemist, one of the few German words she knew.

Two hours later she watched as Jordan, bathed and shaved, sat eating ravenously the meal she'd had sent up, and drinking the wine. He was hollow-eyed and his sunken cheeks made his cavernous face look almost sepulchral, as though he were haunted by death. She had never seen such a horrifyingly dramatic change in anyone. The story he'd told her had been very similar to the one she'd heard from Schmidt about the purge of the SA. Only Jordan added the information that Röhm himself had been summarily executed on the orders of the Führer. Röhm, who had been one of his oldest colleagues, a fellow member of the German Workers' Party in the early Munich days. It was almost unbelievable.

'I tell you Hitler *is* a tyrant,' Jordan said at the end of his terrible tale. 'I now know that he will stop at nothing.'

Rachel realized she hadn't eaten all day and picked at the salad that Jordan had left in his dish, breaking off a piece of cheese to eat with some bread. She drank a glass of wine.

'Don't tell me you're converted,' she said, looking at him askance.

'My dear Aunt, I have seen the light about Hitler, not about National Socialism, which I still passionately believe in. It is said that the SA was going to rise against Hitler because of his tyranny. Someone betrayed them.' Jordan's voice became wobbly and Rachel looked at him with concern.

'Why did you care so much about Röhm, Jordan?'

Jordan's expression became rapturous. 'He was a god. Did you ever see a picture of him? Strong and firm. I followed him with devotion although I never knew him very well. All my friends, the people I dealt with, are probably dead too.'

'What do you mean, "dealt" with?'

'Well,' Jordan looked at her furtively, 'whom I went round with, I mean to say. That's why I had to run for my life.'

'Tell me, how do we get you out of here?'

'Tomorrow you must buy me some clothes, smart, conventional clothes, not the kind I'm associated with. I'll have my hair cut very short, *en brosse* like the Nazis, dyed if I can, and then you must take me with you when you leave.'

'Don't you think I'm in enough danger, too? Herr Schmidt said I should leave tomorrow. People will be looking at me.'

'Then, tomorrow,' Jordan said eagerly. 'As soon as you can.'

'What about Em?'

'Oh, Em can take care of herself.' Jordan offhandedly poured a fresh glass of wine and Rachel realized, with contempt, what a coward he was. Why should she help him? Yet Jordan was Melanie's son, Bosco's nephew, and she had a duty to him. He was family, however despicable; and family came first.

Just as she was going down to breakfast after another disturbed night, with Jordan sleeping on the floor, tossing and turning, muttering and sometimes screaming in his sleep, there was a call from Mr Spence at the British Embassy, who could scarcely keep the excitement from his voice.

'Lady Askham?'

'Yes?'

'I have just had a call *at home* from the German Foreign Office. You are to go to the Chancellery, instead, where someone very important will see you about your daughter. It seems like a breakthrough, Lady Askham. Don't ask me why but strings have been pulled. I have been called *at home*.' Mr

Spence's plummy public school voice positively squeaked with nerves.

'Whom am I to see there?'

'I don't know, Lady Askham, but it is somebody *very* important indeed. They are expecting you at three this afternoon. Please don't be late.'

'I wouldn't dream of it,' Rachel said, replacing the phone. Staring at Jordan who lay, peaceful at last, snoring, she gave him a prod with her foot.

'Why don't you go into my bed? I'll be out all morning.' But Jordan didn't stir; he was making up for lost sleep. Days and days of it.

Rachel spent the morning shopping and wandering round Berlin, which she liked as a city. It was graceful and well planned and she could recall nothing like the Lustgarten, the Opern Platz and the broad leafy Unter den Linden lined with lime trees, interspersed with chestnuts, that led to the Brandenberg Gate. The shops were full of goods, the populace looked affluent and well dressed. Walking along the spacious streets, past the elegant shops and the crowded cafés it was difficult to think that some bloody *coup* had just taken place resulting in hundreds of deaths and, maybe, many others like her nephew, in fear of their lives.

Rachel had great pleasure in buying Jordan an extremely sober suit with a white shirt and neat necktie, which she delivered back to the hotel by lunchtime. Jordan was in the bath and when he appeared seemed rested, recovered and quite pleased with himself, taking a decidedly rosier view of the world than the previous night when his manner had been that of a hunted fugitive. He had got some of his former arrogance, and much of his cheek, back and reprimanded her for being late because he was very hungry.

Rachel ordered another large meal without wondering what the room service of the hotel would think of her. She had already begun to feel apprehensive about her interview at the Chancellery. She dressed for this with care. Though she had few clothes to choose from, they were neat, even elegant, for Rachel; her dress freshly pressed by the hotel staff. Her calf shoes were well polished and the small straw hat she'd bought that morning at a boutique on the Linden sat snugly on her head; her upswept, chignon style had scarcely varied since she was a girl and suited her blonde elegance. Jordan's parting shot as she left the room was to tell her she looked very Nordic. The Nazis would approve.

The Chancellery building, where Hitler had reigned now for eighteen months, was in the process of being rebuilt. There were uniformed men hurrying about, looking busy with papers and orders but, from the moment Rachel stepped inside, she sensed she was expected. She was passed from one suave, uniformed lackey to another, the decorations and gold braid on each growing more profuse the higher up in the echelon of power she got. No one seemed to speak English, so this was all done with the greatest politeness and clicking of heels, until she stood in an ante-room before an imposing-looking door where she was greeted by a man who spoke to her in English.

'Who is it I'm to see?' Rachel enquired. 'Could you give me his name, so that I'm prepared?'

'You don't know?' The functionary looked astonished.

'No, I don't.'

'Then it will be a pleasant surprise for you, Lady Askham.' The man put his finger to his lips as the door opened and another person in uniform beckoned. Rachel's English-speaking companion squared his shoulders, coughed, smoothed his fair hair and stood back to allow her to pass, bowing gracefully as she did.

The room which she entered was vast, beautifully carpeted but sparsely furnished. At the end, under a window, was a large desk behind which sat a man with bent head, writing. As she advanced into the room she was aware of others hovering on the side, and the air of tension and expectation was such that her heart started to beat faster. It was only when she was halfway across the room and the man at the desk looked up that she realized why there was all the commotion. She was looking into the familiar face of Adolf Hitler, Reichsführer and undisputed master of Germany. When he had gazed at her for some moments with his pale, cold eyes, he put down his pen and stood up, reaching over his desk to shake her hand and bid her be seated.

Rachel had read so much about Hitler, seen so many photographs that she thought she almost knew him. Yet nothing had prepared her for the quality of the staring blue eyes, the pallor of his face, the expression of his humourless mouth beneath his toothbrush moustache.

In the past year since Hitler had dominated the world headlines, when his picture was frequently on the front page of newspapers, not least *The Sentinel*, she thought she knew his face pretty well. She had imagined that his demagoguery overcame his insignificance, and that in private he was rather an ordinary man, his only distinguishing features being the familiar slick of hair over his forehead, his ridiculous moustache, both so loved of all the cartoonists.

But now that they were actually staring at each other – was she the rabbit and he the fox? – the effect was strange and compelling, mesmeric. After a minute she looked away and when she glanced up at him again she thought she saw a hint of triumph in the Reich Chancellor's eyes, as though he'd known all the time he was the fox. Then he smiled in a quite pleasant, normal fashion. His lips, however, were unsmiling as he began speaking in a sharp, staccato voice which was quickly interpreted by the English-speaking official who had come in with her.

'Lady Askham, I'll come straight to the point. Normally I would like to welcome such a distinguished newspaper owner, a member of the English aristocracy, to Germany, but in this case I am unable to do so. Not only is your daughter held on criminal charges here, but she and your paper have been responsible for continually printing falsehoods against me and my Party, trying very hard to alienate the English people against me. Happily, you have not yet succeeded, but why do you do it?'

As he was speaking Rachel drew a deep breath, clenched her hands, and knew that, at this critical moment in her life and that of Em, it was essential for her to remain as unemotional and calm as possible. She studied him for a second or two after the translator had finished, and said:

'We are not alone in reporting as we do about Germany, Herr Hitler. It is the country as my daughter, and other correspondents, see it.'

'That is not true, Lady Askham!' Hitler shot out an arm pointing a threatening finger at her, and she thought of Em, maybe languishing in some cell; and she remembered what happened to Röhm. She tried to force a placatory smile. 'It is a lie, all lies, Lady Askham. Other papers, like those of Lord Rothermere, treat me well. They're honest. Many people make it their business to be fair, to try and understand that I have saved Germany from complete collapse; the ruin that began with the attempts of the Allies to humiliate the Fatherland after the War.'

'If I may say so, Herr Hitler,' Rachel replied, good resolutions deserting her because of the need for self-defence, 'many feel that Germany brought her own ruin on herself. It was *Germany* who began the War, not the Allied powers. We ...'

'You had no business intervening.' The finger outstretched again, Hitler got up and, leaning over the desk, shouted at her. She'd heard that this was a frequent ploy of his to try and intimidate his listeners, and not only those in a large audience. She had to remember that this man already had many lives on his hands. How many more would he have before his power came to an end, as one day it must? 'If England had not interfered in our business on the continent by rushing to the support of Belgium in 1914 we would not have had the terrible conflagration we had!' Hitler sat down again, abruptly, looking at those around him for confirmation. Obediently every one of the half-dozen or so heads in the room nodded in agreement.

'Herr Hitler, I am not here to *argue* with you about the causes of the War, or even to defend the Allies, although I believe their cause was just, but to ask you to release my daughter from wherever she is being held.'

'*That*, I'm afraid, is quite impossible.' Hitler vigorously shook his head. 'It is outside my power to release her as she is being held on such grave charges.'

Rachel's heart sank, her bravery evaporated. 'What *are* the charges, may I ask?'

'Conspiracy to overturn the lawful government of Germany by spying for the International Jewish conspiracy ...'

'That is quite ridiculous, sir!' Rachel managed a quite spontaneous laugh. 'My daughter has no interest in anything as absurd as plotting to overthrow Germany. She is here as a reporter, reporting the news as she sees it.'

'Then there is something very wrong with her vision,' Hitler's fist came thudding down on the desk and everyone in the room jumped. 'I wanted to see you to tell you that personally, Lady Askham, and to ask you to stop telling *lies* in your paper against *me* and the *lawfully elected German government*.' As he came to the end of what he had to say, his emphasis on each word grew to a crescendo, then fell to a soft, dramatic whisper: 'Good day to you.'

Hitler, sinking back in his chair, gave a signal to another lackey who came forward to help Rachel up and, with a feeling of utter defeat and despair, she rose. Then, loudly clearing her throat, she said:

'May I say, Herr Hitler, with the greatest respect, that I cannot give any undertaking not to report the facts, as we see them, in my newspaper. However, *if* my daughter, Emmeline, is released unharmed I will undertake not to send another representative of my paper to Germany. After all, if she is home in England she can do no further harm, can she? But if she remains here I assure you that I will use all my influence with the government. This includes a long acquaintanceship with the Prime Minister and Mr Anthony Eden, whom not so long ago you welcomed to this very building. The moment I arrive back in England an outcry will be launched by the press against Germany on her behalf that will far outweigh anything that might happen to my daughter, much as I love her.'

Hitler stared at her again, shook his head and pointed towards the door.

'What you have to say is of no interest to me, Lady Askham. You and your daughter are pronounced Jew lovers, your son is married to a Jew. For all I know there is even more Jewish blood in your family. Certainly I know you are a lover of the Bolsheviks whose ranks are full of Jews. We have obviously nothing more to discuss. Please be out of Berlin by tomorrow, or I might arrest you, too. Good day.'

Rachel turned, heart thumping dully, like a funeral dirge, and walked slowly from the room. As the doors opened those in the ante-room gazed at her curiously, parting ranks for her as she made her way down the broad stairs of the Chancellery and out into the Wilhelmstrasse. Even though it was a short step to the Kaiserhof she felt her legs wouldn't carry her and hailed a cab.

Jordan, looking relaxed and elegant, listened carefully to what she had to say as, nursing a whisky after she got back to the hotel, she gave him an account of her meeting with Hitler.

'You didn't say anything about *me*, did you?' he enquired anxiously when she had finished.

'Oh, yes, I told him all about you here.' Rachel glanced vaguely around her. 'You can expect a knock on the door at any moment.'

As Jordan jumped to his feet she managed to smile, but not for long. 'I tell you I'm frightened, Jordan. Very frightened of what is happening here in Germany. Much, much worse than I thought.'

'Me, too,' Jordan interrupted. 'How, now, am I going to get out if they're watching you? Did you think of *me*, Aunt Rachel, when you argued with the Führer?'

'But are they actually looking for you?'

'I don't know. Not yet, maybe.'

'Then what has made you so frightened? I don't quite understand.'

Jordan hung his head and remained silent. Restlessly Rachel got up and, moving to the window, looked out. It was near here that, in 1919, the Spartacists, led by the Communists Karl Liebnecht and Rosa Luxemburg, had tried to take over the state by proclaiming a German Soviet Republic in front of the Emperor's Palace itself, the Königliches Schloss. Liebnecht and Luxemburg had subsequently been cruelly murdered by the predecessors of Hitler's SA, the Freikorps. Rosa's body had been flung into a canal, not far from this hotel. Rachel knew that Germany had not changed and that there was nothing, now, of which Hitler was incapable. She knew also that she should have placated him, pleaded with him, made any promises he wanted. But her pride, the pride she'd inherited, along with so much else, from the Askhams, had not let her. By, at last, becoming truly a proud, arrogant Askham, used to commanding rather than receiving commands, she may have cost Em her life. Now not only did she have the worry of Em but the burden of Jordan, her nephew. She looked at him helplessly.

'I can't *think* what to do with you,' she said. 'All you can do is take your chance openly, and come with me. I will book you a seat on the train and let's hope for the best.'

'But if they drag me away?' There was hysteria in Jordan's high, frightened voice.

'Then I'll do what I can when I get home, as well as for Em. I suppose one day people will find out how to leave Germany with false passports and so on, but just now I don't think we've the time. We shall just have to brazen it out.' She had begun to feel less pity for the craven, terrified Jordan, riddled with self-love.

Rachel spent the rest of her time in Berlin at the British Embassy trying to get help. But once again the only advice they could give was to leave Germany as quickly as possible, and pull what strings she could once she got home. Everyone was inclined to think that Hitler wouldn't harm Em, that he was trying to teach her a lesson. But no one could be sure. She tried Herr Schmidt again, but he refused to come to the phone, his daughter saying bitterly: 'Why don't you leave us alone or else we'll be tarred with *your* brush?'

After a fitful night's sleep Jordan was despatched down the back stairs of the hotel in his new outfit, cleanly shaved and as wholesome looking as Jordan was capable of. He had orders to rendezvous with her at the station for the afternoon train to Paris.

Rachel was drinking coffee in her room, feeling unfit to face the world and have breakfast downstairs, finishing off what Jordan had left, when the phone rang and a voice speaking careful English said:

'This is the Chancellery. Are you leaving today, Lady Askham?'

'I'm leaving on the afternoon train for Paris. Have you news of my daughter? Oh, please ... is it not *possible* that I could just see her ...'

But the ominous buzzing in her ear told her the line was dead.

Quickly she packed. There was nothing else she could do. Nor was there any time for tears.

It seemed incredible that people were still going on holiday, laughing, joking, meeting relatives or friends and behaving as though nothing untoward was happening in Germany. The station bustled with good-humoured crowds. There was only

586

a sprinkling of uniformed police; true, more than one would see in England, but not excessive.

Rachel had booked two seats in different parts of the train and she soon spotted Jordan nonchalantly reading a newspaper, inconspicuous except for his height and the fact that he carried no luggage. He saw her, but made no sign of recognition and, as she passed him, she kept her eyes straight in front of her, before queueing at the barrier to mount the train. She'd bought him his ticket the evening before.

After presenting her ticket, she walked along the platform to find her comfortable seat by the window. The porter stored her small case in the overhead rack. She watched the platform for a sign of Jordan, but didn't see him again. He could, of course, have mounted the train higher up. Everything seemed terribly normal except the unusual pace of her heart, the tight constricted feeling in her chest, the moist palms which she kept on wiping on the arm of her seat.

After an interminable time the whistle blew and, slowly, the train began to move out. From the platform handkerchiefs were waved, tears were shed. Maybe there were some fortunate Jews on the train, who knew they would never come back. If they had the means to support themselves overseas and were given visas some could still manage to leave; but not everyone had money, or friends overseas to support them, and western countries were notoriously loath to give visas to the Jews. Hitler mocked these countries, saying that if they loved the Jews so much, they should let them come and live there.

Sadly Rachel pressed her head against the cool windowpane as the train slowly gathered speed and began drawing away from the platform. Then suddenly she heard a series of sharp whistle blasts as if by someone with a frantic sense of urgency; a long shrill command to halt the train. Then, to her horror, uniformed men started to run along the platform waving, gesticulating, while with a shudder that sent many people to their knees inside their coaches, the train stopped just as the last carriage was about to leave the platform. Rachel closed her eyes and leaned back as the other people in her compartment began to jabber in German and French. Aware of that menacing, knell-like thump of her heart she remained where she was, eyes closed, not daring to look. She wondered how she would be able to tell Melanie that she had been unable to save Jordan, and decided at once to travel from Paris to Cannes instead of going back to London.

Suddenly the carriage door was opened abruptly and a voice in German called gutturally: 'Frau Askham?'

Startled, Rachel opened her eyes and looked at the uniformed man who was beckoning to her, saying in German: 'Hurry, hurry.' She got up to get her case, but he gave an impatient wave of his arm and, drawing her into the corridor, was babbling in German while propelling her along.

'You can't detain me!' she cried. 'I'm a British citizen.'

Halfway down the corridor her way was blocked by the man who had interpreted for her in the Chancellery. He had on a uniform coat and cap and in his hands was a paper from which he began to read:

'"Lady Emmeline Down is herewith expelled from Germany for activities undesirable in an alien, and will never be allowed back. If she does attempt to return she will be tried as a spy and, inevitably, shot."

'This is signed by the Führer himself, Lady Askham,' the man said gravely. 'He also asked me to tell you that you can repay the kindness and humanity he has shown you by saying something good in your paper about Germany. Auf Wiedersehen, Lady Askham.' Then a hand shot out, opening the door of the carriage next to her, whose blinds had been drawn over the window.

Inside was Em, pale but well, her arms stretched wide open to greet her.

CHAPTER 28

'I wonder if I could touch you for a loan of a few quid?' Jamie said, looking across the table with his customary smile of roguish charm calculated to win over the most critical audience. Only Susan wasn't critical. For some reason she liked her disreputable cousin, seeing in him, perhaps, some of the attraction that had so bowled over Bobby's wife.

Yet no one really liked being asked for money. There was something slightly shameful about this open appeal to one's generosity however much one could afford it and, momentarily, she bowed her head, staring at the thick, opaque glass surface of the table.

Kyril, however, didn't look down, but remained staring at Jamie, an expression of interest on his face.

'Bad as that, is it?' he enquired sympathetically.

'Only a temporary embarrassment,' Jamie assured him. 'Funds, you know, expected from abroad.'

'What exactly is it you do?' Susan said, looking up. 'I never know.'

Jamie pushed back his chair and lit a cigarette, his appetite gone even though the meal was not quite finished, his disregard for good manners typical. Jamie was always bizarre, strange, never did what was expected of him. Certainly he constantly betrayed his aristocratic origins. Some would call him rude and abrupt. Susan never did.

'This and that, using what small talents God has given me, Susie.'

'Yes, but *what*, exactly?'

'Well, I meet a man here or there and do him a favour. Nothing illegal, usually. You'd be surprised what services one can tender when one is well connected and not altogether unprepossessing.' Jamie tried to look modest.

'Yes, I'm sure,' Susan murmured, knowing she would never get an honest answer because she had asked him before. He was quite a frequent guest at the apartment when he was in Paris. He amused her and, for some reason, Kyril liked him. She was due at a reception at her house in the rue Schetter for a new artist that Winnaretta de Polignac, aged but still vigorous patron of the arts, had discovered. Already dressed for the occasion, she rose to her feet. 'I'm terribly sorry but I must leave you. Kyril will discuss with you any needs you have, Jamie dear. I'm sure we can help.'

She smiled at Jamie and then gave Kyril a meaningful look. He nodded and waved his hand, not bothering to rise or see her to the door.

'Amazing woman, your wife,' Jamie said when he was sure she was out of earshot.

'Amazing in what way?' Kyril looked curious and also lit a cigarette. His expression seemed to indicate that he didn't share Jamie's opinion.

'Well, she's quite formidable, isn't she?' Jamie sounded nonplussed for once, sensing the lack of response in his cousin's husband. 'I don't know one half of all the things she does; but she's a great patron of the arts, a connoisseur of this and that, an ...'

'An Askham ...' Kyril finished bitterly. 'The trouble is that my wife is an Askham with all that that means. Come, let's go into the lounge and have coffee.'

Kyril rang a bell which had the effect of bringing a maid immediately to the door. Giving her his orders he linked his arm through Jamie's and strolled with him along the corridor, hung with paintings, which connected the dining-room with the lounge and its bewitching view of Paris across the waters of the Seine. He stood for a few moments, arm still linked through Jamie's, pointing out landmarks of interest, although the towers of Notre Dame Cathedral dominated everything else. Then when he heard the sounds of coffee being prepared he turned, thanked the maid and indicated a sofa.

'Do make yourself comfortable. Brandy?'

'Thanks,' Jamie said, settling into the sofa upholstered in damask with huge soft, plump cushions. 'Tell me, what does it mean; being an Askham?' He drew on the fresh cigarette he'd lit, preferring it to the cigar proffered by Kyril.

'I always think of one word in connection with that family: arrogance.' Kyril bent his head towards his cigar, carefully drawing on it.

'*Susan* is arrogant?' Jamie looked surprised. 'On the contrary, her sympathy and gentleness always surprise me. I must say she has always been awfully good to me, even though one wouldn't necessarily expect it. The business with Hélène, for example ...'

'Ah well, Hélène ...' Kyril shrugged. 'She was always a spoilt girl. No, Susan is at heart a romantic, and a doomed passionate love affair would appeal to her because it would remind her of her feelings for me. These only grew more romanticized the longer we were apart. Yes, Susan is a romantic at heart, but she is arrogant. Very rich people usually are. Take Bobby, for instance ...'

'I can tell you don't like him.' Jamie smiled with satisfaction thinking the mood of the evening, above all Kyril's hostility, were all conducive to the prospects of a loan, hopefully a large one.

Things were going right for him, for once. Hélène was an expensive mistress. She needed things she hadn't needed in the past – if not clothes and jewels then smart restaurants, flowers, proper care taken of her, respect paid to her position as wife of a very wealthy man. She was capricious. If he wanted to keep her he had to do something to increase an income which always hovered around the bread line. In the fringe world of vaguely dishonest business dealings he worked in, debts often remained unpaid.

'I detest Bobby,' Kyril said, placing in front of Jamie a balloon glass, the bottom of which was covered with fine Armagnac; old, if not quite as old as Louis Philippe, which it claimed. The aroma was magnificent. Jamie breathed deeply and with satisfaction, feeling that his fortunes were on the turn. 'I detest him,' Kyril went on, 'because through his mother, an Askham, he has inherited more arrogance than anyone else of that breed.'

'And the Lighterman money, too.'

'The Lighterman money would not have produced that alone. It had to have something else. Blood. Bobby, you know, was responsible for bringing me out of my country without even asking if I wanted to go. That was typical. I have never forgiven him for it. The arrogance of his attitude.'

'I'm sure he thought he was doing you a favour.' Jamie didn't altogether know why he was trying to be fair on behalf of a man whom he detested too – if anything more than Kyril. Bobby, after all, had actually humiliated him, done him harm, stolen his woman – even though, now, he had stolen her back.

'He didn't even ask me if I wanted to go. I was given into his care. Brought here against my will. Do you know I scarcely even remembered Susan? She was not the first affair I'd had and the marriage was a formality. She wished it, to make her feel respectable. It wasn't even strictly legal. I'd almost forgotten that too. You can imagine how I felt...'

'So you do have regrets?'

'Oh yes ...' Kyril paused abruptly, his eyes narrowing, as though afraid of giving too much away, and he turned once more to gaze at the river. 'But there are compensations, I suppose.'

'I understood, however, that you were no longer in favour of the Soviet regime.'

'That is true,' Kyril nodded slowly and faced Jamie. 'To a certain extent that *is* true, and it is also my knowledge of politics and political intrigue that enables me to suggest a slight move against the Askhams which I think will not do them too much harm, but will embarrass them exceedingly – and also, maybe, reimburse you handsomely.'

'Reimburse?' Jamie said with alacrity, sitting up with difficulty among the comfortable cushions.

'I happen to know, you see, because I make it my business to know such things, that a substantial proportion of the armaments shipped legally to France from the Askham factory in Birmingham went secretly to Ernst Röhm's troops in Berlin, just before he fell from power. Somehow Hitler got wind of this – not the source, but the supply.' Kyril laughed with outright pleasure, showing strong even teeth interlaced with plenty of gold. 'Isn't that amusing? What would Lady Askham say, that supporter of Socialism, if she knew that guns supplied to the *Nazis* were making her family even richer?'

'She'd be furious.'

'She'd be furious, and humiliated. They all would. They'd *all* be in very serious straits indeed, as the arms came through Jordan Bolingbroke and Rachel helped to get him out of Germany. The implication, therefore, is that somehow she was very closely involved; maybe a secret Nazi sympathizer herself. I must say I find the whole thing terribly amusing. Don't you?'

Jamie wasn't sure.

'Why, exactly, are you telling me all this?' Jamie moved to one side as Kyril rapidly crossed the room and sat beside him leaning forward, urgently, his voice scarcely above a whisper.

'Because you can help bring their embarrassment about. Now, Jamie, I take it you are a kind of soldier of fortune, your services available to the highest bidder?'

'You can take it like that, if you wish,' Jamie nodded, flicking ash into a large bronze ashtray, also a product of the Tula works. 'Nothing too illegal, mind, or anything that could get me into serious trouble.'

'I assure you that what I am asking you to do need involve neither. In a sense it is betraying your family, but it's my family too ... by marriage. They will recover, after some discomfiture, which will amuse me. You are only very distantly related through your late great-aunt.'

'Oh, I don't give a fig about the Askhams,' Jamie said savagely. 'This will be one in the eye for Bobby, too, if the truth is known. The whole bloody family. They never lost the chance of making us feel like poor relations, and yet they always endeavour to seem so good and kind. I just wonder that you care enough about them to harm them.'

'I care because I hate hypocrisy,' Kyril said sanctimoniously. 'I am also an admirer of Hitler, who will approve of me if the Askhams are publicly humiliated. I will make sure that he knows who was behind it. There is Röhm, being supplied with guns from England, and Lady Askham writing against Hitler. I thought it would be a terrific joke if this could be revealed to the world at large. Hitler will be very happy if she and her brood are made to look foolish. He will know that as a disciple I am trustworthy. It suits me very well. And it can be done. Through you. In exchange, needless to say, there will be a substantial fee with, perhaps, more to come. I can see you are a man who would be very useful to me; a man after my own heart. Influential yet discreet. Should we say, a thousand pounds as a commencement?'

Jamie gave a sharp intake of breath.

'Tell me what it is you want me to do,' he said.

Dr Fraser was the son of the Dr Fraser who had looked after the Askham family since he had first taken up his practice in the district in the 1880s. That Dr Fraser was dead, but his son carried on the practice like his father before him. It was a tradition among those who served the family that son succeeded father, daughter mother; and so it was with the Frasers.

Dr Tony Fraser was as old as the century, thirty-four, a pleasant young man with a good bedside manner, but now, away from his patient, he looked grave.

594

'Had I known you were thinking of having a family so soon after your wife's illness I would have discouraged you, Mr Down.'

'It was not our intention to have a baby,' Freddie said, looking agonized at the doctor's news. 'It just happened.'

Dr Fraser, a family man himself, nodded understandingly. He had been called out in the middle of the night the previous week when Marian suffered a haemorrhage from the mouth and, since then, tests and a visit to the local hospital had confirmed what Dr Fraser had at first thought.

'There is no doubt that the scars on her lungs are tubercular. She has also lost weight rapidly.'

'Is she *very* ill?' Freddie asked with the hopeful expression of a man who knows he has no hope.

'Your wife is quite gravely ill,' Dr Fraser nodded, consulting his notes. 'Normally I would advise a therapeutic abortion ...'

'But I thought it was illegal?'

The doctor looked towards the door, though they were alone in the house except for Marian who was upstairs and the servants who usually had time off in the afternoon.

'Of course, strictly speaking it's illegal, but in serious cases when the mother's life is gravely in danger one can always find a sympathetic gynaecologist. But I think at five months it is too late.'

'I don't think Marian would want it, anyway. She is so keen to have the baby.'

'But do you understand the risks, Mr Down?'

'I understand,' Freddie said broken-heartedly. 'Is there anything else we can do?'

'Only rest; plenty of rest, no exertion at all of any kind. Swiss mountain air would also do your wife the world of good.'

Freddie shook his head. 'She wouldn't go. It is too near Germany. You know she is a refugee and both her brother and father have been arrested by the Nazis. There is no news or trace of them. I think it was worry about them that brought this on.'

'I did hear about it,' Dr Fraser nodded sympathetically. 'It was something to do with your sister?'

'It was *nothing* to do with my sister. She was arrested at the same time as Marian's brother, but she didn't cause his arrest. She was trying to save him.'

'So I understand. Very brave.' Dr Fraser was a medical man unconcerned with politics and began to put his notes into his bag. 'I will do all I can for Mrs Down. I'll come and see her every week and you must call me if you are at all worried. Rest, plenty of rest. And hope.'

He looked kindly at Freddie, held out his hand and, after he had seen him to the door, Freddie made his way slowly upstairs, standing for some moments outside Marian's door before he went in.

She lay as she had when Dr Fraser had visited her, propped on pillows, her face almost as white as the bedclothes, her dark hair like a halo around her. Freddie briefly closed his eyes but when he opened them again she was looking at him, smiling. As he went over to her she held out her hand.

'Bad news, eh?'

Freddie tried to smile but she said, 'I do know, Freddie. He told me everything. I said I wanted to know so that I can be prepared.'

'Oh, darling, you're going to be all right.' Freddie knelt beside the bed and clasped her frail body in his arms. 'You've just got to be very, *very* careful.'

'I think in the old days they called it galloping consumption. It's just a question of whether I can have the baby first.'

'Marian, it's not like that at all!' Freddie squeezed her tighter. 'You just have to rest. There are only four more months to go and then, after that, you can get all the treatment you need, even if it means going to Switzerland because I'll be there with you and it'll be all right.'

'Sometimes I wish I'd stayed in Germany and hadn't caused you all this suffering.' Marian took his hand. 'I'd be dead by now.'

'Marian, must you break my heart?' Freddie looked at her with distress and she held out a slim, pale hand to stroke his cheek.

'Am I sounding very Victorian? Very like Elizabeth Barrett Browning? Well, she went on living, and so might I.'

'You *will* go on living; but we won't have another baby. I wish we never ...'

'But I'm glad we did,' Marian said. 'Truly. I'm glad we didn't plan and plot and try to thwart nature. I'm glad we let our love express itself as it should, as we wanted. We've had the most wonderful months, Freddie,' she began to stroke his head which he pressed to her bosom, 'here in this dream house where your mother and father loved each other, where you were born. I never thought anything like this would ever happen to me. I can really say that, despite what has happened to Peter and Father, it has been the happiest time in my life, these few months when we just had each other, before I became ill again. Whatever happens now we will *always* have that precious time.'

'And your illness will only be a bad memory,' Freddie said, gathering strength from her courage, 'because the good times *will* come again.'

'They say Marian is dying.' Cheryl looked out towards the Grange from her sitting-room window. 'The doctor said she should never have had a baby. Some people do make the most awful mess of their lives.' She walked back towards the small table in the centre of the room where the maid had placed the coffee things. From all round the large house came the noise of banging.

'Chris said the whole thing was beyond him.' Sylvia selected a Marie biscuit and delicately bit into it. 'Freddie comes back married to this girl he hardly knows and then tries to get an annulment. The next thing is they are having a baby! Well, you can't get an annulment on that, *can* you?' She looked meaningfully at her friend, who grimaced.

'The Askhams, as a family, are quite beyond me. Have you ever considered how *really* dotty they are? They never seem to think of anyone but themselves.'

'Well, Chris is all right,' Sylvia said defensively. 'I mean he's a good, sterling sort. He's not at all like his mother, but takes after his father. So he really is a Bolingbroke through and through – good, solid middle-class people.'

'Well, I wish Ralph were good, solid middle-class,' Cheryl said bitterly. 'As it is he has the selfishness of the Askhams with the stubbornness of the Bolingbrokes. I'm afraid he takes after his father *and* mother and, believe me, that is a hideous combination. I never knew his father, of course, and all who did praise him, but that mother ...' Cheryl raised her eyes to heaven. 'She actually *condoned* the marriage of Freddie to that Jewess even when her daughter was arrested and nearly shot in Germany because of it. They're all mad, quite mad.'

'Jordan is a bit like that,' Sylvia acknowledged regretfully. 'Chris's brother. I mean that scatty side of the family is really quite strong in Jordan. Why he ever came out of Germany in all that secrecy is a complete mystery because he was supposed to admire Hitler. Now he's had some sort of breakdown in the South of France and I'm told his mother, who never worries much about anything except herself, is worried to death. She says he's afraid of the Nazis hunting him down. Shooting him.' Sylvia looked, wide-eyed, at Cheryl, and giggled. Then she put her hands to her ears. 'Oh, all that banging's making me deaf. I wonder what Ralph will say when he gets home?'

'I daresay that, to start with, he won't be too pleased. He was always against having anything done to the house so I had to do it while he was away. It won't be finished by the time he gets back, but at least a start will have been made; too late for him to undo anything, thank God.'

'He'll realize then how lucky he is.' Sylvia ingratiatingly got out her diary and started turning the pages. 'When are we next playing bridge?'

Sylvia had become a kind of fixture since the death of the old lady the previous year. When Cheryl was in the country she was always finding some excuse to stay with her, and when she was in town she somehow contrived to be there at the same time too. Soon Cheryl accepted the inevitability of a woman she didn't care for very much being around all the time. She also came to realize that Sylvia wasn't there as a threat or to spy on her; wasn't waiting for an opportunity to reveal at any moment to the rest of the family the fact that Dulcie Askham had collapsed during an argument with her.

No, Sylvia, married to a rather boring man, was a lonely girl who aspired. She aspired to being a lady, rather as Cheryl had; and Cheryl understood this because, at one time, she had been a rather lonely girl married to a boring man in Kenya, George Lee; aspiring to being a lady too. In time Cheryl came to find Sylvia almost congenial in the sense that people with strong, aggressive personalities seem to need others about them to serve as foils. Sylvia was someone who would agree with her, flatter her and listen with sympathy to her endless complaints about members of the Askham family, especially her husband, her mother-in-law and her husband's half-brother, Hugo.

The other members of the family came to regard Sylvia as a rather weak, good-natured woman who was content to be bossed about and patronized by Cheryl. It would, however, never have occurred to any of them to disagree with this arrangement or be concerned about it. It simply didn't interest them very much because, unlike Sylvia, in their own lives they were too busy and preoccupied not to wish to mind their own business.

As soon as Ralph had gone to France with Hugo and Bobby to attend the horse sales, Cheryl had signalled to her designer, who was standing by with his plans ready and squads of workmen, and they descended on Askham Hall. In no time the main reception rooms were stripped bare and the beautiful ornate eighteenth-century plasterwork removed; the furniture was packed up and sent to the sale room, the pictures likewise.

One wall of the main drawing-room was turned into a huge mirror and the others stripped and painted cream and brown in the latest *art deco* fashion. Lacquer and chrome, brass and onyx proliferated everywhere and a centrepiece of the new drawing-room was a long low macasser ebony table by Kaare Klint. Beside one of the huge, upholstered sofas, a marble statue of a naked dancer held a huge lamp between her hands shaped, suggestively, like a cornucopia. In front of the mirrored wall was an off-white cocktail cabinet with concealed lighting and, nearby, a huge Coromandel lacquer screen which reflected in the glass. The electric candles in sconces on the walls appeared like a vast shiny Chinese dragon, accoutrement of a magician whose tricks had transformed the room to fairyland.

Ralph was away just over three weeks and Sylvia had come down to observe his delighted reaction when he returned, a day before he was expected. After their coffee the two women walked through the house admiring the efforts of Neil and his workmen, while those members of the staff who thought differently, and knew better, peeped round the half-open doors, stifling giggles with their hands to their mouths.

'He might not be very pleased at *first*,' Sylvia remarked after their tour of inspection, 'but in time I'm *sure* he'll be delighted. It is so *very* different.'

It was different and, if one appreciated modern ideas of art and decoration, it was very nice. If, on the other hand, one preferred the works of Chippendale and William Kent, the paintings of Constable, Vandyke and Joshua Reynolds, the carvings of Grinling Gibbons, the plasterwork of Bradbury and Pettifer, to walk into one's home and see it completely transformed in the space of a few weeks would come as something of a shock.

Nothing was obvious to Ralph, arriving back that night in January 1935, well pleased with his trip, until he left the hall which, with its panelling and parquet flooring, was difficult to change, and ran up to the drawing-room on the first floor.

Cheryl, cocktail in hand, was waiting for him by the fireplace, which had been stripped and remodelled with gleaming tiles surmounted by glass, and in which now there was a warm fire because it was a very cold winter's day. Sylvia perched on one of the laminated, cantilevered chairs with a curved plywood seat designed by Alvar Aalto, nervously sipping a gin and Martini.

'What the hell is this?' Ralph stood on the threshold, still in his raincoat, the butler hovering behind him.

'A surprise, darling,' Cheryl said brightly, taking a step towards him. She had already fortified herself with two quite substantial cocktails and her face was a little flushed.

'A surprise? More like a shock.' Ralph stripped himself of his mac, and gave it to the butler, who gladly disappeared through the door, closing it sharply behind him. 'A bloody awful shock.'

'Ralph, is *that* very nice the moment you come in?' Cheryl pouted and went over to the shining new cocktail cabinet to mix him a drink. She had carefully prepared herself for the homecoming in a couture frock made of jaska wool with wide revers, that had cost her the best part of fifty pounds, and her make-up was more lavish than usual to conceal her nervousness, the pallor of her face. She didn't expect Ralph to like it. She knew it would be a battle; but she wanted her own way and to show him that, come what may, she would get it.

That was why she had been quite glad of Sylvia's support; she was a useful person to have around. She didn't argue; she ran any number of little errands and did useful jobs, like bossing the servants and arguing with the housekeeper about the rearrangement of the furniture. Cheryl thought of her as a sort of menial, a social secretary which, had she known, would not have pleased Sylvia Bolingbroke very much at all.

Ralph had thrown himself into a chair, his head sunk on to his chest and, when Cheryl tripped over to him with a drink held in her beautifully kept white hand with its brilliant red nails, he took it and downed it at a gulp.

'Well, you got your way, didn't you?' He held up the glass to her face, rudely jerking it, as though he wanted a refill. Without a word she took it and replenished it with whisky and soda, Ralph's drink.

'I knew we'd never do anything while you were here,' she explained.

'*We?* Do you mean you and I, or you and Sylvia?'

'Well "we",' Cheryl smiled vaguely in Sylvia's direction. '"One" that is to say. Nothing would have got done, ever.'

'Nothing needed to be done.'

'There I disagree with you, darling. Even Sylvia thought ...'

'I'm rather tired of hearing what Sylvia thinks, if you want to know,' the tone of Ralph's voice was even harsher. 'You'd think you had no mind of your own but, at every minute, we have to hear what Sylvia says or thinks. Well, I happen to know that you *have* got a mind of your own, that you *are* determined to get your will, at all costs, and that what Sylvia says or thinks is of not the slightest interest to you. You use her. She bolsters up your colossal vanity, the ruthless manner in which you get your own way.'

'Ralph!' Cheryl looked shocked. 'That is a frightfully *rude* thing to say about your cousin's wife.'

'Cousin's wife or no it's true. She's an ass to let you use her.' Ralph swallowed his second drink as quickly as the first and got up. 'Now, I want Sylvia out of here and I want all this junk taken out and the furniture, the priceless furniture, that has been in my family for generations, put back. And I want it done by the time I return. And,' he pointed a finger at her, 'if you've sold it you'd better buy it all back or I'll sue you for theft, even if you are my wife.'

'Ralph!' Cheryl ran across the room, seriously alarmed for once, by an outburst of temper such as she had never seen from her husband. She grabbed his arm. 'Please, *don't* go. You know it's impossible.'

'Why is it impossible?' He tried to shake her off.

'Because all the stuff has gone ... it *is* sold,' she gestured helplessly with her free hand. 'If I'd have known, of course, I ...'

'*You* did this by yourself? On your own initiative?' Ralph seized her roughly by both arms and shook her. 'You threw all this stuff out that is worth a fortune? That was *my* inheritance? What the bloody hell did you think ... Oh, what's the use,' he threw up his hands and collapsed on to the huge upholstered sofa, putting his muddy shoes on the shining pink satin. 'You've won, Cheryl, haven't you? You've been waiting a year to do this. You *planned* and you *schemed* and then, when you knew I was going away, presto!' he snapped his fingers. 'Everything swung into action. I suppose it's all like this. The whole place?'

'Well, not *all*,' Cheryl guardedly glanced at Sylvia, whose face was ashen. 'I mean this *is* just the beginning ...'

'Then let it be the end. Get rid of them, the designer, the workers ... I don't want them near here.'

'But it's half finished ...'

'Let it stay that way. Let it ever be a memorial to my folly in trusting you; the half-finished, half-baked house.'

'You can't just *leave* it.'

'Yes, I can,' Ralph said. 'It's my house and I can do what I want. And you'd better ring up the sale room tomorrow, first thing, and see if you can get anything back. I suppose, in law, I'm responsible for your criminal actions. I shall be staying with Hugo at the farm until all this has blown over; but make sure that my instructions are carried out to the letter. Do you understand?'

'Yes,' Cheryl said, feeling overwhelmed for the first time in her life, her eyes brimming, maybe with hatred, maybe with contrition; but – too late.

'My goodness,' Jamie said, 'listen to this.'

'What?' Hélène turned sleepily in bed, her arm thrown over her lover's chest.

'It's all about the Askhams. They do have a penchant for getting into hot water, don't they?'

'Oh, what?' Hélène sat up and rubbed her eyes, glancing at the clock which told her it was 10 a.m. Jamie was laying on his back reading the paper which his servant had brought when he had discreetly put the morning tea by their bedside. Bobby was in France buying horses with Ralph and Hugo, and the children were in the country with Mabel. It was heaven. She stretched luxuriously and sipped her tea to try and wake up.

'Listen to this.' Jamie tucked his arm behind his head, shook the paper in front of him and read:

'Headline. I quote:

"Red Countess's Family Firm Accused of Rearming Nazis.

"It was revealed yesterday to your correspondent, by an impeccable source, that arms were supplied to Ernst Röhm's stormtroopers, who were alleged to be in a plot to topple Hitler, by Askham Armaments Ltd, a firm near Birmingham. Röhm and many of his co-conspirators were subsequently shot without trial on the orders of Hitler, who said at the time that he was acting on his own authority to save Germany from destruction.

"I am told that Hitler was furious when this revelation was made to him because the stormtroopers, who were forbidden to carry arms, would not have dared act without sufficient weapons.

"The curious thing is that Lady Askham is a well-known supporter of the Bolsheviks and a pronounced foe of Herr Hitler. Her daughter, Lady Emmeline Down, who was formerly a reporter for Lady Askham's paper *The Sentinel* in Berlin, left Germany hurriedly in the summer, under circumstances the cause of which has never been revealed."'

Jamie smiled and looked at Hélène, who was now wide awake.

'But that's *Bobby's* firm. It has nothing to do with the Askhams. It has to do with me!' She sat up abruptly.

'Well, it has their name. Someone's been stirring it up. Bobby's not even mentioned.'

'He'll be furious.' Hélène lay back and chuckled, then, suddenly, she sat up again, drawing the sheet up to her chest.

'Oh, my God!'

'What?'

'My father.'

'Your father what?'

'Oh, my God, I know exactly what has happened.' Hélène sat on the edge of the bed and poured more tea before slipping on a robe and tying it furiously about her as she began to pace up and down.

'*What* happened, darling?' Jamie reached over the bed and playfully tugged at her, but she didn't stop.

'I can't tell you, I'm afraid.'

'But you must. You're obviously terribly upset.' Jamie put his long legs over the side of the bed and, drawing her down beside him, held her close.

'I think my father's involved and ... Jordan, Bobby's cousin. You see Jordan asked Bobby to supply arms to Röhm ages and ages ago. Bobby refused. He was scandalized. I said, in a rather jokey way, that I'd speak to my father. You know I was being clever and mischievous, trying to score off Bobby. As far as I knew, though, nothing more happened because my father refused to take it seriously; at least I thought he did.' Now she looked doubtful.

'Well, someone's going to get it.' Jamie kissed her cheek. 'And the great man comes back today?'

'Yes.' Hélène turned to him, hugging him. 'Oh, how I hate him! You know I'm actually afraid of him. If only ...'

'Yes, my pet?' Jamie kissed her again as she looked longingly into his eyes.

'If only *you* ...'

'Darling, you know that I'm not husband material. Besides, I have no money and I'm still married. My wife will simply not divorce me.'

'But have you asked her?'

'Of course I've asked her. Do you think I want to stay married to her all my life?'

Hélène didn't know. There was so much she didn't know about Jamie. In many ways he was an open book, apparently an extrovert, uncomplicated man, yet, in many others, he was so mysterious.

Yet the fact was that, worthy of her or not, she was besotted with Jamie Kitto. He was, and remained – as far as she knew would remain – the love of her life. They'd been lovers since Dulcie's funeral. Jamie had rung her up a week later, coinciding with another of Bobby's trips abroad. Jamie was exciting and vigorous and she loved him; she had always loved him but, somehow, instead of being satisfying this compromise was frustrating. She was less and less happy with Bobby and more in love with Jamie.

She went into the tiny bathroom next to his bedroom, washed and made up; then she came back in her cami-knickers and silk slip and completed dressing with her usual care, watched by Jamie, lying on his back. It was always a marvel to him that this beautiful, elegant woman waited around for him; was as dissatisfied as she was. She could have got any man she wanted.

After she'd gone he lay there for a long time thinking what a lucky man he was to be desired by many beautiful women, to have time on his hands. Then he pulled the phone towards him, still lying comfortably on his back, and asked for a number in Paris. When, after a few moments, he heard a voice at the other end he said:

'It's in the paper today. They bought the story.'

'I hope they paid you well.'

'I don't want anyone to think I'm taking blood money by betraying my relatives.'

'Very remote relatives,' the voice said in its deeply accented Russian accent. 'It should not worry you. And they only got what they deserved. Now there'll be a stop in the supply of armaments to the Fascist parties in Spain. That's all I wanted.'

'Spain?' Jamie wrinkled his nose. 'Why Spain?'

'Because the next war will be there.' Kyril quietly put down the phone before his wife Susan could ask who he was talking to.

As soon as she got into the house Hélène could tell that Bobby was already home. Before she had closed the door she began to tremble and walked nervously into the drawing-room where he was looking through his letters.

'Ah,' he said, without looking up. 'You're back.' Hélène went up to him to give him the perfunctory kiss of greeting, but he pushed her away. 'Where were you?'

'Shopping, darling.'

'I mean last night?' Bobby's cold eyes stared at her. 'I came back last night. I was a day early.'

'With Cheryl.' Hélène, a practised liar, spoke automatically. 'I stayed the night with her.'

'Why?'

'Why *all* the questions, Bobby?' Hélène stooped to look into the mirror, removing her hat with its little half-veil concealing the upper part of her face, a jewelled brooch at the side. She shook her head, smoothing its neat upswept coiffure with both hands, trying to still the guilty beating of her heart.

'Why not?' Bobby turned over a letter and glanced at the contents. 'You're my wife. I expect to see you here when I get home. No one seemed to know *where* you were.'

'I went to see Marian,' Hélène improvised, 'Freddie's wife, and then I stayed the night with Cheryl.'

'Well, that's all right then,' Bobby looked at her and lit a cigarette. 'How was everything?'

'Fine.' Hélène seemed surprised.

'No disasters or anything?'

'Not that I know. Why?' Hélène began to feel more and more uncomfortable. 'Why should there be?'

'Just asking.' Bobby threw several empty envelopes in the fire and then turned to the paper which was lying on the sofa and shook it open.

'Did you see this?'

'Yes. Awful, isn't it?' She was relieved to think Bobby had a reason for his bad temper besides her. She was just the object of his temper.

'Well, I'm going to get to the bottom of it. Aunt Rachel has already been on the phone and she's spitting.'

'I can imagine.'

'Thank God I wasn't mentioned.'

'Thank God you weren't.' Hélène lit a cigarette, hands still shaking, and gazed at her polished nails. The sinking feeling inside her refused to lift. Everything seemed to be wrong. Everything.

'I don't suppose *you* know anything about it, do you?'

'I?' Hélène looked outraged. 'How could *I* know anything about it? I'm nobody, as you keep reminding me.'

'You're so devious, Hélène, but I don't suppose even you would start running guns. You might know something about it, though.'

'How could I possibly know anything?'

'You were in Germany with me when that little bastard Jordan made enquiries about arms. He is behind it, of course, there is no doubt about that.'

'Are you sure?'

'Of course I'm sure.' Bobby poured himself whisky and soda though it was not yet noon. 'He came out of Germany in a great sweat just after that coup last summer and, according to Mother, he's been in a terrible state ever since, saying people were trying to shoot him. He's in a clinic, nearly out of his head. Mother has already been on the phone about this. So has Ralph ...' He looked at her but she didn't get the significance of Ralph's name and she shook her head.

Rachel said: 'I can't bear another court case; the last one is still too vivid in my mind. It's never worth going to law.'

'Oh, Aunt Rachel, that was years ago,' Bobby said impatiently. 'Some families as big as ours are litigating the whole time. Things are always going wrong. You don't know.'

'Well, I don't want it and I don't like it. It would also mean bringing in Jordan and, according to your mother, he really is quite ill.'

'I'm going to kill the little brute, anyway,' Bobby said furiously and Adam looked at him, gently raising and lowering his hand.

'Cool down, Bobby. Cool down.'

The family conference had been called to discuss the article, everyone gathering in the drawing-room in St James's Square. Rachel, seeing the house again, didn't know what horrified her more: the state of what had once been a beautiful room, with its exquisite eighteenth-century furniture, or the article which once more threatened to expose the Askham secrets.

Present were Rachel and Adam, Ralph and Cheryl, Em, Bobby, Hélène and Christopher Bolingbroke there with his father to give legal advice.

'The point is we know it's half true,' Christopher said in his slow, ponderous way. 'Jordan undoubtedly did get some arms to Röhm. Not that it did him much good. He had to get out of Germany in such a hurry. Jordan obviously stole from the company.'

'Yes, but how? That's where a *private* investigation would be preferable to airing the matter in court,' Rachel said.

'Oh, we'll have an investigation, all right. There's something very nasty going on at my works in Birmingham because I've already had a quick investigation there and was told the inventory control *had* been faulty, but everything was now all right. The point is that Aunt Rachel and, through her, the family, have been libelled by this. I suppose I know how she feels after the libel trial that finished Uncle Bosco.'

'You must go and see the newspaper owner,' Adam suggested after more talk. 'Just like Bosco did and, until you have, we can't really decide what to do. Harvey Oscott is the new owner, a reasonable man I hear, though not one I've ever met. You can threaten him. I don't think he'll be anxious to go to court, either.'

'The main thing is that they apologize to Mother.' Ralph, sitting next to Cheryl, kept on glancing at his mother opposite him. He had never seen her looking so wretched and dejected, as if the past had returned to haunt her.

But even more uncomfortable than Rachel was Hélène who sat at the back of the room, as if she hoped to remain invisible. It was she, and she alone, who knew that somehow her family were implicated in this intrigue and that, if anything, the Askham family was barking up the wrong tree. It was a wonder that no one suspected Alexei. She felt wretched and alone, needing Jamie yet knowing that he had gone to Paris soon after their last meeting. The porter in the block of flats in St James's where he stayed had given her the news, with some pleasure she thought, as if he knew who she was and the clandestine nature of their relationship.

As the family broke up shortly after noon and moved into the downstairs drawing-room for drinks before lunch, Hélène caught hold of Cheryl's sleeve and tugged her to one side.

'Do you think we could have a quick word?' she whispered. 'In private?'

'How mysterious,' Cheryl looked conspiratorially around her. 'Could it wait until after lunch?'

'Now, if you don't mind,' Hélène copied her furtive glance. 'It might be too late after lunch.'

'Dear me.' Cheryl opened the door of her private sitting-room, which had been Bosco's study, then Rachel's. Now it was her den, furnished in the style she liked with a roll-topped desk for her accounts – there were many of these – and prickly, uncomfortable-looking armchairs consisting of broad strips of leather slung between supports of laminated birch. All traces of Bosco and Rachel had been swept well away.

'Now,' she closed the door quietly, 'we mustn't be long. Would you like a naughty gin? One needs it after a morning with the family.'

'That would be nice,' Hélène smiled. 'Why "naughty"?'

'I always think it's rather naughty to keep a bottle of gin in my little den, but I do. For when the Askhams get too much for me.'

She poured two large gins, adding a dash of Martini to each glass, and raised hers.

'Chin-chin.'

'Chin-chin,' Hélène said.

'Now, what's the frightful secret?'

'It *is* rather a frightful secret really,' Hélène quickly adopted Cheryl's rather false style of patter, though her soft Russian accent mitigated the harsh, brassy modern tone, 'but I don't want you to ask me *yet* what it is.'

'Say away.' Cheryl, intrigued, sat on the wooden arm of her chair while Hélène perched on the arm of its twin.

'I would like you to say that I have just been staying with you, if it crops up.'

'Where? Here or in the country?' Cheryl readily replied, with all the aplomb of a woman who is used to deceit and indeed, in Kenya, it had been part of a way of life.

'In the country, for a few days. At the Hall ...'

'Consider it done,' Cheryl quickly swallowed her drink, 'but I'm dying to hear *why*.' She shook a finger roguishly at Hélène and then put the other finger to her lips as she crept towards the door, as though playing a game. 'If they asked *why* we crept away we can say I've been showing you the redecoration. Do *please* say you like it.'

'Oh, I shall! I do.' Hélène was ready to do anything to placate a fellow conspirator.

Hélène was grateful, too, that Cheryl had such a short memory, and bore no malice towards her for her disagreement with her mother.

No one asked where they had been. They appeared not to have been missed, because the meeting – the whys and wherefores of the theft of arms, Jordan and what should be

611

done with him – continued over drinks and subsequently at lunchtime.

'I think he should be despatched to Kenya,' Bobby said in a pause. 'We still have the farm there. Ralph?'

'Excellent idea, providing he wants to go.'

'He will have to go after I've spoken to him,' Bobby said. 'He'll have no option, particularly as he doesn't want to be killed.'

'Personally, I don't think Jordan is in any real danger,' Rachel said. 'It is his morbid imagination, and when I saw him he was in a highly emotional state. I think the Nazis have too much on their plates to run after small fry. Someone planted that story to embarrass me. I flatter myself it might even have been inspired by Hitler. What Jordan did, the little he did, had no serious consequence for Hitler except to cement the impression he wanted to give that there really was a plot, which no one seriously believes. Röhm was even waiting at a prearranged spot for a meeting with his Führer when he was hauled off to prison and shot. Jordan is a problem to himself, and his mother I suppose, not to the Nazis.'

'Jordan would absolutely *love* Kenya,' Cheryl said, a little breathlessly. 'It's just made for a young man like him.'

'But not you?' Em, who'd said little, looked at her with a faint smile.

'Oh, I *loved* Kenya.'

'But not enough to want to go back?'

'Well, not for good,' Cheryl said carefully. There was a lot she didn't like about this practical, plain-speaking girl, who had so much courage that she would even defy Hitler, and so much indiscretion that she fraternized with Jews. 'But Ralph and I were thinking of going there in the summer, weren't we, darling?'

'Were we?' Ralph looked surprised.

'After the decorations are finished.'

Rachel looked with dismay at the modern furniture which had supplanted those delicate works by George Hepplewhite and Thomas Chippendale which had fetched a high price at Sotheby's the previous spring. The table on which they were dining was made of black satinwood lacquered to a brilliant polish. A matching sideboard, on which two alabaster *art deco* statues posed in the nude, also had a complicated brass and glass candlestick which contained electric lights shedding a garish light on the cream painted walls which had once seen a rather priceless William Morris wallpaper. Suddenly Rachel longed for the peaceful atmosphere of Bedford Row which she felt was now more of a home to her than this had ever been.

'But isn't all this finished?' She kept her voice level and pleasant. 'I thought the whole house was done.'

'It is, Lady Askham. I'm talking about the country. It's still a mess there. Ralph is a *little* bit annoyed with me because I've already started there, but I know he'll get used to it.'

'Even if it bankrupts me.' Ralph's smile was forced. Both he and she were making a great effort to keep their recent rift from the family.

'Odd that you didn't mention the redecoration to me?' Bobby looked fixedly at Hélène.

'Why should I? You didn't ask me.'

'Well, if the whole of the Hall is upside down I think you might have referred to it.'

'Hélène probably didn't see it, as I did,' Ralph intervened helpfully. 'The night I got home the whole place was upside down, and she wasn't there then.'

Harvey Oscott, the new owner of *The Evening Globe*, a self-made man and a former journalist who went round the country buying up newspapers and making them pay, was clearly not anxious to go to litigation. But he was as stubborn as the former owner of *The Sentinel and Echo*, twenty-three years before, in refusing to yield to threats. There was none of the 'old boy' network here. Oscott was a grammar-school boy who retained his Lancashire accent whereas Lord Brancaster, who owned *The Sentinel* in 1911, and Lord Askham had been at Eton together.

'You know that we respect our sources, Mr Lighterman. I'm afraid I can't reveal them to you.'

'Even though the person is in grave error? Lady Askham, my aunt, has been libelled. I'm afraid that, regardless of what happened in the past, I shouldn't hesitate to resort to the courts again.'

'Hmmmm!' Oscott read again the paragraph in question and took a long time doing it. Clearly Bobby, with his arrogant, acerbic attitude, irritated him.

'It just says the family of Lady Askham, and that she is well known for supporting Communism.'

'My aunt is *not* a supporter of Communism. She supports the Labour Party in this country, not the Communists. She has even written articles recently criticizing the trials in Moscow very bitterly. Now I think this thing is slanderous, Oscott, and I will have no hesitation in going to court. I am advised very strongly that I have a good case.'

Harvey Oscott knew all about the Askham family, having been well briefed. The daughter, Lady Emmeline, had left Germany rather quickly, and so had the nephew, Jordan Bolingbroke. He had no doubt that he had a good case and that all Bobby was trying was bluff.

'I'd like to help you,' he said at last, 'and I am willing to compromise. I'll print a retraction saying that it was not intended to imply that Lady Askham was involved in this personally. But if I get any more information, I shall use it, make no mistake.'

'I wish to God I knew where you get it from,' Bobby stood up. 'I'd kill the bastard.'

Bobby was on the threshold of the door of the editor's room which led into the large editorial room where the journalists worked. One or two looked up as he spoke, but then Oscott took him by the arm and steered him out of the door leading to the press room, chatting amiably.

'I hope that will satisfy Lady Askham, Mr Lighterman. I have a high regard for her. Dog don't eat dog, you know. We journalists don't like to crucify one another, and I respect your aunt even though her views don't coincide with mine. She's a remarkable woman.'

At the bottom of the stone staircase Bobby thanked Harvey Oscott, shook his hand and said he'd consult with his aunt and solicitors about what to do next.

'I hope you'll accept the retraction. It's sincerely meant.'

Bobby came out of the main entrance of the *Globe* and into the little warren of streets that criss-crossed the bank of the Thames between the Embankment and Fleet Street. It was nearly half past five and people were emerging from their offices, shoulders hunched against the cold, bent on the homeward journey. Bobby intended to stop by at the *Sentinel* offices near Ludgate Circus to report to Rachel on the outcome of the meeting. He was about to cross Whitefriars Street and take a left turning towards the Circus when he felt a hand tug at his arm. He stopped angrily to shake it off, an expletive on his lips, and turned to see a man he vaguely recognized, smiling at him.

'Mr Lighterman?'

'Yes.'

'I have some information you might like to hear.'

'Oh?' Bobby tipped his hat and scratched his head. 'I have a feeling I know your face.'

'I'm a sub-editor on *The Globe*. I was at the desk outside the door and heard the remark you made as you left Harvey's office.' As Bobby continued to look puzzled the man added: 'About the informant.'

'You know *who* he is?' Bobby's bewilderment changed to excitement.

'Of course. I paid him for the information.'

'But why are you telling me?'

'Could we discuss it over a drink?' The man pointed to the brightly lit doors of a public house used by a variety of Fleet

Street workers, many of whom had crowded into the bar on their way home. A mist was rolling in from the river and a little nip of something strong would provide a welcome barrier against the cold journey home. Bobby allowed himself to be led inside, and was asked what he would drink.

'Let me get it,' Bobby said, then lowering his voice, 'I sense you're after money?'

'You sense right, Mr Lighterman,' the man smiled. 'I'd like a double Scotch, please. I can see you're a man of business. Straight to the point, is it?'

They took their drinks to a small table in the corner which had just been vacated by a party of print workers going on to the night shift.

'I can't stay long,' the man said, 'or I'll be missed. I might also be recognized, so I'll talk very quickly.'

'How much do you want?' Bobby said. 'There's no point in beating about the bush with platitudes.'

'A man after my own heart, Mr Lighterman. A thousand pounds.'

'Nothing is worth that to me.' Bobby tossed back his drink. 'You've wasted your time.'

'I thought it might *just* be worth it,' the man said, 'as I understand the person in question is a relation. It might be useful to know that you have a spy in the family.'

'I'm not interested in spies in my family,' Bobby said tersely. 'I'll give you fifty pounds and that's it.'

The man also tossed back his drink and stood up. His pleasant expression had changed to one of meanness.

'That's an insult, Mr Lighterman, and you know it. I won't accept a penny under a thousand and I think you'd find it cheap at the price. You see there may be a *double* treachery and you yourself, never mind your family, might be in danger. I see you don't care. Good day.'

The man took his hat from the table and placed it on his head, straightening the brim. Bobby looked up and, reaching for his arm, pulled him down.

'If I'm going to pay that sort of money I have to know why it's worth it.'

'Your wife is involved, Mr Lighterman.'

The man smiled again, but kept his hat on, sitting back on the wooden chair and feeling in his pockets for his cigarette pack. As he saw Bobby's expression he smiled, showing in the light of the match blackened teeth in need of urgent dental treatment. He was a seedy character, even for *The Globe*. But times were hard, there was a depression and Bobby thought if he got what he wanted he'd try and make sure the man lost his job as soon as possible. Then he would certainly need his ill-gotten thousand pounds.

'Go ahead,' he said.

'A thousand?'

'You have my word,' Bobby nodded. 'I can write you a cheque now.'

'No cheque.' The man shook his head.

'I have about five hundred on me,' Bobby's tone was exasperated, 'and the rest you will get tomorrow, here, at any time you like.'

'Well, I know you're a gentleman, Mr Lighterman, as you'd have to be to marry a Russian Princess.'

'What is it about my wife?'

'Does she know someone called Kitto?'

'Kitto? Kitto's the name of my grandmother's family.'

'Well, this man is very well known to your wife.'

'Jamie?' Bobby said thickly, and the man nodded.

'You can call me Arnold,' he said, 'for identification, though Arnold's not my name. I wouldn't want you to know that.'

'I could find out, anyway. Go on, Arnold, and look,' Bobby pointed a finger at him. 'This is a one-off. No blackmail. I won't be blackmailed because the Askham family has suffered already from stinking little journalistic creeps like you.'

'Come now, Mr Lighterman,' Arnold said. 'You can't compare me to Adrian Hastings.'

'You do know everything, don't you?' There was a trace of admiration in Bobby's voice as Arnold nodded.

'Harvey told me to brief him on the background to your visit. He likes to be well informed. So I spent half a day looking up files on the Askhams and the Askham Libel Trial in 1913. Very interesting, it was.'

'Go on,' Bobby said, 'or I might change my mind. I'm like that, you know. So what about Kitto?'

'Kitto, as I understand it from him ... I met him here as a matter of fact,' Arnold looked amused at the coincidence. 'Well this Kitto wanders all over the world; a bit of a card, soldier of fortune. He thought this information was worth some money.'

'It's not worth all that much,' Bobby said. 'You're probably going to tell me that he told you that Jordan Bolingbroke pinched arms from my firm and sold them to the Nazis. I know it already; but I'll pay you for who told him. That's the person I want.'

'Mr Lighterman, you've got me *wrong*.' Arnold's rather ugly mouth was transformed into an unpleasant leer. 'He told me that your *wife* told him about the arms. Apparently she's a *very* close friend.' Looking at Bobby's face he suddenly drew back and put a hand to his mouth. 'Oh, dear me. I hope I haven't given you an awful shock,' and then, as Bobby hurriedly counted out the notes on the table in front of him, he added contritely: 'I can see I have, dear, dear.'

Bobby threw a thousand pounds on the bed in which Hélène lay reading a book. It was very late and she had expected Bobby home for dinner. She looked up in surprise and put her book down on the bed. She thought he had been drinking.

'What's that for, Bobby?'

'It's for you,' Bobby said. 'And cheap at the price.'

'I don't know what you mean?'

'Don't you?' Bobby sat on the bed and gazed at her. 'It's blood money. A thousand for the informant and a thousand for you. You can share it with Kitto, if you like, because you're not going to get any more for a long time, and I don't know how much they paid him for the information.'

'What on *earth* are you talking about?' Hélène, who'd been on edge for days, looked wildly at the clock. 'It's after one o'clock.'

'I'll tell you.' Bobby stood up and put his hands in the pockets of his trousers. Then he began to walk up and down the room past the bed; up and down. 'I'll make it very brief and very accurate. I went to see the owner of *The Globe* today. He didn't tell me, but someone else did, that a) the information was sold to them by my cousin Jamie and b) he told them that information had been supplied by someone close to *me*. They refused to pay him until he told them who to be sure his source was trustworthy.' Bobby's finger rose and stabbed the air in front of his wife. 'He said *you*, my wife. Now, from this I deduce two things: 1) you are still carrying on with Kitto, as I suspected, or rather I suspected there was someone when I got home and found you weren't here, and not here for some time according to the butler. 2) You were not staying with Cheryl because Ralph Askham didn't see you there. You noticed that I was too polite to question *him* in front of the family at lunch, too proud to humiliate you and me.'

Hélène hung her head, her eyes filling with tears.

'It's no use crying, Hélène, because it won't affect me. I've guessed for some time that you were unfaithful to me but I didn't want to stoop to putting a detective on you. I didn't think it would be that frightful twerp.'

'What's there to be faithful to?' Hélène retorted at last through her tears. 'Don't you have a mistress, *and* a son?'

'How do you know that?' Bobby took a step back.

'I've seen that woman several times. You always denied it, yet the boy even looks like you.'

'It was well before I married you,' Bobby said. 'It has been over for years. The point of all this, Hélène, is that I'm throwing you out. I don't love you and you don't love me, but

I could have put up with a wife who did her best to entertain me and who was faithful. But one who is a slut and a spy *and* an informer to boot ... I've already seen my lawyer. I went straight round to him after purchasing this information. There is no doubt at all. Somehow Kitto got hold of this story and sold it to the newspapers because he is always short of cash. My source at the paper told me that Kitto vouched for the authenticity of the story because of his close relationship with the *wife* of the owner of Askham Armaments.'

'How could I possibly know?' Hélène's voice contained a note of hysteria. 'I know nothing about Jordan or guns or ... how could I know?'

Even as she spoke she could see the hotel room in Berlin in 1933 when Jordan told her of his plans and Bobby, observing her closely, saw the subtle change in her expression. His eyes narrowed.

'You've thought of something, haven't you? You *do* know.'

'It is certainly not me. Why Jamie drew *me* into it I have no idea.'

'I'm leaving you, anyway,' Bobby said shortly. 'The very fact that you would take up again with that bounder disgusts me more than I can say. The whole sad, shoddy business of adultery and betrayal is somehow typical of your family ... of you, and your father ...'

At the mention of Alexei their eyes met.

'Your father,' Bobby went on. 'Now *there's* a thought. There's a muck-raking rascal, if ever there was one; a Jekyll and Hyde of the world of international business and intrigue. You *or* your father I don't care; maybe both of you. All I know is that I want to be rid of the Ferov influence for ever. I despise you and your entire family – a pack of rogues, cheats and liars, always an eye on the main chance. Whoever told Kitto, you or your father, is no longer of any interest to me. A princely family older than the Romanovs. Pah! For all I know probably that's the biggest lie of all.'

'You know it's no lie!' The familiar fire, a look of scorn, returned to Hélène's eyes. 'Certainly *we* don't have a grocer for a near ancestor ...'

As Bobby hit her she staggered across the room.

'A grocer! A grocer!' she screamed. 'And what sort of name is *Lighterman*? People who work on the river. Your origins betray you too much, Bobby. They explain the sort of person you really are. They reduce you to the gutter, the level of the market place. All your money can never give you the breeding you crave because of the grandfather who was a grocer's boy and all the generations of menial ancestors before him.'

As Bobby hit her again she sank to the floor and began to crawl along it, blood streaming from a cut on her mouth.

The sight of the blood frightened him and he knelt by her side, putting a hand on her arm.

'I'm sorry ...'

'You're *sorry*!' Hélène's cry was an eerie sound, more like the wail of a tormented animal than anything human Bobby had ever heard. 'Oh, how funny! Jamie was a beater too. Isn't it *absurd* that I can bring out such violence in men.'

Bobby took a clean handkerchief from his pocket and, his hand trembling, put it to her mouth. As he dabbed the blood Hélène suddenly bared her teeth, plunging them into Bobby's flesh.

Bobby wanted to hit her again, to pummel her beautiful face until it was unrecognizable. But the violence of his emotions terrified him and, clutching his wounded hand, he ran to the door as Hélène began to rock backwards and forwards on her knees, fresh blood from the cut on her lip staining the front of her gown.

As he ran down the stairs to the hall of the large and beautiful mansion with its mirrored walls and Sert murals, that had once contained all his hopes for the future, Bobby could hear the awful wailing start up again.

He fancied that it echoed in his ears as he closed the front door behind him and went into the street to his car.

CHAPTER 29

Everywhere that Irina Ferova looked she saw ruin; desolation all around her. It was, in many ways, just like 1917 all over again. Only somehow it was worse because then they'd seemed to have no chance, they'd made the best of what little they had. Now they'd had many chances and lost them all, thrown them away. Surely those chances would never come again to restore the family fortunes and, with them, the family pride?

As soon as she heard what Bobby had done to Hélène she went round to the Russian Church in rue Darue to light candles in front of the family's icons, candles that never stopped burning at home as well. Kneeling, she crossed herself, stood and kissed the icons, crossed herself time and time again; but when her husband, summoned peremptorily to London, was dismissed as well, candles seemed of little avail even to one strong in her Orthodox faith. She took to her bed for several days; periods of melancholy were interspersed with long fits of weeping.

If Aileen Younghusband had once questioned whether Bobby was indeed a hard man he had, without doubt, grown into one now. That night he dismissed his wife and, with her, his three daughters, little girls he had never really grown to love, not as he loved David. The children were too like Hélène, a constant reminder of her looks and fickleness. They were too like the Ferovs for comfort. They could all go – them and their mother – and it would be many years before Bobby would see any of them again.

It was understood by the family that he had had a very grave shock, but by then everyone knew about Aileen and David. No one could do anything about it. Bobby was a law unto himself – an enormously rich, strong-willed man with little love in his life and no close friends. Bobby always compensated for his cruelty by looking after people from a financial point of view; Hélène and the girls would never want, but then Hélène would never have the riches to which she'd aspired or anything like the luxurious lifestyle she had enjoyed as Bobby's wife. She would get the minimum required by law. She was a cast-off, a divorced woman who had been the guilty party; even in the enlightened year of 1935 that was no enviable thing to be.

In the months between finding out about Hélène and her settling in Paris in the spring Bobby had begun proceedings for divorce. The conditions about her maintenance were made absolutely clear: she would have a house or apartment wherever she chose; she must not try and contact him, other than through solicitors, and he waived visitation rights to the children. Furthermore, if she ever annoyed him in any way he would see that even the small allowances he had given her were severely cut. He knew that the best way to punish Hélène was through her purse ... carrot and stick style.

The family were very divided about Bobby, even though Hélène had placed him in a terrible predicament – if the story going around were true. She had not only been unfaithful to him, thus making a very proud man feel foolish, but she had made the family look foolish too, and none of them much cared for that.

Bobby went about his vengeance with a will after the revelation on that January night. He invited Harvey Oscott to dinner and did a deal with him. He would tell him who had betrayed his confidence, undermined his own trust in his employees, in exchange for a part apology in the newspaper. A very careful compromise was agreed on by the two men, dining in Bobby's London club, whereby Harvey Oscott learned about 'Arnold', whom he was quickly able to identify, and Rachel got an apology printed on the front page of *The Globe*, but so worded that the substance of the story appeared to remain true:

Further to our report about the sale of arms to Hitler's stormtroopers by Askham Armaments Ltd we are glad to point out that this transaction in no way involved Rachel, Countess of Askham, personally, who had no knowledge of it at all. Nor had any of the family knowledge of the matter, and an internal investigation is under way. We apologize for any wrong impression that might be caused, or embarrassment to the Askham family.

Bobby also agreed to hand a very large sum of money over to Harvey personally, which he could use in any way he liked. Soon after that Harvey Oscott bought a large house in the home counties and married again.

Compared to this domestic upheaval the sacking of Prince Ferov seemed rather trivial. He became merely an employee who had lost his job, without compensation. Bobby explained to him that whatever the status of people who worked for him, father-in-law or not, utter loyalty was expected. Treachery deserved no compensation. The Prince was sacked forthwith without a penny and Bobby asked that, henceforward, the Ferov family be rigidly excised from his life.

But one Ferov who remained was not so easy to get rid of: Susan, his sister, as Princess Tatiana Ferova, had husbanded her share of the family fortune by wise investments, particularly in antiques and the growing art market. She was not at all pleased at Bobby's summary treatment of her in-laws, and the first real division for many years occurred in the Askham family ranks. Bobby and Susan ceased to have anything to do with each other.

Susan was generous in softening the blow that had fallen on her father-in-law though, of course, as she explained to Melanie, who was too distracted to take sides, her fortune wasn't a bottomless pit.

But it was in the treatment of his children that the family did unite against Bobby – those little girls summarily removed from a comfortable home to a furnished apartment in Paris, and from regular contact with a father whom they might now never see again.

Melanie, however, was not a woman attracted by the idea of self-sacrifice, of putting herself out for others. In her life Melanie had always come first and this remained her philosophy. She was not, therfore, at all inclined to look after her innocent grandchildren, harshly put out of his life by their father, her son; though she made a weak note of protest that was hardly heard eight hundred miles away on the other side of the Channel.

It was hard to imagine Rachel not taking more sternly to task a son who deserted his children and then, if he did, looking after them. On the other hand, it was quite easy for those who knew Melanie to see how she could distance herself from the predicament of her daughter-in-law and grandchildren and make excuses for Bobby.

On a chilly day in the autumn of 1935 Irina sat hugging herself, gazing mournfully at her grandchildren as they played around her, happily unaware that their lives had taken such a dramatic change for the worse, though, apparently, none of them much missed their father. The eldest, Stefanie, had just had her sixth birthday. Born when her father and mother had still cared for each other, if not much then a little, she was easily the prettiest; tall and dark, the most like Bobby, but still too like a Ferov for his taste. The other two, Natasha and Olga, were fair and greatly resembled the Ferovs. As Bobby, of Melanie's children, had seemed to stand on his own, so Stefanie was different from the rest; more beautiful, more alert, more exceptional in every way. Of the three girls she was probably the closest to Bobby, the one who would miss him the most. But as yet they had no inkling of what had happened except that their mother was sad, and so were their grandparents, and something very disturbing had happened to them all, and Daddy, always a remote figure at best, was no longer around at all.

In a corner of the room, under the icons, sat Alexei, also staring mournfully, in turns, at his grandchildren, at his wife then back again to the children. Occasionally he looked towards the door hoping that it would open and bring him news – of anything just to get him out of this place, away from his memories. Alas, it seldom did.

In the last six months his wife had aged ten years, going from a smart, pretty woman of over sixty to an old lady, taking little care of her appearance, apparently still in the grip of a deep depression. Yet when the grandchildren came she cheered up for them, she took a little more care with her dress and dabbed on the cheeks the rouge, carefully smudged round her eyes the kohl, brushed on her eyelashes the mascara, painted on her lips the colour that had all once helped to enhance her natural beauty.

Hélène lived with the children near the Park Monceau, but she was hardly ever there in the small, cramped flat quite unlike the kind of thing she had grown accustomed to. Yet she was no longer able to spend her days with her wealthy friends in boutiques, or drinking at the Ritz on the Georges Cinq, or lunching in the smart restaurants of Paris. Few of them, anyway, were interested, now that she was known to be on a small allowance. It was extremely revealing, if infinitely depressing, to discover how fickle close friends could be.

Instead, she spent a lot of time with Susan, or with her lawyer trying to persuade him to get more out of Bobby. But lawyers cost money and Susan was free; Susan who now hated Bobby almost as much as Hélène. Susan was good to the children and so was Evgenia, but the main responsibility for them fell on Irina, and most days they were taken over to their grandparents' flat and dumped while Hélène wandered around Paris, smoking countless cigarettes, drinking innumerable cups of coffee – brooding over the way she had been wronged, hoping against hope that her luck would change.

Hélène would leave the children at the door of her parents' apartment near the Gare du Nord, but she never came in; or rather, she never came in when her father was there. He really was the cause of all the trouble, his greed and his foolishness, and she would have nothing to do with him. Even though she was remotely responsible for it, his shoddy little deal to supply arms to Jordan had cost her her marriage, her standard of life. Never, never would she forgive him or speak to him again. She made herself this promise the night Bobby left her, and she'd kept it. Not one word.

As if aware of their grandparents' sorrow, despite the efforts to entertain them, the children were always very good when they were with them, sitting obediently at table drawing or reading; going for walks with Grandmother or Grandfather in the park and, more important, because of their reduced station in life, learning how to cook with old Masha in the kitchen. One never knew when such skills would be useful.

Alexei, reading one of the many exile papers published in Paris, lowered it on to his knee and gazed through his half-moon glasses at his wife. If she had changed he hadn't. He kept a pride in his appearance: his moustache clipped and waxed, his hair regularly pomaded, the grey streaks kept at bay by a black dye, not always skilfully applied, however. His suits were carefully brushed and regularly cleaned, even though he no longer had a personal servant, his silk shirts lovingly washed by Masha, faithful family servant and friend, who had gone from riches to poverty, to riches and back again with the same peasant equanimity she had stoically maintained all her life. Alexei wore grey spats over his carefully polished shoes and always carried a silver-topped cane. He was dapper, a figure to respect, if sometimes also to snigger at. Like an English fictional creation whom he rather resembled, Mr Micawber, he was sure that better days would return again. He never, in short, stopped expecting something to turn up.

As the sound of the old-fashioned doorbell jangling in the hall disturbed their thoughts and labours, everyone in the room looked up; the children from their tasks at the table, Irina from her thoughts of better days and Alexei from his paper. Producing a large ancient timepiece – it had belonged to Czar Alexander III – from his waistcoat pocket, he consulted it.

'Who can that be?' he said in Russian to his wife; the children, as yet, only spoke English.

Irina shrugged. 'What time is it?'

'Eleven.'

'I don't know who it could be.' The Princess got up to draw aside the lace curtain and inspect the street below for a sign as to the identity of their visitor when they heard a familiar voice greeting Masha.

'Kyril!' everyone said in unison, except that the children said 'Uncle Kyril' and they ran to the door to greet him, for Uncle Kyril was a very popular visitor who, besides his willingness to play with them and tell them stories, mostly about old Russia, often brought sweets, brandy for Grandpapa and gifts of food or fruit for Grandmama.

Uncle Kyril had been absent for some weeks on a visit to Spain with his wife and, hearing his voice, Irina was the first to the door, throwing it open in greeting and then falling into his open arms.

'Mamushka,' he kissed her tenderly on the cheek and then opened the other arm to embrace Stefanie, Natasha and Olga, in that order.

'Back so soon?' Irina cried, emotionally burying her face in his chest. 'Oh, we have *missed* you.'

'What a greeting, what a greeting!' Kyril smiled over her head at his father, shrugging his shoulders, because he had no free hand to greet him with. Although their relationship was still formal, based on business rather than affection, the older man was pleased to see him, and as the women of the house fussed about him, relieved him of his parcels.

'Brandy? Oh, thank you.'

'Spanish brandy, Father. It is very good. Susan sends you all greetings.' Speaking in English Kyril came into the room, the little girls still hanging on to him, tugging at him to come and play.

'See this, Uncle Kyril!'

'Look!'

All were anxious to show him what they had been doing.

'The samovar, Masha,' Irina ordered from the door, but the grumbling voice of Masha in the kitchen told her that, of course, it was already on and the tea being prepared.

'Later, later,' Kyril said to his nieces as he sat down, and Olga, the youngest, immediately clambered on to his knee. 'I have come to see Grandpapa about important business, but later I will play. Perhaps today we go out to lunch. Yes? All of us?'

To an ecstatic series of 'yeses' he rose and beckoned to his father, saying to his mother in Russian:

'A few quiet words with Papa alone, Mamushka, if you don't mind. Then I'll take you all out to lunch.'

Transformed by his presence, a contented woman again, Irina nodded and returned to her chair, happier now than she had been for some time because Kyril was back. She set to remembering her days at Askham, yet again, her favourite reminiscence which she could keep going for hours – Askham, and Esenelli, the Caucasus home in summertime, were her favourite memories.

The dining-room next to the sitting-room was small, and Kyril shook his head as, standing back to allow his father first into the room, he perceived how dark it was, and damp. He ran his hand over a patch on the outside wall and shook his head again. From outside came the noise of trains.

'I wish I could get Susan to part with some more of her money. You would not be here.'

'Susan is very generous.' Alexei stooped to put a light to the ancient gas fire which emitted a roar as well as a pungent smell, as soon as it was lit, so that one had to jump back. 'You can't expect her to keep us *all*. She is very good to Hélène and has recently bought all the girls new clothes.'

'Still, she has plenty.' Kyril rubbed his hands vigorously in front of the fire. 'Do the lawyers hold out any hope for more money from Bobby for Hélène?'

'None.' Alexei shook his head and lit one of the many cigars he smoked during the day, lingering over it as though he were in the comfort of his club in London or one of his former gracious homes. He rolled it round and round in his fingers, savouring the aroma, then drew on it appreciatively. 'Besides, Hélène can't keep us and she doesn't wish to. She will have nothing to do with me. I have only myself to blame, Kyril ... It was very foolish to fall into that temptation, when I had so much to lose. Then there was no money to pay me because Röhm's plans failed. I burnt my fingers badly.'

Kyril sat down, bidding his father to do the same. For a few moments he drummed his fingers on the scratched, polished table and then he stared at his father.

'No hard feelings, Father?'

'About what?'

'The past. We have not always seen eye to eye. I know I hurt you bitterly and I regret it.'

'The past is the past, my boy,' tentatively Alexei put out a hand and touched that of his son. 'You have been very good to us since you abandoned Communism. I have no complaints about the past. We all have to learn.'

'Then I think I have work for you.' Kyril sat up straight. 'Only it involves more risks. This time, however, you have little to lose.'

'Work?' Alexei Ferov looked up, his eyes alight; then his face clouded as the meaning of Kyril's words dawned on him. 'Is it something illegal?'

'No more illegal than what you did before. Tell me, did you keep in touch with Duncan Curtis?'

'Of course I am not in touch with him! He is still not suspected and he begged me to have nothing more to do with him.'

'I see.' Kyril nodded, got up, and slowly walked over to the window which looked on to the side of the house next door and also a fire escape, so that the room had very little natural light of its own. Then he turned to his father, leaning against the sill:

'Let me, if I may, speak aloud for a few moments. In Bobby's opinion you managed to deflect supplies of arms, lawfully destined for France, to the German enemies of Hitler. It was only a small quantity but it was enough.'

'Enough to ruin me, not enough, evidently, to help Röhm.' Alexei stooped to try and regulate the spluttering fire – one day, he knew, it would blow up. 'What I don't know, and never will, is how Kitto found out. People say I told him, but I certainly didn't. Why should I?'

A guarded look came over Kyril's face, which the gloom of the room prevented his father from seeing. Kyril knew he was playing for very heavy stakes. He had set up his father, ruined his sister's marriage, to deflect suspicion from himself, to make possible the task the Party had been training him for for all these years – the success of the Spanish Left-Wing Republic, with the aim of ultimately establishing Communist rule in Spain.

A father ruined, broke and disaffected would be very willing to play a double game – to trust him, now his closest son since Dima practised as a doctor in Nice. Alexei, having tinkered with the fire to his satisfaction, sat back again, and Kyril said:

'Kitto is and always was a fool. It was through Duncan Curtis that you really got the supplies, and there are more to come, obviously.'

'I'm not sure. After the enquiry he has to be very careful.'

'Yet he has no time for Bobby because of the way he treated his daughter Aileen.'

'None at all.'

'In fact he hates him?'

'I would say so. Yes.'

'Good. Now the position is this, Father. I did not go to Spain only for a holiday. I went to establish liaison with the Right-Wing forces of the Falange there because, believe me, there will soon be war in Spain.'

'You are *really* on our side, after all?' Alexei's trusting eyes sparkled.

'Have no doubt of it, Father. The Nazis think well of me. I have been very close to sources close to Mussolini in Italy, and he will help the attempt to topple the government in Spain all he can. Now, I feel, it is time for me to come out into the open, as I could not before, when you asked me to help you.'

'I understand, my boy,' Alexei smiled gratefully. 'Believe me, I'm relieved.'

'You said could I help with Röhm and I said "No". Frankly, I did not believe in Röhm. I didn't think he would win. I was right. Nor did I trust young Jordan, a dangerous hot-head. I sympathized, but I didn't think I should directly intervene. But in Spain things are different.' Kyril leant forward and lit a cigarette which he had been twirling in his hands. For a moment the flame illuminated the deep scar on his thin, serious, dedicated face. He'd cut it as a boy when he fell down a rock on to the beach at Batum, and Alexei thought now how odd it was that it had not seemed to fade with time, but got deeper. 'In Spain,' Kyril went on, extinguishing his match, 'things are very hopeful indeed, because the Army are against the Republic, and the Army always wins.

'There is a man called General Franco who was manipulated by the government and is disgusted with it. He was used to put down the miners in the Asturias, and they said he was too harsh. What I want you to do, Father, is to go to Spain as my emissary and set up a base there in Madrid or Barcelona; Madrid, I think. I will tell you how to make contact with the Nationalist rebels and discover their needs. You will find that Askham Armaments supplies arms to the lawful government of Spain, so there is a channel. Then I want you to contact Curtis again and see what you can do.'

'But it will be very dangerous.' Alexei looked distinctly nervous.

'Oh, *very* dangerous; but well rewarded. What have you to lose?'

'Exactly,' Alexei said with resignation, though also he had the strange feeling that fresh blood was finding a course through his clogged-up veins and making a new man of him again.

'In Spain the CEDA is the monarchist party and I will give you the names of the top people there. I tell you, you must go soon, because there isn't a moment to lose.'

For Alexei it seemed once more the end of a nightmare, the beginning of a new life. His optimism, his conviction that something good would happen, were justified. What was more, this talented son of his appeared to have been working for years on the monarchist cause in Spain without even letting him into the secret! What a man of discretion – unlike himself: what vision! In the further discussion they had before they went to lunch Kyril told him that Spain was the battleground of the future and, on it, the Germans and Italians wanted to try out their new weapons of war in case the conflagration extended to the rest of Europe because of the expansionist policies of Hitler and Mussolini. There, in Europe, they might well give fight to their old enemies the Bolsheviks. Who knew, it might even one day be possible to envisage the restoration, in a liberated Russia, of the Ferov wealth and estates. What dreams!

It was a happy, exciting day in which the charge generated by Kyril in his father seemed to infuse and affect the whole family. There was lunch at a nearby bistro, a walk in the park and then tea and games on the return home, Kyril content, apparently, in the bosom of his family; Alexei excited about an imminent trip to Spain, the prospect of generous expenses, the opportunity to recoup his lost fortune, the chance of getting his own back on Bobby. It never occurred to him once to question the integrity of his son – his own blood, flesh of his flesh.

Just as Kyril was about to return home at five, standing in the hall saying goodbye to the family, the bell went and he found himself face to face with his sister, Hélène.

She stared at him hard before kissing him warmly on the cheek. 'I didn't know you were back. Susan is here?'

'We returned early. I had some business with Father.'

'Oh, I *must* go and see Susan,' Hélène's eyes lit up and she, too, seemed happier than she had been the second before. 'I missed her so much.'

'Come in, come in,' Kyril stood back, but Hélène shook her head.

'No, thank you. I just came to collect the children. If you like, you can run us home. Have you your car?'

'Of course. Wait a minute. I'll get them for you.'

While Hélène waited outside Irina came to greet her and give her a report on the day, how productive and happy it had been, even the change in her father.

'He is to go to Spain,' Irina said but, coming quickly behind her, Kyril tapped her on the shoulder and whispered in her ear.

'Shh! It is a secret. You must be *very* discreet, Mamushka.'

'Oh! *Shhh!*' Irina pretended exaggeration as she put her finger to her lips, her excited eyes wide with mischief.

On the way back to the centre of Paris Kyril said: 'By the way, you should make it up with Father.'

'Why?'

'It's silly not to.'

'He ruined my life.'

'Yes, but you helped to ruin it, too. It was very silly to go back to that fool. Incidentally, he's back in Paris. I shouldn't tell you, I suppose.'

As she didn't reply he looked sideways at her profile and smiled. In the back seat the children strained forward to hear what they said but, as they were talking in Russian, the meaning still eluded them.

'Where is he?'

'I wouldn't tell you if I knew. He's done enough harm.'

'Do you think so? I'd just like to tell him what I thought of him. That's all.'

'Still, I don't think it's wise. Forget about Kitto. Think of the future.' He reached out and touched her hand. 'You never know. It might be better than you think.'

Hélène rang the downstairs bell but there was no answer. Then she rang another bell and, on being asked who she was, said she was a florist and was given entry to the apartment block where Jamie had had the same *pied-à-terre* for a number of years. It had not been too hard to imagine he might use it again, as he was a creature of habit.

In the paved hall Hélène stopped to catch her breath, though she had not even started to climb the stairs which led to Jamie's third floor apartment. There was no lift in this old block, built many years before.

As a drowning person is said to view his or her life in those last moments, or a prisoner mounting the scaffold, so did Hélène Lighterman look back over the years as she slowly climbed the stairs towards Jamie's flat, like someone being propelled towards inevitable doom because she didn't know whether she would ever descend them again. She reflected that, in her whole life, her only real happiness had been as a child before the Revolution.

She paused, listening to the slow, quiet thump of her heart, on the first floor landing; then started towards the second. It was Jamie who had ruined her life with his pretend love, his deception – about his means, about his occupation which, as far as she could see, was really spying. It was Jamie, her first and only love, who had forced her into a marriage with a man who could give her those riches she had missed since she left Russia, forced her family to live dependent on Bobby, forced her father to take to dubious deals involving selling arms to Fascists. None of that would have mattered if they had stayed together; but Bobby had offered a chance of escape. Who could resist it?

She paused on the second floor and, as she began the last ascent, she fingered the small gun in her pocket she had taken

635

from the bureau in her father's room when he was out. It hadn't been difficult because she knew he kept a gun. It was very dramatic, this; just like a story – a thwarted, frustrated, bitter woman seeking revenge for all the evil that one man had brought on her and her family.

For now the Ferovs were just as they had been just after the Revolution: penniless beggars forced to live in demeaning circumstances, with three additional mouths to feed.

She gazed at the number on Jamie's door and then, banishing her fear, rapped sharply on it with her clenched fist.

'Who is it?' he called sharply.

She leaned against the door and whispered, 'Your true love.'

She could hear the door being unlocked, the chain removed. Jamie was obviously very suspicious, very uncomfortable. Good. He opened the door gingerly and peered through the crack.

'Oh, it *is* you?'

'Who else would your true love be?' Hélène sauntered past him, her hand in the right pocket of her loose coat.

'Well, I didn't expect to see you again, I'll admit.' Nervously Jamie ran his hand over his unshaven chin. He had been in bed and the room smelt vaguely of unwashed body and drink. The pallor of his face was awful and his eyes were glazed and bloodshot, as though from dope. His gown was closely wrapped round his body as if to show he had nothing on underneath. 'I'm terribly sorry about what happened,' Jamie said, indicating the only chair in the room which was empty. The others were covered with clothes and suitcases as though he were just moving in, or moving out. 'I had meant to apologize, but I didn't think you'd understand.'

'Understand about what, Jamie?' Hélène didn't sit but remained standing in the centre of the room.

'Well, you know, the whole thing was so terribly confused. I didn't think you'd be involved in any way. How could I?'

'Yet you read me the piece from the paper as though it was

636

a complete surprise to you. Perhaps, though, you were proud of it?'

'Well, that *was* rather theatrical, wasn't it?' Jamie yawned, blinked his eyes and grinned ruefully. 'I wanted to know what you thought. Look, I *am* terribly sorry. I only just got in, and I'm leaving later today.'

'What a good thing I caught you, then.'

'Why?' Jamie didn't seem at all suspicious. 'I haven't any money, you know.'

'You were very lucky, Jamie, to have got off so lightly, don't you think? Named as co-respondent, yet no damages. Bobby hasn't finished with you yet, you know.'

'I bet he hasn't,' Jamie said. 'That's why I'm moving on. Quite a lot of people don't like me. The trouble is, Hélène,' he looked at her with his old appealing charm and leaned against the wall, his hand still awkwardly clasping his gown, 'I've never *really* been able to make it. I'm thinking of going back to India and getting a decent job on a plantation, maybe making it up with my wife. The country there is lovely and I'm tired of running. I was never at all mixed up in this business with the arms but I *was* stupid enough to accept your brother's bribe to sell the information to the papers. He knew I would sink low enough to betray my own family for a few pounds...'

'My brother?' Hélène's sharp exclamation stopped him abruptly. 'You mean my *father*?'

A smile played on Jamie's ruddy features. 'Oh? Is that what they told you? Your father, was it?'

'*Wasn't* it my father?'

'Well, maybe he has reasons of his own ...' Jamie appeared to consider something – maybe the opportunity of fresh blackmail – and then went on, 'Well, your father, or whoever. Maybe I got it wrong on the telephone. Ferov, Ferov ... you know. The point is that with all the trouble it cost I didn't get too much from *The Globe*. And for what?' He held out his hands appealingly, the practised hands of the professional beggar,

'I didn't mean to ruin you, or your father, or whoever …' that calculating expression came into Jamie's eyes again.

'I know my *brother* wouldn't be involved. It's no use trying to drag him into it, no one would believe you.'

Hélène immediately dismissed from her mind a suggestion whose implications were only to be recalled by her again many years later.

Jamie didn't want to pursue the matter. Maybe he'd said too much already. More money might be forthcoming from that source, although somehow he doubted it. Kyril, having used him and got what he wanted, was quite capable of discarding him as abruptly as he took him up. How carefully he'd covered his tracks, too. 'Perhaps you're right,' he said, and yawned.

Watching him, Hélène, almost unbearably tense in case he did something unexpected, unclicked the safety catch of the gun in her pocket.

'What's that?' Jamie, startled, put his hand to his mouth, stifling his yawn.

'What's what?'

'I thought I heard a click?'

'I think it came from outside.' Hélène cocked an ear towards the door. 'So,' she said, turning to gaze at him again, her face grim and unsmiling, 'how does that leave me?'

'You?'

'What am I?'

'I don't know. What are you?'

'I'm a divorced woman, with a slur on my name. My husband has punished me by depriving me of the things I enjoyed, which you enjoyed too – like money and good living, a life of ease. We both tried to get it dishonestly, Jamie, and we both lost.'

'I haven't lost,' Jamie said. 'But then I'm not so greedy. Bobby always was a swine. Everyone in the family knew it, even me.'

'But Bobby would never have known about us if it hadn't

been for you. The biggest lie of all was that you told the paper you had the information from ME...'

'It sounded more credible...'

'Regardless of the circumstances...'

'How could I know they'd tell? Journalistic secrecy, you know. I never dreamt Bobby would find out, naturally.'

'You played a wicked, deceitful game. You, and only you, are directly responsible for what has happened to me and my family.'

'I'm sorry, darling. I couldn't help it, really. I'm terribly weak – you knew that.' Jamie got up from the wall, looked at his watch and rubbed his face again. 'I want to go back to bed. Care to come with me?'

Hélène never knew if he saw the gun emerge before she shot him clean through the forehead with all the ease of a practised marksman.

Rachel first heard of Jamie's death over the wireless, sitting in the lounge of The Grange where she had gone to visit Marian and her grandson, Paul, born the previous spring. The whole family had rejoiced at this event, and the fact that Marian not only survived the birth but grew stronger after it, thus confounding even most of her doctors. She still had to keep to a careful regime and they advised Switzerland, if only for a few months. Marian, however, believed that she now had a charmed life, and nothing would induce her to leave her husband or infant son, a dark-eyed, dark-haired tiny baby, resembling her.

Rachel called out when she heard the news:

'Quick! Oh, my God!'

'What is it, Mother?' Freddie was in the next room making a train for Paul, who was asleep with his mother upstairs. It was a quiet September afternoon and The Grange, always that oasis of peace, seemed the very last place in which to hear of such a violent act, especially concerning the family. When Rachel told him what she'd heard he said:

'Are you *sure*?' and started fiddling the knobs of the set.

'*Perfectly* sure. It was just a news item. But it said Jamie Kitto, brother of Lord Kitto, had been found shot in Paris, and Princess Hélène Lighterman, who was found with him, was arrested. I'm afraid it seems to make sense. Jamie ruined her.'

'It doesn't make sense to me. None of it. I can't understand why there's all this intrigue.'

'I'm afraid, darling, that is part of exile politics, of all politics to be truthful; but the émigrés, with their various groups and factions, do seem to go in for it in a big way. Unfortunately Jamie Kitto, who was a weak man with a very greedy side to him, couldn't keep out of it. Yet his only crime seems to have been to sell a snippet of information to the papers which did us no good at all, either. Thank God Daddy wasn't alive to hear this. Though, of course, if he were it wouldn't have happened. The business would still have belonged to him.'

Rachel picked up the knitting she had embarked on for Paul, but Freddie sat there, his head bent, hands joined in front of him. She looked at him.

'What is it, Freddie? There's nothing we can do about it. I must say I'm sorry for Irina, who never did any harm to anyone, and is a genuinely nice person. She's suffered enough.'

'It *is* very worrying, Mother.' Freddie got up and went over to the window where the Hall was just visible between the trees. 'At a time like this it might sound selfish, but I'm rather worried about myself.'

Once again Rachel put down the knitting. 'But I thought you were the happiest man alive.'

'I am and yet I'm not,' Freddie turned round. 'I'm the happiest man in the world with Marian and Paul but, do you realize Mother, that I'm a complete idler? I am twenty-seven years of age and I have never done a job of work in my life.'

Rachel turned off the wireless and removed the spectacles she now needed for close work.

'Darling, a lot of men of your class don't work. I don't like to use the term, but it's true. If you have your own income ... and you have, and you are quite happy, why feel guilty?'

'But I do absolutely *nothing*, Mother, and I can't help feeling Marian doesn't respect me for it.'

'Freddie, I think Marian absolutely adores you. All the signs are that she does. I'm sure she has no ambitious ideas for you at all.'

'But you, Mother, what do *you* think of it?' Freddie looked at her anxiously and Rachel smiled at the man, still a boy to her, she had always adored, the Honourable Freddie, true to the soubriquet the papers had given him – feckless, irresponsible and fun. Yet he had shown a great deal of courage and responsibility towards his wife, and he was a loving father who enjoyed doing things for little Paul himself in a way that Bosco wouldn't have dreamed of. If Paul cried in the night it was Freddie who got up. The couple had no nanny and lived quite frugally at The Grange, with a single resident maid plus a woman who came daily from the village to clean.

'I think, if you want to get a job, then get one. But up to now your concern has been Marian, and living here is good for her. It's so peaceful and the air *is* splendid. There's no question of her living in London. What could you do here?'

'I could help Ralph and Hugo.'

'But would you like that?'

'Not much.' Freddie looked rueful. 'I'm not all that keen on farming. The only thing I would really like to do is what Father did.'

'Business?' Rachel looked surprised.

'No, before that. I'd like to go into the Army or something.'

'Darling, you've left it terribly late.' Rachel looked doubtful, also quite shocked. 'Too late, I think. Besides, Marian...'

'Oh, it's out of the question with her as she is; but it's what I'd like to do, nevertheless. I like the idea of travel, though I don't suppose there'll be a war for years.'

'Some people doubt that.' Rachel resumed her spectacles and started recounting her stitches.

'Or what Em does.'

'Journalism?' Rachel looked up, dropping a stitch. 'I could easily get you a job there, darling; but, again, you have the question of Marian. Freddie,' Rachel finally abandoned her knitting and leaned back. 'I do know how you feel and I want you to realize I *am* sympathetic; but you have married a woman who is very sick.'

'Mother, she's ...'

'She *is* sick, Freddie. She keeps her head above water, but you know the doctors thought her survival a miracle. Thank God she survived and so did Paul, and I trust she has many more years to live. But you are to have no more children and, really, she must lead the life of a semi-invalid. It's a pity you don't like farming or stables because it's just about all you could do here. But the Army or journalism ... it would make Marian very very upset to lose you, and then who would stay with her?'

'I thought her mother. She desperately wants to get her out of Germany.'

'You mean her mother would come here and you'd go away? But where to, Freddie? And what would Marian say?'

'Marian already suggested I should go away,' Freddie smiled. 'She never thinks of herself, you know. She's the most amazing woman. She's like you, Mother, selfless; she has many of your qualities.'

'Oh, Freddie.' Rachel felt a rare sensation of weakness. It was many years since such a remark had brought the colour to her face.

'No, it's absolutely true. Marian said that it would do me good to get away and we talked about it. She would love to have her mother here and I ... well, I think I might like to write, Mother.' Now it was Freddie's turn to blush. 'I mean, maybe it's in the family, but over the years I've written lots of things which I've been too shy to show you.'

'Oh, Freddie! Why, you *must* show me!'

'Well, maybe I will, one day; but I thought I'd like to go and try and write a few articles, that sort of thing. It was Em's idea. She thought we should go to Spain together.'

'But Em has gone.'

'Yes, but we talked about this in the summer. I said I couldn't go then, but I can now. A lot is going on in Spain.'

'A *lot*!' Rachel said gravely. 'And, unfortunately, that too may lead to war.'

'Then I'll be in the perfect place, won't I, Mother?' Freddie's smile was radiant.

That night they went over to the Hall for dinner. It was usually a weekly event, whether Rachel was in the country or not. Cheryl tolerated her sister-in-law, and the feeling of uninterest was mutual. The two women hardly ever met, apart from the formal dinner parties at which their husbands, brothers and devoted to each other, could be present.

There was a lot of talk that night; first of all, excitedly from Marian, about the prospect of getting her mother out of Germany.

'I thought Jews weren't allowed,' Cheryl said suspiciously. 'Isn't that why Freddie had to marry you?'

'They can leave if someone gets them a visa,' Marian smilingly avoided the implication of Cheryl's remark, 'if they have a place to go to, and someone to support them. My mother now is on her own because my father is in the concentration camp and my brother, well ...' she paused and the tears, always close to the surface, came into her eyes. 'You know he disappeared. One day I hope ... but in the meantime...'

'*If* we can persuade your mother to come, and I'm not sure we will, and the authorities will let her,' Rachel said, 'there will be no difficulty. One day, I'm sure, you will all be united. A lot of people are still trying to find out what happened to Peter.'

'I know he's dead,' Marian said. 'I'm sure the Nazis killed him. We were so close that we used to have the same thoughts, but now I have not shared thoughts with Peter for two years. I know he is dead; killed by those murderers.'

The word 'murderer' struck an awkward note. Rachel had rung Cheryl and Ralph to tell them about Hélène but, so far, the subject had not been mentioned. But that word served as a reminder and Cheryl looked round to be sure none of the servants were present. Ralph had put a stop to her worst excesses in the house and the dining-room was as it had always been. It was a cosy, comfortable room, not the main dining-room that was used for big occasions in the past, but the smaller dining-room on the ground floor where the family always ate when they were alone. It always brought back memories to Rachel when she dined there, and she felt happiest there in this house she had never lived in.

'It's frightful about Hélène,' Cheryl's cheeks coloured slightly. 'Such a blot on the family.'

'What family?' Freddie asked. He didn't like his sister-in-law and never tried to hide it.

'Well, *your* family ... *our* family, I suppose,' she looked doubtful.

'I don't see why?' Freddie, sitting across the round table from her, gazed at her.

'Well, the Askham name *is* always in the news, isn't it?'

'The Askham name isn't involved at all, as a matter of fact,' Rachel pointed out. 'If anything it will be Lighterman and Ferov.'

'That's what I mean.' Cheryl looked nervously at Ralph who said:

'I must say I feel awfully sorry for Bobby. He is bound to be involved.'

'I can't, in my heart of hearts, say I feel sorry for Bobby.' Rachel accepted more wine from Ralph with a smile. 'I've never been able to forgive him for the way he behaved about those children. I can understand a man being wounded by infidelity and wanting a divorce ... but those girls! What a way to behave.'

'What will happen to them now?' Everyone gazed at one another as the implication of Marian's remark became clear. 'I mean she might ... die, mightn't she? Don't they have the guillotine in France?'

'Too frightful to think about,' Rachel sipped from her glass. 'I'm afraid the day the Ferov family came into our lives was bad news for the Askhams, the Bolingbrokes and the Lightermans. And, I suppose, in a way I'm to blame. I was there.'

'Where?' Freddie looked at her in surprise.

'I was in Russia in 1921 when Susan met Kyril.'

'But you couldn't help that! It was her fault, not yours. She ran off with him.'

'Yes, but maybe I could have stopped it. Difficult to tell. Cheryl, this lamb is beautiful. Is it from the home farm?'

'No, Mother,' Ralph replied, 'we don't have lambs, although Hugo would like to extend the land. He is a first-class farmer.'

'I thought he might be here tonight?' Rachel looked up.

'The Bey is very ill. Didn't you know?'

'Oh dear, I *am* sorry,' Rachel frowned. '*Very* ill?'

'Dying, I think. He said, though, that whatever happens, he won't leave the farm. His life is there now, not with Nimet.'

'I'll keep my fingers crossed,' Rachel said. 'But, to return to the Ferovs. Hélène, I have always felt, a sad girl, unhappy, out of place. Kyril is an enigma. I don't understand him at all. I think he's a fanatic of one sort or another. Alexei,' she shrugged as if finding it hard to make an appraisal, 'I think he suffered from always feeling out of place, bereft of a fortune, a means of keeping his family in the style to which he, and certainly they, were accustomed. Irina I was, and am, very fond of. I shall write to her tomorrow because this business must devastate her. Your grandmother was devoted to Irina, and genuinely.'

'Even though Irina blatantly sponged off her.' Cheryl calmly helped herself to cheese.

'You may have thought that, but I didn't,' Rachel glanced at her daughter-in-law with dislike. 'I think she was exceedingly fond of Dulcie, she was devastated by her death; but then I suppose you find it hard to like her after what happened between you.'

'I thought she was a parasite, I'm sorry,' Cheryl shrugged her shoulders.

'But didn't you like Hélène?'

'Not much. I knew she was unfaithful to Bobby too. You didn't have to be a detective to realize that she couldn't keep her eyes off men. Frankly, I think that the wrong person got killed. There's something evil about those Ferovs. Even Susan is now tainted with their brush, refusing to speak to her own brother. Like the Jews, they're always making trouble. I wouldn't mind if the whole lot of them were shipped back to where they came from.'

And opening her eyes wide, unaware of any *faux pas*, she looked round, as if waiting for agreement.

'You always put people's backs up,' Ralph said later as they undressed, he speaking from his dressing-room through the door. 'You seem to enjoy it. Why did you have to say all that about the Ferovs?'

'Because it's true,' Cheryl shouted back. 'They were a lot of penniless parasites.'

'Yes, but why say it in front of Mother?'

'Nothing I say in front of your mother pleases her or you.'

'And then that about the Jews. Freddie was furious.'

'He doesn't like me, anyway. At least in Kenya they had the sense to ban Jews at the Muthaiga Club.'

Cheryl stood at the door in the nude as if to provoke him, wriggling her head through her crêpe de Chine nightie. Ralph looked at her, his eyes rising to her face.

But the stinging reply didn't come. Once again he failed to rise to the bait. Despite everything that happened between them, the poor state of their marriage, the tension, their

646

inability to communicate, he still wanted her. She noted with satisfaction the expression of lust she had deliberately provoked and strolled across the bedroom, stretching out on the bed, smoking a cigarette, when he came in tying his pyjama cord. Then he sat on the bed and leaned on his arm.

'I would like us to get on, darling.'

'So would I,' Cheryl replied with a brief sarcastic laugh. 'Do you think I like living in this vast empty mausoleum in a permanent state of war? But what can we do? It's hardly *my* fault.' Angrily she stubbed out her half-smoked cigarette. 'Your family are determined not to like me whatever I do, and never have. I can't do or say anything right.'

'That's not true.'

'It *is* perfectly true, Ralph. Your mother *never* stays here, but always at The Grange.'

'She knows you don't want her.'

'I don't mind if she prefers that little Jewess to me ...'

'Now that's another *very* provocative remark, Cheryl,' Ralph sighed. 'The kind you seem able to make almost without thinking. Even *I* find that offensive.'

'Well, that is true too,' Cheryl paused to light a fresh cigarette. 'She is a scheming little German Jewess, just like the Ferovs, battening on your family, feeding on the fat of the land. Hitler, at least, has the good sense to try and get rid of the Jews, and I can't say I blame Mr Stalin for doing the same to people like the Ferovs. For your mother to say Irina was *not* sponging ... she helped herself to thousands, if you ask me ...'

She paused as Ralph jumped off the bed and stood at the foot of it, his hands on his hips.

'I really can't stand this, Cheryl. I must call a halt. To say things like that about the Jews is absolutely contemptible. Thousands of them are being herded into these concentration camps, Marian says.'

'It's all lies, if you ask me.' Cheryl was completely without contrition. 'People exaggerate. She can get her mother out quite easily if she wants to ... oh come on, Ralph. Let's go to sleep. I'm tired of these flare-ups every night.'

Ralph stared at her then, turning back the bedclothes, got into bed beside her. He lay for a while with his hands on his chest staring at the ceiling.

'I do *so* hate these arguments.'

'Why do we have them?' She turned and looked at him.

'I don't know, something always seems to start them.'

'Maybe we should have separate rooms, Ralph. Then we shan't see so much of each other.'

'We don't see much of each other *now*.'

'True,' Cheryl conceded. 'But we *do* share a bed and as you say every night ... row upon row.'

'It might change,' Ralph reached out a tentative hand. 'I mean you call this a big, empty house. With children...'

'Oh, Ralph, don't start *that* again.' Crossly Cheryl threw his arm back and straightened up. 'The number of times you talk about that.'

'But, Cheryl, I *want* children. We've been married six years. You have always promised...'

'Why don't we have them, then? Why? Why?'

She stared at him with such a wild expression in her eyes that Ralph suddenly felt afraid.

'What, you mean ...'

'I mean *I'm* not stopping them. *I'm* not taking any precautions. Did you ever think of that?'

'No, I ...'

'I don't think you even know the facts of life, Ralph Askham. Neither of us is trying to stop a baby coming yet none come. There's nothing else we can do...'

'I thought you were taking precautions, I'm sorry,' Ralph said, embarrassed. 'I thought you didn't like them, didn't want them.'

'How could I take precautions without you knowing?' Cheryl flung out an arm, almost hitting him in the eye.

'I really don't know an awful lot about it.'

'No, because you're a fool, Ralph. *You* don't really know much about *anything*, I suppose it's my fault for marrying a boy...'

'I was twenty-four...'

'Yes, but younger mentally. Much younger. The trouble is that you and Freddie have been mothered to death. You're practically both retarded. What sort of work does he do? Nothing. And you pretend to be a farmer ... really, Ralph, in my book you're a pair of good-for-nothing idlers. I think I even preferred George Lee. At least he and Freddie produce children. Whereas you, you can't produce anything. Have you ever thought of that, Ralph? *I'm* not preventing a baby. I've already had *two*. You're sterile, don't you realize that? Useless. No good...'

Ralph leaned over Cheryl and grabbed hold of her throat, stopping her flow of words which had assumed the proportions of a torrent. He started to bang her head rhythmically on the pillow while she tore wildly at his hands.

'Shut up,' he cried, 'shut up. If you don't stop I'll kill you, just like Hélène killed Jamie. God help me I will – and for as good a reason.'

Then with a final bang he released her, jumped out of bed and ran from the room leaving her sobbing, gasping for breath.

CHAPTER 30

The situation in Spain [Em wrote] reminds me of Germany, before Hitler came to power. Only here it is difficult to see the emergence of a strong leader on one side or the other. I think it is because, unlike the Germans, the Spanish people abhor discipline and authority. They hate being told what to do. Hence, for so many years politics in Spain has been chaotic and, since the elections, it seems to me even more so. In addition there is terror in the streets. Supporters from the right and left make forays with guns in fast cars, murdering their opponents with impunity.

For all that, Madrid is fun and Freddie in seventh heaven. I think he's going to write a novel.

Em's letters to her mother were interspersed with accounts of the deteriorating situation in Spain for *The Sentinel* – reports which Rachel duly printed, glad to put Germany on the inside pages.

But what Em didn't tell her mother or, naturally, the readers of the paper was that, for the first time in her life, she found herself deeply committed not only to a cause but another human being: a man, Felipe Barrio. For the first time in all her twenty-eight years she was in love.

It was not quite true to say that Em had never had a relationship with a man in her life. In the course of her job she met many congenial souls, and several she had found attractive and some were attracted to her. But journalism was an ephemeral profession, much of it conducted in conditions that were either solitary or overcrowded. So much time was spent on railway stations or, more recently since the advent of commercial airlines, in airports that in her years as a correspondent Em had found little time for romance.

Nor had she seemed to need it. She knew she was an independent woman, not too feminine, who liked dressing in trousers or the functional garb necessary to her profession. She did not aspire to being a top mannequin as her sister Charlotte now was; nor would she wish to be. Of all Rachel's children she was most like her mother who, although emotional and once deeply in love with her husband, had always given a high priority to the intellect and her work.

But Em couldn't even confide in her mother about Felipe. For once it was, unusually for her, an experience she found difficult to put into words.

But the situation couldn't be hidden from Freddie, who'd arrived in Madrid just after the February elections in 1936, that returned the Popular Front to power, and a wildly jubilant Em and her new Spanish friends on to the streets to celebrate. The leader of the Republican Left, Manuel Azana, became Prime Minister and one of his first acts had been to open all the gaols and release the political prisoners who had languished there since the Revolution in October 1934. Another of his acts was to banish the generals who had supported the rising in the Asturias, Generals Franco and Goded, to outlying parts of Spain: the Canaries and the Balearics.

Felipe Barrio was no relation to another republican leader Martinez Barrio, but was a fervent supporter of the Left though not, he told Em when they first met, a Communist. He believed in a Spain ruled by Spaniards and not by some outside foreign power like the Comintern, nor the Nazi Party in Germany who supported the Spanish Right: the Catholic Party and the Monarchists.

A miner's son from the Asturias, Felipe had come to Madrid to seek work and, although he did work as an electrician, he spent most of his time in cafés discussing politics, which was where Em first met him. Felipe was a stocky man, rather on the short side with receding hair, not the romantic type that a woman – even a mature one – might choose for her first love. But he had a strong, clever face and a mellifluous voice and,

651

although his English was poor, Em, who had a gift for languages, had almost mastered Spanish in the nine months she'd lived there since she had first gone to report on the Spanish situation the previous summer and offered to take Freddie.

Em had never met on equal, familiar terms the son of a labourer, such as a coalminer, and Felipe had never met the daughter of an aristocrat. But their lack of a social base seemed unimportant because they had everything else in common. They loved to talk and argue far into the night, and Felipe was interested in Em's experiences in Germany; whereas he could tell her so much she didn't know about the situation in the working-class areas of Spain, particularly the Asturias. There the miners had been terribly repressed by General Francisco Franco, who had previously commanded the Foreign Legion before being sent to quash the rebellion.

Felipe loved Em's dedication, her practicality and lack of convention. To her he became that embodiment of everything she had understood, and loved, about her father: bravery, humanity, manliness.

Freddie had arrived from England in the middle of the night to find that his sister had a companion in her bed. He was surprised by it, but Em was neither ashamed nor embarrassed and Freddie soon accepted Felipe for Em's sake and was glad.

But he thought Felipe was a strange man for his independent-minded, headstrong sister to fall in love with. He was very dogmatic, and Em seemed to accept what he said without much argument. He also believed that the man was to be waited on in the home, even if it wasn't his. Em found this a novel experience, and didn't mind, because she was used to having people wait on her. She liked getting up at dawn to wake Felipe and see him off to work, though this was really the only conventional part of the day, because they hardly ever got home again until midnight after the elections, when it became obvious that things wouldn't settle down as everyone hoped, but would get worse.

The supporters of the Government were convinced that the parties of the right, the Monarchists, the Catholics and the landowners, were out to topple the lawfully elected government and, in its place, put either a new dictator like Primo de Rivera, whose son had founded the Falange, or restore the monarchy. It seemed vital to protect the Republic, that government elected by the people for the people.

Freddie had left Marian and Paul with Marian's mother, who had joined them after Christmas. She was a sad, almost broken woman but overjoyed to be reunited with her daughter, and she soon settled down in The Grange, promising to look after both daughter and beloved new grandson. It had, she assured Freddie, given her a purpose in life. So he took off happily, allowing himself three months in which to find a new profession.

Over the years Freddie had written stories, poems and articles – above all a diary – which he kept secret from all the members of his family except Em. Em knew about these ambitions in Germany; but maybe she feared a rival, or maybe she didn't think it was very important because she didn't take a lot of notice of Freddie's ambitions. She didn't even ask to see his work.

Freddie settled down with Em and Felipe in the flat off the Calle de San Bernardo near the University which belonged to friends.

Everyone in Spain tried to behave as though everything was normal; and normal things like marriages, visiting friends and holidays abroad continued because, for so many years, the situation had been as unstable as it was now.

And yet still it got worse; there was no use denying it. Em learned from her new friends and other journalists that, though there was not the air of menace there had been in pre-Hitler Berlin, there was a typical Spanish atmosphere of frenzy which was the counterpart of the prevailing German atmosphere of gloom and doom.

Freddie, an inveterate student, registered at the university for a course to learn Spanish, and went there every morning, usually returning in the afternoon to work, sleep, and make notes. He didn't feel like a married man with a son, but like the irresponsible young man he'd been in the heyday of the 'Honourable Freddie'. He could quickly slough off responsibility and become a youth again. And yet he missed Marian.

'Do you think,' he said one day when the three were having the customary late Spanish lunch at about three in the afternoon, for once at the flat. 'Do you think Marian could come and live in Spain?'

'Why not?' Felipe dipped his bread in his tortillas and washed both down with a glass of white wine.

'Well, everyone thinks there'll be a war.'

'There'll be no war,' Felipe said authoritatively. 'We shall win without a war. You think the Spanish people have gone through all this to have war?' He shook his head and Em shook hers too. She didn't like always to agree with Felipe, especially in front of Freddie, but there was no doubt he was always right. Theirs was not strictly romantic love; they didn't touch much, and they wouldn't have dreamt of holding hands, or kissing in public, but it was a deep, sensual attraction that made its ultimate physical expression paramount in both their minds. When she was not with him Em felt haunted by Felipe; even the sight of him walking along the street, a cigarette in the corner of his mouth, his head buried in the socialist party paper, *Unita!*, made her heart lurch. She couldn't understand how every other woman didn't find him equally devastating. Freddie said she was sick. He shook his head now, seeing her again agreeing with Felipe, and wagged a finger at her. She knew what he meant, but Felipe – rather self-absorbed – missed its significance.

'I thought I could take my wife to the coast,' Freddie said. 'The air might suit her better by the sea. She's ill, you know.'

'I know.' Felipe nodded, but he didn't look sympathetic. A sick woman, like a sick child, would be a nuisance to a man like him. He didn't expect to have any trouble like that with strong, sturdy Em. She reminded him of a robust countrywoman, of the kind he was used to – with large bones and broad hips. Except for the female part of her, she was very like a man, with a man's mind, a man's ideas.

'Do you know who I saw yesterday?' Em said suddenly. 'I meant to tell you, Freddie. Kyril Ferov is here.'

'How curious. Did he say why?'

'He said the family are considering moving to Spain. They find Paris intolerable with Hélène in prison.'

'Then who's going to visit Hélène?' Freddie looked curious.

'I don't know that they think about that much. They've had enough with all that fuss. Susan won't go, of course, just the father and mother, and the girls. And there's Charlotte and her sister, Evgenia. She won't be alone. Anyway, I gave him our phone number.'

Hélène's trial had dominated the papers in France and England for several days, even though she pleaded guilty in order to save her family distress. Her counsel, Maître Deribe, made a great thing of the extenuating circumstances which involved many unkind references to Bobby, their children, and the bad way she had been treated. No one had a good word to say about Jamie. There was no reference at all to the armaments business, which would have been considered irrelevant to the case, even if Hélène wished to introduce it – which, emphatically, she didn't. There were too many irons in the fire already. It was regarded strictly as a *crime passionnel* and some thought the judge, who was clearly sympathetic, would let her off completely. But she got five years, although everyone thought she would be paroled after two. Rachel and Charlotte attended the trial every day with Irina and Evgenia, and sometimes Susan, though Alexei and her other brother Dima didn't go at all. Strangely enough Kyril didn't go either – no one quite knew why, unless it was that he was the one who had told her Jamie was in Paris. That much was known, no more. It was as though both families were divided into sides based on gender; the women in sympathy, the men against. That was not the whole story, of course.

Em was explaining to Felipe about Hélène when the telephone rang and Freddie got up to answer it in his halting Spanish. Then Em heard him exclaim:

'We were just talking about you! What a coincidence. Yes, Em said she'd seen you. Yes, we'd love to. Tonight?'

'Can we meet Kyril for dinner tonight?' he looked over his shoulder and Em nodded. Freddie said 'Where, Kyril? OK. Em will know it. She has a boyfriend. He'll come too. Felipe Barrio. No, no relation to Martinez.' They chatted for a while longer, then Freddie said goodbye. 'What a coincidence. Good old Kyril.'

'I don't think he's good old Kyril,' Em said. 'You've a very short memory. There's a lot I'd like to know about that man. I don't trust him a bit. The way he changed sides was so funny – first a Communist then a Fascist. Odd, if you ask me.'

Kyril, however, was waiting for them at a restaurant on the Plaze de España, not far from where they lived. He looked extremely respectable and eminently trustworthy, a quiet, almost nondescript man, a good husband and father, sipping a sherry just inside the door of the restaurant. Freddie introduced him as Prince Ferov and Kyril looked annoyed, but it was a conversational opener, though maybe a mistaken one, as Felipe retorted:

'*Prince* Ferov? What is this? A monarchist gathering?'

'I must say that is where my sympathies lie,' Kyril acknowledged. 'But it is not why I am in Spain.'

'I don't think I want to eat with this man,' Felipe said to Em, refusing the chair Freddie offered.

'Oh, *Felipe*!' Freddie took his arm. 'Be reasonable. He's my cousin's husband.'

'I'm afraid I don't eat with princes.' Felipe put his evening paper under his arm, turned his back on them and left.

'Oh dear,' Kyril wrinkled his nose. 'I am sorry; but surely *he's* not your boyfriend, Em?'

'He is, as a matter of fact,' Em looked after Felipe as though wondering whether to follow him but Freddie held her arm.

'Do let him go, Em. He behaved badly. He's a bit wild, you know. If you go after him now he'll tread all over you.'

'I don't know what you mean by that?' The colour leapt to Em's face.

'I mean that he's got to learn how to behave, even if he is the son of a miner.'

'Oh, Freddie, what a revolting thing to say.' As Em shook her napkin in annoyance, Kyril smiled.

'So? Mixing with the working classes, are we?'

'Well, we're trying to,' Freddie said. 'I must say I find Felipe rather hard going; but he is Em's choice, so he can't be all bad.'

'I'm afraid, if you go on like this, I'll have to go too,' Em said. 'I do dislike personal remarks.'

'Sorry. Please don't go.' Freddie called for the waiter, jovially insisting that the dinner was on him. Then the conversation became general, where was Kyril staying and how long was he here for and so on.

'Are you really looking for somewhere to live?'

'For my parents,' Kyril said carefully. 'It is cheaper to live in Spain than in France. The worst thing is the possibility of war, or perhaps, not *precisely* a war but a "coup" – where the monarchists will seize power and restore the Bourbons. But some say it will be over in a day or two.'

'It's a good thing Felipe didn't stay to hear you say that,' Em said. 'He's so left he's almost a Communist.'

'Really?' Kyril looked towards the door as though somehow expecting to see Felipe return. 'Then you should look out. Don't become too involved with him.'

'I already am,' Em replied, defiantly tilting her chin.

'I see,' Kyril gazed at his well-manicured hands. 'I really wanted to see you on family business – to talk about Hélène. Oh, don't misunderstand me, I know that your mother, Charlotte and Susan are doing all they can; but there is the question of the children. Bobby doesn't pay enough towards their upkeep and my parents are feeling real hardship.'

'Kyril, we can't affect Bobby!' Em cried. 'We never see him. He wouldn't listen to us if we did. I agree he's behaved very badly towards the children but, I assure you, the whole family is putting all the pressure on him it can.'

'Bobby is an evil man,' Kyril said. 'Even Susan hates him.'

'If Susan didn't hate him so much she might do more to help the children,' Freddie retorted. 'You can't expect reason from someone you can't talk to.'

'Yes, but ... oh, I didn't mean to have a family brawl,' Kyril looked embarrassed. 'I thought you might be able to do something. I see you can't. The children will come with my parents to Spain ... if they come.'

'I think it's a very bad idea, if you don't mind my saying it. I'm toying with the idea of bringing my wife, who needs a warmer climate, but people are against it. The situation is really quite dangerous. I'm sure Bobby wouldn't be too pleased if his daughters were brought here.'

'Really?' Kyril gazed at them with a curious expression. 'I'm intrigued to know he cares. You'd think that, with their mother in prison, he would at least take an interest. There's a heartlessness about the man I, frankly, can't stand. If anyone ever did any harm to Bobby I wouldn't blame them. Not at all.'

And, looking at them cryptically, Kyril held up his glass in a toast.

'To the Revolution ...' he said.

'The Revolution,' Em echoed but, later, she thought that maybe they both meant different things. Meeting Kyril that night somehow seemed to disturb her. She couldn't have said why.

'He's such a funny man,' she said to Freddie when they parted after the meal. 'You know he told us absolutely nothing.'

'I think he was fishing.'

'What about?'

'What we knew about politics, about Bobby; why we were here. I don't think he was so concerned with Hélène at all. He never even went to the trial.'

'I don't suppose Kyril will occur very much again in our lives, but it *is* worrying about the girls. After all, they're our cousins, Aunt Melanie's grandchildren. You'd think *she'd* care.'

There was no sign of Felipe in the flat when they returned, and for several days after he didn't appear. Em tried all their old haunts, but no one had seen him and she became more and more worried until, one day, he just turned up again, refusing to answer questions about his whereabouts.

Em found this unsatisfactory and told him, but he said it was none of her business. He reserved the right to come and go, and not answer to a woman. Freddie advised her to fling him out. 'You've chosen a very funny man for your lover,' he said at last. 'You let him tread all over you. I'm amazed at you.'

Freddie's opinion mattered to her, the scorn on his face, and on those of some of her friends, as Felipe became more eccentric, more secretive and, somehow, more dangerous. Yet she loved him. She didn't want to lose him.

In April a judge was assassinated for condemning a member of the Falange to thirty years in prison, and a bomb was flung at the President at a parade in honour of the fourth anniversary of the Republic.

Em sent daily reports of all these events and others to *The Sentinel* and a long account of the traditional working-class march through Madrid on May Day. The youth of the Socialist and Communist parties had amalgamated and gave the clenched fist salute to the sound of the Internationale. Manuel Azana became President of the Republic and Cesares Quiroga, a leading Socialist, became Prime Minister.

Freddie was returning to England in May, and urged Em to come with him. The people who owned the flat, anyway, were talking about needing it again.

'It's just to get me away from Felipe,' Em said to him.

'You're right, it is. I was all for you falling in love and now I'm all against it. I don't know what Mother would say about Felipe ...'

'Please don't tell Mother,' Em said urgently. 'I don't want her to know.'

'But she will know, if ...'

'If?' Em looked at him. She was sitting by the window typing her article and Freddie was deciding what to pack to take home. He intended after all to try and persuade Marian to come back with him and go to the South of Spain. He probably wouldn't return to Madrid.

'Well, aren't you going to marry or anything?'

'Why should we?'

'I just wondered.'

'A love affair isn't for life, you know. Not necessarily.'

'I see. Good. I thought it seemed quite serious.'

'You don't like Felipe at *all*, do you, Freddie?'

'Not much.' Freddie was reluctant to admit it. In all their years together they'd never even had an argument – not identical twins, but very, very close. 'I don't think he's worthy of you. I know you're my sister and I'm prejudiced; but I can't, honestly, see him fitting in with your life when you come home, if you bring him with you, of course.'

'Who said I was going to go home?'

'Aren't you?' Freddie looked amazed. 'I thought ...'

'I like Spain. I like the people and I do love Felipe, warts and all. He is very different with me when we are alone. Very tender.'

'Then it's just as well I'm going,' Freddie said.

'Oh, I didn't mean that!' She flung her arms round his neck. 'Darling Federico, I don't want to get *rid* of you. I mean when Felipe and I are really alone ... you know.'

'*I* know,' Freddie ruffled her hair. 'In the sack. You and I are a funny pair. We've each fallen for very unlikely partners. All I can say, old thing, is that I hope in your unlikely choice you're as happy as I've been.'

That night Freddie was sent for to return home urgently, because Marian had been taken seriously ill.

Rachel and Marian's mother were at the hospital when he arrived after a non-stop journey. Marian had had a lung haemorrhage and had not regained consciousness. It was very sudden, in the night, and she was almost dead before her mother, waking on an impulse, went to see that she was all right and found her lying in a pool of blood.

Freddie had flown from Spain, his first air journey, which he had not enjoyed. He had hardly slept at all since the news came, and when he heard what had happened he blamed himself for ever having left her.

'But, darling, you could have done nothing to prevent it.' Rachel had not had much sleep either and held the hand of her stricken son.

'I should never have gone for all that time.'

'But she knew you were due back. She was so looking forward to it and, maybe, returning with you. I know what you wrote. Marian was really well. There was no cause for undue apprehension.'

'But I shouldn't have gone,' Freddie said. 'Don't you see, Mother? I should never have left her. We could have had these three months together instead of apart.'

When the doctors allowed Freddie in to see Marian he thought she was already dead. Her face was as white as the pillow and the halo of her dark hair was so familiar that he fell on to his knees beside her and wept. The doctor with him urged him not to cry because even the unconscious could sometimes apprehend what was happening outside their silent world, and such despair might upset her. Freddie nodded, dried his eyes and sat on the chair beside her, taking her limp pale hand and squeezing it, trying to induce life into it.

But, during the course of that long day, Marian's life slowly, quietly ebbed away, rather as she had lived – as though she were determined, by her end, to give as little trouble and offence as she had in life.

When the doctors announced that she was dead two of the people she loved most in the world were with her, her husband and her mother. A third, her infant son of just fourteen months, was in his cot at home in the protection of a nanny his grandmother had hastily engaged, blissfully unaware that he was motherless.

Bobby Lighterman was a sad, chastened man; but one with his head well above water. Throughout his life he had been a realist and he remained one, despite the criticism of those dear to him.

When Bobby decided to put his daughters out of his life together with his faithless wife, it was because he felt as little affection for them as he did for Hélène. He had once loved her, or so he thought, certainly desired her strongly; but he had never got to grips with his relationship with three very small girls, one still almost a baby. He calculated that his life in the future would not make him very close to them either and that, therefore, or so he reasoned, their best interests lay in not seeing a man who had no paternal feelings towards them.

The financial arrangements he made for them would increase in generosity the older they got. That way Hélène, or the Ferovs, would have less chance of getting their hands on his money. So now they were not well off, but when they were grown up they would be. Each of them would be an heiress and well worth marrying. All his life Bobby Lighterman had thought that money was the answer to everything.

By the winter of 1936 Bobby felt that all he had left, besides money and ambition – he still had plenty of both – was an abiding love for his son David, now nine years old and still living with his mother in Harrow, preparing to go to the big school on the hill.

Those who were closest to him might have included among their number his mother, his grandmother, his brother

Christopher and maybe his wife Sylvia, but certainly not his sister, Susan, with whom he had quarrelled bitterly on account of her championship of Hélène, or his half-brother Jordan, still a sick man languishing in a nursing home in the South of France in daily anticipation of attacks from the Nazis. These former were people whose opinions he might, or might not, heed, but their importance in his life was nothing compared to that of his son. It seemed that in that dutiful, rather lonely boy, virtually fatherless as he had been all his life, he saw himself – a young boy striving for recognition and success, for the love of his mother, as once he had.

Bobby stopped his Rolls at the door of the modest suburban house and stayed there for a few minutes alone in the driving seat, looking at the shabby gentility of the tree-lined street, wondering how Aileen, or David, could have stuck it for all those years. He got out of the car and locked the door. He no longer drove an Askham, too sad a reminder of his one major failure, a terrible blunder, and now what cars remained were museum pieces.

As he opened the gate and walked up the path he saw the lace curtains in the front room fall and, a few seconds later, the front door opened and Aileen stood there, so trim, fresh and pretty one would have imagined his arrival had been announced beforehand, which it hadn't. He often wondered how much time she spent by those curtained windows because, whenever he arrived, the door opened for him before he reached it. Bobby removed his hat and kissed her on the cheek in the affectionate way he customarily did, on the few occasions in the year when he now came to see her.

'Were you expecting me?' Bobby enquired, going into the hall.

'No. Should I?'

Aileen closed the door and looked at him, a pleasant, anticipatory smile on her face.

'You just look all ready for a guest; or do you always look like that?'

'You never know who will call.' Aileen flung open the door of the lounge. As usual, like her, it was neat and tidy, not a thing out of place, ready for whoever might call. In fact very few people did call, but it was just as well to be ready. 'May I get you coffee?'

It was eleven in the morning and Bobby thought coffee would be nice. While she was out he peeled off his gloves, removed his overcoat and sat in a chair opposite the fire, crossing his legs.

'You look well, Bobby.' Aileen glanced at him as she set the tray on a small, conveniently placed table.

'I feel well,' Bobby said. 'Thank heaven, now all that business is over.'

Aileen grimaced sympathetically. 'You *did* have a bad time, didn't you? Fancy her turning into a murderess.'

Bobby stroked his new moustache which he had grown, perhaps to make up for the sad but undeniable fact that his hair was receding, although he was only thirty-seven. *Tempus fugit*. No longer beautiful Bobby, but distinguished, handsome maybe. He hoped so, and his hand stole over his thinning strands of hair at the front of his head.

'The whole family was unbalanced, you know,' he said.

'I suppose they must have been,' Aileen passed him his cup and saucer, set on a neat doily. 'Cheating, lying, killing. Do you miss the little girls?'

'Not a bit,' Bobby said firmly and held up his hand. 'Now don't you criticize me, *please* ...'

'I wouldn't dream of it,' Aileen looked offended. 'It's hardly my business.'

'It was a conscious decision, made in their interests. That was, of course, before I knew that their crazy mother was going to go and kill somebody. Even then I decided they were happy enough with their grandmother and that to see them again would be cruel. Don't think I neglect them. I don't. My lawyer is always accessible to Princess Irina. Charlotte and Susan, I know, keep an eye on them and all in all I think it's for the best. That, really, is why I'm here.'

Bobby sipped his coffee, looking at her over the rim of his cup. Neatly smoothing her skirt under her Aileen sat on the edge of the sofa, carefully breaking a biscuit before putting a piece of it daintily into her mouth.

Aileen had worn well with the years, Bobby thought. She was nearly forty – pretty, cool, attractive and with a good, clear skin: a sensible woman. In another time, another place, he might even have married her. He smiled.

'I think what I have to say will please you. I hope so.' He coughed and placed his cup carefully on the table by his side. 'I have, as you know, always had a warm affection for David. I may not see as much of him as I should, or do the normal things a father does, play football, walks in the park and so on. As David gets older I think he will see the reason for that, and that I am a very busy man.'

'He knows it now, Bobby. He never grumbles.' Aileen kept the pleasant, docile smile on her face; but when she put her coffee cup carefully down on its doily anyone more observant than Bobby would have noticed that her hand trembled.

'I have a proposition now,' Bobby said, joining his hands as if he were at a board meeting, 'which I hope you will accept. As I have said, I love David. He reminds me of myself as a boy and I am very conscious of the fact that, as I was, he is at present, to all intents and purposes, fatherless. I had the love of my family, particularly Sir Robert and Mabel, my grandparents who virtually brought me up. But my memories of my youth, while pleasant, because I was always surrounded by wealth and the things wealth can bring, are of a lonely boy who lacked that special love that only a father can give. My father, as you know, was killed at Omdurman and I was a posthumous child. But I have no such excuse as far as David is concerned. Here I am in the flesh, yet I hardly ever see him. He doesn't know me. I'm a stranger who visits. I would like to remedy that.'

Bobby unjoined his hands and cleared his throat again, gazing directly at Aileen.

'I would like formally to adopt David. To be his guardian, as well as his natural father, and to give him my name. I would like him to grow up with me – oh, I know he will go to Harrow in due course, but his home will be with me. Naturally, I will groom him as my heir, to inherit my fortune as my grandfather groomed me. Only it will be a much, much larger one than Sir Robert left. David will one day be a very wealthy, very fortunate young man.'

Bobby was so intent on what he was saying that he might not have seen the expression on Aileen's face change from anticipation to surprise and, finally, shock. When he finished she was staring at him open-mouthed. It was a very unladylike expression for one who had always taken a great deal of care about appearance, especially in the lonely years when she had waited behind her lace curtains in Harrow on the off chance that Bobby might call, like today. In those years she'd had to live through his business successes, setbacks, his marriage to another when she was about to have his child – and finally his divorce, the scandals attached. It seemed there were always scandals – or threats. Finally he had called and, as he began to speak, she thought that, at last, he'd brought with him a proposal.

But proposal it was not. It was a proposition.

'Is all well, Aileen?' Bobby enquired after a moment or two of this open-mouthed inspection. It was most disconcerting. 'I thought you'd be pleased.'

'And what about me?' Aileen said.

'You?' Bobby looked at her, lowered his head then raised it again. 'What about you?'

'What happens to me?'

'Why,' Bobby laughed, 'nothing "happens" to you. I thought you liked this house. You have enough money. Of course David will come to see you, stay with you. If no …'

'And *I* am to wait *here* as I have for the past *eight* years on the *off chance* that *you* and now my son will come and visit me? Maybe take me for a drive in your large car and tea at some boring café in the town? Do you think *that's* what *I* want to endure for the *rest* of my life, Bobby Lighterman? No, thank you.' Aileen stood up and, putting her hands on her hips, leaning towards him, hissed: 'No *bloody* thank you! David is my son, mine, borne by me and brought up by me. Neither you nor anyone else is taking him from me. David's all I've got, do you know that, Bobby? Apart from him I have nothing else in life worth living for...'

'Oh, come now, Aileen,' Bobby looked indignant. 'You're exaggerating. You've had a very nice life, without having to work for it. You've had every comfort, better than you'd have had on a secretary's pay. I am offering David the chance to be a very important man. You can't deny him that.'

'And what if I say no? Will he still be important then? Won't you leave him *any* of your stinking money when you die?'

'Look, Aileen,' Bobby stood up. 'I have no need to tolerate this, but I do have rights, and if you go on being intransigent I will assert them.'

'What will you do?' Aileen took a step nearer him as if threatening him. 'What will you do? Tell me that?'

'I'll have to see my lawyer. I don't know exactly what rights you have. It has never come up. I didn't think it would. I didn't think you could possibly be so unfeeling, so selfish.'

'Selfish and unfeeling, is it, Bobby Lighterman?' Aileen bawled at him in tones reminiscent of a fishwife. 'Selfish and unfeeling. The words you've always used to me to describe me before have been self*less* and generous. Self*LESS*, Bobby, that's the complete opposite of self*ISH*, in case you didn't know. Now, how generous do *you* consider you've been all these years? Oh, generous in *money* maybe, but not very, considering all you've got. I mean we've had all we need, nothing more.'

'You've got the house!' Bobby expostulated.

'The house!' Aileen jerked her head in the direction of the window. 'You can have the bloody house; this stinking little *box* in the middle of nowhere – middle-class, suburban, horrible.' Aileen shuddered.

'All right, what is it you want? Do you want to travel, go abroad? Would you like to live in the South of France? Tell me what you want.' Bobby juggled the small change in his pocket impatiently and looked at his watch, always a sign that he was short of temper or time, or both.

'I want you.' Aileen suddenly moderated her tone of voice. 'You may not believe it, but I want to be Mrs Bobby Lighterman, received in society, the best restaurants, by the nobility, your perishing mother Lady Melanie, your condescending Aunt Rachel – people like that, people who matter. You may think that your Hélène was the only sort of person people like that received. Well, look what happened to her. She's now in a French gaol, and all her life she will bear the stigma of a murderess. That's what your flirting with the aristocracy did to you, *Mr* Lighterman. Cost you your reputation.'

'I didn't flirt with the aristocracy,' Bobby sounded dangerous. 'I *am* aristocracy. You're over-reaching yourself, my good woman.'

'Oh, yes, *your* mother and *your* grandfather and *your* blooming grandmother. Earl of this, Countess of that, Lady this, that and the other. But what about your aunt who drowned herself, poor wretch; your half-brother who slept with boys and smuggled arms to the Nazis; your cousin the high and mighty Earl himself, who works as a farmer knee deep in mire half the time, and his father with the fancy name who slept with a Cairo prostitute and had a kid no one wanted? What about *them*, Bobby Lighterman?'

'What about them?' Bobby sounded deflated.

'Not very distinguished, is it? Not a very nice legacy for your son. And what happens, finally, to your wife, mother of three daughters? She goes and kills someone and then what do you do, *on* top of all the awful, selfish things you've done already – like cause the death of your cousin's husband who wanted to retire – you abandon your three little girls. In "their" interests, mind you. What do they think of it, may I ask? Why have *they* deserved *that*?'

'I told you …'

'*You* told *me*, but you didn't convince me. How do *I* know that *you* won't do the same to David, once you've got over the kick of taking him from me? Oh, no, Bobby. I won't part with David, however much you pay me, whatever you do to try and bribe me. Never, never, never. Never unless you make me your wife too. Now those are my terms and that's all I have to say.'

'I see.' Bobby took a deep breath and walked over to the French windows, gazing out at the wintry skyline, the few brown leaves on the trees etched forlornly against the sky. He was shocked by what Aileen had said, by the depth of her venom, the coarseness of her tone; but somehow he was not surprised. He turned and looked at her and what he saw filled him with reluctant admiration.

In many ways she was right; many of the things she had said were true. She *was* a fine looking woman, still on the right side of forty and, in a way, in her dress and apparent air of breeding, she could hold up her head with duchesses. He could go away and think about it – but he was a businessman, a man of action used to taking quick decisions about important matters.

Bobby sat down at last, his hands deep in his pockets, his feet stretched out before him.

'Very well,' he said, looking at her, a half smile on his face. 'We have a deal. For the sake of David I *will* marry you. It will have many advantages, legitimizing my own son. It will be nice for him to grow up with two parents; but I want you to know this, Aileen, and know it well: as far as you and I are concerned our passion is long passed. I'm not saying I will have other women, but I might. If I do I don't want any objections from you. You may have my name, your share of my possessions –

which are vast – my house in Mayfair; Manchester Square and Robertswood when I inherit them.

'But, please, *don't* expect my love. You and I have an arrangement, call it a business partnership, by which we both gain. You have what you want, and I have David.

'I have tried once to combine love with marriage but, for me, it was a dreadful failure. I expect you to be faithful and not to make a fool of me because, if you do, I shall do what I did to Hélène, only I will keep David. Never fear of that. Above all, I have absolute control over our son without consulting you – his schooling, his career. Lastly, if all this proves too much for you, you must not sue for divorce for at least five years and if and when you do you will only receive a pittance. I'll have an agreement drawn up in writing. Is that understood?'

For a while Aileen didn't reply, didn't smile, didn't cry. Then, her face ever impassive, she nodded.

'Understood. I agree to abide by the rules. I might not be very happy, but nothing can be worse than this. I might be exchanging one stultifying life for another, but I don't mind. I'll keep the rules, never fear.'

'So be it,' Bobby said, as though he were in church. 'David will be awfully pleased to have both of us together.'

Aileen thought that, for once, he was thinking of someone else besides himself – his son and his happiness.

Or, was he really only just thinking of Bobby? Was Bobby once again getting, by his usual unscrupulous methods, just what he wanted? A servant, bound to him body and soul under the legalistic name of wife?

CHAPTER 31

The sun beat down on the hot Castilian plain and Freddie, his hat tipped over his eyes as protection against the harsh light, his bandit-style bandoleers criss-crossed over his chest, peered once again down the sights of his rifle. The man creeping along by the white wall of the house in the village of Villaneuva de la Cañada seemed aware of his unseen, silent enemy and paused, looking fearfully around. Freddie got into a more comfortable position, taking care not to make his move too obvious, and his finger slowly pressed the trigger. The man was about his age, bearded like Freddie, roughly the same height. He could be his brother.

Freddie took his finger off the trigger. He was somebody's brother, somebody's son. Not for the first time in this terrible war he lowered his gun. To kill this man who was trying to escape with the rest of the departing Nationalist troops was not merely war, it was murder. Maybe he would live only to be killed another day, but today his death wouldn't be on Freddie's conscience. In the instinctive Spanish gesture, although he wasn't religious, he crossed himself and settled against the wall, separated from the rest of his unit, to await events.

The object of the attack was the little town of Brunete near Madrid, towards which the Republican forces had advanced from the Corunna road with the object of isolating the Nationalists encamped in the Casa de Campo and the University City in Madrid. Since his arrival in Spain the previous November, 1936, Freddie had been active in the defence of Madrid, especially the battle for the University City which gave him his first taste not only of war but of acts of unparalleled ferocity, citizen waged against citizen, neighbour against neighbour, friend against friend, brother against brother.

Freddie had killed many men in that time, but none in such cold blood – as would have been the case if he had shot his defenceless brother creeping along by the wall desperately looking for a bolthole. Freddie had been hounded too, often found himself in almost impossible positions. But it hadn't made him savage or revengeful. It increased not only his bitterness, but his sadness at the terrible tragedy that was being enacted in Spain since Franco had raised the flag in Morocco in July of the previous year.

Freddie had been in England when Franco gave the signal for the carefully planned attempt to overthrow the democratically elected Republican government. Within two days he thought he would be master of Spain; but such was not the case. The citizens of the Republic rallied to its defence and soon men from many nations began to stream to Spain to join the International Brigades.

Rachel had begged Freddie not to leave his baby for a war in which he had no experience, and which was really of no direct interest. But Freddie had insisted it was. Em and Felipe were heavily involved on the side of the government, Em sending inflamed despatches to *The Sentinel* which Rachel's new managing editor had heavily to edit. The English government under Baldwin set about trying to agree a non-intervention treaty and the new King, Edward VIII, arranged his Coronation for the following year. Ramsay MacDonald had finally turned Conservative and lost his seat in the election of 1935. Even Rachel, increasingly a moderate, regarded him as a traitor to the cause.

Freddie's adversary soon disappeared out of sight and, as the sun blazed down, Freddie got into a comfortable position, his rifle slumped over his lap, and thought about home, particularly his mother. More than anything he regretted his estrangement from her. He'd never seen her so angry or so desperate as she pleaded with him not to go, not to leave Paul, just in case anything should happen. Even the way he assured her nothing would happen – and at that early stage no one knew just *what* would happen – terrified her, because it reminded her of the reassurances his father had given her in 1915 before he went back to the war, long before he was fit.

But Freddie, the 'Honourable Freddie', soon came to think that he had a charmed life. Like his father before him, although he didn't know it, he was convinced that he would emerge unscathed from the fray; that good luck would see him through. And, indeed, in these six months he had been in many terrible situations yet he had never received a scratch. Even Em, in besieged Madrid, had faith in Freddie and in Felipe who, as a senior commander on the Republican side, was helping to direct operations in the north.

'I think we're about to go in,' a voice called behind him and, turning, he saw Randy Tucker move over a boulder and crouch beside him. 'Why did you let that bastard go?' Randy tipped his hat back on his head and looked curiously at Freddie.

'No point. I don't like killing for the sake of it,' Freddie said. 'He made me think of home – brothers and sisters and that. I felt I *was* him, for a moment – caught in a trap.'

'You're a crazy pommy,' Randy said. He was an Australian who had joined the British Battalion, now commanded by Fred Copeman, an ex-sailor. In command of the regiment, which was part of the XVth International Brigade, was the eccentric Major George Nathan, a very brave but foolhardy English officer.

In fact everyone had to be slightly mad to fight in this savage war, where rules of combat were largely ignored. There were many defections, and summary shootings as the harsh punishment for cowardice, even though the British had tried to negotiate different conditions for their troops.

Randy was a soldier of fortune, who claimed to have fought in the Russian Revolution, but no one believed him because he would have had to have been about ten at the time. He had certainly been to Russia, and had become enthused by the Communist experiment. Some said he was a high-powered agent of the Comintern, which had a huge finger in the Spanish pie; but Freddie thought he was just an ordinary bloke, a man with a wanderlust, a craving for adventure. He was one of his best friends in the British Battalion and the two were never very far apart.

Gradually the other members of Freddie's platoon crept up behind him and Sergeant Randolph Tucker, and they started to move towards the village, just as a bombardment began from the artillery corps to their left flank. Then the flack started to fly and bullets whizzed past them from the remnant of those defending the village and, just for a moment, Freddie wondered if the man whose life he had spared were among them. This last ditch stand by the enemy had not been anticipated.

By nightfall, however, the village was in the hands of the Republicans, and those villagers who had stayed behind and not fled either to Madrid or along the Corunna road came out to offer them food and shelter. That was on 10 July.

The next day there was confusion as the brigades, entering the Nationalist lines, were mixed up with one another, and much unnecessary slaughter ensued. At one stage Freddie found himself isolated, appearing to be in retreat while the others went forward, and he was terrified in case someone should observe him and think he was deserting.

However, eventually Freddie rejoined his Battalion and, that day, two more villages fell – Villaneuva del Pardillo and Villafranca del Castillo. The objective now was Boadilla which had been a battlefield the previous winter.

George Nathan had been blown up by a bomb and, as he lay dying, he asked his comrades surrounding him to sing. It was one of the most moving experiences of the whole war, and so was his funeral that night under olive trees near the River Guadarama when George Watkin, the Brigade Commissar, gave an oration that moved many of those listening, including Freddie, to tears.

Dug in now in trenches around Boadilla Freddie wrote a letter to his mother in which he said:

This is a terrible war, Mother, but not a fruitless one. That is why it is being fought with such bitterness on both sides, and there is a kind of holy dedication that was probably the same during the Revolution when the Bolsheviks fought to keep out the Whites.

I feel this has been the experience I was lacking in life, Mother, the 'job' I needed and, although I bitterly regret hurting you the way I did and the rows we had when I came away, I feel that I was right and you were wrong.

You once told me that you thought Father found himself in battle after the humiliation of the trial, and I think the same thing is happening to me; that Father's spirit *is* with me. I wish I'd known him well, or could remember him. I often think of him, especially on days like today when we are busily digging trenches round the ruined town of Boadilla, so many times fought over, as was the case in Flanders when Father was there, ground fought over time and time again.

I am still unscratched, Mother, and feel this is the way it will be with me. God knows how long this war will last. Our arms mainly come from Russia for, since the non-intervention treaties by the other democratic powers, including England, we are getting none from elsewhere. Our lines are also full of Russian fighters and helpers, and I am told that they regard Barcelona almost as their country and are much disliked there. I have not met any personally, but they are unpopular, in the same way that we hear from our captured prisoners how much the Nats dislike the Nazis and the Italians who are helping them. The German Condor Legion is quite savage and bombs and machine-guns towns and fleeing civilians without mercy. You will have heard what happened in Guernica. I have heard nearly 2000 civilians were killed there, regarded as target practice by the Germans who are building up their crack squad of pilots. What for, Mother? I think Em was right. Germany does want war.

Em said she caught a glimpse of Kyril Ferov in Madrid and wonders what he was doing there, because the city is still held by the government; but I think she must have been mistaken. If he is anywhere he will be with Franco's forces at their headquarters in Seville. I must say I dislike the fellow, even though he has always been very pleasant to me. He's such a Nazi.

It is getting dark now, Mother, and we are due to go into the attack again at dawn. There are two hills in front of us occupied by the Nats and in the twilight I could see figures stealthily moving up, bringing reinforcements. At times like this I am conscious, in a funny way, and I don't mean religious, of the power of the universe – of some mysterious force that overlooks us all. Does it sound soppy?

Mother, when I come back I will make some arrangement for Paul because I do want to get a job. I may go into the Army because the life really does suit me. I seem to feel no fear. All I fear is boredom. If Trudi will look after Paul, be a second mother to him, all well and good; but you say she won't, that she wants to join her sister in Switzerland in order to be near Germany. Don't worry about it. I will always love my son and provide for him and look after him. I won't rely on you. How I miss my darling little Marian. I miss you too, Mother, and send you all my love.

Freddie

That night, after sunset, Freddie went into Boadilla, largely ruined, with a bunch of friends including Randy, an Englishman he had known at Oxford called Simon Roy and two Spaniards from El Campesino's 46th Division. There was a makeshift meal being served to the troops and, as he sat down with his plate on a bench under some trees, a man passed him talking rapidly in Spanish, but his tone made Freddie look up.

'Kyril,' Freddie said, and the man stopped, looked behind him and went on again, as though he hadn't heard. Freddie watched Kyril as he walked up the street, still talking rapidly, and then two or three of the more senior commanders who had joined him. They had towards Kyril an air of deference, which puzzled Freddie, because it seemed to him that they regarded Kyril, who was in military dress, with some respect, as though he were a senior commander. Kyril kept on looking behind uneasily, as though he wondered where the voice calling his name came from, but he went on talking, gesticulating, as though giving orders. Then someone produced a map, cigarettes were lit and a lamp and, in its glare, Freddie had no doubt at all that the man was his cousin Susan's Russian husband. He had that clear, deep scar on his chin.

After he finished his meal Freddie sat for some time on the bench looking at Kyril, thinking he must put a footnote about this extraordinary coincidence in the letter to his mother. Then the group round the table broke up and Kyril strolled back the way he had come, with Joe Hinks who had taken over the British Battalion after Copeman was wounded, another Englishman whom Freddie didn't know, and two or three Spaniards. Kyril was still talking to them, lecturing them; in fact, there had been a lot of desertions, mainly by the Spaniards, in the height of battle. Maybe the commanders were getting a ticking off about this. One thing was clear: Kyril was in charge – Kyril, supposedly the right wing, anti-Communist, was directing pro-Communist, Republican troops.

Freddie was about to let Kyril pass again, and then, his curiosity overcoming him, he stood in his path, hand outstretched.

'Hello, Kyril,' he said. 'The last bloke I expected to see here.'

Kyril stared at him and, in the glare of the lights, Freddie saw as deep a fear on Kyril's face as he had ever seen on that of an ally, or an enemy in battle. It was most extraordinary. Kyril looked as though he were wondering whether to acknowledge him or not and then, saying something in rapid Spanish to Luis Ortega, the senior commander of the Brigade, he took Freddie's shoulder and moved him to one side, away from his comrades.

'Freddie, you must not call me that here. I am known as "Serge".'

'Oh, I see!' Freddie laughed, but his laughter lacked humour. 'Undercover, is it?'

'Something of that sort, which I will explain to you later. Where will you be?'

'Well, I'm in a trench,' Freddie scratched his head. 'Difficult to pinpoint it. We are hoping to find barracks in the town.'

'I will get you somewhere to sleep. Meet me here in,' Kyril consulted his watch, 'one hour's time, that is 21 hours. Here, at this spot.'

He made another authoritative gesture, and then the men, who'd been looking at him curiously, gathered round him obediently again and they continued on their way.

Freddie spent the next hour smoking and talking to his friends, who asked him about Kyril.

'I thought it was someone I knew,' Freddie said. 'Now I'm not so sure.'

But he was sure. What he didn't know, yet, was what right Kyril had there. Was he friend or foe? Republican – or a spy?

When the time came for Kyril to return Freddie moved off so as to encounter him away from the others. He hung around for another hour, but Kyril did not return. Then one of the corps commanders of Colonel Jurado, a Republican regular officer, came along, looking at the faces of those standing or sitting about and calling: 'Down. Corporal Down?'

'Here, sir, here.' Freddie sprang off the ground where he had been sitting and the officer glared at him and said in Spanish: 'Come with me.'

He then led him out of the reassuring lights of the square, down a dark street and into a hut where Kyril sat with his military-style jacket off, and only a shirt and breeches on, his revolver tucked into a strong leather belt. Kyril nodded to the corps commander and stood up to welcome Freddie, shaking him by the hand and drawing him to a rickety chair next to his.

'Sorry about that, Freddie. You understand, strict military reasons.'

'What I don't understand,' Freddie said, taking the cigarette Kyril offered, 'is what *you're* doing here, so far behind Nationalist lines. Seems cock-eyed to me.'

'Ah,' Kyril smiled and Freddie saw how deep the lines were on his face, by the side of his eyes and around his mouth. His hair was beginning to turn grey and his face was sunburnt and weatherbeaten. The scar looked livid, as though it were quite fresh. But Freddie knew it went back to his boyhood. It was like the mark of Cain, Freddie thought, yet without knowing why he thought it – a mark that one carried through life, distinguishing a person from everyone else. Without the scar Freddie wasn't altogether sure he could positively have identified Kyril. He would have let him pass.

'If you're a spy I'm in a spot,' Freddie said, beginning to feel nervous. 'I suppose you'll have to shoot me.'

'Freddie,' Kyril clasped his arm in a comradely manner. 'I am no spy. I have never betrayed my Party ever since I left Russia. I have always been . . . one of you.' He looked earnestly at Freddie observing that, at last, understanding was dawning.

'You mean you *pretended*?'

'Yes.' Kyril nodded and gave a deep sigh.

'All the time?'

'Yes. I wanted to go back to Russia, but they told me I was in a unique position to be of service to my country. They could see war in Spain coming, quite a long time ago, to say nothing of the takeover of Germany by Hitler. I was very valuable in Europe to the Russians.'

'But after all *you* went through in Russia? I simply don't understand.'

'I have always believed in the Revolution, Freddie. I think you have too. You must have, to fight in this war on our side. I didn't know you were so much one of us.'

'I'm no Communist,' Freddie said. 'Don't misunderstand me. I just didn't like the lawful government of Spain, elected democratically by the people, being overthrown by the Fascists. I didn't like what was going on in Germany and I know what they're like. Frankly, Kyril, now that I've seen the worst excesses of the war on both sides, I don't know that there's much to choose between them. I have seen the aftermath of the terrible massacres committed by the Republic, as well as unmentionable outrages by the Nats. I have heard of appalling things. But here I am, and here I'll stay, until we win.'

'Good man. But will you be one of us when this is over?'

'I shall probably go home and join the regular Army. My wife died, you know, and I rather like the life.' Freddie gazed at his relation by marriage – a Ferov, so closely interrelated now with his family, yet a comparative stranger; an elusive, oddly alien man. 'Tell me truthfully, old boy, why did you have to *pretend* to side with the Fascists? We all thought you were frightfully right-wing. Devious, I must say. Then when we met you in Madrid you told us those whopping lies. Whoppers!' Freddie looked as though he had a sense of schoolboy outrage at the very idea.

'I consider life as a permanent battle, Freddie,' Kyril said, returning his gaze quite calmly. 'The world is in a perpetual state of revolution as far as I'm concerned. No holds are barred. I was working for my country, as you suggested, as an undercover agent. My case was vital, no one must know. The end justifies the means. For a long time we have been preparing for Communism to triumph in Spain. I was with General Berzin helping to make provisions for the war which, we always knew, would come. By making myself seem a staunch supporter of the right I provided a very effective, useful smokescreen. It was unfortunate meeting you in Madrid. Even more unfortunate seeing you here.' Kyril stopped talking and in the silence the only sound was of distant cicadas which had somehow survived the battles – God knew how – and the laughter of a group of men nearby playing cards.

'Does Susan know?'

'Of course not!' Kyril roared with laughter. 'No one knows. Not a soul – not my father, nor my mother, certainly not my upper-class English wife with all her society friends, her money, her lavish way of life.'

'You sound bitter.' Freddie put his head on one side – anxious to know more of this peculiarly idealistic, but certainly corrupt and perverted, man.

'Oh, I'm not bitter! I'm realistic. You see, I'm a soldier in battle – always; always fighting a war, even in peacetime. I use what means I can.'

Nervously Freddie licked his lips. 'But, now that I know – aren't you afraid I'll split?'

'Of course I'm not afraid, comrade,' Kyril thumped him on the arm again reassuringly. 'You are a staunch Republican, fighting for the cause. When this is over, and we have won, you will be convinced of the justice of the Communist cause. You will be one of us. You *are* one of us. Now, as you see, Freddie, I am here for a purpose, which is to direct the relief of Madrid. We have had stalemate there for too long now. Tomorrow we will resume the attack on Brunete. Already too many people have been killed. Remember, don't tell anyone about me, or talk about this conversation. The man who brought you here will take you back. You are to have lodgings with your battalion who are already grumbling about the battle. You must inspire them with your fire. I will see you in Madrid, Freddie, in a free and independent Spain. And remember – I trust you!' He gave him his straight palm, which Freddie clasped.

'Trust me, old boy!' he said. 'The old mouth will remain closed as an oyster. See you in Madrid, and, *mucho suerte!*'

Kyril shook Freddie warmly by the hand for so long that his arm ached. He thought there was a sad, distant look in Kyril's eyes, but maybe he was tired. Outside, the same soldier waited for him, and escorted him along the deserted streets of the village to where his platoon had bedded down for the night.

Reveille sounded before dawn. The plan was to capture the two hills occupied by the Nationalist commanders, Sáenz de Buruaga and Colonel Asensio. Freddie had not slept well because he kept thinking about Kyril and his cynical manipulation of the family. Because of the dark he had not had the opportunity to write a note about Kyril to his mother and decided, anyway, it was better not to, even to her, though he didn't doubt it would be a story hard to keep to himself when he got home. When it was time to wake up he had only just fallen asleep, so it was with considerable exhaustion that he got to his feet, performed the perfunctory ablutions which were all the battle-fatigued troops had time for before the call came to advance stealthily towards the hill.

By mid-morning the sun was blistering. There was desperate thirst and fatigue throughout the brigade. Many of the men were openly talking about deserting, but Freddie said that this day would surely be the last – for a while. He tried to cheer his friends on.

'The last in this world,' Randy said, licking his parched lips. The terrain in front of them was uneven, blocked by ruins of farms and once prosperous houses. Freddie thought they looked like the bones of skeletons bleached in the sun.

As the attack on the hill gathered momentum, the artillery came up to support the infantry who swept forward, encouraged by their commanders. Those on the hill who had the advantage began to fire into the swarm of Republican troops, many of whom staggered, lost their directions and fell.

From the shelter of a half-demolished building Kyril, who knew of the plans, indeed he had helped to draw them up, and had been in his position before dawn, watched the Republican advance, keeping an eye on the tall eye-catching figure of Freddie, hoping that the Nationalist guns would do his work for him. However, Freddie continued, as was his custom, to defy death and, as the Nationalist retreat began, he was in the vanguard of the pursuit, running after them, his long gangling figure distinctive against the harsh terrain.

It is impossible to know whether Kyril Ferov felt any remorse as, at last, peering from behind a wall, he took aim at his quarry before he could outdistance him, or disappear from sight. Freddie appeared to falter for a moment, and look behind, as if aware of his unseen assailant, of the bullet in the barrel that was meant for him. The moment gave Kyril an advantage, his eye unerring, his finger steady and one shot, straight through the back, felled the only man still alive who might betray him.

It was a chance, but the only chance he couldn't take.

As Freddie pitched forward Kyril watched for a while, to make sure he didn't move. Then, as the dead man's friends began to gather round him, one looking towards the ruin, he swiftly moved away – silently, stealthily, deceitfully, as he had all his life. He doubled back through the troops to rejoin his command in the town before planning the next strategic step in the battle for Brunete which, however, finally ended in stalemate on 25 July.

Yet both sides claimed victory in the battle which had cost so many lives. The dead were buried on the field of battle, among them Corporal Frederick Down. There were too many for tears, but Randy Tucker removed his friend's effects from his pockets and his last letter to his mother, addressed but without a stamp. One day, Randy promised himself, he would give it to her personally and tell her about her brave son who fell so unexpectedly when the immediate object of the attack had seemed to be within moments of victory.

Over the years there had been many gatherings in the little church at Askham which held the family vault. But this time there was no body to inter with its ancestors or with the frail little wife who had died the previous year. The large congregation, gathered for the memorial service to Freddie, were piously reminded by the Rector not only of the futility of war, but also of the heroism of those who volunteered to give their lives that others might live. But who exactly had benefited by Freddie's death? As yet the issue was unclear.

It was September 1937 and the leaves had started to scatter on the ground of the huge park and woodland surrounding Askham Hall. In two more years the whole nation would be engulfed by war, but no one knew it then.

For Rachel, who had lost a husband in war, the death of Freddie was one event for which Bosco's own end had been a grim rehearsal. Bad as that had been, Freddie's was infinitely worse, intolerable. She remembered how she had argued with him, as though she had foreknowledge, and he said that it wouldn't be a proper war. It was fun, Mother. Probably it would be over by the time he got there. How she regretted those hot, wounding words they had exchanged before his departure.

Next to her was Ralph, her hand in his, and on her other side Em, who had grieved more than anyone for her twin – the half of her that was now dead. She had tried so hard to get Freddie's body to be buried in England. But on that battle-scarred plain no one could find it. There were little, pathetic mounds of stones marking the last resting places of the unknown dead.

Charlotte stood next to Em, and then Bobby, his wife Aileen and their son David, now part of the family. Cheryl was on the other side of Ralph and next to her were Christopher, Sylvia and Hugo.

Missing from the large congregation were any members of the Ferov family, something that would have been unthink-able for many years past. The Russian family had been part of their lives for nearly fifteen years. Now, since the divorce and the murder of Jamie, it was as though they had never existed except for Susan, of course, who was in Venice with her children, Kyril who was on some mysterious business in Spain, and, of course, the three little girls, to all intents and purposes orphans.

Susan had not felt herself terribly close to Freddie but, more than that, she had no desire to see her brother Bobby or, for that matter, any member of the family. She felt that, with the possible exception of Charlotte, they had not done enough for Hélène; they had been frankly unsympathetic about the plight of Alexei and poor, devastated Irina. Whether she was right or not it is difficult to say, because she was so partisan. As she grew older Susan increasingly saw things in sharp colours, rather than muted tones, and where right and wrong were concerned she thought there was no in-between. Like many very wealthy, spoilt men and women used to their own way, she'd become increasingly intemperate and dictatorial. Oddly

684

enough she and the brother she had broken from grew more and more alike, as though their separation accentuated similarities.

Standing there, at about the same time in the morning that Bosco's memorial service had been held twenty-two years before, Rachel reflected that on that day Freddie had been just eight, too young to attend. He and his twin, Em, would have been playing in The Grange where now Freddie's orphan son was at home with his nursemaid. Only a week before Freddie's death Trudi Klein had gone to Switzerland because there was news that her husband, a sick man, might be released by the Nazis.

The congregation sang the same hymn that had been sung at Bosco's memorial service but Rachel's eyes now, as then, were dry, though many of those in the church were not.

> 'He'll fear not what men say
> He'll labour night and day
> To be a pilgrim.'

Then, once again, they all streamed out into the sun, though this time there were no medals, no purple cushion with the Victoria Cross. The boy who had carried it on that day, Ralph Askham, was now a man of thirty-one, not a soldier as his father or brother had been, but a farmer. He took his mother's arm and said to her:

'Do you want to ride or walk?'

'Walk, I think.' Rachel glanced up at the sky. 'We walked, do you remember, back from your father's memorial service? I want everything to be today as it was then.'

Only it was not as it was then. Many of the people present in 1915 were dead, including Bosco's much beloved mother, Freddie's grandmother, and his Aunt Flora. Others who had been there had also died, some in the War, tenants and workers on the estate now much reduced.

And people were there now who had not been then, like Cheryl, Sylvia, Susan's son Sasha, Charlotte with her eldest son, Hugo and many Kittos and members of the family, some not born in 1915. Arthur Crewe was also there with his family. He had wanted to go to Spain but, as a member of the British serving forces, it was strictly forbidden by the non-intervention Treaty.

Rachel wanted to walk home through the park with her children; her surviving son and two daughters, just the family. Arms linked, saying little, they sadly made their way through the forest, round the lake and up the other side where Cheryl awaited them, with her customary false, social smile, at the vast open door of the Hall already filled with people.

How familiar it all was, an Askham reception. How familiar and yet how strange. It was strange because the Hall no longer seemed the place it was, as though Dulcie in departing this life had, somehow, taken with her the spirit of the place she'd loved so much, lived in for so many years, filled with parties, gaiety, children, interesting people. Now it seemed like an isolated shell – cold and unfriendly, like its chatelaine who, having done her worst to it, scarcely ever lived there. She and Ralph led largely separate lives – Cheryl in London, he on his farm. It was rather as though the place were permanently in mourning for the gay spirits who had once inherited it and were now no more.

Familiar, and yet strange. As Rachel walked alone up the staircase to the crowded reception rooms on the first floor she thought of the little boy who'd always loved the place – playing hide-and-seek with his brothers and sisters, his numerous cousins, and who had now joined the ranks of the departed – his father, his grandmother and grandfather, his uncle and aunt – who had lived there too. How strange it was to be mourning with them, her son, her Freddie, her baby.

Rachel gave a gulp as she reached the landing and went into the room crowded with mourners, the subdued murmur of people with only memories to exchange. For once, there was no representative from the Royal Family. The new King, reported to be in emotional trouble because of his relationship with Mrs Simpson, was not of the generation that remembered Askhams. Queen Mary had sent a personal note to Rachel and a wreath, but no one could remember when an occasion like this had not been graced by Royalty or its representative. It seemed like a sign of the changing times, or perhaps too many thought Freddie had died for a wrong cause and on the wrong side.

Hugo had not walked back with Rachel and the others because, at a time like this, he felt that, strictly speaking, he was not one of them. He felt his separateness, the fact that he was Bosco's son but not Rachel's. He couldn't help her in her grief, like the others could.

Hugo circulated, helping to entertain the guests, talking knowledgeably about the farm, the crops, the stable and the stud. To those who enquired he also said that his mother, now a widow, had left England and was living once again in Cairo. Charlotte was trailed around by Arthur Crewe who wanted to marry her. But she liked her independence, her status as one of the most famous mannequins in Paris, and was reluctant to give it up. Everyone said how elegant and sophisticated she was, how beautiful in her grief, mourning Freddie.

Ralph and Cheryl moved separately around the room and Em remained sitting most of the time. People remarked on her pallor, as if she felt she was responsible for luring Freddie to Spain and bringing about his death.

The Duchess of Quex had finally died, though most people had assumed she would live for ever, but all the other Askham friends were there, including the Crewes, the Anstruther-Grays, the Partingtons, the Gore-Whites, the Plomley-Pembertons, the Bulstrodes and the Fford-Frenches. The Kittos were there too, though not in such force as on previous occasions, understandably. Jamie's was a name mentioned by no one.

Adam was in America, a guest of the Supreme Court, and Melanie had thought it too far to come. She was scarcely ever seen in England these days, enjoying vaguely poor health while Denton gambled her money away in the casino, and Jordan remained out of sight in his expensive private nursing home. In many ways it seemed as though the family had broken up. Everyone tried to avoid talking about Freddie, but not his mother. She wanted to talk about Freddie all the time, never to forget for a single moment that, unlike Bosco, whose grave was known, or Arthur or Flora, he lay in an unmarked grave on an arid plain in Castile, somewhere near Madrid. His only known resting place was thus in their memories.

People said, as they always said about Rachel, how brave she was, what an example to others. But Rachel felt fragile, and was glad when they started to drift away. It had not been one of the very big Askham parties held on previous occasions. Cheryl couldn't be bothered; she didn't see why she should put herself out for all these people she hardly knew. Anyway, she wanted to go up to London, and drove herself off with the last of the guests so that only the real family was left. They were glad.

Bobby and Aileen had been married nearly a year. The family liked Aileen; she was polite, not ingratiating, a good hostess, a skilful needlewoman, a homemaker. The kind of companion Bobby seemed to need after Hélène. It was observed that she and Bobby did not appear to be too much in love, and there were no signs of further children, maybe because of her age; but they seemed a compatible pair. Bobby went up to kiss Rachel and took her hand in his.

'I don't feel I've spoken to you enough. May I come and see you in a day or two?'

'Of course,' Rachel kissed his cheek. 'And thank you *very* much, thank you for everything, your support, Aileen's support.' She kissed Aileen affectionately, and warmly shook

David's hand, saying what a big boy he was. The family liked David too, had welcomed him.

They were escorting Bobby and Aileen to the door when a man whom Rachel had seen, but not spoken to, came up and, bowing to her, presented her with a letter.

'I hope you won't mind me giving you this, Lady Askham. I found it on your son's body the day he died. I hope it's not a shock. I was with him that day. He was a very brave man, a real sport. My name is Randolph Tucker...'

Rachel held out her hand for the letter, her face registering astonishment, then grief. For the first time she nearly broke down, clinging to his hand.

'Randy Tucker ... Freddie mentioned you. Oh, Randy, how *kind* of you to come.'

'I wanted to bring you the letter personally, and I have a few other memories of Freddie, Lady Askham, things I found in his pockets. I hope it doesn't upset you too much. I didn't quite know what to say.'

'Very *good* of you to come.' Ralph came from behind Rachel. 'Have you anywhere to stay?'

'I thought I'd go back to London, sir. You must be Freddie's brother.'

'We'd like you to stay with us,' Ralph said, 'if you could spare the time. It would help us all to know about Freddie's time in Spain. It would help us so much.'

Randy Tucker stayed for two days and he did help. Freddie had been happy, confident, never afraid.

'He really was an example,' Randy said in his drawling Australian accent. 'We were all so sick of the war that troops were deserting like flies. One time old Major Nathan, who was killed too, went after the fleeing Spaniards with his gold-topped swagger stick and drove them all back. It's a terrible war. Believe you me, I was glad to get out. I'm sorry to tell you that. It simply wasn't worth it. Freddie's death wasn't worth it.'

'It was worth it for Freddie,' Rachel said, in the pause that followed. They were sitting in The Grange after a late family lunch, Charlotte preparing to go back to Paris accompanied by Arthur, who had leave. Hugo was in charge of the farm, while Ralph stayed with his mother. 'It was worth it for Freddie because it was what he wanted to do. He wanted to feel worthwhile, and fighting in Spain did that for him.'

'There was some bloke he saw there the night before he died,' Randy said. 'It was a bit of a mystery, really. I thought he was a relation or something. He didn't seem to expect to see him, and they went away for an hour or two. He wouldn't say anything about him. I thought it broke him up a bit.'

'What sort of bloke?' Ralph asked, mystified.

'Someone he knew from the past. He said he'd tell me later, but he never did. He was a Spaniard of some kind I think; anyway, a foreign fellow. I often wondered if it had anything to do with his death, but it couldn't have done.'

'Why on earth do you say that?' Em leaned forward, slipping her hand into her mother's, pressing it tightly.

'He said he didn't sleep well, but then none of us did – and he was just so quiet. Unlike Freddie, not as buoyant or ebullient as usual. Maybe his concentration slipped, but maybe it's my imagination.'

'I'm *sure* it is,' Charlotte looked anxiously at her mother. 'Can we give you a lift back to London, Randy?'

'That's very kind of you, Lady Charlotte,' Randy said perkily. 'I'm sure I don't mind if you do.'

Paul was heavily asleep. Em and Rachel went to peer over his cot, and Rachel stayed to croon a little song. Ralph went back to the farm and, when she got downstairs, Em was sitting waiting for her.

'You look tired, Mummy. You've taken it all so marvellously. You always do.'

'That's all one can do,' Rachel said, 'take things as they come. I've found that in life.'

'Can you bear a shock then, Mummy, or have you already guessed?' Em looked at Rachel, who said:

'I think I guessed. Women get a funny shape when they're four or so months pregnant. Am I right?'

'Do you mind terribly?'

'I don't mind! But do you?'

'I'm quite pleased though, of course, it wasn't planned. Felipe doesn't actually *believe* in marriage or anything like that, but I think he's pleased too. You know, Mummy, this war really is awful, and how do I know if *he* will survive it, either?'

'Well, you can't go back as you are, that's for sure,' Rachel said. 'I'd already decided that when I suspected. You must stay here until the baby is born. You can help look after Paul.'

'But, Mummy, I'll *die*,' Em groaned. 'I'll be so bored I won't know what to do.'

'You can go through all Freddie's writings, if you can bear it,' Rachel said gently. 'I would like to publish something, as a memorial to him, and you can do a little biography of him to accompany it, just for the family. Would you like that?'

'Mummy, it's the nicest thing you've thought of.' Em lay back contentedly on the sofa and put her feet up. 'I'm so glad, you know. But won't you have an *awful* lot to do?'

'How do you mean?'

'With me and my baby, Uncle Adam's children, little Paul.'

'Oh, I'll cope,' Rachel said. 'Everyone says I always cope and, unfortunately, I always do.'

'Unfortunately?'

'Well, sometimes I think I'd like to break down or go mad or throw things about, but somehow I never seem to. I'm that awful sensible type that everyone relies on. Believe me, sometimes I wish I weren't.'

'Mummy, I love you.' Em reached up for her and Rachel bent down and took her in her arms, holding her tightly for a few moments. She was close to tears. Freddie dying ... and Em, his twin, giving life. Suddenly it seemed too hard to take.

As Em settled back to have a nap Rachel wandered out into the garden, where the resident family of blackbirds, who had lived at the Grange for generations, had started their evening calls. Lenin, following her, looked up at them, but it was a formality. Lenin and the blackbirds were old foes and, like old adversaries, treated one another with respect. Lenin yawned and stretched his legs. He slept a lot these days. One of the gardeners up at the Hall had lit some early leaves and the smoke spiralled through the trees, against the background of the setting sun, its pungent nostalgic smell tickling Rachel's nostrils, somehow reminding her, too, of the past. She stooped to pick up a twig and then trailed it along the ground for Lenin who looked at it lazily and strolled past it without interest. After all, he was at least seventeen. Then he sat on the edge of the lawn and began to wash himself in his stately, arthritic way, with all the time in the world – and, indeed, he *had* all the time in the world. Lucky cat.

Rachel threw the twig away and sniffed a late flowering rose. Then her eyes did fill with tears because somehow it reminded her vividly of Freddie, who had planned and nurtured the rose garden for Marian – who loved roses – in the short time he'd lived here. The place was full of Freddie. She looked towards the window where his son slept in his cot and then towards the window where his twin, harbouring new life, also dozed. She stooped to stroke Lenin, and then wandered through the garden gate down the path towards the bench by the lake where Bosco had proposed all those years ago, and Freddie had told Marian he loved her.

As she sat down, Lenin, who had sauntered after her, jumped on to the bench and in a rare display of affection, got on to her lap, and started pawing her skirt.

'You're a silly old cat,' Rachel said, ruffling his ears. Lenin purred.

Looking about her at the familiar scene, with the dear old cat on her lap, Rachel thought that life, though it consisted mainly of pain and heartache, was punctuated by moments of pure happiness – moments like this with Lenin, the smoke rising through the trees, the sun slowly sinking out of sight.

These little pockets of contentment could suddenly transform life from gloom to gaiety, depression to joy. They occurred at the most unexpected moments – like now, two days after Freddie's memorial service, sitting on the bench she'd shared with his father years before he was born. It was as though Freddie were there.

It was these moments that gave strength, enabling one to continue; to decide that, perhaps, life was not lacking in purpose, after all. That, maybe, Bosco and Freddie, Marian, Flora, Dulcie, Paolo and Margaret weren't dead but, united somewhere out of time, were waiting for them.

Gently she put Lenin on one side and, getting up, walked slowly back up the path towards the house where, already, she could see Em on the lawn waiting for her, Freddie's baby in her arms. Life, after all, renewed itself, again and again. Rachel waved.

This life; so precious.

SELECT BIBLIOGRAPHY

Best, Nicholas, *Happy Valley: the story of the English in Kenya*. London, 1979.

Bielenberg, Christabel, *The Past is Myself*. London, 1984.

Blixen, Karen (Isak Dineson), *Out of Africa*. London, 1979.

Bolton, Kenneth (also editor), *The Lion and the Lily: a guide to Kenya*. London, 1962.

Briszat, Martin (trans. John W. Hiden), *The Hitler State: the foundation and development of the internal structure of the Third Reich*. London, 1981.

Bryant, Louise, *Six Red Months in Russia*. London, 1918.

Buchanan, Meriel, *Recollections of Imperial Russia*. London, 1923.

Bullock, Alan, *Hitler: a study in tyranny*. London, 1962.

Cederholm, B., *In the Clutches of the Tcheka*. London, 1929.

Court, William, *Power and Glory: a history of Grand Prix Motor Racing 1906–1951*. London, 1966.

Cunnington, C. Willett, *English Women's Clothing in the Present Century*. London, 1952.

Dietrich, Otto (trans. Richard and Clara Wilson), *The Hitler I Knew*. London, 1957.

Duranty, Walter (selected and arranged by Gustavus Tuckerman, Jr), *Russia Reported*. London, 1934.

Fitzlyon, Kyril and Browning, Tatiana, *Before the Revolution*. London, 1977.

Fox, James, *White Mischief*. London, 1982.

Galitzine, Princess Nicholas, *Spirit to Survive: the memoirs of Princess Nicholas Galitzine*. London, 1976.

Gold, Arthur and Fizdale, Robert, *Misia*. London, 1980.

Goldman, Emma, *My Disillusionment in Russia*. London, 1925.

Grant Duff, Sheila, *The Parting of Ways: a personal account of the Thirties*. London, 1982.

A Handbook of Kenya Colony and the Kenya Protectorate. London, 1920.

Hauner, Milan, *Hitler: a chronology of his life and times*. London, 1983.

Hills, George, *The Battle for Madrid*. London, 1976.

Hoare, Sir Samuel, *The Fourth Seal: the end of a Russian chapter*. London, 1930.

Isherwood, Christopher, *Mr Norris Changes Trains*. London, 1947.

Kessler, Count Harry (trans. Charles Kessler), *The Diaries of a Cosmopolitan 1918–1937*. London, 1971.

McCauley, Martin, *The Soviet Union since 1917*. London, 1981.

Metternich, Tatiana, *Tatiana: five passports in a shifting Europe*. London, 1976.

Paustovsky, Konstantine, *Story of a Life*.

    Vol I *Childhood and Schooldays*. London, 1964.

    Vol II *Slow Approach of Thunder*. London, 1963.

    Vol III *In That Dawn*. London, 1967.

    Vol IV *Years of Hope*. London, 1968.

    Vol V *Southern Adventure*. London, 1969.

    Vol VI *The Restless Years*. London, 1974.

Porter, Kathy, *Alexandra Kollontai: a biography*. London, 1980.

Rado, A. (compiler), *Guide-Book to the Soviet Union*. Berlin, 1929.

Rubin, Jacob, *Moscow Mirage*. London, 1935.

Snowden, Mrs Philip, *Through Bolshevik Russia*. London, 1920.

Sokolova, T.M. and Orlova, K., *Russian Furniture in the Collection of the Hermitage*. Leningrad, 1973.

Thomas, Hugh, *The Spanish Civil War*. London, 1961.

Troyat, Henri (trans. Malcolm Barnes), *Daily Life in Russia under the last Tsar in the year 1903*. London, 1959.

von Eckhardt, Wolf and Gilman, Sander L., *Bertold Brecht's Berlin: a scrapbook of the 'twenties*. London, 1976.

von Meck, Galina, *As I Remember Them*. London, 1973.

Webb, Sidney and Beatrice, *Soviet Communism: a new civilisation?* 2 vols. London, 1935.